LIZANDRA'S DEEPEST FEAR

LIZANDRA'S DEEPEST FEAR

TESHOVAR BOOK II

JASON DOROUGH

This is a work of fiction. All the characters and events portrayed in this novel are fictitious.

LIZANDRA'S DEEPEST FEAR

Copyright © 2024 by Jason Dorough

Cover design by Franziska Stern

All rights reserved.

No part of this book may be reproduced in any form or by any electronic or mechanical means, including information storage and retrieval systems, without written permission from the author, except for the use of brief quotations in a book review.

A 908 Press Book

ISBN eBook: 978-1-7366140-8-2
ISBN Paperback: 978-1-7366140-6-8
ISBN Hardcover: 978-1-7366140-9-9

For my first reader and best friend, Celeste

LIZANDRA'S DEEPEST FEAR

PART I
STORMBREAK

CHAPTER 1

The twelve bells of Bachali rang just before midnight with the clanging cadence that signaled danger. Every citizen of Tresa knew the ancient bells by number and rhythm, even though it had been decades since they rang in warning. Three times, then twice, and twice more, before starting the pattern over again. The clamor crashed through the city, startling the citizens out of their beds, but nowhere did it seem louder than in the halls of the governmental seat, seven stories directly below the bell tower.

Guards rushed through the pale stone corridors to secure all exterior doors, and the city's barracks emptied as soldiers ran into the streets, some still strapping their regimental armor over their orange uniforms. They moved to block the four bridges spanning the canal that surrounded the square walls of the capitol building as chains released to drop the massive portcullis across the front archway that framed the main entrance. The ground shook as the huge, latticed grille slammed into place, drowning the bells for an instant with its thunderous boom.

Alexia Rhandolph had overseen the city for three mayoral terms, but nothing like this had touched her reign until now. The white-haired woman watched the chaos from within the grand foyer, just a short walk down the entryway from the front gates. The floor here was light stone, and the orange banners of

Tresa flanked the room, the white lion's head emblazoned on each. Stairs ascended either side of the enormous chamber, with open doorways punctuating all but the south wall where an arch led toward the front entrance. Just before guards dragged the doors shut, two soldiers unhooked the counterweights from the portcullis, securing the tons of iron in place. No one would be getting in or out until this mess was sorted.

"Madam Mayor," a voice called. It took her a moment to realize that the voice was addressing her, and she pulled her eyes away from the barricaded exit. It was one of the household guards, dressed in the uniform orange tunic, its edges trimmed in white. The white lion's head stood bright across the young man's chest, and the older woman raised a hand to her own chest, her fingers touching the dark and ordinary fabric of her suit. Rhandolph had not been in her official garb when the alarm sounded.

"What is the meaning of this?" she asked, her thin, white eyebrows drawn close together and her aged eyes holding the guard in place.

"I don't know, Madam, but you should be headed to the saferoom by now."

One eyebrow raised, and she drew her head back. "You presume to tell me what I should be doing, do you?"

The guard cast a glance to the left, surely wishing he could swap his place with any of the other soldiers and staff hurrying through the foyer as the bells continued ringing. He stammered, "It's the protocol, Madam."

She sighed and flicked her wrist away from her chest, gesturing toward the doors leading deeper into the building. "Fine, then. If you're so determined to lock me away, you can be my escort."

"Of course," the guard said, his eyes shifting enviously toward the other staff, who had not decided to approach the mayor.

He made a crisp turn on his boot heel to lead her through the left door at the back of the room. She followed and watched the thin sword strapped to the guard's right hip. He either was left-handed or had put on his belt backwards. The blade bumped against his thigh as they crossed a smaller room and went through a discreet doorway that opened onto a landing.

"This way, Madam." And they were down the stone stairs, headed into the basement levels now. The air became cooler as they descended, and they left the noise of the capitol behind. No other guards or staff were down in this part of the building. The woman's upper lip twitched, and she shot an anxious look back up the stairs at the receding door.

"It's just down this hallway," the guard said, extending his arm to point. The left one, she noted with a satisfied huff of her breath. "Would you like for me to wait with you?"

"Unnecessary." She made the shooing motion again, and the guard snapped her a sharp nod before heading back up the stairs. "Guard," she called as an afterthought, stopping him.

"Madam?" The guard paused on the fifth step and turned.

"Do you know what this is all about?"

"I do not, but whatever it is, you'll be well protected down here. No one else will have access to the saferoom. Once you're inside and lock it, that door can't be opened until you unlock it again."

She nodded and shooed the man for the third time. This time, the guard made his ascent at a faster pace than before. Should she have ordered him to stand guard in the hallway? It was too late for second guesses now that he was gone, so she looked back down the hall at the closed door at the end. Was she the first to arrive?

The door was ajar, and she heard voices inside as she neared the end of the corridor. She scowled. She should have been the first.

She pushed her way into the room, and the conversation died as the other two jerked their heads toward the door. The slim man standing to the right exhaled and let his shoulders drop. "Alexia. Thank the High Lord, it's only you."

"You expected someone else, Dimano?" she asked and left the door open behind her. There was still one more coming.

Dimano wore his orange and white tunic with his sash of rank draped across his shoulders. The white lion's head was at the center of the sash, overlaid atop an orange icon of a coin, symbolizing the city treasury. He raked his fingers through his yellow hair and adjusted the arm of his eyeglasses. "Either you or Bogan. Or whoever caused this lockdown."

"Did you hear?" the woman on the other side of the table asked. There were enough chairs for all of them, but both Dimano and Golchin stood. Dimano continued fiddling with his glasses, while Golchin cupped her elbows as her eyes darted between the mayor and the open door. She, too, wore her uniform of office, the gavel of lawkeepers emblazoned in orange behind the white lion on her sash. Why were they still uniformed so late in the night, and did Rhandolph's lack of a uniform reflect poorly on her own work ethic?

"Hear what?" she asked as she approached the table. It was round and wooden, just large enough for a company of five or six to sit around it comfortably. There'd be only four tonight. There would have been a fifth if Rhandolph had appointed a new city commissioner after Krezlin died last year, but she hadn't gotten around to it. And so the city of Tresa rested on the shoulders of only four people, all of whom would soon be hiding in this subterranean locked room while their subordinates ran through their emergency routines above.

Dimano said, "Murder." The way he said it, the word dripped with drama, and the corners of his mouth quivered. The treasurer looked as if he found this whole thing more exciting than disconcerting as he waited for the mayor's reaction.

"Murder," she repeated. "In the capitol building?"

Golchin nodded, and her black bangs shook against her forehead. "A page found the body, and they got the bells ringing just after."

"Surely you've heard more than that."

"Not yet," Dimano said. "Golchin and I had only just finished executing the contract when the bells started. That beastly mercenary always insists on late meetings. Otherwise, I'd have been in bed long ago." That explained the uniforms, then. Dimano paused and chuckled. "Come to think of it, he's probably locked in the building, too, even now."

"We were hoping you might know more," Golchin said. "Surely Bogan will have heard something by the time he gets here. What's keeping him?" Golchin looked through the open door and into the empty hallway. Bogan should be along shortly, and then they could lock the room.

"Perhaps he's been murdered as well," Dimano said with a wicked grin.

Golchin's eyes widened, and a tremor made the skin hanging at her throat waggle. She, at least, seemed to take this more seriously than Dimano.

But no, Bogan yet lived, his perseverance proven by his thudding footsteps and his huffing breath. The short guildmaster rambled his way toward the saferoom, the man's round head tucked down, sweat shining on his bald scalp. His hunched shoulders rocked with every step, and he seemed ready to topple to the floor and roll the rest of the way to the vault. He looked to have been roused from sleep and still wore his dressing gown, its dark sash at the waist swinging in time with the guildmaster's gait. Rhandolph was no longer the most underdressed for this occasion.

"Golchin thought you'd been murdered," Dimano said with a laugh as Bogan trundled through the door.

He wheezed to catch his breath as he shook his head. "Not me. It's the…" His voice trailed into silence as his round, dark eyes flicked across the room.

The door slammed shut behind him, sealing the room, and the new silence consumed the unending pattern of the bells, turning them into faint and distant tones. The mayor's key turned in the primary lock before the deadbolt slid home.

Bogan watched her movements with an open mouth, and Dimano prompted him. "It's the what? What did you hear?"

The guildmaster worked his lips and finally found his voice again. "Not what I heard. I saw it. I saw the mayor dead upstairs. They had her body in the council chamber."

Dimano laughed again. "As you can see, our mayor is alive and well."

Bogan had backed as far away from the white-haired woman as he could within the small confines of the saferoom. He shook his head, never taking his eyes off her face. "I know what I saw," he said. "And that is not the mayor."

Golchin looked from Bogan to the woman by the door, fear spreading across her face. The table was between her and the mayor, but she took a step backwards, anyway. Dimano wore a smile when he looked to Rhandolph for a response, but it faded as soon as he saw the woman's face. "What in the ageless realm?" he asked, and he blinked through the lenses of his spectacles before removing them altogether, as though he could no longer trust them.

Nahk knew they saw her now. She'd seen the looks of bewilderment, fear, and understanding so many times before. The change wasn't a physical one, and she felt no difference when the face she presented stopped being Mayor Rhandolph's and became her own. It was clear that her Veil had dropped, though, as it always did when too many people looked at her with too much suspicion.

The aging politician was gone, her pasty and wrinkled skin having tightened and darkened to a light tan. Nahk's face showed now, sharp and angular, a divot dimpling her pointed chin just below her thin lips. Rhandolph's thick upper lip had disappeared, as had the white eyebrows, replaced by Nahk's thick and dark ones, matching her short, black hair. The mayor's dark suit, the one Nahk had seen the woman wearing when she killed her, was no longer the same, having disappeared into Nahk's tight-fitting black shirt and trousers, the sleeves covering her arms to her wrists, where she wore a thick brown bracer on each forearm. Most telling, though, were the mayor's pale eyes, which Nahk knew had vanished to reveal her own peculiar gaze. No longer hidden behind her Veil, Nahk's eyes glowed violet in the dim gaslight of the saferoom.

Dimano was closest to Nahk, and she flicked her right arm at him first. The bracer on that arm clicked and released its small steel blade. It shot out straight and true, piercing him at the center of his throat. Nahk turned to the right, and the cable that attached the tiny knife to her bracer pulled taut, yanking the blade free and spraying the table with the treasurer's blood. Dimano fell to his knees, his hands slapping at his throat, and that was when Lawmaker Golchin opened her mouth to scream.

Nahk threw her left arm at the terrified woman and let the

LIZANDRA'S DEEPEST FEAR

cable unspool, sending the knife out from the left bracer even as the other blade retracted on its cable into the right one. Nahk tugged, altering the left knife's flight, and the cable spun once about Golchin's neck. Nahk's fingers wrapped around that cable, and she gave it a hard pull to unwind the loop, dragging the blade in a tight orbit with it. Golchin spun away and was dead before the scream could leave her throat.

Guildmaster Bogan was the last one left, and Nahk leaped atop the table just as the blade slipped back into her left bracer, retracted by its zephyr spool. Nahk avoided slipping in Dimano's blood as she pounced across the tabletop, clearing the chair on the other side. Bogan had fallen back against the wall, his knees pulled tight against his belly, and he held his hands up in supplication. He might have been crying, but it was hard to tell amid the sweat that already bathed his face.

"No more!" Bogan begged between hitching breaths.

Nahk stood over him, her hands relaxed at her sides but ready. The first two had dropped so quickly she'd hardly had time to think about them, but this one would have to be deliberate. More cold blooded, and she didn't like that.

Bogan took her hesitation as a sign of mercy. If only it could have been that simple. But then he began babbling. "I told them not to deal with you. I knew this would come back on us." He wheezed, his chest rising and falling faster now. "I was the only one against it, and now look. Look at this."

Nahk had drawn her right hand back, ready to strike the killing blow, but these words arrested her movement. "Not to deal with me? I don't know you, Guildmaster." Her speech had shifted from Rhandolph's trilling pitch down to her own quiet voice, deeper than most people expected when they saw her true appearance.

"Not you," he said, still gasping. "Your order. They've doomed us all. So goes Tresa." He winced, and his hand jerked toward his chest, fumbling at the edges of his thin gown.

It was Nahk's turn to blink. She lowered her right hand and squatted to grab the back of the man's neck. She yanked his face close to hers, her eyes lighting his skin pale purple, and hissed through her teeth, "Tell me exactly what you mean."

Bogan opened his mouth, perhaps to comply or perhaps to swallow one more labored breath. Whatever he was attempting, he failed, and his eyes rolled upward, showing nothing but the whites. He jerked in Nahk's grasp, and his mouth convulsed into a grimace.

"Bogan!" Nahk shouted in his face and shook him, but it was no use. She released his neck, and he slumped back against the wall, his head lolling to rest his chin on his unmoving chest.

∼

Outside the saferoom, Nahk pressed her back against the door and closed her eyes. Her hands spread against the hard wood, and beads of blood dripped out of the bracers, wetting her fingers. The flood of adrenaline had passed now, and exhaustion tried to press through. Her breathing slowed, and she forced herself to regulate it, inhaling through her nose, exhaling through her mouth. Her stomach lurched once, and she swallowed hard, forcing herself not to vomit. It had been many years since she'd thrown up after killing, but the urge was still there every time.

Behind her closed eyelids, she saw Dimano and Golchin. Neither of them had had time to realize they were dying, but they'd had plenty of time for the fear and threat of danger to grab them before Nahk threw her knives. It was different with Bogan. He saw the others fall, and he knew what was coming for him. With Nahk's hesitation, he had an instant to hope for mercy, and then he'd died anyway. It was his own heart's betrayal that did him in, but Nahk counted the guildmaster's death as her responsibility as surely as the other three had been that night.

The mayor, then the treasurer, then the lawmaker, and finally the guildmaster. In one night, she'd removed the entire leadership structure from Tresa. Certainly, other bureaucrats would hasten to fill the void, and the city was likely to be back in operation within a week, but the new leaders would not soon forget this brutal evening. They would continue the Empire's work, and they'd keep scraping to the High Lord's will, but they would remember their predecessors' fates. They'd be waiting for their own knives. That's what the rebellion intended, and that's what Nahk delivered. The mission was successful, but there was no sense of victory. It was quite a thing, hating what you were best at doing.

The hallway was empty, the bells continuing to toll far overhead. For the second time, Nahk questioned the wisdom of letting the guard go. He'd learn the mayor had been murdered, and surely he'd tell someone he'd just escorted her eminence down to the saferoom only moments ago. It was a risk Nahk shouldn't have taken, but it was done, and there was no use regretting it. She'd taken four lives on that night and had no desire to add a fifth. Naecara wouldn't approve, but Naecara wasn't the one holding the blades.

Protocol mandated that all the leaders retreat to the saferoom whenever the twelve bells sounded danger, and that's where everyone would expect the three remaining politicians to remain until they felt safe enough to emerge. The captain of the guard was likely to come down to tell them it was safe to open the door, but that wouldn't happen for hours yet, provided the guard who'd escorted Nahk down didn't alert him earlier. And, after that, it would be even longer before anyone had the temerity to break through the door and find the bodies.

Nahk pivoted to face the door and slid Rhandolph's key into the outside lock. She turned it and heard the heavy bolt slide home. The only other keys to that door were inside, hidden somewhere on each of the three corpses. None of the staff could unlock the door unless they got their hands on Rhandolph's key. After sliding the lock home, Nahk chopped her right bracer down against the metal setting. The key broke flush with the door, and its head dropped to the floor with a soft ping. Nahk kicked it and watched it slide back under the narrow gap beneath the door, back into the room with the bodies.

She hesitated before making her next move. Naecara had ordered her to get out of the capitol and leave Tresa before anyone realized the extent of the assassinations. But Naecara hadn't heard what she had heard.

"Your order," Bogan had said as Nahk stared into his soft,

moist eyes with her glowing violet ones. There was no mistaking what he meant by that. He thought the Nightingales had sent her to double cross the Tresa leadership. Before Bogan arrived, Dimano and Golchin had talked about having just finished executing a contract as the bells began ringing. Someone who insisted on meeting at nighttime and someone Dimano had called a beastly mercenary. Someone who was likely still locked in the government building, just a few floors above where Nahk stood at that very moment.

There was a Nightingale in the capitol with her. Another Nightingale. She touched her fingers to her face, just below her eye, and realized too late that she was smearing Dimano's blood on her cheek.

There was no decision to make, and she had no choice. Nahk sniffed and swallowed hard once more before she turned and headed back up the hallway, hurrying toward the stairs.

∼

By the time Nahk reached the foyer again, she moved behind a new Veil, this one looking like the household guard who had led her to the saferoom. When she spoke, she knew listeners would hear that man's voice instead of her own, just as they'd heard Rhandolph's voice earlier in the night.

She hesitated in the doorway. There were still too many people moving through the area. The guards were sweeping the entire building, room by room, and she would probably encounter more than she could hold at one time. Maintaining the illusion required her to focus on every person she wanted to trick, dividing her efforts among different individuals when more than one person was present. She could usually hold it for up to three observers, but she always lost the thread and revealed herself when she tried to deceive more. Nahk knew she'd have been able to hold it for as many as ten or more observers if she'd had a chance to finish her training, but she worked with what she had.

In the years since she'd been on her own, she'd practiced her skills and even developed a few tricks of her own. She had even worked out how to Veil someone else, altering the way others saw them, as long as that person was within a couple of feet of her and as long as only one or two people needed to be tricked. Even with its limitations, that maneuver was something she felt sure even the average Nightingale with full training couldn't pull off. Nevertheless, she knew her skills were lacking in other areas, but she'd prefer that to having finished her lessons. Killing was one thing she suspected she could do as well as any proper Nightingale, and she needed to do it one more time that night.

Nahk had known the still-tolling bells would signal the leaders to scurry into their saferoom, making it easier for her to finish all of them in one place after she'd killed the mayor and left her body to be found. The downside to that plan was that the bells would also lock the building down, making her escape through traditional exits more difficult. She'd planned for that, though, and knew the ballroom on the second floor afforded the best opportunity for escape while the rest of the capitol building was in turmoil. If the other Nightingale had gotten locked in with her, as she suspected, they would have the same idea. She only hoped they hadn't already effected their escape.

During a brief lull in traffic, Nahk slid out the door and into the foyer and made a brisk pace across the light stone to the stairway on the right. The blueprints she'd found had not shown where the saferoom was, but they had shown the way to the ballroom. She didn't encounter anyone as she took the first flight of stairs and turned at the landing, but a soldier was jogging down the steps toward her as she ascended the second flight. She nodded to him with the guard's head, and he didn't respond, his attention focused on getting downstairs as quickly as possible.

The second floor was dark, but Nahk heard voices and footsteps down the corridor to the left. They were still searching for the murderer, and she hoped they'd already cleared the rooms to the right. She passed three doors on the left before coming to the one she'd marked and memorized on her map. Five doors on this hallway led into the grand ballroom, and she pushed through the first one, stepping into a huge, black space. Her eyes adjusted to the gloom faster than an ordinary person's would have, and she could see the shapes and details in the dark, all tinted pinkish purple.

Round tables and chairs circled the dance floor, checkered with a bright-colored wood and varnished. That broad square took up most of the space in the room, with three grand chandeliers hanging above it. None of them were lit at that hour, but moonlight entered the room through the back wall of glass and aided Nahk's enhanced vision. Windows covered the entire wall, as the blueprints had indicated, but seeing it in person was a more marvelous sight than Nahk had imagined.

The capitol stood on a hill that dropped precipitously toward the sea, and through the glass she could see the waves sparkling and rolling toward the dark horizon. The sound of the everclanging bells reverberated through the room, and Nahk wondered whether she might have been able to hear the water crashing onto the rocks below if that blasted alarm had been silent.

"It was you, wasn't it?" The voice cut through the bells but was soft. It echoed from all the hard surfaces in the ballroom, monotonous and ageless. Where was it coming from?

Nahk dropped into a crouch and turned her head, searching for the speaker. He wasn't by the windows, not on the dance floor, nowhere near the doors to the hallway. Still bent low, she crept between two of the round tables, acutely aware that the Nightingale could be watching her even now, her form silhouetted against the white tablecloths that hung nearly to the floor. He'd be able to see through her Veil, just as she could see through other Nightingales', so she dropped the illusion. It didn't matter whether she hid her eyes here; they would shine just as bright for the other person. But that meant the other Nightingale would be showing his eyes as well. She just had to find them.

"Rhandolph," the voice said, and Nahk pivoted on her heel, ready to defend herself, but no one was there. "You killed her, didn't you? Who sent you? This was not part of our arrangement."

Nahk was about to backtrack her steps when she saw the eyes. They shone purple across the dance floor, and the Nightingale now stood before the great wall of glass, no longer in hiding. The moon backlit the man so that he appeared to her as a black and featureless form with glowing eyes. She could make out no details, despite her extraordinary night vision. With a start, Nahk realized this person had never been hiding. She just hadn't seen him. He stood at ease, waiting for her response. This Nightingale thought she was one of them.

Mirroring his casual demeanor, Nahk pushed up from the floor and stood between the tables. "You startled me," she said, her voice even and calm but projected to carry across the room. She walked toward the wooden floor, her steps sure and at ease, her thundering heart threatening to betray her.

"Who sent you?" the other Nightingale asked again.

"Rhandolph was unrelated to your contract," Nahk said. There was no way the Nightingale could know she'd also killed the other three politicians. She spoke carefully, so as not to give him any more information than he already had. "You should have been gone by now."

"I would have been if you hadn't brought the whole Tresa guard down upon us."

Nahk was midway across the dance floor now, her footsteps silent by habit, despite the hard, smooth surface beneath her. "We both know how to get out of here. It's not a problem."

The other Nightingale waited for her, and something about the way he tilted his head almost imperceptibly to the left stopped her in her tracks. "Who sent you?" he asked for the third time.

Had she slipped up? Not overtly, but her just being there was enough to make the other assassin suspicious. Her refusal to answer that simple question was enough to push the Nightingale from suspicion to certainty. Things were about to get ugly. Before it started, she asked, "Does Moghadan still live?"

Rather than answer, the Nightingale shifted his weight and pushed back one side of his dark coat. It was floor length, something Moghadan never would have allowed when Nahk knew him. But time had passed, and ways had changed. Perhaps Moghadan no longer cared whether his minions got tripped up in their own clothing. Perhaps Moghadan was dead, and his replacement had more of a penchant for the dramatic.

The Nightingale straightened his arms in a quick motion, and batons slid down from the coat's sleeves and into his palms. Nahk was already in motion, sprinting directly toward him. Before he could come at her, she arrested her own approach, planting her feet and letting the momentum of her leap unleash both knives from her outstretched bracers. The cables made a zipping sound that was barely audible over the clanging of the bells.

With perfectly synchronized flicks of the batons, the Nightingale swatted Nahk's knives away, the impact flickering a quick bloom of orange sparks. The Nightingale sprang forward then, and Nahk crossed her forearms in front of her chest as the cables retracted, and she gave them a hard pull, hoping to trip her attacker from behind. The Nightingale was too fast and leaped clear of the blades just as they swept beneath his feet. He was barely five feet away when the zephyr spools clicked as the knives slipped back into place. Too close for another attempt with them.

The Nightingale thrust the tip of a baton at Nahk's head, and she weaved to the right. She felt the breeze as the club rammed past her face, nearly close enough to brush her cheek. If she'd been an instant slower, it would have speared through her eye.

The second baton swung in from her right, and there was no dodging that one. It cracked into her side, and she stumbled left with the blow, hoping no ribs were broken. The Nightingale left her no time to think about that, as he spun with her and aimed another swing at her head. She ducked forward under that one and planted her hands on the floor, pushing herself up and ahead into a front handspring. She bent her legs as they passed over her head, and then she slammed them forward. Nahk felt the soles of her feet impact with something, likely the attacker's chest, and for once she wished for heavy boots with metal soles instead of her usual shoes made from light fabric and built for stealth.

The Nightingale grunted and staggered backwards a half step, but his hand closed around Nahk's right ankle before she could finish her movement. She had just enough time to marvel at his speed before the man gave a hard turn that dragged Nahk along with it and flung her across the dance floor.

Nahk spun in the air and threw one of her knives out, hoping to anchor her on something, anything, but there was nothing to catch her. She hit the floor with her right shoulder, and her skull cracked against the wood an instant later. She slid three feet on her side, her head already throbbing. Blazes, this person was not only fast but strong as well. Was that a natural ability, or is this what she would have been like if she'd completed the training?

Nahk rolled onto her back and kicked up to her feet as the Nightingale came at her again. Her vision blurred, and she stepped from one foot to the other to regain her balance. Then the assassin was upon her, both batons slapping at her in a flurry of blows. She blocked most of them with her leather bracers, but a few hits got through. Nothing hard enough to truly injure her, but the pain from the ongoing beating was adding up.

Nahk wasn't used to this. She was the silent and invisible blade that appeared only at the last second, disappearing again after making her cuts. She wasn't accustomed to this level of resistance, but she was not ready to admit she was outmatched.

Between two blows, she dropped the knife from her left bracer into her hand, and she followed the next block with a fast horizontal slice. The Nightingale saw it coming and leaped back just in time to avoid a slash across the chest. He swung the baton in his left hand, and Nahk danced back. The key was to stay out of the Nightingale's range, but not so far as to let him dodge the cables.

She jogged back two more steps and swept her left hand in a wide arc. The knife shot out of her palm and past the Nightingale, and she twirled her body to the left. The cable arced, and the blade turned back, coming in behind her assailant. He grunted once more as the small knife lodged in his back. For a thrilling instant, Nahk thought she'd drawn blood, but no. The Nightingale spun on one foot, throwing off the coat. Nahk's blade remained embedded, likely in a hidden layer of padding or soft armor. The assassin wrapped the coat tighter around the knife before throwing it to the floor, and then he leaped over the discarded pile, coming after Nahk again.

Nahk fell back another step and yanked at her cable, but the knife was stuck fast in that heavy coat and dragged it along the floor, slowing her retreat. She deflected two hits with her right bracer but had lost the ability to maneuver with her left hand tethered to the discarded garment.

The Nightingale took his chance, and Nahk knew the fight was finished. He spun the batons in both hands once before extending his arms wide to the sides and then swinging them together as if he were about to clap his palms together. Nahk's head was in the middle of that clap, and she managed to block the baton coming from her right. Her left bracer came up too slowly, weighed down by that cursed coat, and the length of the baton slammed into her left temple.

Nahk's vision reduced to a pinpoint, and her balance disappeared in the roar that filled her ears, drowning even the sound of the incessant bells. The ballroom tilted, and Nahk's head bounced on the wooden floor for the second time that night. Her body settled with her right arm pinned beneath her, and she knew she had to get up, but her limbs would not obey. She was about to die.

The Nightingale stood over her then, and her slowly recovering vision allowed her to see the two menacing eyes glowing down at her. She could still make out no features and knew nothing about this person. How humiliating, to be bested and destroyed by an absolute stranger. But the deathblow did not come. Not yet, anyway. The Nightingale squatted, his feet spread wide and both batons held in his right hand, that elbow resting on his right knee.

"Moghadan lives," he said. "What is your name? I'll report your death to him the next time I see him."

If Moghadan had trained this Nightingale, his lesson about not monologuing and finishing the target with all expediency had not stuck.

Without a word, Nahk closed her left fist over the still-extended cable and gave it the hardest tug she could muster. At last, the blade came loose from the wad of fabric behind the

Nightingale with a low chunking sound. Squatting over her, the Nightingale had no time to move or to even turn before the knife shot forward and between his feet. It caught at the back of his right foot and dug deep as it made the turn and sliced forward along the inside of that foot before finally finding its home in Nahk's bracer once more.

Nahk heaved a relieved breath and thanked Moghadan for at least making sure this fool adhered to the standard light footwear. Anything heavier, and the knife wouldn't have penetrated far enough. As it was, Nahk believed she'd nicked the bone.

The Nightingale howled in pain and fell backwards, away from Nahk. He tried to stand, but his right foot betrayed him. Nahk pushed her left hand against the floor and managed to crawl backwards half a foot and drag her right arm out from beneath her injured ribs. Perhaps they were broken after all. That still didn't matter. Only survival mattered at this point.

She flicked her right hand at the Nightingale and allowed that knife to fly free for only an instant before she jerked it back into its sheath. Just long enough for the knife's tip to puncture the assassin's right thigh as he tried to scramble to his feet.

Blood pattered on the floor now, and the roaring in Nahk's head had diminished enough for her to take satisfaction in knowing she'd seriously injured the Nightingale. She still might die, but she'd at least left him with scars he was likely to carry for the rest of his life. He would not forget this fight.

Nahk attempted to get her feet under her legs, but her head swam, and her balance was nowhere to be found. She tumbled to her hands and knees and shook her head, trying to clear it. Doing that brought a fresh wave of pain into her skull. It felt as if everything from her sinuses outward to her temple was ready to explode out the side of her head. Her vision dimmed once more, and as she tipped forward into unconsciousness, her last thought was that she would at least never have to kill again.

∽

Nahk was not dead, but the splitting headache she felt upon waking caused a small part of her to beg for peaceful obliteration. The rest of her shoved past that tempting surrender and reminded her she'd just wounded a Nightingale and learned that Moghadan was alive. She couldn't die yet. She had work to do.

The bells continued ringing, far overhead in their tower, and the droning tones vibrated her skull. How long would they keep those damned things tolling? For that matter, how long had she been unconscious, and why wasn't she dead?

Nahk pushed herself up to a sitting position and winced as a new pain shot through her left temple. She felt the side of her head and flinched again at the throbbing soreness her fingers traced. She was sure to have some lovely bruises on the left side of her face. Hard to hide those without makeup or a prolonged Veiling, neither of which sounded easy or pleasant just then.

She dropped her right hand to the floor and supported her weight there as her left hand felt along the right side of her torso. More bruises would grow there as well, but her prodding fingers found her ribs to be intact. At least one or two should have been broken after that beating she took, but she wasn't one to question this fortunate outcome. It was amazing that she had survived the encounter with the Nightingale, much less that she'd gotten away mostly unscathed after gifting him with some significant wounds.

Nahk stabilized herself until she was sure her balance was no longer compromised, and she moved up to her knees and then to her feet. It was still nighttime, and the moon remained in relatively the same position outside those enormous windows. It couldn't have been more than a few minutes since she'd passed out on the dance floor.

Why hadn't the Nightingale killed her?

The answer was a few feet in front of her, where a wide and dark puddle marred the wood. Servants would thank their blessings that the floor was so well varnished when they had to clean that up later, lest the blood leave a stain. From the size of the puddle, it was clear the Nightingale had fallen and then hesitated, likely to have inventoried the damage Nahk had done. But then the blood continued in irregular drips and splotches, trailing away from the puddle and toward the back of the ballroom. Toward the windows. Had the Nightingale flown into the night so easily? Nahk should have been dead, but perhaps she'd hurt the other killer worse than she'd realized.

Nahk took two uneasy steps to the left, rounding the blood without stepping in it. She kept her eyes scanning the room as she moved, anticipating a trap and an attack from the darkness, but none came. She shifted another step and stumbled over a lump on the floor. The Nightingale's coat lay in a pile where he had dropped it. That coat had likely saved Nahk's life.

"Have you checked in there?" The voice came loud and clear through the closed doors of the ballroom, jolting Nahk out of her careful progress. The guards had arrived, and they'd be storming into that room shortly. She had no desire to be present when they came inside. She already had too many lives on her hands for one night.

Nahk scooped the coat off the floor and threw it around her shoulders. As it went on, something dropped to the floor. Not armor or padding, as she'd guessed, but a small pack with a leather strap the Nightingale must have been wearing on his back. That's what she'd stabbed and what had held onto her knife. Nahk grabbed the discarded satchel and held it to her side. She wouldn't be able to fool more than three or four people with a Veil, but the coat would be a convenient cover, even if it was no good for fighting in. She followed the trail of blood off the dance floor and directly to the far wall, where the Nightingale had broken a single, large pane of glass.

From her research the previous week, Nahk knew the drop from the window to the ground was about ten feet. No problem for her when she was intact, but who knew how that would go when she might be nursing a concussion? No time to worry about that, when the alternative was having to slaughter a room full of Tresa guards. Nahk paused at the window and leaned out, her left hand holding the frame, and she saw the grass below, barely lit as the moonlight filtered through the surrounding trees. She knew that beyond the trees was a steep cliff that descended to the sea, and she'd considered coming and going that way by boat. She thanked her earlier wisdom for abandoning that plan. There was no way she could rappel down a cliff in her present state.

One of the ballroom doors banged open behind her, and she threw herself out the window, preparing to tuck as she fell. The ground rushed to meet her, and she came down in a roll, distributing the impact across her body. Not as graceful as she could have done it, but not bad, all things considered.

When Nahk came up from the roll, she had to steady herself with a hand on the rocky wall beneath the ballroom as her injured head threatened to tip her off balance. She could hear the waves now that she was outside, and a salty breeze cut through the trees, ruffling the long coat so that she had to pull it closer with her free hand. The other arm held the satchel pressed into her side, and its pressure felt strangely good against her bruised ribs. She made a quick search of the grass below the window, but there was no sign of blood. Where had the Nightingale gone? It was almost as if he truly had taken wing and swooped out the window without touching the ground. No time to dwell on that now, though, as he was likely too injured to be waiting to ambush her.

Those cursed bells continued ringing, louder than even the waves out here, but between the gonging tones she heard more voices above. Light bloomed from the windows, and she knew they'd lit the gas chandeliers. They'd be finding the signs of her fight with the Nightingale soon, if they hadn't already, and that would lead them straight to the broken window above. It was time to go.

The cliff curved west as Nahk moved north. She ran fully under the cover of the trees now, and it would have been impossible for anyone without her vision to see in that darkness. She was banking on that advantage as she sprinted the last few feet to the edge of the stone wall, which then descended away from the city's government sector. Nahk could feel her heartbeat thudding inside her sore head, and she forced herself to slow her pace and control her breathing before she made it to populated areas. She also had to deal with her eyes.

Nahk dropped to a knee and fished a small, hinged box from just inside her left bracer. Before opening it, she sat the Nightingale's parcel on the grass and wiped her right hand on the edge of the cloak. Not clean by any means, but that would have to do for now. Inside the case, two tiny reservoirs held water that she was careful to not spill. She dipped her right index and middle fingers in, one to each, and then lightly touched her fingertips to her eyeballs. The colored shields adhered to her eyes, and she blinked twice to settle them in place. She didn't entirely understand how those discs worked, but they hid the glow at the same time as they diminished her night vision. She would now have normal, dark brown eyes without needing a Veil.

She snapped the box closed and slipped it back into the bracer before picking up the satchel. She was ready if she encountered people now, and it didn't take long for her to find them. It was late, but the taverns were still open, and she pulled open the door to the one that looked least crowded. No doubt the whole city would be under curfew after word spread about the murders in the capitol, but for now it was business as usual, even with the bells of Bachali announcing danger. The drinkers and gamblers and hustlers and bards didn't care what might be happening in Tresa. Their loyalties were fluid, and they would blow in whichever direction this new wind might carry them. As loud as those places could be, Nahk needed light, now that her eyes were shielded, and a tavern was the most likely place to find it this late.

She stepped around a loud man holding a beer in each hand and found her way to a seat in a dark corner. It was on the opposite side of the room from the small stage where a bard was leading the patrons in song, but the singing was loud enough to make her head throb again.

"The birds flew in with wings of red,
Their sharp beaks aimed to take his head,
But he stood tall and firm instead,
A-ki-thar!"

Nahk groaned and dropped the packet onto the table in front of her. Every bard in every inn was singing the same songs now, all about the wizard that freed Klubridge. They knew to change the lyrics when Imperials came near, but the crowd seemed fearless on this night. She just wished they could save their bellowing for when her skull didn't already threaten to split itself in two. She tried to ignore the singing as she rested and considered her next course of action.

Nahk had to report her success back to Naecara, but taking a brief break to find out why a Nightingale was in Tresa wouldn't delay that message. Going after the Nightingale again on her own would, though, and she might not survive a second encounter when she was already battered from the first one. Dying in vain at the hands of one of them wouldn't do her any good, either, now that she knew Moghadan waited for her blades.

Nahk looked at the packet on the table and saw where her knife had punctured the front, just under the clasp. The clasp itself was intact, and Nahk undid it and opened the top. Inside, she found a pair of black leather gloves, cut through the middle. That's what her knife had held onto when she was fighting. She pushed the gloves aside and found a few papers folded beneath them. The first three were blank, parchment waiting to be filled. She recognized this paper as the kind Moghadan sent for contracts, slick and slightly oily and yellowish in color. The fourth and final paper was of the same stock but was covered in writing.

It was a contract, just as she suspected, and it had all the standard legal terminology Nahk had learned many years ago. She always found it ironic that such a culture of technicality and propriety surrounded the occupation of professional murder. The Nightingales were born of the Empire but lived both within and without it, so it made a kind of sense that even that order should be steeped in bureaucracy.

Her eyes traveled down the page and past all the standard requirements, disclaimers, and warranties until she reached the details about this specific contract. The high seat of Tresa, acting in accordance with and on behalf of the High Lord Peregrine and the Empire of Teshovar, sought the services of the Nightingales, to be rendered with as much expedience as possible. The terms of the payment followed, a combination of seri and some minor properties that would be transferred to the order upon completion of the contract. All very standard agreements for a high-value contract. Nahk skimmed the rest to see which politician or lordling Tresa might move against in secret but under the auspices of Imperial mandate. When her eyes tracked across the target's name, she huffed a noise halfway between a laugh and a gasp. She had to read it twice more before it made any sense.

Nahk looked around the tavern, wildly certain that everyone else would be reacting to the contract the same way, but they all remained focused on their mugs or their games or whatever ridiculous song the bard was singing now. Nahk packed the contents back into the satchel and shoved herself up from her seat. She could have used some more time to rest, but that was no longer in the offing. There could be no delay in getting this message to Naecara, and it was a long journey back to the Stormbreak Sanctuary.

CHAPTER 2

Caius Harrim swore and dumped his mug over the side of the ship. The craft pitched above a wave, and he staggered but kept hold of the cup.

"You'll regret that," Samira Tandogan told him with a raised eyebrow. "It's the only stuff that's kept me from being sick the whole journey."

"I'll be fine," he said and glanced up at the stars one more time before following her toward the front of the deck. The bow —was that what they called the front of a ship? Caius knew as much about sailing as he did about casting spells. Or about leading rebellions, but apparently that was something everyone expected him to learn.

Ergo Drass was already in his office when Samira and Caius came through the door. They'd been here with him before on more than one occasion, the most recent being when they had negotiated transport for the whole theater crew in exchange for an obscene amount of seri. That plan had fallen through, and Caius had returned to renegotiate the passage for all of them except himself, handing over a package full of Imperial blackmail documents as the payment. Caius didn't know what Drass would do with those documents, but he'd expected himself to be dead or at least in an Imperial dungeon by now, so he had given little thought to the old sea dog's motives.

The office was spacious and ornate, the walls covered in a red fabric that should have been mildewed after spending so much time at sea but somehow still held the same color Caius remembered from the first time he'd seen them. Drass' long desk, a menacing piece he'd found somewhere and affixed to the floorboards with huge iron nails, dominated the room. Sculptures of birds' skulls adorned the four corners of the desk, marking it as Imperial property, but Caius had never inquired about its origins. There was a black safe at the far side of the room, probably secured to the flooring like the desk had been. Caius had no doubt Drass had locked those blackmail papers inside as soon as he'd taken possession of them. Several lanterns swung from the ceiling on chains, but only one burned just then. Drass had ordered most of the ship's lights extinguished by the time Caius came up to the deck for the first time, having finally awakened from his involuntary slumber of several days.

Shadows shifted across the office as the single source of light rocked back and forth with the motion of the ship, casting an eerie sense of movement around the walls, ceiling, and floor. Caius craned his neck and watched a peculiar shadow scamper across the back corner of the room before sliding down to hide half of a wardrobe pressed against the wall to Caius' right. He was about to speak when his eyes refocused in the dark and met another pair of eyes staring back, flickering the reflection of the lamplight. Caius jerked back with a gasp, and that caused Samira to flinch as well.

Drass chuckled and beckoned to the figure in the shadows. "Don't let her scare you. I'm beginning to believe she enjoys doing that."

The woman came forward without a word, her gaze locked on Caius', and she stepped to the side of Drass' desk. She stood slightly shorter than Samira and scrutinized them with gray eyes flecked with blue. The little skin Caius could see around her eyes was light in color, with thick and tightly groomed eyebrows over them, perhaps light brown or dark blonde. That was all he could see of the woman, the rest of her face hidden behind a thin black scarf that revealed the shape of her nose and lips, but no details about either. The scarf disappeared around the sides of her head into a hood patterned in shades of patchwork brown that concealed her hair and neck, connecting to the long and shapeless robe she wore, also of the same patterned material. Caius could discern nothing about her age, her shape, or anything else beyond those piercing eyes.

"You're the spy," he said.

"Aether," Drass said, "meet Caius Harrim, known to the world as The Great Akithar."

Caius felt Samira stiffen next to him at the mention of his real name, but he touched her hand and nodded to Aether. "There are many people who believed you were me."

Her eyes darted from Caius to Drass. "Have you told him what is needed?" Her voice was even, emotionless, and without accent. She could have been from anywhere.

"I have, and Samira here has, but our good friend is the reluctant hero, as ever."

Her cold eyes were back on Caius now, and she hadn't moved otherwise since approaching the table. "Reluctance is a luxury we can't afford. You are a part of this now."

"They told me stories have spread. That people believe I defeated the Kites and that I—"

"It's true," Aether said. "The name of Akithar is on tongues throughout Teshovar, as far north as Tresa and as far south as Inport and beyond. The rebellion has never had a symbol like you. Someone the people can rally behind."

"I'm not a symbol," Caius said. "What they're saying isn't even true. I'm not even a mage."

Aether held his eyes for a long moment before she said, "Of course you aren't a mage. Let that be the last time you say those words to anyone."

"But—"

"Allow me to simplify your situation for you. What happened in Klubridge has made you a hero, and everyone knows your name. Many know your face by description. When you stood in that plaza, you wore no stage makeup, no magician's finery. They know your name as Akithar, but they know the face of Caius Harrim. They know your cohorts by name and description. Samira Tandogan. Apak Brem. Lizandra Daedan. Reykas

Kozic. Everyone knows all of you now, and that includes the Empire. Do you know what Peregrine does when he perceives someone to be a threat? And make no mistake, Caius Harrim. You are a threat. Do you know?"

Caius had no answer and turned his head away from Aether to look at Samira. She watched the exchange with her eyes wide and her lips pressed together so tightly the skin around them was white.

"There are already bounties on all of you," Aether said. "Substantial ones that won't be ignored. The military will be looking for you, too. There is nowhere in Teshovar that any of you will be safe as long as Peregrine rules."

"And what, you can keep us safe? You'll hide us until you bring down the High Lord?" Caius laughed at the absurdity of it. "He's immortal, and the entire world is terrified of him. What could you possibly hope to do to him?"

"Not the entire world." Caius thought her voice softened then, but it still did not come close to anything he'd call warm. "What do you know of the world?"

Caius frowned. Was this a trick question? Something to trap him in semantics? "I've lived in it for thirty-three years. I know a good bit."

"You know Teshovar," she said. It was a statement, not a question, and Caius felt the line deepen between his eyebrows.

"I do know Teshovar. What else is there?"

Aether's eyes moved to Drass, and he sighed as he slid a long scroll onto his desk. A prop in a performance they'd rehearsed for just this moment. Caius disliked surprises when he was not the one revealing them. The older man unrolled the paper and dragged small stone weights over the four corners to hold it open. The lamplight flickered across the yellowed parchment and the black lines and letters that covered it.

"A map," Caius said. A first glance at the map showed nothing recognizable. It was a crudely drawn illustration of a few islands, all the features out of proportion with each other. His eyes stopped scanning at the midpoint. Something about the central island's eastern coastline was familiar. It followed a path similar to...

"That's Teshovar," Drass said, jabbing a finger at the recognizable border, and the land bridge at Sandwallow became apparent, a tiny hook on the edge of the drawn island. No, not an island. A continent. A central continent surrounded by others.

Caius couldn't stop his hand from reaching to touch the map, as if it were some sort of ephemeral artifact. His fingers pressed against what must have been the Madigus Sea, the very water across which they traveled even now, and the map was tangible and real. He trailed a fingertip east and traced the edge of a foreign coast. "This is a world map."

"It is," Drass said and leaned against the back of his chair, his hands folded across his belly.

"Is this accurate?"

"It is," Drass said again and looked at the map. "And, before you ask, no, I won't tell you where I got it."

"All this is the blighted land, then," Caius said. When Peregrine rose to power, he'd scorched everything he didn't control. There was nothing left inhabitable, and there'd been nothing worth charting outside Teshovar. Nothing worth mapping meant there were no maps. "I never imagined there was so much out there. So much devastation."

"There isn't," Aether said. "None of that is true. Peregrine never scoured anything. There is no blighted land."

Caius frowned down at the map, and Samira took a step closer to the desk. "That's impossible," she said. "With this much land, there would be other people out there. Other realms."

Drass breathed a chuckle but said nothing.

"All of it is populated," Aether said. "All of it is alive."

"How?" Samira's mouth worked the word out as her eyes lingered on the map. "How is that possible?"

Drass sat forward again and propped his forearms on the desk. "When Peregrine took over, he cut off Teshovar. Killed who he needed to, drove out the rest. It had been ruled for generations as a monarchy by a dynasty called Tamrat. He assassinated the ruling family and hunted their descendants to extinction. He took Teshovar and made it his, and he walled it off from the rest of the world."

Caius blinked. "There's a wall?"

"Not a literal one. He keeps everyone in by making us believe there's nothing else out there. Nothing worth looking for. He tells us we're all alone after he burned the rest of the world," Drass said.

"But the rest of the world has to know we're here," Caius said. "They have to know about Teshovar."

Drass inclined his head. "They do, and they give us a wide berth. I've seen the foreign ships. They're shaped different, fly strange flags. I see them on the horizon, and they turn away when they spot us."

"They fear Teshovar's magic," Aether said. "In the early days of the Empire, the ones who'd been pushed out tried to return. Peregrine repelled entire armies, navies, and anyone else bold enough to sail west. He wouldn't let anyone in, and he wouldn't let anyone out, so the world moved on without us."

"That's impossible," Caius said. "After all this time, out of all these people across all this land, there would have to have been someone who could face Peregrine. Someone with magic to rival his."

Drass shook his head. "Teshovar's unique. There's magic elsewhere, but not like here. Either Peregrine took Teshovar because of its magic, or it has its magic because he took it. Nobody's sure about that. But what they are sure about is that the magic is weaker everywhere else. Rarer."

Caius glanced at Samira. Was she thinking the same thing he was? In a world where magic was so rare that it was confined to a single continent, and on a continent where the population of mages had been decimated, Samira was among a dwindling few. With her abilities to both heal and protect, she was now among the most powerful people in the entire world.

"Do you see your importance in this, Caius Harrim?"

He looked back to Aether and waited.

Her pale eyes held his. "This is not just about ridding Teshovar of the Empire. This is about bringing Teshovar back into the world."

He studied what he could see of her for any sign of deception, but she was hard to read. She'd probably have been just as hard to read, even if he'd been able to see her entire face. Drass was more discernible, and his eyes showed no lies. This was the truth. This was the world. Whether it was the rocking of the ship or Caius' own legs going wobbly, the room pitched just enough for him to place a palm flat on the desktop to steady himself. He looked at Samira again, and she swallowed. "I believe them," she said.

He did, too.

"None of this answers my question," he said, looking back to Aether. "Peregrine has kept Teshovar isolated for centuries. Maybe longer than that. How can you even imagine you could defeat him?"

Aether spoke slowly, as though to a child. "The rebellion has a plan, Caius. A plan that many believe has a better chance of working than anything anyone has tried before."

"Many believe," Caius said. "But you don't. You don't think it'll work."

"What is the plan?" Samira asked after Aether offered no reaction.

"That's not for me to divulge. But the rebellion needs allies if it's to work, and we can't get those allies unless the people of Teshovar have hope." She took a step closer to Caius, and he resisted retreating to maintain his distance from her. "You give the people that hope."

"That's all you want from me?" Caius asked. "To wave at the people and act the part of a hero while you go against an omnipotent god king?"

"You won't wave at anyone. You will be hidden and safe at Stormbreak while we enact the plan. All we need from you is your name while you remain in protection. As long as Teshovar knows you live and frustrate the Empire's efforts, our chances increase."

Caius' head had begun aching midway through the conversation, and he closed his eyes and wiped a hand down his face. "I don't know. I just…"

Drass cleared his throat and said, "There's nothing to know. What other choice do you have? You can't go anywhere else."

Caius looked to Samira. "We could, though. We could go into

the mountains. Or the swampland near Acleau. There are so many places we'd never be seen. We could head east and leave Teshovar entirely. See what's on the other side."

Samira was looking at the map as he spoke, and even as he waited for her response, he knew what it would be. At last, she looked up at him, and her eyes were tired, as tired as he felt. "We can't," she said. "We'd spend the rest of our lives waiting for them to catch us. And how would we live? All we know is performing. There's no stage you could stand on in Teshovar without the Empire coming for you. And it's not just you or just me. We're responsible for all the others now. Oreth and Fairy, too." Her face dropped again. "Aquin."

Caius pressed his fists against the top of the desk, and he stared down at them, feeling the frustration swirling in his gut. He let it play out and forced a slow breath in and then out. He turned to Aether. "What information are you bringing to the rebels? What caused all this madness that pulled us into it?"

She blinked back at him and finally moved, shaking her head just once. "No. That's not for me to tell, either."

"Of course it's not," he said and sighed. "What happens, then? We're your prisoners until you win your war?"

"You are not prisoners," Aether said.

"So we're free to leave," he said.

"I would advise you not to do that."

"Caius," Samira said, her voice a warning, this time with her hand squeezing his arm.

Caius glanced at her face again before looking back to the spy. "What happens to us if you fail? If your plan doesn't work?"

"Then you'll either be dead or we will no longer be there to protect you. Neither option is one you want."

Caius pulled his hands back from the desk and paced past Samira. This was ludicrous. They were theater performers. They knew nothing about rebellions or politics or wars. None of them should even be on this ship. But they were, and it was all because of their loyalty to him. Their belief in him. How ironic that he had tried to protect his friends for more than a decade by pretending to be a magician, and now it was that very attempt that had dragged them all into the wrath of the Empire. He'd gotten them into this, and he was the only one who could get them out. The only path was clear, as much as he hated it.

He faced Aether again. "We all need new clothes. Our friends need the assurance that this will not be permanent, that they can have lives after this is done."

Aether bobbed her head in one slow, stilted nod. "Done."

Caius nodded back, and the weariness took hold. He'd been sleeping since Klubridge, but the exhaustion still had him in its grip. He placed a hand on Samira's shoulder, and she looked to him. "I'm going back to my cabin. If you accidentally throw the spy overboard while I'm sleeping, I won't tell anyone."

When Caius awoke, the ship was still rocking, but his headache was gone. How long had he been asleep? He lay for a quiet moment and listened for voices but heard none. It must have been the middle of the night, but he was wide awake. He sat up on the small bed and slid his bare feet off the side, checking the floor beside the cot before standing. Showing up at the Stormbreak Sanctuary with splinters in the soles of his feet would make for an inauspicious entry into the rebellion.

He was midway to standing when he stopped and looked back down at the floor. The cabin was completely dark, and no light shone from under the door, but he had been able to make out the flooring with no trouble at all. Even now, he could see his pale feet resting on the wood, as if lit by some colorless illumination. He blinked and turned his head around the cabin and could see the chair across from the bed, where Fairy had sat when he first woke on the ship. He saw the tiny desk built into the wall next to the head of the bed, and he could make out the door to the cabin and its metal handle. All of it was faint but visible to his eyes.

Before Caius could ponder this visual phenomenon, a shock of pain shot through his belly. His arms wrapped around his midsection, and he leaned forward in agony as his stomach groaned a wail unlike any he could remember hearing from it before. How long had it been since he'd eaten? The Imperials had fed him breakfast in his tower cell the morning before they took him down to the plaza, but there had been nothing since then. And how long ago had that been? Two days, three? He was no longer certain about time after his long slumber following his nearly dying at the hands of the Herons. One thing of which he was quite certain was that he needed food, and badly.

Once the stomach cramp had subsided, Caius stood and steadied himself. He still wasn't used to being at sea after having spent his entire life on land, the past decade of it mostly in one city. With his legs firmly under him, he padded to the cabin door. Surely the ship had a kitchen, or did they call it a galley? A mess? Somewhere he could find something to eat, at least. As if summoned by his longing, the scent of something delicious wafted into the room. He couldn't identify it, but it seemed both savory and spicy, and his stomach gurgled once more in response.

More eager than ever, he grabbed the handle to the door and gave it a pull. It wouldn't budge. He tried pushing, but it remained in place. Was the door stuck, or was he locked in his cabin?

"Aether," he mumbled, and the name came out as a croaking whisper. The spy had either locked his door or otherwise secured it shut. There was no question.

"Hey!" Caius yelled at the closed door and pounded on it with his fist. "I'm locked in here!" He hammered at the wood until he was sure either his skin or the door would split, but neither gave way. He growled in frustration and backed away. The scent was stronger now, permeating the cabin as if it were taunting him.

"Hey!" he tried once more, but there was no answer. Surely someone could hear him. Where was Samira? Or Apak, for that matter. Not everyone on the ship was in league with Aether. Had she incapacitated everyone else as well?

Another cramp derailed that line of inquiry, and Caius fell to his knees, his arms wrapped around his stomach until the pain passed. What was this hunger? It was keener than anything he could remember. He'd been hungry before, but this was a completely foreign experience. The hunger felt like a being inside him, gnawing to get out. To get at whatever it was that he could smell.

Still on his knees, Caius looked toward the cabin door but realized that wasn't where the scent was the strongest. It came from the other side of the cabin, through the opposite wall. Wasn't that the outside of the ship? There should have been nothing but sea and sky through that wall, but he was positive whatever he was smelling was just on the other side. Caius clambered across the floor and pressed his cheek against that wall, listening for a sign of something other than the water, but he heard nothing. But the smell intensified until he could stand it no longer.

Caius turned his head and pressed his face against the wood and pushed his mouth into the boards at the bottom of the wall. His teeth elongated into fangs, and he gnawed through the timber, slivers of wood falling off his chin.

"Caius."

His eyes came open, and it was dark, but he knew he was in the cabin, still in bed. His hand flew to his mouth, and his fingers probed his teeth for any signs of damage or wood. What in the ageless realm was that? A dream, to be certain, but it had been so bizarre and yet so realistic.

"Caius," the voice said again in a whisper, just to his right, near the chair. Faint light came into the cabin through his door, now standing open past the foot of the bed. It was still dark out there, but the moon and stars provided enough of a scant glow for him to see Drass was the one who had woken him. If he truly was awake this time.

"I'm up," he said, pushing up onto his elbows, and his voice sounded more like his own. Not the guttural growling he remembered from the dream. And, while he realized he was hungry, it wasn't the ravenous torture his dream self had felt. It was a reasonable protest from his gut, complaining about not having been fed in recent memory.

"Take these," Drass whispered and pressed something into Caius' chest.

Caius took it with one hand but couldn't make out any

details in the gloom. It was a package of some sort, something wrapped in fabric, or perhaps thin leather. "What is this?"

"It's what you gave me. The blackmail from Klubridge," Drass said and glanced at the doorway. "I don't know the spy. Never met her before this trip. I know you, though, and I know you'll do what's right."

"What's right? What do you mean?" Caius was fully awake now and sat up in the bed to try and look at the parcel he now held in his lap. It was still too dark to see it, but he recognized the familiar weight of the papers he'd brought Drass a few days ago. A week ago? His sense of time eluded him, even outside of the dream.

"I'm taking you to an abandoned dock in a cove west of Tresa. That's as far as I go when I make runs to Stormbreak."

"You've never been to the rebels' hideout?"

"I have not. Now, listen. Carriages will take you all from there to wherever the rebels are set up. You will keep that parcel with you, and you won't let the spy know you have it."

"Why don't you trust her?" Caius asked.

"Do you trust her?"

"No."

"Well, then," Drass said, as if that explained everything. "When you get to Stormbreak, give those documents to a man named Yannis Heriot. He leads the rebels, and he's one I do trust."

"Yannis Heriot," Caius said.

"He's former Empire. He'll know what to do with that information. The spy might give it to him. She might sell it to him. She might keep it and sell it to the Empire. Who knows? You take it to Heriot."

"How do you know I'll even go that far? I could slip away and disappear into the wilderness, never to be seen by rebels or Imperials again." And the truth was, he'd considered doing exactly that.

"I know it," Drass said, "because you're another one I trust." He sat back on the chair and sniffed twice before saying, "I know I've taken you for a ride once or twice, and you've had reason to not trust me. But I've always liked you, and Samira too. You're good people, and I know you'll do the right thing, just like I know Heriot will. We might not see each other again after you leave this ship, so you need to know that."

Drass didn't wait for a response. He clapped Caius on the shoulder and slipped back out of the cabin, pulling the door shut behind him. Caius sat in the darkness, now entirely awake, and he weighed the packet of contraband in his lap. He rubbed at his eyes and leaned his back against the wall behind the bed. It appeared he was going to be a rebel after all, at least for now.

∼

The ship dropped anchor at an old dock in the middle of the northern wilderness, just as Drass had told him. It was a cold morning, and Caius believed they had to be somewhere at least as far north as Tresa. The chill wind whipped around him as he stood on the deck with Samira and Apak, watching the sailors work. It had to have been late autumn by then, but it felt like they had sailed directly into winter. No snow touched the trees that surrounded the landing, but they would soon be dusted in white. There had been enough warm clothes stowed on the ship for all of them, and Aether had assured Caius she'd fulfill her end of the agreement by seeing they received more once they got to Stormbreak. Caius rubbed his hands together and blew into them, hoping some thick gloves would be in the offing.

The newcomer, Magra, joined them at the railing and stood silent, her arms hugged around her body inside the heavy brown shawl she wore. Magra was a halflock Samira had found and freed while breaking Aquin out of Imperial custody back in Klubridge. Caius remembered her as one of the three Imperial mages the Kites had stationed in his cell to prevent him from using his magic. He glanced at her now and saw a cunning intelligence in her eyes that was missing while she stood sentinel over him. Caius had to admit Magra was at least as good an actor as he was.

Caius knew he'd missed a lot while he was in that cell and then afterwards when he was unconscious, and he was learning more about what had happened with every new day. Some of it he was glad to hear, some not so much. More than a little of it was horrifying. He wanted to talk with Apak about that in private, but there hadn't been a chance while they were on the ship. Bringing it up while stuck in a carriage with him, Samira, and Magra wouldn't be the right time, either. Perhaps once they reached the Stormbreak Sanctuary, wherever or whatever that was.

Another carriage had already taken the rest of their group away. There had been little time for plans or goodbyes as Aether hustled Lizandra, Reykas, and Fairy down the ramp and off the ship. Oreth had elected to go with them, as had Aquin. Neither Apak nor Samira had said anything about those departures, but Caius could read plenty in their faces as they stared down the dock at the dirt road that disappeared into the forest. Their group was fracturing, just when it most needed to hold together.

Aether wouldn't tell them where the sanctuary was located or even how long it would take them to reach it. Based on the supplies strapped to the back of the first carriage that left, he guessed it was far away, at least as long a trip as the journey by sea had been. And so it was. After the four of them departed in the second carriage, Caius lost track of time again. They rode for days and nights, sometimes stopping in old, dilapidated barns for the night. Other times, they rode on through the darkness, forced to sleep facing each other on the jolting seats of the carriage. The sleep was fitful, and Caius knew he dreamed, but none of the dreams stuck with him upon waking like the nightmare on the ship had done.

The air grew colder the farther they went, and Caius knew they had to be headed even farther north and west. What was north and west of Tresa? Not much that he knew of, aside from frozen mountains. Accompanying the four passengers were a driver and what Caius presumed to be a guard who sat next to him up front. Those two men never gave their names and never spoke to their passengers unless they were telling them to get in or out of the carriage. They grumbled to each other while changing the horses at some of their stops, though. There were fresh horses waiting with grooms in remote stables that must have been part of the rebel network, and the carriage left those barns faster than it had arrived.

It was just after leaving one such stop that Apak looked across the carriage at Caius and asked, "What are you hiding?"

Caius had just woken from another restless sleep and had to blink twice at his friend. Apak's black beard had grown slightly longer than Caius was used to seeing it, and the gray patches in it showed more prominently now. Caius rubbed a hand across his own chin and felt the stubble that was now turning into a proper short beard of his own. When would he have the chance to shave again?

"What do you mean?" Samira asked from the bench seat next to Caius before he could answer for himself. They faced forward in the carriage, and Apak sat next to Magra on the bench facing them. The pale morning light flickered through the frost-speckled windows in the doors on either side as they drove onward through forests and hills that were turning into craggy rock formations. The sunlight seemed weaker this far north as it tried to push through the frequent clouds.

Apak nodded toward Caius and touched the rim of his small spectacles as they threatened to slide down his nose. "He has been carrying something under his coat since we left the ship. I believed he was waiting for an opportune moment to share it with us, but I am beginning to believe he has no such intention. And so, I am curious." He looked back to Caius. "What are you hiding?"

Samira looked at Caius then, and so did Magra. They all had their eyes on him, and it felt like an accusation. Like he'd betrayed them. "Apak's right. I was going to tell you, but I hadn't yet." And why hadn't he? Too late to worry about that now. He pulled back the right side of the wool coat Aether had given him and untied the green scarf he'd bound around his waist. Out of the bundle came the packet of papers. He handed it across the car to Apak.

"What's that?" Samira asked, her voice calm but her eyes showing hurt. He really should have confided this to her, even before they'd left the ship.

"It's the blackmail papers from Klubridge," he said. And then, to Apak, "The ones you took from the library."

Apak had opened the packet and riffled the edges of the documents with his thumb. He looked up from them to Caius. "Why do you have these?"

"Drass gave them to me the night I first awakened, after Samira and I met the spy. He doesn't trust her, so he didn't let her know about them. He told me to hide them until we reached Stormbreak and then give them to a man named Yannis Heriot."

They rode in silence for a moment as Caius' companions considered what he'd told them. Apak was the first to speak. "Do you know anything about this Yannis Heriot?"

"Drass said he's the leader of the rebellion, and he trusts him." After a brief hesitation, he added, "He used to be an Imperial."

Apak snorted. "Ergo Drass is a pirate and a scoundrel."

"Why doesn't he trust Aether?" Samira asked.

"He thinks she's too mercenary, and he doesn't know her. She might not deliver the documents, or she might try to sell them back to the Empire. Who knows?"

"I am uncertain about this, Caius." Apak closed the packet and handed it back. "But I trust you will consider your actions carefully, as they impact all of us."

Magra rolled her big, dark eyes toward Caius, and he felt a prickle of unease at the base of his neck. She could read minds, the one aspect of her magic the Empire had left intact after it hollowed out and muted the rest of her abilities. "The surly one's right," she said. "Better to work with the one you know than the one you don't."

"We know nothing about Aether," Caius said. "Not even what she looks like or who she really is. All we know is that she's a spy and has information she's bringing to the rebels. Probably to this Yannis Heriot, so it's all the same if I wait and give these papers to him myself."

"We know the Empire has no love for the spy," Apak said. "They upended Klubridge to find her before she could leave with whatever information she carries. That does not seem like something they would do if she were likely to betray the rebellion."

Magra nodded at that, but Caius felt his fingers close tighter around the packet. He looked at Samira, and her expression had softened. He still recognized disappointment in her eyes, but she said, "Keep them hidden for now. You don't have to decide anything until we get there. After we've met this Heriot person, then you can decide what to do."

Caius nodded at that and looked at Apak for a response. His friend opened his hands and gave a small shrug before settling back into his seat to watch the wilderness passing outside. Caius exhaled and bundled the papers back into the scarf and bound the whole package up in his coat again. The four of them were exhausted from the long trip, and conversation didn't resume after that until Caius leaned forward and peered through the glass in the left-hand door, out his side of the carriage.

"Snow," he said. The others leaned toward the windows as well. A thin layer of white now topped the scraggly bushes at the sides of the road. As the carriage continued its bumpy way between them, frozen flakes whipped past the glass, individual snowflakes occasionally sticking to the windows for an instant before blowing away again. They were well and truly into the mountains by then, the road angling upward and the forest to the left quickly dropping away to leave a steep hill. With every passing moment, that drop was becoming less hill and more cliff.

"I haven't seen snow since..." Samira trailed off, one hand against the glass on the right side of the carriage.

"Ordport," Caius finished for her.

"Has it been that long?"

"Longer for me," Apak said. He watched through the window next to him but did not comment further.

"What about you?" Caius asked Magra. Her big eyes flicked back and forth as she tracked the passing landscape.

"I don't know. I haven't seen snow in my recollection," she said. "Not since I've been like this."

Caius knew she meant since she's been a halflock. "How long ago was that?"

She shrugged and drew the corners of her small mouth tight. "Hardly matters now."

"And there's nothing at all left from... before?"

She chuckled and shook her head. "Wouldn't be a very effective procedure if they left anything, would it? I'm lucky to have my wits at all."

Caius remembered the version of Magra the Empire had sent to his tower cell as being anything but intelligent. But that had been the game she'd played for however long the Empire had held her. She'd pretended to be like most of the other halflocks, robbed of their memories as well as their wits. He imagined life was easier for her when her keepers expected less of her. She had probably been afforded more freedoms, when the Imperials didn't think she knew enough to make good use of it. She'd kept up the charade until Samira had broken into the keep and given her a way out.

The snow continued falling, at first light and then growing in intensity as they climbed higher. That night, the carriage stopped in one of the old barns that Caius was growing to recognize as rebel waypoints. As the group sat on the ground around a perfunctory fire and prepared to eat another dinner of dried rations, Caius asked the driver, "How much farther is it?"

The man, wide with a thick, dark beard over what looked to be a face heavy with lines and wrinkles, eyed him for a long moment before mumbling, "Not as far as it was." He turned to go back to tending to the horses, but Caius stopped him again.

"Did our friends come through this way ahead of us?"

The man shook his head. "Different way." He didn't wait for any more questions and headed back to the carriage.

Having the carriages take different routes made sense. The location of Stormbreak was the rebellion's most closely held secret. Changing up the paths and varying the directions could make it harder for Imperials to track caravans with any consistency. Reykas and the others could already be at Stormbreak by now. The thought gave Caius some comfort as he imagined his friends in a more hospitable setting than this rundown barn with brittle straw covering the rocky floor. The driver's answer to the first question was less satisfying, though. Was it another week? Another month? How much longer would they be living out of a carriage before reaching their destination?

The answer came sooner than Caius expected when Samira nudged him around noon the following day. They had been back on the road early, and he had fallen into a light sleep with his head resting against the window. He jolted as he woke and nearly banged his forehead against the glass, but Samira's hand on his shoulder steadied him, and his gaze followed her finger toward the window.

Sometime while Caius slept, the left shoulder of the road had fallen away, and the trees now stood far below, a layer of fog making them hazy from that distance. The road was now a narrow path clinging to the side of a sheer cliff face to its right. From within the carriage, it was impossible to see the top of the mountain on the right side. As the cliff face curved to the left ahead, so went the road, visible all the way around the great gap until it disappeared with a distant right turn into a split in the mountain. Just past that split rose a strange and massive rock structure that looked naturally formed but loomed above in the unmistakable form of a massive bird.

"Crowspire," Apak said, leaning across Magra to see the formation.

"I've heard of that," Caius said. "An early Imperial garrison, wasn't it?"

Apak nodded, continuing to watch the bird structure as the carriage made slow progress toward it, the horses treading with care on the soft snow that now covered the narrow road. It looked less like a bird as clouds shifted and sunlight hit it from a different angle, but there was no denying the rough resemblance of a massive creature sitting sentinel at the end of the roadway.

"One of the earliest Imperial structures," Apak said. "When Peregrine was establishing his rule, he built fortresses and outposts throughout Teshovar. Crowspire was the northernmost."

"Why would he build something all the way up here?" Samira asked and leaned across Caius to look down into the canyon below. "There's nothing here to protect."

"The fledgling Empire constructed this keep thousands of

years ago. Much has changed since that time. There could have been settlements here. Cities that would have stood in opposition to Peregrine's rise," Apak said. "Cities that are here no longer."

Caius said, "The Empire hasn't used the castle here for a long time. Hundreds of years, probably. That's what I know about it. Do you see the face of the bird?" He pointed toward the top of the rock structure, and Samira nodded. "Part of that collapsed during a storm. The way I heard it, the rocks destroyed the castle, and the Empire abandoned it."

Samira ducked her head to look at the giant birdlike formation once more before she settled back on her side of the seat. "And now it's the Stormbreak Sanctuary. The rebels came up and claimed it as their own."

"It's smart," Caius said. "The Empire isn't likely to check its own castles when it's looking for the rebels. Especially castles that are supposed to have been destroyed."

"Especially ones up here in the bum end of nothing," Magra added.

Caius watched Crowspire loom larger as the carriage closed the distance, and he knew they had nearly completed the journey. Somewhere around that curve to the right would be the remains of the castle and whatever the rebels had done with it to build their Stormbreak Sanctuary. A sudden dread gripped him, and he said, "We have to stick together."

Apak had been looking out his window but turned toward Caius. "Pardon?"

"When we get there, we don't know who or what we're going to encounter. We have to find our friends and remain united if we're going to get through this. Just like we always have."

"Of course we will," Samira said. Apak nodded his agreement before turning his attention back to the window. Magra's only contribution was another rolling of her eyes.

The carriage soon made that turn to the right, and they were in the shadow of the giant bird. It seemed even more immense as they rode beneath it, and a chill ran down Caius' spine. He shifted in his seat and pressed a hand against the packet of blackmail material hidden beneath his coat as the horses pulled them onto a covered bridge built from mortared stonework. The wheels didn't jostle as much here as they had on the roads leading to this point, but Caius felt more unsteady than ever. The sunlight disappeared as they passed through the tunnel-like construction, abruptly reappearing when they emerged from the other side.

And then, with no further warning, the journey ended. The carriage rolled through the arched doorway of a coach house, built from the same rocks as the bridge. It came to a halt as soon as the back of the carriage had cleared the entrance. The car shifted as the driver and guard climbed down, and the doors opened outward on both sides.

"Out with you, now," the driver said, his voice as much a terse grumble as ever.

Caius climbed out the left side, followed by Magra, while Samira and Apak came down from the right. Caius wrapped his arms around himself and tucked his hands into his armpits. It had felt cold inside the coach, but it was nothing like the freezing temperature outside it. A gust of wind blew snow through the open doorway, and Caius' chill of worry mingled with a genuine shiver of cold. He stepped back to the door and looked down the path toward the tunnel they'd crossed. A single horse had just emerged from it and trotted their way. Caius squinted through the falling snow and stared in confusion as the rider came into view.

"Aether?" he asked as she pulled the reins once she was inside the coach house. Had she been following them this whole time? How had she made the trip that far on her own, exposed on a single horse?

She answered none of the questions in his mind. Instead, she slid down from the saddle, her entire head and body still covered with a hooded robe, this one gray but covered in similar patterns to the brown one she'd worn on the ship. "This is Stormbreak," she said and handed the reins to a teenage girl wearing a thick, black coat with mismatched stitching holding it together. "An attendant will take you to your rooms. I'm sure you'd like a night in a normal bed."

Caius hadn't even considered that he would be getting

proper sleep that night, but after Aether mentioned it, he couldn't think of anything else. He glanced back to find Samira as a man came through a door on the other side of the stable. His tight-fitting black suit showed him to be thin and around Caius' height, if not an inch shorter. He had dark hair that looked to be shoulder length, but he'd pulled it back from his long and angular face and bound it into a tight ponytail behind his head. His skin was pale, nearly as white as the snow falling outside, and his dark eyes moved from one newcomer to another, as though he were taking inventory. His eyes locked with Caius' for a moment, and his thin lips twitched at the corners, nearly a smile but not quite. And then his gaze moved on to Aether, and the smile was gone.

"Welcome back," he said to the spy, ignoring everyone else for the moment. "I hear you have something for me?"

"I have something for Naecara," Aether said. "What she does with it is none of my concern."

Caius felt the lump under his coat where the blackmail documents pressed into his body, and he kept his cold hands tucked away, afraid that any movement would betray his parcel. Was this Yannis Heriot?

The long-haired man's mouth closed, and he stepped back to allow Aether past him and out the door through which he'd entered. He watched her go, and his eyes lingered on the empty doorway for a few seconds after she'd left. At last, he sighed and turned his attention to the newcomers, the almost-smile more forced now. "My name is Micah Vaino. Welcome to the end of the Empire."

CHAPTER 3

"General, the Council is gathering."

Tenez Bekam had been staring out the window on the second floor of the Robdwell Building in the government square of Aramore. Politicians, clerks, and military mingled below, already wearing their warm coats and scarves and hats against what promised to be an early winter. Few paused to talk in the large quad formed by the surrounding legislative houses. The grass remained green, but the leaves had already dropped from the trees, and the civil servants' paces along the paved pathways had quickened with the falling temperatures.

"General, the—"

"I heard you," Bekam said, pulling his eyes away from the window to look back at the page dressed in black with white sleeves showing beneath her vest.

She ducked her head and said, "Apologies, sir."

Bekam looked back to the window to check his reflection in the glass. He ran a finger along his thin mustache and smoothed his hand along the right side of his black hair, ensuring the part in the middle was sharp and defined. The colors of his uniform were muted in the window, but he knew the signature deep blue of the Aerie like he knew his own cold blue eyes. Like the commanders who reported to him, Bekam wore the emblem of the Kites on his chest, but the silhouette of the bird with its wings outstretched on his uniform matched the yellow of his tabard's trim, unlike the black bird on the chests of every Kite beneath him. He lowered his hand from his face to touch his chest for an instant before turning to the page.

"Lead me," he said, and the page bobbed another nod before moving through the door.

The general knew the way to the council chamber, of course. He walked those same hallways every time he came to the building for the quarterly meeting with the Security Council. Wandering into the meeting without an escort would be unseemly for someone of his station, so he followed behind the page as she headed down the hallway and wound toward the assembly. And the quarter had not yet ended. This mid-term summons was an unusual one, but there was only one thing the Council could want to discuss. This would be about Klubridge.

The Council was ostensibly an oversight committee for the martial workings of the Empire, but everyone knew the thing it kept most secure was the Imperial purse. It took seri to run the Kites, the Herons, the regimented military, and all the other official operations of Teshovar, and the Security Council was the source from which the money flowed. The fountain that filled the Council's chalice was taxation, and it was hard to collect taxes from a city in revolt. The rebels had held Klubridge for nearly a month now, and these puffed-up bursars would want to know what Bekam was doing about it and when the money would start flowing again. If only he had a simple answer for them.

When they reached the chambers, the page went inside first. Bekam waited just outside the door until he heard her announce him: "General Tenez Bekam, Director of the Imperial Kites and Martial Appointee to Aramore."

He waited the additional breath, as was appropriate, before coming through the familiar doorway and entering the chamber. The room was tall and circular, the walls formed from pale stone that had been cut and smoothed until it reflected the light of the gaslamps hanging in clusters from the ceiling. A gilded railing rounded the room, matching the gold of the wall sconces that provided additional light.

A long table built from dark wood and fashioned into the shape of a ring was the focal point of the room. The Security Council already sat in their positions around the table, and Bekam moved to his customary seat nearest the door, separated from the table where the ring was broken with a wide gap near the entrance. The seat reserved for those testifying before the Council was hard and deliberately isolated, sitting apart from the committee and adrift in the room with no table or desk before it. The Council had designed the arrangement to be intimidating, and Bekam couldn't fault them for exercising what little power they held over him. They all knew he'd leave the meeting with his requested allocation of seri granted. If the Council wanted to feel superior to him for a few moments while they went through the formalities, so be it.

Bekam paused, his hand on the back of the chair, and frowned at the empty second chair next to his own. This was the first time there'd been an additional seat before the Council. He sniffed and gave the room a brief bow, not more than a slight bend at the waist, and he sat on that hard chair to the left of the empty one.

Fifteen chairs lined the outer edge of the table, but it was unusual for more than five of them to be filled for the routine quarterly meetings. Today, eleven of them were taken. Bekam recognized most of the faces, but at least three were new to him. He tried not to study the Council's expressions, their postures, their glances at each other and at him, but his curiosity was too great. He settled for watching them with as much discretion as he could muster. Why were there so many? Why was there an additional chair beside him, and what was that shared look on so many of their faces? Was it consternation? No, not that. It was hunger. They were here with intent, and he was the meal for which they'd been whetting their appetites.

The chamber door opened behind Bekam with a clank, and the Council's attention shifted behind him. Bekam half turned in his chair to see a new page standing in the doorway, his head raised proudly as he announced the newcomer. "General Qae'lon, Director of the Imperial Herons and Martial Appointee to Bria."

LIZANDRA'S DEEPEST FEAR

Bekam exhaled and managed to not curse when the ethereal form of the sorcerer glided into view behind the page and then into the Council chamber. The man was tall and thin, nearly gaunt, and his pale skin stretched across his protruding cheekbones to an ageless smoothness. His white hair hung past his shoulders in a straight, shimmering sheet that turned silver when he came through the door. Qae'lon wore one of his customary robes, this one off-white from his throat down to where it nearly touched the floor, with golden ornamentation decorating the panel that descended the middle of the front. The mage's white fingers, long and slim, were all that showed of his hands, concealed within his voluminous sleeves.

"General Bekam." The voice pulled his focus back to the Council, and he inclined his head to the speaker, a woman sitting diagonally to his left and wearing a rumpled tweed suit. The Council rarely arrived in uniform, but their colors tended to align with their positions or home districts. Her suit was threaded with dark purple, and Bekam would have recognized the designation of Ordport, even if he hadn't already known the speaker.

"Commissioner Prusik," Bekam said, ignoring Qae'lon as the other general lowered himself onto the neighboring chair, the fabric of his robes settling with a shushing whisper. As much as Bekam loathed the mage, having him here in the next chair was a good sign. The blame for Klubridge was to be spread, then.

Prusik stared at Bekam over the half-lenses of her eyeglasses, her round jowls hanging motionless and her too-red lips pressed together so that her mouth looked like a rouged dot in the pasty skin midway between her nose and her chin. She was waiting for him to say something more, but he waited her out. He knew better than to feed into whatever this was. He would learn what he could before speaking again.

The voice that broke the silence came from the right. Bekam looked toward the other side of the table ring, where a heavyset man with a shaved head and a short gray beard sat. This one did wear his uniform, all in black and bearing medals of rank from Military Command. Dark freckles marked his light brown skin, and his heavy cheeks pushed his eyes nearly shut so that Bekam could see only the slightest glimmer between his eyelids. Bekam knew this man, both from countless meetings with the Council and from campaigns to the west when they both were younger men.

"We've received word from Tresa," the man said, his voice pitched higher than one might guess, based on his stature.

Bekam's eyebrow twitched. Not about Klubridge, then. "My courier sent the payment, as ordered, General Milev."

"You haven't heard, then."

"Heard what?" Bekam asked. Qae'lon made a soft noise that might have been a chuckle, but Bekam ignored him and kept his attention on the Council.

"The leadership in Tresa were murdered," Prusik said. "Shortly after they signed the contract with the Nightingales, they were all slaughtered in the capitol building."

"All—"

"All four of them. The mayor, the guildmaster, the treasurer, and the chief lawmaker." Prusik scowled and stared at Bekam. What kind of response did she expect?

"I've heard nothing of this," he said.

"No one has," Milev said. "The Nightingales informed us last night. The deputy mayor is trying to contain news of the assassinations until he's installed replacements for the bureaucracy. Even now, he is scrambling for supporters in secret."

"Talonak will install his own people to push his own agendas," Bekam said. "Tresa will descend into liberal anarchy. Was this his doing?"

Milev shook his head. "Unlikely. According to the Nightingales, it was a rogue member of their own order. They're taking this into their own hands and will hunt down the assassin."

"For free?" Bekam asked and huffed. "That hardly sounds like the way of the Nightingales."

"The Nightingales do nothing that does not benefit them," Prusik said. "They seek the assassin to recover the contract. She stole it after it had been signed."

"Surely it's still binding," Bekam said. "We paid them what they asked. The land deeds are in transit even now."

Prusik waved at the air. "None of that is of concern. The

contract stands, and the Nightingales are honoring it, but the document itself is in the assassin's hands now."

Bekam blinked, finally understanding. "My name is on it. I'm the one who signed for the Empire." He looked from Prusik to Milev and back again. "Do you think she's coming for me?"

"Unclear," Prusik said. "We merely thought it prudent that you be informed. This is not the purpose of our meeting today. Our primary concern is the disposition of Klubridge."

Bekam opened his mouth to speak again but shut it just as quickly. The possibility of having a Nightingale after him was a terrifying notion, but there was nothing he could do about that at the moment. Klubridge was another matter.

It had been nearly a month since the rebels had taken the city, and reports were still arriving about how things had gone wrong. Bekam had been piecing it together, but the shape of the events was becoming clearer with every refugee who found their way to him in Aramore.

Prusik said, "We understand you sent the Scarlet Kites to the city, and the entire unit was lost when the city rebelled. Is this true?"

"I sent the Scarlet Kites, and we believe none of them survived the insurgency. None of them have returned to us or sent communication, at least."

"And why did we have to learn about these developments from secondary channels? Why did you not report this to us yourself?"

Bekam wanted to remind Prusik that he reported to the Council only when it was time for them to pay him, and he otherwise took no operational orders from them and owed them no explanations. Instead, he said, "My apologies, Commissioner. I was waiting to get a clearer view of what happened before informing you. I didn't want to bring an incomplete report."

Prusik pressed her glasses up the bridge of her nose and tapped her pencil against the desk three times before saying, "This seems like the moment, then. Regale us, General. Why did you send the Scarlet Kites to Klubridge?"

How dare these glorified accountants speak to him as if he

were beneath them? On any other day, he could have any of them jailed for such insolence. On this day, however, he inhaled slowly and quelled his disdain. "As you know, Commissioner, we had received intelligence that a rebel spy was sowing discord in Karsk."

"We are aware," Prusik said, her voice dry.

"You're also aware of the information the spy stole. We were told they were bringing this information to a contact in Klubridge. From there, they would take it to the Stormbreak Sanctuary. I sent the Scarlet Kites to intercept the spy, both to prevent the transfer of information and to learn the location of Stormbreak."

"And did you learn that location?"

"We have yet to receive a confirmation that—"

"Did you ascertain the identity of the spy?"

"Again, we have yet—"

"Answering in the affirmative or the negative will suffice, General."

Bekam's eyes narrowed. This was more than a mere inquiry. They were scapegoating him for what happened in Klubridge. "Negative," he said.

"You at least prevented the transfer of information, I suppose?"

"That is unclear at this time," he said. Of course the information was transferred. The rebels owned the whole blasted city now. If they wanted to accept information from a spy or take the spy to Stormbreak or treat them to a four course dinner atop the Imperial tower, there was very little he or anyone else could do to stop them.

"Why did you send the Scarlet Kites?" This time it was a man almost directly to Bekam's left, sitting near the closest end of the table, just before the break in the ring. Bekam certainly knew this one, dressed in a blue doublet, the cream-colored sleeves of the shirt underneath exposed. This was Teka Lacar, an ambitious soldier Bekam himself had raised into the government only four years earlier. So much for appreciation and loyalty.

"As I just told the commissioner, I sent the Kites to Klubridge to intercept the spy."

"You misunderstand me, General," Lacar said. "My question was not why you sent Kites to the city, but rather why you sent the Scarlet Kites. Klubridge is under the purview of the Azure Kites, is it not?"

"It is," Bekam said. "I had reassigned Commander Tereth and his unit to Karsk to locate the spy and quell the growing unrest."

"But Tereth could not identify the spy," Lacar said.

Bekam forced his jaw to relax and said, "His Kites quelled the rebellion in Karsk, but the spy appears to have escaped the city."

"And so your blue Kites failed as well, though not as spectacularly as the red ones," Prusik said, staring at him now through her thick lenses. Qae'lon crossed his legs, and Bekam managed once again to keep from acknowledging his presence.

"What can you tell us about this Akithar person?" Milev asked. "Is he a mage? A rebel?"

Of course they knew about Akithar. Anybody who'd been within earshot of a tavern that month knew about him, the courageous wizard who faced down the wicked Kites. "Akithar worked as a stage magician in Klubridge. He is a mage and appears to have hidden his true abilities behind his stage performance."

"How was he connected to the spy and all this other nonsense?" Prusik asked, and Bekam bristled at her tone but did not rise to the provocation.

In truth, it wasn't clear how Akithar was connected to everything. He couldn't have been the spy without traveling, and, by all accounts, he'd been a fixture in Klubridge's theater district for at least ten years and rarely, if ever, left the city. But placing him as the spy's contact made little sense. The contact was the one providing passage for the spy out of the city and into Stormbreak, again a role that necessitated travel. So how did Akithar fit into the equation? He was unquestionably an insurrectionist, but Bekam suspected he was not directly connected to the spy or any of that business until Nera Mollor and her incompetence pulled him into it. That wasn't an admission Bekam was prepared to make, so he said, "Akithar seems to have been operating a rebel cell within the city. He was not the spy or the spy's direct contact, but he was instrumental in organizing their meeting. He had been working in the shadows for many years until my Kites identified him as a threat."

"Do you believe he is still in the city?" Lacar asked. It was a reasonable question and one Bekam had been asking himself.

"That is unclear," Bekam said. "Once the rebels occupied Klubridge, it became difficult to insert Imperial agents and gather any sort of valuable intelligence."

Milev's gaze shifted to the side, toward the accursed wizard sitting next to Bekam. "General Qae'lon. You had Herons in the city at the time it fell, yes?"

Bekam kept his eyes ahead, but he saw Qae'lon nod in his peripheral vision. "I did, General Milev. General Bekam's Kites requested Herons in order to silence the mage Akithar."

"How many did you send?"

"A company of four, along with the requisite guard."

"And how many returned?"

Bekam's heart thudded at that question, and he couldn't keep his eyes from darting to the right, toward Qae'lon. The wizard took his time in answering but finally said, "One, so far."

"So far?"

"There could be others. I have learned of only one confirmed killed in the chaos."

"What does your Heron say?" Prusik asked. "What happened in Klubridge?"

Qae'lon was silent for a beat too long, and Bekam angled his head toward the other man. The mage caught Bekam's eyes and gave him a knowing smile, his white teeth barely visible between his thin lips, before he said. "It would seem Akithar rained destruction upon the city, killed many Imperials, and incited the revolt."

"Is he still in Klubridge?"

"That seems unlikely."

Prusik sat back in her chair, and Bekam watched Qae'lon from the corner of his eye. The wizard was lying. If a Heron had come back to him, Qae'lon would know the truth. He'd know Akithar had been no mage, and the city had fallen because of Nera Mollor's incompetence. The blame for the revolt lay on the decimated shoulders of the Scarlet Kites, and Qae'lon had to know it. Why was he withholding the truth? Why wasn't he throwing Bekam to these eager wolves?

Milev cleared his throat, and Bekam's attention shifted back to the general, who now sat forward, his forearms resting on the table. "There are many questions to be answered," he said, "and they all seem to begin in Klubridge, which begs the question. What is your solution for retaking the city, General Bekam?"

Bekam's mouth would have dropped open if he hadn't clenched his jaw. He kept his voice even when he responded, but he could feel the edge in his reply and was certain the Council could hear it as well. "General, you know that is neither my purview nor my priority. The Kites maintain the order of the realm by ensuring no mages go unaccounted for. They find carriers of magic and carriers of disease. They provide safety to the populace and to the government. They are not an army equipped for holding sieges or overthrowing enemy invaders."

Milev's eyes never left Bekam's. "I am indeed aware of the Kites' duty and mandate. At this moment, anarchy reigns in one of the Empire's most profitable harbors. Countless loyal citizens are held hostage by the rebels. The longer Klubridge remains in open rebellion, the more tempting it will be for other cities to slip the Imperial yoke as well. An unpaid Empire is not a happy Empire, as I am certain you can understand. And an unhappy Empire's purse is apt to remain closed. How will you win the city back?"

Bekam looked from Milev to Prusik and then to Lacar. To all the faces that waited for his answer. They were threatening his funding and his very rank. Surely this was a bluff. He ignored the bead of sweat that escaped down the back of his collar and said, "With support from a battalion—"

"You will have your Kites as your support," Prusik said. "Further resources are unavailable until Klubridge returns to Imperial control. How will you win the city back?"

They expected him to conquer a city the size of Klubridge with a handful of mage hunters and no siege engines. How many Kites could he even pull away from their usual duties, and how long would it take for them to mass outside Klubridge? Even if they could block the roads, there was the harbor to worry about.

There was no way he could set a blockade without naval units, and it was clear the Council was affording him no favors in this task.

"No?" Prusik said, something like satisfaction in her voice, and she looked at the other man. "General Qae'lon? What is your plan for retaking Klubridge?"

Bekam's eyebrows raised. This was it, then. Whichever of them could reclaim Klubridge would earn the Empire's amnesty, and the other would bear the blame for the revolt. He opened his mouth, but Qae'lon was quicker.

"I am confident I can present a solution to the Council within a month's time."

"As can I," Bekam said quickly. "I will meet with my advisors, and you will have my plan within..." He hesitated but then added, "Within the month." It was a ridiculous promise, and everyone in the room knew it.

"Unnecessary," Prusik said, placing her pencil on the table before her with precise care.

Bekam frowned. "Commissioner, I assure—"

"General Qae'lon says he will present us with a solution, and I am inclined to believe him. His task will be the reclaiming of Klubridge."

The implication hung heavily in the chamber. Bekam didn't want to rise to the provocation, but the question had to be asked. "And my task, Commissioner?"

Milev was the one who answered. "You will return to your original mandate. You sent your Kites to Klubridge to find the spy that would lead us to the Stormbreak Sanctuary. You will pick up the thread where your Kites dropped it, and you will locate the sanctuary."

Bekam swallowed his urge to protest. The Empire had been searching for the Stormbreak Sanctuary for decades, and the Council now expected him to deliver it to them. The retaking of Klubridge was suddenly the more appealing prospect.

"You will find the rebels, and you will destroy them," Prusik said. "You will report your progress to us within a month's time."

That's how it was done, then. Whichever of them had not accomplished their task by the end of that month would be

LIZANDRA'S DEEPEST FEAR

blamed for what happened in Klubridge and politically ruined, if the Empire didn't decide it would be more expedient to quietly execute them instead.

Teka Lacar's eyes were down now, and he was thumbing through some papers. Bekam felt Qae'lon's eyes on him, but he didn't acknowledge the gaze. Prusik's eyes shifted between the two men, and she gave Milev a subtle nod.

"We will reconvene in one month."

∼

Bekam shoved through the front door of the Elliswell Building, a short walk across the quad from the Security Council's assembly room. Since being elevated into his present position, Bekam had made a habit of taking that walk only four times a year. They always enjoyed waving their momentary and monetary superiority over him, but this was the first time he'd felt substance behind their implications and threats. This was the first time he'd considered the ramifications of the Council not granting him the Kites' budget for the winter. As secure as he always felt at the top of the chain of command, the past hour had shown Bekam exactly how narrow the gap was between being funded and losing everything. All it would take was one quarter without adequate seri to pay his commanders and their subordinates, and all the respect he'd grown in them would blow away like today's leaves on tomorrow's breeze.

The directness of the threat had caught him by as much surprise as the Council's pitting him against Qae'lon had done. He was used to dancing around implications and subtle hints from the bureaucracy and rival officials, and he was accustomed to being the most direct person in the room. Not this time. He'd managed to keep his civil tongue, lest he make the situation even more dire for himself. When interrogated, he'd told what he knew about Klubridge and the fate of his Kites. He'd told a version of it, at least.

Now he needed a plan for picking up the path of the spy that had eluded the Scarlet Kites, and that necessitated his understanding what had truly occurred in Klubridge after Nera

Mollor and her soldiers arrived. It was the urgency of that question that drove Bekam up the stairs to his office, two steps at a time.

Cillan waited in the anteroom and looked up from a ledger he'd been studying as Bekam burst through the door. The smaller man's yellow eyebrows twitched beneath a clammy forehead, and he scooped his eyeglasses off his desk and shoved them onto his face. With the faint mustache that matched his brows, Cillan looked every bit the bureaucratic tool that he aspired to be. Bekam withheld any fondness for that type, but he knew Cillan was unfailingly loyal to him and, therefore, was useful.

Cillan held out his hands to take Bekam's overcoat and carried it to the hooks to the right of the door. "Did all go as expected, General?"

"It bloody well did not," Bekam said and halted in the middle of the room, just before the white lacquered door to his own office. "Is she in there?"

"She is, sir. She's been waiting for the better part of two hours."

"Who else knows she's here?"

"No one, sir, just as you ordered."

Bekam nodded and reached for the doorknob before stopping again. He half turned to Cillan and said, "Send for the marshal as well."

Cillan bowed his head, showing the pink patch of scalp from which his wispy hair had already retreated. "I already took the liberty, and he should be here shortly."

Bekam grunted his response and finally turned the knob and pushed the door open. Its bottom scraped lightly across the dark blue carpet within, and he pushed it shut behind him as he entered. A woman stood from the chair in front of his desk and turned to face him. She was small, barely as tall as Cillan, and slim, but she held herself straight and strong, and no one would mistake her for anything but a soldier. Her dark eyes sat wide apart, the lower lids pronounced, and her mouth was narrow, the upper lip larger than the lower and pressed into a tight frown.

Bekam guessed her age to be somewhere around twenty, maybe even younger. She was a fresh recruit, but she looked as if she'd had a rough time of it. Her black hair was shoulder length and crinkled at the ends on the left, as if it had been burned. A freshly healed cut ran from the outer edge of her right eyebrow and angled back toward her ear.

"Your name is Shoy," Bekam said as he made his way around his mahogany desk and stood before the blue upholstered chair behind it.

She turned to face him as he walked, nodding but not sitting again. "Kalina Shoy, General. I was assigned to Commander Mollor and was training with her Kites."

"You say you're a Kite, but you come to me with no uniform."

She glanced down at the baggy gray trousers she wore and the long-sleeved green shirt with a tear down the left arm. "I'm sorry to come to you in this state. I had to abandon my uniform in Klubridge. They were killing anyone who looked like an Imperial."

"They?"

"The citizens. The city went into revolt, and they all turned against us. I barely made it out alive." Shoy's right hand strayed toward the cut in her left sleeve, but she dropped it back to her side before it got there. "They were killing everyone. Kites, Herons, even the local constabulary."

None of this was news. Everyone had heard about Klubridge falling into chaos and freeing itself of the Empire's order. Bekam knew all of this, but there were details he didn't know. "Where are your fellow Kites, Shoy?"

"Dead," she said, and her head dropped. "I think they're all dead."

"All killed when the city fell?"

"Kela died before that. And Eyral, too." She looked up again, and her brows drew down in anger.

"It was the wizard, Akithar?" Bekam asked, settling into his chair. He watched for her response from beneath his dark eyebrows.

She shook her head. "He was at the center of it, but Akithar was no wizard."

The statement hung between them long enough for Bekam to take a breath and release it. The sureness in Shoy's face left no room for argument or denial. He'd already known Akithar was no mage. The news from Klubridge had been scant, but that much had reached him. And, if a Heron had truly returned alive, Qae'lon knew it as well. Akithar was no mage, and the entire campaign that sent Klubridge into chaos had been in folly.

"Akithar was the man I sent the Scarlet Kites to find," Bekam said, leveling his gaze on this woman's face. "A highly skilled band of soldiers, all trained specifically to contain mages, and a single man undid all of you? This is greatly disappointing."

"It wasn't him, but he led the ones who did," Shoy said. "They are mages, but he is not. But he is ruthless, all the same." She stopped to turn her head away, something like disgust playing at her mouth. "He burned Eyral to death, and he arranged for Kela to be torn apart in the streets. I believe he even killed a young boy who worked for him. He murdered him in front of Lieutenant Gieck."

This was the first he'd heard about a boy being killed. Bekam had arranged the assignment for Gieck, and it was his own fault the lieutenant had been in Klubridge to begin with. He was sure to hear from Gieck's wealthy parents before long, and he needed answers for them. "What about Gieck? Did Akithar kill him as well?"

Shoy hesitated, and Bekam felt the edge of something new, something the rumors hadn't told him. At last, she spoke, her eyes cast down. "No, General. Commander Mollor killed him."

Bekam exhaled and sat back in his chair. Over the past month, he'd heard many stories coming out of Klubridge, but this was indeed a new one. "Why would she do that?"

"I don't know, sir, but I saw it happen, right there in the city square. The ritual had already happened. The Herons tried to take Akithar's powers, but it didn't work, and his friends started blowing up buildings and killing people. Everything was in confusion by then, and I was too far away to hear what they said, but I saw the commander and the lieutenant fighting. It didn't last long, but she knocked him down and cut his throat. She disappeared into the crowd after that, and I tried to help him,

LIZANDRA'S DEEPEST FEAR

but it was too late. He died there on the cobblestones." Her lips trembled, and Bekam thought at first that it was from sadness, but then he saw the renewed anger in her eyes. "She murdered him, General."

It had been bad enough that the Scarlet Kites, entrusted with enforcing the Empire's will and suppressing magic, had fallen and lost the whole city to insurgents. That was enough to condemn Bekam as an incompetent leader. But the truth that they had begun murdering each other even before Akithar and his band had their way with them? That was more than Bekam could tolerate. More than his career could tolerate.

"Aside from Lieutenant Gieck, all the others were killed by Akithar, yes?"

"By him and by his people. He had many people working with him."

"All of them mages?"

"Some mages, some who weren't. He ran a theater in the city, and Commander Mollor believed his whole troupe was in league with him. There was an acrobat girl who worked for him, and I saw her in the plaza that day, fighting the Herons. He also had a woman who wasn't a mage working for him. Samira Tandogan."

Bekam glanced past Shoy and saw Cillan standing in the doorway, scribbling the name into his ledger. He'd slipped in behind Bekam and closed the door again so soundlessly Shoy didn't even seem to know he was there. "Who else?" Bekam asked.

"There was another woman who worked for the university library, Aquin Mirada. She was in some sort of relationship with Tandogan, and she was likely working with Akithar as well. The commander arrested her not long before everything fell apart."

"Tell me about that. How did everything fall apart?"

Shoy sighed and looked past Bekam, staring out the large picture window behind his desk as she spoke. "Lieutenant Gieck was the one who arrested Akithar. He caught him in a pub in the city, and they took him back to the Henburn Estate."

"The castle," Bekam said.

"Yes, sir. Commander Mollor believed he was a mage and

stationed three halflocks in his cell to make sure he couldn't use his magic to escape. Then she called for the Herons."

"Four were sent, I understand?"

"Yes, four. They took Akithar into the plaza that day. Commander Mollor wanted it made public, so they shackled him to a platform, and the Herons started the ceremony."

Bekam had seen that ceremony performed four times. It was never pretty, but it was always effective. Less effective when the subject was not a mage, apparently. "What happened then?"

"I don't know, sir. The Herons were chanting, and it looked like it was working. Akithar collapsed on the platform, and I heard one of the Herons say he was no mage. That was when his people came into the plaza and began their attack."

He could make this work. "They attacked the citizens?"

"No," Shoy said. "They attacked the Kites, the Herons, anybody in a uniform. That's what started the people revolting. Everyone was coming after us. And then they created a monster."

Other survivors of that day had described a monster, but Bekam had taken it to be the product of mass hysteria and panicked imaginations. "You saw this creature, then?"

"I did. It was enormous, like a huge cat, but its head was like a snake. Some sort of reptile, at least. It was loose in the square in the middle of the crowd."

Bekam snorted. "What you're describing is a chamir. I'm certain you're aware chamirs do not exist outside of children's stories?"

Shoy inhaled and nodded, looking less certain now. "I know what I saw, General. I don't know how it was made or what happened, but I saw the creature. I saw it kill Asil, and it ate one of the Herons."

"Asil?"

"She was another of our Kites, General."

"Ah." Bekam sat back in his chair and propped his right elbow on the arm. He ran his index finger across his thin mustache for a moment before asking, "And what ultimately happened to the commander?"

"She died."

"How did she die?"

"It... It was in the plaza. Everything was in chaos, and the monster was loose. One of Akithar's people was blasting apart buildings and—"

Bekam stopped her with a gesture. "You didn't see her die, did you?"

"I... No, General. But she was at the central dais when the beast attacked there, and there was a huge explosion. One or the other got her."

The general stared at Shoy, and she held his eyes for a moment longer than he'd expected she could tolerate it, but then she broke away and looked at the floor. He held his tongue, waiting for more from her. Given sufficient time and silence, there was always more.

"That's all I know," she said at last, still studying the deep blue carpeting. "I barely made it out of the square, and I exchanged my clothes shortly after. Then I headed for Aramore. I couldn't send a bird ahead of me after the city had fallen. There were no messengers left, and I couldn't get into any of the governmental buildings, anyway. So I left."

"And it took you a full month to make your journey."

"It was difficult, sir."

Bekam studied her sullen face, her beaten posture, and her ragged appearance. That was all she could offer him, at least for now. "Cillan," he called past her, and the secretary's head bobbed up from his note-taking. "Is the marshal here?"

"Just outside, sir," Cillan said, motioning through the door.

"Call him in, will you?" Bekam instructed. And then, to Shoy, "You say Commander Mollor, Lieutenant Gieck, and all your fellow soldiers were killed in Klubridge. It would seem you are the final Scarlet Kite standing, eh?"

"I believe so, sir."

"Therefore, by battlefield rules, the Scarlet Kites are yours to command, such as they are. Congratulations on your promotion, Commander. Note this down, Cillan."

"I am, sir, and I will file the papers."

Shoy looked up from the carpet, once again meeting his gaze, this time with confusion. "General?"

The marshal was at the door now. He was a thick brute of a man and reminded Bekam of Gieck, though hopefully less psychotic. Bekam shifted his eyes from the doorway back to Shoy. "Field regulations also specify that the ranking officer in a unit bears responsibility for the actions of the unit. As such, the failure of the Scarlet Kites now is your failure. Compounding that unfortunate turn of events, you also abandoned your fellow soldiers and discarded your uniform, thereby proving yourself a traitor to the Empire. It is for these crimes that I order your arrest."

And then, to the marshal, as the man's huge hand closed on Shoy's trembling shoulder, "Take her to the cells with the rest of the Klubridge survivors."

~

It had been a week since the meeting with the Council, and Bekam was no nearer anything like a plan. Picking up the trail in Klubridge would require getting into the city to investigate. The rebels wouldn't look kindly upon an Imperial regiment marching through their streets, and Bekam wasn't about to go there alone, even in disguise.

Klubridge was an enormous city with no fewer than eight gates in its walls. The rebels had organized themselves enough to keep all eight entrances covered, and they had blockades and checkpoints at all of them. Even if Bekam managed to get inside the city, he might be stranded there in enemy territory. He'd have no better luck with the harbor. The Kites were not a seafaring force, and it was clear he could expect no support from the Imperial Navy. Laying siege to Klubridge would be impossible.

A direct assault, then? A charge through one of the gates with the full force of the Kites? Bekam snorted, and his breath blew out in a white vapor in the cold air. Driving through any of those eight gates was an excellent way to leave his forces trapped and susceptible to being flanked and obliterated. No matter which way the battle went, it would be a bloodier affair than he could afford, and fighting from street to street was never advisable. And once the fighting had started, trying to get any sort of information about the whereabouts of the spy or Akithar and his gang would be folly.

Time passed him at a sprint, and every day that ended without a strategy was another day Qae'lon could be advancing on the city, poised to bring his victory to the Council. The mage had promised that he'd deliver the city within a month. Was that even possible? Was he simply posturing, waiting to see what Bekam would do?

Not for the first time that week, Bekam cast a wary glance over his shoulder. Just as he had his agents at work, Qae'lon would have his own informants prowling through Teshovar. Bekam shuddered and tugged his coat tighter, wrapping his arms around his body.

The first flakes of snow fell that day, and the lawn in front of his mansion shone with a dusting of white, glowing under the moonlight as Bekam approached the front walk. A tall fence of black iron surrounded the property, the gates topped with spikes that curved outward. It had been a long time since anyone had been foolish enough to try and gain entrance to the grounds over that fence, but Bekam still felt safer with the barrier than he would have without it.

Being a man of some prominence in the Empire and having engineered many a downfall, Bekam knew his destruction was the topic of dinner conversations across tables throughout the Imperial city and beyond. No one had shown the temerity to move against him in recent years, and it seemed doubtful that any of his rivals would be direct enough to try to assassinate him in his home. All of them had heard some version of the fall of Klubridge by then and expected they'd see the demise of his career in a month or so without their acting at all. In that expectation, Bekam looked forward to disappointing them.

Two guards, both wearing blue uniforms of the Aerie, stood at the front gate, one inside and the other out. In the dark of the early evening, they were indistinguishable from each other, their faces hidden in the shadows beneath the narrow brims of their regulation hats and their shapes made blocky and indistinct under the bulk of the winter uniform coats. Even though they were out in the cold on a night-long post, this was still a cushy assignment. There was little chance of their having to do anything more than watch the gate or patrol the grounds, and these guards got meals and pay beyond the experience of most others of their rank in Aramore. They stiffened at Bekam's approach, and the one outside dipped his head in a courteous bow. "General, we weren't informed you'd be home tonight."

What the guard meant to ask was whether Bekam's wife knew he'd be home that evening. These household guards the Empire had assigned were more hers than his, and he spent more nights in the apartments at his office than he did under this roof. Marjiel enjoyed the luxuries being the wife of a high general afforded her, but he suspected what she enjoyed the most was having to see him only when absolutely necessary. The feeling was mutual, but having a guard treat him like an interloper in his own home still raised Bekam's hackles.

"Open the gate," Bekam said, "and report to Otero in the morning for reassignment."

The guard had already reached for the gate, and the additional order gave him pause for only a moment. Bekam suspected he was weighing the likelihood that the general even knew who he was. Apparently having decided, the guard gave a quick nod as he pulled the gate open and said, "Sir." The truth was that Bekam didn't know any of his wife's household staff, much less this guard unlucky enough to be assigned to gate duty on the rare night when the general came home.

Bekam walked through, and the guard on the inside kept their head down and their eyes on the ground as he passed. They stayed out of his way, but how long would it be before the two were gossiping to each other, complaining about him behind his back? He paused a few steps inside the gate and looked over his right shoulder at the second guard. "You'll report to Otero, too. Tell him I said to find both of you something more entertaining to do."

Would they go to him? Maybe so, and maybe not. Either way, Bekam felt better as he continued his march up the pathway to the house. If the guards feared him enough to go to Otero, Marjiel would have to replace two of her staff, and causing her minor inconveniences had become something of a hobby over the last few years. If they didn't follow his orders, they'd live in fear of his recognizing them later and punishing them for their insubordination. Either outcome was acceptable.

His house stood three stories tall, the outer walls built from quarried stone the builders had ground and compressed into huge bricks. The mansion had to have been three or four hundred years old, but careful maintenance and occasional repairs had kept it looking less than a century old. The grand wooden doors at the entrance were considerably newer, and the one on the right swung inward as Bekam approached. An old man in butler's livery waited in the doorway and gave a slight bend at the waist. "Welcome home, sir. Shall I take your coat?"

Bekam shrugged out of his long jacket and dropped it into the butler's hands as he came inside. "I trust my wife is here?"

"She is, sir. She sits with the young mistress in the library. Would you care for dinner?"

"Not now." Bekam passed through the foyer for the first time in a month and noted the new tapestries hanging at the ceiling and an urn in the far right corner that he didn't recall seeing before. He tested Marjiel by toying with her staff, and she got him back by spending his money with reckless abandon. At least his family's portraits still hung in the hallway instead of in some midtown pawn shop. Ordinarily, he might allow himself to engage her in this petty game, but he would not be distracted from his purpose that night. He didn't relish meeting with her, but she was as invested in the success of his career as he was, and there was no denying the strength of her cunning. As much as they might despise each other, they made a formidable pair.

Despite its being called the library, bookcases lined only one wall, just to the right of the doorway. There had been more, but Marjiel had seen them carted out to other parts of the house and a fireplace built into the outer wall of this room, where histories of the realm previously collected dust. Making the changes had annoyed Bekam, but he hadn't protested. He hadn't known then that the dismantling of the library would be her first play in their ongoing game of challenging and usurping each other's power, long before she had a daughter just to spite him.

Leonie sat on a black rug near the fireplace, her long black hair pulled back from her pale face but otherwise looking nothing like her mother. She had none of Marjiel's beauty, and she'd shown no signs of developing intelligence like either of her parents. If not for the fortune she would inherit, Bekam had no idea what the Empire might make of his daughter.

She wore a dark dress with a white collar that looked more appropriate for a younger child, but Marjiel oversaw their child's wardrobe, and Bekam had neither the knowledge nor the inclination to interfere. Leonie had been staring at the dark wood paneling on the nearest blank wall with her dull blue eyes when he came in, but her head cocked toward him as he entered. "Papa!" She leaped up and ran toward him but stumbled over her own feet and sprawled onto the floor midway there.

Bekam sighed and placed a hand on the back of her head as she got herself back up. He'd have thought it was a ploy for attention if she hadn't been like this for all of her eight years. In addition to being homely and dense, Leonie was also a clumsy little girl. "Go to the kitchen. Cook will have you some sweets."

Her father now forgotten, she bounded out the doorway with a whoop. She'd probably knock both of her knees on the way there, but nothing would keep her from the pastries.

"Must you encourage her? Nanny has a hard enough time getting her to bed without a bellyful of jam."

Bekam watched the empty door for another moment before placing his hands behind his back and facing his wife. She was more than a decade younger than his forty-six years but looked as if she had stopped aging altogether nearly a decade before that. That evening, she wore a black gown with white trim that nearly matched her daughter's. Her unlined skin was white, like Leonie's, but her eyes were a deeper blue. Leonie's were icy like her father's but failed to discern a quarter as much as his had at her age. Why had she inherited those ghastly eyes and not any of his other traits?

Marjiel stared at Bekam over the top of the book she'd been reading, waiting for an answer. He saw her face touched by a hint of powder, and she even had rouge on her lips at this hour, and at home, no less.

"Expecting company?" he asked.

"Clearly not you," she said and slid a purple ribbon between the pages before closing her book and placing it on a side table. "What do you want, Tenez?"

He always hated this part in the exchange. Marjiel was intelligent enough to know it was coming, so he dispensed with equivocation and got straight to it. "The Security Council meeting didn't go well last week."

"Oh?" She raised an eyebrow but otherwise remained unmoved, her forearms resting on the arms of her chair.

"They've been trying to sort out the mess with the Scarlet Kites since it happened, and—"

"And you're their scapegoat. Interesting."

Bekam watched her face as her eyes flicked to the side quickly, and then back to meet his own. That was as long as it would take her to evaluate the situation, question whether she could bend his downfall to her gain, and calculate that remaining allied to each other would still be the best play for both of them. "Have they denied your budget?"

"Temporarily," he said. "They want me to find the Stormbreak Sanctuary and bring down the rebellion. They've simultaneously charged Qae'lon with reclaiming Klubridge for the Empire."

The corners of her mouth twitched, and he knew it was an effort to keep the smile off her face. His doom would be more amusing to her if she wouldn't be dragged down with him. "They've pitted you against each other. Whichever one succeeds will be regaled, and the other will bear the blame for losing the city in the first place. They gave you the impossible task. It's no secret where their expectations lie."

Bekam leaned forward to protest that charge, but Marjiel was not finished speaking.

"They've always favored Qae'lon. After you've been dismissed in dishonor, they'll send a properly outfitted army to take the rest of Klubridge back without you. You'll be exiled and blamed for everything. The Council will install a new general, and the Kites will carry on without you." She thought about it for a moment and nodded. "It makes sense. It's what I'd do." And then, to him, "What resources do you have available to you?"

He released his hands from behind his back and came to sit on the matching chair that sat at an angle to Marjiel's. "I have the remaining Kites. Some of their commanders may have friends in military command that would join, but the Kites are the only ones we can count on."

"The only ones you can count on," she said, both because it was an accurate correction and because she abhorred referring to Bekam and herself as "we" or "us."

He let that pass and said, "We know the rebels who overthrew Klubridge intended to travel from there to the Stormbreak Sanctuary. I need to start my search in Klubridge, but I have no way in. I can't lay siege to the city. I haven't the bodies to mount an assault."

"Mercenaries?" she asked.

"With what money?" he responded. "I don't suppose your father would be inclined to buy me an army."

The bastard could afford to do exactly that, but Bekam taking back the city himself armed with only a paring knife would be easier than prying a single seri out of the old man's palsied grasp.

Marjiel knew that as well as he did, and she ignored the suggestion. "You wanted to pick my brain to see whether there's a way for you to get out of this without fighting. Without dashing your soldiers against the rebels, failing, and losing your station and possibly your life." She touched a black-painted fingernail against her lower lip. "Do you suppose I'd still get your pension if you died in military action? Probably not, if they're determined to pin all the wrongs of the past year on you."

Bekam was used to this game, and he waited her out. As always, she had inferred his every intention in coming to see her. After all, her shrewd intelligence feeding his capability to maintain their money and position was the only part of their relationship that remained functional and thriving. "Do you see a way to get into the city and avoid armed conflict or the risk of capture?"

"They want to make a point of this. They want to make an

example of you. I'd imagine the Council would prefer that you not demolish the Kites in the process. They're going to have to pay a lot to rebuild the red ones. It makes economic sense that they wouldn't want to pay to replace the rest of them at the same time. No, you're the one they want. If you can give them an alternate way to dispose of you without wrecking the Kites, I believe they'd approve."

Bekam pulled his mouth tight. "A plan that results in my disposal is just as bad. Perhaps there's a way to reason with them and make myself useful."

Marjiel shook her head, but he could tell her brain was turning now. Her eyes were focused past him, at the window behind him that looked out onto the blackened rear lawn. At last, she looked at him and said, "I see two options. The first is that you go above the Council and find an ally at a higher seat."

It was Bekam's turn to shake his head. "I could try bypassing them on this, but I'm not going to change the whole structure of the government and the military. In another month and a half, I'll be back to them and asking for money again. By that time, they'll have a grudge, and nothing ever will go the same after that."

"The second option, then," she said. "The Council wants a scapegoat. They've settled on you, and they've positioned Qae'lon alongside you, but they don't want him." Her eyes shifted to meet Bekam's. "He's the one who'll get the Kites if you fail, isn't he?" She'd already discerned the answer and didn't wait for his confirmation. "You could give them someone better. Someone who—" Marjiel looked to her right, where the butler waited silently in the doorway.

He stood with hunched shoulders that could have been either in supplication or purely age curving his spine. His eyes lowered, and he extended a cream-colored envelope in both hands. "Apologies, my lady. An urgent message has arrived from the General's office."

Bekam half rose from his chair to take the envelope, but the butler went straight to Marjiel and placed the message in her hands. Bekam blinked, both shocked and indignant, as the old man turned and left without another word and without even acknowledging him. Marjiel had already torn open the flap and was reading the letter.

"The impertinence," Bekam said, looking back at the doorway through which the butler has disappeared.

"Shut up, Tenez," Marjiel said, and that got his attention. They jabbed at each other, but direct rudeness was uncommon. She had finished the message and held it out to him, her eyes wider than before. "Read this."

He took the paper, and his indignation evaporated as his eyes moved across the words. Before he'd even finished reading, Marjiel was talking again. "Go, Tenez. You must see to this tonight."

He was nodding as he stood, his eyes still on the message. "Where do—"

She was standing, too, and she grabbed his sleeve before he could leave. He looked up from the paper and met her eyes for one more brief moment of sincerity. "I was saying you have to find someone better to blame for this. For Klubridge." Her eyes dropped to the paper in his hand and then jumped back to his face.

"What are you thinking?" he asked.

"Go look into this," she said, touching the message. "And then find the mage the rebels are singing about. Use his celebrity against him, and the Council can't deny you. It's too public now. Akithar is the one you blame."

CHAPTER 4

"Get down from there!"

Fairy blinked as she dangled upside down and tried to find the voice. There it was. An old woman was pointing up from below and waggling a finger at her. "You'll fall and break your bleeding head!"

"I'm fine," Fairy called down and closed her eyes. If she couldn't see the old woman, she wasn't there.

"Look at her," the voice was saying to someone else, and then another voice started yelling at her, this time one she recognized.

"How many days do I have to pull you down from the walls?" It was the guard who'd been chasing her all over Stormbreak. He looked dreadfully old, probably into his forties, and it was hard to tell where the fur wrap around his head ended and his own scraggly hair and beard began. Fairy hadn't believed him when he'd told her he was coming up if she didn't come down that first day. But he'd called her bluff, and he was up on the ledge and yanking her back across to the walkway before she knew it. He didn't look the sort, but he could climb like he was born to it.

"All right," she groaned and hoisted herself up with her legs. "I'm coming, I'm coming."

Fairy had her knees hooked over a thick beam that stretched the length of the dining hall, and she grabbed the wood as she sat up and hopped her feet up on top of it. She'd been hanging there for probably fifteen minutes before that old bat spotted her. Who knows how long she could make it if everybody would stay out of her business?

"Careful, now!" the guard called up, and Fairy looked down at him. The rock floor was about three stories below her, with all the wooden dining tables and benches arranged in grids, and more people were looking up from their food to see what the commotion was. It was bad enough when just that one old woman and the guard were after her, but now half the blasted rebellion was going to see her. Her cheeks burned from the scrutiny as she scurried along a rafter. She grabbed her cloak off a nearby joist where she'd hung it and leaped across two crossbeams and onto the wall.

"Careful!" he yelled again, but she ignored him, already shimmying down a big and blocky chunk of wood that stuck out from the back corner of the room. By the time the guard was over there, she was gone and out the side door.

Fairy pulled on the cloak the rebels had given her when she first arrived and shrugged the hood up over her blonde hair before she stepped into the cold. The gray fabric was thick enough to keep her warm but too thick to allow her to move like she wanted to. She was away from Klubridge for the first time in her life, and she had no intention of just doing nothing, even if it appeared there was nothing to do. These people were supposed to be rebelling, but all she saw them doing was sitting around and complaining or swinging swords at nothing in the practice yard. She had to keep herself busy somehow, and there were worse ways than exploring this huge and weird castle up in the middle of nowhere.

She stopped at the corner of the dining hall and looked back toward the door she'd exited. When Fairy saw the guard wasn't following her out, she leaned against the rough bricks and blew between her lips. The cold air turned white in front of her mouth and spiraled away in puffs and swirls like she'd never seen before. She'd known there was more to Teshovar than Klubridge, but she hadn't thought about little details like this.

Who'd have imagined the air changed colors other places? Not Fairy, that's for sure!

That same deep voice dragged her out of her thoughts, and she realized the guard had come from the opposite door and rounded the building to cut her off. "How old are you, girl?"

Fairy turned to run back the other way, but his hand was on her shoulder now, holding her in place, and there was no escape. She sighed, creating another little puff of fog that amused her, and said, "Fifteen." She knew she looked younger and could have gotten away with as low as twelve, but she told the truth this time.

"That's old enough to know better. You can't go climbing all over this place. You'll fall and kill yourself, and who'll be responsible for that?" He stared at her, waiting for a response. "Who's going to scrape up your brains?"

She rolled her eyes but humored him. "You?"

"Me, that's who. Just last month, somebody fell off the south path, never saw him again. You want that to be you?"

"I wasn't on the south path," Fairy mumbled and didn't break his gaze.

The guard's eyes pinched closer together, and he squeezed her shoulder tighter.

Fairy looked past the guard's shoulder and called, "Apak!"

The little engineer stopped with a jerk and craned his head to see who had called his name. The guard looked back in that direction as well but did not release Fairy.

"Apak!" she called again, and he saw her that time. The recognition in his eyes gave way to confusion and annoyance, and he stepped off the path he'd been following to trudge through the snow in their direction. Was he annoyed with the guard for grabbing her or annoyed with her for creating a scene? Or was he just annoyed at the world in general? The more she got to know him, the more Fairy thought the latter was most likely.

He wore a woolen vest over long sleeves and trousers, a heavy scarf wrapped around his shoulders. It was another outfit the rebels had given them, but it wasn't that different from Apak's own clothes he'd been wearing the first time Fairy saw him when they were on the boat and leaving Klubridge together.

"Apak is my guardian and mentor, and he can take responsibility for me now," Fairy said and tried to wrench her shoulder out of the guard's grip, but he held fast.

She could tell Apak was about to protest, but the guard cut him off with a sharp shake of the finger like the one he'd given Fairy inside the dining hall. "This is the last time I'll fish her down from the ceiling. Keep her on the ground." And he shoved Fairy towards Apak before he headed back around the corner of the building.

Fairy took Apak by the elbow and guided him away from the building as he watched after the guard. He took a few steps before yanking his arm away. "What is this, Fairy?"

"I was exploring, and the guards don't like when I go up high because they think I'm going to fall and break my neck."

Apak frowned at her. "It would have taken only one fall. And you lied to the guard."

She shrugged. "Well, I didn't fall. And I didn't lie." She'd been thinking about this next part for most of the week since she'd been there and nearly all of the five days since Apak had been there. "See, I want to be your apprentice."

At that, Apak stopped in the pathway so a trio of soldiers had to walk around them. "My apprentice? Whatever gave you that notion?"

"It's just... Since we've been here, everybody else has fit in somewhere and had something to do. I haven't. I've tried to find something, but all I keep doing is getting myself in trouble. Which is fun on its own," she said with a flash of a grin, but it vanished just as quickly as it came. "I need to be useful, though. And I know you can teach me things. Engineering. Chemistry. Whatever! I'm already good with numbers."

"Fairy, I have no workshop. I have no equipment. All of it is lost, either destroyed or abandoned in Klubridge."

"But they've got a workshop here," she said and realized with surprise that she was sounding like she was begging. "It's out back from the main keep, through the smaller courtyard."

"I have seen it," Apak said, his voice quieter now.

"Of course you have! Oreth's been back there in the supply depot just about the whole time. That's right next to the workshop." But, now that she thought of it, she hadn't actually seen Apak in the workshop or anywhere near Oreth since they'd all reconvened at Stormbreak.

"I cannot teach you these things, Fairy."

"But—"

"I will not teach you," he said, more forcefully this time. His eyes held hers until he finally gave her a small nod, and he moved away from her, back down the path the way he'd been headed.

This wasn't fair. She had nowhere to go and nothing to do, and these people had brought her here. Maybe it really would've been better to stay in Klubridge, Imperials or not. Until that moment, she hadn't realized how badly she'd wanted Apak to guide her or even why she wanted that. But then, in desperation, she shouted the truth after him. "You taught Dorrin!"

That stopped Apak, but just for a moment. His head half turned, as if he were going to look back at Fairy, about to say something else. But no, he turned away and left her in the snow, alone once more.

∼

The snow fell heavier for an hour before it tapered to nothing. Fairy squinted up at the bright, glaring sky. The edges of the sun looked hazier than they had earlier in the day, but that could have just been because her eyes had gone dry after she'd run out of tears. She wiped the back of her hand across her nose again and tugged her hood down tighter around her face. It was cold outside, but at least it wasn't cold enough to freeze her snot.

After Apak rejected her, she'd squeezed herself between some bushes and the wall of some stupid building, and there she'd sat in her misery. Fairy couldn't explore the castle. She couldn't climb. She couldn't even get Apak to teach her. Nobody wanted her to do anything, and nobody wanted her in their way. Maybe she could just sit there in the ice and brambles and get herself covered in snow. Maybe that would keep her far enough away from everybody.

There was a footpath on the other side of the bushes, and the shrubs weren't very tall, so most of the people passing during the last hour had noticed her. She must have looked like such a mess, some strange blonde girl covered in dirt and snow and sobbing in the bushes, but none of them had spoken to her. A few had picked up their paces after glancing her way and stomped past at double-time. Fine with her. See if she cared whether anybody wanted to talk to her or check on her or even acknowledge her bloody existence.

She'd just bowed her head and pulled the hood even tighter when somebody said something to her. She sniffed hard and looked up at an older boy standing over her. He looked vaguely familiar in the way all these various rebels did: dark hair, drab winter coat, nose red from the cold. She thought she'd probably bumped into him or climbed over his head when she was in the rafters or done something equally humiliating in his presence. "What?" she asked, a little harder than she'd meant to.

"I asked if you're okay." He shot a quick look down the path, like he was already regretting stopping to talk to her.

"I'm fine," she said and heard her voice thick and nasal from the remnants of her crying.

"You're the girl what came in with the wizard, aren't you? From Klubridge?"

Fairy exhaled a foggy plume of air and pulled her knees up under her chin. She'd longed for somebody to pay her some sort of attention, and now she wanted nothing more than for this nosy boy to leave her alone. What was wrong with her?

"Can... can I help you?" He sounded like he was concerned about her but knew he was in over his head, so he probably felt relieved when she just tucked her head down again and pressed her forehead into her kneecaps. That blocked out the brightness of the snow and the sound of all the annoying questions, and she could pretend she was alone, even if this boy wouldn't leave. But she finally heard him say, "Okay, just wait there. I'll get you some help." And she looked up again at that, but of course he was gone that time, and she didn't know in which direction.

Fairy groaned and shuffled her feet to get some feeling back into them so she could stand up. She'd been fine behind the bushes, but she would not hang around back there and wait for that boy to bring back another guard or worse, and that was a fact. She'd just wander back to the bedroom they'd given her on the second floor and throw herself onto her bed, fully clothed and dripping wet with snow. Who cared if the mattress and sheets soaked through? Not her, that's who.

The pathway was stone and would likely be covered in a slick sheet of ice if somebody hadn't poured gravel over it. The little rocks crunched under Fairy's feet as she headed back toward the keep, and she wrapped her arms around herself as she walked, partly to keep herself warm and partly to hold herself together.

The natural wall of the mountain loomed on her left side, and she knew that giant bird would be standing over her if she looked up. Instead, she looked to the right, where the outer wall of the castle had crumbled a long time ago. Somebody had told her part of the bird fell off and broke through it, and that didn't make her like the idea of the rest of that huge thing standing up there, just waiting to fall on top of all of them at a moment's notice. Sure, it had been ages since the first part had come down, and it wasn't likely a wing or some other part would break off anytime soon, but that's probably what those other people had said just before a big rock bird's head had ruined their day. She gave a little shiver and looked out through the missing section of the wall, across the tops of the snowy trees far below. Her stomach gave an uneasy lurch at that, and she swallowed hard, resolving to look neither up nor down while she was outside in this place.

"There she is!" The voice snapped her attention back to the path ahead, and the boy who'd talked to her at the bushes had just come out the doorway from the keep. Her pace hitched, and she would have turned back the other way, but it was too late now, and the person he'd gone to fetch was coming out now as well.

"Oh," she said and sighed.

"Fairy?" Caius blinked at her, taking in the whole dirty, sodden mess, and seeming as unsure about this interaction as she was. "What happened to you?"

"I'm dice," she said and angled off to the right, away from the living quarters. She didn't know what was down this way, but it seemed as good a time as any to find out. But, naturally, Caius fell into step next to her.

"Do you know that boy?"

She glanced back and saw that he, at least, wasn't following them. "No."

"He said you looked upset."

"I told you everything's fine."

"I can see it isn't." He frowned and looked ahead at what seemed to be an infirmary. "Where are we going?"

Fairy stopped in the middle of the path, and Caius had to backtrack a step to stay with her. "I don't know, all right? I don't know where to go or what to do. Nobody wants me here, and I'm stuck, and I can't…" Her voice trailed off into nothing, and her throat tightened. "Everything is not dice. Is that what you want to hear?"

She didn't want to look at Caius' face, but she did it anyway. If she'd seen pity or judgment there, she wasn't sure what she would have done. Probably crawled back under some other bush or buried herself in the dirty snow outside the castle walls. Instead, what she saw looked more like understanding.

"I saw Apak a little while ago. He mentioned seeing you," Caius said. His voice was lower now that he wasn't trying to keep up with her as she dragged him all over Stormbreak. "He was upset, too."

Fairy bit at her lip and scrubbed her boot through the wet gravel. Some of it stuck to her toe, and she tried to scrub it off but only succeeded in getting more on there. Her voice came out even lower than Caius'. "I asked him to teach me, but he won't."

"To teach you?"

"How to build things or fix things or… I don't know, just something. But he doesn't like me. Nobody does. I shouldn't have come."

"That's not true, Fairy. I like you. Samira does. We all do. Even Apak." He looked just past her and nodded to a metal bench that miraculously wasn't covered in snow or ice. She dragged her feet but went along with him and sat, her elbows on her knees and her head hanging low again. The seat was hard, and she could feel the cold on her legs, even through her cloak, but she admitted it was better than huddling on the ground again.

Caius said they all liked her, and she knew they did. That wasn't what this was about. But it was easier for it to be about that. "Then why wouldn't Apak teach me?"

Caius didn't answer, and Fairy looked over at him. For the first time since they'd all reconvened at the Stormbreak Sanctuary, she saw the dark circles under his eyes and the lines on his forehead. Had he looked that tired the whole time they'd been there? Had she just been so wrapped up in herself that she hadn't seen? He hadn't seemed so worn down on the ship, at least. And not when she saw him in Klubridge, even when he was locked up in the Imperial tower. "Are you all right?" she asked him.

He looked at her for a moment before he attempted a weak smile. "I haven't been sleeping well. Not since we left Klubridge."

"Not since they tried to scoop magic out of you," she said.

He managed an honest chuckle at that. "I suppose not." But then the smile faded, and he asked, "This is about Dorrin, isn't it?"

It had been there all along, but hearing him ask it still hit her in the chest like a mallet. Her throat tried to close again, and she felt the burning tears trying to betray her eyes, but she kept herself solid this time. She couldn't say anything, but she nodded.

"I miss him, too," Caius said, his voice quieter than ever. "That's why Apak won't teach you, you know. He taught Dorrin, and I think there's still a part of him that wonders whether Dorrin would still be alive if he hadn't done that."

"He thinks he'll get me killed if he teaches me?" Fairy asked and frowned.

"I don't think it's that simple. He's dealing with what happened, just like the rest of us are."

"It's not his fault," Fairy said. "I'm the one who told Dorrin to leave and find something better. He wouldn't have even known you all if it hadn't been for me."

"He might have been no better off if he'd stayed. This wasn't your fault."

Fairy wanted to protest, but there was truth in what Caius said. If she hadn't told Dorrin to run away, it was only a matter of time until Skink would have killed him. Skink, now dead himself down in the basement of Scrounger's den. And Scrounger just as dead, too. And neither of them would have died if Dorrin hadn't left. It was all a tangled ball of twine, and she didn't know where the end of the thread was or if she should even try pulling on it. It was no wonder Apak was so prickly about the whole thing.

"Did you live your whole life in Klubridge?" Caius asked.

Fairy nodded. "At least as much of it as I can remember."

"I was only there for ten years, but it was home." He looked down the pathway toward the infirmary and whatever else was in the building beyond it. "This isn't. Not yet, and hopefully we won't be here long enough for it to ever feel like home."

"How long are we staying here?" As she asked it, Fairy realized she had tied her fate to those of Caius and his friends. They were a unit now, and she'd go where they went. She didn't know anybody or anywhere else.

"I don't know. No longer than we have to." The lines were back in his forehead now, and Fairy realized the white dots in the beard he'd been growing weren't just from the snow.

They sat quietly for a few minutes, just two people watching strangers pass them by. She broke the silence with, "I miss him. I know I won't see him again, but it doesn't feel that way. It feels like he'll be coming back anytime now."

Caius rubbed a hand down one side of his face and heaved a deep breath. "Losing someone you care about is never an easy thing. Had you ever lost anyone else?"

"Not anyone I truly cared about before Dorrin," Fairy said. "After him, though? Everybody. Everybody I ever knew is gone." Dorrin stung the worst, but she also thought about Miri. She'd done her best to take care of the little girl after Klubridge started falling apart. That was after Scrounger was gone, after Dorrin and Skink and everybody else. Miri was the last one she'd held onto, and then even she was gone one morning, probably having wandered off looking for food in the night. Fairy hoped that she'd survived and was still okay somewhere in Klubridge, but she'd never truly know.

"Samira and I grew up together," Caius said. "We had a friend named Henrik. I was only a little younger than you are when he died."

"How did he die?" she asked and looked up at him quickly, unsure whether she should have asked that.

But Caius answered. "He was sick. We still don't know what happened to him, but it was enough to put him in danger." His voice was sad, but he sounded like he'd found a way to accept it and to talk about it without falling apart. She wasn't to that point with Dorrin and didn't know whether she ever would be.

"In danger from the Kites?" she asked. She'd seen the Scarlet Kites in Klubridge and knew they came after mages. On the journey to Stormbreak in the carriage with the others, Lizandra had told her about how they also came after the ill. She'd been afraid they were coming after Reykas.

Caius nodded. "We took him and ran. That was soon after we knew Samira was a mage, so they'd be coming for her as well, if they found out. She could heal with her magic, but she couldn't heal him."

He looked sadder than ever now, and Fairy felt like she should hug him or pat him on the shoulder or tell him something encouraging, but she didn't know him well enough for that. Instead, she just nodded to show him she understood, and she tried to turn it over in her head. Is this what life was? Loving people and losing them? What kind of junk was that?

She thought she had nothing else to say, but then she asked, "What happens to them? After they die?"

Caius raised his eyebrows. "What do you mean?"

"When somebody dies, they just stop. But that can't be it. There has to be more to it. They can't just all go away like they never existed."

"Nobody knows the answer to that. A lot of people have different ideas, but there's no way to know for certain."

"What ideas do they have?"

"Some people think a part of the person goes on living somewhere else. Some people think everything does just stop. It depends who you ask."

She looked at him, and she could tell he tried to look away, but her eyes held his. "What do you think? What happens to them?"

He broke her gaze, and she thought he might not answer, but she waited him out. At last, he said, "I think it's important to help people and to do what you can to take care of the ones you care about while you're alive. Then, when you're gone, part of you stays with them. You've made a difference in their lives, so they remember you, and that's how you go on."

She tried to wrap her brain around that, but it felt more like something she needed to wrap her heart around instead. It wasn't completely satisfying, and it wasn't everything she wanted to hear, but somehow it felt like it might be enough, for now. "Is that how Dorrin goes on? We just remember him, and he's still here?"

"In a way," Caius said. "But we have to go on, too. When we lose somebody, we need to live for them since they can't do it anymore. We can be sad, and we can miss them, but we have to find a way to carry on."

"That's what I've been trying to do," Fairy said. "That's what I was doing when I saw Apak earlier. Nobody wants me to do anything here." She scowled and looked down again. "Makes it pretty hard to carry on."

"What have you tried doing? Other than asking Apak to train you?"

She wrinkled her nose and glanced at Caius. "I've been exploring some. And climbing."

Caius laughed, and she couldn't help but smile at how ridiculous it sounded. "You helped Oreth after he got hurt, when we were on the boat," Caius said.

"Yeah?"

"Have you talked to him much since we've been here?"

"Not really." She'd seen him around and knew he'd been at the supply depot a lot, but she suspected that had more to do with the girl with the big, curly hair who worked at the depot than it did with Oreth actually doing any work there himself.

"You might want to try. He's been having some trouble with Apak, too."

Fairy cocked her head toward him. "Apak won't teach him now, either?"

"I think it's a bit of the opposite. Oreth doesn't seem to want to talk to Apak after what happened to him in Klubridge. Maybe you could be a friend to him? It could help him to have somebody to talk to."

And it would keep Fairy from swinging from quite as many rafters, if she had something more productive to do with her time. Caius didn't say that, but Fairy knew he meant it, and that was fine and fair. She was big enough to recognize when she'd been making herself a nuisance. Truth be told, she felt a little more embarrassed about all that after talking with Caius and after throwing her feelings out there into the frozen air for both of them to examine.

"I'll try," she said, and she would.

~

Fairy wasn't about to march herself into the supply depot and strike up a conversation with Oreth while covered in mud and snow sludge. The level of acceptable grime seemed significantly lower at Stormbreak than it had been in Klubridge while she was running with Scrounger's gang. Back in the East Ward, they reserved clean clothes for whenever they needed to look presentable and fit in among higher-class marks for their pickpocketing, and baths were luxuries most of them had never known. Things were different up here, where there was a lavatory on the very same floor as Fairy's bedroom.

The castle seemed ancient and not like the kind of place that would have amenities of any sort, but somebody had rigged up running water at some point, so Fairy had more access to a bath there than she'd ever had in her life. Once back in her room, she decided she wasn't quite filthy enough to require a full submerging, though, and she settled for washing her face and hands and digging a clean change of clothes out of one of the drawers in the old wooden chest that was pushed against the wall opposite her small bed. She didn't have an extra cloak, so she had to hope the quilted blue vest and wooly, cream-colored shirt under it would be warm enough.

It turned out to be plenty warm once she went back out of her room and into the second-floor corridor. The floor was smooth stone here, and the wall with the door to her room was brick of a brownish, reddish color. The opposite wall was some kind of carved stone with decorative holes in it that looked out into the courtyard at the center of the keep. She'd explored the whole building her second day there and found that the inner keep was a square building with all the rooms tucked into the outside walls and surrounding a big, open area at the center. The swirling designs in the walls were pretty enough, but Fairy would have traded all those holes for something more effective at not blowing an icy wind through the hallway. Although she had bundled up from the neck down, she scowled at the breeze she knew was reddening her cheeks even then.

Fairy took the stairs down at the turn in the hallway and emerged into the courtyard, where some soldier-looking types were doing drills with wooden sticks near the tall tree that grew out of the middle of the quad. A low brick wall surrounded the tree, and Fairy thought she saw Lizzie sitting on the edge of it with her back to her, but she didn't stop to talk. Fairy was on a mission and wouldn't be deterred.

Deep down, she'd known what had been bothering her, but she hadn't wanted to deal with it in ways that would have been effective. Talking with Caius had adjusted her outlook, and she was starting to think making better friends with Oreth really could be a helpful tactic. After all, he was only a few years older than she was, and there weren't that many others around their age that she'd seen in the castle. Maybe rebelling against the Empire was an old folks' hobby. Whatever the reason, this new need to connect with anyone who could help her move forward was a pressing one, and if she could help Oreth in the process, then he was as good a choice as anybody else.

An alcove tucked into the back corner of the courtyard led Fairy down a short passageway with no doors on either end. It took her through the rear wall of the keep and out into a second, smaller courtyard that backed up to the central building. Shorter outbuildings surrounded a little cobbled plaza, and she headed straight for the squat building on the right, the one with a sloped wooden roof and barn doors standing open to the elements. She passed the workshop beside it and frowned into it. Apak should have been in there, doing whatever he did in such places.

The light from a fire flickered inside the supply depot, and Fairy wondered why they'd have put a wooden roof on the top of a building with an open furnace. It seemed dangerous to her, but what did she know about architecture?

"Oreth!" Fairy called as she came through the doorway. He was midway across the room, sitting at a table made from raw wood that had been nailed together. Nothing fancy, but it looked plenty sturdy. He'd been studying some papers spread in front of him, but his head came up at his name. "Why won't you talk to Apak?"

He was slender and lanky, and Fairy had heard somebody say he was eighteen, but he didn't look any older than sixteen, just a year older than she was. His pale, freckled head poked up out of a too-big brown shirt with the sleeves rolled up. His hands were pale, too, and rested on the table, holding down whatever he was reading. She noticed he kept his left arm at a slight angle, bent toward him. That's the one he'd nearly blown off and that Samira'd had to fix for him.

"Fairy! What do you mean?"

She stepped over an open crate of apples and wove her way between two overstuffed shelves until she was at Oreth's table. Papers of all sorts lay here and there, some looking discarded and others like they were in the midst of being scribbled upon. Lots of numbers and lots of lists of vegetables and grains and whatnot.

Fairy hopped up on the edge of the table and looked down at the paper Oreth had been studying. "Caius thinks you have a problem with Apak. Do you?"

He sighed and ran his right hand through his shock of red hair. It had been looking unruly when she first saw him on the ship, but by now it had grown truly wild, no longer content to poke out over his ears but now hanging down toward his neck and over his forehead. The light ginger facial hair he'd been working on hadn't made quite as much progress.

"I don't have a problem with Apak," he said. "It's just, I'm not ready to deal with him yet."

"Deal with him?"

"He can get a little…"

"Intense?"

Oreth nodded but didn't look comfortable talking about this. "I just need some time after what happened to me. You know what I mean?"

"Compre," Fairy said. She knew all about the explosion in the Downsteps. She'd been helping tend to Oreth for the first couple of nights aboard the ship, and there had been plenty of time to listen to him moan about dropping that cylinder off the table. He didn't even know most of the story, seeing how he'd been unconscious and nearly dead. She'd gotten the rest of the details from Samira and thought she might even know more about what happened to him by now than Oreth himself did. She took a breath before continuing. "But, just for the sake of argument, let's say you did have a problem with Apak. Let's say you blamed him for dragging you back into his workshop, and you felt like he was the reason you were in there and blew yourself up." Fairy angled her head at him. "I wouldn't think you were wrong. But it's not going to do either of you any good if you stay that way."

Oreth slid back on his stool and looked at her, probably trying to figure out why this annoying child was trying to give him advice about something that was none of her business. But Fairy wouldn't back down. She'd found something she felt like she could actually help with, and it was worth making herself and a few other people uncomfortable for a little while if she could help sort things out.

After Oreth had said nothing for a few seconds, Fairy looked back at the papers on the table. "What are those?" They looked like ledgers of some sort. There were lists down the left side and numbers in grids all along the right. Fairy knew numbers, one of the few useful things she could thank Scrounger for teaching her.

"It's supplies. I'm helping with keeping track of what comes in, what we need, who's using what," Oreth said. He looked away from her toward the papers. "It takes a lot to keep this place going."

"What kind of stuff?"

"Food, weapons, clothing, just about anything you see around here had to come from somewhere." He stood from the stool and moved toward the other end of the table, where a thick blue logbook lay open.

"I like your leg thing," Fairy said as he walked.

He glanced back at her, his eyebrows up, and then put a hand down to his left leg. She couldn't tell whether it was a move of embarrassment, but she hoped not. The thing he was wearing truly did look awesome. There were two bands wrapped around his upper leg and two wrapped around his lower. Fairy guessed they were leather or something sturdy like that. Bolted onto the straps were four shiny, flat rods made of metal. Two were on the outside and inside of his upper leg, and two matching ones on the lower. Between the rods on the inside and outside of his leg were round things that looked like hinges, one on each side of his knee. It all bent and moved with him as he walked, and she guessed it helped keep him upright after his leg had been so blasted up. Samira had fixed the worst of what had happened to him, but her magic wasn't perfect.

"Glad you like it. I made it," the girl said, sweeping into the room like she owned it. Which she might. Fairy had seen her in here enough to make it a possibility. And then, to Oreth, "Do we need more grain?" But before he could answer, she turned to face Fairy and put her hands on her hips. "Who are you?"

She was thin and somewhere around Fairy's height. It was hard to tell for sure because the girl's hair gave her an extra few inches. It was dark brown and bloomed out from her head in big corkscrews like a wild arrangement of springs. She wore a tan smock over drab green coveralls, and there were smudges of something black all over both. Her hands, presently cocked on her hips, were hidden inside yellow-brown gloves that looked a few sizes too large for her. She wore an old pair of goggles pushed up on her forehead, and her thick eyebrows crinkled downward below them.

"I'm Fairy. I came here with Oreth and the others." The girl didn't look much older than her, probably around the same age as Oreth, but something about her intimidated Fairy.

"I'm Leyna." She cut her eyes over at Oreth and then looked back at Fairy. "You're friends?"

"We just met on the trip from Klubridge," Oreth said. He was thumbing through the logbook on the table, but he had a goofy smile on his face now and kept stealing glances at Leyna when she wasn't looking.

Leyna made a "Hm" sound and looked back at Fairy. She had blue eyes, and her eyelids hung heavy, the kind that made a person always look either sleepy or bored. But Leyna didn't seem like she was either of those things just then. "We're working, Fairy. Something you need?"

"I…" Fairy hesitated and looked at Oreth. Why hadn't he said they were friends? And why was Fairy letting this other girl get to her? "I came here to see if I could help. I'm good at numbers. I can help with the supplies."

Leyna chewed on her lower lip as she looked Fairy up and down, and then she shook her head. The curls bounced with the motion, and she said, "Nope, sorry. We don't need help."

Oreth's eyes widened, "But Leyna—"

"We're all good," Leyna said and took a half step to her left, positioning herself precisely between Fairy and Oreth. Oreth leaned to his right and gave Fairy a half shrug from behind Leyna's back.

Annoying as a second rejection might be on that day, Fairy felt like she'd worked out a puzzle. "I'll just see myself out, then," she said and couldn't keep from grinning as she backed out the door. What had Oreth gotten himself into?

CHAPTER 5

Caius lit a second lantern and sat it on the wobbly table next to his wardrobe. It was meager lighting, but it helped dispel some of the shadows that had gathered in his quarters, even with a shaft of dusty midmorning light cutting through the narrow window set in the back wall. This was a far cry from the meeting room in the back of the Chamberlain, but it would have to do.

He glanced at the four others he'd gathered before he reached into the back of the wardrobe, past the heavy coat that hung inside. "We need to talk about this." Caius pulled the packet out from where he'd hidden it and tossed it onto the table, where it landed with a heavy thud, making the lantern next to it flicker.

"What is that?" Lizzie asked, leaning forward in her chair. One hand was in her lap, the other on Reykas' leg beside her. He reclined on the bed, his back resting against the wall behind it. Caius hadn't asked whether the sickness had come back after they'd arrived at Stormbreak. He hadn't had to ask.

"It is the blackmail material we recovered from the vault in Klubridge," Apak said, a line forming between his eyes. "You have not delivered it to Yannis Heriot."

"Heriot's dead," Samira said and sat on the corner of the bed, careful to not jostle Reykas.

"Dead." Apak's frown deepened.

"Wait," Lizzie said. "Why do you have those papers, and who is Yannis Heriot? Was," she amended. "Didn't you give those to Drass?"

"I did, and he gave them back to me. He didn't trust the spy to deliver them, so he told me to bring them directly to the leader of the rebellion. He knew the leader to be an ex-Imperial named Yannis Heriot."

"But Heriot's dead," Samira said again. "We were suspicious after we'd been here a few days without hearing anything about him, so I poked around. He had led the rebellion for many years. Everybody I spoke with had nothing but glowing opinions of him."

"Was he killed?" Lizzie asked.

Caius shook his head. "A sickness." He realized too late that his eyes had strayed to Reykas, but the other man's head was turned to stare toward the small window. "He died a few months ago, and Micah Vaino assumed leadership."

Samira added, "It sounds like Heriot trusted him. They'd known each other for a long time. They'd been in the Empire together, but both defected."

"I know who Vaino is," Lizzie said. "I've seen him around the keep."

"He welcomed us when we arrived," Apak added. "The spy did not seem to trust him."

"That's why I called you all here," Caius said. He tapped the top of the packet of papers. "We have to decide what to do with these."

"You were planning to give them to the leader of the rebellion," Lizzie said. "That's Micah Vaino now. Shouldn't they go to him?"

"I do not trust him," Apak said. "I do not appreciate the notion of delivering these documents that we liberated from the Empire to another Imperial. We paid too dearly for them."

"Ex-Imperial," Samira said. "And Yannis Heriot used to be Imperial as well. Drass trusted him."

Apak wrinkled his nose, and his eyeglasses tilted forward. "I do not trust Ergo Drass, either."

"All right," Caius said, looking from one face to another. Reykas was the only one who hadn't spoken, but his eyes were unfocused, and he seemed far away from that room and that conversation. "What are our other choices? What do we do with this if I don't give it to Vaino?"

They sat in silence for a long moment before Lizandra spoke again. "There's a woman some of the rebels seem to follow. I've heard people talking about someone named Naecara."

Samira nodded. "Naecara Klavan. She's the one Aether took her message to, instead of Vaino. I haven't met her, but I know who she is. I've seen her in the courtyard."

"What do we know about her?" Caius asked. "I've heard her name mentioned, too."

"What I've heard makes her sound like a leader. At least some of the rebels respect her," Lizandra said.

Apak frowned. "There are two factions within the rebellion, then. This is not a good thing."

Caius took a breath and wanted to disagree, but Apak was right. Yannis Heriot had led the rebellion and had earned the unified respect of the rebels. After his death, something had fractured the movement, and now some of them followed Micah Vaino while the others followed this Naecara Klavan. "We need more information. We need to know about Klavan. We need to know how she's different from Vaino and why the rebellion has two leaders now. Why does the spy trust Klavan and not Vaino?"

A rap at the door halted any answers or speculation that might have been coming. Caius shared a quick glance with Samira before he crossed the room and pulled the door open.

Micah Vaino smiled from the other side. He wore another black suit, like the one he'd worn the day they had arrived at Stormbreak, but this one had decorative silver embroidery at the collar. His dark hair hung loose, and a gust of wind through the courtyard wall tugged at a long strand.

"Good, you're in!" Vaino said. "I was hoping to speak with you." His eyes moved past Caius and toward the others gathered behind him. "I hope I'm not interrupting anything."

"No," Caius said. "Nothing at all."

Samira and Caius followed Vaino into the corridor, where the midday sun shot narrow beams of light through the holes in the decorative wall that overlooked the courtyard. The patchy spots of warmth felt strange on Caius' exposed face and hands in the midst of the day's chill. It had been cold enough when they'd arrived at Stormbreak more than a week ago, but the temperature had been continuing a steady crawl downward since then. It was hard to imagine what this place would be like at its coldest.

"I apologize for not taking the time to properly meet with you both before now," Vaino said, half turning as they walked. "I'm sure you can imagine how hectic things can be."

"We've been well taken care of," Caius said. "Thank you for taking us in and for providing the clothes, food, everything we need."

"It's the least I could do for the hero of the rebellion," Vaino said with a sharp grin. That meant something, but Caius didn't know this man well enough to decipher what the implication might be.

Caius stepped aside to let a woman carrying a basket pass in the hallway. "I had wanted to ask you about the message the spy brought on the ship with us."

"Aether?" Vaino said and looked back again, this time his expression less pleased. "You're entitled to know about that message, given all the trouble it caused you. I understand the Kites believed you were the spy, and that's how you ended up here?"

"More or less. Ergo Drass helped us get out of Klubridge and brought us north."

"I've never met the man, but he provides a great service to our cause."

"Drass is no friend to the High Lord."

"I don't believe anyone is." And there was that strange smile again. His eyes shifted to Samira. "I saw your theater when I was in Klubridge. It was many years ago."

"The Chamberlain," Samira said. It was impossible to miss the note of regret in her voice.

"Did you come inside?" Caius asked.

"Alas, I was only in town for the one night and was otherwise occupied," Vaino said. He hesitated, drew a breath, and said, "Imperial business."

None of them spoke for a moment as they rounded the corner to head toward the stairwell.

"The message," Caius said again.

Vaino slowed his pace as the stairs approached and glanced back at him. "I'll tell you what she brought, but it wouldn't mean anything to you until after this. I'm taking you to meet someone, but the three of us need a word before that happens. I need to prepare you."

"Prepare us?"

Vaino stopped just before the stone archway that led to the landing. He looked from Samira to Caius and back again before he asked, "How much do you know about Teshovar?"

"What do you mean?" Caius asked.

"Everyone knows the standard bits," Vaino said. "The Imperial propaganda. Teshovar is where we live. Teshovar is all. Teshovar is ruled by our magnanimous High Lord. All that tripe." He paused for a breath and asked, "What do you know beyond that? What do you know about the actual history?"

"About it being a monarchy before Peregrine came?" Caius asked. "And that the rest of the world isn't as scourged as we've been led to believe? That sort of thing?"

"That sort of thing," Vaino said, a hint of a smile playing at the corners of his mouth. "I assume you had conversations with the spy on your journey."

"Not her," Samira said. "Ergo Drass."

Vaino tilted his head, considering. "That does make more sense. Aether is less... forthcoming."

"Do you trust her?" Caius asked.

Vaino huffed a low laugh, and his breath plumed in a pale vapor. "More than she trusts me, it would seem."

"Why didn't she give you her message directly?" Samira

asked. Caius inhaled, afraid she might have overstepped with the question, but Vaino seemed to take no offense.

"I haven't had this position for long. Only a few months. My predecessor was beloved and was far more adept at this job than anyone could have expected him to be. After his passing, I stepped into the role. That disappointed some who believed they were better suited to it, and they've chosen to be... difficult." His expression turned contemplative. "I tell you this so you'll understand the landscape of this place. You're likely to hear from some who are dissatisfied with me. I'd like you to understand the origin of that dissatisfaction in advance. I am a good leader, and I'm doing the best I can with what we've been left to work with." He waved a hand. "Aether is not what's important right now. When you spoke with Drass, how much did he tell you about the rise of the Empire?"

Caius shrugged. "Just that it supplanted the monarchy. The High Lord pushed out the old guard and closed off Teshovar from the outside world. He claimed to have destroyed everyone and everything outside of Teshovar, but Drass said that was a lie."

"It is," Vaino said. He resumed walking, Caius and Samira falling into pace behind him. "What do you know about the Aescalan?"

Samira shot a querying glance at Caius, and he said, "They're giants. Folklore creatures." He chuckled. "My parents said they'd carry me away if I didn't do my chores."

As he climbed the stairs, Vaino glanced over his shoulder. "They're not folklore. They're not myths. The Aescalan were very real, and they lived in Teshovar before the days of Peregrine. Before the Empire."

Samira's mouth dropped open, but she followed up the stairs. "What—"

"The Empire lied about burning the world, and they lied about the Aescalan. They lived here, and they were among the first the Empire pushed out. They fought back, but they lacked the tenacity and the sheer power of the early Imperials. They were fierce opponents, but the battles were no contest. The Empire drove them east and into the sea."

Caius asked, "You know all this because you were an Imperial?" They rounded the third floor landing and took the next flight of stairs upward.

"I know it because the Aescalan are not dead. They were defeated but not exterminated. There's a nation named after them due east of here, directly across the Madigus."

Caius blinked and hesitated, his right hand on the rail and his left foot midway between two steps. Drass had not elaborated when he'd told them there was more to the world than Teshovar. Of course there were more people and more lands out there, but it had all been abstract until now. He shook his head and hurried up the next couple of steps behind Vaino. "The Aescalan. They're not like the stories, then? The Empire spread those tales so we wouldn't believe they were real. So we wouldn't know what Peregrine had done. They're not giants."

Vaino stopped before a thick wooden door at the top of the stairs and quirked an eyebrow up at Caius. "You can be the judge of that. You're about to meet one of them."

~

Cold air whipped through the door and past them. Caius squinted against the white light the covering of snow reflected into his eyes. Flakes were falling again, and he looked up as they emerged from the doorway onto the roof. His feet crunched into the snow, and he cast a wary look to the side. There was no wall or railing along the inside of the walkway. Slipping on a patch of ice and tumbling into the courtyard far below would put an inauspicious and abrupt end to whatever plan the rebellion had for him.

"You've probably noticed the snowfall is irregular," Vaino said, pulling the door shut behind them.

Caius nodded and pulled his eyes away from the distant flagstones. "Almost never at night."

"There's a reason for that." Vaino stepped perilously close to the inner side of the walkway, and Caius' heart thudded in his throat as he watched Vaino's boot nudge a clod of snow over the edge. Vaino pointed toward a tower that jutted up a couple of stories higher than the keep, just beyond the far side of the keep. "Two mages are in there. They can form invisible shields in the air. Nothing can get past them."

Samira's eyes were wide, and Caius put a steadying hand on her arm. She could form those shields as well.

Vaino continued, "The Empire built most of its castles with focusing stones inside."

"Focusing stones?" Samira asked, and Caius could tell she was fighting to keep her voice even.

"That's what most everyone calls them. They're about this high," he said and held his hand up to his collarbone. "Conical and made from some sort of rock we haven't identified. There's one in that tower. When our mages project their barriers into it, the stone amplifies the magic and shields the entire castle. No one can get in or out as long as that barrier is up. That's how the Empire maintained security in its early fortifications. How it still maintains it in some places. Salkire has Herons on guard duty for just that reason."

"And it keeps the snow from falling at night, when the barrier is up," Caius said and looked up again as the flakes continued falling.

Vaino nodded. "Our two mages work in shifts. We keep them active during the night, but raids seem less likely during the middle of the day, so that's when they usually rest."

Caius looked at Samira again, but her eyes were locked on that tower. She had told no one at Stormbreak that she was a mage, and he would not be the one to let her secret slip. "You have more mages here?" Caius asked. "More than just those two?"

Vaino gave a faint smile over his shoulder. "We have all sorts of people here." And then he nodded across the open space of the courtyard, to the next section of the roof rimmed by battlements. "He's already arrived. He can be prickly."

From that distance, Caius could make out the shape of an enormous man standing with his back to them. Perhaps not as massive as the Aescalan of children's stories, but there was no doubt what had inspired those tales.

He was leaning against the top of the battlements that capped the outer wall, looking away from Stormbreak, across the descending slope of the mountain and toward the distant flatlands. As they began walking again, Caius saw the wind ruffle the furred collar on the man's wide and rounded shoulders. He was wearing a heavy cape that sat high and obscured anything else about the man's appearance from that angle.

They rounded the corner of the walkway, and Caius' impression of the man's size was correct by only half. From across the roof, the Aescalan had seemed broad, but now Caius saw he was also much taller than he'd looked while leaning on the wall with his head bent. He stood to his full height and turned to watch the group as they approached. Caius heard Samira's intake of breath just behind him, and he felt like gasping as well.

This man had to be seven feet tall, probably closer to seven and a half. His bright orange hair stood out from his head and hung wild around his face, descending into a thick beard that he'd braided at the bottom with beads that glimmered blue and green and red in the sunlight. The little of his face the hair didn't cover was tanned by the sun or the wind and deeply lined. Bright blue-green eyes squinted down at them.

The man now looked every bit the Aescalan Caius had read about as a child. Not the height of two men, but that hardly mattered. He wore furs and hides from neck to toe, all sewn together into thick padding that seemed as much like armor as it did a garment. The cape draped over his shoulders was of light brown fur, nearly the color of sand, and it rode high, covering his neck and the back of his head.

"Dekan Hama," Vaino said, "This is—"

"The wizard," Hama said. His voice rumbled but was clearer than Caius had expected. He eyed Caius with something like an appraisal, but just shy of suspicion, and grunted. His gaze shifted to Samira. "Who is this?"

"Samira Tandogan," Vaino said before Samira could answer. A flicker of annoyance passed across her face.

"The woman can speak for herself, can she not?" Hama asked, and Vaino's lips pressed together, either in annoyance or chagrin.

Hama's voice was accented, but it wasn't something Caius

recognized. There was a strange lilt, and the vowels were softer than he'd have guessed they'd be. The stories cast the Aescalan as warriors, hardened from a culture of conquest and battle. Dekan Hama dressed the part and stood like the giants of the legends, but something about him was softer than the Aescalan were supposed to be. More real, Caius supposed.

"My name is Akithar," Caius said.

"It's not, but that'll do for now," Hama said, showing the ghost of a wry smile. He looked at Vaino and asked, "Why've you called me up here to freeze my arse off? Surely not just to meet your wizard."

"You had asked to meet on the roof," Vaino began, but Hama's glare halted his protest. Instead, he continued, "You needed to meet him. You needed to meet both of them, if you and I are to do business."

Caius shifted and frowned back at Samira to see she hadn't liked that phrasing any more than he had. "What sort of business —" Caius began, but a sharp look from Hama stopped his query as surely as it had stopped Vaino. The shiver that shook Caius' shoulders had nothing to do with the cold. This enormous man could swat him off the edge of the roof if he took half a notion to do it.

Caius swallowed his fear and asked, "Why are you here?"

Hama scowled at that and favored Caius with a stare that was more curious than angry, but the line between the two seemed thin. "I'm here for what's mine," he said. "Mine and my people's." At that, he turned away from them and rested his forearms on the wall, his gaze moving back to the distant lands.

"There's a prophecy," Vaino said. He spoke slowly now, almost gingerly, and he kept his eyes on Hama's back. "Thousands of years ago, the ancient Aescalan were defenders of the realm. They aligned with the Tamrat dynasty and protected the bloodline."

"Tamrat," Caius said. It was the name Drass had told them.

"That was the monarchy," Vaino said. "Aescalan history shows they ruled in peace for many generations."

"Hardly mattered in the end," Hama said, his voice a low growl on the wind.

Vaino said, "When the Empire arose, its armies drove the Aescalan out of the city we now know as Aramore. That was the capital of Teshovar and the seat of the Tamrat. They butchered the royal family and burned the city to the ground. The Aescalan fought back, but, in the end, they were pushed to the sea."

"And that's when Peregrine's rule began," Samira said.

Vaino glanced at her with that same strange look he'd given both of them earlier, but that didn't stop his story. "The Aescalan have been waiting across the sea all this time—thousands of years. They know how they came to be there, and they are still loyal to the Tamrat."

Caius frowned but didn't ask the obvious question. If Peregrine had exterminated the whole family, to whom were these people loyal?

Vaino nodded as if he could see the question on Caius' face, and he said, "The prophecy tells them the dynasty hasn't ended. It says there's a Tamrat scion that will rise and lead the Aescalan back into Teshovar."

Hama grunted and half turned. "If you're going to tell it, tell it right."

Vaino inclined his head. "My apologies, Dekan Hama. If I have it wrong, please correct me."

The bigger man made another grunting noise and shifted to face them but kept his weight against the battlements. It was like watching a mountain turn, and that chill ran through Caius' body again as Hama caught him in his gaze once more.

"Vaino's got the right of it, to a point. The scion lives and is here in Teshovar. He'll lead us back into our homeland, and he'll see us bring down the Ruinbringer."

"That's their name for Peregrine," Vaino interjected but closed his mouth again when Hama's gaze shifted his way.

"After we destroy the Ruinbringer," Hama said, "we come for Teshovar next."

His words settled into silence, and Caius asked, "You'll resettle in Teshovar after you depose Peregrine?"

Hama snorted and spat over the edge of the battlements. "We have no interest in settling here. We have our lands, and we have no use for these." He shifted his weight off the wall, and his cloak fell back, exposing something brassy and with a wooden grip hanging from his belt. Caius studied it in the brief moment it was exposed and could have sworn it was a firearm, but unlike any he'd seen in Teshovar.

"What, then?" Caius asked, looking back up to Hama's face.

"We kill the Ruinbringer, and we burn the realm. Teshovar will be no more, little wizard. We go home, and then we rest." He sniffed at Vaino. "We are finished here. I have met your wizard."

Hama passed his eyes over each of them once more before he turned and made his way to the opposite stairwell with a heavy but brisk pace, his huge feet shuffling through the snow that had collected on the walkway. After he had ducked through the door and shut it behind himself, Caius blinked at Vaino. "How have we not seen him before now?"

"He keeps to himself. Him and the others. They're staying in makeshift quarters at the back of the keep. None of the regular beds were large enough, so we had to make provisions."

"There are more of them here?" Samira asked, still watching the door through which Hama had left.

Vaino nodded. "Eight of them. Nine with Dekan Hama. They arrived a couple of weeks ago as a diplomatic detachment. They slipped through the blockades on a small ship."

Caius asked, "Why are they here? Did you send for them?"

"I did. We've made an agreement with Hama to form an alliance between his people and the rebellion."

"Does Hama know that?" Samira asked, pulling her eyes away from the doorway. "It sounded less like he's interested in cooperation and more like he has an invasion in mind."

Vaino smiled his sneaky smile again, still as inscrutable as the first time he'd done it. "Their entire society is based around their hatred of Peregrine and worship of the Tamrat. It's their long-standing generational tradition. Every Aescalan child learns about that prophecy. They grow up believing the Tamrat line still lives and that a surviving scion will lead them back to Teshovar. That they'll defeat Peregrine, and only then will they lay waste to the entire realm."

"And you feel like dealing with these people is a good idea," Caius said.

"You don't know the size of their armies. The numbers they can raise. I visited their lands two years ago. Their military is like nothing Teshovar has ever seen, and what they've accomplished with ballistics is…" His voice trailed off in wonder.

After a moment, he cocked his head toward Caius again. "There are pockets of resistance throughout Teshovar. Local armies that oppose the Empire. None of them will rise on their own, but they would join with us if they believed we had a chance of winning. The Aescalan bring that chance. They have agreed to cross the sea with their entire fighting force, well trained and well armed. All we have to give them is the Tamrat scion."

Caius' forehead creased. "If they're so powerful and hate us so much, why haven't they come before? Why haven't they just taken Teshovar on their own?"

"The prophecy," Samira said.

Vaino nodded. "The prophecy is everything to them. They probably could invade Teshovar and burn it all to the ground, just like Hama wants to do. They could do it at any time, but their prophecy tells them they'll only succeed if they have the Tamrat scion on their side."

Realization dawned on Caius and he huffed a half-laugh. "That's the message. That's what the spy brought and what the Empire wanted from us. You've found the scion."

Vaino smiled and cut his eyes toward Caius. "His name is Hyden Gressam. He lives on a farm a couple hours west of Bria. He probably has no idea about his ancestry."

"Do you believe this prophecy?" Samira asked.

"No," Vaino said. "But it doesn't matter whether I do or don't. All that matters is that the Aescalan believe it."

Samira watched Vaino for a long moment before asking, "Why did you say Dekan Hama needed to meet us? You told him he needed to meet us if you were to do business with him."

Vaino's mouth pulled tight, and he rested a hand on the battlement where Hama had been waiting for them. "Hama knows we're hunting for the scion, but he doesn't know we've found him. I'll have to tell him soon, and he'll want to go after the man on his own, maybe with the other Aescalan." He sighed.

"I don't think Hyden Gressam will be receptive to a band of giants showing up on his farm and telling him he's their savior."

"And you need Gressam. Without him, you don't get the army," Caius said.

Vaino nodded. "That's why I need you," he said to Caius. "Akithar is the face of the rebellion. He's a hero that's inspiring Teshovar. He's the sort of man a farmer just might be inspired to follow."

"You want me to travel to Bria with the Aescalan and convince Gressam to come back to Stormbreak." Caius shared a perplexed look with Samira. "My face is known! There are bounties on our heads."

"I've seen the pamphlets," Vaino said. "The likenesses leave something to be desired. You'd be traveling back roads and staying out of sight as much as possible anyway. The Aescalan would not escape notice on the main roads and in cities." He looked back at Caius and held his gaze. "This is your best opportunity for winning freedom for yourself and your friends. Help us retrieve Hyden Gressam, and we can do the rest."

Caius ran a hand through his hair and exhaled. "How can you believe any of this is a good idea? Even if this works, you'll have opened Teshovar to a foreign army that wants to destroy everything."

"They won't do that," Vaino said. "They'll only turn their forces against Teshovar itself after they've fulfilled their prophecy. In order to do that, they would have to destroy Peregrine."

"You want them to rally their armies and attack the Empire, but you don't believe they can kill Peregrine."

"I know they can't," Vaino said. His eyes twinkled, and that knowing smile reappeared. He leaned closer. "The High Lord Peregrine doesn't exist."

CHAPTER 6

Lizandra sat in the courtyard, where she'd spent so much time since arriving in Stormbreak. The snow was falling once more, but she knew it would stop again soon enough. She'd visited the tower on her third day there, and she'd met one of the mages who stood sentry, keeping the focusing stone fed with power. When they fed the stone, the barrier went up, just like the ones Samira could make, but impossibly larger, big enough to surround the entire castle. With the barrier up, snow settled on top of an invisible dome, waiting to fall in when the mage's shift ended. She'd seen it come down a few times, usually in soft splashes of white powder but once as a terrifyingly solid dome of ice. It had been late at night that time, and the ice had shattered over the castle with a sound like glass breaking from everywhere, in all directions.

The mage she'd met was a small, dark woman named Beghran Tajer. She was short where Lizandra was tall and impossibly thin and frail, where Lizandra was slim and strong, and it was hard to guess how old she might have been. Lizandra had heard about some mages looking younger than their years, and she wondered whether that might be the case with this woman and whether it might eventually happen to Lizandra herself. Tajer had large, dark eyes that reminded Lizandra of that blasted halflock Magra's, and she wore a heavy jacket that looked like it had been intended for a child.

Tajer had been gracious in meeting Lizandra but apologetic that she had to concentrate on her duty. And she had seemed pleased—eager, even—to spend the entire day in that tower, channeling magic into a stone. Lizandra hadn't told her that she, herself, was a mage, and she wondered whether any of the others had revealed their secrets to the rebellion. If they had, the rebels would surely put them to work in one way or another. But Lizandra knew little about what the others had or hadn't been doing. She'd isolated herself these past days, focusing only on her own duty.

"Lizzie."

She jerked at the hand on her shoulder and nearly slid off the low wall where she was sitting. "Samira! I'm sorry. I just…"

"Your mind was back in Klubridge," Samira said with a sad smile. She gestured to the space on the wall next to Lizandra. "Do you mind?"

"Not at all. Sit," Lizandra said and brushed at the snow that had collected there. Her mind had been elsewhere, but it hadn't drifted as far as Klubridge. All her concerns were at Stormbreak.

"Have you talked to Caius?" Samira asked as she sat. Her voice was low, and Lizandra had to lean closer to hear her over the noise of the courtyard. Someone was always coming or going, and the sounds of practice weapons striking each other punctuated the rumble of constant conversation. It was a busy place, but Lizandra welcomed the bustle.

She shook her head. "Not since yesterday when we were in his room. What did Vaino want?"

Samira sighed and looked toward the nearest cluster of rebels, two men and a woman huddled together in discussion. "He wants Caius to lead an expedition to Bria."

"Bria?" Lizandra nearly laughed, but it was obvious that Samira wasn't joking. "The whole point of coming here was to hide and stay safe."

"It's a long story," Samira said. "He's convinced that Caius is the only one who can do it, and I think he's beginning to have Caius convinced."

"He's not going, surely. He can't go south. Everybody knows who he is now! They'll be hunting for him and probably the rest of us, too."

Samira opened her palms and sighed again. "You can try telling Caius that, but I suspect you'd make the same progress I did."

"He's going, then?"

"Unless something convinces him otherwise." Samira hesitated. "If he goes, I should go with him."

"Samira!"

"He hasn't been sleeping. He's not eating, either." Samira's eyes dropped. "I put my hands on him yesterday, but I couldn't find anything to heal. I think what happened to him in Klubridge left more of an impact than we realized."

Lizandra dropped her own eyes to her hands, where she'd been picking at the edge of a thumbnail without realizing it. A dot of blood rose to the skin, and she pressed it against her cold lips before Samira could spot it. "Will Aquin go with you?"

After a moment of silence, Samira said, "That'll be up to Aquin. I suspect she'll want to stay here." She'd taken longer to answer than she should have, and Lizandra watched her face for any sign of what she wasn't saying. Samira caught her eye and leaned in closer. "Vaino told us something else yesterday. I don't know what to make of it."

Lizandra still had her thumb pressed to her mouth, but she lowered it, waiting for Samira to continue. When she did, her voice was even lower. "Micah Vaino claims the High Lord doesn't exist."

This time, Lizandra did laugh. It was an absurd little chuckle, and she swallowed the next one before it could escape, but that had not been what she was expecting Samira to say. Samira didn't smile back. "What do you mean?" Lizandra asked, her own smile faltering.

"He claims the Empire made up Peregrine. Or maybe he existed once, but he hasn't for centuries, at the very least. He's a contrivance... a tool they use to control Teshovar with fear."

"That can't be true," Lizandra said. "Someone would have found out. After all this time, somebody would have known."

Samira shrugged. "Vaino says most of the Empire believes Peregrine exists. Only the top leadership knows the truth, and they use him to control their underlings just like they control the rest of the realm."

"Do you believe him?"

Samira stared at her for another long moment before looking away. "I don't know. I don't know what to believe."

"How does this make any sense at all?"

"I think Caius believes him," she said, but her tone said she was anything but convinced.

"He's lived for thousands of years, Samira. He's probably locked himself away somewhere and just gives orders to his underlings. That makes more sense than all of it being a lie."

"But Vaino was one of those underlings. Yannis Heriot, too. They should have known if he existed, and Vaino says he doesn't."

This was nonsense, and it had Lizandra picking at her thumb again. She wrapped her fingers around it to stop herself. "How certain is Vaino?"

"Certain enough to wager all our lives on it," Samira said, her gaze drifting toward the rebels again. "All our lives, all theirs, and all of Teshovar."

Lizandra blinked at that and opened her mouth to question it, but Samira spoke first. "Reykas is getting worse, isn't he?"

Lizandra looked away from Samira, the sudden heat of anger flushing in her cheeks. Her heart thudded so hard her chest should have heaved. She squeezed her fingers tight around her thumb and forced herself to breathe twice and swallow once before she answered. Her voice dropped even lower than Samira's had been. "It started on the ship. His hand was shaking, and I thought it would be just like it always is."

"But it's not."

She met Samira's eyes, even though she knew her own were about to betray her with tears. "He's been weaker every day we've been here. The fever's started now, too. I don't know what to do."

"There's an infirmary in the castle," Samira said. "They have doctors here."

"I know that. I've told Reykas, and he won't go. He says it's no use. He says they won't be able to do anything."

"He doesn't know that."

"Don't you think I've been telling him that every morning and every night?" Lizandra's tone was sharper than she'd intended, but the words were out now. And, after she'd said the first part, the rest of it came loose and poured out faster than the tears that still threatened the corners of her eyes. "He won't see a doctor. He won't tell any of the rest of you that he can hardly walk now. That he can hardly even sit upright. He... I think he's given up." And then the tears did come. They ran down her cheeks, hot in the cold air, and she wiped at them with the back of her hand. One furious swipe to obliterate the evidence.

Samira watched her, but the pity Lizandra had feared wasn't there. Instead, Samira reached her left hand to cover Lizandra's right. She squeezed and said, "He'll see the doctor. Take me to him, Lizzie."

~

The infirmary was bigger than it had looked from the outside when Lizandra had found it on one of her aimless walks through the castle. It opened onto an outdoor path with a single door, and that door led into a small entryway that, in turn, fed into a hallway. Doors lined both sides of the corridor, some closed and others open, all of them seeming to house small rooms for patients. Some rooms had a single bed, but most of them seemed to have two or even three. Many of the ones with multiple beds had curtains hanging from the ceilings, separating the beds and giving the patients a measure of privacy.

Just as the facility itself was larger than she expected, there were also more patients being treated than Lizandra had anticipated. As she walked down that long hall, she heard murmurs from behind several doors, coughs and groans from behind others. A man carrying a small satchel emerged from a door on the left as she passed, and he stepped back to allow her to pass. She glanced past him and into the room he was leaving and saw a young girl in a bed, the sheets pulled up to her shoulders and a canister of some sort of yellow fluid suspended from a rail at her bedside. The girl was pale and had her face turned away from the door, and Lizandra saw her draw a shaky breath in the instant before the man closed the door behind him.

She continued down the hallway to the door on the right that she knew to be Reykas'. As she'd promised, Samira had convinced him to seek help at the infirmary. Having him there was a relief, but Lizandra could admit to herself that Samira's ability to coax him with one conversation stung after a week of Lizandra's own entreaties had failed to move him. Still, he had agreed, and that was what mattered.

Lizandra and Samira had gotten assistance the day before, and an attendant had left the infirmary to help them transport Reykas down the stairs and out through the courtyard to the facility. They had raised him onto a wheeled cart after they got him down the stairs, and that had helped the process, but the ride to the infirmary had still been slow and bumpy, with the wheels jostling over patches of snow and uneven stone. Once they'd gotten him inside, the attendant had wheeled him through the facility to the room where Lizandra now hesitated before turning the doorknob.

The room was dim and windowless but had a gas lantern burning on a hook on the far wall. Its light was sufficient for Lizandra to be able to see, but it was faint enough to not disturb Reykas. Two beds were in the room, and he lay in the one on the right. The man in the bed on the left had been asleep when they brought Reykas in the day before, and he slept when Lizandra arrived this time. There was no curtain between the beds in this room, and Lizandra had caught herself watching the motionless form on the other bed the day before. She wondered whether he had awoken at all in the time between, and for an instant she felt a dizzying certainty that the man was dead. But then his back moved with a slow exhalation, and Lizandra released a breath in time with him.

Reykas' eyes opened enough for the lamplight to flicker as a white speck in each, and the corners of his mouth turned upward. "You came back," he whispered, and Lizandra pushed her fingernails into her palms to keep herself from crying again.

His voice had diminished so much since just yesterday. He was fading away before her very eyes, and she could do nothing to stop it. At least he was in this facility and could have the care of a doctor for what she imagined was the first time in his life. She had never seen a doctor herself. Let even the suggestion of a physician slip, and the Empire came running with their chains and their cages. How had this doctor even learned his trade?

"Of course I came back," Lizandra said, her voice under control and the tears at bay for now. "Did you think I'd just abandon you here?" She came to his bedside and considered sitting there, but this bed was so narrow, much smaller than the one in their quarters in the keep. The bed back there felt far too big last night when she'd slept in it alone, and now this one was far too small. She settled for taking his hand in hers as she stood at his side. "Have you seen the doctor yet?" She hoped not. They'd said the physician would come around noon, and she'd timed her visit to be there when he saw Reykas.

Reykas parted his lips to answer just as a quick knock came at the door, and it opened again before either of them could answer. It was the man Lizandra had passed in the hallway, and he still had the satchel in his hand. He wore a gray coat belted around the middle with a dark green sash. His brown hair had receded far enough that the flickering gaslight reflected off the top of his head. He wore glasses that reminded Lizandra of Apak's, but these were larger and thicker, the lenses housed in a solid black frame. His face was clean-shaven, and he rubbed a hand over his mouth as he came into the room. "Reykas Kozic," he said and sat the satchel on the floor at the foot of the bed. He stared at Reykas for long enough that Lizandra had to break the silence.

"I'm Lizandra Daedan," she said. "I'm here with Reykas."

He glanced at her, and his words came at a fast clip. "I'm Sila. Can he speak?"

"You're the doctor?"

He nodded once and looked back to Reykas. "Can he speak?"

"He can," Reykas said, and his voice came as a whisper again. Every day he sounded weaker than the day before.

"What have you found?" Lizandra asked.

The doctor spread his hands. "I examined him last night. The symptoms are fairly common. I see this at least two or three times a month. It's always people who can use magic. You're a mage, I presume?" he asked Reykas.

Reykas nodded back. "I create portals in—"

"The specifics are irrelevant," Sila said and brushed at the air. "This is a condition that affects only mages. It's hard enough to learn about ordinary diseases without running into trouble. You can imagine how much harder it is to learn about ones that are specific to magic."

Knowing nothing about medicine or sickness beyond what she'd experienced with Reykas, Lizandra couldn't imagine, but she asked, "This is magic?"

Sila shook his head. "We believe it's a regular disease. Something persistent, chronic. Ultimately terminal. But you know all this, I suspect."

Lizandra took a step back toward Reykas and put her hand on his warm shoulder. "You don't know what's wrong with him." She fought to stand upright even as her stomach and heart felt like they tripled in weight and tried to shove her to the floor.

"I have seen this before, and frequently. In that respect, I know what it is. What caused it? How to cure it? No, I do not know." Sila's lips pressed together, and his eyebrows drew downward. His brusqueness faded into something else for that moment. Disappointment? Frustration? Whatever it was, it passed soon after, and he said to Reykas, "I can give you something for the fever. Something to keep you comfortable. It will make you drowsy. You'll sleep most of the time. I cannot save your life. Do you understand?"

The directness of that final pronouncement wobbled Lizandra's knees, but she remained standing, holding strong. She had to. One of them had to.

Reykas swallowed before responding, and his throat made a dry clicking noise she hadn't heard before now. "I understand," he said.

Sila nodded, satisfied, and stooped to gather his satchel. He undid the brass clasp at the top and withdrew a small brown paper that had been folded over like a makeshift envelope. He handed it to Lizandra, and she took it in silence with a hand that she managed to keep from trembling. "One pinch of this powder with water, twice a day. No more than that. Yes? If you are unable to administer it, you can leave it for one of the attendants here."

She stared at the package in her hand and couldn't say anything in response. The doctor didn't wait for a reply. He snapped his bag shut again and was out the door as quickly as he'd entered. Lizandra stood beside the bed, staring at the packet of powder in her hand, unmoving. Reykas had to say her name twice before she could pull her eyes away and look at him.

"He doesn't know what it is," she said.

"I know," Reykas said. "I heard him, too."

"He doesn't know, so he doesn't know that it's terminal."

"Lizandra."

"He doesn't know anything!" she insisted and closed her hand over the packet, hiding it from her view but being careful to not squeeze the contents out. "You might not even need this... this stuff."

"Lizandra," Reykas said again, his voice gentle this time and sounding almost like it had before. Before all this. "We both knew this was coming. It has been coming for a long time, and now it is here."

"No!" she said and shook her head. "He doesn't know."

"He doesn't, but I do."

The voice startled Lizandra, and she nearly dropped the packet. It was the man on the other bed, no longer asleep, if he ever truly had been asleep. He lay on his left side now, looking across the room toward them. He had light skin made sallow by whatever afflicted him. His hair was dark and cropped short but still looked a tangled mess from his time in bed. He turned his face toward his mattress to cough and then looked back toward them. "It starts with trembling hands, doesn't it?"

Reykas' eyes opened wider, and he turned his head on the pillow to face the stranger. "It does."

"And then you have sweats and feel weak. Dizzy. It gets worse, and then it gets better. Something like that?"

"How do you know?" Lizandra asked, but then it made sense.

The doctor had said he'd seen this condition many times. "It's what you have, too, isn't it?"

The man nodded and said, "I'm Pelo Foyen. Former jeweler, lately rebel, lifelong mage."

"How long have you been sick?" Lizandra asked.

"Years." He paused and frowned. "I don't rightly know at this point. Long enough that it doesn't matter anymore. I come from Craydon. My da had a jewelry shop and taught me the business. I'd been at it on my own for about five years when I came into possession of a ring the likes of which I'd never seen. Have you seen the rings with compartments on them? Little doors that swing open?"

Lizandra shook her head, unsure where this story was going or what it had to do with the illness this man Foyen shared with Reykas.

"Eh, hardly matters. They're popular among assassins and folk like that. They like to secret their poisons away in them and then drop it into a drink. But these rings always open somehow, so they can hide things inside or get them out. I could tell that's what this one was, but there was no way to open it. The clasp was stuck shut, and there was no mechanism to let me in." He stopped and let out a series of rough coughs and sucked in a deep breath before he went on. "I beat my head against it for days until I realized how to open the thing. Magic."

"Magic," Lizandra repeated.

"It was built so the only way in was to trip a tiny lever on the inside, and the only way I could figure to do that was with magic. And I could do that. So I opened it, and that's where my trouble began. Whoever had loaded that ring had put the illness inside. It's a viral thing. Do you know viruses?"

She shook her head again. The word was vaguely familiar, but she had no frame of reference for it.

"It is an infection," Reykas whispered. "It sickens anyone exposed to it."

"Right in one," Foyen said and gave Reykas a sad grin that made his thin face even more skeletal. "Except this one doesn't sicken just anyone. It only affects mages, and even at that, it only affects some mages. Not all. You and I were the lucky winners, my friend."

"How do you know all this?" Lizandra asked. "Reykas wasn't exposed to any rings or anything like that."

"Didn't have to be a ring," Foyen said. "It could have been something else that got him. It was just the ring for me. They set it up that way, so the ring had the virus, and only a mage could get at it, so it was more likely to infect someone."

Lizandra blinked and looked at Reykas and then back at Foyen. "You're saying this was intentional? Someone wanted you to be sick?"

"Wanted your friend to be sick, too, I'd wager," he said. "There's nothing natural about this illness. It was created and spread to infect us. To kill mages."

"Who would do such a thing? And why?" she asked, but the answer was obvious.

"The Empire," Foyen said. "Hardly matters who in particular. They wanted a way to cut us out of the population, so they targeted us. It was our poor fortune that it's worked on us. Fortunately for you, it's an imperfect formula. It hasn't affected you."

"Are you saying it spreads?" She looked at Reykas again with wide eyes. "That he could be infecting other people?"

"That, I do not know. I'm sure they'd have built it that way if they could. But if no other mages have been falling ill around him, I'd say it's isolated to him."

Reykas had listened to the exchange in silence, but now he spoke. "If this was built, there must be people who know how it works. There should be people who know how to counter it, yes?"

Foyen tilted his head to the side and pulled the corner of his mouth tight. "Yes, and no. There is a cure, but it's not one you'd want. It's not one I wanted. I didn't even tell Sila about it. Nothing he could do, anyway, aside from making us comfortable."

"A cure," Lizandra said, and it came out as a breath that she heaved into the room. Sudden hope rushed in to fill the space where the air had left her.

"After I caught this thing, word got around. They try to make you sick enough that other people will find out, and someone's always sure to call the Kites. That's what the real goal is. If they can't kill you with it, they want to catch you and turn you into a halflock. So I fled. I ran for a long time, going from city to city and doing odd jobs. Eventually I ran into someone else who'd been hit with our particular affliction, and she told me the same thing I'm telling you. But she'd been cured."

"How do you know she had been ill?" Reykas asked. He was usually reserved, especially when the sickness had him, but his interest swelled the hope that was growing inside Lizandra. She felt it like a tangible thing in her chest.

"She recognized what I was going through," he said. "And I knew her… well. For a time. She had been ill, I assure you. But she went to Karsk, and she came back cured."

"What's in Karsk?" Lizandra asked.

"There's a man in Karsk named Jod Padar. By her account, he's a chemist. He has the means to produce and administer a cure to this disease. And it works."

"Why have you not gone to him?" Reykas asked. He was tense now, the muscles in his neck and shoulders taut and not just from the strain of the virus, as Foyen had called it.

Foyen exhaled and rolled his head on the pillow so he was staring at the ceiling. "I did go to him. I went to Karsk, and then I left."

"You left without the cure?" Lizandra asked.

Foyen glanced to the side and favored both of them with that sad smile again. "The price was too precious. I turned him down."

"What did he want?" Reykas asked.

"More than I was willing to give. The Empire gave us this thing, and the Empire takes it away."

"The Empire? Padar is Imperial?"

"Not directly, but close enough. He's connected to the Empire and provides them information. Who knows what else he does? He's a villain. That's all I know for certain."

"But your friend gave him what he wanted," Lizandra said.

"She did. I never asked her what she gave. It's different for everyone, but I know it would be more than you'd give. Either of you."

"How can you know that?" she asked, her forehead creasing in frustration.

"You're both here in Stormbreak. You're already at odds with the High Lord and his servants. I know you're allied with the mage from Klubridge. Whatever Padar asked of you would go against everything you believe. He'd have you betray your own principles to get that cure. That's not something anyone trusted by the rebellion would do."

"But how do you know? How do you know what he'd ask of us?" Lizandra's voice raised. She looked to Reykas. "There's a cure."

He met her eyes and glanced once at Foyen before looking back to her. "We can't do it, Lizandra."

"If there's a chance of you getting well—"

"No," he said. "I am not giving anything to the Empire. I value my life more than to leverage it in a bargain with Imperials."

"Reykas," she said and held his arm with both her hands. Weak though he'd become, she still felt his thick muscles and knew they could be strong again. "This is what we've looked for. This is the answer! You can't just dismiss it."

"You heard what the man said," Reykas said. "This is not something we should pursue."

"We could at least go and see what he says. We could always turn him down," she said, desperate now. If she could get him to agree to that much, they'd be that much closer to his agreeing to the whole deal.

But no, he shook his head once more. "I do not want this. I couldn't travel to Karsk now, even if I did want it. But I do not. We won't discuss this again. Please, Lizandra."

She bit the inside of her cheek to keep from screaming at him in frustration. The solution was right there, and his pride and sense of duty to these people wouldn't let him grasp it. But she knew better than to press the issue. Just like his dogged refusal to go to the infirmary until Samira stepped in, Reykas would dig in his heels about a trip to Karsk. Lizandra made herself nod, and she touched the side of his face, now burning hot again. He would have to take the medicine the doctor had left for him. That would help in the short term, at least, but it would put him to sleep. She had so much to do before then, so much to figure out.

But, for now, she leaned forward and put a gentle kiss on his forehead, her lips coming back salty with his sweat. She wouldn't push him just now, but the issue was far from resolved. Hope had infected Lizandra as surely as the virus had infected Reykas, and it would not leave her any more readily than the illness would leave him.

CHAPTER 7

It was nearly midnight by the time Quentyn Wickes reached Sandwallow. He had started this journey more than a month ago, with a tip from a drunk sailor at a tavern in Plier Gleau. The old man was halfway into a tankard of some disgusting concoction, and Wickes had made sure he got the rest of the way into it before the end of the night. With his lips loosened, the sailor had sent Wickes west and then north to Dushouca.

A few seri into the right palms in Dushouca's less reputable hideaways confirmed that a man with black hair and a beard going gray had indeed come through looking for sturdy laborers who were out of work. His name wasn't Dhasho, though. He'd been going by Chatham, according to an intimidating barmaid with arms bigger than her head. Blaine Chatham. Wickes had smiled at that. Dhasho knew enough to keep moving and to use a different name, but not enough to keep from calling himself by the name of the first ship he'd crewed.

The barmaid said Dhasho—Chatham now—had found the capable bodies he was looking for and then left with the first light the next morning. She didn't know where he was headed, but Wickes knew. Dhasho had gotten himself a crew, so he had to have a ship of his own. The closest port was at Plier Gleau, but he'd just been passing through there, according to the old sailor. He must have come from Acleau to the north, the next most accessible town between there and another port. And the next harbor? Inport, just northwest along the coastline from Plier Gleau.

Wickes did not relish the trip through the swamp from Acleau east, brushing so close to his own people, so long after he'd left them. He kept to the main road, though, and soon found himself in Inport. The harbormaster had dealt with a Blaine Chatham earlier that same week. In fact, this Chatham still had his ship docked on the fourth pier, even now. He'd left with some of his crew for a meeting north, across the land bridge to Sandwallow, and had said he'd be back within eight days. Wickes undoubtedly would meet him on the road if not in Sandwallow itself, the harbormaster had told him.

And that was how Quentyn Wickes found himself weary from the road, hungry for a meal, and ready to be finished with this business that late night in Sandwallow.

The town hung on the edge of a huge sandbar that had attached itself to the mainland on the north and west, with two natural bridges. None of its structures stood taller than a couple of stories, and they had all been cobbled together from weathered boards, many of the earliest buildings seeming to have been built up from scavenged driftwood. The sandy foundation surely couldn't support anything larger or heavier than that. It wasn't much of a town, and it would be a surprise if it still existed in twenty years. Either the brigands that populated most of Sandwallow would have burned the place down, or the sea would have reclaimed it. Either way, Teshovar was likely to be better off without the place.

Wickes had been there before, but it seemed like a lifetime ago. In reality, it had only been four or five years, but so much had changed since then. Not in Sandwallow. That was still the same decrepit pile he remembered. No, Wickes was what had changed, and it was hard to say it had been for the better.

He remembered the saloon at the edge of town. It had no name posted on the sign out front, possibly because most of its patrons couldn't read. Instead of text, there was a worn illustration of a duck, much of the paint having washed away and one leg missing where a chunk of wood was missing. He pushed through the batwing doors at the front, and it was just as dingy inside as he remembered.

A few flickering gas lanterns hanging from the low ceiling lit the front room. There was a bar along the left wall with several drinkers propping themselves up on their stools with steady rounds of booze. Four round tables crowded the rest of the cramped room. Two men and a woman were gambling at one table, and the other two tables had been pushed together to accommodate a bedraggled group that had turned to watch Wickes make his entry. He stood just inside the door for a moment, breathing the acrid stench of old beer, and showing the others he wasn't there to cause trouble. They lost interest in him one by one and went back to whispering and muttering to each other.

Wickes passed between the empty table and the one with the gamblers to get to the bar. There was an abandoned stool at the end, and he settled onto it and waited to get the barkeep's attention.

"You Navy?" The short and round man asked him. He sniffed and wiped the back of a thick hand across his sweaty forehead.

"Not Navy," Wickes said. He was used to hearing that question asked with suspicion every time he arrived in a new place.

"Uniform looks Navy."

"The uniform is Navy. I'm not."

The barkeep studied him for another moment. "I don't need trouble with the Empire."

"I'm not bringing trouble. I'm looking for an old friend. Have you had a man pass through here calling himself Blaine Chatham? About my age, maybe a little shorter?"

"Dark like you?"

"Not dark like me. Light-skinned but with dark hair and a beard going to gray. He'll have a crew with him."

The barkeep sniffed once more and looked past Wickes. Wickes glanced over his shoulder and saw one of the younger men getting up from the tables that had been pushed together. They'd gone quiet and were watching him again. The man pushed out through the saloon doors, and Wickes sighed. He turned back to the barkeep. "It's like that."

"Looks like it. You getting a drink?"

"It appears I'm not."

"Get out, then."

Wickes hesitated only briefly before rising from the stool. He had a good idea of what would be waiting for him outside that door, and he was ready for it. Ready to finish this task Tenez Bekam had set before him three years ago. It was so close to being done, and he'd be free of the obligation. He exhaled and pushed between the tables again, making his way back to the door.

"The gods damn you, you filthy sea rat."

He froze just short of the door and turned back to see a woman sneering at him, filthy hair hanging down to obscure one of her eyes. She bared her dirty teeth at him and cackled. "You heard me. I know who you are. Word of traitors gets around."

That was another thing he'd heard many times over the past few years, and it never got easier. There was no retort, nothing he could say to defend himself. She was right. All of them were right. He'd betrayed everything he used to stand for, and he was about to do it one more time, as soon as he got back out on the street. Trying to answer her would only cause more problems, so he kept his mouth shut and his head down, and he shoved the doors open.

"Hello, Quentyn." The man was waiting right there, in the middle of the darkened path. Wickes walked out to meet him. The road was little more than grainy dirt, and his boots shuffled through the sand as he stepped off the walkway and into the street.

"Dhasho. You're looking well." The sailor was much as Wickes remembered him, but that was years ago. He still had the beard but had put on a few pounds. He was sturdy now in the way success and hard labor can build a man.

"Staying busy does that for me," Dhasho said. "I've heard you've been busy as well."

Wickes tilted his head. "Busier than I'd like to have been."

"What about Rutland? I haven't heard she's been handed over."

"She's dead," Wickes said. "They killed her when they brought me in."

"And yet here you are, alive." Dhasho ran a thumb across his beard. "For now."

Wickes heard a boot scrub through the dirt behind him and had time to spin away from the attack. It was the young man who'd left the saloon to report to Dhasho. His filthy purple shirt hung on him like a rag, and he'd missed Wickes by a mile with the unwieldy piece of wood he'd swung. Before he could lift it for another try, Wickes kicked at his hands and connected hard enough to send the makeshift club flying. The attacker flinched away to hold his injured hand, and that gave Wickes the opening he needed. A quick punch to the side of the head and another to the throat, and the young man was down. That wouldn't be all of them, of course.

Two more were coming after him from opposite sides. He thought they might have been in the saloon as well, but it was too dark to be certain. One of them had a knife and was making a lunge with it even now. Wickes slid back from the stab and caught the man's wrist as the knife sliced past him. He twisted the man's arm hard and pulled forward, using the momentum of the thrust to drag the attacker off his feet. The third man was upon them now, and Wickes turned, still holding the second one's arm. The third man ran into them at full stride, and the knife sank into his belly to its hilt. Wickes shoved both of them away before the blood began to pour. Bekam would have something to say about his ruining this damnable uniform if he stained it red.

As he expected, the man holding the knife had already gotten more than he was being paid for. He scrambled to his feet and ran into the night, cradling his twisted arm, and leaving his partner on the ground with the knife still in him. Wickes stepped over the moaning body and moved toward Dhasho with a deliberately slow pace. There might be more coming, but he doubted it. Even if Dhasho had brought more of his crew with him, they weren't getting paid enough to tangle with a man who had already dropped three of their cohorts. It was just Wickes and Dhasho now.

"Now, Quentyn," Dhasho said, holding up a hand. "Do we really need to—"

Wickes dropped him with two fast punches, one to the nose and the other to the jaw.

∽

The lights of Inport glimmered off the starboard bow. Wickes watched the tiny points of flame in the distance, his arms resting on the railing. He looked down and could barely make out the shining crests of waves hitting the sides of the boat as they sailed southward. The sea was black beneath them, but he knew it wasn't empty. Somewhere down there, she waited.

Wickes glanced to the right, making sure the crew was elsewhere and busy. They wouldn't understand what he was saying anyway, but they were likely to recognize that it was Aevash. Whenever they heard him praying, there was taunting and embarrassment. If he'd been able to pick his own crew, it would have been different. These were Imperial men, though, and they didn't believe. She was a superstition to them, no more than a fairy tale. They didn't know that she could reach a hand up from the depths and crush them as easily as he'd swatted down the thugs in Sandwallow.

He shuddered at the thought of the massive, coral-encrusted goddess lurking somewhere down there, hiding in the deepest crevices of the ocean, her skin bleached white and her eyes black and smooth. One night she would take him, just as she had taken so many other sailors. Perhaps this would be the night, perhaps not. For once, he hoped not tonight. Not when he was so close to the end of this awful task.

Wickes closed his eyes against the dark and listened to the water and the wind, the two elements she controlled. He smelled the sea in the air and tasted the salt on his tongue. She was all around that night, and being so close to Inport and the swamps beyond made him feel closer to her. A chill traveled down his arms, and he stopped it by clasping his hands. He began to pray in the old tongue.

LIZANDRA'S DEEPEST FEAR

By the time he'd finished, he was ready to check on Dhasho. Wickes filled a mug from the cask that had been secured to the deck just outside the cabins. When he brought the watery grog through the door, Dhasho woke on the floor with a start. He blinked fast as he looked around the cabin. He tried to move but didn't get far before the bindings on his wrists held him down.

"Are you thirsty?" Wickes asked, nodding to the mug.

"You broke my nose," the other man said and tried to sniff. Dried blood caked the lower half of his face.

Wickes sat on the edge of the bed, the only piece of furniture in the room. He held the mug down and shook it so the prisoner could hear it slosh. "Here. This will help."

Dhasho leaned toward the mug and looked in, but it was too dark in the cabin to see anything other than the lamplight reflecting off the surface of the drink. "You're trying to poison me."

"If I wanted you dead, you'd be dead in Sandwallow, not tied up here. Drink it."

The bound man stared at Wickes for a long moment but finally allowed him to tip the mug up for him. He swallowed down a sip and recoiled, spilling some of it down his shirt. "What is that? It tastes like piss."

"Been drinking a lot of piss since the last time I saw you?" Wickes laughed and took the mug away.

Dhasho leaned his head against the wall and pushed back with his feet so he could sit up straighter. "Last time I saw you, as I recall, you were in much the same condition I am now."

"I bought you an extra three years. You should be grateful."

"Grateful?" Dhasho barked a hoarse laugh and flinched in pain. "Grateful, you say, after what you've done."

"You'd have done the same," Wickes said. His voice was low and measured, though he struggled to keep it that way.

Dhasho shook his head. "I never would have. We were family, Quentyn. You, me, Weylis, the rest. I never would have done what you're doing."

"You don't know until you have to do it."

"How many more of us are left?"

Wickes sat the mug on the floor and leaned his elbows on his knees. "You're the last."

Dhasho's breathing was a keen whistle through his broken nose. He took his time to reply but finally asked, "How much are they paying you for me? I have a ship. I have seri now. I can pay you, and you just let me go."

"It doesn't work like that, Dhasho."

"How much? A thousand seri? Two thousand? I can pay you, and you can tell them you killed me or I was already dead or whatever you have to tell them. For old time's sake, Quentyn."

"I told you." Wickes leveled his stare at the man he used to call a friend. "It doesn't work like that."

Dhasho blinked at him, and Wickes could see that he understood. "They're not paying you at all. This is how you're keeping yourself out of the very noose you're slipping around all our necks, isn't it? Bring in your old mates, and you get to live. Is that it?"

"Something like that," Wickes said. He forced himself to hold Dhasho's gaze.

Dhasho spat at him, but he was weak, and he ended up just drooling down his own chin. What was Wickes feeling? Some form of pity? Remorse? Shame? A mixture of all of those? He knew he'd pay for what he was doing, if not in this life, then in what came after. She would drag him down and deal with him.

"You were the best of us," Dhasho said. "And now look at you. You've killed your family. All of us but me, and I'm set for the hanging. Look at you. Are you proud of yourself? Has it been worth it?"

Dhasho's eyes turned wet, and Wickes couldn't hold the gaze any longer. He looked away, out toward the deck. "I'm not proud. I'm alive, and soon I'll be free of this burden. That's all I have."

"You're right about that. I hope this life of yours is worth your reputation. You had honor. You used to mean something." Dhasho hissed at him through gritted teeth. "No longer. Everyone knows what you are now. No matter how long you keep yourself alive, everyone in the Madigus Sea knows what you've done. And I know what you fear."

Wickes looked back at the other man, his eyes suddenly wide. He was right. Of all people, Dhasho did know.

"That's right," Dhasho said, his cheeks wet now. "Just try and enjoy this life you've bought yourself with our blood. You may have escaped the Empire's noose, but you haven't escaped her. I hope she haunts you every night you're on this blasted sea. Sooner or later, Ikarna will have you, and she does not treat well with traitors."

∽

Wickes left Dhasho alone for the rest of the trip to Troshall Landing. There was no point in talking with him or even seeing him again before they arrived. They had been as close as brothers once, but that time had gone. Ripped away by the very Empire that Wickes now served.

It was true, everything Dhasho had said. Wickes had chosen his own life and his own survival over those of his crew. It was despicable, and it was made worse by the length of time it had taken him to complete this task. He'd been sent to hunt down all his shipmates that had escaped when Wickes himself was captured, and that had taken most of three years. It had taken him up and down the coast countless times, and he'd been in and out of innumerable towns in the interior. He'd spent long enough traveling to enough places that word got around.

Quentyn Wickes, feared captain of the *Gaillardia*, was now a hound for the Imperial Navy. Getting leads had become more difficult, the more the word spread. Few wanted to help a bounty hunter in the best of times, but no one wanted to help a turncoat. Thankfully, the chore was done now, and he didn't have to run down any more poor souls. He was finished, and the Empire would be finished with him, provided Bekam kept his agreement. But what kind of life would that leave for Wickes?

There was nowhere along the coast that he could travel inconspicuously. He'd always be looking over his shoulder, waiting for that dagger from family or friends of someone he'd turned in. Maybe even from one of his own old cohorts who wasn't a part of Bekam's list. There would be no way to know until it was too late, and if he died, then what was the purpose of all this? He wasn't ready for Ikarna's condemnation. Not yet. Perhaps he could head northwest and lose himself somewhere in the wilderness beyond Karsk. Better to freeze to death up there than to drown out here, anyway. He knew he couldn't head east, farther across the sea. There was nothing out there past the horizon but blasted land, all uninhabitable after the High Lord arose. But regardless of where he went, it would all lead to the same destination.

Wickes set aside his thoughts of the future as his ship slid into the harbor alongside one of the docks reserved for Imperial business. Across the way, he could see merchant ships along another pier, and even farther away was a dry dock where workers were hammering and sawing on the bow of a new ship.

It was a busy day in the harbor, and dockhands were already tying Wickes' craft down. The crew were readying themselves to disembark. Wickes caught the arm of a helmsman who'd been assigned to him for this hunt. He hadn't learned the man's name throughout the entire voyage. Wickes had learned to keep to himself on these trips and didn't see a need to involve himself in any more of these sailors' lives than was required.

"Is the prisoner ready for transfer?" Wickes asked him.

The helmsman jerked his arm free and scowled back. "Go find out for yourself, you filthy pirate."

Wickes considered protesting but held himself back. He was the captain and could have enforced the order, but it wasn't worth it. Not this close to the end.

With a sigh, he turned back to the cabins and found Dhasho still shackled, but this time his hands were in front of him, and he was sitting on the edge of the cot.

"End of the line, eh?" His voice was nasal now, his injured nose fully swollen and darkened.

"Come along," Wickes said, and motioned to the door.

Dhasho grunted at him but came as directed. He ducked the low frame of the door and walked ahead of Wickes out onto the deck of the ship. When he emerged into the sunlight, he gave a bitter chuckle. "Should have figured we were on *Gaillardia*. They let you keep her, eh?"

"They did."

"You didn't get yourself half a bad deal."

Wickes began to argue, but he held himself back once more. He knew Dhasho was right. No matter how miserable Wickes might feel about it all, he was getting to keep his life and even his ship, not to mention his freedom after this. Those were three great steps ahead of what awaited Dhasho at the end of that dock.

The Naval offices were in a three-story building they could see from the deck of the ship. It was painted white, like most of the buildings in Troshall Landing. The summers got hot here and bled into the autumn, and dark colors were a sure way to sweat yourself into a faint. There would be no fainting for the upper crust of the Empire's southern reaches, though. This is where they lived in their splendor, displaying their wealth in ostentatious manor houses and presiding over plantations that stretched for dozens of miles inland. The servants outnumbered the southern landed here, but even the servants lived in elegance, at least as seen from the outside.

"Walk," Wickes said and prodded Dhasho in the back. The other man grumbled something in response and trundled across the gangplank, unable to move faster than at a shuffle with the leg irons weighing him down.

Two soldiers met them on the dock and escorted them up to the Naval house. Neither of them spoke to Wickes, but they both watched him with keen glances the whole way up from the harbor. It was enough to make Wickes wonder whether they knew who was the prisoner and who was the captor.

The front doors stood open to the midday breeze blowing in from the sea. Once inside, one soldier pointed up the stairs, but Wickes already knew the way. He'd been up and down those steps more times than he wanted to count. This would be his final ascent.

He nodded to Dhasho and indicated the stairs, but Dhasho didn't move this time. Wickes grabbed him by the arm and pulled him up the first few steps until he finally moved of his own volition. They turned right at the top, and Wickes knocked at the door. The nameplate on it was brass, tarnishing at the edges, and had "CMDR. DARBY MEDIEAN" engraved with steady block letters.

Wickes expected another soldier to answer the knock, but it was Mediean himself who pulled the door open. The commander was well into his sixties but still stood over six feet tall, only perhaps an inch shorter than Wickes. His tightly trimmed hair had gone white, as had his neatly manicured goatee. Wickes remembered seeing Mediean decades ago, when the Navy man was in his prime. He'd been broad shouldered and thick around the middle, but all that had disappeared during his years behind a desk. He was now thin, his brown skin pulled tight across a face that had become gaunt. His dark eyes were tired, dragged down by bags that hadn't been there until the last year.

"No more uniform?" Wickes asked.

Mediean touched the front of his black suit, more appropriate for bankers or solicitors than career Navy men. "No need for it if I'm not on the sea. Bring him in."

Dhasho didn't need prodding this time. He dragged his bound feet through the door and stood to the side of Mediean's conservatively small desk. Wickes watched his old friend's eyes taking in the room. The certificates on the wall, the oversized painting of Mediean's first ship, the map of the eastern coast and much of the Madigus Sea. They'd spent years running from this man's reach, attacking his vessels, and stealing his supplies, and now they stood with him in his office. It wasn't right, and they both knew it.

Mediean walked to within a foot of Dhasho and studied his face. "This is Dhasho Keats?"

"Blaine Chatham," Dhasho mumbled.

"What's he saying?"

Wickes shook his head. "He's been calling himself Blaine Chatham."

Mediean pulled the corners of his mouth tight and looked at him again. "You are Dhasho Keats. You stand accused of piracy at sea, violence against the High Lord's Empire, theft, conspiracy, and so forth. You will be held here until your trial in three days' time. You will have the opportunity to speak for yourself before judgment is rendered."

"Lot of good it'll do me," Dhasho said and shot a look at Wickes. The weight of his situation had begun to press on him. Soon he'd start begging again, and Wickes couldn't handle more of that. He had to get out of there.

"We're done?" Wickes asked.

Mediean was still talking to the prisoner but halted mid-sentence. "Done?"

"This is the last one. You'll tell Bekam we're square now."

Wickes had Mediean's full attention, and a mean smile played at the corner of his mouth. "Done," he said again. "Square." He looked to Dhasho. "Do you think Captain Wickes and the Empire are done? Are we square, Mr. Keats?"

Dhasho's building dread for his own situation had a momentary reprieve as he clocked the same thing Wickes was realizing. "No," Dhasho said. "I expect you're not done with him, and he'll never square his account with you." Dhasho started laughing then, and Wickes felt the water closing over his head.

"We had a deal," Wickes said. "I've given you everyone Bekam asked for. I did it exactly like he told me, and you have them all now. We're finished. That was the agreement."

Mediean rounded his desk and sank into his chair. The wooden spindles at the back creaked from age, certainly not from his meager weight. "You are a good hunter, Wickes. I'm not too proud to admit that, even to you. Make no mistake, however. There is no deal. I do not make agreements with pirates." He leaned forward on the desk and propped his elbows on the surface. "You are in Imperial custody, the same as this man you just brought me. The only difference is that General Bekam has elected to give you tasks to perform. You'll serve us until he tells you we are finished. And I assure you that we are not yet finished."

Wickes swallowed hard, and he forced his anger down for the third time in the past half hour. He'd been swindled, but it would not do to let his temper control him here, of all places. "What more do you want, Mediean?"

The older man's face cracked into a smile. "Now, that's a

better attitude, isn't it?" The smile disappeared, and he pushed a small stack of papers across the desk. "You're going to sea again, and you're going to catch us one more fish."

Wickes reached for the papers. "There's no one left. Dhasho was the last of my crew."

"Your crew is finished business now. Bekam has a new task, and I believe it will be more engaging than the last."

"Who am I hunting?"

"I trust you've heard the songs and the stories? You're going to find us the mage called Akithar."

CHAPTER 8

The snow came down in thicker flakes, pelting Nahk's head and shoulders as her horse took the mountain path at a slow and steady pace. This was the first true, hard snowfall of the season, and it came earlier this year than last. It wouldn't be long before full winter was upon them, and they'd all be frozen into that blasted castle together. The thought of being trapped behind the ice for a full season made her urge the horse ahead a little faster, but she knew better than to encourage him into a run with the mountain face to their right and the sheer cliff dropping into the endless cold fog on the left.

Nahk looked up at the giant shape of the bird in the rocks as they neared the turn. She hated that thing, but she'd come a long way to see it again. She'd left Tresa in chaos, the bells still chiming in the night and the people none the wiser about their city's government having been wiped out. Nahk was on foot then, her face and her ribs still aching from the fight she'd barely survived. She'd gone west, intending to cut back to the north and take the shorter way to Stormbreak, but the Imperials had a blockade north of the crossroads. She hadn't risked getting close enough to see what was happening there and instead turned south. Aramore was the Imperial seat, but there was no avoiding it unless she wanted to go through those checkpoints. She could have fooled a few Imperials with her Veil, but more than a few, and she'd have had to fight her way out. So Aramore it had been.

Nahk had passed through the city easier than she'd expected and came out the western gates without incident. She'd thought there would be trouble in the Imperial city, but it didn't catch up to her until she was half a day outside Aramore and headed into the first foothills of the mountains to the north. She'd taken the horse from a gang that had tried to rob her, and she'd gotten a purse full of seri as well. The horse had gotten her through the hills, and the seri had replaced her worn shoes with sturdier boots once they reached Esterburgh on the western side of the pass. The air was freezing by then, so she'd bought herself a heavy cloak as well, careful not to spend too much money with one merchant and cautious not to make herself too memorable to anyone in the town.

And then she'd ridden north, the sky becoming grayer and the ground becoming whiter as the elevation rose and the pathway transitioned from dirt to rock. It was a long trip under the best conditions, and Nahk's brush with the Imperial barricades had made it even longer. She'd made it, though, she and the shaggy brown horse that had made a better travel companion than she could have hoped to find on that journey.

As she rode under the shadow of the giant crow, Nahk felt the magic. It buzzed in her head, vibrating her back teeth with a subtle resonance she doubted most people could feel. Something about what they'd done to her had attuned her to this sort of thing, a byproduct of her Veil that she doubted even her creators knew about. The buzzing came now, and it was strong enough to set her on edge, her neck and shoulders tensing as the source neared.

Nahk saw a pale face peering through a narrow window in the guardhouse beside the path a moment before the wooden door opened and a young woman swaddled in several layers of wool and leather leaned out. She stared at Nahk with a mixture of confusion and curiosity for several seconds before she said, "We're not expecting anyone."

"Let me through," Nahk said. "I'm on rebel business."

The guard looked back into the guardhouse, no doubt

wishing she could retreat into it and shut the door against the cold. But she looked back at Nahk and shook her head. "Nobody's supposed to be here just now. The barrier's up. I can't let you through."

Nahk wasn't surprised the guard didn't know her. She spent as little time at the Stormbreak Sanctuary as possible, and when she was there, she kept as low a profile as her work would allow. She shifted herself off the saddle and slipped down to the ground next to her horse, the reins still tight in her hand. "Naecara Klavan is expecting me. Describe me to her, and she'll tell you to let me in."

The guard looked inside her shelter again and then back at Nahk once more before she nodded and headed into the covered passageway that would lead to the keep. Once she was gone, Nahk took a step forward, closer to where she knew the invisible wall of magic would keep her out of the castle. She looked at the ground and saw the rim, where it curved through the snow, a larger pile of powder sloping against the outside of the barrier than was held inside it. She extended her hand and placed her palm against the shield. Through her glove, it felt solid and smooth, like a sheet of slick glass arcing up and away into the sky. The vibration was stronger here, but she felt it only in her head, reverberating in her sinuses and at the back of her throat, not in the hand that laid against the barrier or in the arm attached to it.

A few more minutes passed before there was movement at the opposite end of the passage. Nahk lowered her hand to her side. The figure approaching the other side of the barrier was not Naecara, and it was not the guard.

"Vaino," Nahk said, her nose crinkling and her upper lip pulling up involuntarily to expose her teeth.

He'd left his dark hair hanging loose, and it swayed with his steps as he drew closer. He wore a black coat that hung nearly to his feet, and it looked warm despite its lack of bulk. It was cut lean and fitted to his slender form, just like all the fancy outfits he'd brought north with him. A green scarf wound once around his neck and hung down his chest, the fringe at the end moving in time with his hair. When he was only a foot away from her, he stopped and snorted, a cruel smile twisting the corners of his mouth upward.

"You're back," he said. There was something in his tone, but Nahk wasn't sure whether it was malice or amusement.

"Let me through," she said and shifted her weight. Her horse prodded at the ground behind her, likely sensing her tension.

"Did you come from Tresa?" he asked.

"I did."

"It's done, then?" His eyebrows raised, and he eyed her with interest now.

"I don't report to you." She kept her own tone even, but it was difficult.

"And yet you beg for entry onto my property." He extended a hand back toward the passage to the castle, as though beckoning her through the impassible magical shield.

"I beg for nothing," Nahk said, "and this is not your property. Unless you're claiming it for your Imperial masters."

Vaino snorted again and lowered his arm. "I may have worked for the Empire, but they didn't build me."

"I had no choice in that," she said. "You did. You took Imperial coin for a long time, Vaino."

"And then, when presented with a proper choice, I committed myself to the rebellion. Can you say the same?"

"I can, and I do."

"And you say you don't report to me. That seems at odds with your supposed commitment to the rebellion," Vaino said. He'd narrowed his eyes now, a look Nahk had seen many times before. He wanted to humiliate her before he let her inside.

"The rebellion is not yours, Vaino. Yannis Heriot was a good man, and he was a proper leader. You're pulling down everything he built."

Vaino pursed his lips and crossed his arms, pinning the green scarf to his chest. "He was indeed a good man. He taught me how to resist the Empire, and I'm continuing his work."

Nahk sighed, blowing a breath of warm steam against the barrier, where it dissipated on the invisible surface. "You're continuing nothing, Vaino. Yannis didn't want to build an army. He didn't want to go to war. You were useless to him outside his chambers. Why do you think he never gave you more to do than organize his maps and warm his bed?" Nahk's cheeks burned, but it was too late to take back what she'd already said and too soon to stop. "Naecara supported him the whole time he led Stormbreak, and she earned the respect she's gotten. Naecara is who I'm here to see, and you'll let me through to see her."

Color rushed into Vaino's white skin, his ears turning pink, and his breathing quickened just enough for Nahk to notice it. She doubted anyone else would have sensed his anger, but she knew she'd scored a hit on his ego. This might not be the most productive way of getting her message delivered, but she'd traveled a long way and had no patience for this arrogant pretender's nonsense. Her frustration had been building, and this had been a long time in coming out.

At last, Vaino spoke. "I'm not inclined to let you through. Tell me what you're here to tell her, and I'll consider it."

"You'll let me through, or I'll stand here until Beghran tires."

"Beghran is not in the tower," he said, his words coming clipped.

"Adonar, then. Or whoever you have casting this shield. They'll stop eventually, and I'll come inside, and you'll have impeded the delivery of an important message." Nahk crossed her arms, the reins hanging from her hand over her left bicep.

"How secure do you feel, Vaino? Will your people like to hear how you left me out here in the cold out of spite? How you kept me from delivering an urgent message? And I thought you took the rebellion's best interests to heart." She clucked her tongue at him and shook her head in mock disappointment. She was pushing harder than she needed to, and she might regret it later, but for now, it felt good to see the uncertainty forming around his eyes.

Vaino would never admit it, but he knew his place. He knew precisely how tenuous his hold on the rebellion's leadership was and how many people supported Naecara as its rightful commander. He would have let her through, even if she hadn't pressed. But she had, and Naecara wouldn't be happy about it, and Nahk would answer to the consequences later.

Vaino broke his stare and glanced toward the door to the

guardhouse, still standing open. He looked at Nahk once more. "The sooner you're in, the sooner you'll be back out. You never stay long." And he waved a hand toward the doorway.

Nahk couldn't see the mage inside, and nothing visibly changed, but she felt the vibration change as a doorway opened in the barrier. She led the horse through and passed Vaino without another word. She'd said enough for now, more than she'd ever said to him before. Nahk still had more she'd like to say, but time was short, and she was already running late.

∽

The great irony was that Vaino would have welcomed Nahk back to the Stormbreak Sanctuary if he'd known the contents of the contract she carried. She'd opened and reread that paper so many times during her journey that the edges were becoming frayed. It was the one time her goals might align with his, but she wasn't about to let him know that before she'd reported to Naecara, the true leader of the rebellion and the one who paid Nahk for her services.

Beyond that, Naecara understood Nahk, as well as anyone could. Vaino saw her as nothing more than a leftover assassin, created and discarded by the Empire that made her. And maybe there was truth in that, but he didn't know why she came to the rebellion or why she stayed after he treated her the way he did. He had no interest in her remorse, her anger, and her commitment. To be fair, she had no understanding of Vaino's own motivations, beyond his desire to spend the rebellion's seri on new outfits to keep him fashionable in the frozen north of Teshovar, and she had no desire to get to know him better. They fell into each other's lives as fate dropped them, and the best either of them could do was to move forward from there.

The shield still encased Stormbreak when Nahk emerged from the covered passageway, so it wasn't snowing there. The sun hid behind clouds, but its light still came through the invisible dome, casting odd shadows on the ground where clumps of snow suspended on the barrier blocked it. All that snow would drop whenever Vaino's mages released the shield.

LIZANDRA'S DEEPEST FEAR

Nahk handed her horse off to a stable hand and gave the flank a quick pat before she headed into the keep. Before entering the building, she pulled the hood down from her head and brushed away the snow where it had settled on her cloak at the shoulders. Her short hair exposed the back of her neck, and she shivered at the sudden chill as she moved into the courtyard.

Naecara wasn't there, so she must have been in her office, diagonally across the quad from where Nahk entered. She wasn't sure whether Naecara's office being placed on exactly the opposite side of the keep from Vaino's was intentional, but the symbolism was not lost on her.

She crossed the open ground and passed rebels at work, resting, and training without recognizing any of them. She'd been gone for months, and it was likely that many newcomers had arrived in her absence. It was just as likely, though, that most of these people had been at Stormbreak every time Nahk had been there and she'd simply avoided interacting with them. By design, she knew few of the rebels beyond Naecara and Vaino. It suited her to not become familiar with or attached to these doomed people and for them to not know her.

Nahk held no illusions about this ragtag group being able to overthrow the High Lord, especially not if they followed Micah Vaino's plans. He'd already convinced half of them Peregrine didn't even exist. They didn't even know what they were up against. If and when they failed, it would do her no good to be connected to or identified by any of them. The best hope for the rebellion's success was that they'd realize the value of Naecara's leadership, but that tide shift was slow in coming. Nahk needed to accomplish her own goals before the whole thing fell apart.

As Nahk neared the opposite side of the courtyard, the door to Naecara's office pulled open. A short man with dark, curly hair looked out one way and then the other, and he slipped into the quad with the practiced hesitancy of one used to moving below the notice of others. Like recognized like, and Nahk nodded to him when their eyes met. Without acknowledging her, he pulled a drab brown hood over his head, hunched his shoulders, and headed in the opposite direction from her.

Naecara Klavan managed an extensive network of spies and

information brokers who ranged far and wide through the realm. Vaino had had access to his own sources of information during his time on the Imperial payroll, but those avenues had closed to him once he'd followed Yannis Heriot into the indignity of revolution. Vaino hated that Naecara now controlled the flow of intelligence, but he surely recognized her value. That might be the key factor that had, so far, prevented his scheming her expulsion from Stormbreak. Naecara was a more legitimate leader than Vaino, and she had better eyes and ears on the Empire than Vaino did.

Nahk didn't know how many rebels still hung on Vaino's every word, but she suspected the bulk of them were those who were hungry for battle. They were the ones who thought change could be made through traditional warfare, as the rebels amassed an army and threw it against the Empire's. They were the ones who believed Vaino's nonsense about Peregrine not existing. Of course he existed, and he'd smite any army that moved openly against him before it even arrived on the field of battle.

Naecara favored a subtler touch, poisoning the Empire from beneath and from within. She reasoned that the High Lord's structure could not stand on weakened legs, so she plotted and identified points of vulnerability, and then she sent her agents to hit the government where it would hurt. That was how Nahk had found herself in Tresa and how she'd made similar visits to so many other unsuspecting hosts over the past year.

The short man had pulled Naecara's door fully shut, so Nahk rapped her knuckles against it as she turned her shoulder into it, letting herself face the courtyard. Keeping her back to the wall was instinct by now, even within this keep that so many called a sanctuary. But Nahk knew all too well, and better than most, that the dagger that killed you was the one that got you when you weren't watching for it.

Nahk turned back to the door as it opened, and she nodded to Naecara. "It's done. Tresa—"

"I know it's done," Naecara said and scanned the courtyard over Nahk's shoulder. "I got word days after you'd finished. It was good work, but I worried you'd been caught."

"I was delayed coming back," Nahk said. "A roadblock I had to go around." She glanced back, following Naecara's gaze, and saw Vaino across the way, leaning against the brick column next to his office and watching them. "He didn't want to let me in," she said. "He tried to keep me outside the shield."

Naecara huffed something that sounded halfway between amusement and frustration and stepped backwards into her office. "Come in."

Nahk had been in the office countless times, and its lack of a chair still struck her every time she entered. Naecara was a woman of action and motion, and Nahk couldn't imagine her sitting behind a desk. Nevertheless, it felt like every office needed a chair, and this one felt odd without one. The floor was mostly open, giving Naecara the room she needed to pace or, as she often did, to spread innumerable papers and maps across the wooden floor. Most of the rooms in the castle had their original stone floors, but Naecara had brought planks into her space and helped install them herself. The result was a cozier room that felt less like it had been hollowed out of the side of the mountain than the rest of the keep.

She'd pushed tables against three of the walls, and two stools sat at angles to each other against the fourth. That was where Naecara sat when she absolutely had to have a conversation without standing and moving, but she didn't offer a seat to Nahk just now or take one herself. Instead, she pushed the door shut and exhaled a breath that sounded like she'd been holding it for a while.

It was then that Nahk saw the tiredness in her eyes. Naecara didn't let many people see her when she wasn't at her strongest, but she'd known Nahk long enough and trusted her enough to let the seams show. She walked to the nearest table and leaned back against it, allowing her shoulders to slouch.

"Micah was giving you trouble," she said.

Nahk considered complaining about him, as she'd done before, but this time she said, "No more than usual."

Naecara said, "Hmm," and Nahk knew that meant she didn't believe her and didn't appreciate Nahk's holding back details on account of sympathy for Naecara's exhaustion.

"He wanted me to tell him about Tresa before I came to you," she said at last. "He threatened to leave me outside the shield."

"And you had none of that," Naecara said.

"I did not. I might have gone a bit farther than I should have, but you know how he is."

"And I know how you are," Naecara said with a smile. Her face soon fell, though. "He's been worse lately."

"The Aescalan?"

"That and the group from Klubridge."

"What about Klubridge?"

Naecara's eyebrows raised, and she started to say something, but Nahk saw her change direction before she said, "We've had refugees arrive. You've heard of the wizard Akithar?"

Nahk couldn't help but laugh. "You're joking. He's here?"

"He came with others. Micah has been working him over, bringing him into the fold. I haven't had even a moment to approach him myself."

"That figures," Nahk said. "I'm sick of hearing every bard from here to Plier Gleau sing his praises. It's no wonder he's enamored Vaino."

"It's not just that," Naecara said. "We had news while you were gone." She moved from her perch to the table on the wall to her left. She shuffled through a few papers scattered atop it and pulled one free, handing it to Nahk. "Aether brought this. I made a copy for myself before passing it along to Micah."

Nahk took the paper and read it twice before she realized what it meant. "They found him. The Tamrat heir."

"They did." Naecara slid her index finger under one line and then the next. "This is his name, and that's his location. Micah is eager to go after him, and I've heard he's recruited the wizard to travel there with the Aescalan."

That took Nahk by surprise, and she looked up from the paper. "He's sending Akithar after the scion? Why would he do that?"

"I'd wager he thinks the wizard's reputation will be enough to convince this Hyden Gressam to join the cause."

"He's more likely to get the wizard killed. The man's no more than a stage magician, isn't he?"

Naecara gave an exaggerated shrug. "Who knows how much of what we've heard from Klubridge is true? The stories say—"

"The stories are rubbish," Nahk said. "They say he resisted a silencing by the Herons, wiped out an entire squadron of Kites, and killed a chamir with his magic. A chamir."

"Well, we at least know the magic part isn't true. Akithar is no mage."

That stopped Nahk mid-thought. "He what?"

"Aether was in Klubridge when the city turned, and she came here on a ship with him. She said he's no mage. He'd been playing coy with that subject the whole time he'd been in the city, according to her. A decade, at least."

"To what end?" Nahk asked.

"He was a stage magician, and the mystery helped draw the crowds. As to why he maintained the charade after the Empire was after him, I have no idea."

"There are too many accounts of his using his magic to defeat the Imperials. Not all of them could be wrong."

Naecara opened her hands and tilted her head. "Mage or no, he's Micah's problem now."

"He could be our problem as well," Nahk said and reached inside her cloak to withdraw the well-worn contract she'd carried from Tresa. "Read this." She pushed it into Naecara's hands, and the other woman looked at her for a quick moment, the lines between her eyebrows creasing, before her eyes turned down to the parchment.

"Hyden Gressam," she read aloud. "That's a name we've been hearing too frequently."

"The Empire has hired the Nightingales to find him and kill him," Nahk said. Her pulse quickened, and she leaned closer. "The Nightingales, Naecara."

The taller woman met her gaze and held it long enough for it to feel uncomfortable before she sighed. "We can't do anything about this, Nahk."

"We can and we will. Vaino will even approve this one. No need to skulk about in secret if we're saving his precious scion from—"

"This isn't about Vaino or the scion."

Nahk's mouth hung open, and she blinked at the other woman in disbelief. "You promised me, Naecara. This is the deal you made with me. If I stayed here and helped you, you would help me." She grabbed the paper, nearly tearing it out of Naecara's hands and shook it. "This is the first lead we've had on the Nightingales in half a year. The first time we've ever intercepted one of their contracts before they executed it. We know who they're going after, and we know where he is."

Naecara waited for her to finish before shaking her head, a slow and sad shake, but a refusal, nonetheless. "Nahk—"

"This is politics," Nahk snapped at her. "You've used me, and now you won't act on this because it would help him. Because Vaino wants the scion."

"Nahk," she said again, but the younger woman's fury was unabated.

"I should have known. I should—"

"Nahk," Naecara said once more, this time with a firmness that silenced her protests. "Under any other circumstances, we could do this, but something has happened. I need you with me. We'll give this to Micah, and he'll pursue it, but..." Her voice trailed into silence, and for the first time since she'd come into the office, Nahk saw the sadness in Naecara's eyes.

"What is it?" she asked. "What's happened?"

Naecara studied the floor for another moment before she walked to the table on the south wall and pulled a slip of paper from beneath a book. "After Akithar left Klubridge, the city fell into chaos. The citizens revolted and overthrew the constabulary. They closed the city to Imperials, and we've heard that some of the loyalists and nobility that were trapped inside the city walls were executed."

"I heard pieces of that," Nahk said. Where was this going?

"We knew the Empire wouldn't let this stand. It took some time, but they have exacted their revenge."

"They retook the city?"

"No," Naecara said and handed her the message. "It happened earlier this week, but I just got this message moments before you knocked at my door. It took time for word to reach me."

Nahk read the text and shook her head. "This makes no

sense. What does this mean?" She read it again. "How reliable is this?"

"Reliable," Naecara said. "And it means just what it says." She took the paper and looked at it once more before dropping it back on the table. "The city is in ruins. Klubridge has been destroyed."

PART II
PIERCING VISION

CHAPTER 9

Bekam saw smoke on the horizon before he could smell it in the air. It was midday, the sky the kind of blue streaked with thready white clouds that always felt heavier than they looked. The sun shone directly overhead as he climbed the low hill, and his boots crunched on the brittle grass that was making its transition from bright green to a duller shade. Before long, winter would be upon them, and the whole hill would be brown.

A smear of gray marred what he could see of the sky past the top of the hill. It reminded him of Marjiel's attempts at art, when she would construct the easel and stare at the blank canvas for what seemed like hours. At last, she would dip a fat brush into black paint and drag it across the surface, the stroke more about the motion than the result. She would step back from the easel, disappointment clenched in her jaw and the brush dangling from her fingers, paint dripping on the hard floor, before she would sigh and abandon the project. He'd seen it happen enough times to remember that single, dramatic flourish that ruined the painting before it had even begun, and that's what marred the sky as he approached the crest of the hill. The thick stroke of black faded against the blue, the edges jagged from the uneven bristles of the brush.

Bekam hesitated, his right foot planted ahead and at an incline. He shouldn't have been able to see so much of the sky.

He'd been up and over that hill so many times in the past, and he was used to the view, used to seeing the tower rising to split the horizon. He should have seen the spire at the top before he even began his ascent, and by now he should have been able to see the ornate and curved walls of the tower beneath it, the tallest structure in the city by far. It rose from the middle of the Henburn Estate in the center of the city's Imperial complex and was the most easily identifiable structure in all of Klubridge. But it wasn't there. It was gone, replaced by that streak of smoke across the sky.

Bekam had left Aramore as soon as he'd received the message, but as he traveled south and east, he'd questioned its accuracy. "Klubridge is destroyed." What could that even mean? The rebels had taken the city and torn down the Imperial leadership. Perhaps it was metaphorical? But no, he knew it would be more than that. He knew it was something literal, something substantial. All the way from Aramore, he'd pondered the message, but he'd known it meant exactly what it said. Klubridge was destroyed, and only one man could be behind its doom.

He forced his legs into motion, and then he saw the Imperial tower, or what remained of it. The white stone column climbed upward from the city as it always had, but now it ended at a severe angle, as though the upper half had been sheared from the lower. The line where the tower stopped existing was abrupt, so even and straight it called to mind a knife cutting through a hot loaf of bread, bisecting it into two parts. It was as if something had sliced the tower apart just as easily and just as precisely. Sections of the wall had crumbled inward, leaving jagged holes, but those had come after whatever had done the initial damage.

As the rest of Klubridge came into view, he saw it wasn't just the tower and wasn't just the Henburn Estate. What lay before him looked nothing like the city he'd known. Bekam stood atop the hill now and stared at the destruction ahead of him. Parts of the city walls still stood, at least on this western side, but most of them had fallen, cut down as cleanly as the tower had been. The still-standing pieces of wall formed strange angles and looked less like defensive structures and more like odd sculptures, carved by a demented creator.

Beyond the walls and through the gaps where they had once stood, he could see the rest of the city that was no longer a city. What still stood resembled chunks of rocks, pebbles thrown and scattered by a giant child at play, the buildings cut and torn, toppled just as the walls and tower had been. For a dizzying moment, Bekam imagined his daughter Leonie looming above the city, that vacant stare in her eyes as she swung a massive cleaver at Klubridge, rending the city with clumsy but powerful swipes.

He shook his head and banished the thought. Of course it had been nothing like a massive and maladroit child, but something had come upon the city and sheared stone, torn apart wood, and sliced marble in a way he'd never imagined possible. This was not the work of an army. This was magic.

The High Lord Peregrine.

Bekam's mouth twitched as he coughed a nervous laugh between his lips. Peregrine did not exist, of course, but this was exactly the sort of vengeance the Empire would blame on him. They'd say he had descended upon the city and unleashed his immense power against Klubridge as recompense for its disloyalty. He'd excised it from Teshovar as easily as a man cutting the pit from a peach. This act would bolster the people's belief in the phantom that ruled over them, and fear of the High Lord would increase, as it always did after every new and barbaric act. Bekam had seen this sort of strategy before, but the physics of it eluded him. He'd seen powerful magic before, but nothing that could have rent this much disaster from what he presumed to be a single mage.

A sudden breeze tugged at Bekam's cloak, whipping the yellow-bordered blue fabric away from his shoulder and allowing a cold wind to cut through. The smell of Klubridge rode the wind and came to him all at once, nearly staggering him backwards. The cold air carried the scent of burning, so similar to the small logs that had been crackling in Bekam's own hearth the night he'd departed Aramore. But between and beneath that familiar and sooty smell lay a different odor. It was a rancid smell that forced him to swallow, and he raised a hand to pull the edge of his cloak around the front of his face, covering his nose and mouth.

"It comes from the corpses," Qae'lon said as he approached. His voice was soft in volume but high in pitch, formal and polite, but more familiar than Bekam liked.

Bekam glanced at him, his own mouth pulled tight now as annoyance cut through the dread bubbling in his gut. "This was you, then?"

Qae'lon was tall, taller even than Bekam, and slim, his face long with the cheekbones pressing out from beneath his pale, almost silvery skin. No wrinkles lined his forehead, but his hair had gone white, and a golden clasp at the back of his head held it back from his ears. Bekam couldn't begin to guess at this man's age. He could have claimed to be in his twenties or in his seventies, and Bekam would have believed either.

He wore something akin to a gown, the material white and silky, the shoulders pushed out to points from which white feathers sprouted in a downward arc that made Bekam think of the tassled epaulets on his own formal uniform. Gold braiding lined the front of the robe, where it closed with golden clasps all the way down the front, stopping just above the ground and hiding Qae'lon's feet. He seemed to float on the hill, nothing visible beneath the hem of the robe to support his weight. It was like the robe Qae'lon had worn in the Council chamber but even more ornate here on the hill overlooking the carnage he had wrought.

Another breeze rolled across the hill, and Bekam shivered in its path, but the mage stood motionless as the thin fabric of his robe rippled, revealing an ornate pattern sewn into the white material that shimmered as it caught the sunlight from different angles.

Qae'lon cut his eyes to the right, meeting Bekam's gaze, and they were as pale as the rest of him, the light blue of his irises nearly as white as the sclera. "The smell," he said. "It's the bodies they are burning."

Bekam pulled his eyes away and looked back toward the city, and he saw it now, the source of the smoke on the horizon. He'd assumed it was a remnant of fires that had broken out during Klubridge's destruction, but it was too regular and contained for that. These were intentional flames that someone was maintaining, each curling a thin line of black into the air. There were too many to count, and the lines of smoke mingled above the city, casting a dirty haze beneath the clouds. These were bonfires, and Bekam could see the flickering orange of the nearest one, just outside the crumbled wall. People worked around it, pulling kindling from a wagon and tossing it onto the blaze. No, not kindling. They were burning bodies. The bodies of the people who died when the city fell.

Motion to the left drew Bekam's attention, and he watched another cart, this one led by a weary horse and loaded high with bundles and boxes that at least were not corpses, as it made its way out from the city, a bedraggled man walking alongside the horse and a woman following behind, limping every few steps. Behind them came another small group, this one parents with two young children, and another group behind them, these too filthy for any details to be discerned. The line continued ahead and behind, slow and heavy as it pulled out from Klubridge like defeated soldiers making their way home from the battlefield.

But these people were leaving their homes. They were refugees, displaced by whatever Qae'lon had done to Klubridge, and they'd be heading for Gramery, Deakem, anywhere that would house them. The towns nearest Klubridge had already been dealing with an influx of nobles and Imperials displaced by the rebellion, and now they'd be truly overwhelmed when the commoners arrived behind them.

"What did you do?" Bekam asked, despite himself. The question pressed its way past his reservations.

Qae'lon touched his thin lips with spindly fingers that bent like the legs of an alabaster spider, the nails grown long enough to resemble small claws. His lips pursed as his eyebrows raised, his forehead somehow still avoiding creasing. "You haven't heard? It was the High Lord himself."

Bekam's eyes narrowed, and he frowned at the mage.

But Qae'lon carried on. "He was here!" He gestured toward Klubridge, his hand sweeping upward. "He appeared from nothingness, a shade clad in black. Shadows gathered in the sky around him, terrible and great. He announced his judgment against the people of Klubridge, and he summoned forces from the sky like they have never seen."

Qae'lon's eyes stared blankly ahead as he spoke, and Bekam studied them for a twitch, a tell, anything that would reveal what the true story might be. But there was no wavering. His eyes remained fixed, his breathing steady and slow, and his smooth face showed no sign of deception. Was he mad? Did he truly believe what he was saying? That the High Lord had come down from the clouds and torn Klubridge apart with magic?

The mage's eyes flicked back to meet Bekam's again, and a grin cracked across his face. His laugh was a trill that spread goosebumps up Bekam's arms. "I nearly had you," he said. "Of course it was me."

Bekam's stomach gurgled again, and his right foot shifted back a half step. This madman had truly destroyed Klubridge. "What did you do, Qae'lon?"

Qae'lon cut his eyes toward Bekam, and his lips parted, baring his small white teeth in a narrow grin. "Do you know what this is?" From within a fold in his shimmering robe, he withdrew something round and smooth, just large enough that he had to spread his fingers to hold it in one hand. The marbled surface was slick, the sun reflecting off it in a wicked glare. It was black, but red veins ran through it, and beneath those ran orange ones, creating irregular patterns unlike anything Bekam had seen. No, he did not know what the ball was.

"Have you heard of the Eye of Kelixia?" Qae'lon asked, glancing back at Bekam, one corner of his mouth now turned upward in a smirk.

Bekam snorted at that. "Every fool knows what the Eye of Kelixia is. It's a children's story."

"Oh, is it?" Qae'lon asked, his voice quiet and airy, his brows drawing down now, his mouth twisting into a more savage grin than before. He clasped the orb in both hands then and extended his arms out from his chest. The sound was quick, something like the sound Leonie made when slurping soup from her spoon, but more abrupt than that. Bekam flinched back, and a flash accompanied the sound, a blinding stab of colorless light that erupted from the man's entire body and then disappeared.

The orb glowed for an instant longer than Qae'lon did, and then the light leaped out of it, shooting away and down the hill. Bekam barely had time to turn his face away from the light, and that's how he saw a cluster of refugees explode. He could think of no other word to describe what happened to them. One instant, they were walking along the path in line with the rest of the displaced unfortunates. The next, their upper halves had left their lower. Some of them lost their heads, some their arms, and some evaporated into nothingness altogether. The ones that didn't entirely disappear fell in a sudden and horrifying tumble of limbs and rucksacks. The refugees in front of and behind them began screaming, and the terror spread up and down the line as panic unfurled itself. Survivors scrambled, dropping their belongings, abandoning their friends, and fleeing in all directions. What had been a slow and orderly line was now a mass of chaos with fresh carnage at its center.

Bekam clasped a hand across his mouth and staggered back a step. "What did you do?"

"A demonstration," Qae'lon said, as he slipped the artifact back into his robe. He favored Bekam with another smile, this one less manic. "Retaking the city should be much easier now, wouldn't you say, General? I believe I have fulfilled the task the Council set before me."

A new cloud of screams arose as more refugees came upon the bodies of the ones Qae'lon had slaughtered. The rising mayhem pulled Bekam's attention away for just long enough for him to draw an unsteady breath. When he looked back to Qae'lon, Bekam found himself standing alone again, once more shivering and confused atop the hill.

∼

Cillan caught up to Bekam when he was more than halfway down the other side of the hill and headed toward the ruined city of Klubridge. Bekam was glad he had approached from south of the road, given the chaos continuing to unfold as one group of refugees after another discovered the bodies of the ones Qae'lon had mutilated. Would someone eventually move the corpses and take them to the fires? Or would they lie on the road until they rotted away, a lingering reminder of terror for all the survivors who were fleeing the city? Surely the carts would come for them before dusk. That's what Bekam told himself as he moved closer to the edge of the city and forced his eyes away from the brutality.

"Was he a mage?" Cillan asked, breathing hard as he jogged down the hill, his slick shoes sliding on the grass every few steps. Bekam had brought him along on this trip, but Cillan had come ill-equipped for travel. He was a creature of office life, comfortable in his suits and roaming the governmental hallways of Aramore. It was rare that he left the Imperial city and even rarer for him to balance his descent down a slippery slope in the wild.

Bekam glanced at his secretary and let out a breath. "Did you see where he went?" Bekam asked.

Cillan shook his head. "He was standing beside you, but he was gone after I looked away for just a moment."

"It was Qae'lon," Bekam said.

Cillan stumbled again, more likely from his slick shoes hitting another patch of long grass than from surprise. "Of course," he said. And, after a brief pause, "He reports directly to the High Lord, just as you do." His voice wavered somewhere between awe and fear.

"Something like that," Bekam said. Cillan was a believer, and if he had heard the rumors of Peregrine's nonexistence, he chose not to believe them. "He also destroyed Klubridge." Cillan nearly came to a full stop at that, but Bekam grabbed his sleeve and pulled him along. "He showed me an artifact that seems capable of having done it."

"I saw what he did to the people on the road," Cillan said, nearly at a jog to keep up with Bekam.

"He claims it's the Eye of Kelixia."

"But that's—"

"A myth, I know. Whatever the thing he has is called, it's dangerous."

They were off the hill by then, and as they approached the ruins of its walls, Klubridge loomed above them, even in its state of destruction. The smell of death was stronger there and grew less tolerable the farther they went, but Bekam forced the stench out of his mind. He heard Cillan swallow more than a few times, no doubt fighting the urge to vomit as the smell of bodies, burning and otherwise, washed over them with the breeze. The wind lost its chill the closer they came to Klubridge. It was warmer now, the heat of the fires and of the press of so many people overwhelming the insistent approach of winter. The odor intensified in the heat, and Cillan finally lost his battle, staggering to his knees and retching into the grass.

Bekam waited for him and stared at the city. Someone had swung the massive gates shut when the attack had commenced, and they remained shut even then. Ironically, the section housing the gate structure was one of the few intact portions of the wall that still stood on this western edge of the city.

The procession of travelers leaving the city stumbled over the crumbled blocks of the walls to the left and right of the gate. Their exodus was slow and seemed eternal. How long had people been leaving? How many more people could there be in the city after so long an evacuation? Was it like this at the city's other gates?

Those were questions Bekam knew would answer themselves in time. Before then, he had other worries.

Through the gaps in the wall, he could see the outer edge of what had been the Financial Quarter. Bekam opened his mouth to speak to Cillan, and bitter ash settled on his tongue. He spat into the grass, his gorge rising as he recalled the bodies were the only things in the city that were burning. Bekam spat once more and looked to Cillan, still kneeling on the ground behind him. Cillan was not prepared for this kind of reality, with buildings blasted apart and their inhabitants slaughtered. He'd be of no use for at least another quarter hour. Bekam coughed another flake of ash out of his mouth and wiped at his lips with the back of his hand before he turned back to Klubridge and studied the devastation.

The walls and buildings had been sheared at odd angles, just as it had appeared from above when he stood on the hill. From where he now stood, the city looked less like a jumble of tossed stones and more like a field of enormous and jagged black teeth. He remembered Klubridge as being a colorful city, bustling with constant business and thriving on its arts. When it fell, all the color went with the life. The remaining structures hung heavy and gray, the facades ripped away, the roofs blasted apart, and the stony innards spilled forth in a mess of dark rock.

Nevertheless, some buildings still stood. As he looked through the space where the wall had been, Bekam saw that some of the smaller buildings even appeared to be untouched by Qae'lon's attack. They hid among the rubble of their larger neighbors, still standing, but for what purpose? Klubridge well and truly was destroyed. There was nothing worth salvaging for the Empire. Innumerable people had died within those walls, peasants and nobility alike, and sorting through the carcasses of citizens and buildings was not a task Bekam imagined the Council had any interest in pursuing. Qae'lon had said he'd made it easier to retake the city, and it was true. Bekam imagined the Empire could march a small squadron to Klubridge and reclaim the whole place within a day. The rebels were finished there, but so was the city.

Any answers about Akithar's destination when he left Klubridge were lost in the ruination.

"There's nothing for us here," Bekam said and held his hand out to Cillan.

The other man took it and rose on shaky legs. "General?"

Qae'lon had done this to him. The Council had given both of them jobs, but the mage had known their priority was quelling the rebels and discouraging other cities from repeating Klubridge's transgression. Qae'lon had struck fear into the rebellion, and he had rendered the reclaiming of Klubridge moot. Would the Council overlook the loss of the city's revenue in the face of such a show of Imperial strength?

But someone had to answer for all that had happened in Klubridge, and Bekam would find no answers in the ruined city. There was nothing remaining that could bring him closer to finding the rebels, and he would have nothing to report to the

Council. Bekam would bear the full weight of the blame for the fall of the city, the loss of an entire unit of Kites, and now the utter destruction of one of Teshovar's key urban centers. The city was lost, and with it went the seri it generated and the entertainment it provided to keep the citizens compliant. So much gone, lost beyond recovery.

Cillan wavered next to Bekam, and he still looked queasy, but he said, "This was all his doing."

"Whose doing?" Bekam put a hand on the man's shoulder to steady him.

"Qae'lon. It was the Herons. They failed to silence the mage, and then all this happened. It's one thing after another, and it was Qae'lon behind it all along."

Bekam released Cillan's shoulder and ran his fingers over his mustache and his thumb across his chin. Qae'lon. Of course, the mage had not been behind the failed silencing. No one who hadn't been in that plaza knew what had really happened there, but there was no question in public opinion that the Herons were the ones who could not quell Akithar's magic. And Cillan was right. That was when the city fell. It wasn't when Bekam's Kites had been investigating and identified the wizard as a rebel. They'd been in the city for weeks without incident. It was only after the Herons arrived that everything turned sour.

And then Qae'lon had come to Klubridge himself and used a weapon of illegal origin to decimate the city and its inhabitants. The Empire could have recovered Klubridge, but now it was a lost resource, all at the hands of Qae'lon.

Bekam breathed faster, heedless of the surrounding stench, as the plan formulated. He had already sent the pirate after Akithar, and he'd use that thread to find the rest of the rebels. That would take time, though, and likely longer than the allotted month. In the meantime, the Council needed someone to blame for this disaster, and that would not be Bekam.

CHAPTER 10

Samira looked into the bowl, and her own tired eyes stared back from her reflection in the broth. It was some sort of vegetable stew, and it smelled better than most of the meals she'd had since they'd arrived at Stormbreak, but she hadn't even dipped her spoon into it. Voices rumbled and chairs dragged against the hard floor behind her, the sounds of cutlery and bowls scraping together echoing through the dining hall, but she sat in silence.

Ten years in Klubridge. Ten years of refining the stage show and putting together the perfect company. Ten years of remodeling and upgrading the Chamberlain Theater to become one of the most prestigious in the Theater District. Ten years of family.

All of that was gone now, wiped away by the messages that had been arriving at the rebel keep for the past few days. It had started with the initial news that the city had been destroyed, but nobody really knew what that meant. Had the uprising been quelled? Had the Empire retaken Klubridge and destroyed its temporary insurgency?

Was it a metaphorical destruction? That was how Samira had initially interpreted the news. It was all too easy to imagine lines of Imperial soldiers marching through the streets and shoving the citizens back into line. Perhaps more Kites had come, maybe the blue ones filing back into Klubridge now that the red ones were finished. The Kites would be going through her theater, ransacking more of her belongings and trashing more of her memories, and those thoughts had filled her with a quiet and impotent rage. There was nothing she could do, sequestered in this remote hideout tucked into the frozen mountains, farther north than she or anyone else she knew had ever been.

But then the additional reports arrived, and it quickly became apparent that none of what Samira had imagined was accurate. "City walls fallen" read one message. "Bodies being burned in streets" read another. Piece by piece, the picture of what had happened at Klubridge assembled.

"Not hungry?"

Samira blinked up from her bowl to see Caius watching her across the wooden table. Concern filled his eyes, but the dark circles below them betrayed his own exhaustion. "Do you think it was Peregrine?" she asked.

Caius frowned and leaned in. "Peregrine?"

"At Klubridge." She found she couldn't say more than that. Just thinking about the city—her city—laid to waste dried her mouth and soured her throat. Who knows what would have happened if she spoke about it aloud?

Caius shook his head. "Vaino got a new report today. Witnesses saw someone with a weapon. They think it was a mage."

It was Samira's turn to frown. "And Vaino still doesn't believe Peregrine exists."

"No," Caius said and dropped his eyes to study his own bowl. He'd gotten the spoon into it but had gotten no farther than that.

"He says Peregrine is a phantom."

"Something like that."

They had talked about it in the days after Vaino had made his revelation or claim or whatever it had been, but they hadn't truly discussed it. Not to the extent that any of it sat right with Samira. "What do you really think?" she asked.

Caius looked up at her again, and he seemed even more tired than before. His shoulders sagged, and he'd missed another couple days of shaving. He gave a slight shrug. "I don't know. It makes sense, in a twisted kind of way. We've always been told about the High Lord and his powers, but there's never anything specific. Have you ever heard about him actually appearing anywhere? Actually using his magic to do anything during our lifetime?"

She shook her head. What Caius was saying seemed reasonable, but it didn't sit well with her. Had they truly lived their whole lives oppressed by a manufactured rumor? Her conversation with Lizandra lingered. "But how could the Empire suppress that? Surely more people would be talking about it, if they knew he wasn't real."

"Maybe he did exist at some point. Maybe he was the origin of all this mess we're living with now. But then, once he was gone, the people closest to him just kept it going. They perpetuated what he started, and they held onto their power. I don't think everyone knows about this. The way Vaino said it, it seems like only those in the highest ranks knew the truth. They used it to control their underlings, too."

"How high was Vaino placed in the Empire?" Samira asked. She knew he'd been part of the government, but it sounded as if Caius knew more than she did. Of course he would, though. He'd had Vaino's attention since that first meeting.

"Vaino attended the Academy. He was a strategist. Competent and well respected, from what I can tell. I don't think he had much political standing on his own, but Yannis Heriot did. He was a governor or high magistrate. Something like that."

"Yannis Heriot," she said. The man who had led the rebellion prior to Vaino. Or at least this incarnation of it. The more she learned, the more it sounded like the rebellion was an ever-evolving thing that had taken various forms over thousands of years. Its history had fragmented as it had failed time after time, only to be resurrected by other hopeful revolutionaries. But it had never come to more than a minor annoyance to the Empire in the past. What made them think this time would be any different? The tension between Vaino and Naecara Klavan seemed ready to tear Stormbreak apart, and if that didn't do them in, perhaps bands of marauding Aescalan would finish the job.

"Whatever the truth," Caius said, "something has happened to Klubridge. It sounds bad."

Samira traced the rim of the bowl with her finger and couldn't meet his eyes. "It was bad enough that we had to leave everything. When Lizzie and I came back to the theater that night and saw the Kites had taken it, I knew we'd never get it back. But at least it was still there. At least there was hope we might see it again, somehow. But now..." She dropped her hand to the table. "I just can't imagine everything being gone. Destroyed. And all the people. Everyone we knew in Klubridge." Her breath caught, and then she did look up at Caius. "The rest of the company. Zerva, the others. Do you think..."

"I don't know," he said, and there were lines beside his eyes she hadn't seen before. He exhaled and looked away, toward the others having their lunches across the room. He and Samira had taken their seats far from the rest of the rebels, an unspoken agreement passing between them that they had no desire to interact with anyone but each other just then. When he looked back at her, he asked, "How's Reykas?"

She was grateful for the change of subject, but this one would be just as hard as the other. "No better," she said. "I saw him this morning, and he seemed weaker again."

"Is there nothing that can be done?" Caius asked. "There are doctors here. Real doctors."

"There's a doctor, but he doesn't know anything. He just gave Lizzie some sort of powder to give Reykas. To ease his suffering." Her voice had dropped to a whisper by the end.

Caius said nothing in response to that but slid his hand across the table and placed it over hers. They both knew what that powder meant. The doctor couldn't do anything, and that meant no one could do anything. Lizzie continued to protest and fight against what was coming, but Samira saw no real way to help Reykas. She squeezed her eyes shut and forced her thoughts away from her friend, who even now lay dying in a bed that wasn't his, surrounded by people he didn't know.

He deserved better, and she couldn't help feeling responsible for all of them ending their journeys here, so far removed from the world and hunted by relentless forces they could never escape. Perhaps she could have done something different in Klubridge. Something that wouldn't have drawn the Kites to the Chamberlain.

If she hadn't taken pity on Dorrin that night when he was thieving in the streets. If she hadn't let Caius protect her and the others all these years. There were too many ways to say "if" and "maybe" with any of them surely leading to a better outcome than this one. But she had done what had seemed right at the time, as they all had done, and this is where their combined efforts had taken them. To the edge of the world and likely the ends of their lives.

"I think I'm losing my mind."

Samira's eyes came up, and she tilted her head at Caius. "What? What do you mean?"

He pulled his hand off hers and propped his forehead against both of his palms, his elbows braced on the table. "I feel like I'm going mad. There's something wrong with me, but it's nothing you can heal. You tried it three times, and there was nothing. It's not my body. It's my mind."

"You're not going mad," she said. "We're all unmoored. Nothing has been right since we left Klubridge. And even before that, we were living in fear of the Kites. We've all been in turmoil."

"It's not just that," he said. He rubbed a hand down his face and sighed. "I have nightmares every night now. I don't know what they mean or where they come from. They're bizarre and horrifying, and they feel so real. Sometimes I can't even tell whether I'm awake or asleep."

"But they're just dreams. I'm not surprised you've had trouble with sleeping."

"The night before last, I woke in the middle of the night, and I was standing on the roof of the keep. I was dressed for bed, standing in the cold of the night, and I have no idea how I got up there."

Samira frowned at that. She'd known Caius nearly her whole life, and this was more unusual than some bad dreams. "You've never sleepwalked before."

"No."

They sat together in silence for a long moment, and Samira finally said, "You're not alone. This is awful. None of it is anything we should be involved with, but we're going through it together. You know that, right?"

"I know. But knowing doesn't change this. I dread going to sleep every night. But I do sleep, and then I'm tired every day. And I can't let anyone else know."

"Why not?"

"Because they all need me to be something I'm not. Something bigger, stronger, nobler. I'm supposed to be a hero of the rebellion, whether I like it or not."

"That's not you. That's Akithar."

"I'm not sure where he ends and I begin." He took a deep breath and sighed once more, and Samira knew that topic was finished for now. She'd had enough talks with Caius to read his breaths and his postures, and just then they said, "No more."

She watched a group of rebels finishing their food, laughing, joking with each other, and she wondered where they had come from. What had brought them to the Stormbreak Sanctuary, so far away from everything else in Teshovar? They didn't have the haunted look she knew that she, Caius, and the rest of their friends carried. These people didn't look like the Empire had hounded them into hiding, so why were they here? Had they come of their own volition, out of some idealistic desire to fight against tyranny? Was their presence based on anything more than emotion and speculation? She wondered whether she'd ever laugh like that again, after what they had been through. After Klubridge, the Kites, the journey. And now Reykas.

Samira winced from her own thoughts just as Caius asked her something. "Sorry?" she said.

"I asked if Oreth is still avoiding Apak."

"As far as I know, he is," she said. "I suspect Oreth blames him for his injury."

"How is he now?"

"He's walking better, but that's thanks more to the leg brace he's wearing than anything I was able to do for him."

"You saved his life," Caius said.

Samira angled her head in agreement but said, "Apak seems like he doesn't know what to do with himself."

"Fairy tried to get him to apprentice her, but he refused."

"Because of Dorrin?" Samira asked.

"Because of Dorrin and Oreth, I suspect."

"What happened to them wasn't his fault," Samira said.

"It wasn't any of our faults, but we still live with it."

Samira wanted to argue, wanted to carve off some piece of the blame and shove it into the hole she felt in her heart, but she knew he was right. It wasn't their faults. It was the Empire, and that's why they all were here. She cast a quick glance back toward the others and lowered her voice to a whisper. "I'm thinking about offering to help with the shield," she said. "I could take shifts in the tower."

Caius raised his eyebrows. "Did you tell anyone about what you can do?"

She shook her head. "But I feel like I should. I feel like I should be doing something."

"You're trying to find a place to fit in here," he said.

She hesitated. "I already have a place."

Caius gave her a few seconds before he asked, "Have you talked with her?"

She shook her head again, this one a slow shake that dropped her eyes back toward her stew, now cold and congealing in the bowl. "She's hardly been out of her room. I've barely seen her since we arrived."

"She's probably hurting like the rest of us. Maybe even worse. We have each other, but she's on her own. She doesn't really know anybody here but you."

Samira looked up at him again, and she could feel the desperation in her own eyes. "What should I do, Caius? I've tried to give her space, but it feels like she's never going to speak to me again." And maybe Samira deserved that. She'd dragged Aquin away from her home and embroiled her in a conflict she had nothing to do with. Aquin was even more of an innocent in this mess than Caius and the rest of them were. She wasn't even a mage and shouldn't even have interested the Kites. Again, it all fell on Samira's shoulders.

"It's not your fault," Caius said again. Samira knew he had no magic, but sometimes she could have sworn he knew exactly what she was thinking. "If Aquin hadn't come with us, she would have been in Klubridge when..." He didn't have to finish the sentence, and Samira had already been thinking the same thing. Aquin would probably be dead, a corpse thrown into a cart like so many others, if she hadn't come with them when they left the city. That didn't make the circumstances feel any easier, though. She'd been forced out of her job, her home, and her life against her will. How much did her survival in an icy fortress matter to her, matched against the loss of everything she held dear?

"What should I do?" Samira asked him again.

He held her eyes as she waited for an answer, and he finally said, "Talk to her."

~

Caius was still brooding over his uneaten stew when Samira left him in the dining hall. His words gave her the push she had been needing and wanting, and she was afraid they would fade from her ears if she delayed acting on them. Her heart fluttered with a mix of excitement and fear as she pulled the door open and emerged into the bright cold. Snow was settling on the invisible dome, and the clumps that had collected overhead cast mottled shadows on the ground. The effect was surreal, like transparent gray leaves appearing at her feet as she walked.

Samira had seen Aquin from afar a few times, but she'd kept her distance. She'd thought Aquin would come to her when she was ready, but the sightings had been fewer over the last several days, and they still hadn't spoken to each other since they had left the ship. Their time at sea had been less than productive, with Samira spending most of the first days aboard hurling her meals over the railing and into the sea while Aquin sequestered herself in her cabin below the deck. Once the ship had docked near Tresa, Aquin had made certain she was in the first carriage, leaving Samira behind with the others.

Aquin's being upset with her for dragging her into this mess was understandable, but how deeply did the upset run? Was there any hope for reconciliation? Samira swallowed that question like a piece of dry bread stuck in her throat and forced herself to think positively. She knew where Aquin's room was, on the second floor of the keep, around the square hallway and on the opposite side from Samira's own quarters. She took the short flight of stairs two steps at a time and felt her heartbeat thrumming in her neck and chest again when she emerged from the stairwell.

Aquin's door was the third on the left. Samira stopped before it and raised her hand to knock but arrested the movement before her knuckles met the wood. Aquin would have come to her if she'd been ready to talk, wouldn't she? Or was she waiting for Samira to come to her? Samira frowned and backed away from the door, her momentum vanishing with every step. By the time she pressed her back against the wall, she knew she would not be knocking on that door. But she couldn't just leave, either. What did that leave?

Samira's eyes stayed on the door as she slid down the wall, and she came to rest sitting against it, her knees bent in front of her and her arms resting on top of them. The wind blew a cool gust through the decorative pattern in the wall, and Samira shrugged the collar of her coat up to cover her neck. A strand of her dark hair blew loose, and she reached to tuck it behind her ear but otherwise remained motionless. She would sit there, Aquin's door in front of her and the courtyard behind her, for as long as it took. Eventually, Aquin would leave her room if she was already in there, or she'd come back to it if she was away. Either way, she would have the opportunity to talk to Samira, and Samira would accept whatever she had to say. She would wait for a month if she had to.

As it turned out, Samira only had to wait for half an hour before the sound of the doorknob startled her to her feet. She smoothed her hands down her front, rubbing warmth into them and pressing the wrinkles down and out of her coat. Her stomach lifted with that familiar feeling of butterflies, a sensation she'd had every night before Caius went on stage in Klubridge and that she hadn't felt since his final performance.

LIZANDRA'S DEEPEST FEAR

The door swung inward, and Aquin was halfway out before she froze, her hand still on the door and her body seeming to resist the last step into the hallway.

It had been weeks since Samira had spoken to her, and her breath still caught, as it did every time. Aquin wore donated clothes, just like everyone else had been given, but she'd managed to make even those look elegant, in the absence of her usual silks and patterned dresses. A long, light tan coat that contrasted with her dark skin hung nearly to the floor, and Aquin had tied it at the waist with a thick violet sash. A matching violet wrap of thinner material hung from her left shoulder and passed diagonally across to her right hip, where it looped back around her back. Aquin had pulled her long, midnight-black hair back and bound it away from her face. Her pale blue eyes stared at Samira without expression.

Samira hooked her fingers between the openings in the stone behind her and held tight, lest her legs give way. "Hi."

Aquin blinked but didn't look away. "How long have you been out here?"

"Not long. I was looking for you."

"I gathered that much." She looked down the hallway, toward the stairs. "I was on my way out."

"Can we talk first? For just a moment?"

Aquin tensed and looked back at Samira. "What is it?"

Samira wanted to ask so many things and to tell her so many more, but the question that forced its way out first wasn't the one she'd intended. "Do you hate me?"

Aquin's eyes narrowed, and her head gave a slight tilt to the right. "Hate you? Of course not. How could you ask that?"

"I know you don't want to be here, and you think it's my fault. I never would have forced this on you. Please, just don't hate me."

"I said I don't hate you. I'm unhappy, and I'm scared, and I'm angry, but I don't hate you. And you did force this on me. I told you I wouldn't leave Klubridge. Couldn't leave it. But you have me here anyway."

"If we'd left you—"

"If you'd left me," Aquin interrupted, "I'd have gone back to my home and worked in my library and continued my life. By the time you all were finished with Klubridge, hunting for me would have been the last thing on the Empire's agenda. You brought down the whole city."

Aquin hadn't heard about Klubridge. Of course she hadn't. She hadn't connected with any of the rebels and had kept to herself in her room. How could she have heard any news? "We couldn't just leave you there." Samira hesitated. "I couldn't leave you there. You were hurt, and we didn't know what was going to happen. There was so much chaos."

"Even the constabulary was shut down. The Empire has no hold on the city anymore. It's free, and I could still be there instead of…" She gestured into the air, at the empty hallway, the courtyard behind the wall, the room behind her. "This place, wherever we are."

"Aquin," Samira said, dreading the other woman's reaction to what she was about to tell her. But she had to know, and keeping it from her would only do more damage. "The Empire came back to Klubridge. They attacked it. We've heard the whole city has been destroyed."

Aquin's jaw fell open, but her eyes remained locked with Samira's. She blinked twice before speaking again. "Destroyed? Destroyed how?"

"Caius said there are witnesses who saw a mage with a weapon. Probably some sort of artifact. Something with an enchantment, maybe. They used it to bring down the walls and destroy the buildings."

"Why would they have done that? The Empire could have taken the city back from the rebels. This makes no sense."

"I don't know," Samira said. "Many people have died there. If you had stayed…"

"I might be dead," Aquin finished for her and finally dropped her eyes to the floor. She studied the stonework at Samira's feet for a moment before raising her gaze again. "Do you want me to thank you? Do you need me to congratulate you for rescuing me?"

"You were hurt!" Samira said with more force than she'd intended. "I couldn't just leave you behind."

Aquin leaned a shoulder against the wall in her open doorway and asked, "What do you want, Samira? What do you expect me to say or do?"

Samira hung her head and wiped her hand down her face. "I don't know, Aquin. I'm scared, too. And lost. I lived in that city for ten years, and now everything I knew is gone. I can never go back to the Chamberlain again, or to my house. They're probably gone, and all the people I knew who stayed there could have died in the attack. At best, they're probably homeless now. I don't know what to do. And I'm angry, too. I'm feeling all those things you're feeling. I just don't want to feel them alone."

"What about Caius?"

"What about him?"

"Can't he help you?"

"Caius is here. He'll always be there for me, but he's not you. You're the one I want to be with."

Aquin watched her for a long moment before saying, "I don't hate you, Samira. I care for you, just like I did before. It hurts that you had to ask me that." Samira started to speak, but Aquin held up a hand. "I need time. It's not just that you brought me here. You also lied to me."

"I didn't—"

"You did," Aquin snapped. "I asked you if Caius was a mage, and you told me he was. And you never told me the truth about what you could do until you had to reveal yourself. You didn't trust me."

How could Samira respond to that? Every word of it was the truth, which was a lot more than Samira had given to Aquin.

Aquin's eyes softened. "Things are different now, and I need to understand how I feel and what I think before I can be any good for you. Before we could be any good."

"Different?"

"I just need time. Can you give me that?"

Samira met her eyes. The two women stood, staring into each other for what felt like hours but probably was a handful of seconds, before Samira said, "I can give you that."

∼

It had been less than an hour since she'd left Caius in the dining hall, but Samira felt as if she left Aquin with the weight of years piled upon her back. She'd promised to give Aquin time, and she would abide by that promise, but how much time would she need? Another day? A year? The uncertainty was the hardest part of it.

But everything was uncertain now. They were staying at Stormbreak after fleeing Klubridge, but it was no home. And, even if they could leave at some point and seek a life away from this chaos, their true home was gone. Klubridge was no more. If a single mage could do that kind of damage, what hope did these rebels have against the whole Empire? Against just the High Lord, if he even existed?

Those were the thoughts rolling through Samira's mind when she almost collided with Apak at the bottom of the stairs as he was ascending. She stepped away, nearly tripping back up the steps, and the shorter man caught her arm with his strong hand. "Careful," he said, his voice tight and scolding.

"Sorry," Samira said and blinked at the courtyard past him. The inner walls of the keep had fallen into shadow, and the ground had dimmed, not just beneath the limbs of the great tree at its center, but all around. "I thought it was still early."

Apak squinted at her over the rim of his glasses and glanced back toward the tree. "It is the accumulation of snow on the dome. I question the decision to keep such a dome in place, the obstruction of lighting aside."

"You don't think it will protect us?" Samira frowned at that and took a step away from the stairwell to look up towards the invisible shield. From beneath, it looked as if they stood inside a sphere made of ice, with occasional holes showing through to the sky where the snow had yet to stick.

Apak followed her into the courtyard and waved a hand at the sky. "It seems unnecessary to maintain the magic as constantly as Vaino demands. It would be a better use of his resources to post additional sentinels who could call for help if an enemy approaches. At that time, the shield could be raised. There is no need to keep mages working tirelessly like this."

"There are two mages working in shifts."

Apak raised an eyebrow at her. "Has Vaino asked you to help them?"

Samira shook her head and lowered her voice. "He doesn't know what I can do. None of them do." She cut her eyes at him. "Have you told anyone what you can do?"

"I have not." He watched Samira for another moment, but when she had no response, he looked to the sky again. "Aside from the impracticality of working mages beyond the limits of reasonable labor, keeping that barrier in place for so long is doing all of us within it more harm than good."

"How do you mean?" Samira studied the underside of the snow again and imagined it all tumbling into the courtyard in a thick blanket whenever Beghran or Alev released their hold on the magic. She wondered how something so heavy didn't damage the massive tree every time it fell, but then she noticed the blunt stumps of branches and limbs high on the trunk that looked like they'd been broken away as the snow had poured in time after time.

"The barriers you create," Apak said. "Do you know how permeable they are?"

"Permeable?" She remembered the way Nera Mollor's blood had spattered her shield in Klubridge on that day that seemed so long ago now but truly had been only a month. A few months? More? Time had become an uncertain thing in the secluded keep. "They block out liquids, like…" She hesitated but then said, "water. Heat, too," she continued, thinking of the blinding flash of light that had swallowed her when Apak had ignited his weapon just seconds after the bubble had sheared Mollor's arm off.

Apak grunted again and nodded. "I would wager that it also stops the transmission of gases. Breathable air, for instance."

Samira's brow wrinkled as she tried to recall whether she'd ever tested her power in such a way. "I don't know. I could hear you through the shield in Klubridge when you called to me."

He shook his head. "That means only that it can transfer the vibrations of sound. It answers nothing about the question of gas permeability, and that is where my concern lies for this barrier that holds us even now. Is it slowly starving us of air? If it remains in place long enough, would we all suffocate? Very troubling," he said.

Why had that never occurred to her? She could create these same shields, and she'd never stopped to consider how long she could survive inside one of them. "Surely Vaino knows about that. He has to have considered it."

Apak pinched his lips together and snorted through his nose. "Vaino is a fool. I would put little faith in his having considered much beyond his own wardrobe for the day." He looked up at Samira. "What do you think of his claim that the High Lord is fictional?"

"I don't know."

"Preposterous," Apak said, his mouth contorting down and his nose wrinkling.

"You don't believe him?"

"I do not, and I am not the only one. I have been talking with Naecara Klavan, and she is of a similar mind."

"You've been talking to Naecara Klavan," Samira said, her eyes widening. "When? How did you—"

But Apak pressed onward. "Vaino's insistence that Peregrine does not exist is not only misinformed, but it also is dangerous for everyone in this rebellion."

That was at least something Samira had considered. Caius seemed far more willing to accept what Vaino had told them as fact. Or, at the very least, he was willing to consider it as a strong possibility. If Vaino were correct, the rebellion he was building had a chance of succeeding where all others had failed. If he were wrong, though, he was marshaling forces against entirely the wrong enemy.

Apak had been watching her for a response, and he seemed satisfied with whatever he saw on her face. Given his usual difficulty in reading her, whatever he'd just seen must have been blatant indeed. "I am concerned about Caius and his devotion to Vaino," Apak said.

"He's not devoted to Vaino," Samira said, perhaps a little sharper than she'd meant to. "He's not devoted to any of them. He just wants to find a way to get all of us out of this and away from the rebels. And away from the Empire," she added, almost as an afterthought.

The edges of Apak's mouth turned down again at that, and he ran a hand across his chin, stroking his dark beard. "I am not certain that is the best choice," Apak said.

"What do you mean?"

"I believe Klavan has the right of this, and her leadership very well could turn the tide against Peregrine."

"Really," Samira said, her eyebrows going up. "I didn't realize you were that invested in this rebellion."

"We all should be as invested," he said. "The Empire hunts us all, and we will not know peace until it ends or until we do."

"There has to be another way. This can't be the rest of our lives." And it couldn't, could it? When they'd had to flee Klubridge, that choice had come quickly but was not an easy one. They had known the Kites would find them if they stayed, and they had done everything they could to escape. But what came after that? They'd thought no farther than leaving, but there had to be something more. Somewhere that would be home again.

Apak crossed his arms and exhaled as he looked at the ground. "I believe this could be my life now, Samira."

"You don't mean that."

"In Klubridge, I was prepared to do whatever I had to do in order to avenge Dorrin. On the day of Caius' silencing, I knew I might die in that plaza."

"But you didn't. None of us did. We were able to rescue him and escape." Samira touched his shoulder, and she felt his arm stiffen. Apak had been in a dark place after Dorrin died, but they hadn't talked about it. Had any of them taken the time to talk with him? Her chest tightened. She'd been so consumed with worrying over Aquin that she had ignored Apak and what he'd been through.

He gave a slight smile, but his eyes didn't meet hers. "I do not know that that is true. I feel a part of me remained there, in that plaza. A part of me perished alongside the Imperials."

"You're here now," she said and moved in front of him. "Things are different now, and everything's uncertain, but we still have each other. We can get out of this, Apak. We can have lives away from this conflict."

And then he did meet her eyes, and she saw the sadness she expected, but there was something else. Determination? He said, "My life is entwined with this conflict now. It is as it must be."

Samira's hand dropped from his shoulder. "You've been talking to this Naecara a lot?"

"We have Ikarna in common. She was raised to worship differently than I was, but we have her in common. More than that, we have a common belief in how this rebellion might succeed."

"I know you're hurting, but this doesn't have to be the way. You seem so certain about this."

"I am certain. For the first time since this began, I feel a measure of certainty and intention."

Samira sighed and looked away. "I don't know how you can be so sure that you want to be embroiled in this. This isn't who we are, Apak."

"It is because of loss." He uncrossed his arms and clasped his hands behind his back, at last looking up again. "First, Dorrin, and then the accident with Oreth. And now Klubridge. All of these losses, all laid at the feet of Peregrine and his Empire. It is too much to bear without recompense."

"Oreth is still alive," Samira said. "I know things are tense with him, but he just needs time. He's still healing."

"Oreth's wounds will heal with time, but I am unsure that his respect for me will. There is a fracture that I have been unable to repair. I do not know whether I ever will be able to mend it, but I can make those responsible address it. There is a part for me to play in this rebellion, and I have to play it." And then, through clenched teeth, he said, "I want to play it."

That was when Samira recognized what she saw in his eyes beneath the sadness. It was rage. Apak practically shook with fury, and it had taken her this long to realize what was driving him. She took a step toward him and said, "Apak, I know you're angry—"

He slid a half step back and met her gaze once more, a hint of a smile playing at his lips. "Angry," he said. "I am enraged. I do not expect for you to feel as I do or to understand why I feel this way. It is carried by the ghosts of the things I have lost. The friends I have lost. Loss and the anger to address it are what I have." He took a deep breath and looked away from her. "I pray to Ikarna that you never understand this anger, Samira. I pray you never know this loss."

CHAPTER 11

Lizandra had not given the medicine to Reykas. He hadn't asked for it, and she hadn't offered it, and it had lingered between them, an unspoken finality tucked into a packet she carried in her pocket throughout every day. The doctor forbade Lizandra from sleeping in the infirmary, so she found herself banished back to her quarters every night. The room felt empty without Reykas, and she hardly slept, her eyes vigilant on the crack at the bottom of the door where the morning's first light would appear. As soon as the faintest glow crept beneath, she was up and out again, headed back to visit the hospital on the other side of the keep.

Reykas lay in the bed in the room with the other sick man. At first, he had been able to sit up and converse every day when Lizandra arrived. As time passed, she could see the illness taking hold, and one morning he could only raise himself onto one elbow. The next day, he lay motionless, exhaustion pinning him to the thin mattress. He could still speak, but his voice came weaker every time she saw him.

She was watching Reykas, the man she loved more than anyone or anything else in the world, wither and die before her very eyes. Sometimes the others came to visit, usually Samira, but they stayed for only a few minutes at a time before they had other concerns, other business pulling them away. Was everyone else truly that busy, or was lingering at Reykas' bedside something they could only endure in small doses?

She had held her tongue every time she'd come to see him, and she'd sat beside his bed, sometimes holding his hand and sometimes leaning so she could rest her head on the pillow beside his. She hadn't mentioned the cure in Karsk since he had ended that conversation on no uncertain terms. Nevertheless, it remained on her mind as a constant presence, a weight that pulled her down, dragging her shoulders forward and curving her spine. Some days she felt as if it would pull her completely prone to the ground and even through the rocky floor of the castle and down into the unknown depths and caves within the mountains beneath her feet.

There was a cure, according to Pelo Foyen. Something existed that could save him and that could save Reykas, and Foyen had turned it down.

What price could the chemist ask that would be more precious than Foyen's own life? The betrayal of a family member? A loved one? Lizandra knew she'd never betray Reykas, so she could understand having that as a line she would not cross. But not pursuing this cure felt like the highest betrayal. There was a chance for Reykas to live—for both of them to live the life they'd longed to have. If such a chance existed, shouldn't they pursue it? Even if only to know what the price might be?

"What are you thinking?" Reykas asked, and his thumb stroked along the back of Lizandra's hand. She sat on the chair next to the bed, and it was one of the days when the weight of her burden had pulled her down so that she felt it as a physical thing, her head pressed against the scratchy white linen that covered the pillow. Her hand rested on his chest, and his hand covered hers, and he'd turned his face toward her.

Her dark blue eyes stared into his deep brown ones, and she studied the lines and specks in his irises as if she hadn't already memorized every trace of them years ago. She felt his breath on her face, still coming regularly and still keeping him alive, but for how much longer? Lizandra took her own breath and held it for a long moment before she answered him. "I'm thinking about Karsk."

"Karsk?" His right eyebrow raised, and she realized he hadn't been thinking about any of this like she had. Karsk and whatever it held had not been on his mind as he lay in his sickbed day and night. What else could he have been thinking about, if not a way to prevent the end that crept closer with every passing day?

"What Foyen said," she whispered. The man in the other bed was asleep, his back turned to them and his shoulders rising and falling with regular breaths, but she kept her voice low. The last thing she wanted was to draw him back into the conversation.

Reykas' eyes flicked to the right, and then Lizandra saw the recognition come into them. He truly hadn't been mulling over the cure, over a way that it might be turned in their favor. A way they might yet get it and make it work.

"What were you thinking?" she asked him.

Instead of answering, he said, "We will not go to Karsk, Lizandra."

She'd been afraid to broach the topic again, because she knew he would put a stop to it, just like he did last time. She wouldn't have said anything just then if he had not asked what she was thinking, but now it was spoken, and she had to choose her next words carefully. "Perhaps there's a way to get the cure without paying anything."

"What do you mean?" Reykas spoke in a whisper, too, but that was less from a desire for privacy and more from the weakness now pulling at his voice.

"We could find out the price, and if it's too much…" She had looked away from him but now met his eyes again. "We could just take it."

His mouth curved upward, and Lizandra felt her heart thud in her chest at the sight of a smile from him, now rarer by the day. "You want to steal it? Have you become a master thief in the past month?"

"Foyen said he's a chemist. We could, I don't know… We could intimidate him."

"And now you intimidate chemists."

Reykas' tone was light, but Lizandra knew him well enough

to see that she was making no progress in swaying him. She closed her mouth and turned her head downward on the pillow, looking toward their hands, still resting on his chest. She turned hers over so that her palm pressed against his, and her fingers threaded between his fingers, squeezing just tight enough to reassure herself that he was still there, still alive, still within her ability to help him.

"If you were well," she said but stopped herself. She started again. "If you didn't have this condition, what would you be doing?"

Reykas didn't answer at first, and she looked up to see whether he'd fallen asleep. He was still awake, but he'd turned his face toward the ceiling, his eyes seeming to study every angle and texture in the stonework above them. He was thinking. She gave him time, and when he turned his head back toward her, he said, "I would be making myself useful to the rebellion. I would be helping however I could to ensure they are successful."

"That's what Apak is doing," she said. Her cheek pressed hard against the pillow now and pushed her mouth into a pout. "He's been spending a lot of time talking to Klavan."

"The woman who opposes Vaino."

"I don't know that she opposes him, so much as that a lot of people think she'd be a better leader, so they pit her against him."

"And Apak agrees?"

Lizandra gave a half shrug. "He seems determined. Sometimes it seems like he's the only one of us who's found a place here. Something that suits him."

"What does Caius say about this?"

"I haven't heard him say anything, but I know he doesn't want to be here. Samira, either."

Reykas ran his thumb along the side of Lizandra's hand again, and it sent a warmth up her arm that spread through her body. She shifted to bring her right hand up to the pillow and put her chin on it so she could look at Reykas more directly. "If we found a way to help you, you could help the rebels."

"Lizandra."

"Don't you think you could be an asset to them? That you

could be of service?" Joining the rebellion held no appeal for her, and she wanted for the two of them to be far away from this conflict and away from Stormbreak, probably as much as Caius did. But she would follow this path if it led to his agreeing to pursue the cure.

"We have discussed this. I'm not willing to pay the price. The others would agree."

"They wouldn't," she said, and she knew she was right. "If the others knew there was a chance, any chance at all, they'd do whatever was necessary to get it for you."

"Foyen said—"

"We don't know him," Lizandra said and pushed herself up so that she was propped on her elbow on the bed. "We do know our friends. Just let me tell them about it, and you'll see."

"They have enough burdens. I won't be another one."

"You think you would be a burden to them? They are our friends, Reykas. They're our family. They want you to be well. To survive!" She fought to keep her voice low, but the last came out louder than she'd intended, and Foyen shifted on the other bed. He still had his back to them, and the regular motion of his back resumed after a moment. She lowered her voice again. "Please let me tell them what Foyen said. Even if we don't go after this cure, knowing that it exists and that the Empire has a chemist in Karsk could be useful." She struggled for something to convince him. "Useful to them. To the rebellion."

Reykas waited for her to stop, and his smile was sad now. "I know, my love. Samira would march to Karsk on her own, if she thought I wanted this. But this is not what I want. I will not have our friends putting themselves in danger for me. And going to see this chemist would be dangerous. The Imperials do not know where we are, but going there would expose us. It would expose you. I can not have that on my conscience. I will not."

"Reykas," she said, but she already knew she'd lost again.

His fingers pressed against hers, a soft squeeze that was so unlike the strong, firm grip she knew. He turned his head away from her, and he slept.

∼

LIZANDRA'S DEEPEST FEAR

Lizandra always stayed at Reykas' bedside for as much of the day as possible, leaving only when necessary or when the nurses ran her out of the infirmary at the end of each day. That day, she left early, unable to sit quietly beside Reykas as he slept while her frustration built. He would not agree to seek out the cure or even to learn more about it, and he had no interest in finding out what its infamous price might be. He didn't want her to tell any of the others about the cure, not even Samira. He refused talking with Pelo Foyen any more about it. As far as Reykas was concerned, the subject was closed, and he was content to remain untreated. He was content to die.

And yet, his dedication to their friends and sudden conversion to the cause of the rebels remained staunch. It made no sense. If Reykas continued to refuse treatment and embraced his end, wasn't that a betrayal of the things he claimed were important to him? Shouldn't he be willing to try anything he could, just to survive? To have a chance to help Caius and the rest of them and to be a positive force within the rebellion? Shouldn't he be willing to live with her? For her?

She scowled at that thought as she pushed her way out the front door of the infirmary. Was this selfish? Was she trying to force him to live just so that she didn't have to live without him? That was a part of it, but that was not the whole. The world was a better place with Reykas in it. It was impossible to imagine a world without his strength, his smile, and his gentle way within it. She didn't want to imagine that. Yes, part of her determination was driven by selfishness, but it was undeniable that Reykas' very existence was important to so many people other than Lizandra.

She rounded the corner of the keep with that thought in her mind and collided with a smaller woman headed in the opposite direction. Lizandra staggered back a step and was about to apologize when she met the huge, dark eyes staring up at her.

"Magra," she said. The rebels had given the halflock clothes, just like they'd given them to the rest of the Klubridge refugees, but Magra had kept the ugly gray dress she'd been wearing when Lizandra first met her. She wore it under a drab overcoat, but the hem was visible at the bottom, the edges fraying from the garment being worn all the way from Klubridge up to Stormbreak and presumably every day since they'd been at the castle. She hadn't changed her clothing, but she'd made sure to keep the back of her head trimmed smooth, just like she'd had it that first day in the bank. The rest of her hair hung in black and greasy strands, but the back of her head lay bare to the cold wind.

Magra blinked at her, wide eyelids sliding down over those enormous eyes and back up again, and Lizandra fancied they made a wet smacking sound, but surely that was her imagination. Lizandra had first met the halflock when Magra had helped entrap her with the Kites back in Klubridge, when the woman had invaded Lizandra's mind and shared her thoughts with Nera Mollor. She'd expected that to be the only and final time she'd meet this creature, but then she'd shown up on the ship as they were leaving Klubridge, Samira having somehow rescued her from the Imperials. As if Magra had need of rescuing.

She had been a prisoner and had endured terrible surgeries and likely other indignities and atrocities. But, at the end of it all, she had chosen to betray her own fellow mages, just to save her own skin. Lizandra didn't know how the others didn't find her actions as reprehensible as she did, but they had embraced Magra as one of their own, and so Lizandra had been obligated to endure her presence. That didn't mean she had to enjoy it.

"You're not listening to him," Magra said, her voice low and her pale lips barely moving. Her eyes flicked to the sides, more aware and cunning than she'd pretended in Klubridge, but the frantic and addled act she'd presented seemed like it still lingered somewhere just below the surface.

"Who are you talking about?" Lizandra asked. She wanted nothing more than to return to her quarters and bury herself facedown on her mattress without encountering anyone who knew her, but her luck had decided otherwise.

"Reykas," Magra said and turned her eyes back to Lizandra. "You're not listening to him. You're doing what you want, not what he wants."

Lizandra gasped and slid a pace backwards, away from the halflock. She felt the power flowing into her arms, wanting to lash out, but she squeezed her hands into fists and quelled the magic. "You read my mind," she said, her own voice going low to match Magra's, but anger laced her tone while Magra's words had lacked any trace of emotion, as though she were commenting on the cold weather rather than tearing insights from Lizandra's brain.

"Not read, really," Magra said. "It's more like you shouted it in my face. Can't ignore that." She sniffed and pulled her coat tighter around her body as she glanced away.

Lizandra's face flushed, and the heat stung her skin in the brisk air. She jabbed a finger at Magra. "You know nothing about Reykas or about me. You'll stay away from both of us."

Magra shrugged. "Hasn't been hard to avoid you. You keep yourself locked away in the infirmary all day, every day. Not likely we'd cross paths."

"What else would you have me do?" Lizandra asked, her face ever hotter now, her rage at this spy—this interloper—daring to criticize her, flooding her body. It had been bad enough when Magra had informed on Lizandra to the Kites, but now she dirtied Reykas' name in her traitorous mouth.

"Something useful, like the rest of us are trying to do." Magra's voice carried no sign of malice. She spoke plainly, and Lizandra knew the woman was not trying to anger her, but every word struck Lizandra like physical slaps.

Lizandra wanted to hit her, to scream at her, to shake her, but none of that would help. Magra was an awful blight upon the rebellion and had no place at Stormbreak, but attacking her would do no good. The Empire had cut open the halflock's head and stirred its contents around. It was no wonder she trespassed so readily and spoke with such unknowing and unintentional malice. Unintentional or not, it was still malice, and Lizandra had no capacity for responding to it at that moment, nor any desire for politeness. This was the woman who had nearly gotten Lizandra killed, and that was not something she could forget or forgive so soon.

Lizandra ground her teeth together to prevent her from saying something that would worsen the situation, and she sidestepped Magra. Her shoulder knocked against the other woman as she passed, another unintentional aggression between them, but she didn't slow to apologize. She didn't slow for anything until she was on the second floor, through the door to her room, and falling onto the mattress, her cheeks already wet with the tears she wouldn't let the halflock see her cry.

∾

The confrontation with Magra was the capstone for Lizandra's days and nights spent worrying about Reykas, and the result was a concoction of depressed exhaustion that made her body too heavy to move from the bed. It kept her prone atop the sheets even when it was mealtime, even when her stomach growled and cramped, even when the cold of the night became more than she thought she could bear. But she didn't go to find food, and she didn't pull the blankets over herself. She lay cold and empty, in every sense of the words. At some point, sleep finally claimed her, and she fell into a dreamless black void that held her in an unconscious slumber that provided no rest.

Voices in the courtyard and footsteps passing her door eventually roused Lizandra. She opened her eyes in the gloom of the bedroom that she was accustomed to not being able to see upon first waking. That morning, she could make out the meager furnishings and every detail of the wall beside the bed. And then she could see the pitted rock of the ceiling above as she rolled over to her back, and her eyes found the space at the bottom of the door that usually admitted that faint sliver of light before she was up and away to visit Reykas. Rather than the customary dim crack of daylight, bright sunlight poured beneath the door, reflecting up and casting shadows all around the room.

She squinted at the light in confusion for a moment before her breath hitched. How late had she slept?

Lizandra bolted upright on the thin mattress and swung her feet off the side. She had fallen into bed fully clothed and hadn't even removed her shoes. She felt dull and achy and sticky now from the night of restless sleep, but none of that mattered. She swiped a hand through her tangled hair, wincing at the snags and pulls that tugged at her scalp, but didn't take the time to look in the mirror on the room's opposite wall. She pulled the door open and was out and halfway down the hallway within a minute of awakening.

Sunlight dappled her face and made her squint as it stenciled its way through the designs in the wall on her left. The smell of something cooking wafted up from the courtyard, and Lizandra heard the sounds of people talking, laughing, all the noises of a keep up and about long before she was. She'd slept through the entire morning!

It must have been nearly lunchtime, and she scowled at the top of the stairs as she recalled running into Magra. Reykas' refusal to listen to reason had upset her, but she'd have walked her frustration off and maybe sulked in her bedroom for a while if she hadn't encountered the halflock. Lizandra's cheeks flared again as she remembered the woman's words and the casual way she'd delivered them.

"You're doing what you want, not what he wants."

Lizandra stopped at the bottom of the stairs, before heading into the courtyard, and forced her jaw to unclench and her fingers to relax from the fists into which she'd balled them. Magra was a damaged and self-serving tool of the Empire. She had no power over Lizandra that Lizandra didn't grant her. Magra knew nothing about her or about Reykas, just like Lizandra had told her. Magra might not have intentionally invaded Lizandra's thoughts, but she had not been welcome to them any more this time than she had been when Lizandra first met her at the bank in Klubridge. The woman had no sense of boundaries or respect, and nothing she said was worth listening to.

Lizandra's head ached, and she felt grimy in the same clothes she'd worn the day before, but she had stifled her thoughts about Magra by the time she'd reached the front door to the infirmary. She wasn't even sure what she'd felt upon waking. Anger? Embarrassment? A tiny voice in her head asked whether it might be shame, but what would Lizandra have to be ashamed about? She was trying to protect and save Reykas, and Magra had trespassed into their lives. Whatever the emotion, it now sat pushed down within Lizandra, where it wouldn't show itself on her face when she went in to see him. He didn't need to know about any of that or about the state Lizandra was in the previous night.

She glanced down at her clothing again and hoped he wouldn't notice she hadn't bathed or changed, but it was too late for that. Too late, by far, as she pushed the door open and entered the facility hours later than she'd been arriving every other day.

As she came inside, the attendant at the front desk glanced up and gave her a small smile. Lizandra smiled back and hoped it looked more honest than it felt. She'd pushed her emotions down, but what did that leave other than exhaustion?

"You made a wise decision," a voice said from Lizandra's right, arresting her movement as she headed for the hallway that led to the patients' rooms.

She turned halfway and saw that the doctor had been lingering to the right of the doorway, a pair of glasses midway down the bridge of his nose and a stack of papers in his hands. "I'm sorry?" she asked.

"It's for the best," he said. "He is resting soundly now. When I arrived this morning, I found it where you'd left it, and I administered it for you."

The doctor looked back down at his papers, but Lizandra took two quick steps back the way she'd come, toward him. Her mind spun, but his name eluded her. She'd seen him only that first time when he'd proven himself as useless as everything else at Stormbreak. His entire solution for Reykas' illness was to drug him senseless so that he'd die in his sleep.

Lizandra's eyes widened, and she slapped a hand to her pocket. She'd been carrying the powder there, keeping it on her person at all times, but it was gone. Her fingers dug into that pocket and then the other, finding nothing but emptiness and lint. The medicine was gone.

And then she remembered. Yesterday, when she'd visited Reykas, she had wanted to put her head on the pillow beside his. When she'd leaned into the thin mattress, the packet in her pocket had pressed against the metal frame of the bed. She'd been afraid the package would rupture and spill the powder, so she'd removed it and placed it on the small table next to the head of the bed. She'd told herself she would pick it up again before she left. But she hadn't picked it up. She'd left so abruptly that she hadn't even thought about that powder until now. She might have remembered it later, if Magra hadn't accosted her, but she'd ended up spending the entire night in a stupor while that package of medicine lay unclaimed on that little table.

Lizandra glared at the doctor then, her eyes as wide and round as Magra's, but only for an instant. She spun away from him and ran into the hallway, her feet pounding the path she'd walked back and forth every day since they'd taken Reykas there. A moan tried to escape her throat, but she was breathing too hard and too fast to let it out. It lodged there, feeling like a physical lump above her collarbone that threatened to betray her despair as she rushed down that hallway that now seemed interminably long.

She shoved her way into the room, and Pelo Foyen lurched in his bed, startling awake as the door banged open. But Reykas didn't move.

"No," she whispered. "No, no, no." Her left hand covered her mouth, and her right reached out toward him, as if she could forestall what had already been done to him. She wasn't aware of her feet carrying her any farther than the doorway, but then she was at his bedside, falling to her knees, her hand on his brow.

His skin was warm but not burning, and his chest rose and fell beneath the white blanket. He lived, but he wasn't there. Lizandra bent her face next to his ear and whispered to him, pleaded, and tried to remember the names of the old gods her parents had taught her. Her eyes stung, and she squeezed them shut after a single tear wet the pillow beside Reykas' head, a small and perfectly round attestation to her sorrow made manifest.

CHAPTER 12

No one told Fairy anything. They'd let her in on the big stuff, like when Caius pulled her aside and told her Klubridge was gone. Apparently, the whole bloody place had just blown away somehow. But there weren't any details, and she didn't know whether that was because they didn't know the details or because they just didn't want to share them with her.

And then there were the little things. Something was going on between that woman, Naecara, and the man who seemed to be the leader of the rebels. Or, at least, he fancied himself to be the leader. Maybe the woman was the actual leader? Just another point of annoyance where everybody else seemed to know things Fairy wasn't allowed to know or wasn't worth the time to explain it to.

Surely a whole city couldn't just disappear, especially not one as big as Klubridge. The thought of the entire city simply not existing anymore baffled her. It was where she had lived her entire life, or as much of it as she could remember, before she'd joined up with Caius and his friends and they'd taken her away with them. If it hadn't been for Dorrin catching Samira's attention that night outside the theater, she would still be in Klubridge now. Or destroyed along with the city, she supposed. Fairy placed a hand against the brickwork along the edge of the

LIZANDRA'S DEEPEST FEAR

eastern wall at the side of the courtyard and leaned her weight into it as she pondered the situation.

So many things had happened because Dorrin met Samira that night. Dorrin was dead because of it, for one. Fairy didn't blame Samira, not in the least, but she couldn't help thinking through everything that had led all of them to where they'd ended up. That chance encounter had caused so much destruction, it was hard to not see it as the single moment when everything in her world changed. When everything in everybody's lives changed, as far as she could tell.

Fairy's brows pushed together, and she blew a loose strand of yellow hair out of her face. Was whatever happened to Klubridge connected to all that as well? She'd heard enough to know the city had gone into full revolt after the Empire had failed to take away Caius' magic, and now the city didn't even exist anymore. That had to be related, didn't it? If so, it all traced back to that one chance meeting between Dorrin and Samira. That one night Scrounger had felt spiteful and sent her out with Dorrin and Skink to lift purses together in the theater district. It all tied together too neatly, and Fairy didn't like it. Things weren't that tidy in real life. Not for her. Not for anybody.

If she hadn't climbed the tower that night, fully intent on murdering Caius, she wouldn't be at Stormbreak now. She'd likely be dead in the rubble of Klubridge, just like everybody else there probably was. Fairy thought about the rest of Scrounger's gang, those remaining kids who had spread to the winds after he died. She'd tried to keep them together, but it was all in vain. She didn't know where any of them had ended up, except for Dorrin and Skink. No idea about Gad, Till, Rafe... Miri. Fairy swallowed hard and forced herself to not think of that little girl who'd disappeared in the middle of the night, the last of the gang she'd been watching over. Miri had to have gotten out before the city fell. She had to be okay.

Fairy bit at the inside of her cheek and slipped out from behind the wall and walked across the courtyard in an attempt at a nonchalance she didn't feel. Her shoulders were tight under her cloak, and she felt like her feet were huge and clunky, smacking and crunching along on the slushy snow. But the woman she was following didn't turn her head. She didn't acknowledge Fairy and didn't seem to know she had anyone trailing her as she passed through the gate at the back of the keep, headed out toward the area where Fairy knew they'd set up an archery range. Fairy had tried to get one of the rebels to teach her to use a bow, but he'd just sneered at her, and she'd backed away with a rude gesture.

That's how everything was going for Fairy these days. She'd try to become interested in something and would try to get involved with something other than herself, and she'd be turned away. It had happened with Apak when she'd asked him to apprentice her. It had happened with Oreth when she'd tried to help him with supplies. Caius seemed to take her more seriously than any of the rest of them, but even he had no time for her after he'd cozied up to the man Fairy assumed was the leader of this thing. Vaino, was that his name?

She had stopped her climbing and exploring of her own accord, most definitely not because any guards had told her not to. She had simply found everything that seemed worth finding in that place, and none of it had been very interesting. For a castle hidden up in the icy mountains underneath a giant rock that looked like a bird, Stormbreak had ended up being surprisingly boring. There were plenty of places to roam and clamber and sneak, but all of them were the same after a while. Just a bunch of old, gray rocks piled up in the snow.

Fairy had been on the verge of doing something truly desperate, like approaching Oreth again, when the new woman had arrived and caught her attention. She looked a few years older than Fairy, but not by much, and she might even have been a little shorter, but Fairy hadn't gotten close enough to know that for certain. Her skin was the color of the sand Fairy had seen on the narrow beach at the eastern edge of Klubridge, almost like copper and not quite like anyone else she remembered seeing. Her hair was black and chopped short, haphazardly uneven in places like she'd cut it herself without a mirror. Ever since she'd arrived, she'd been wearing the same tight-fitting black clothes, or maybe she had several sets of the same clothes. Either way, she usually wore a black cloak over the outfit, sometimes with the hood up, sometimes with it down.

She wasn't like any of the other rebels, and not just in her appearance. She had a way of leaning against walls or crouching next to furniture that made her blend with the environment. She did it with the casual grace of someone who could be comfortable just about anywhere, like she could make herself disappear at a moment's notice. Fairy admired the woman's way of skulking about without looking like she was skulking about, and the guards said nothing to her. Nobody did. Nobody seemed to even notice her, but Fairy saw her. And her way of sneaking about wasn't even the most interesting thing about her.

Fairy had spotted her when she'd first gotten to Stormbreak, and she'd seen the woman go straight into Naecara Klavan's office. Since then, she'd spent a lot of time with the woman, both in that office and out, and the two often had their heads bent together. She spent more time whispering to Klavan and getting whispered back to than anybody else Fairy saw, and that made her even more interesting. Whatever was going on in the rebellion, whatever the conflict was that brewed between Klavan and Vaino, this woman had to know all about it and was probably getting to play a part in it. That's what made her the most interesting.

Who was this woman, barely older than Fairy, who looked so ready for anything and who seemed like she could come and go at will? What was going on between her and Klavan, and why was she at Stormbreak, anyway? Fairy was determined to find out, and she'd been following behind the woman, watching where she went and what she did. She'd been after her for the better part of three days now and was no closer to understanding anything about her, but Fairy was undeterred.

Fairy passed through the gate at the outer edge of the keep and emerged in the open pathway between two rows of supply barns, and she stumbled to a halt. The woman had been just a few feet ahead of her, but now she was gone! None of the barn doors were open, and there was no sign of her farther along the path, toward the archery range.

The only person on the pathway was an old man she'd seen a

few times during her explorations. He wore a straw hat over his longish white hair and gave Fairy a suspicious eye as she came out from the keep. It was the treatment Fairy had gotten used to, but she still gave him an exaggerated snarl and stuck out her tongue before turning her attention back to the empty row in front of her. The woman hadn't had time to get into one of the barns and close the door without Fairy hearing it slam shut. Had she somehow gone up and over one of the buildings?

Fairy turned in a circle, her eyes scanning the rooftops, but she stiffened when the old man's hand clamped on her arm. His voice was raspy, just like she'd expected it would be, when he asked, "Why are you trying to spy?"

Her whole body tensed, ready to bolt, as she turned to face the man, but she didn't flee or even give him a rude retort. In fact, the old man wasn't even there anymore. It was the woman with the short hair and the strange black outfit who had her fingers wrapped around Fairy's upper arm. Fairy looked from the firm grip up the arm to the shoulder and to the face above it that didn't look pleased. Her hood was down, and the glaring sunlight on the woman's black hair made it look almost blueish silver.

Up close, Fairy saw the woman was just about the same height as she was, but she was so much more intense, so much more intimidating, and it made Fairy feel about three feet shorter. The woman's eyes were brown, and there was something strangely flat about them, not quite reflecting the day's light in the right way. This was an entirely weird woman, and in that instant Fairy realized she wanted to be just like her.

The woman shook Fairy by the arm, jarring her out of her daze, and asked again, this time in a decidedly less raspy voice, "Why are you trying to spy?"

"You're a mage," Fairy said. It was the only thing that made sense. The woman had spotted Fairy and shifted her shape into that of the old man in order to catch Fairy unaware. Was there even an old man? Had that really been this woman every time Fairy had seen him? No, it couldn't have been. Fairy had been spotting the old man long before this woman had come to Stormbreak.

"I'm no mage," she said. "I'll ask you nicely one more time why you were trying to spy, and then I'll ask less nicely."

"I wasn't spying," Fairy said and gave her arm an experimental tug. The woman held fast, and her fingers even tightened. Whatever she was or wasn't, this woman was strong, and that was a fact!

"I didn't say you were successful at it. I asked why you were trying." And the way she stared at Fairy brooked no argument. She'd been caught, and coming clean seemed the safest route out of the predicament.

"I don't know. I'd seen you around, and I was curious." Fairy's eyes had dropped to the ground, but she looked back up then to see how the woman took her response.

"You were curious enough to follow me around Stormbreak for two days—"

"Three."

The woman frowned. "What?"

"Three days," Fairy said. "I've been following you for three days."

The woman frowned at that, but it wasn't an unkind frown. Not the kind that came before a beating, and not the kind you needed to argue with. It was a thoughtful frown, like she was reassessing Fairy. Like she might not go that "less nicely" route after all. She released Fairy and said, "My name is Nahk."

Fairy rubbed at where Nahk had been holding her arm and thought there'd probably be a bruise showing up tomorrow. "I'm—"

"Fairy," Nahk said.

Even though she was no longer being held in place, Fairy hadn't run, and after hearing her name said back to her, all thoughts of fleeing disappeared. She squared her shoulders at Nahk and asked, "How did you know that?"

One side of Nahk's mouth pulled up in a smirk, and she shrugged. "I asked around when I saw you following me. You came with the group from Klubridge. With the wizard." When Fairy didn't answer, she said, "I was told you grew up on the streets there, in a gang."

Fairy scowled. "What about it?"

Nahk laughed at that. She actually laughed. It was a low chuckle, but still a laugh, and that made Fairy's scowl deepen. "I wasn't criticizing you. You'd know that if you saw where I grew up. I was just curious... Do you know the name Raseul?"

Of all the things this Nahk woman could have said, that name had to be one of the least likely. Fairy remembered the only time she'd heard the name Moeply Raseul, back in Klubridge, when she was hiding behind the ratty curtain with all the other kids. The Kite woman had said it, just before she left. Just before the other one had killed Scrounger, and then they'd killed Skink. Moeply Raseul.

Fairy hadn't said anything, but she could see in Nahk's face that the woman had spotted the recognition in Fairy's eyes. Or maybe in the way she'd stopped breathing or in the swallow that had gotten stuck midway down Fairy's throat. There were a dozen different ways she could respond to hearing the name, but the one that came out was, "He's dead."

Nahk raised an eyebrow at that. "You're certain?"

"I saw him die. One of the Kites killed him. He choked him with a..." She made a motion at her wrist, like she was pulling at something. "A cable thing."

"Like this?" Nahk asked and pulled back her sleeve. There, strapped to her arm, was a dark band of leather, and she pulled the end of a cord from it, the same kind of cord the Kite had used, making the same high-pitched zipping noise as it slid out of its holder. The Kite's cable had ended in a blunt, metal weight, but Nahk's had a small, pointed blade attached to the end. When Fairy nodded, Nahk said, "It's a zephyr spool. Kites don't carry them. Nobody does."

"This one did," Fairy said. And then, "You do."

"I'm no Kite," Nahk said and let the cable slip back into its housing with another quick zip.

"What are you, then?"

Nahk looked up from her zephyr spool and shrugged her sleeve back around it while holding Fairy's eyes for a long moment. Instead of answering, she asked, "How did you know him? Raseul."

LIZANDRA'S DEEPEST FEAR

"He called himself Scrounger. It was his gang."

"I was going to kill him myself," Nahk said, as easy as she might have commented on how cold it was at Stormbreak.

"Well," said Fairy, and she didn't know what to say after that.

Nahk looked at her again and asked, "Do you know what he was?"

"Scrounger? He ran the gang, but that's all I knew. All any of us knew. When the Kites came, they talked about some kind of arrangement he had with them, but that's it." She tilted her head. "Was he Imperial?" That would explain why this strange rebel woman knew about him and wanted to kill him, at least.

"Not Imperial in the way you mean," Nahk said. She glanced back at the gate through which Fairy had exited before blowing out a long sigh. The tension melted from her shoulders, and she leaned back against the barn where she'd been lurking. It wasn't a stealthy lean like Fairy had gotten used to seeing from her. This one was more relaxed, almost like she was becoming comfortable talking to Fairy. Nahk scratched at the side of her nose and tilted her head back against the wooden wall. "He was what they call a finder."

Fairy took a tentative step toward Nahk and then another. When she was about a foot away, she turned and leaned against the wall next to her. Just a casual conversation with the shapeshifting lady. Everybody could relax. Everything was dice. Fairy swallowed again and cut her eyes to the right so she could keep Nahk in view. "A finder?" she asked.

"You know about the Kites. And there are the Herons. You know them?" Nahk glanced at Fairy.

The white carriages they'd arrived in were hard to forget. "They were in Klubridge, too."

Nahk nodded and tilted her head back again. "There are those, and then there are others the Empire doesn't talk about as much."

"Secret groups?"

"Something like that."

A shiver ran down Fairy's spine, and it wasn't from the cold. If the Empire had secrets like that, they had to be even worse than the Kites and the Herons she'd already seen. Was that what had happened to Klubridge? Had the Empire used one of its secret weapons there? Fairy was about to ask about that when Nahk started talking again.

"Kites are raised up through the military. They get special training, schooling, all that. Very public and ordinary. And the Herons are the mages the Kites don't catch. They turn against their own, turn themselves in, and agree to serve." She inhaled through her nose and held the breath for a moment before saying, "The others are different. There's no official source for recruiting. No way to conscript people in, no visible training. That's because the Empire gets those recruits when they're children." She rocked her head toward Fairy. "The Empire uses finders to locate kids who don't have families, aren't attached to anything, and are ripe for the taking. That's what Raseul was. A finder."

Fairy squinted back at her. "You're saying he was going to turn all of us over to the Empire? He was recruiting us for secret things?"

"No. Raseul recruited for the Nightingales. It's a very select group, very small. Elite assassins that operate on the Imperial charter but beholden to ways that are far older than the Kites or the Herons. It's rare to find someone suitable for recruitment. At most, he would have given one of you to them, and they'd have paid him handsomely. It's unlikely he'd have found more than one among you they'd want. Was there anybody in your gang that he paid special attention to? Anybody with unique talents? Someone who stood out from the others?"

Fairy's chest grew heavy, and her breath caught. It all made so much sense now. The way Scrounger had kept him close, tested him, protected him from the Kites. It was like a piece falling into a puzzle Fairy hadn't known she was assembling. "Dorrin," she said, and her voice was quiet, barely more than a whisper. She looked back at Nahk with wide eyes. "It had to be Dorrin." Sweet, brave Dorrin, who had died protecting his friends. Dorrin, who never would have become an assassin of any sort, no matter what Scrounger might have intended for him.

LIZANDRA'S DEEPEST FEAR

"What was special about him?" Nahk asked.

"He was a mage, for one thing," Fairy said.

"Wasn't him, then. Mages can't be Nightingales."

Fairy frowned at that. "We didn't know he was a mage until... until just before he was gone. I don't think Scrounger knew—"

"If Moeply Raseul had a mage under his watch, he knew it," Nahk said. "If he had anyone with potential, it was somebody else. Was there anyone Raseul spent extra time with? Anybody he gave special instruction or tutoring to? Mathematics? Reading? History?"

With every word, Fairy felt her stomach dropping more, her knees growing weaker. It hadn't been Dorrin after all. Nahk was right, as improbable as that had seemed. Dorrin wasn't the one Scrounger had tutored, the one who had learned to keep the accounting for the gang, the one who had studied cartography under Scrounger's instruction. "It was me," she whispered.

Nahk watched Fairy as the realization settled over her. After a moment, Nahk gave a satisfied grunt and said, "I thought it might have been you."

Fairy blinked at her and said the most obvious thing she'd spoken all day: "You're one of them, aren't you? A Nightingale."

Nahk pulled the corner of her mouth tight and said, "Was, am, wasn't, who knows? They wanted me to be, at least. I didn't finish the training. I was never a full Nightingale." She hesitated but then finished, "I'm not sure what I am now."

Fairy's brain still hadn't resolved what Nahk was telling her, but she blurted out the next most obvious thing she'd said that day. "I want you to show me how to be like you. You have to teach me what you know!"

"Can't do it. I wouldn't know where to start, and even if I did, I wouldn't do that to you."

"But you could show me what you know. Help me be like you."

Nahk pushed away from the wall and stood to her full height. She moved in front of Fairy and made sure she had the girl's eyes before she said, "You don't want to be like me. I don't know if you believe in Khealdir or Ikarna or any of that, but if you do, you should thank them for sparing you. The things they did to me aren't things you want done to you. And the things I've done aren't things you want to do."

"But I have nothing else," Fairy said, and her eyes burned, and she was embarrassed about that, but there was nothing to be done about it. She kept talking. "Everybody I knew was in Klubridge. They're all probably dead by now, the ones I don't already know are dead for sure. I came here with these people, and none of them has time for me. Nobody cares. And now you're telling me I almost had something. I was going to be special, and then Scrounger died, and all of it went wrong." Tears had betrayed her by the time she was finished, but she no longer cared about that. She let them roll down her cheeks, the breeze chilling them on her skin. "I need this."

Nahk watched her cry without looking away like most people would. There wasn't sympathy in her eyes. There wasn't anything, really. They just stared at her and let her get it out, and somehow that was okay. It might have been better than okay. Still not good, but better. After the tears weren't as fresh and Fairy was pretty certain she was done with that, Nahk said, "You don't need this. I can't teach you this, even if I wanted to. Anyway, I'm probably leaving soon."

"Leaving? For where?" Fairy's heart thudded with the possibilities. "Take me with you!"

"I'm not taking you with me. Things are happening right now. Both here in the rebellion and elsewhere in Teshovar. I suspect Naecara and Vaino are both going to be taking action soon, and that's not the kind of thing you can come along for." She paused and studied Fairy for another moment. "You need something, though. What have you tried?"

And so Fairy told her. She described her attempts at finding something to fill her and coming up empty. She spilled it all out without shame or embarrassment at being the one who couldn't get anybody to help her. Something about talking to Nahk made that easy, maybe because she didn't seem like she had somewhere more important to be or maybe because the two of them shared some kind of weird connection through this Nightingale thing. Whatever the reason, Fairy was out of breath by the time

LIZANDRA'S DEEPEST FEAR

she'd finished, and she realized it had all come out in a rapid string of words and sentences and accusations, with scarcely a pause throughout.

She could tell Nahk had listened to the whole thing, though. She finally nodded and said, "I know Leyna. She's probably taken a liking to your friend and thinks you're after him, too. You're not, are you?"

"No!" Fairy said and almost laughed at the notion. The objection probably came out too forcefully, and she thought that might have made it sound like a lie, but it was true. She had no interest in Oreth beyond hoping he'd be her friend.

"Give it until tomorrow," Nahk said. "I'll get it sorted out. Go back to see your friend tomorrow."

Fairy's brow crinkled, and she stood up straighter. She looked toward the keep and then back to Nahk before leaning closer. She whispered, "You're not going to... kill her."

Nahk's own eyes narrowed, and she took a half step back. "What?"

"Leyna. I don't want you to kill her!" Fairy said, and she regretted saying it as soon as the words were out.

Nahk's shoulders raised, and she folded her arms, taking another step away from Fairy. "That's not the only thing I can do," she said, and her voice was harder again. Fairy felt whatever connection they'd made fraying, so soon after it had formed. She was about to say something when Nahk said, "Tomorrow." The woman who wasn't quite a Nightingale turned then, pulling her cloak tighter around her shoulders, and disappeared into the keep.

~

Fairy went back to the workshop the following day, just like Nahk had told her to do, but she didn't expect to find anything different. Not after she'd insulted Nahk like that. Why in the world had she said that, implying that Nahk would off Leyna just because it might help Fairy out?

Nahk had said she'd started training as one of those Nightingale things and that they were assassins, but that didn't mean

Nahk was itching to commit murder for some desperate orphan she'd only just met. Fairy'd had to open her big mouth and spoil everything, just when she'd found somebody she could get along with.

But, still, Nahk had told her to go see Oreth the following day, and she hadn't taken back her offer to help, so Fairy felt obligated to at least show up. She wasn't surprised as she approached the front of the supply depot and saw Leyna standing in the big, open doorway. The quick smile that came to Leyna's face was plenty surprising, though. Fairy nearly stumbled on the paved path but kept herself walking until she was just outside the entry.

"Hey," Fairy said.

"Hey," Leyna said back. She pursed her lips as she studied Fairy.

"I'm not here to cause trouble," Fairy said.

Leyna shook her head, and her mass of brown curls shook around her face. "None of that. I owe you an apology."

Fairy had stopped a few feet away from Leyna, not so far away as to make talking to the other girl awkward but not quite within arm swinging distance, just in case. "An apology?"

"I was harsh with you when you were here before. You didn't fit, but Naecara explained things, and now you do."

Fairy's forehead creased as she tried to work that out. "Didn't fit? I'm... I'm not after Oreth. I don't want any trouble there."

Leyna waved a hand as if she were shooing away a fly. "That wasn't the issue."

"Wasn't... You're not interested in Oreth?"

"Well, yes, of course, but I meant you didn't fit, aside from any of that." Her tone was even and direct, and she didn't even blush at the admission. Fairy knew she'd have been bright red by then. Before she could say anything else, Leyna continued. "You came in with the mage from Klubridge and all his people. All of them worked with him, were friends with him, knew him. All of them made sense. You didn't. Whenever something doesn't fit, I have to find out why it doesn't. That was you. You didn't fit with them."

"I hardly knew them. Hardly know them still," Fairy said, and the admission made her ache. Had it really been such a short time since she'd been in Klubridge, living in Scrounger's hovel with Dorrin and Skink and all the rest of them? And now all of them were gone, and she was the one left. She was the one traveling to strange castles with a group of theater people—mages, for the most part—that she barely knew.

"But you fit now," Leyna said. She turned halfway, heading back into the doorway. "You make sense, and you're not magic." She paused and cut her eyes back at Fairy. "You're not magic, are you?"

"I'm not," Fairy said, shuffling to keep up with the other girl but stopping again when she'd stopped. "You don't like magic?"

Leyna pushed her lips together and crinkled her nose. "Who really likes magic? It's been nothing but trouble for anybody I've ever heard about using it. Or being around it. Or even thinking about it," she added with a quick frown.

Fairy wanted to protest, but she considered Leyna's words. Maybe she was right. If not for magic, the Kites wouldn't have chased Caius and the rest of them out of the city. Dorrin wouldn't have died, the rest of them wouldn't have had to flee, and Klubridge itself probably wouldn't have been blasted away, or whatever had happened to it. Come to think of it, without magic, there wouldn't even be a High Lord to keep causing all this trouble, and that was a fact. But Fairy still frowned. "You don't like magic, but you like Oreth."

"I do," Leyna said and turned her back again, leading the way into the workshop.

Fairy followed, and it took a few seconds for her eyes to adjust to the relative gloom. She'd already said, "But, you know, Oreth is a mage," by the time she saw Oreth himself sitting on a bench toward the middle of the back wall, his head bent over some project that had his attention. "Oh," Fairy said. "Hi, Oreth."

He looked over his shoulder at her and grinned. "Why don't you spill everybody you know's secrets while you're at it?"

Fairy clamped her teeth tight. She shouldn't have said anything. That really had been Oreth's secret to tell or not tell, and she'd just blabbed it right out. But he didn't seem upset by it, and Leyna confirmed it when she said, "I already knew."

"She says it's not real magic anyway," Oreth said and turned around on the bench to face them. He was wearing the brace Leyna had built for him, and it made his left leg look like some kind of machine, the way the rods moved when he bent his knee and swiveled.

"What do you mean?" Fairy asked. She followed Leyna around the big central table and leaned back against it, propping her palms on its surface.

"The type of magic he has," Leyna said. "Oreth can't do anything by himself."

It was subtle, but Fairy saw Oreth wince at that last bit. Things were going better with Leyna, strange though the other girl might be, but Fairy couldn't just let her say something like that. "He can do plenty by himself." It was a weak retort, but it was something.

Leyna tilted her head. "In general, yes. With magic, no." She squinted at Fairy. "Do you even know what he can do?"

Fairy opened her mouth but then shut it again. Everything she knew about Oreth, she'd learned on board the ship, when she'd been helping take care of him in the aftermath of Klubridge. He'd been unconscious a good portion of that time, so there had been little time to quiz him about whether he could make fire or levitate. She shook her head.

Oreth glanced at Leyna before looking back to Fairy. "I can change other people's magic. Make things they do a little stronger, a little different. Change directions, change colors, things like that."

"What do you mean?" Fairy asked.

"Let's say somebody," he said, pausing for emphasis like Fairy was supposed to know who he meant, "was able to throw magic energy like knives. I could make them go faster. I could change their direction, make them curve, all kinds of things."

"That's amazing!" Fairy said, and she meant it. She knew everybody but Caius and Aquin could use magic, and she'd heard most mages could only do a few specific tricks. She had pressed none of them for details on what they could do, but she'd gathered that Samira had access to some sort of healing power and had brought Lizzie back from the brink of death.

And, based on what he'd told her, she knew Dorrin had been able to create threads from nothing and had used them to pull himself along, even through the air and over roofs. She'd wondered about what the others could do, but she hadn't asked or gotten answers until now.

"Leyna's right, though," he said. "I'm pretty useless unless there's somebody else doing something I can modify."

Leyna gave Fairy a tight smile. "So, you see, he's not going to cause trouble. He's hardly a mage."

Fairy wanted to say something else in Oreth's defense, but she could see Leyna hadn't meant that as an insult. Still, it didn't sit right with her. She looked from Leyna to Oreth, and he was smiling at her.

"It's okay, really. If I had a choice, I wouldn't even have this thing. Just like Leyna says, it's never anything but trouble."

Fairy started, "But—"

Oreth was still smiling but cut her off. "You didn't come back here just to talk about magic."

"No," she said. "I still want to help here, if I can. I thought maybe there'd be something I could do."

Oreth scratched at his cheek and glanced back at the ledger he'd been working on when Fairy had arrived. There were a bunch of black scribbles tumbled across the top of the yellowed page in front of him. He looked back at Fairy. "You're welcome here. You can come hang around anytime you want. I just don't know that there's anything you can do to help right now."

"I know math and maps," Fairy said, a sudden desperation pushing the words out. She couldn't be rejected again. Not when she was so close!

"It's not that," Oreth said. "There just isn't that much to do right now. When we start getting more supplies in and start organizing wagons to go down the mountain, then we could use some help with loading, inventorying, all that sort of thing. But, until then, there's not a lot to do."

"Oh," Fairy said. It was disappointing, but it wasn't quite a rejection. Not like everything else had been, at least.

"There isn't even enough for me to do now," Oreth said with

a shrug. "I've resorted to tinkering. But you can stay here all you want. And when there is more to do, you can help. Really."

Leyna tilted her head and favored Fairy with a sudden grin that was as disconcerting as it was sincere. Fairy raised her eyebrows, and Leyna said, "I'm glad we're friends now."

CHAPTER 13

Quentyn Wickes didn't know what to expect from Klubridge. It had been more than a year since he'd been through the city, and when he'd left it, it had been every bit the bustling metropolis it had always been. The streets had been crowded with merchants, bankers, urchins, and actors, the pubs full of drunkards and university students in equal measure and sometimes overlapping. That's how Klubridge had looked and sounded and smelled for all Wickes' life and likely several more lifetimes before his own. It was a city always in motion, always at the center of some deal or scheme, and it had never occurred to him that it would ever stop.

That was before the uprising, before the rebels shoved the Empire out of the city, and before the Empire returned and exacted its vengeance. Whatever had happened to Klubridge was recent enough and unprecedented enough that nobody seemed to understand the source of the destruction or its magnitude. Rumors floated north and south along the coastline and surely penetrated into the mainland, all providing conflicting versions of what had befallen the city.

Some said it was the Imperial military, bringing its full complement of soldiers and armaments to bear. Others claimed it was the Herons, brought to the city by their handlers to lay waste to the one place that had successfully opposed the Empire.

And still others said it was the High Lord Peregrine himself, unleashing his immense power to obliterate the largest city to ever revolt against his unchallenged authority.

Wickes wasn't sure which rumor to believe and thought it likely that none of them were true. Still, something had happened in or to Klubridge, and he'd be seeing the aftermath soon enough. It had been a long trip back up the coast, and the Empire had insisted that he fly Imperial flags with the blue crest of the High Lord's aerie whenever he was about his Imperial business. Given the turmoil and changing of hands in Klubridge over the past weeks, sailing up to the remains of the city in an Imperial-marked vessel could be tantamount to suicide. A day out from port, he had the Imperial colors lowered and his original flag of nonalignment flown. It was a black banner with the outline of a white circle at the center, recognized throughout Teshovar as the flag of a ship with no port and no master beyond the one commanding the deck. In some waters it was the pirates' flag, and Wickes suspected it would be more welcome in whatever remained of the city than any governmental flag would have been.

There was no hiding the ship itself, and Wickes knew the *Gaillardia* had a reputation now. It had spent the last three years running down the very crew who used to work its sails, and that was every bit as disreputable as being a fully branded ship of the Empire. Maybe even worse. At least the Empire would stab you in the front. He hoped the chaotic state of Klubridge would help him sail in and out without incident, but he'd be equally ready for things to not go his way.

As the crew raised the flag of piracy, Wickes changed out of his uniform and into plain clothes that wouldn't raise suspicions the way naval epaulets would. The last thing he needed was to have any surviving citizens mistake him for one of their attackers and set upon him and his crew. He stowed the uniform in his cabin and was standing on the deck as they neared the port.

Even from a distance, it was clear that Klubridge had changed. The city still existed in some form, but gone were the familiar shapes of its skyline, replaced by irregular forms and

LIZANDRA'S DEEPEST FEAR

geometries that left a heaviness in Wickes' gut. He pulled one hand off the rail of the ship to rub at the back of his neck and cast a quick glance down at the surface of the water, shimmering in the midday sun. Between the white crests of waves that approached and crashed against the ship's hull, there was the deep green that obscured what lay beneath. Wickes inhaled and tore his eyes away from the depths.

The docks, formerly an orderly row of wooden structures extending out from the port, now jutted into the water at odd angles, some bucking upward and twisting against their pilings while others dipped beneath the rolling wake. The piers farthest south had been sheared away, all at the same angle, like some great reaper had swung a massive scythe across them. Despite the state of the docks, a few ships had anchored there, most of them to the north, where the damage seemed less severe.

Klubridge's devastation revealed itself in stages as the *Gaillardia* crawled nearer to the city. The stairways leading up from the port had been torn away, and jagged wood still clung to the side of the city wall that faced the sea, where remnants of the steps remained. In place of the old stairs, someone had assembled rickety ramps and landings, some of them secured to the walls and some supported by ropes that suspended the walkways from makeshift cranes above. Whatever had happened there, enough people still lived and inhabited the city to have begun these haphazard repairs.

Above the port and beyond the seaward walls, the city's easternmost structures now tumbled together, some buildings cut off midway with the same sort of enormous strokes that had severed the piers and some having lost their foundations and fallen into their neighbors. It was still identifiable as a city, but it was nothing like the Klubridge Wickes remembered. He stared at the bleak edge of the city and the black smoke that curled into the sky beyond and imagined the state of the rest of the place. Candlestick would be to his left, the university to his right, but he knew that was no longer true. The districts no longer mattered. The Downsteps, the Financial Quarter, all of it was as one now. If he traveled into the city itself, he'd see it all crushed together into one sprawling collage of misery. The old lines of class and property no longer mattered, when the buildings that defined those lines no longer existed.

He had no desire to go any farther into Klubridge than he had to, though. He had no inclination to investigate the extent of the destruction. His business was confined to the port, and he pulled his gaze down to the building that used to house the harbormaster's office. It was a bulky structure at the far north end of the docks, and it resembled a vast warehouse more than anything else. Being situated as it was, it had been spared the bulk of the demolition that had shredded the southern piers.

Two columns of smoke arose from somewhere in the city, one to the north, toward the Henburn Estate where the huge tower once loomed over the city, and the other to the south, probably somewhere in the Downsteps or the East Ward. Something was always burning down there, but the fire uptown was another sign that disaster had come. It really was true. Klubridge had fallen, and neither the rebels nor the Empire had a hold there anymore. After hearing about the uprising, Wickes had thought Klubridge might be a suitable place for a former pirate to disappear and start over again. Whatever razed the city had destroyed that notion along with it.

Even though there were fewer ships, workers still waited at the dock to wave the *Gaillardia* in, and they set about securing it to the moorings before preparing to receive the ramp the ship's crew extended. Even amid disaster, life carried on, and someone had taken control of the docks. Wickes waited on the deck, one hand on the railing, and watched the ropes pull taut, the dock hands yell to each other, and the business of the port operate as if the city hadn't mutinied just a few short weeks before and been destroyed shortly thereafter.

As workers tied the last of the knots and slotted the ramp into place, a fair-skinned man with a recent sunburn on his neck and cheeks mounted the walkway and came up to the ship, his hands sliding along the metal handrails as he climbed. His hair was blond and cut short, as was the beard on his square jaw, and he wore a white shirt with the sleeves rolled midway up his large forearms. He had the look and demeanor of a man who'd

LIZANDRA'S DEEPEST FEAR

worked the docks, but not one who was accustomed to doing business with the captains.

"Permission to board," he called, and Wickes gestured him onto the deck. The man climbed over the railing and extended a hand. Wickes shook it and felt the hard calluses ahead of the firm grip. "Name's Marfont," he said.

Wickes released his hand and asked, "You run the docks now, I suppose?"

"I do. What's your business?"

"I'm trying to find someone. He left Klubridge the day the riots happened."

"You got no cargo? No trade? No passengers?"

"I do not."

"Can't help you, then. On your way." Marfont turned to leave, but Wickes stopped him.

"I have seri for the docking and your time. I suspect you can help me, and maybe I can help you."

Marfont was ready to climb back over to the ramp and already had his hand on the railing, but he paused at that and looked back. "How much seri we talking?"

The negotiation was swift, and it only took a few minutes for Wickes to head down the ramp and up the long pier with the new self-appointed harbormaster. According to Mediean, the wizard Akithar had been in contact with the rebels and most likely left the city immediately after the failed silencing ceremony. Imperial intelligence expected he'd headed from there to the Stormbreak Sanctuary, in the company of a rebel spy. The Empire had wanted him before he'd brought down Klubridge, primarily because they thought he could lead them to the rebels' famously hidden headquarters. After Klubridge, though, they needed to bring him down as a symbol of revolt. Akithar was on everyone's tongue now as proof that the Empire was fallible and that the High Lord could be beaten. They wanted Stormbreak, to be sure, but Wickes thought they might want the man himself even more now than before.

The Scarlet Kites had locked down the city for weeks prior to the silencing, and the gates hadn't reopened until the citizens had stormed them as a mob, a day or more after the rioting started. It was unlikely that Akithar and his compatriots had hung around long enough for that to happen, so it stood to reason that they'd left by sea. Wickes was gambling on the likelihood that the port records hadn't been cleared out when the Imperial harbormaster had been disposed of and hadn't been destroyed in the ensuing attack. Judging by the intact state of the warehouse at the north end of the port, Wickes expected the logs were safe and had fallen into the hands of this new fellow, Marfont, after he installed himself in his new position.

"Yeah, all the books are here," Marfont said and looked toward a door at the back of his office. "Don't know what all's in there, but I haven't moved any of it."

"Would you mind if I had a look?"

"You mind if I take a few more seri?"

Wickes had anticipated the greed and slid the coins across the desk. Without waiting for further permission, he stepped around Marfont and went into the back room. It was an orderly storeroom with racks of books along two walls. The ledgers showed date ranges on their spines, and all of them sat in chronological order. Wickes pulled the final one from the bottom shelf and noted that nothing else had been logged after that one. The new order didn't seem to care about keeping records, and he was thankful for once that the Empire had been fastidious.

He opened the logbook on the table near the back window and flipped through the pages, passing days and weeks and months of ships coming to and going from the port. Would the harbormaster have even logged ships on that day, while the riots were starting up? Or would chaos have already descended by then, upending any semblance of record keeping?

Wickes' fingers stopped flipping pages when he reached the final completed record in the book. It was all blank sheets after that one. On the final day, there were records of ships going in and out of the harbor, all with their times noted. Conspicuously, the records ended just prior to noon, the time Medican had said the silencing had been scheduled to happen. Wickes knew the Kites and the Herons had dragged Akithar into the city's main plaza at midday and tried to take his magic away. He'd withstood the ceremony, apparently a historical first, and he'd destroyed his enemies in what the stories described as a spectacular fashion. There had been explosions, screaming, stampedes—all the hallmarks of a good revolt. It had, no doubt, been big enough to disrupt the port just a few blocks away, and that had been the end of the records and likely the end of the Imperial harbormaster.

That meant the ship Akithar took when leaving Klubridge had to have been in the port at the time the revolt began in earnest. Wickes trailed his finger down the page and read the names of all the ships that were still docked when the records ended. Seventeen vessels in all. It was highly unlikely that Akithar had taken an Imperial ship when he departed. Of course, it was possible that he'd compromised a captain in the Imperial Navy, but that seemed doubtful. No ships of the Empire had been reported missing after the Klubridge riots. Wickes paid attention to that sort of news and would have heard if a craft had dropped out of the roster.

He went through the list of ships again, eliminating the ones logged as naval vessels or ships officially logged as Imperial property. That left six. Wickes recognized two of them and knew their captains to be Imperial loyalists. He'd conferred with them during his long quest to incarcerate his own crew, and he knew those two would have never given passage to a fugitive when they could have turned him over to the Kites for a profit.

So that left four. Four ships that might have given passage to Akithar and his gang, any of which might be docked at Stormbreak even now. Wickes tore a blank page out from the back of the ledger and grabbed a stubby pencil from a side table. Its tip was blunt, but it would do. With careful block letters, he copied the names of the four ships onto the paper: *Pilchard*, *Echuca*, *Sephare*, *Moray Firth*. He read the list and then read it again, committing the names to memory, before he folded the paper and slipped it into his pocket.

～

After leaving Klubridge, the *Gaillardia* sailed south to Redwater. The crew didn't ask Wickes any questions about what he wanted there or what he'd been doing in Klubridge. They didn't care. They weren't even his crew, in truth.

Medlean supplied sailors whenever the Empire sent Wickes on an errand, and the crew didn't need or want to know anything beyond their immediate orders, as long as they continued getting paid. Even when the crew stayed behind, there was always one soldier assigned to shadow Wickes, likely to make sure he didn't try to disappear into Teshovar and abandon his mission. He was lucky to still own his ship, and he suspected that might be a temporary arrangement that would end in the *Gaillardia* being seized and hauled into an Imperial port for refitting as soon as Bekam had no more use for a seafaring hunter.

Even if he would never be comfortable with it or like it, Wickes had gotten used to the arrangement, and he didn't bother telling his new first mate anything other than giving him the order to set sail for Redwater. The other officers didn't enjoy sailing under a pirate flag, so they ran the Imperial colors back up the mast without consulting Wickes. Having his orders countermanded or outright ignored was another thing he'd grown used to, and it wasn't a surprise to have the ship rebranded without his orders. He was the captain only as far as they needed him to be for the hunt. And he knew he was a better hunter than anyone else on that ship or any other.

Redwater was another port city and did twice the business of Klubridge, despite being a quarter of its size. Where Klubridge had catered to its wealthy upper class and had hardly any exports of its own, Redwater was a hub of commerce and attracted merchants and industry that its northern neighbor shunned in favor of the arts, education, and finance.

When the *Gaillardia* arrived at Redwater, it was just one among dozens of similar vessels, unlikely to raise any eyebrows. And it was among company, docked beside countless other ships flying Imperial colors. After Klubridge had slipped from the

LIZANDRA'S DEEPEST FEAR

Empire's grasp, an exodus of Imperial loyalists had followed, and many of them had ended up here, stuck in Redwater until they felt safe to return home after the Empire had reclaimed the city. That would never happen now.

Wickes' Imperial escort into Redwater was a broad and surly man he knew only as Jalla. Jalla stood nearly a full head shorter than Wickes and had a clean-shaven scalp above a full and gristly beard. It looked as if his hair had slid off the top of his head and gathered at his chin. He'd said fewer than ten words to Wickes on the journey from Klubridge, and Wickes didn't expect to hear many more than that now that they had reached their destination.

Jalla followed Wickes into the city and lagged behind him as he wound his way past factories and warehouses until he found the address he was looking for. It was a low and narrow house, squeezed between two shops along a back road called Clove Lane. Someone had painted the front door green, but now the paint was flaking away to show the brown underneath. Wickes studied the dark window beside the door and wondered whether someone inside might be staring back at him.

"This'll go better if you wait out here," he said to Jalla but didn't wait for a response before he approached the front door and knocked twice. When he glanced over his shoulder, Jalla had crossed the street and was crouching to sit on the curb to wait for him.

Wickes turned back to the door and raised his hand to knock again when he caught movement in the window. She was looking out at him, and his breath caught. They stood like that for a long moment, her inside and him out, staring at each other through the glass, before she moved to the door, and he heard the lock disengage.

"You've been to Aramore," she said as she opened the door. She didn't open it wide enough to let him in.

"Last month."

"And he told you where to find me."

"He did."

She frowned and cursed under her breath. "You've known

where to find me for a full month. I should have moved again after the last time I saw him."

"You should have," Wickes said. He had been expecting this conversation for three years but didn't know where to begin. So he said, "It's over, Weylis."

Her frown deepened. "I should have expected. It was only a matter of time."

This was going wrong. He shook his head and started again. "I'm not here to take you. All that's over now."

She blinked at him and looked past his shoulder, like she didn't believe him. Like she thought he'd changed his mind and really was there to take her. "What do you mean, it's over?"

"I got Dhasho. He was the last one. It's over now."

She looked past him again before she stepped back and pulled the door wider. "You'd better come in."

He followed her through the entrance and pushed the door shut behind him. They were in a small kitchen, and Wickes could see the bedroom through the open door in the far wall. The whole house was only two rooms, maybe three, if she had a bath. Nothing was baking at the moment, but the scent of fresh bread lingered in the air.

Weylis Rutland sat at her kitchen table, a rough piece of furniture that looked like she'd scavenged it off the street, and she nodded to the chair. Wickes pulled it back and sat across from her, the table between them.

"You look good," he said, but even he could hear the falsehood in his voice. It had been three years since he'd seen her, and those years had clearly been hard ones. She still looked as strong as ever, but her long hair was going gray where it used to be brown, and her skin was pale where it used to be tanned. The sun-seared creases still lined her forehead and the corners of her eyes, though, and without the tan, they just made her look old and tired. Nevertheless, his chest tightened, and he tensed, startled by the familiar ache his heart had almost forgotten.

"What do you want, Quentyn?" Her voice sounded as tired as she looked.

"To tell you it's finished. The Empire won't be looking for any more of the crew."

LIZANDRA'S DEEPEST FEAR

"They still think I'm dead?"

"It's what I told them, just like I promised you. The rest of the crew thinks it, too."

"Not for long," she said. "I'd be surprised if the Empire suffered any of the others to live, and Dhasho will be swinging by the neck shortly, if he hasn't already." Her hands were on the table, and she was picking at the nails on her left hand with the right. "So, what now? You're free of your burden? Released to go do whatever you please?"

"It's not that simple," Wickes said.

She chuckled and raised her eyes to meet his. "It never is. I believe someone told you that before you started betraying and murdering all our friends and ruining your own honor and reputation. The Empire's never finished with you until they're finished with you."

She was right, just like she'd been right when they got caught. He'd told her the deal he'd been offered, and she'd told him he was mad to accept it. Part of him had known, even then, that Bekam wouldn't live up to his end of the bargain. Agreeing to the terms had saved Wickes from execution, but the cost was the lives of the rest of his crew. At least he'd saved her, too, for whatever good it had done her.

"Why can't you just stop doing whatever they're telling you to do now?" she asked. "Sail to Plier Glau or take a coach to Bria or go anywhere else, and they'd never find you."

"They would," he said. "There's always someone following me. And even if I could get away from him, where could I go? My name and face are known everywhere by now."

"Quentyn Wickes, infamous pirate captain, or Quentyn Wickes, cowardly tool of the High Lord?"

"Either would be enough. I can't be free until they free me."

"And they won't free you."

He knew she was right again, but he didn't say it. Instead, he said, "They have me looking for Akithar."

"The magician from Klubridge. That figures."

Wickes drew the crumpled piece of paper from his pocket and slid it across the table to Weylis. "He left the city on one of these ships, likely headed for the Stormbreak Sanctuary. Do you know any of these?"

She looked at the list, and her eyes tracked down the names, and she looked back up at him. "And, what? You're going to find him and turn him over to your masters?"

"That's what they want," he said.

She exhaled slowly, her eyes still on him. It was the first time he'd ever heard disappointment expressed so profoundly in a single breath.

Weylis looked at the list again and tapped it, sliding the paper back across the table with her finger next to one of the names. "This is the one. *Sephare*."

"That easily? How do you know?"

"The captain is Ergo Drass. He's been supplying the rebels for years. I sailed with him briefly, long ago."

Wickes read the names of the ships once. "You're certain it's this one? Not one of the others?"

Weylis shrugged. "You came to hear what I know, and that's what I know. Drass is a good man. Find out what you need to find out, but don't hurt him."

"I won't hurt him," Wickes said, perhaps too quickly. He saw that Weylis knew the truth. He'd do whatever it took to get answers out of the man, but he'd at least try to do it without hurting him. "Where can I find him?"

"He used to have a house at Inport. He'd dock there to resupply and would stay for a few days, usually once every month or so."

"Inport?"

"Not your favorite, I know. But that's all I know about him." Weylis sat back in her chair, and Wickes knew that's all he'd get from her, even if she did know more.

"Thank you, Weylis. I—"

"Was it worth it?"

He frowned. "How do you mean?"

"Betraying everything you stood for. Hunting all our friends and sending them to the gallows, and now you're still dancing on Bekam's strings."

"I did it for you, Weylis. All of this was to keep you safe and alive."

Her lips drew tight, and her eyes pressed him back in his seat, her breath deep and steady. "You did this for me. You killed all our friends for me. Is that what you've told yourself?" She shook her head. "You did none of this for me, Quentyn."

"But I—"

"No," she said, and her tone was sharp enough to cut off the rest of what he'd been about to tell her. She rose from her seat, her eyes never leaving his. "You did this to save yourself. If I could trade my own life and bring back all the ones you've doomed, I'd do it in an instant. I won't allow you to blame me for the past three years."

Wickes wanted to protest, to tell her he wouldn't have—couldn't have done all this if she hadn't been his priority. That knowing she was safe somewhere outside the interest of the Empire was all that had mattered. But her words had struck true, and he couldn't do it. He couldn't tell her something he was no longer sure of himself.

"Was it worth your trouble?" she asked.

He willed his eyes to break her gaze, but they betrayed him. Had it been worthwhile? The betrayals? The deaths? The ruination of his own life in the service of ruining the lives of nearly everyone he'd loved? Weylis knew the truth. It had kept him alive, and that made it worth it. But, even now, he couldn't say that to her. Not when this was likely to be the last thing he'd ever say to her. He opened his mouth to speak, but the lie still wouldn't come. He finally said, "I don't know."

She nodded and pushed her chair against the table, taking a step back and folding her arms. Wickes stood and dragged his own chair back into place. It scraped across the uneven wooden floor before resting in the silence between them. Wickes finally dropped his eyes to the table. He picked up the paper with the list of ships and folded it once before sliding it into his coat pocket. "Thank you," he said again.

Weylis already had the door open and held it as she stepped out of his way. "Don't try to find me next time, Quentyn. Never again."

CHAPTER 14

Apak twisted the screwdriver and felt the screw turn into its home with a satisfying smoothness, despite the crude nature of his drilling. The facilities at Stormbreak were rudimentary, when compared to the workshop he'd seen destroyed in the Downsteps and even when compared to his backstage tinkering station at the Chamberlain Theater. His fingers twitched at the thought of the delicate instruments and precision tools that were lost to the flames when the Kites had forced him to abandon his home.

It did no good to think of that now. What was lost was lost, and there was no going back for any of it, now that the entire city had fallen. Apak scowled at the piece of metal in his hand and grabbed the rag to his right. He scrubbed at a smear of grease along the top of the metal, wiping at it with such ferocity that the edges began to fray the cloth.

He dropped the cloth onto the table and placed his work atop it. Even if the Empire had not destroyed Klubridge, there would have been no going back. Not after what they had done in the service of rescuing Caius. Not after what he had done.

Apak pulled his glasses off and rubbed at his closed, weary eyes with his thumb and middle finger, first gently and then so hard it made dark stars sparkle behind his eyelids. Even then, he could see the faces of the guards turning from determination to terror as they recognized the bizarre fate that awaited them. And Apak had delivered that fate without hesitation. He had built a machine for that specific purpose.

Before going into the plaza, Apak had told Samira, Lizandra, and Reykas that he would provide a distraction for them. Samira had warned him not to cause any unnecessary damage or violence, and he had agreed. He had known what awaited all of them within that plaza, but his assurance to Samira had not been a lie. The destruction of the Scarlet Kites had been necessary. Their utter defeat was essential.

When Oreth had lain unconscious on what very well might have been his deathbed, Apak had sworn vengeance. He had promised the boy that no Kite would leave Klubridge alive, and he had gone to save Caius under the weight of the knowledge that either he or the Kites might leave Klubridge alive, but not both. Possibly, neither would survive the conflict.

But Apak had survived, and he had bought that survival and his revenge in blood. The violence he had wrought had tamed his anger only momentarily. The Empire had killed Dorrin and had nearly caused Oreth to die as well. It had sent mage hunters to hound all of them to their own deaths or to imprisonment or worse. And now it had driven them from their city and, capping the indignity, laid waste to it.

The fury arose fresh in his chest, and his face flushed with it. Apak took the grease-stained cloth in his hand again and squeezed it, his fist mangling it into a tight ball of dirty fabric. He had saved his friends, and the anger remained. He had killed to fulfill his promise, and the anger remained. He probably had lost Samira's trust after she saw him destroying the Imperials, and the anger remained. Was there any end to it, and what must all of them think of him after Klubridge?

"I think that's wrung out."

Apak opened his eyes. The halflock, Magra, stood beside him at the table, her peculiar eyes trained on his hands. "I did not hear you enter," he said.

She shrugged and reached in front of him to tug at the edge

of the cloth dangling from his fist. "I think you can let that go. Whatever was in it's out now."

He looked down at his hands and forced his fingers to relax. The cloth dropped to the table once more, crinkled and torn where his nails had dug into it. "What do you want, Magra?"

"What were you doing?" She leaned over the table and peered at the contraption he had been building. She would not understand what he had been assembling, so there was no use in trying to explain it. In truth, Apak did not understand, himself. He simply knew that his hands needed movement, and his brain needed to feel productive. He had gone for too long without finding diverse pieces and constructing them into something new. It hardly mattered whether the construction yielded anything useful. The benefit was in the process. He had avoided coming into the workshop at Stormbreak whenever he knew Oreth was next door in the supply depot, but he was elsewhere that day, helping the girl with other duties. The tools and facilities were free and open for Apak's use.

"I am working," he said and placed his glasses upon the bridge of his nose once more.

Magra stood beside him without speaking for a long moment but then said, "I'm mad, too, you know."

Apak turned his head toward her again, an eyebrow raised, but he said nothing.

"Not loony mad," she said. "I'm angry. Mad as can be, and I can see it in you, too."

Denying the woman's observation might hasten her departure, but Apak held his tongue. Perhaps the way forward with his friends could begin with this newcomer. "I am angry," he acknowledged. "I seem unable to stop being angry."

"It's about Klubridge, isn't it? And the Kites and all that business." Magra had been a prisoner of the Empire until Samira had freed her, while Apak's slaughter had commenced in the center of the city. Apak did not know how much she knew or had surmised about his own role in initiating the chaos that day, but he resolved not to deny anything this woman might have learned. If talking with Magra was the start of his way forward, then honesty would be its catalyst.

"It is," he admitted. "The Kites also killed someone dear to me. A young boy."

"Dorrin," she said, and Apak glanced at her. It was unsurprising that she would have heard the boy's name, perhaps from Fairy, but hearing it spoken continued to prod at the wound that had not yet healed. Perhaps it never would, no matter how much destruction Apak brought to the Empire.

"Dorrin," he said, his voice low. He forced himself not to look away from Magra, unsettling as her round, dark eyes might be. "How long were you a prisoner?"

"I don't know." She looked away, and the corners of her mouth turned downward, as though she were trying to recall. "I can remember only as long as I've been a halflock. Who knows how long they kept me chained up somewhere before that?"

"How long have you been as you are, then?" Apak asked. It seemed strange that he felt uneasy calling her a halflock after she had spoken the word herself, but he refrained from saying it.

"Too long," she said, still staring away, but then she looked at him again, and her mouth contorted into something unlike a smile but not quite like a grimace. "And not long enough." She had been standing but now dragged a nearby stool from under the table and sat on it. "Do you know how they make us? What they do to us?"

"I have heard rumors, but I doubt their veracity."

She snorted at that, and Apak realized it might have been a laugh. He saw no humor in what he had said, but he remained silent. Magra said, "When they round you up and decide you're a mage and want to make you into a halflock, they have all kinds of bureaucracy around it. They say it's to make sure they get it right and there aren't any mistakes, but it's all just a show. They drag you to one of the courts. Aramore, somewhere fancy like that. And then, all it takes is three people testifying you're a mage, and you're done for."

"The Empire brings witnesses against potential mages?" This was surprising. Apak's experience with the Empire had shown it to be uncaring about evidence or truth. It did what it wanted, and it claimed whatever it needed.

Magra shrugged. "Like I said, they say it's so everything's fair, but it's not so. They have safeguards in place to protect themselves. If somebody tries to say a noble's a mage, they put a stop to it. The testimonies have to come from the higher ups themselves. Imperial officers, nobility, landowners. You know the type. If one of the three says you're not a mage, they cut you loose."

"I imagine that does not happen for those who are not already in favor," Apak said.

"Just so. Drag one of us up there, and it's all over before it starts." She scratched at the side of her face. "Once they've got you and put you through all that mess, then they cut open your head and stir up your brains." She rotated on the stool and turned her head enough for Apak to see the horseshoe-shaped scar ringing the back of her skull. The incision had healed as a wavering pink line, the skin puckered at the seam. Magra's black hair should have grown back there to cover it, but she had kept it shaved to the bare skin so the scar was a visible and obvious remnant of what the Empire had done to her.

When Magra turned back around, Apak said, "I always have been curious. How does this surgery remove your abilities? Has the Empire found a physiological component to magic?"

She shrugged again. "They didn't remove it. They just changed it, or that's how I hear it told. I don't know what I could do before they scrambled me up, but afterwards I can hear thoughts. That's the limit of it. After the surgery is when they clear your head. It's some kind of magic that does that, not cutting."

Apak leaned forward, intrigued. "The amnesia they inflicted upon you was not an effect of the surgery?"

She shook her head. "Separate thing. They cut you up and tame you, and then they use magic to make you forget about it. One or the other is what makes most halflocks go crazy. I was one of the lucky ones." Her tone was sarcastic, but there was no doubt she was sincere. When Samira found Magra, she had been pretending to have lost her sanity. It must have been easier for her to survive in captivity if her captors thought she had lost her footing in reality.

LIZANDRA'S DEEPEST FEAR

"How do you know all this?" Apak asked. "I gather you cannot remember the process as it was done to you?"

"I can't," she said. "But I've seen enough mages taken in that I know what happens to them. To us. Trust me," she said, and her eyes drifted again, now filled with something Apak did not recognize. It could have been fear or despair or even guilt, but it was a foreign thing for him to diagnose.

Apak let his shoulders fall. "What was done to you was inhumane. Intolerable."

She inclined her head and nodded. "It was, but I learned to tolerate it. You have to, or you really will go mad after a while." She glanced at him. "You'll learn that, too. Things get better. You don't always have to be that angry."

When Apak gave no response, she said, "It's better here, anyway. It's cold as a garfak's udder up here, but it's been better here than it was there." She sniffed. "Except Lizzie. She hates me."

Apak raised his eyebrows and pursed his lips. "I understand she has reason for that." Lizandra had told them all about Magra and how she had helped the Kites trap her in the bank in Klubridge. To Apak's knowledge, no one had discussed that situation with Magra herself.

"I had to do things for the Kites," she said. "If I didn't show results, it would've been worse for me."

"You informed on Lizandra," Apak said.

"I did, but I kept her biggest secrets."

"You knew she was a mage," Apak said. "From the very beginning, you knew she had power, and you did not reveal it to the Kites."

She waggled her hand back and forth and said, "I thought she might be, but I wasn't sure. I wasn't about to tell them. They'd have hauled her away to turn her into another one of me. But I did inform on her. I know she's sore about that, and I don't expect she'll get over it soon. Even with everything else," she said, almost as an afterthought.

Apak found himself trusting this woman more than he had expected. He surprised himself when he said, "I have trouble with Oreth. He blames me for his injury."

"Are you to blame for it?"

"Partly," Apak said. He rested his hands on the table and studied the smudges of grease that had worked their way into the creases around his fingernails. "I did not properly protect him, at the very least."

Magra tilted her head again, and her impossibly big eyes held something else now. Was it pity? No, it looked like compassion. She placed one of her small, pale hands atop one of Apak's thick, dark ones and said, "That's another thing that'll be okay. Give him time, and he'll come around. He'll get better toward you while you get less angry." She patted his hand once before withdrawing hers and standing from the stool. "That's what you need to work on. Get yourself busy so you won't have time to be mad. In either sense of the word."

Apak's nature was to scoff at such platitudes, but something held his reflex in check. The truth was that talking with Magra had helped. He felt slightly less angry, but it was not gone. The anger no longer roared, but it simmered, and he knew she was right. He would find a way to occupy himself. He would be of service to the rebels.

The door to Naecara's office stood partway open, and Apak nearly rapped his knuckles against it but hesitated when he heard the voices inside. One of them was Naecara, but the other was unfamiliar. Apak stepped to the side, just far enough to look through the narrow crack in the door, and he saw Naecara Klavan standing with her back to him, her arms crossed and her feet standing as wide as her shoulders. Past her, facing the door, was Micah Vaino, his face contorted into a mixture of frustration and disbelief.

Apak stepped back before either could see him, and he waited to the right of the door. He had no desire to intrude on whatever argument they were having, and he was content to wait patiently until it had played itself out.

"Apak." The voice was soft and tentative, and it took half a second before Apak was certain he had not imagined it. But it came again, and that was when he saw Lizandra lurking in a dark alcove, diagonally across the walkway from where he stood.

"Lizandra," he said, careful to keep his voice low enough that it would not carry through the open door to his right. "Hello."

She moved out of the shadows, and the light of the courtyard illuminated her face, revealing the red in her eyes and the dark skin ringing them. Her hair hung in straight and unwashed strands, and flakes of dried skin marked her lips. It had been only a few days since he had seen her in the keep, but somehow her face looked unnaturally gaunt, lending to her fractured appearance. She shuffled a step closer and asked, "Have you seen Samira?"

Apak shook his head and studied Lizandra's face. Should he comment on her state? Would that be appreciated? Would it seem rude? Instead, he said, "I have not. Perhaps she is with Caius."

"Where is he?" Lizandra asked. Her voice was as ragged as her appearance.

"I do not know that, either," Apak said. He wanted to ask about her wellbeing, but he was unsure where he stood regarding his friends. What would be an agreeable response? He ventured a question of his own. "How is Reykas?"

Lizandra blinked at him, and it seemed to take her eyes longer than it should have to reopen. When they did, they still were red but now were wet as well. "Not good," she said, and a tear escaped down her cheek. She did not provide elaboration, and Apak felt he should not ask for more. Perhaps inquiring at all had been a mistake. He closed his mouth and looked to the right, willing the voices to conclude their conversation.

"What are you doing out here?" Lizandra asked and stepped closer. Her shoulders sagged, and her feet slid along the floor, as if she lacked the energy to lift them.

"I am waiting to speak with Naecara Klavan," he said. He watched her face and tried to read her reaction, but there was no change. Her eyes remained expressionless, and she looked as if she had nothing but exhaustion filling her.

"Can I sit with you?" she asked. Without waiting for a

response, she stepped into place beside Apak, to his left, and she slid down the wall until she was on the floor, her knees bent in front of her face and her forearms resting across them. She looked up at him. "What do you want with her?"

Apak took two steady breaths before answering her. Unsure as he was about his standing with the rest of them, Lizandra seemed unconcerned by what she had seen him do in Klubridge. She had been injured in the fighting, so she had missed things Reykas and Samira were likely to have seen, but she still had been there and had been a part of the chaos. And she did not flinch away from him. She trusted him enough to sit with him when she seemed at her most vulnerable.

"I wish to join her," Apak said at last.

"Join her how? As a rebel?"

Before Apak could respond, the volume from the office raised again, and he glanced toward the door once more. Vaino's voice carried through the opening. "We're going after the scion, Naecara. There's no argument to be had."

Apak had tried not to eavesdrop, but it was impossible to avoid hearing every word being argued at that point. Naecara responded, "The Empire has the ability to destroy an entire city, Micah. They have a weapon that took down Klubridge. Klubridge! They could use it anywhere next. Even here at Stormbreak."

"They don't know where Stormbreak is."

"And if they do find out?"

"We have protections here," he said, but he sounded unsure.

"Your mages can't hold those shields forever. The Empire has a bounty on Akithar now, and how long will it be before they track him here? If they come with that weapon, we're finished."

"I won't abandon the scion," Vaino said. "And I can't go after him and after this weapon at the same time."

"Then go after the weapon," Naecara said. Her tone was urgent, insistent, almost pleading with the man to see reason. "Finding that one man will do nothing. But if we can find out how they destroyed Klubridge, we can prevent them from doing that anywhere else."

There was a pause in the argument, and Apak looked down

and to his left. Lizandra's head was cocked toward the door, and he knew she was listening to every word, just as he was. He looked back toward the doorway as the conversation resumed. It was Vaino now: "You would sacrifice an innocent man? Just let him die?"

"If it means saving countless other lives, you know I would. And you know it's the right thing to do, Micah. It's what Yannis would do."

When Vaino replied, it was louder than before. "Don't presume what Yannis would have done. You didn't know him like—"

"Like you did? No, but I knew him better and for longer, and he wouldn't stand for this war you're building."

"War is the only way to end this."

"You put too much faith in the Aescalan," Naecara said. Her voice was softer now, and Apak leaned toward the door to hear it. He had avoided listening at the start, but he now was resolved to hear how this would end.

"And you don't put enough. They'll follow us anywhere, as long as we have this one man. They've practically built a religion around him."

"This weapon—"

"There's no time for that!" Vaino snapped. "Maybe after we've found Gressam, but he has to be the priority. Even Nahk agrees on this. The Nightingales have his name now. They'll be ahead of us if we don't start now."

"I spoke with Nahk, and she understands the significance of finding this weapon," Naecara said. "We can get the scion after we've ensured the Imperials won't be razing any more cities."

Another moment of silence, and then Vaino said, "You still don't believe we can defeat them at all, do you?"

"Not in open warfare. If we even try to face them on the battlefield, Peregrine will—"

"Peregrine does not exist," Vaino said, exasperation at the edges of his voice. "There is no High Lord. There is no almighty mage to arrive at the final hour and lay waste to our armies. Aligning with the Aescalan and bringing their force to bear against the Empire is our best plan. It's the only plan. What would you have us do?"

"You know what I'd do. Strategic strikes against targets of opportunity," Naecara said. "Making small and precise attacks will destabilize their infrastructure. We sow uncertainty among their ranks. That's how we break them, Micah. Not on a battlefield where they'll always have superiority, no matter how many Aescalan we bring across the sea."

"You're condoning terrorism," Vaino said. "Your way would have us being the ones attacking urban centers. How many innocent people are you willing to kill? Gressam and how many others?"

"There will be collateral damage either way. Innocents will die in your war, just as surely as they might die in targeted strikes. You have to accept that truth, and we both have to accept the consequences of our actions. We have to do whatever it takes to see this through. If we're not prepared to do that, what are we even doing up here on this frozen damned mountain?"

There was no response, and Apak expected Vaino to return with another cutting reply, but nothing came. An instant later, the door to the office swung open, and Vaino stalked out, passing both Apak and Lizandra without seeing them. He was halfway across the courtyard, headed toward his own office, by the time Apak realized Naecara stood in the doorway beside him. She watched the other man's retreat and shook her head. "I imagine you got an earful of that," she said.

Apak shifted his feet and said, "I attempted not to listen, but it was rather loud."

Naecara allowed herself a low chuckle before favoring Apak with a tight gaze. "I'm sorry you had to hear it. You were waiting here to see me?"

"I was," Apak said. "I would like to help you. To help the rebellion."

"You mean you agree with my way of thinking," she said.

"More than I agree with Vaino's."

Naecara watched him for a moment, and Apak felt her eyes weighing and evaluating him. Apparently satisfied, she nodded. "Come in. We can talk."

He looked back to see whether Lizandra intended to accompany him all the way into the office, but she was gone. He looked down the corridor and saw no sign of her presence or her departure. With a heavy breath, he followed Naecara into her office and pushed the door shut behind himself.

CHAPTER 15

The ride northwest from Klubridge had been long, and Bekam had allowed the carriage to stop in Deakem for rest and supplies, but he had pressed the driver hard after that. The roads were rough and uneven, and Bekam's back ached by the time they reached the outskirts of Ornamen. Cillan sat beside him on the padded seat inside the carriage, both of them facing ahead.

The narrower man took less space on the bench but still bumped shoulders with Bekam every time the carriage rocked to and fro. And, every time they collided, Cillan delivered a furtive apology, his eyes downcast. Cillan had his arms wrapped around his leather pack, clutching it as though his life depended on it. And it very well might, as Bekam had no idea what the little man carried around in it with him.

Bekam watched Cillan from the corner of his eye and adjusted himself on the seat once more before asking, "You've heard nothing else of Qae'lon's recent business?"

Cillan had been staring at the floor but jerked as though he'd been napping and suddenly found himself awake. He looked at Bekam, his eyes small above the rim of his spectacles, and he shook his head. "I know nothing of him more than his reputation, sir. I'd never seen him in the flesh before today."

"You've been to Heron assemblages."

Cillan bobbed his head. "That's just been mages and bureaucrats. Qae'lon leads the Herons, but he never comes to those meetings."

"And he is a mage himself," Bekam said, more to himself than to Cillan, but the secretary bobbed another nod.

"A powerful one, if the demonstration at Klubridge was any indication, sir."

Bekam drummed his fingers on the windowsill beside his seat. "How will the Council react to what he's done to the city? Surely they won't overlook this slaughter."

Cillan closed his mouth and pushed his glasses up his nose with the middle finger of his right hand. His eyes narrowed, and Bekam could imagine the thoughts churning in his head as he considered the possibilities. At last, Cillan shook his head again and said, "I can't be certain. The Council issued its challenge but did not specify a means for accomplishing it. It's impossible to know whether they will consider this a job done. Or perhaps they'll punish him for ruining any chance of recovering the city intact." He shook his head. "Hard to say, sir."

The situation remained as unsure as Bekam had expected. Qae'lon was a problem but was just as likely to bear the wrath of the Council as Bekam was. That made things simpler, at least. Bekam could blame everything that happened in Klubridge on Qae'lon and his Herons, from the botched silencing to Akithar's escape to the very destruction of the entire city. There had to be more, though. Oddities like Qae'lon always had something else to hide. Bekam had seen the pompous sorcerer in meetings on many occasions, but their meeting outside Klubridge was the longest direct exchange the two had ever shared. Despite their mutually long tenures in service to the Empire, Bekam knew next to nothing about the other man. It was time for that to change, and that's what had them arriving in Ornamen less than an hour later.

Bekam descended from the carriage and considered telling Cillan to wait there for him, but the smaller man needed a break from the road as badly as Bekam did. He didn't need to witness Bekam's business in the city, though.

"Where are we going, General?" Cillan asked as he slid down

from the carriage and planted his feet in the thin layer of mud that covered the roadway. He still held his satchel against his chest and looked like nothing more than a terrified schoolboy.

Bekam glanced from him to the driver, standing next to the carriage's open door. "Driver, this is my man. Take him to an inn, and see that he's fed."

"But sir—" Cillan began, but he stopped when Bekam cut his eyes toward him.

"I will find you when my business is finished."

"Yes, sir," Cillan said and ducked his head. Bekam left him standing in the roadway and didn't wait for the driver to collect the little man back into the carriage.

Ornamen was a larger city than Deakem, but certainly smaller than Aramore and Klubridge. Local nobility had held these lands for centuries, and Ornamen had grown from a collection of farms and mills into a thriving agricultural center at the heart of the Empire. It sat southeast from Aramore and due east from Salkire, perfectly positioned to provide supplies to the key governmental complexes, and that arrangement had kept it in favor for as long as anyone could remember.

The last noble who had held the city was a duke, descended from the original landowners who had developed the properties. Bekam had never heard the full story, but this duke supposedly liked his drink and enjoyed his gambling, and both somehow drove him into disfavor. Representatives from Salkire had come and taken him away a few years ago, and Ornamen had been under the direct control of the Empire since then. To Bekam's mind, it was more likely the Empire had tired of sharing the collected taxes with a self-important noble, and it finally found an excuse to oust him. Whatever the reason, Ornamen now sat securely within the grasp of Teshovar, and its population had become more martial and less agrarian in the years since the change.

With the influx of Imperials came all manner of resources, and Bekam knew where to find the one he was seeking. A turn to the right, past a storehouse, and then a turn back to the left between two taverns, and he was in an alleyway lined with empty bottles, broken glass, and other refuse that had spilled from the drinking houses into the streets. He stepped over a particularly wicked shard that had broken off the top of a jug, avoided a suspicious patch of something dark and wet-looking, and found himself before a plain gray door at the end of the passage. The door had no markings and nothing to identify it as anything other than the back entrance into whatever business faced the opposite street. Bekam knew he had the right place, though, and he rapped three times on the door. His knuckles rang against the metal, unusual material for such an unusual door in an otherwise nondescript alley.

It took half a minute for the door to open, and when it did, a large man with close-cropped hair stared out at Bekam. His tired eyes didn't blink beneath the bushy dark brows, and he waited for Bekam to speak.

"The third flower reminded me of Mother," Bekam said.

The man shifted out of the doorway and pulled it inward. He beckoned to Bekam by twitching his fingers toward his palm but said nothing. Now that the door stood fully open, Bekam could see that the doorman was huge. His shoulders spanned nearly the entire width of the passage, and his hands looked bigger than Bekam's face. Spies needed their protection, and it was hard to imagine doing better than this behemoth.

Bekam squeezed past and followed a dark hallway to its end, where light flickered from an open door on the right. He stopped at the entrance to the room and willed his eyes to adjust to the gloom, but the most he could make out was a table at the center of the floor and a woman sitting behind it. The nearby candle threw shadows across her features and turned her face into an ever-shifting landscape that Bekam knew he'd be unlikely to recognize if he saw her again outside this building.

She wore a brown tunic with a dark, hooded cloak thrown across her shoulders, but those were all the details Bekam could make out. Her skin could be anywhere from pale white to dark tan, or perhaps even darker than that, and there was no hint of her hair or its color beneath that hood. Even her age was a mystery, as the candlelight smoothed a face that might just as easily have been lined.

"Sorrel?" Bekam asked, still lingering in the door.

"Come in," she said, and her voice was even and unremarkable, just as unlikely to betray any details as the rest of her had been. She gestured to a chair across the table. "Have a seat, General."

"You know me," he said as he rounded the chair. He squinted into the dark, but the shadow of the hood hid her eyes.

"By reputation. I assume that's how you know of me as well."

"You're a well-kept secret," he said, and then he added, "I've known where to find you for a long time."

"And here I am," she said, her gloved palms turned upward on the table before her. "What brings you to me?"

His lip twitched, and he debated taking the long way around. But this was an Imperial spymaster. Behind all her drama and spectacle, she was an agent of the Empire and beholden to the same goals as he was. She would do what he wanted. "I need information about Qae'lon."

The name hung in the air between them, and after a long moment of silence, Bekam nearly felt it as a tangible artifact, dangling there and waiting for a response. At last, Sorrel leaned back in her chair and shook her head. "I can't help you."

"Can't or won't?" Bekam asked.

"Won't," she said. "Qae'lon has ways of knowing things."

"You're afraid of him."

"You would be, too, if you knew what he was capable of doing."

"And what is he capable of doing?" he asked.

She clasped her hands and shook her head again. "I don't know. I know everything, but I don't know what he can do. Of course that frightens me."

"He destroyed Klubridge."

"I do know that," she said, and Bekam heard the truth in her words.

"All I need is a weakness. Something that can be exploited."

"And that's supposed to be an easy ask? Something I would feel comfortable getting for you, after what I just said?"

Bekam huffed a laugh and asked, "Do you think he's here in this room? Do you think he's listening in on us this very moment?"

LIZANDRA'S DEEPEST FEAR

"I don't know what he can do," Sorrel said again. "I wouldn't have held this position for as long as I have if I were not a smart person, and smart people practice self preservation. I have no desire to have him show up in Ornamen with a grudge to settle."

Bekam had expected resistance and had come prepared. Given the apparent extent of Sorrel's fear, though, he was no longer certain this would be enough. Still, he had to try. He slipped a hand into the pocket inside his jacket and withdrew it with his fist clasped around the trinket he'd brought. He placed his hand on the table and opened his fingers, and the metal disc dropped onto the wood with more of a thud than a clink. Sorrel didn't move, but Bekam knew her eyes were on the disc, and he knew she recognized it and its meaning.

"Take this," he said and pushed the coin toward her with the tips of his middle and index fingers. "Get me information on Qae'lon, and I will owe you."

"What will you owe me?" she asked. She still had not moved, but her tone was flat now. Some of the resistance had left it, and Bekam knew he had her.

"A favor," he said. He gave the coin a shove, and it slid across the smooth tabletop, stopping at the edge in front of Sorrel.

She sat motionless for another long moment, and Bekam could smell the trail of her reasoning. She didn't want to risk being on the bad side of a homicidal wizard, but how likely was it that Qae'lon really would learn she was looking into him? That was a remote possibility, assuming she did her job properly. And she always did her job properly. On the other hand, she could be owed a favor by Tenez Bekam, one of the highest-ranking officers in the Imperial military. That was no small prize, especially for one with her fingers tied to strings in every corner of Teshovar. The decision would ultimately be a simple one based on probability. It was far more likely that she'd benefit from having Bekam in her debt than that Qae'lon would find out about her.

Her hand passed across the table, and the coin was gone. "I'll see what I can do," she said.

Bekam nodded. "How will you contact me?"

"You'll know." And that was the end of the negotiation.

By the time they headed back to Aramore, there was more snow on the ground than when they had departed. The fallen leaves had left the roadside trees bare, standing as stark guideposts for the journey. Nevertheless, it felt good to be going home, especially amid such turmoil. There was a vulnerability to being away, and, while Bekam didn't truly fear being waylaid by bandits or assassins on his travels, being away from his estate and office for so long did leave him uneasy.

He had collected Cillan from the tavern only a couple of brief hours after sending him there. Despite Cillan's clear exhaustion and his own heavy eyes, Bekam put them back on the road again instead of staying the night in Ornamen. The business with Sorrel was done, and Bekam felt no urge to linger as she began her inquiries into Qae'lon. The threat of Qae'lon himself arriving in Ornamen held no weight for Bekam, but Sorrel's nervousness had infected him. The sooner they were away and headed for home, the better. She could fret on her own, as long as she got the job done.

Bekam knew she'd find anything there was to find about the strange mage, and she'd deliver it as soon as she had it on hand. Sorrel knew the significance of holding a marker from someone in Bekam's position, and she wouldn't tarry in making good on her end of the deal. But would she rush to trade the coin back to him for a favor? Custom and honor dictated that he'd drop whatever he was doing to see to her request, and he was duty bound to follow through on his promise, if he wanted his word to continue carrying weight in the darker sectors of the Empire. But he hoped she'd be slower to bring the coin back. If the information she found proved useful, he'd have busy weeks ahead as he built his case against Qae'lon and prepared to present it to the Council. He hoped it would be months or years before he laid eyes on that coin again.

Although the temperature had fallen and sections of the road had begun to ice, the weather didn't impede the carriage's progress northward. They made stops at inns along the way for food and sleep and to change the horses, and worry was a constant companion until Bekam recognized the southern edges of his city passing outside the carriage windows. Aramore welcomed him through the city gates, and he allowed himself to relax into the seat for the first time since he'd headed south through that same gate.

"Home now, sir," Cillan said.

Bekam nodded. "So we are." He had instructed the driver to take him home first and then to deposit Cillan wherever he lived, and they were headed up the main thoroughfare toward the estate even then. They had both traveled light and bought what they needed along the road, paying on the Imperial coin, so there was only one bag for the driver to unload outside the gates of the estate. Cillan was in the process of bidding Bekam farewell when the driver shut the door. The secretary's voice disappeared mid-sentence.

"I'll get him back where he belongs," the driver said to Bekam with a quick bow before climbing back into his seat and urging the horses forward once more.

Bekam watched the carriage disappear at the end of the lane before he made the walk up the path to his house. No guards stood at the gate, and Bekam frowned, puzzled, until he saw the truth. He'd ordered both of the gate guards to seek reassignment from Otero. It had been dark, and he hadn't even known their names, so he'd had no reason to believe they would actually follow that order. How would Bekam have even known if they were still there, given how rarely he was at the house? And yet, the gate was unguarded. They had left, as he had ordered, and Marjiel had deigned not to replace them. In the end, she had turned his jab at her back on him, as it so often went. With a heavy sigh, he searched his pockets for the gate key. Finding it and pushing against the cold iron, he grunted as he picked up his own bag and toted it the full length of the path. No one had tended to the walkway as they had done to the streets, so he had to watch for icy patches as he went. Despite the cold, he'd broken a sweat by the time he reached the steps leading up to the front of the house.

As he ascended, the front door opened, and the ancient butler peered out at him. It was nighttime, and Bekam certainly wasn't expected, but the man seemed wholly unsurprised by his arrival. The old man had probably been watching his strained progress up the path and had not even offered to help with the bag. Bekam snarled, an insult ready on his tongue, but the butler spoke first. "Good evening, sir. Your wife and daughter are in the dining room."

"Dining room?" Bekam asked and looked up to the dark sky, where hazy snow clouds obscured the moon and blotted away all signs of the stars. "It's the middle of the night."

"Shall I take your luggage, sir?"

Now that he'd lugged the thing all the way into the house, the butler offered to take it the final few feet to his bedroom. Typical. But Bekam dropped the bag in the foyer and glanced back at the butler. "The dining room?"

But the butler didn't answer. He had picked up the valise and was headed up the stairs with it, his attention deliberately not on his master. Such impertinence would be addressed, but the weight of weeks away from home pressed down on Bekam's shoulders just then. He had no desire to deal with the old man that night and instead would find out why his family was eating this late at night before he collapsed into the upstairs bed he so infrequently used.

Bekam wiped a hand down his face and stifled a yawn as he came through the door to the dining room. "Why in blazes are —" The words died on his lips, and his hand lingered in the air, just below his face. He'd lost the presence of mind to lower it and instead stood just inside the door, his mouth agape.

The dining room was an elegant part of the first floor, the walls smooth and painted a light cream that reflected the light from the two chandeliers that hung along the center of the room. A single dining table ran the length of the room, its dark wood surface covered by a fine, blue cloth Marjiel had had imported from somewhere in the south. She'd said the blue would make the right impression for any guests expecting to see signs of the High Lord's Aerie on display. And there was room for plenty of guests. More than twenty high-backed chairs surrounded the table, though Bekam couldn't recall seeing more than half of them in use at any of the occasional dinner parties that had taken place in his house.

At present, Marjiel sat in one of the chairs at the far end of the room, on the left side of the table. Leonie sat across from her mother, uncharacteristically still and quiet. The plates were set before both of them but remained empty, as did their glasses. Their forks and knives and spoons all lay in their formal array around and between the plates, but none of the utensils had been moved. Marjiel and Leonie stared across the table at each other, and neither acknowledged Bekam's arrival. He would have wondered whether they even breathed if he hadn't seen the regular rise and fall of his wife's chest as she sat upright and unmoving at her place.

At the far end of the table sat Qae'lon. The mage wore the same white vestment he'd worn on the hill outside of Klubridge. He practically glowed beneath the light of the candles above him.

"General," he said, rising from his seat and extending a hand toward Bekam. "So good of you to join us. Please do have a seat."

An additional place had been set at the near end of the table, where Qae'lon gestured. Bekam closed his mouth and opened it again to protest, but no sound escaped. Compelled by a force that was not his own, he took one step forward into the room, and then he took another. He willed his legs to stop moving, but they continued, heedless of his desires. Soon, he had crossed the short space to the table and was lowering himself into the seat. And there he sat, staring ahead at Qae'lon, just as silent and motionless as his wife and daughter.

Trapped as he found himself, Bekam's mind remained free, and it spun with questions and groped for options. This was magic, something he understood all too little about. Being the man with the most singular responsibility in the realm for halting the use and spread of magic, Bekam considered these abilities and powers daily, but it was rare for him to encounter them in person, outside of the weakened fumbling of the halflocks who passed through his dealings. True magic at its full potential was alien to him, and he would have shuddered at its invasive touch if any physical movement remained under his control. As it was, he could move not a muscle, and he realized with mounting terror that he continued to breathe and his heart continued to beat only because Qae'lon willed it so.

"I heard a rumor," Qae'lon said. He was up and moving around the table now. He passed behind Marjiel and made a slow pace halfway down the room, toward Bekam. Bekam's eyes followed his progress, but not because Bekam wanted them to do it. He tried to look back at his wife, but his eyes remained locked and focused. Qae'lon wanted Bekam watching him, and there was nothing Bekam could do to resist the pull.

"I heard a rumor," Qae'lon said again, "that you've taken up a new hobby. A new interest, as it might be. I heard a rumor you're interested in learning about me, of all silly things." He smiled then, and his teeth were white and straight, unnaturally bright in his pale face when they should have seemed dim against his alabaster skin. His smile widened, and he said, "If you'd wanted to know more about me, all you had to do was ask."

He waited then and stared at Bekam. After a moment, he frowned. "Nothing to say, General? I was sure you would have questions for me, after all the trouble you went to, traveling to Klubridge and back. And, somewhere along the way, you made your inquiries, didn't you?" He waited again, and when no response came, he tapped his fingertips against his forehead, a mean glint in his eye. "How daft of me. You can't speak, can you? Allow me to help with that." He flicked his hand toward Bekam as if he were shooing away a fly, and the general's mouth fell open.

Sensation returned to Bekam's face, to his tongue and his throat. He gasped and groaned before he could speak. "Why are you here?" he managed after he remembered how to form words.

"To help you, of course," Qae'lon said. "You traveled so far and asked so many questions about me. I thought the least I could do was to come here and make it easy for you to get your answers."

"Let them go," Bekam said, surprising himself. If pressed, he would have expected his first request to be self-serving, but there he was, asking for his family to be released first.

"I think not," Qae'lon said. "Not just yet." And the mage's eyes left Bekam's face to look to his right. Bekam's own eyes could move then, and he could turn his head. The butler stood in the doorway, having deposited the traveling case upstairs and returned. His eyes stared forward, his expression as blank as Marjiel's.

"You have need of me, sir?" the butler asked, his voice strained, and Bekam knew he moved and spoke entirely at Qae'lon's will. Bekam's thoughts turned back to the front gate. Perhaps the guards had not left, after all. Perhaps Qae'lon had merely compelled them to wander away from the gate. Perhaps he had made them lie facedown in the snow and smother themselves.

How long had he been here? How had he arrived ahead of Bekam and Cillan? Their pace had been brisk all the way from Klubridge to Ornamen and then from Ornamen to Aramore. There was no reasonable way Qae'lon could have overtaken them by enough time to lay siege to Bekam's entire household. And yet, here he was, with at least four people under his complete control.

"I have no more need of you," Qae'lon told the butler. The old man's mouth fell open, and he stumbled one step forward. A low wheeze escaped his lips, his right hand clutched at his chest, and he curled forward to tumble onto the floor. Bekam knew he was dead before he even hit the carpet.

"You don't need to do this," Bekam said, even though he now had a better measure of the other man. He now knew it didn't matter whether Qae'lon needed to do this. He was a sadist, and he wanted to do this. He wanted to show Bekam how easily he could kill a man, and he didn't even need to use the weapon he'd brought to Klubridge.

Qae'lon studied Bekam's face, and Bekam knew he saw the understanding there. The mage nodded in satisfaction without answering the question that by then was entirely rhetorical. Instead, he said, "If you don't have any questions for me, allow me to ask one of you. I know you made inquiries, and I believe you have set someone on my trail. Sate my curiosity, General. Who is it?"

Of course the wizard wouldn't know the specifics about the stop in Ornamen. Even if he had heard that Bekam had someone making inquiries, he wouldn't know who directed the questioning. The Herons had no need for plumbing the Empire's intelligence networks, and Qae'lon was unlikely to have ever encountered one of the hidden spymasters. The Herons made a big show of getting by on the strength of their own magic, and they had no use for the more mundane intrigues that ran the rest of the Imperial apparatus. Bekam's eyes narrowed, and, still under Qae'lon's control as he was, he finally had a piece of leverage.

"I don't know what you're talking about," he said. "You have trespassed in my home, endangered my family, and killed one of my servants. I'll see you answer for this."

"Endangered your family?" Qae'lon asked with a mock gasp, his fingers splayed on his chest. "Not yet, I haven't." He angled his head a fraction to the left, and a silver fork rose into the air from the table before Leonie. It bumped against the rim of a plate as it rose, its soft tink the only sound in the room. The fork hovered, motionless, and then it began a slow approach toward Leonie, its tines angled toward her face. The fork made a smooth and direct journey over the rest of her place setting until it slowed less than an inch away from her, the metal points crawling closer to her left eye with every passing breath. The little girl stared ahead, still unmoving, waiting patiently for the sharp metal to graze her eyeball.

Bekam watched the motion of the fork with dread. This was a game for Qae'lon. He wanted the name of the person who had agreed to spy on him, and he was willing to maim Bekam's family to get it.

"What was the name of the person you consulted?" Qae'lon asked. He continued watching Bekam as the threat to Leonie played out behind him and down the table. It seemed of no consequence or interest to the mage. "Tell me, and I'll be on my way."

Bekam's eyes moved from Qae'lon back to his daughter. The mage watched him, expectant eagerness in his face. Would he even keep true to his word if Bekam did reveal his source? Were they already doomed, regardless of what he told this man? He had to at least try, didn't he? He couldn't allow this to happen to Leonie. Qae'lon would disassemble them piece by piece, just for his own amusement, for as long as Bekam refused him.

The fork was a hair's width away from piercing Leonie's eye when Bekam looked back at Qae'lon, ready to speak. But when he saw the smile playing at the corners of the mage's mouth, Bekam's resolve hardened. He would not bend to this creature's will. He would not humble himself for this man's mirth. Not for anything. Not even for his daughter. She was young enough to forget she ever had two working eyes, anyway.

Qae'lon's smile dropped, and Bekam knew he'd read the defiance in his face. He wouldn't be getting the name. Qae'lon grunted and said, "A pity."

Qae'lon tilted his head back to the right. In an instant, the fork spun away from Leonie. It made a quick turn in the air, and it flew down the length of the table, faster than Bekam could understand its flight. There was a flash of light gleaming on the metal, and then there was darkness. Before he felt anything, Bekam heard a soft and wet sound that went something like "pock." And then everything was pain, and he would have collapsed from the agony if the magic did not continue to hold him upright. Behind the pain, he became distantly aware of something wet pouring down his left cheek. His hands wanted to rise, to explore what had happened, to make repairs where they could, but they lay flat on the table, unmoving. When the initial wave of hurt had passed, Bekam realized the vision in his left eye was hazy, dimming, and that was when he realized what Qae'lon had done.

Bekam wheezed and gasped as searing heat flooded into his left eye again. The fork was still in it, and then it wasn't. It retracted, pulling away about a foot and hanging in front of Bekam's face. Qae'lon waited through all this, his face expressionless now as he watched Bekam's agony. Bekam sought his gaze with his good eye and found him past the hovering fork. "You... you..." he said, and it was all he could get out. His breathing was fast now, no longer under Qae'lon's control, and his heart beat hard in his chest. The mage wanted him to feel this. To experience it in every way he could. To remember it.

"The name," Qae'lon said. There was no malice in his voice. No hatred, and not even a threat. His was the voice of patience.

The fork twitched in the air, and it dragged Bekam's attention back to its wicked tines that now shone wet with something clear that even now dripped onto the blue tablecloth. There was no blood, only clear liquid. A cold comfort of sorts, but a comfort, nonetheless. "Please," Bekam whispered as the pain threatened to give way to panic.

"The name," Qae'lon said again, and the fork began to move. It drifted toward Bekam's face, angling toward his right eye now, the tines growing larger and larger until they were the only thing he could see. He tried to move away, to shut his eyelid, but the mage still had control of him. His eye remained open, and the fork drew nearer.

"Sorrel," Bekam said. His voice came clear and urgent now. "Sorrel. Her name is Sorrel. She's the spymaster in Ornamen. You can find her there. Please. Please."

Qae'lon made a sound in his throat that could have been satisfaction or disappointment. Either way, the fork arrested its movement and dropped with gravity, hitting the plate in front of Bekam with a clang and tumbling off the table to the floor. Bekam had control of his right eye again, and it darted around the room, seeking the next threat, but there was none. His wife and daughter sat unmoving, and Qae'lon remained to his left, his face now smoothed into a smirk. "You are a terrible father."

Qae'lon's hand dipped into a pocket in his robe, and he withdrew something small that he placed on the table. Bekam tried to track the item, but it was too close to him, and he couldn't move his neck to look down far enough. Qae'lon walked away, up the table, and passed behind Marjiel. He rounded the head of the table and stopped behind Leonie.

"What are you doing?" Bekam asked, and the strength had

left his voice again. It was a rough rasp now, the words barely more than gasping coughs.

Qae'lon glanced once at Bekam before turning his attention to the girl. He placed his right palm against the back of her head, and his fingers glowed with golden light for less than a second. Seeming satisfied, Qae'lon pulled his hand away and smoothed Leonie's hair, the gesture almost an affectionate one.

"What did you do to her?" Bekam wheezed and struggled to keep his focus as the pain in his left eye surged back, nearly replacing all reason.

Qae'lon favored him with a smile that could be mistaken for a friendly one as he came back down the table. He placed a hand, the same one he'd pressed against Leonie's head, on Bekam's shoulder, and he leaned close enough for his lips to brush Bekam's ear. "You need to understand your enemies before you choose them," Qae'lon whispered, and then he was gone, departed through the door behind Bekam.

There was no sound of the front door opening and closing, but Bekam knew the man was gone as soon as his own muscles spasmed. His arms and legs twitched, and only then was he able to bend at the waist and hold his face in his hands, his fingers covering but not daring to explore his ruined eye.

Bekam was aware of Marjiel and Leonie stirring at the far end of the dining room, both released from Qae'lon's control at the same time he had been freed. One of them was sobbing, possibly both of them, but Bekam couldn't sit upright enough to see them. He groaned and leaned his forearms against the edge of the table, his forehead pressed against them as fluid continued to leak from his wound. Still no blood, and that became the mantra that repeated in his brain and kept him from spiraling into madness over the next few moments. *Still no blood.*

When the pain had dulled again and his breathing had slowed, Bekam pushed himself back from the table. He still couldn't sit upright, but he was able to raise his head enough to see the rough shape of the object Qae'lon had left on the table. He groped for it and knew what he would find even before his fingers closed over it. Bekam dragged it in front of his face and squinted his right eye at it, trying to understand, to make sense of it in light of everything that had just happened.

Next to Bekam's plate lay his promise coin, its metal edges burned and melted smooth so that its features had muddied. The stamped details were still visible at the coin's center, though, and between the letters and the grooves was where Sorrel's blood had collected and dried.

CHAPTER 16

Lizandra made her way down the hallway to the room Pelo Foyen shared with Reykas, as she did every morning. She pushed through the door with her usual care, afraid that she might wake Foyen. She no longer worried about disturbing Reykas.

She'd made sure the doctor wouldn't administer any more of whatever that powder had been, but one dose had been enough. Reykas was unconscious, and no one acted as if they thought he would ever wake up again. They were wrong, and Lizandra knew she would see his eyes flutter open once more. That was why she spent every waking moment at his side and feared leaving for even an instant. The nights, when she was not allowed inside the infirmary, were torture, and she hurried back to his bedside every morning before the sun had even risen. And the sun was coming up slower now, as winter descended upon Stormbreak in earnest.

She had to be at his bedside at all times. She had to be there when he woke up. And she would be there if he... did not. But he would awaken.

As she came into the room now, her eyes adjusted quickly to the dark and sought Reykas' face. He still lay in the same position in which she'd left him, his head on the pillow and his closed eyes facing upward, looking for all the world like he was simply taking a nap. Like he was resting after one of their particularly arduous acrobatic routines. Like he would awaken at any moment. And he would! She would be there to see it happen.

Lizandra stepped to the foot of his bed, and she placed a hand on top of the sheet that covered his feet, which now splayed at odd and unmoving angles upon the mattress. One day he'd be back on those feet, standing again and running and jumping. They'd find another place to perform, with or without their friends. And, even if they didn't find a theater, just being together would be enough. It was time they struck out on their own and got out of this rebellion mess, anyway. It would all be for the best.

She smoothed her palm along the sheet and felt the warmth of Reykas' leg beneath it. The heat was reassuring. As long as it was there, he was there. A single tear had escaped her eye, and she swiped at her cheek with the quick practice she'd picked up over the last few weeks. Crying came easily to her, but she had no desire to be a spectacle to anyone else in the keep. Not when she needed their help in getting assistance for Reykas. Not when she needed their confidence and respect in order to solicit that help.

Lizandra made one final swipe at her cheek with the back of her hand and sniffed. If Foyen had been awake, he'd think her a fragile fool. She sniffed again and forced a smile onto her face before she turned to look at the other man.

Pelo Foyen was dead.

Lizandra knew it without even approaching his bed. He lay on his back, and his head rested on a pillow identical to Reykas', but Foyen's face was turned to the left, facing her. The flickering candlelight sparkled with a dull reflection in his half-closed eyes, and his mouth hung open, slack. The tip of his tongue protruded as if he'd died while licking his lips.

She backed away from Reykas' bed, her feet sliding across the smooth floor, and she tried to look away from Foyen's dead gaze, but she couldn't turn her head. Her heels banged against the door, and her hands scrabbled behind her back, attempting to gain purchase on the knob. It took several tries before she got the door open, and even then she banged it into her heels again as she pulled it. At last, she forced her eyes away and sidestepped so she could get the door the rest of the way open. She leaned into the hallway and called, "Help! Someone, help!"

The doctor who had been tending to Reykas wasn't there, but the nurses summoned another physician Lizandra didn't recognize. The woman was short and serious, her dark hair held back in a tight bun. She frowned over Foyen, poked at his neck, squeezed his wrist, and held a hand before his face. All the prodding and maneuvering turned Lizandra's stomach, and she looked away from the corpse for the second time since her arrival. She was sitting on the chair next to Reykas' bed by then, and she focused her eyes on the floor in front of her feet, even as her hand slid under the thin white blanket and sought his. She found his arm and followed it down, interlocking her fingers with his and pressing her cold palm into the warmth of his hand. He lay unresponsive, but the heat meant he was still there.

If Reykas didn't wake up and Lizandra wasn't there to see to him, this was the treatment he'd get. An anonymous doctor would poke and squeeze at him and make humming noises in the back of her throat as she examined him as if he were nothing more than a body. As if he were not Reykas. That was unacceptable. She wouldn't leave his side, and he would awaken.

Within just a few minutes, the infirmary staff had pulled the white sheet up and over Foyen's face, and they had transferred him over to a cart similar to the one they'd used to bring Reykas into that very room. But now they used it to wheel Foyen away, and Lizandra looked up and watched his departure. The man deserved the respect of being seen away, even if she had no idea where they might be taking him. What happened to people when they died at Stormbreak? Was there a graveyard somewhere? Were they burned? Those questions gnawed at the back of Lizandra's mind, but they were questions she didn't truly want answered. She could live with the ignorance of what Stormbreak did with its dead, and she hoped against hope that she'd never have a reason to dispel that ignorance.

She settled back into her chair and rubbed her thumb along the back of Reykas' hand, feeling the tendons that stood more prominently now. He'd lost weight since being there. She had, too, but it was more noticeable on him, particularly when she was so accustomed to the feel of his thick, strong hand in hers. He was disappearing by ounces, and she would put a stop to it.

The door swung inward once more, and Lizandra looked up from her thoughts. "Samira," she said, and her own voice startled her. It was hoarse now, both exhausted from her constant vigils and strained from her screams for help after finding Foyen.

Samira came into the room and closed the door. She wore a dark green woolen dress that reminded Lizandra of the nicer one Samira had had to leave behind when they'd fled Klubridge. That one had always been Samira's lucky dress, and now it was abandoned in the theater, or in whatever remained of the theater after the attack on the city. Samira was pale, her eyes wide, and she nearly stumbled as she came near Reykas' bed. She extended a hand and steadied herself on its wooden frame.

"I came after I got your message," she said. "But when I got here, I saw... They were taking..." Her voice trailed into silence, and Lizandra understood.

"You saw them taking the cart away, and you thought it was Reykas."

Samira hesitated but nodded. "I was so afraid, Lizzie. I thought I was too late."

"It was Pelo Foyen. He shared this room with Reykas. Did you meet him?"

Samira looked toward the empty bed, its sheets now wrinkled and pulled aside for a patient who would never return. "I spoke with him briefly a few times when I came to see Reykas, but nothing at length." She looked back to Lizandra. "Were you here when..."

Lizandra shook her head. "He was already gone when I got here. I found him," she said. She couldn't say more about it and didn't want to. The rest was obvious and didn't need to be stated.

"I'm so sorry, Lizzie."

"That isn't going to happen to us," she said. She looked at Reykas' face, more gaunt than it had been when he first came to that bed, and she turned back to Samira. "They won't be taking Reykas out of here like that."

Samira frowned, and a line appeared between her eyebrows. "What do you mean?"

"Foyen had the same illness as Reykas," Lizandra said. "He'd had it for a long time. Long enough to find out it wasn't natural. The Empire created the disease."

She'd expected Samira to protest or to look surprised by this revelation, but instead she looked from Lizandra down to Reykas. She approached the opposite side of the bed and traced her fingertips along his still forehead.

Lizandra continued, "They made it to kill mages, but for some reason, it only works on some of us. You and I haven't caught it. Apak and Oreth haven't. It was just Reykas. He was vulnerable to it for some reason. Just like Pelo Foyen was. But Foyen found a cure." She watched Samira's face again for a reaction, but there was nothing but sadness. Samira's eyes were on Reykas' resting face as Lizandra continued. "There's someone in Karsk who has the cure to the disease. He's just waiting there, and I'm going to get it. But I can't leave Reykas alone. I need your help, Samira."

At that, Samira looked up, and Lizandra saw the shimmer in her eyes, the brimming tears she'd been holding back. Samira took a deep breath and said, "Reykas told me about the disease, Lizzie. The cure, all of it."

Lizandra blinked at her and opened her mouth and closed it again twice before finally asking, "When?"

"A couple of weeks ago? It was after you'd spoken with him about it yourself. You know that isn't what he wants, Lizzie."

The revelation hit Lizandra in the chest like a fist. Reykas hadn't told her he'd spoken to Samira about this. He'd hidden it and even lied to her about not telling anyone.

Lizandra tried to force her voice to be even, but it came out angry. Angrier than she knew it should have been. "He can't tell us what he wants! He can't speak, Samira. Look at him!"

"I am looking, and he told me he didn't want to go to Karsk, and he didn't want you or anyone else going there on his behalf.

He said there might be a cure there, but he wasn't willing to pay the price for it, and he wouldn't have anyone else pay it for him."

In that moment, Lizandra hated Samira. She hated her and this keep, and a little part of her even hated Reykas just then. He had chosen a rare moment when she wasn't at his side, and he had confided all this information to Samira. Aside from Lizandra, Samira had been his closest friend, ever since he and Lizandra had arrived in Klubridge, but that hardly mattered. He'd gone behind her back and stolen the little hope he might have left her.

"I'm not letting him die, Samira. How can you even entertain this?"

"This isn't my choice. This is what Reykas wants. We have to respect that, Lizzie. Can't you see that?"

Lizandra's face burned, and she knew her cheeks must have been glowing pink, but she doubted Samira could see it in the dim light of the single candle. "What I see is that the man I love is dying, and I have a chance to save him. He's supposed to be your friend."

"He is my friend," Samira said, her voice now as sad as her face looked. Lizandra couldn't keep looking at her, or she'd find it harder to hate her. She looked back down at the floor in front of her feet as Samira continued talking. "This is the last thing we can do for him. He made his wish clear, and he asked me to make sure it was followed. He knew it would be too hard for you."

"You won't help me. You won't help him," Lizandra said. The hatred and anger had flared but now simmered, filtering down through her body and leaving even more exhaustion in their wake. She made her eyes meet Samira's, and she said, "If you won't help me, I'll go to Caius. I'll go to Apak. Micah bloody Vaino, if I have to. Someone will help me."

Samira shook her head. "They can't do anything to help, and they wouldn't if they knew that wasn't what Reykas wanted. His wish was to die—"

"He never wished to die," Lizandra snapped, the fury rising again.

"He wished to go in peace," Samira finished. "He didn't want anyone to risk their lives or the safety of the rebellion on his behalf."

"He's been sick! He didn't know—"

"He did know," Samira said. "He's known all along that this was coming. You've known it, too. I am so, so sorry this is happening, especially here, so far away from everything and everyone we know. But going to Karsk would be for you, Lizzie. It's what you want. That's not something you'd be doing to help Reykas."

Lizandra kept her mouth closed and glared at Samira for another moment before she turned her eyes down again. She wouldn't fight with Samira, not with Reykas lying right there between them. She squeezed her fingers again and felt the reassuring resistance of his hand beneath the sheet.

"Caius can't help you with this," Samira said. "Even if he wanted to, he's not well. I don't know what's happening with him, but he hasn't been sleeping properly since we left Klubridge, and he's been hallucinating."

Lizandra glanced up at that but said nothing. He'd seemed fine enough to her when she'd encountered him around the keep.

"There's trouble brewing in the rebellion," Samira continued.

"I heard Micah Vaino and Naecara Klavan arguing," Lizandra said.

Samira nodded. "They're pulling the rebellion in opposite directions, and I don't know what the outcome will be. Apak is sympathetic to the woman, Klavan. And Vaino wants to send Caius on some sort of insane quest. I'm doing everything I can to keep him safe."

"What about Aquin?" Lizandra asked.

Samira winced and recovered quickly, but it was enough for Lizandra to notice. Samira gave a weak smile and said, "We'll see."

"So that's it, then," Lizandra said. "All of you are too wrapped up with these new people we don't even know, and you won't help me save Reykas."

"Lizzie," Samira said and took a step to the side, as if she were about to come around the bed. The very last thing

Lizandra could tolerate at that moment was having Samira placate and patronize her. Petting at her and hugging her, poking and squeezing like the doctor over Pelo Foyen's corpse.

It was too much, and it was not enough, and Lizandra had to be up and away from Samira before she began screaming or crying again or both. She pulled her hand away from Reykas and was on her feet and out the door before Samira could say another selfish word.

∽

The wind hit Lizandra as soon as she emerged from the infirmary, and she wrapped her arms around herself and squinted up toward the sun. It hid behind a layer of hazy clouds, but the day was still bright, and the sky was a pale blue that held more promise than Lizandra felt. Stormbreak's protective shield was down, and snow drifted out of the sky in fat and lazy flakes that stuck to her hair and shoulders and tickled her nose. She wiped at her face and roamed away from the hospital, moving as quickly as she dared on the icy ground, hoping to put as much space between herself and Samira as possible.

In truth, she knew Samira was her friend and cared about her. Samira thought she was giving the right advice, but she was wrong. It must have been easy to see things in such simple terms when she wasn't inside the situation herself. Reykas was her friend, yes, and Lizandra knew Samira cared about him, but she didn't love him. Not like Lizandra did.

No one else cared for him the way she did, and no one else felt the emptiness as keenly as she did. He still lived, but it felt as if he were already no longer there, the space he'd occupied now a gradually hollowing hole in her chest. It hurt like a physical ailment, and she pressed her fist against her sternum to try and quell the ache.

Lizandra had lived with her parents when she'd first met Reykas. Her family traveled, part of a circus that moved from town to town and didn't linger in one place for long. It felt like it had all been so long ago, and the girl she was then seemed so young now. Of course, she had been young when she met

Reykas, only fourteen. That was younger than Fairy was now. That was five years ago, nearly six, but it felt like a lifetime. And it had been, hadn't it? What had her life been before Reykas came into it? And what could it be if he left it?

She clutched her hands into fists again, the front of her coat balled into her fingers. She wouldn't cry again, not out here where anyone could see her. But then she realized she couldn't cry, even if she wanted to. She felt dry from the inside to the outside, the grief having already pushed out all her tears. All she had left was that growing emptiness and the awareness that she had no one who cared about the loss she was experiencing. The avoidable loss.

A cure waited in Karsk, and, according to Foyen, he'd seen it heal someone already. It seemed impossible, but she believed him. Even though he had shunned the cure himself and died alone up in this cold wilderness, she believed him. She didn't understand him, but she trusted his word that someone south of here could heal Reykas.

The price hardly mattered. Foyen had said it would be more than they'd be willing to pay, and Reykas had agreed, but that was the one part Lizandra didn't believe and couldn't believe. What price could be too great for a life? What price would be too great for Reykas' survival? She couldn't imagine such a thing. She would give her own life if it would keep Reykas alive, but that wasn't the offer and wasn't the question. Reykas hadn't wanted the cure. He'd said he was not willing to put others in danger for his health, and he'd even told Samira to make sure his wishes were followed.

But surely he'd have changed his mind by now. If the doctor had not given him that powder and put him to sleep, Reykas might even now be agreeing to let Lizandra take him south. It would be a hard journey, but he'd have decided it was worth it, wouldn't he? He wouldn't simply leave her alone like this, not if there was a chance to save himself. He'd said he wanted to help the rebellion and to help their friends. Reykas wouldn't leave so much undone, just to protect his own sense of pride and honor.

Or would he? Lizandra kicked through a gathering pile of snow, and it wet the toe of her boot but didn't soak through.

Was Samira right? Was Lizandra pushing for this cure more for herself than for Reykas? Of course it was for her, but it was for him, too. He had so much more to do. So much more he could give and experience and learn. He couldn't be finished now. This couldn't be the end for him.

But what would he actually want? To fight for a chance to live or to die a pointless death, sequestered away from everything he knew while the rebellion fell to pieces around them? His way had always been to sacrifice for others, to give of himself so that the ones he cared about would be taken care of. But what good would this sacrifice do anyone now? Reykas wasn't charging into battle to rescue a friend, like they'd done together in Klubridge. He wasn't pursuing some noble cause that would benefit everyone else. He was lying unconscious in a bed where he would stay until he simply expired.

And that's what he'd told her he wanted and what he'd told Samira he'd wanted.

Lizandra bit her lip and turned her head up to the sky again. Should she let him go? Was that the right thing to do? Even considering that path sent a fresh thread of agony through her core, but she was getting used to that pain. She was finding she could endure nearly anything after being subjected to it for long enough. But not losing Reykas. Surely that was a pain that would never subside. But perhaps that was what she had to endure. Perhaps he wouldn't have changed his mind, and the right thing was to let go. To let him have his peace and then to try and survive whatever her life would be in the aftermath.

A noise ahead pulled Lizandra out of her thoughts, and she watched two men in brown jackets with fur at their collars as they dragged open the huge double doors to a building that looked more like a warehouse than anything else. It sat just outside the keep's eastern wall, and she found her feet had carried her all the way outside the castle itself. As she watched, they pushed something ahead of them on a cart. Pelo Foyen. This was where they'd taken his remains.

"What is that place?" she asked a woman sitting on a bench near her.

The woman was looking toward the workers as well and

said, "Ice house. The ground's too hard for burial, so they'll keep him there until the spring." She turned her head to fasten her wide eyes on Lizandra's.

Of course it would be Magra. Every time Lizandra wandered through Stormbreak and let her feelings swallow her, it was always Magra who appeared in her path. Lizandra broke the eye contact and looked back toward the ice house. They'd pushed the cart all the way through and were closing the doors behind him now. That's where Pelo Foyen would wait out the winter, likely stored on a cold slab somewhere inside like he was a piece of beef. And then, what? They would pull him back out in the spring and try to put him in the ground fast enough that his frozen body wouldn't decay too much. And then that's where he'd be forever, covered in unfamiliar dirt on a mountain no one cared about.

"You're worried that's what will happen to Reykas," Magra said. She'd read Lizandra's thoughts again.

Lizandra's eyes snapped wide, and the empty space in her chest flooded with rage. She spun on the other woman and screamed into her face, "Stop it! I told you to stop!" Before she even knew she was doing it, Lizandra had Magra's shoulders in her hands, and she was shoving her hard, pushing her off the bench. The halflock's eyes opened even wider, either in shock or fear, and she tumbled backwards into the snowy bushes that lined the pathway.

Lizandra recoiled, pulling her hands back as if she'd burned them, and she spun away from Magra without seeing how the woman had landed. Her feet pounded the pathway, and she crunched through the newly fallen snow, heedless of any patches of ice that might have formed. All she cared about was putting the ice house behind her, just as she'd put Samira behind her on the way there.

She couldn't rely on her friends, and she couldn't rely on the rebellion. Reykas truly would die if she didn't intervene, and she would not let that happen now. Not here, not this way. If he wanted to choose some other noble way to go out later, that would be his choice. This would not be the end.

Half mad from her dizzying run back to the keep, Lizandra

stopped just inside the courtyard and propped her forearm against the cold stone wall as she caught her breath. Across the quad and past the solitary tree at its center, Naecara Klavan spoke with another rebel. She was showing him a bow and pointing to where the string attached, telling him something about its construction. Lizandra had heard the argument she'd had with Micah Vaino while she'd waited outside the office with Apak.

We have to do whatever it takes to see this through. If we're not prepared to do that, what are we even doing up here on this frozen damned mountain? That's what Naecara had said, and it had pierced Lizandra straight through. She hadn't even been able to wait with Apak any longer and had rushed away in shame. Keeping Reykas alive was worth any price. It was worth betraying any wish and even worth betraying herself and ruining her own honor. Saving him was all that mattered, and she was prepared to do whatever it took.

She would take Reykas to Karsk herself, and she needed no one else's permission to do it.

CHAPTER 17

Quentyn Wickes leaned over the railing and watched the white crests of the waves roll beneath the ship, some of them simply disappearing beneath the craft and others crashing against the hull. How many times had he stood, staring down at the water like this, waiting and dreading?

He'd been at sea too long. The longer he was out there, the more he felt Ikarna's judgment weighing him, and he knew he would be found wanting whenever she deigned to address those scales. Until then, he watched her and knew she watched him. She stared up just as he stared down, and they kept their mutual vigil with unknown fathoms of water between them.

Wickes looked up to the horizon and saw land, and the dread gripped him harder. It was bad enough to tempt fate on the open water, but it somehow felt even worse on the approach to Inport. He'd been in and out of the city many times during his career of piracy, and he'd been back several times over the past few years while wearing the Imperial yoke. It never got easier, coming this close to the place that spawned him. The place that molded him and taught him the true meaning of fear.

Beyond Inport, just to the west, lay the swamps. A single road disappeared from the edge of civilization into that mire, and Wickes remembered it well, even this many years later. It wound between the trees that dripped with vines and sprouted lichen, disappearing into darkness before you were scarcely five steps in. The brown water covered the roadway in some places, and fallen logs blocked it in others. It was all but impossible for carts or horses, but a person could clamber over the sickly wetness of the logs' bark and continue deeper into the madness. And that's what it felt like, descending to the heart of the swamp. It was a place of madness and terror, and it had created Wickes. It was home.

Perhaps, after the ship docked, he should walk through Inport and out the other side. Perhaps he should take that cursed road into the swamp and never come back out. He could let the mosquitoes decide his fate, stinging and biting at him until he dropped into the waters, allowing it to cover and claim him as Ikarna finally pulled him down. Wickes would have his place beneath the ferns and under the twisted roots of the skinny gray trees that wound their way up from the unseen depths. He deserved no better than that after the choices he'd made. He deserved nothing but strict judgment for all the betrayals and all the deaths that had come at his hands.

He'd not been lying when he told Weylis he'd done it all for her. He'd condemned himself and every one of their crewmates so that she'd have a chance to live. She thought he did it out of selfishness, to preserve himself, but that hardly mattered. He'd have done anything to keep her alive, but he no longer knew what to believe about his own worth. Ikarna should just drag him and the whole *Gaillardia* down now and be done with them all, but he knew she would wait. She was patient, and she would take him when she was ready. And, though dread still filled him, he knew today was not that day.

"Who did you see in Redwater?" Jalla asked.

Wickes had heard his boots on the deck as he approached, but he hadn't turned to acknowledge him. Now he clasped his hands on the rail and looked past them, toward the water once again. The sea looked black today, the tops of the waves lightening to a hateful blue just before cresting white. Then they all went back to black again.

"I'm talking to you," Jalla said.

Wickes considered continuing to hold his silence and seeing

what Jalla would do. The other man couldn't very well pitch him overboard when the Empire was relying on him for this mission, could he? But there were other things that could be done, all of them unpleasant. Wickes licked his lips and tasted salt on them from the spray in the air. Of course he wouldn't betray Weylis to this buffoon, not after everything he'd done to protect her. But did Jalla already know about her? Was this a test of Wickes' loyalty? If Wickes' Imperial shadow had worked out that Weylis was alive and in Redwater, the Empire would have already rounded her up by now, and this line of questioning would be merely a test, a way to see whether they should dispose of a disloyal wretch like Quentyn Wickes after they reached Inport. But, if Jalla didn't know about her, admitting the truth would condemn her.

Wickes had already bent to the Empire too much. He remembered Weylis' words when she told him he'd never be free of the Imperials, no matter how many ghastly errands he ran for them and no matter how many lives he ruined. He'd never be free, and he knew it. Wickes would be damned one way or the other, and he'd rather be damned while holding true to his loyalty for at least one person.

He tilted his head toward Jalla and said, "An exporter I knew there."

"Exporter," Jalla said and spat over the railing. "Pirate, more like."

"An exporter I knew from many years ago," Wickes said. "He has knowledge of all the ships putting into harbor up and down the coast."

"And he said to come here? To Inport?"

"He did."

"What are we doing here?"

Wickes considered withholding the rest of the information, but what good would it do at that point? Jalla would follow him every step of the way and would know their target soon enough. "When Akithar and his allies left Klubridge, it was on a ship called *Sephare*. Her captain has a home in Inport. We're here to find him."

"You know where he is?"

"I know where he may be."

Jalla grunted, and Wickes knew that meant he was satisfied. It hadn't been a test, and Weylis remained safe in Redwater. No, not in Redwater, not anymore. She'd have already moved on by now, and he did not know where she would go. He could find out again, if he put his mind to it. Quentyn Wickes was the best hunter on the seas, and he knew it. But maybe he'd let her go this time. She'd told him not to come back, and maybe this should be the time he listened to her.

~

"Quentyn," the small man behind the counter said with a careful smile. His head was shaved, and his ears protruded from the sides of his head like little, round petals on a dark and strange flower. The man's forehead was scarred, nearly down to his eyebrows, and his bottom jaw had more gold than teeth in it. His upper teeth were gapped at the front, and it gave him a friendlier appearance than the man deserved.

"Tyreck," Wickes said and made a point of looking around the shop instead of continuing to look at its proprietor. Tyreck had run this place since Wickes was but a boy, and sometimes it felt like he'd still be selling fishing lines and lures from this same store long after Wickes was gone. Selling lures and hauling supplies along that twisting, wet road into the swamp every month, an enormous pack strapped to his back.

"You coming by home this time?" It was the same thing Tyreck said every time Wickes saw him, which was every time he had to pass through Inport.

"You know the answer to that," he said.

"Your dad misses you."

Wickes raised an eyebrow and looked at Tyreck then. "The day that old man misses me is a day neither you nor I will see."

"But he does," Tyreck said, insistent now. "He's an old man. He has regrets."

"He told you that, did he?"

"I know the way of old men." With that, Tyreck gave him a

nod, as if he'd imparted some sage knowledge or observation. "I'm bringing him whitefish this month. Shall I bring him a message as well?"

Wickes shook his head and said, "I'm not here for him. I'm looking for a sea captain. Ergo Drass. You know him?"

Tyreck put his palms on the counter and stretched his shoulders forward. The veins standing on the backs of his hands showed both his age and his strength. He'd never stopped working the lines and rowing the boats himself, long after younger men would have given it up. Tyreck was born to the water, just like Wickes had been. Few of them left the swamp to work the sea. Of those, Wickes was the only one who'd never come home.

"By reputation," Tyreck said. "Never met him myself. He's not a fisher." He said this last with a disapproving tone. Anyone who sailed and didn't reap the bounty of the sea was spurning Ikarna's gifts. Wickes was no fisherman himself, not for a long time now, and he wondered what Tyreck must think of him. Probably nothing worse than the rest of Teshovar thought of him at this point.

"Do you know where I can find him?"

Tyreck scratched at his cheek, and his short nails scraped against the stubble. "He's got a house up Fleet Row. Here," he said, and scribbled the directions on a torn piece of paper. He pushed it across the counter and said, "No charge." He smiled when he said it, but Wickes knew the truth in it. Anybody else would have had to drop a seri or two into the old man's palm for this kind of assistance.

"I appreciate it, Tyreck." He reached to pick up the paper, but the fisherman kept it pinned under his fingers.

"Go see your dad," he said, his eyes finding Wickes'.

"We'll see," Wickes said, and that was enough to get Tyreck's hand off the paper. Wickes had no intention of visiting the swamp today or any other day, but one more lie piled up with all the rest couldn't matter that much, could it?

Wickes found Drass' house easily enough. All the houses on Fleet Row had identical wooden post boxes mounted at the front, all painted white, and all stenciled with the owners' names in black. Drass was the fifth one on the left, a small place that looked little different from the other houses around it, but Wickes could tell it was the sailor's house from the first glance. While the neighbors kept their places maintained and clean, the white paint was flaking off the front of Drass'. Curtains were drawn over the window to the left of the front door, but the window itself was almost too dirty to see through. Behind the grime, the blue curtains looked old and ratty. The window to the right had a crack in the glass, right in the corner, as if a pebble hit it or maybe a bird flew into it. It didn't look like recent damage. The post box itself hung slightly askew, the lid propped up by a wad of envelopes that had turned brown and begun decomposing from extended exposure to the elements.

The person who owned that house didn't see it as home. He hadn't been there to collect his letters in a long time, and he hadn't kept the place up. This was just a stopover when he couldn't be at sea. His ship, the *Sephare*. That was home. This was a begrudged obligation.

Just as certainly as he recognized the look of the forlorn house, Wickes was sure Drass wasn't there. Still, he went past the postal box and knocked at the front door. Jalla waited in the street in front of the house, his arms crossed and his eyes not leaving Wickes for an instant.

"You'll want to get away from there," an old man called from across the street.

Wickes turned to face him, and Jalla half turned before stepping back to keep Wickes in view. "Excuse me?" Wickes asked and came down the two steps to stand on the front walk.

The old man sat in a chair in front of his own door, a hat pulled low to block the sunlight. He had to have been there when they came down the street, but Wickes hadn't noticed him. "I see you," he said, louder than he needed to. "You won't get anything under my watch."

Wickes looked at Jalla, and the shorter man looked back. Wickes gave his head a slight shake before he came into the street and crossed to where the old man was sitting. "You have me wrong, friend. I'm here to visit Ergo Drass. Do you know him?"

The old man scowled and squinted up at Wickes from his chair. His skin was leathery and browned from the sun, and what hair Wickes could see beneath that hat was white. "Who's asking?"

Wickes glanced at the old man's house and saw the ornament on the door: a small, iron anchor, affixed with a nail. "You were a sailor," he said.

The man huffed a breath and followed Wickes' gaze to the anchor. "So?"

"I sailed with Drass many years ago. I bring news for him from friends." The lies came so easily now. They'd been harder at the start, but they were second nature after the years Wickes had spent hunting his own people. "Do you know where he is?"

"You don't know him," the old man said, still scowling.

"His ship's called *Sephare*," Wickes said. "I sailed with him and helped move some sensitive... cargo." Wickes raised his eyebrows and gave the old man a knowing look. If he'd known Drass long enough, he'd know what that look meant.

It took a moment, but the scowl finally faded. "Can't be too careful. Not since they stopped patrolling around here."

"Stopped patrolling?"

"The city watch. The bleeding Empire. They took the money away, and there's nobody to watch the neighborhood now. I keep an eye." He tapped his temple next to his right eye and gave Wickes a nod. "Thought you were trying to get in over there. Not like the old cuss has anything worth taking."

"Do you know where he is now?"

The man grunted and said, "Never know where he is until he's here. He's a good one, though. Helps me out when I need it." He turned a sharp eye on Wickes. "Said you had a message for him?"

"News," Wickes said. "Do you know when he's due back?"

"Not for another week, maybe two." He chewed at his lips and then nodded. "Two weeks, more like. He's not here much."

"Two weeks? You're sure about that?"

"Sure as can be," the old man said. "He's not here often, but his schedule's regular."

Wickes turned and saw that Jalla's eyes were still on him. "Two weeks," he said.

"I heard," Jalla said and started back up the street. He jerked his head, and Wickes had no choice but to follow.

∞

The Brass Cabin was a cheap inn only a few blocks away from Drass' house. Jalla had wanted to go back to the ship, but Wickes had convinced him they needed to stay in the city so they'd be ready when Drass returned. The thought of sleeping on his docked ship for two weeks, surrounded by an Imperial crew that knew and hated him, was even less appealing than spending those nights in Inport. Tyreck knew the owner of the place and arranged a room with two beds for Wickes and Jalla. Jalla wasn't happy about staying in the city, where it was harder to keep watch on his prisoner, and he wasn't about to agree to separate rooms. So the two men spent the first three nights as awkward and unspeaking bunkmates.

Tyreck seemed genuinely happy to have Wickes back in town, and he came by every day to bring him a meal and to find opportunities to mention Wickes' father. Tyreck's generosity made it difficult to rebuff him day after day, but Wickes held firm and hoped the fisherman would give up. But there he was each day around noon, showing up with more reasons Wickes should visit his family. And, every day, Wickes made the walk back to Fleet Row with Jalla at his heels. He also made daily walks back to the harbor, but the *Sephare* wasn't docked yet, and there was no sign of Drass' return. Wickes had hoped the old man's two-week estimate would prove to be an exaggeration, but with each passing day, it seemed more likely to be accurate.

When he wasn't fending off Tyreck's pleas and doing his best to ignore Jalla, Wickes pondered the coming confrontation with Ergo Drass. This was a man who had run cargo and served as a smuggler for the rebels for a very long time. Weylis had sailed with him and vouched for his loyalty, and Wickes didn't imagine he'd be the type to betray them easily. But he knew where Akithar was, and, perhaps more importantly, he might know

LIZANDRA'S DEEPEST FEAR

where the Stormbreak Sanctuary was. That was information Wickes could use, and he might leverage it to buy his own freedom. Even as he thought that, he knew the folly of his optimism, but he couldn't help considering it. Finding the rebels' base was a task that had eluded the Empire for decades, and he might be the one to pry it from the old smuggler's mouth.

Drass would not give up that information willingly. Under ordinary circumstances, convincing Drass to loosen his lips wouldn't have been a problem for Wickes. He'd known how to make men talk even before the Empire had its boot on his neck. But these were not ordinary circumstances. He'd given his word to Weylis that he wouldn't hurt Drass.

What was one more broken promise? Weylis had told him not to look for her again, and he didn't know where she might be by then. If he respected her wishes, he'd never see her again. And, living in hiding as she'd have to do, it was unlikely she'd ever see or hear from Drass again. Wickes could beat the information out of the smuggler, and she'd have no way of knowing.

But Wickes would know. He'd done all this for her. That's what he told himself, and that's what he knew, no matter what Weylis thought. Was he going to reach this point, at the end of all of it, and break his word one more time, now to her? No. If his word would ever carry weight again, it would start with her and with this promise. He'd told her he wouldn't put a hand on Ergo Drass, and that was one promise he'd keep.

Wickes spent the next two days dodging Tyreck while he tried to come up with a plan for dealing with Drass. He was accustomed to using fear and violence as his tools. Fear, he could still employ, but violence was off the table. Something told him fear would be less effective on Drass than violence, but there had to be a way to make it work.

He was mulling over the problem while poking at a plate of haddock when Tyreck found him in the tavern adjacent to the Brass Cabin. Jalla was across the table, staring into a huge mug, and raised his eyes when the loud little man spotted them.

Tyreck took the seat next to Wickes and launched into an account of the last time he'd taken supplies into the swamp, how Wickes' father had seemed, and how the village was getting along. Wickes did his best to focus on the fish in front of him and to let Tyreck's voice fade into the background noise, but he looked up at the little man between bites.

Wickes interrupted the story with a quick question. "Colm?"

Tyreck blinked. "What?"

"Colm is still alive?"

"Well, yes, the last time I saw him, he was."

Tyreck waited for more, and Wickes held his eyes for another moment before looking back at his food. His appetite for lunch had fled, and he pushed the plate away with the backs of his fingers.

He had a plan now, and it would work, but it wasn't a good one. As long as he didn't speak it, no one would know he'd even thought it. But when he looked up and saw Tyreck's expectant smile, those gold teeth shining dull in the tavern light, he knew he was going to do it. Damn it all, he was going home.

∼

Jalla had protested leaving Inport and the docked ship, but he wasn't about to let Wickes make the journey on his own. After Wickes made it clear that he wouldn't be dissuaded, the two departed the city by the western road and headed into the wilderness. The main ways out of Inport led north to Sandwallow and south to Acleau, but they took a less-traveled path that had weeds covering it and bumps and puddles where the path hadn't been kept up. They went on foot, as the trip was not a long one, and horses would be of no use to them once they reached the swamp, anyway.

It might have been winter and snowing in the north, but the land this far south felt like it was still in the throes of a hot summer. The sun beat hard on Wickes and Jalla as they trudged out of the city and past the tall grasses, and Jalla had to wrap a scarf around his head to keep the shaved top from burning. Wickes was more accustomed to this weather, even though he'd made a point of not returning home for many years. All that avoidance would end today. Before the sun set, Wickes would have faced his father again, and the thought of looking into those cold but fevered eyes made him clench his jaw to keep himself from shuddering.

The day only felt hotter the farther they got from Inport and the closer they came to the edge of the swamp. The first sign that they were nearing their destination came with the buzzing of the mosquitoes that liked to play in their ears and land on their necks. Wickes swatted one away from his face as they followed the track left around a bend. The farther they went, the rougher the road had become until it was nothing more than a hint of a dirt trail.

Past the hill where they turned, the trees sagged, and the foliage faded from a vibrant green to a sickly olive color. It was more common to find still water sitting in the ruts of the path here, and that brought more mosquitoes and other stinging bugs. Wickes passed through the winged clouds with occasional waves of his hand, but Jalla stumbled and cursed, swatting at the things with every other step. Perhaps he'd be bled dry before they even reached the village. Wickes could only hope for such luck.

Before long, the ground sloped downward, and the trees clustered closer together, and they were walking into a canopy that blocked the worst of the sun but did nothing to deter the insects. The path was softer here, muddy in some areas, with patches of soggy grass sprouting from puddles here and there. They had reached the edge of the swamp. Wickes walked at the front, his steps sure and direct, but every step deeper into the green made him question the whole plan. Surely there was another way to deal with Drass. A better way to get him to talk without resorting to violence, and without facing what waited at the end of this road. Perhaps it was better to ignore the promise after all and to just beat the information out of him.

But no. Once Wickes had decided to honor his word to Weylis, he knew he wouldn't go back on it. And, besides that, Ergo Drass was likely made of sterner stuff and wouldn't bend as easily as most of the others Wickes had questioned over the years. Alternative means were needed for the old captain, and the best chance for that was ahead of Wickes and not behind.

Swamp birds screamed in the distance, and the canopy of

trees closed tighter until it seemed they were walking through twilight instead of the middle of the day. Wickes looked up, and specks of sunlight winked through the tiny gaps in the branches above, casting odd and disorienting shadows on the ground below. Something croaked to the right, and when Wickes looked toward the sound, the ridged back of something slipped off a log and into the water. There had been stories from his youth about travelers who wandered off the path and ended up as food for the reptiles that ruled that shallow and murky sludge. Three wrong steps in either direction, and there was no doubt he'd meet one of the beasts himself.

Wickes glanced back at Jalla and saw the man staring off to the right, probably seeking whatever that creature had been. It was no use. He'd never see the thing if it didn't want to be seen. Not until it had its teeth around his ankle and its tail whipping to knock him over.

They made the entire walk mostly in silence, as had become their way. Wickes had nothing he wanted to share with Jalla, and Jalla cared only to make sure Wickes didn't slip away from him. They trudged forward in a wordlessness that was not at all companionable but was at least not awkward. Each man knew where the other stood, and they needed no words to acknowledge their places.

The sun had begun its descent by the time they neared the center of the swamp, and it truly looked more like night than day at that point. If Wickes hadn't been leading them along the long-familiar route, he had no doubt Jalla would have already wandered off course and lost himself in the gut of some hidden predator. But Wickes kept them directed and true, and just when it seemed there wouldn't be enough light to carry them any farther, he spotted the twin flames in the distance.

"There," he said, pointing. "That's my village."

"About bloody time," Jalla said and scratched at his neck. The mosquitoes had left Wickes mostly unmolested, but red dots speckled the side of Jalla's face and the backs of his hands.

As they neared the entrance, the flames resolved into torches mounted on poles at either side of the road. A primitive fence of woven sticks and wire extended to both sides, and Wickes knew it surrounded the entire village. It looked ramshackle, but it was sturdy enough to keep undesirables, both human and otherwise, from roaming among the population. A single guard stood sentry at the center of the path ahead, blocking the opening in the fence and barring entry to the town. He took a step forward as the two men approached but said nothing.

Wickes studied the man's face but didn't recognize him. He was young, his dark skin as yet unlined and his black hair pulled into tight braids that fell to his shoulders. He would have been nothing more than a child when Wickes left. The guard wore a dark brown shirt and black trousers that made him nearly invisible in the eternal twilight of the swamp. He wore no armor, for who would be interested in invading this place? The guards kept watch here more as a formality than anything else.

Wickes held his hand behind him, the palm down, and Jalla took his meaning and stopped. "I am Quentyn Wickes," he said. "I'm here to see my father."

The guard frowned at him, the torchlight hiding and again revealing his face as the flames flickered on both sides of him. "Who is your father?"

"Elder Kosah," he answered. "Kosah Enwickesan."

The younger man's eyes widened just enough for Wickes to see recognition there. The boy didn't know Wickes, but there was no doubt he knew of him. The errant son of their leader, the one who'd strayed from home and shamed his kinsmen. When Wickes had left, he'd thought he was headed for something better and didn't know that was just the first of many times he would shame and disappoint those who saw him as their son, their brother, their friend, and their lover.

"You are not welcome here," the guard said and stood a little firmer, his hand reaching out for a staff Wickes now saw stood upright in the mud beside the entrance. The man's voice was thick with the accent of the southlands, an accent Wickes had worked hard to lose after he'd taken to the sea. It hadn't been hard to do, but hearing it spoken again reduced him to the scared boy who lived inside the fear of that little village. The very fear he expected to face at the end of his present journey.

"Inform my father that I'm here. He'll want to see me,"

Wickes said. Even as he said it, though, doubt clouded his mind. Would his father truly want to see him after all this time? Had Tyreck been exaggerating? Had he been outright lying? Why would his father have any interest in seeing the son that had failed him? That had failed the whole community?

The guard's hand closed around the staff next to him, and Wickes tensed his muscles without visibly moving, getting ready for a fight. He hoped it wouldn't come to that, but better to be prepared if it did. He cut his eyes toward Jalla and saw the other man watching the guard just as closely. "Was this your plan, Wickes?" he asked.

"Quiet," Wickes said, and, to Jalla's credit, he closed his mouth. The three men stood in silence and motionless, appraising each other in the dark of the swamp. Something chittered in the distance, a high-pitched whirring that sounded four times and died away into an echo. When the guard still had made no indication of going inside, Wickes said, "Tell my father I'm here. Tell him I'm ready to return."

"Return," the guard said.

"To take the rites again."

The younger man's forehead creased at that, and he looked from Wickes to Jalla and back again before taking a cautious step backwards, through the opening in the fence. He called over his shoulder, but Wickes missed the name he'd shouted. A young woman soon appeared behind him. She wore similarly dark clothing and had a keen glare just like the young man's. Wickes would wager they were both guards and, furthermore, were related. Probably siblings. Most everybody inside that fence was related to each other in some way, some more insidiously than others.

"Who's this?" she asked. Her voice carried the same familiar accent, and Wickes wondered whether either of these people had traveled outside the swamp in their lives. Probably not.

"Says he's the Elder's son."

At that, she stared at Wickes, taking in his face, his hands, his rough boots, all of him in a slow study. Her eyes returned to his face and lingered there for another few seconds before she said, "He has the look."

"Says he wants to return. To take the rites again."

She snorted at that but hadn't taken her eyes off Wickes. "You wait here," she said to him. And then she was gone, sliding out of sight and into the village. The first guard still hadn't moved and had his hand on the staff, ready to swing it out of the mud at the first provocation.

"What is this, Wickes?" Jalla asked in a rough whisper.

"Quiet," Wickes said again, sharper this time. Jalla grumbled a response that sounded petulant but said nothing after that.

They remained there, the three men unspeaking, for what must have been ten minutes or more. Wickes' joints were growing sore from not moving, and he shifted his weight on the soft ground. The guard's eyes flicked down, and his fingers tightened on the staff, and Wickes held steady again. The guard looked back up at him and kept his eyes locked until the young woman was there again and put a hand on his shoulder.

"Elder says let him in."

If the order surprised him, the first guard gave no sign. He stepped back and to the side, moving out of the way so Wickes could pass him.

"Not that one," the other guard said, and the first one stepped back into place, blocking Jalla.

"Now, just a minute," Jalla said, nose to nose with the guard, whose height outpaced his own by a good several inches.

"It's okay," Wickes said. He turned back to Jalla and spoke past the guard's shoulder. "Wait here for me."

"Wait here? In the bleeding swamp?" Jalla asked. His first concern was about the surroundings, but then his eyes widened. "You're not leaving me here, Wickes. You're staying in my sight, you hear me?"

"This is the only entrance to the village. I can't get out any other way. Just wait here, and you won't lose me."

"This was a terrible idea." The last was directed at himself, and Jalla looked truly miserable.

Wickes almost felt sorry for his jailer at that moment. He said, "Just wait, and I'll be back for you."

Without giving Jalla another chance to protest, Wickes turned and followed the young woman farther along the path.

They were within the fence that surrounded the village now, and he remembered these sights as surely as if it had been just yesterday that he'd left. The place had aged, buildings had been patched or painted, and paths had been recovered and smoothed, but it was otherwise much like the place he had left. The village had no name, and it appeared on no maps, as far as Wickes knew. It was remote and hidden, and it had no interest in being found or visited by any outsiders. The few faithful, like Tyreck, who did live outside its borders, made infrequent trips back to bring supplies, but they rarely brought news of the outside world.

Wickes hadn't even known there was an outside world until he was fifteen, nearly sixteen. All he'd seen and all he'd been taught was within those flimsy walls. Inside was safety. Inside was the embrace of Ikarna's favored. Outside was danger. Outside was the swamp, with its monsters and snares and temptations, all waiting to lead an impressionable young man off the path and into the depths where he'd be consumed. And he'd believed it for so long that it had taken a lot for him to even consider that there could be something different beyond the reach of the swamp, much less something better. He'd finally made his way out, and the swamp had let him go. Just as surely as the village had loosened its grip on him, though, Ikarna had tightened hers and still had not let go.

The village sprawled back and away from the entrance, meandering rows of squat houses ringing the center of the town, where they grew berries, nuts, and rice in the marshy soil. Hunters went outside the fence to bring back meat from the birds and reptiles that prowled the area, but the center of the village was where most of the food grew. It was there that the young woman was taking Wickes, and it was there that he knew he'd find his father.

As they passed, unfamiliar eyes followed their progress. Wickes studied the faces, trying to seek out any he recognized, but he didn't know these people. Whether they had just aged beyond his recognition or arrived after his departure, he couldn't say. They were strangers to him, but it was evident that

LIZANDRA'S DEEPEST FEAR

he was no stranger to them. Word had traveled fast. The Elder's son had returned. The heretic was back.

Wickes followed close behind the guard, but every step he took felt slower and heavier than the last. Dread crawled up his spine and into his brain. As they walked, the years shed off him like skin from a snake. They passed the chapel where the villagers congregated and spoke in Aevash to their sunken goddess. He was fifteen again, slipping out back and avoiding his father's sermons. Another few steps, and they were near the town storehouse, where he'd hidden from his father when he was ten. And then they were passing the well into which his father had dangled him when he was eight, one hand wrapped around his ankle and the other pointing toward the distant reflection of the water at the bottom.

At the end of this walk, he'd be looking into eyes he'd hoped to never see again, and for what? To save an old rebel smuggler from getting a beating? Was that truly worth enduring this visit? This recommitment? Which was worse, betraying his word to Weylis that Drass would go unharmed or betraying his promise to himself that he'd never set foot in this forsaken bog again?

No one spoke to Wickes as he made his silent and sure way directly through the town and into its center, his face impassive but his mind turbulent. There was no backing out at this point. As soon as he'd come through the front gate, he'd committed himself to this course. Perhaps even before that. Weylis was the one person he wouldn't betray, even if it meant making a liar of himself. Besides, he doubted he'd even make it out of the village alive if he changed his mind before seeing his father and going through with the whole ordeal. These people were still and quiet now, but if they were anything like the townspeople he'd known as a child, every one of them would have a knife or a club ready at hand, and they'd be eager to finish him off once and for all and send him down to Ikarna whole or in pieces.

One final turn around a low wall, and there he was, standing at the end of the path. Kosah Enwickesan, elder of the village for at least half a century now, stared at his son with eyes that were as cold and dark as the rest of this place. He looked older, which shouldn't have surprised Wickes as much as it did. He'd been gone from this place for nearly three decades, but somehow his father's face had continued threatening the back of his mind just as he'd looked on the day Wickes had left and abandoned these ways. His hair still hung in tight braids, but they were gray now instead of black, and they reached near his waist when they'd previously come no farther than his shoulder blades. The man still looked strong and broad, even in his old age, but there was more roundness to his shoulders, and his head drooped forward on a neck that had grown tired of supporting it. His dark face was a map of lines now, extending from the corners of his eyes, drawing deep cuts across his forehead, and pulling downward from his nose so that his mouth hung in an eternal scowl.

Wickes' father had had a beard the last time he'd seen the man, but now his face was shaven clean, just a hint of white stubble showing on his upper lip and at his chin. He held the end of a cane in his right hand, not quite leaning on it but not quite stable, either. The walking stick twisted its way to the ground, looking like nothing more than a piece of wood someone had salvaged from the edges of the swamp, and that was probably exactly what it had been. It was dangerous for the community to make itself known outside of its own swamp, and they foraged and scavenged what they needed from the surroundings instead of going into towns to trade.

The one thing that hadn't changed was the ceremonial robe he wore. The baggy gray material draped over his shoulders and hung loose off his back, the hood dangling back there, a dark blue stripe lining the edges of the whole thing. Underneath, Kosah wore a tunic banded in gray and blue with Aevash runes embroidered into the lighter spaces. Wickes hadn't thought about that tunic in over twenty years, but now he knew he would have been able to recite every rune off it, if pressed. Some memories never left your mind, even when you didn't remember they'd been there to start with.

The pathway ended at his father's feet, and there was nowhere else to go. Others had stopped their work, standing far enough away to not interfere with this meeting but close enough to hear and see everything that was about to transpire. Wickes came to an awkward stop, and the guard moved aside, leaving the two men facing each other with scarcely three feet of space between them. Wickes could hear Kosah breathing at this distance, each breath coming hard through the old man's nose. He waited for his father to say something, but there was nothing but silence and the stare of those dark and empty eyes. He was waiting for Wickes to speak, and he was waiting for a specific thing to be said. It tore at Wickes' guts like physical claws, and he resisted, but he knew in the end he had to say it. He'd come this far, and his pride would do him no good now, if it was all for nothing.

"I'm sorry, Father," Wickes said, and he bowed his head. "I was wrong, and I'm back. I want to make it right."

He waited there, his head down and his eyes on his father's feet. The old man wore sandals that looked identical to the ones he'd had when Wickes was a boy. For a moment, Wickes thought they might be the very shoes he'd worn then, and everything else had spun backwards in time as well. He was a kid again, bracing himself for harsh words in Aevash that he wouldn't understand and then even harsher ones he did understand. But no, these were different sandals, made in the same ancient woven fashion, and shoved onto the same dirty feet. Time had passed since Wickes had run away from this cruel place, and now even more time passed as he waited to be brought back into it.

"Where have you been?"

Wickes flinched at the voice more than the question. It had been decades since he'd heard it, and it was older now and strained by time, but it was the same man and the same voice, now asking Wickes what had become of him after he'd fled everything he'd known and gone out into the bigger world. For the first time, Wickes realized his father probably knew nothing about what he'd been up to. Just as surely as the village didn't trade with the outside world, it also shunned news of outsiders and knew nothing of politics or wars or rebellions, other than what little bits of essential information agents like Tyreck might bring them. They needed to avoid discovery and assault from the Empire, but nothing else was of consequence to them. Kosah knew nothing of Wickes taking to the sea, earning a name as a brigand, and subsequently betraying everything and everyone he'd met in that life, just as surely as he'd done to everyone and everything here. The old man might see the irony in the pattern and find a mean humor in it. Wickes did not.

"I went to Inport," Wickes said. But what if his father did know something? What if he had heard about his son's reckless life at sea? He'd hedge the truth just close enough to not give himself away. "I worked ships," he said. "I sailed for many years but am finished with that now."

Kosah grunted, and Wickes risked raising his head. The old man continued staring at him, but his expression was as unreadable as ever. He said, "You were at sea."

"I was."

"And you return now. Why?"

"I am older, and I have seen the waters. I know Ikarna better than I did when I left. And she brought me back here, to our people. To you."

Wickes stopped talking and watched his father's inscrutable face. This was the moment that would determine everything. If his answer hadn't been good enough, all of this was for naught. Kosah let the moment linger and stretch until Wickes felt it tightening throughout his body. At last, the old man spoke again. "You were at sea, and she did not pull you under."

"She did not."

"You have no place here now. You left our ways and are not one of us."

Wickes swallowed hard before saying, "I'm back now, and I want to return."

Kosah took a few more deep breaths through his nose, his forehead wrinkling even more. He was weighing Wickes then, trying to find any sincerity in what he undoubtedly believed to be nothing but lies. "Your initiation is null," he said.

"I'll do it again."

A low murmur rippled through the onlookers, but Kosah silenced them when he raised his left hand. When they were quiet and still once more, he lowered his hand and asked, "Do you know what that will entail?"

"I do, and I'm ready to do it now."

"Now," Kosah said, not quite asking but not sounding like he believed it either.

"Now," Wickes said again.

His father stared at him for another long moment before turning his head to a woman at the edge of a paddy to his right. He nodded to her and stepped away without another word to Wickes.

∼

Just past the paddies, beneath the boughs of a gnarled and ancient tree, a square hole gaped in the ground. Four rows of white bricks, one stacked upon another, surrounded the hole, looking as weathered and aged as the tree that drooped over them. A set of stairs, constructed from the same white bricks, now slick and green from untold decades of submersion in the swamp, descended into the hole. The first three steps were visible, but everything below that was lost from sight, swallowed by the murky brown water that filled the rest of the hole.

Wickes stood before the stairs and before the assembly of what must have been the entire village. He turned his head first right and then left, scanning the masses of people surrounding and watching him. He recognized none of the faces that looked back at him, but they all stared expectantly, waiting for him to make his first movement toward the stairs.

He was naked now, robed acolytes having taken his clothes when he reached the edge of this ceremonial cavern. The humidity of the swamp pressed against him from all sides, but a chill still settled on his skin, sending a shudder through his shoulders. It wasn't modesty or embarrassment that inspired the shudder, and it wasn't even dread or fear, though he surely felt the latter two. It was that uncanny feeling of being unstuck in time. He was nine years old, standing before this pit for the first time. He was twelve, returning to it once more. He was seventeen, looking down into the water with apprehension, now that he knew exactly what was down there. He was forty-seven, back for a fourth time and about to walk down the steps into the hole he'd sworn he'd demolish and fill with dirt if he ever laid eyes on it again.

A robed priest stood behind Wickes, the dark hood obscuring his face as he painted across Wickes' bare back. The white paint was cold and wet on his skin, but Wickes hardly felt it. His focus was on the task at hand and how he could best survive it one more time. There had been a great amount of ceremony the first time he'd gone in, but the pomp had lessened with every time he had gone back into the hole. Most people did it only once, affirming their commitment to the village and its way of worshipping Ikarna. The only ones who had done it multiple times were the troublesome ones. The ones who needed reminding about who she was and why they lived for her as they did. Wickes had known of a few who had done it twice and one other troublemaker who'd gone down three times, but he knew of nobody who had done it four times. To his knowledge, nobody else had survived past the third visit.

And yet, there he was, voluntarily returning to the site of his trauma, painted once again in runes that he could sound in Aevash but didn't understand their meanings. The water would wash the runes away, leaving them down there with Ikarna and whatever she brought with her this time. That thought pulled Wickes' eyes back to the surface of the water just as the priest finished his painting and stepped away.

Did the water move? No, it was just his imagination. The water remained still and calm and dark, waiting to claim him.

He looked back at the crowd one more time, and his father was there now. The old man stood at the edge of his people, the cane in his hand and his eyes on Wickes. He waited with the rest of them, and Wickes knew he didn't believe he'd go through with it. That certainty was what propelled Wickes forward, first with his right foot and then with his left. His eyes remained on his father's face as his bare foot touched the first step and felt the softness of the slime that covered it. He planted his heel firmly enough that he wouldn't slip, and he took another step. Algae broke loose from the second step and caught between his toes. He ignored it and focused on the old man's eyes. They remained expressionless as the Elder watched his son's descent.

One more step down and then another, and soon his feet were in the water, and then it was up to his calves. The water was warm, just as he remembered it. As its surface passed his knees and climbed his thighs, his left foot disturbed something that had been resting on the next step. It retreated with a panicked leap beneath the water, brushing past his toes once before diving down into the murk where he'd soon join it.

Wickes looked down as he took the next few steps, looking up when the surface had reached his chest, and by then his father and all the other onlookers were gone from his view, blocked behind the bricks surrounding the hole. They wouldn't linger there, anyway. After he was fully submerged, they would make the short walk to the other end, where they'd wait to see whether he came out. It was a short walk for them, but it would be a much longer ordeal for him.

The water touched Wickes' chin, and he'd never felt more alone or more vulnerable in his life. Not when he'd left the village with no allies in the world outside. Not when he'd shunned life on land and taken to the sea aboard ship after ship, throwing himself at Ikarna's mercy year after year. Not when he'd traded his dignity to the Empire and agreed to hunt down the only people who had ever cared about him. Not even when he'd left Weylis in Redwater and seen the certainty in her eyes that she was done with him.

No, this was deeper and older and more primal than any of those times. He'd felt something similar to this aloneness before, every time he'd gone into the water here, but the previous times he'd descended, it had been with the mind and body of a child. He'd lacked the worldliness and knowledge and experience to truly understand what it meant to be alone and to have his head pulled up and his neck bared, helpless to stop the blade that might stop his pulse at any instant.

None of that innocence accompanied him this time. He'd seen the world and its cruelty, and he'd added to it. He knew what it could do, and he knew Ikarna hated him. He'd been raised to believe in her, and he did. She lingered in his mind, as surely and truthfully as when his father had planted her there. Wickes knew she was real, and he knew she wanted him to suffer. He'd also been raised to respect and love her, but those lessons were gone. What was left was terror, an old and spiraling horror that coiled itself into his gut and waited. He knew Ikarna hated him, and, though he'd never speak it aloud, in that moment he hated her right back.

With a deep and final breath, Quentyn Wickes plunged his head beneath the sickly water and dove to meet his goddess in her own realm.

It was too dark for him to see down there, even if he'd kept his eyes open. But he closed them now, just as he'd done on the other three occasions. Despite all feelings to the contrary, he knew he was not alone, and there was an absurd comfort in placing his thin eyelids between his eyes and whatever he might encounter.

As he swam downward, his hands brushed the slick stone of the entrance, but it soon gave way to the bumpy and unyielding masses of tree roots that clogged the watery passage. He recalled those roots from when he'd been there before, and he even remembered exactly how he'd gone above, below, and around them to proceed through the underwater cave, but none of those memories would help him now. Each time he'd gone through this, the passage had somehow changed. The previous turns were gone, blocked by new obstructions, and he'd had to feel his way through the wet darkness as the breath he held in his lungs became heavier and heavier.

His hands grabbed the edges of what felt like a sunken log, and he pulled himself forward, moving past it and deeper into the cave. Something brushed against his face, and he swatted at it before realizing it was grass waving lazily along the floor beneath him. He angled his body so he could pull himself forward, his chest inches above the swamp's floor, his hands grasping the tough grass and hauling him ahead like insubstantial rungs on a horizontal ladder. His feet kicked behind him, propelling him forward, and his right heel struck and dragged across something hard.

He jerked upward, and the top of his head hit the firmness as well. Another root, crawling out from the tree, no doubt. Spirals bloomed behind his closed eyelids, and his head throbbed, but he pulled himself forward once more. He lowered his head this time, and the reedy plants tangled in his whiskers and pulled at his cheeks. There had to be less than two feet of space between the roots above him and the ground below. A sudden wave of dizzying claustrophobia tried to claim him, but he fought it, grunting with the effort and losing precious air as bubbles poured from his nostrils and tickled his lips.

If he panicked, he would die, and this is not where he would end. Ikarna would have him, but not here, and not now.

Wickes shot forward through the water, and his right shoulder banged against something firm, sending him to the left, rotating off course. He reached for the grass, but it was gone now, the ground having dropped from beneath him. His hands sought the roots above, but they had left as well. He flailed and found no purchase, nothing around him but empty water. Wickes felt himself turning, and he fought to correct his direction, but which way had he been going? His momentum was gone, all sense of positioning abandoned somewhere behind him. In that instant, his eyes blinked open, and the dirty water flooded in, stinging them and trying to force the rest of the air out of his lungs. His head throbbed now, and the tendons in his neck bulged with the effort, but he kept the air. His lungs burned, but he held it.

Something brushed his left foot, and he jerked away and looked down, but of course there was nothing to see. He floated in absolute blackness, and there was no sound other than the muffled thudding of his own heart echoing in his ears, now filled with the filthy water. And then the feeling was back, of something sliding along the top of his foot. Before he could move away again, it was at his shin, and it wrapped around to his calf, sliding ever upward even as something else swam over his right arm, winding about his biceps and slithering down, gliding beneath his armpit and around his back. His mind tried to tell him it was Ikarna, reaching up from the depths with tentacles to drag him down, but his rational mind knew what it was, and the truth was no less unsettling.

Even as the third one found him and slipped around his neck, brushing just beneath his chin, he knew he had bumbled into a nest of water snakes. The serpents twisted about him, investigating him, wondering why he was in their territory, and it wouldn't be long before one of them sensed a predator in him and struck. There were too many to track now. They swam swiftly, twirling around one hand and then the other, nudging against the backs of his knees, searching and probing along his belly. He willed them to lose interest, but they remained and moved now with more frantic energy. Wickes forced himself to remain perfectly still, and he couldn't tell whether he might be sinking or rising at that point, or perhaps he was upside down now. His head pounded with the breath he still held, and his equilibrium abandoned him, giving no indication of what was up or down.

Countless serpents lived in the swamp, and most of them had venom. If he moved and they attacked him, his muscles would seize, and he'd stay there, dying a quick but agonizing death beneath his father and the rest of the village's feet. But he was just as likely to drown if he did nothing. His lungs were strong, but he couldn't hold that breath forever. His time was running out, and he had to decide.

Wickes closed his eyes once more and tried not to feel the scales and the bodies as they twined around him, moving more urgently now. He imagined himself as seen from afar, a vaguely man-shaped mass of writhing black serpents. That thought sent another shudder through his body, and his eyes flicked open once more. An immense pair of blazingly yellow eyes stared back at him in the darkness.

Wickes opened his mouth and released the rest of his air in a scream, and he saw the serpents unwinding themselves from his body and fleeing from the light. Even untethered from the snakes, he couldn't move, transfixed and motionless in the wild, bright blaze of the eyes. This was how he would die, frozen in Ikarna's vengeful gaze.

His body tried to gulp for air, and he shut his mouth, but water flooded into his nose. His sinuses stung, and his head swelled, and the blazing eyes disappeared as all sense left him. His limbs convulsed, and he had the feeling of spinning, as if he were lying on a disc that turned faster and faster, trying to fling him away. Wickes' fingers closed, and there was something in his hand. Something firm, and he pulled, and he was moving again, moving forward but still spinning, lights flickering behind his now-closed eyes, and he knew nothing but the forward movement as he pulled and reached with his other hand, the last of his strength waning. Something else—a root? Another gnarled form in his other hand now, and movement, water flowing past his face, his hair flattened to his head as he sped forward.

And then his forearms hit the hard corners of bricks, and he knew he had made it. Almost there, if he had the strength to pull himself up. The surface was just above his head now, nearly within reach. He slapped at the bricks beneath the water, all his strength gone now, but the momentum carried him upward. The stairs scrubbed against his chest and then against his side as he turned, and then they were on his back as his face broke through and his lips opened to taste the foul miasma of the swamp. Rank air flooded his lungs, and he gasped and coughed, and delirium sent him sprawling up and out of the hole, tumbling forward and at last collapsing in the dirt. Collapsing at his father's feet, those filthy feet in those familiar woven sandals.

As strength returned to his limbs, Wickes pushed himself up to his elbows and then to his knees, and he forced himself to rise on shaking legs to meet his father's eyes.

"My son has returned," Kosah said and reached one hand to hold Wickes' shoulder. "By the grace of Ikarna, my son is welcome home again." The old man's mouth twitched, and something shimmered in his small, squinting eyes.

Wickes tried to speak, but his throat was raw, either from the water he'd ingested or from the scream he'd released. He coughed, and more water poured down his chin, but he held his father's eyes. "I have returned," he said, his voice little more than a croak. "Is Colm here?"

Kosah blinked at that, his forehead creasing. "Colm? The halflock?"

"Is he here?" Wickes asked again.

"Colm is here." The voice came from the left, and Wickes

recognized it before he even turned his head to look at the other man.

He knew Colm on sight, even after all these years. The man was thin, his skin pale as ever, his eyes dull with dark bags beneath them. He wore a robe like the acolytes had worn, and its long sleeves hid his hands. He sought Wickes' face, but it was impossible to know whether any recognition sparked in those haunted eyes.

Wickes looked back to his father. "Now reinitiated, it is my right to claim a boon. Is that not true?"

Kosah's near-smile had faded now, and suspicion had returned. "What is this?"

"Is it not true that I am due a boon? Is that not the right of all who pass the initiation, as decreed by Ikarna?"

His father took a deep and noisy breath through his nose before answering. "It is true."

"I claim Colm as my boon."

"That is—"

"I claim Colm as my boon," he said again.

Kosah's hand dropped from his shoulder, and the guard who had brought him into the village was there now, her fingers tight around the staff she held in both hands. She moved forward a step, but Kosah stopped her with a gesture. "What is the meaning of this?" he asked. "What is your intention?"

"My intention is to take Colm, collect my clothing, and never see you again."

Kosah shook with fury. "You think you have swindled me. You have come here to desecrate a sacred ritual. Ikarna blessed you!"

"Ikarna blessed me, and you can't touch me now. Not as long as I'm in the village." Wickes wanted to say something else. He wanted to end things with a final retort, something to give his memories closure. Something to forestall his father and leave him with a final, stinging regret for the way he'd treated his son. But there was nothing. The words would not come, and Wickes instead turned to Colm. "You're coming with me."

Colm didn't look to Kosah. He nodded and followed Wickes back along the path to the other end of the tunnel, to the place where Wickes had gone into the water. The crowd parted in silence, no one moving to stop them. Wickes had survived by the grace of Ikarna, and he had claimed his boon, as was promised to him. Nothing he'd done was punishable by the village's laws or by Ikarna's decrees.

Without taking the time to dry himself, Wickes grabbed his clothes off the table where the attendants had left them in a pile. The material clung to his arms and legs as he pulled the shirt and pants onto his body, and he knew he'd regret the damp later, but haste was more important just now. The villagers had no right to stop him or attack him, but the likelihood they'd ignore what was legal and right increased with every moment he lingered. Wickes was still buckling his belt over his trousers when he passed through the narrow gate a moment later, Colm trailing behind him.

"Why are you wet?" Jalla asked. "Who is this? Is that a halflock?"

"Walk," Wickes said. He glanced back to make sure Colm was still with him, and he saw the angry eyes of the entire village filling the space behind them.

"What? Where are you going?"

"Inport," Wickes said. He looked back once more, and he saw his father pushing through the mass of villagers. He stood just inside the gate, his weight leaning on that crooked cane, as he watched his son leave once more.

The old man's jaw was thrust forward, his mouth clamped tight, and he raised his chin in challenge to the child who had taken advantage of him and spurned him once more. As Wickes walked away, he saw his father's hand tremble at the top of the cane. It was one quick motion, but it was enough to betray something beneath the anger. Something weaker and more desperate that showed that the old man now knew he would die alone after having believed he'd regained his heir for just a few brief minutes. It was a quick motion, and it was the last one Wickes ever saw from his father.

CHAPTER 18

Nahk knew she'd been too harsh when she'd left the girl and stormed away, but it was too late to revise that conversation. She'd spoken to Naecara, just as she'd promised, and perhaps that had done Fairy some good. There wasn't much she could do or was inclined to do beyond that.

She could hardly blame Fairy for assuming that murder would be Nahk's response to everything. All the girl knew about her was what Nahk herself had told her, and the largest substance of that was that Nahk had been a Nightingale and that Nightingales were assassins. The assumption that she was good at and relished a good kill was a fair one to make, even if it was only half true.

Nahk sniffed the air in Naecara's quarters. Was that cinnamon? She crossed the darkened room to the far window and pushed it open, careful to do it slowly so that it didn't make noise and so that its motion wouldn't attract attention. The smell came stronger now, wafting up from somewhere below. She leaned her head partway out the window and peered down, satisfied that the dark of the evening would hide her curiosity from anyone who might happen to be wandering below that side of the keep.

How long had it been since they'd had cinnamon at Stormbreak? It must have come on one of the recent supply wagons, and a cook was making it into rolls or some other confection in one of the kitchens. Nahk's stomach rumbled, reminding her she hadn't eaten since lunchtime. She spent more time away from Stormbreak than she spent there, and she was used to better food than the rebels offered her. She wasn't one to complain about free meals, but there was something to be said about dining in all corners of Teshovar and sampling foods she'd never imagined as a child.

She ducked her head back into the bedroom and pulled the window shut. Creeping around a darkened room in a castle was something she'd become accustomed to doing as a child, but the younger Nahk would have been surprised to learn that she was there to deliver information rather than slaughter the occupant. She'd been raised to kill, and they'd made her good at it. The skill had come with many beatings, much deprivation, and torment that had seemed endless, but it had come, nonetheless.

By the time she had turned ten, she'd already chosen the spools as her weapon and had been training with them for two years. The other kids had picked bigger weapons, showier ones. Long blades, bows, scimitars, staves. But she'd seen the utility in the spools even at that young age. She'd already learned that the goal was to open a vein and release the red, and the small blades allowed her to do that up close or from afar, when she flung them on their cables.

The years after that had taught her to predict their trajectories, to pull the cables to correct their flights in mid-air, and to make quick and efficient killing strikes from any distance and at any angle. Nahk had learned the weaknesses in the throat, the chest, just under the arm, along the inner thigh, and all the other places where she might send her small knives to do their work. She'd become skilled with her weapons, and she'd been poised to complete her training and become a full Nightingale in more than just a training capacity. She might have even enjoyed it, but her memories of that part of the training were blessedly vague.

What she remembered was being betrayed by her own during a torrential downpour, the rain soaking her through and roaring all around her. She remembered the pain and the blood and the shock as she fell off the bridge and into the culvert,

Treg's blade still jammed between her ribs. She remembered the splash when she hit the water that surged through the tunnel and swept her beneath the bridge, and how she'd tried to turn herself in its flow to prevent her back from hitting the round walls and driving the dagger even deeper. That night, the flood had nearly drowned her, but much later she'd realized the rain had saved her life. If she'd hit dry stone beneath the bridge, she'd have been dead on the spot. And if the waters hadn't carried her away, Treg would have come down and found her and finished whatever the first stroke and the fall hadn't already done to her.

But it hadn't been Treg who'd found her soaked and more than half dead at the bottom of a drainage ditch. It hadn't been Treg, and it hadn't been Moghadan, and it hadn't been death itself. It had been a woman passing through Deakem in the guise of a bard, a lute she didn't know how to play slung over her shoulder and a pack full of papers secured to her back and hidden by her cloak. Naecara must have thought she'd found a dead girl, and Nahk could only imagine what a fright she must have looked, fourteen years old, washed up and unconscious, her skin sallow and blood leaking out her back. The dagger had been gone by then, taken by the storm, but the wound remained, and Nahk knew she'd have bled out there in the ditch if Naecara hadn't dragged her up the side of the embankment and dressed the cut then and there.

Naecara hadn't raised Nahk; the Nightingales had seen to that. But Naecara had seen the ways they'd shaped her, and she'd done her best to mold her in the other direction. She'd taught her right from wrong and tried hard to instill a sense of self into a girl who'd so far thought of herself as nothing more than a part of a whole. Those had been hard times, and something in Nahk had longed to go back to the Nightingales, not to seek vengeance but to simply return and reclaim the life she was used to living.

But Naecara had kept her near and kept her safe, and morality had wormed its way into her skull and into her chest, despite her best efforts to ignore everything this imposing woman wanted to teach her. But worm its way in it had, and a desire for a return to the Nightingales had changed over time

LIZANDRA'S DEEPEST FEAR

into a desire to find them and make every last one answer for what had been done to her. Not just for that betrayal on the bridge in Deakem. That was the impulsive act of one jealous boy who'd known no better than he'd been taught. No, she wanted answers and blood from the ones who had carved her into a weapon and set her about the task of killing in their name. The ones who had built her with a void where her scruples should have gone and where loathing and shame now made a home.

By the time Naecara had joined with the rebellion, Nahk was old enough to realize she hated the killing, but she was good at it. It was the one skill she had that eclipsed all others, and it was the one advantage she'd have when she finally moved against the Nightingales. And so she'd agreed to come with Naecara, and they'd worked together on the side of the rebels. Naecara knew how Nahk felt about the killing, and she'd asked her so many times if she was sure she wanted to keep doing what she was doing. Every time, Nahk had said she was sure. And she was, but it wasn't that she wanted to continue killing. It was that she needed her skills sharp for that day when she would finally fling her blades at her real targets. She'd had that chance in Tresa and come up short, but that wouldn't happen next time. And that next opportunity was coming soon.

Nahk had been squatting under the window, staring into the dark, when she heard the doorknob turn, and she hopped to her feet, silent and still crouched but able to move quickly now if she needed to. She knew those footsteps, though, and relaxed even before she saw Naecara come through the door.

"I'm in here," she said, softly but loud enough for her voice to carry across the room.

"I know," Naecara said, not bothering to match Nahk's low volume. "You left the window in the hallway unlatched."

Nahk cursed under her breath. She was good, but she would never be good enough to catch Naecara unaware. The woman had eyes like a bloody eagle. But, instead of lingering on her error, she said, "Vaino is gathering people. He's going to send an expedition after the Tamrat heir."

Naecara had lit the gaslamp mounted on the wall near the

door and glanced at Nahk, the flame's light dancing on the side of her face. "We knew he'd be doing that."

"It's sooner than we thought," she said. "He's already talked to the wizard."

"Akithar?"

Nahk moved out of the darkness so Naecara could see her and nodded. "He thinks he'll make a more convincing envoy than the Aescalan."

"Micah is sending Hama?"

"And all his people," Nahk said. "I suspect the woman will go with them. The wizard's friend."

"Samira Tandogan," Naecara said. "How did you learn about this?"

Nahk opened her mouth, and the full answer nearly came out, but she held back at the last instant. Naecara had taught her to hold her sources and her secrets close, and that was one lesson that had stuck. "It's true," she said, "and they're leaving soon. Maybe as soon as three days' time. They're supplying, and then they're heading out."

"Leyna told you," Naecara said.

Nahk sighed and turned her head to the side. There truly was no keeping anything from this woman. Nahk knew she'd tipped her hand on that one when she'd mentioned the supplies. Of course, it had to be Leyna who'd known about Vaino's crew asking for rations and mounts and blankets and such. No matter. This next part was more important, and she had to ask. "I want to go with them," Nahk said. She'd tried to keep the pleading out of her voice, for all the good that would do with Naecara.

Naecara had pulled her gloves off by then, and she paused after laying the second one atop her dresser. "You think they're going to encounter the Nightingales."

"You know they will," Nahk said. "The Nightingales have a contract, and they're not going to ignore it. They'll find Hama and Akithar and the rest of them, and they'll follow them to the scion, and they'll kill the lot of them."

"But this isn't just about protecting them," Naecara said.

"Of course not. I need to do this. You promised you'd help

me find the Nightingales and hunt them down, and we know where they're going. For the first time in years, we know where to find them."

"One of them nearly killed you in Tresa," Naecara said.

Nahk's face and ribs had healed from that encounter, but she could feel the ghosts of those bruises even now. "They didn't, though, and I'll be ready for them this time. They won't know I'm coming, but we know they'll be there."

Naecara rested a hand on the edge of her dresser and sighed. "I can't let you go, Nahk. The Empire has a weapon capable of destroying a city as big as Klubridge. You know we can't let that remain in their hands."

"You can't do this to me, Naecara." Nahk stepped toward the other woman, closing the space, but her movements were tentative. "You promised me. Was it a lie? Did you lie to me?" She spat the last at her, her anger and frustration rising. Naecara had made those promises when confronting the Nightingales seemed like a distant possibility. But now that she could make good on her word, she was denying her, just like Nahk should have expected.

The eyes Naecara turned on Nahk were soft, though, and Nahk saw no lies there. She saw compassion and sadness, and it was impossible to hold on to the anger when she could see as clear as anything that Naecara hated doing this to her.

"As long as the Empire has that weapon, they can do anything," Naecara said. "We don't know where it is or who has it. It could be on its way here, for all we know. Or to Tresa to clean up what you did there. We just don't know. And we'll never know, and none of us can rest until we find out. Getting that weapon out of Imperial hands is imperative, Nahk. You have to see that."

Nahk did see it, but she didn't like it. She remained silent, and Naecara said, "This is critical for saving Teshovar. We will get the Nightingales. I promised you that before, and I promise it again. But this has to come first. Will you help me?"

With that question, Nahk knew Naecara wasn't forbidding her from going with Vaino's expedition. She'd made the choice Nahk's own, and she'd asked for Nahk's help instead of demanding it. That's the way Naecara was, wholly different from the way Nahk had been raised.

Nahk sighed and looked back toward Naecara. "What's your plan?"

Naecara smiled at her, a tense smile, but a smile, nonetheless. Her shoulders relaxed, and she said, "I've been recruiting as well. I knew Micah would be sending a party after the scion, so I've been putting together my own to find the weapon. We need to leave before Micah's group departs. He'll be too busy coordinating them to stop us. If we wait too long, we'll have his full attention, and that would be a problem."

"Who do you have?" Nahk asked.

"Alev Adonar has agreed to go with us."

"Adonar? Vaino's shield mage?"

"One of his shield mages," Naecara said. "Beghran is staying and wants no part in this, so Stormbreak won't be left defenseless."

Nahk knew Alev on sight but had never spoken to them. They were big and strong and Teusan, everything Naecara might need as muscle for whatever scheme she was putting together. "Who else?"

"Apak Brem."

"Who?"

"He came with Akithar's group from Klubridge. He's an engineer, and the stories I've heard place him at the center of the uprising."

"For all the good it did them," Nahk said. She had accepted that she'd be going along with Naecara's plan, her own desire for revenge delayed once again, but she was still allowed to sulk. "I know the one you mean. Little man with glasses? Dark skin and a beard? He built a weapon of his own, from what I hear."

"That's Apak," Naecara said. "I've spoken with him, and he's eager to help us."

"To help us or to help the rebellion?" Nahk saw the fine distinction in that question and knew Naecara would, too. There was more than one force in this rebellion, and knowing someone's loyalty told Nahk most of what she needed to know about any given person on that mountainside.

"To help us," Naecara said. "He's angry, and he doesn't trust Micah. He sees things our way."

"He has problems," Nahk said. She'd heard the talk about the little man from Klubridge, even in the taverns of Aramore. If that day of revolt had made a hero of Akithar, it had made an enigma of the engineer. Nobody quite knew what to make of the man. "Are you using him?" The question was a harsh one but a fair one, and Nahk knew she'd get an honest answer.

Naecara closed her mouth tight and looked like she was giving her answer some real thought. At last she shook her head. "I don't know," she said. "We need him. He understands machines and weaponry. Whatever this thing is, he would be an asset to us. But I don't know. I leveraged his anger to make him see the importance of what we're doing, but he already didn't trust Micah. I didn't force him to come with me."

"You're going on this outing yourself?" Nahk asked. "I thought you'd stay behind and manage things from here."

"I'm not Micah Vaino," Naecara said, and that was enough of an answer for both of them. "Will you come with us, Nahk? We're going with or without you. I'd rather have you with me."

Nahk watched Naecara for a moment and weighed her answer, but she already knew what she would say, and she suspected Naecara had known it all along. "I'm with you. Damn it, you know I'm always with you."

∽

Even through the intensity of the conversation with Naecara, Nahk couldn't banish the smell of cinnamon from her mind. Just as it had done every time she'd smelled it before, the spicy aroma reminded her of the old woman. She didn't know who the old woman was or where she was or even how Nahk knew her. She just knew there had been an old woman with hunched shoulders and white hair and a kind and toothless smile. Wrinkles spread from the corners of her tiny eyes and wrapped down her lips and creased her forehead and everywhere else Nahk could see.

She couldn't remember how she knew the old woman, but

she knew she was kind. The only thing Nahk knew for sure was that the old woman had baked and had carried a basket that smelled just like the cinnamon that even now wafted up from the kitchens below. And every time Nahk had seen her, the old woman had a cinnamon bun set aside just for Nahk.

That was all Nahk had from her life before the Nightingales. Everything else was a blank and dark haze, time and people and places that Nahk knew existed, but she could remember none of it. None of it but the old woman with the cinnamon buns, and every time she smelled that familiar scent, her mind climbed and reached, desperately trying to grasp some other hint. There had to be some other shred of memory around the periphery, but after a lifetime of trying, Nahk knew there was nothing else to remember. She didn't know why it was gone or what had happened to those memories, but this was all she had left.

Nahk had learned to accept that blankness and to stop straining toward something she knew would never come to her, but that didn't dull the ache of a phantom life that she might have led. It was that ache that pulled her down the hallway after she left Naecara's room, down the stairs, and around the stone corridors until the scent grew heavier.

Just ahead and to the left, the flame of a hearth flickered through the open door to one of the keep's kitchens. The smell of baking bread drew her through the doorway, and she stopped in front of the closed oven. It was huge and black and metal, a hulking fixture in the middle of the north wall, fire visible through the grate toward the bottom. Nahk inhaled and basked in the sweet smell and the warmth that poured out of the oven. The buns weren't finished yet, but she could wait. She had nothing better to do with the rest of her night. This was probably the warmest room in the keep, anyway.

Nahk perched on the edge of a wooden bench just a few feet away from the oven and wiped a hand across her eyes. She'd been snooping on Vaino and his allies more than she'd been sleeping lately, and it was catching up to her. She should have been in bed even then, but her exhaustion wasn't a compelling enough reason to pull her away from that kitchen. Nahk would stay there until the cook came back in, and the conversation would keep her alert long enough to see the pastries delivered onto one of the nearby tables for cooling.

She glanced to her left, toward the nearest table, and her heart thudded hard enough that its dull echo flooded her ears. She was on her feet in an instant, and her hands flicked out to her sides, blades ready.

Past the table, partially hidden in the dark corner of the room farthest from the heat and light of the stove, lurked a man. Nahk squinted and could make out his form, even without the benefit of her enhanced vision. He had dark hair and was tall. Nahk stood just short of five and a half feet, so most of the men at Stormbreak were tall to her, but this one had to be six feet. He stood motionless, his back to her, the striped fabric of what looked like thin pajamas draping his shoulders.

Nahk shifted to the right, her feet silent on the hard floor. Her body tingled now, adrenaline making her breaths come faster but not overwhelming her so much that she couldn't keep her wits about her. How had she not seen this man before now? No one could sneak up on her. Had he truly been that still when she came in and in the moments since she'd sat on the bench?

She took a cautious step toward him, her right hand ahead of her and her left pulled back, ready to snap into action. But the man didn't move. As she neared him and came around from the side, she realized he stood so close to the wall that his face nearly brushed the oak beam in front of him. What was he doing?

"You there," she said, and her voice didn't shake. She gave him a moment, but the man didn't respond. She said it again, louder this time. "You there!"

The man inhaled a sharp breath, and his arms shook. Nahk's knees dropped her into an instinctive crouch, but the man made no move to come at her. Instead, he shook his head and turned it to the left and then the right before shuffling his feet on the floor and backing away from the wall with a shakiness that was almost as disconcerting as his previous stillness had been. His feet were bare and must have been freezing on that stone.

Nahk waited for him to turn around, and when he finally faced her, his face looked as confused as Nahk felt.

"Akithar?"

He blinked and rubbed at his face with his left hand, and then he pulled the hand away and studied it as if it were something foreign. "Where," he said and stopped. He began again, his eyes finally finding hers. "Where am I?"

"You're in the kitchen."

"The kitchen," he said, and uncertainty colored his eyes.

"At Stormbreak. You're in the kitchen. Are you all right?"

The man flexed his fingers a couple of times before letting his hand drop to his side. He looked down, just now appearing to see that he was wearing ridiculously baggy pajamas, his toes poking out from beneath the voluminous cuffs of the pants. He put his right hand on the table nearest him and stood there another few seconds, blinking and looking around the dark room. Nahk had seen him around the keep over the past weeks, but she'd never interacted with him. She'd expected their first encounter would come sooner or later, but this was the farthest thing from what she could have imagined.

"Do you need help?" she asked and only then realized she still stood ready for attack. This man looked like anything but a threat. Naecara had said he was no mage, and her blades wouldn't do much if he did have magic and wanted to use it on her. But that didn't seem to be on his mind at the moment as he took inventory of the room and himself, as if he still didn't know where he was or how he'd gotten there. Nahk lowered her hands and stood from her crouch.

Akithar looked back at her, and an uncertain smile twitched at the corners of his mouth before he said, "Your name is Nahk."

"It is," she said. It wasn't surprising that he'd heard her name. They'd all been corralled together in a relatively small keep for a long period of time. It was only natural that an inquisitive person would know as much as possible about everyone else.

"That's Aevash," he said. "It means 'nine.'"

"I know what my name means," she said, and she did. It was the name they'd given her when she was small, after she'd come to Moghadan. It hadn't been the name she'd been born with, but that, like everything else, was lost to time. She was Nahk, the ninth child brought into that sinister creche.

"My name is Caius," he said. "Caius Harrim."

She'd known Akithar had to be his stage name, but she hadn't expected him to volunteer his true name so readily.

He gestured to the bench where she'd been sitting only a moment before. "Do you mind if I...?"

Nahk looked from his hand to the bench and realized he meant to sit with her. She took a step back and nodded. He came away from the wall where he'd been standing, and as he came closer to the stove, the light illuminated his dirt-stained feet. How long had he been roaming about the keep before she'd found him here? As he lowered himself onto the bench with a heavy sigh and held his hands out toward the warmth of the stove, he seemed so much smaller than he had just moments before. Nahk felt nothing but pity for this confused man, lost in the kitchen in the middle of the night.

"What were you doing in here?" she asked. She stood several feet away from him, no longer worried he was a threat, but she couldn't bring herself to relax enough to sit alongside him.

He rubbed his hands together with slow motions and seemed to consider her question before he could give her an answer. "I haven't been sleeping well since we left Klubridge," he said. "Apparently I've been sleepwalking, too."

"This is the first time you've done that?"

He gave a small shrug and smiled at her, but his eyes remained dull, almost haunted, dark skin betraying his weariness below them.

"Do you want me to get someone?" Nahk asked.

He shook his head. "No, I'll go back to my bedroom. I need to get warm first. I seem to have forgotten my shoes." He looked down again and chuckled. "And the rest of my clothes."

This was Akithar. This man, Caius Harrim, sitting in the dark and warming himself in a half stupor, was the man who had brought down the Empire in Klubridge. This was the wizard the songs heralded. Those damned annoying songs she'd suffered in every inn between Tresa and Stormbreak had celebrated this sad, tired man who wanted nothing more than to warm his hands and go back to bed. In that moment, Nahk's disdain for him melted.

"I heard you're going on Vaino's quest," she said. She hadn't meant to say it, but she couldn't stop herself.

"I don't know that I'd call it a quest," he said. "But yes, I've agreed to go."

"He's using you. He wants you to go because he thinks the Tamrat heir will have heard of you. He thinks you'll be able to convince him to come back with you."

"I know why he asked me to go," Akithar said. Or was it Caius? The more the man spoke, the more Nahk felt like the two might as well be separate men. "I'm supposed to be a symbol of the rebellion. Everyone's supposed to rally around me." He looked away from the oven and smirked at her. "Hurrah."

"You're not what I expected," she said.

"I don't think I'm what I expected," he said. "Not anymore."

He stopped talking at that, and his face fell with sadness. Nahk didn't question what he meant, because she could see the disappointment and defeat he carried within him. No matter how thoroughly he'd defeated the Kites and the Herons and whoever else had been in Klubridge that day, the man sitting before her was broken, perhaps himself defeated by what he'd experienced that day.

"Don't go," she said, too quickly to stop herself. "Vaino is wrong, and he's going to get you killed. You can't trust him."

"I don't trust anyone but the people I arrived here with," he said, but his voice was weak, and his eyes were uncertain now.

"How did Vaino win you over?" she asked.

He wiggled his fingers and folded them into fists once more before laying his hands on his lap. He looked down at them and said, "This is what I have to do to make it safe for us to leave this place. My friends don't deserve this. I don't even deserve this myself."

"Vaino is keeping you hostage?" She leaned forward, her brow creasing.

"No, not really. We might as well be hostages, though. There are bounties on all of us by now. Klubridge is gone, but we couldn't have gone back, even if it were still there. We all have to start new lives somewhere, and we can't do that as long as the Empire is hunting us. We need them to lose interest in us."

"And you think finding the scion will do that."

He raised his shoulders in a weak shrug. "I have no interest in fighting a war or in being any sort of hero or whatever they've tried to turn me into. I just want to live my life and help my friends find their new lives. If finding this Gressam fellow is what will make the Empire forget us, it's what I'll do."

"It won't work," Nahk said. "The Empire can seem single-minded, but it's not. They'll continue hunting you. They'll just add this poor sod to the roster alongside you. You can't trust Vaino," she said again, this time with what she hoped was more emphasis.

"I told you I don't trust him," Caius said. "Not like I trust my friends. This plan is sound, though, and it's the only thing I can do to help. I'm not going to just sit here in this keep for the rest of my life, and I'm not going to have that for my friends."

Nahk hesitated. Why did she care so much about whether this man went off on Vaino's fool mission? She didn't know him and had despised him by reputation prior to this encounter. But now she saw that the man and the legend were so dissimilar. This wasn't the wizard Akithar. That man lived only on the stage and in the hearts of the rebels. The real man was a frightened refugee who'd gotten caught in something he never meant to be involved with. All he wanted was to unwind himself and the ones he cared about from these strings the Empire had wound around him, and now Vaino was binding him even tighter.

"I was in Tresa not long ago," Nahk said. "I found a contract there. The Empire is sending Nightingales after Hyden Gressam. And they will find him. Or they'll find you and follow you to him. I don't know whether you're a mage or whether you're a liar. If you do have magic, even that might not be enough to stop them."

Caius dropped his head and laughed another quiet chuckle, and Nahk said, "I'm serious. These are assassins."

"I've heard of the Nightingales," he said. When he looked up again, the laughter was gone from his face. "Rumors of them, at least. Are you saying they're real?"

Nahk considered telling him about her childhood. About the training she'd endured, and about the many ways she'd learned to kill a person. About the shadowy murderers who had been the closest things she'd had to family, and about the arcane abilities that had been forced upon all of them. Instead, she simply said, "They're real, and they'll be coming for you."

He studied her face, and she let him. She watched him as his eyes searched for any sign of a lie. At last, he asked, "How good are they?"

"The best," she said, and she didn't look away from him. She knew he believed her now. "You can't go on this journey. They'll find you, or they'll find the scion. Neither of those ends well."

"They have to have weaknesses," he said. "How do we handle them if they do find us?"

She was certain then that he believed her, and he was still planning to go. She knew there was no dissuading him at that point, so she moved another step closer to him and squatted so that she could look directly into his eyes and ensure that there was no uncertainty about her next words. "There is no handling the Nightingales," she said. "When they find you, you're done."

CHAPTER 19

Samira watched Reykas, hardly believing he was still there, until she saw the slight movement of his chest beneath the white sheet. His breaths were shallow now, and they came farther apart than seemed possible, but they still came. And, as long as the breaths came, her friend still lived.

She touched the foot of the bed, her fingers cold on the frame, and she looked across to the empty bed where the other man, Pelo Foyen, had died. Lizzie had been so certain he'd known the secret to Reykas' illness and known how to cure it. But now he was gone, along with any secrets he might have held. Just as Reykas soon would go.

Samira closed her eyes against the tears that wanted to come. She pushed them back, and her eyes ached with the effort, but she wouldn't allow herself to cry here, standing over Reykas while he was still alive. He needed her strength and her reassurance. He didn't need her grief. That was for herself, for later.

She came around his bed and lowered herself onto the chair where Lizzie had kept her vigil for weeks while his health had declined. She'd been there night and day, for as long as the doctors would allow it, and she'd come back after Reykas had lost consciousness, and she'd kept watch over him in solitude. Samira placed her hand on the side of the bed, where she'd seen Lizzie place her own so many times, and she wanted to reach for

Reykas' hand, to feel some warmth, some other sign he was there. Her fingers twitched, but she didn't reach for him. This was for Lizzie, not for her. Lizzie was the one who should be with him, seeing him through his final days.

Samira looked away toward the wall, and it was harder to hold the tears now. She closed her hand on the sheet hanging off the edge of the bed, and the fabric crinkled in her fist. This was all so unfair. Reykas had been her friend since the day he and Lizzie had arrived in Klubridge. He'd shared her love of reading, and they'd made a game of sharing books with each other. Sometimes the writing was brilliant, and sometimes it was... less than brilliant. The most recent one from Pandridge had been the last book they'd shared. A laugh slipped past Samira's lips when she remembered how polite he'd been about hating that thing. And now there would be no more books to share, no more talks in the theater balcony, no more Reykas.

She released the sheet and covered her mouth with her hand, pressing it against her lips as though they had betrayed her by allowing her to laugh. But that was nonsense, and Reykas would have told her so. He had loved her, Caius, all of them. He'd been loyal first to Lizzie and then to all the rest of them. They were his family, and he was in that bed and unmoving now because of that loyalty and because of Samira's loyalty to him.

What if Lizzie was right? What if his disease had been engineered somehow by the Empire, and what if there was a cure waiting in Karsk? She longed for all of that to be true and for there to still be a chance to save her friend, but she pushed that hope down, shoving it away alongside the tears she refused to cry. Even if it all was true, Reykas hadn't wanted the cure. He'd said he was tired of fighting this, something he surely had never told Lizandra. He'd told her the price of the cure was too great, and he wouldn't survive the journey, anyway. Samira didn't know what the price might be, but the latter seemed to be true, at least. Samira doubted Reykas would even survive being taken outside this very room. He looked so small and frail now, his head barely pressing into the pillow.

Apak had told Samira she'd understand his rage once she'd experienced more loss, but she felt no rage just now. What she

LIZANDRA'S DEEPEST FEAR

felt was emptiness and doubt and sadness and regret. She'd never know whether she'd done the right thing by ensuring that Lizzie didn't go after that cure. It was what Reykas had wanted, so surely that made it the right thing, didn't it? But uncertainty remained, and Lizzie would never forgive her. No matter how all this turned out, things would never be the same between them again.

The door clicked and slid inward, and Samira flinched. She brought her hand up from her mouth and wiped at her eyes, swatting away the tears that had never come. She squinted through the darkness at the face that peered around the edge of the door. The relative brightness of the hallway beyond cast his face into shadow, but she would always recognize him, even in pitch blackness. "Caius?"

"How is he?" he asked as he pushed the door shut.

She looked at Reykas and didn't want to speak, sitting so close to him, but Reykas always appreciated the unvarnished truth. "I don't think he has much time," she said and smoothed her hand over the edge of the sheet where she'd crumpled it.

"Where's Lizzie?" he asked and glanced to the other side of the room, as if she might be hiding somewhere over there, among the shadows where the other man had died.

"I don't know. The last time we spoke, it… didn't end well. I haven't seen her since then."

Caius looked down at their friend and rested his hands on the frame at the foot of the bed, but he made no motion toward coming any closer. Samira watched him in the gloom and knew from the set of his shoulders and the angle of his head what he was thinking and, more importantly, what he was feeling. They'd known each other so long that they didn't need words.

"This isn't your fault," she said.

He sighed and shook his head. "I know, but it feels like it. We shouldn't even be here."

"If not here, then where? We couldn't have stayed in Klubridge, and this was the only other option."

"And we can't leave here in safety. Not as long as the Empire has bounties on us."

"Are you sure? Couldn't we go somewhere far away from

here? Far away from Klubridge? Maybe we could go back to the south. You liked it there."

"We were in Plier Gleau for too long. People there would still know us. They'd turn us in for a purse full of seri."

"We could change our appearances. You did it every night in Klubridge."

"Is that really the life you want? Disguising yourself every day and living in fear?" he asked.

"Of course not, but it has to be better than staying here. We can't live here forever."

He drummed his fingers against the bed frame a couple of times, light enough that it didn't make a sound. "Micah says it'll be safe to leave only after the Empire is no longer a threat."

"You mean until his rebellion defeats Peregrine."

"He says Peregrine doesn't exist."

It was the same conversation they'd had over and over again, but it still wasn't clear where Caius' beliefs fell. Either the High Lord was real, or he wasn't. Whatever the truth was, there was a very real Empire standing between them and freedom. "Do you think this rebellion stands a chance?"

"At defeating the Empire?" Caius shook his head again and huffed a low laugh. "Not a chance."

"So, what, then? Do you have a plan?"

"I always have a plan," he said, and it was true. "I can't swear it's a good one, though."

"Tell me," Samira said.

Caius left the end of the bed then and came around the side. He squatted in front of her chair and leaned his back against the hard wall. The flickering light of the room's solitary candle finally lit his face, and Samira wanted to reach out, to place a hand on his shoulder, but she held back. In the candlelight his skin was sallow, his eyes puffy, and his jaw speckled with stubble. He looked worse, even, than when she had seen him the day before. He still wasn't sleeping properly. How much longer could that continue?

"You know that Vaino wants me to go south with Dekan Hama and his people."

"To find the Tamrat heir."

He turned his eyes toward hers and nodded. "Micah thinks I'd present a more compelling argument for this man to come back to Stormbreak than they would. Hama has insisted on going, but Micah wants me to lead the expedition."

Caius was in no condition to lead any sort of expedition, much less with only fanatical strangers to accompany him. But she wouldn't say that. She'd tried talking with him about whatever was happening to him, and every time it had left him seeming more depressed than before. Instead, she said, "I know you want to go. What's your angle in this?"

He rolled his neck to the right and stretched before answering. "The Empire has sent assassins after the scion. Nightingales."

"Those are real?" She was less surprised than she might have been before coming to Stormbreak. The Nightingales were folk legends, tales to scare children into behaving. They didn't exist any more than the Aescalan were supposed to have existed. And now, here they were in a world where both seemed to have materialized from the tales at once.

"They're real," he said. "And it sounds like they're every bit as dangerous as they're supposed to be."

"You can't go, then!" she said, sitting straighter in the chair. "You can't put yourself in that kind of danger for this."

"We need Hyden Gressam," he said. "We need to get him and bring him back, and we need for the Empire to know we got him."

Samira leaned forward, her elbows on her thighs. "You think the Empire wants him more than he wants us."

"It seems like a safe bet. They want to punish us for what happened in Klubridge, but they have to know I'm no real threat to anything. Not like the last remaining heir to the dynasty the Empire upended. He's a real and true symbol of something existing beyond the Empire, and they have to know that. If they know the rebellion has him, they'll put every resource into recovering him."

Samira frowned. "You're suggesting we sacrifice this man to the Empire. He could be an innocent in all this. That's not our way, Caius."

"The Empire is already on his trail. He's already in this," Caius said. "If we don't find him, the Nightingales will."

She quirked an eyebrow at him. "So trading our fate for his is altruistic now?"

"It's practical. He might not want to be a part of this any more than we do, but he's already stuck in it just like we are. Finding him before the Empire does will help us, but it'll also save his life."

"Having the Empire go after him doesn't mean they'll forget about us," Samira said. "The Empire has enough resources to go around." But there was a kind of logic to what he was saying. The Great Akithar had stood against the Kites and Herons in Klubridge, and his was the name on the tongues of the bards and the discontented populace. That kind of fame didn't last, as long as something bigger eclipsed it. And, if everything she'd learned since coming to Stormbreak was true, this Gressam was a compelling candidate for distracting the people of Teshovar.

"It's all we have," Caius said, his voice lower now.

Samira spoke quickly, hoping to pull him back up before he sank again. "I think you could be right. This is an awful plan and a dangerous plan, but I think it could work." And it really could. There were so many ways it could go wrong, but, as Caius had said, it was all they had. Would it be enough to pull the bounties off their heads? Enough to refocus Teshovar on a new figurehead for the rebellion? Perhaps.

"I'm going with you," she said, before she'd even considered it and talked herself out of it.

"This is going to be dangerous," Caius said. "You were right about that."

"That's why I'm going with you. The Nightingales are bad enough, but I don't trust the Aescalan, either. I'm not letting you go off on your own with Dekan Hama." She didn't have to add "not in the condition you're in" and hoped he wouldn't detect the unsaid worry in her tone.

Caius' eyes opened wider. "You think Hama plans to betray Vaino."

Samira stared back at him, and that look was enough of an answer.

"I don't want you risking your life for this," he said. "It might not even work."

"How many times have we been in that situation together? Sometimes it works, and sometimes it doesn't. The important thing is that we'll be watching out for each other, just like always."

"Samira—"

"If you're going, I'm going. There's no changing my mind," she said. Worry and doubt wanted to gnaw at the back of her mind, but she kept them at bay for at least long enough to press the matter. And, behind that fear, she felt something else that buoyed her. Was it hope? Could this thing really work? At the very least, it would get them away from the pointless bickering and scheming that had become a constant in that castle.

Caius' eyes reflected the flame as he looked at her, and she knew he was trying to decide whether it was worth arguing with her. She knew he'd see that having her along made more sense than leaving her behind, and he finally nodded. "If you're sure."

"How soon do we leave?"

"Soon," he said. "Within the next few days."

She did put her hand on his shoulder, then, and she rose from the chair, her joints sore from the cold. "There's something I need to do before we go."

The library at Stormbreak was a far cry from the one Samira was used to visiting in Klubridge. Where the one at the university had been a soaring monument to education and literacy and creativity, this one was a single, long room with a low ceiling that spanned the entire eastern side of the keep's third floor. Windows in the outer wall provided enough light for navigating the stacks but not enough for reading, so a collection of small lanterns sat on a wooden shelf near each of the two entrances.

Samira didn't plan to read that day and left the lanterns where they sat. Instead, she trailed her fingers along the spines of the books on the middle shelf to her left and rounded the corner to see a long and narrow path before her. Bookcases lined both sides of the aisle, and she could tell at a glance that the selection was a mere fraction of what she'd been used to seeing in Klubridge. The tomes here were old, many of them moldy, and even more of them with pages spilling out from broken spines that hadn't been mended. There was no telling how long these books had sat here. Many of them looked like remnants of the old Imperial guard that first built the castle at Crowspire and then abandoned it when the mountaintop fell.

Her eyes roamed along the volumes as she made slow progress through the room. She was interested in the collection, but a larger part of her wanted to forestall the conversation she knew waited at the end of the walk. That part of her turned the titles and authors' names into a blur of gilded text that meant nothing, even though she still guided her gaze along them. The only name that mattered was the one she spoke when she passed the last bookcase before encountering two rows of tables in the middle of the room.

"Aquin."

Her head was down, her black hair swept to one side so that it wouldn't block the lamplight as she read. Samira saw she'd been immersed in some ancient and massive book, but she glanced up at the sound of her name. The light caught her eyes, and their pale blue stole Samira's breath, just as it had done when they'd first met. It seemed like forever ago, but it also seemed like less than a week. Aquin's eyebrows raised as she looked up, but they lowered again, surprise giving way to annoyance, and Samira felt the disappointment gather at the center of her chest. What had she expected?

"I asked you for time," Aquin said. She dragged her fingers back along her temple, pulling a loose strand of hair behind her ear.

"I've tried to give it to you," Samira said. "I didn't want to bother you. I didn't want to come to you before you were ready."

"And yet you did."

Aquin had looked down at the text again, but then she looked up and met Samira's eyes. The gaze wasn't cold, exactly, but it wasn't warm, either. It wasn't the kind of look they'd shared for those brief couple of weeks in Klubridge before everything went wrong.

"I had to find you. Micah Vaino has asked Caius to go on a mission for him."

"A mission?" Aquin's eyes narrowed, and she folded her hands on top of the open book.

"He's going to be traveling south with the… with some of the other rebels." Had Aquin met the Aescalan? Did she even know about them? Best to keep things simple for now. No sense complicating an already tense conversation by telling her a mythological race was real and part of this rebellion. "I'm going with him. I'd like for you to come with us." She hesitated. "If you would."

"This is something to help the rebellion," Aquin said. It came out flat, not exactly a question.

"It is. We're going to find someone and bring them back here. It's someone who could be more interesting to the Empire than we are. It could be our way out of this predicament—out of this place. And it would help the rebels."

Aquin pushed the book away from her, just far enough that she could prop her elbows on the table, and she said, "Samira, you're not a rebel. I'm not a rebel. We have no part in this."

"We do now," Samira said. "We're in it, whether we like it or not."

"You, maybe. Not me."

"You mean you don't have to be a part of it because—"

"Because I'm not a mage." Aquin winced after she'd said it, and Samira knew the other woman regretted her words as soon as she'd spoken them, but there they were, said and lingering in the air between them.

Samira opened her mouth with a retort but closed it again. That would do no good. Instead, she said, "The Empire wants you now, too, regardless. They know you're with us, and there's probably even a bounty on your head. You can't leave here any more easily than the rest of us can."

"And if I could, where would I go? Not Klubridge."

Heat flared on the back of Samira's neck, and she gripped the back of the chair in front of her. "We all lost Klubridge, Aquin."

"And so many besides us. How many people died because you and Caius and Apak and the rest of you lived there? How many, because you had to have the fame and the money and that theater? Because you couldn't go somewhere safe, somewhere you wouldn't hurt anyone."

"That's not fair," Samira said. "You know that's not fair. I came back for you, and I took you out of that interrogation room myself."

Aquin's eyes narrowed, and she slid her chair back. "I wouldn't have been there if they hadn't been looking for you. Do you know how long you left me there? Do you know what that Kite did to me? You haven't even asked."

"I didn't think you wanted to talk about it! Not with me, at least."

"I didn't," Aquin said, her voice hard now. This wasn't going at all the way it was supposed to. For the second time in as many days, Samira had tried to talk with a friend and ended up in a fight. It was this place. This rebellion. It twisted everything, made everyone quick to anger.

Samira tried to hold Aquin's eyes but finally dropped her own gaze to the table. There were illustrations in the book she'd been reading. They were upside down from where Samira stood, but she could make out what looked like leaves and a flower in the dim light. "I miss you," she said. "I'm sorry for what happened, but I can't change any of that. I can only try to do things right in the future. And I want to start by spending time with you. I'd like you to come with us."

"You want me on this journey for the rebellion. You want me tagging along with you and Caius, when I can hardly even look at you?" Aquin shoved the chair back again and stood. "I told you I need time, not to go on some fool's errand with you."

"It's to help the rebellion—"

"The rebellion can burn, for all I care," Aquin said. "I told you I have no part in it, and I want no part in it."

"This is the only way—"

"The only way to defeat the High Lord? The only way to bring down the Empire?" She snorted and slammed the book shut. "These people can't even organize themselves, much less

LIZANDRA'S DEEPEST FEAR

overthrow a government. Can't you see they're doomed? And now I'm a part of it, just like I fell into the midst of the same thing in Klubridge. None of this is my fight, Samira. I was happy. I had a life."

"We have to work with what's left," Samira said. "It's not how we want things to be. None of us should be here, but this is what it's all come to. And now we have to find the best way back to our lives. Caius thinks this mission is the way to do that, and I agree with him."

"There's a bleeding surprise," Aquin said. "When has he had a thought you haven't agreed with?"

"That's not fair," Samira said again.

"I think it's at least as fair as you knowing me for two weeks before destroying my entire life." Aquin's voice had risen but stopped at that, her lower lip trembling, and her eyes dropping. "I'm sorry. I didn't mean that."

"You meant it," Samira said. "And I can't even say you're wrong. If we hadn't met, you wouldn't be here now. You wouldn't have gotten wrapped up in all the business with Kites, and I wouldn't have had to rescue you and drag you onto that ship. But if you'd stayed, you'd have been there when the city…" She couldn't finish. Knowing Klubridge had fallen was hard enough. Thinking about Aquin remaining there and dying in the attack made it even worse.

Aquin pinched the bridge of her nose and closed her eyes for a long moment. When she spoke again, her tone was softer than before. "I know you didn't mean for any of this to happen. And, despite all this, I don't regret knowing you. I don't hate you, Samira." She opened her eyes and looked around the room. "What I hate is this. This place. These people. This situation. We'd all be better off if the Empire had just come here and destroyed this place like it did to Klubridge. We'd have an end to it, at least, and Teshovar could go back to the way it's always been. There's no fighting them and winning. You have to know that. We just endure it, and we survive. Like you did with Caius for so long, before you even knew me."

"You don't hate me," Samira said, her voice barely more than a whisper.

"What? Of course I don't hate you. How many times do I have to tell you that? I care about you. But I can't think about that or doing anything constructive with that as long as we're here. As long as this is our life."

Samira swallowed hard before she could continue. "That's what we're trying to fix. If we go on this journey and bring this man back to Stormbreak, that could divert the Empire's focus from us. That could be the thing we need, if we're ever going to have normal lives again."

Aquin's fingertips rested on the closed cover of the book as she looked at Samira across the table. She took one breath and then another before she said, "I think that journey could be a good idea."

Samira's eyes widened. "You do?"

"I think you should go with him, and you should do what you need to do. Get it finished, and be done with it."

"But you won't come with us," Samira said.

"I'm not going. I still need time, and I'm not a part of this. No matter what you say, I'm not. You think appeasing the rebels is our way out of this. I say we won't be clear of this mess until the rebellion is destroyed. And we both know that's going to happen, sooner or later. Once the rebels are gone, the Empire will lose interest in the Great Akithar. There'll be nothing for him to inspire. It'll all be done, and we can go back to living."

"That's not—"

"It is. That's the way it is, Samira." Aquin reached a hand halfway across the table, and Samira moved to take it, but then Aquin pulled back. She looked up from where they'd nearly touched, and her eyes were sad. "Be careful," she said, and she was gone, retreating down the aisle and toward the opposite door.

Samira watched her go and said nothing. There was nothing she could say. Aquin was staying at Stormbreak, but at least she didn't hate Samira. That had to count for something.

"Let her go."

Samira flinched and half turned to see the shorter woman standing behind her in the gloom of the darkened stacks. "Magra. How long were you there?"

LIZANDRA'S DEEPEST FEAR

"Long enough. She'll come around on her own, or she won't. You'll do no good forcing the issue."

Magra pressed her lips together and nodded her head, and Samira knew she was right. There was nothing more to be done, for now. "You heard all of that?"

Magra tilted her head toward her right shoulder, and she looked for all the world like an unusually large owl. "Go and do what you need to do. The space will help. I'll watch after her while you're gone."

"Watch after her?"

"Someone's got to make sure she doesn't burn the whole blasted place down herself."

CHAPTER 20

"This is most irregular." The woman peered over her glasses.

"The doctor said there's nothing more that can be done for him," Lizandra said and affected her most sympathetic expression. She knew she already looked a disaster after the past weeks of sleeplessness and stress, but a little extra sadness around the eyes and a little droop at the corners of the mouth couldn't hurt. "I just want to have him with me so I can watch over him. So I can make him comfortable and be with him when..." She let her voice trail off, the tragedy itself unsaid. It was easier to talk about these things now. It was easier to think them now that she knew she'd make sure it didn't come to pass. Reykas was going to live, as long as she could pull this off.

"But where would you even take him?" The woman was the administrator at the infirmary, the organizational side of the operation, removed from the doctors and concerned only with making sure she didn't misplace any patients or medications. It had taken half a day of asking and pressing before Lizandra finally found herself seated across the desk from this woman whose name she still didn't even know. All the nurses she'd spoken with just called her "the administrator" and that's how Lizandra thought of her now. Not as a person who might complicate this project, but as an obstacle she had to overcome.

"I've moved to new quarters," Lizandra said. "I spoke with the castellan yesterday, and he was able to find a larger room where we could stay. There's room for the special bed, and it's just off the courtyard." And it was true. She'd found the man in charge of managing the castle and all its rooms, and he'd turned out to be an older, portly fellow with white whiskers that fluttered under his nose while the overhead shield was down and the cold breeze blew through Stormbreak. He'd been happy to accommodate her when she'd explained her situation and asked that she be moved to a larger and more accessible room. He'd been apologetic that the new room would not be as well appointed as the previous one, but she'd assured him it was no trouble, and that was that.

"I know the layout of the keep," the administrator said, her voice sharp, and her eyes sharper. Her dark hair was pulled back from her face and secured in a bun so severely tight that she nearly looked bald from the front. "How would you care for him?"

"He's still taking water when we give it to him," Lizandra said.

"And his cleaning? His toilet?"

"I can take care of him," Lizandra insisted. And she was sure she could do all those things, if she had any intention of actually staying in the castle with Reykas. She hadn't fully worked out the details of how she'd keep Reykas clean and content on the road, but that was a problem for another day. Being pampered in this castle would do him no good if it only led to him having a clean corpse. She would see to it that he lived, even if it caused both of them a bit of discomfort along the way.

The administrator watched her with doubtful eyes, still looking over the rim of her spectacles, and for a devastating moment, Lizandra thought it would end there. This woman had the power to keep Reykas in his hospital room, locked away from any chance of getting real help, and a word from her would kill Lizandra's hope as surely as it would kill Reykas. But, after an interminable pause, the administrator finally sighed and rested her hands on the desk. "I'll have someone help you move him. Is that all?"

And, just like that, it was done. A young man arrived moments later, bundled in a brown coat that looked like it had been made for someone twice his size. He spoke little and kept his eyes down as he loaded Reykas from the bed onto a cart like the one they'd used to bring him into the hospital. It was another bumpy trip, but this one was less urgent than the first one. For all these people knew, there now was no rush for Reykas at all.

Lizandra pulled her coat tight around her with a fabric belt she'd found discarded in the keep's laundry, and she kept a hand on the rail at the side of the cart as the young man rolled Reykas out of the room where he'd slept for the past weeks and where Pelo Foyen had died after denying himself the salvation Lizandra would not deny to Reykas. A nurse in the front room pulled the hospital doors open wide enough for the cart to pass through, and then they were out of that sterile and constrictive place, out into the cold whiteness. The shield was up just then, so no snowflakes fell, but Lizandra could see them speckling the invisible dome above them.

She looked down from where the snow seemed to settle in mid-air and scanned the paths and doorways around them as the cart's wheels crunched through the icy slush. Rebels were milling about, but she recognized none of the faces. What would Caius say if he saw them just now? Or Samira? And what would she say to Samira, for that matter? They hadn't parted on friendly terms, but Lizandra had tried to push that conflict out of her mind. Samira thought she was doing the right thing, that she knew what Reykas would really want. Even though she'd been his friend ever since he'd arrived in Klubridge with Lizandra, Samira didn't know him as well as Lizandra did. She couldn't know him that well. No one but Lizandra could. And she knew he wanted to live, his stubborn excuses for avoiding this cure be damned.

Still, it was best to avoid any familiar faces for now. Best to avoid all faces, in fact. Would Micah Vaino even allow her to leave Stormbreak? As far as he knew, she might be a spy, heading straight to the Imperials to inform on him and all the rest of them for a bit of seri. She'd be able to lead the Kites or

LIZANDRA'S DEEPEST FEAR

worse straight back to Stormbreak, the castle they would have known as Crowspire. She'd never do that in a million years, but Vaino didn't know her, and she couldn't blame him for expecting the worst, just like she couldn't blame Samira for doing what she thought was best for Reykas. Neither of them truly knew Reykas, and neither of them truly knew her.

The journey would be a tough one down through the mountains with snow and ice underfoot, and having Reykas unconscious for the whole trip would complicate matters further. But Karsk wasn't that far away, if she really thought about it. Not as far as they'd come from the docks after Drass let them off the ship. She could make the trip, locate the cure, and get Reykas back to Stormbreak before any of the rebels would even know she'd gone.

The cart bumped up and over a row of low paving stones at the end of the path, and they were into the keep itself. "Our room is just ahead, on the left," Lizandra said, pointing. The young man nodded, still not quite looking at her and still not speaking. She kept her right hand on the edge of the cart. It felt good to have her fingers wrapped around the metal rail, ready to hold the cart steady, even if it wasn't needed. She looked at Reykas, his eyes closed and his face still and oblivious to everything happening around him.

Doubt sparked in her mind for a horrible instant. Would he even survive the night, much less a trip all the way out of the keep and through the wilderness? He looked so fragile now, so ready to let go. But no, he would hold on. She'd make sure he did, and they'd make the trip together. The risk of taking him away from Stormbreak was no risk at all, in truth. Staying there was the way to nothing but a certain death. Taking him to Karsk was the only chance he'd have at living. If he died along the way, at least she'd have tried. At least they would have tried, and they'd be together, just like they would be if they stayed in the relative safety of the castle.

Taking the journey was worth the risk, but she had to move soon. Every day she lingered in worry and indecision was a day closer to the unthinkable. She had to get him out of the castle and south to Karsk as soon as possible.

In the corridor next to the courtyard now, Lizandra looked toward the keep's exit at the opposite end. There was a gate in the way, and she remembered the covered bridge they had crossed when they'd arrived at Stormbreak. It was likely to be guarded, and there were attendants around to take care of the horses and carriages when they'd first gotten there. And, beyond that bridge, there was the invisible dome of magic that kept everyone inside just as much as it kept everyone else out.

She'd need a way to transport Reykas, too. They couldn't make the journey on foot, even if Reykas had been in full health. The season had turned, and the bitter cold would get them before they'd made it halfway down the hillside. She needed a horse and a cart, at the very least. Supplies to see them through the trip would help as well, but the cart for Reykas and the horse to pull them were essential.

A horse, a cart, and a way through all the barriers between Stormbreak and the outside world. Lizandra squinted at the gate at the end of the walkway one more time as she pushed open the door to her new quarters. She needed all that, and she needed it in secret and as quickly as she could get it. It was a tall order, but Lizandra knew where she had to go next.

∽

It was nearing lunchtime when Lizandra sat on the edge of a short wall across the walkway from the workshop and the supply depot, but she wasn't hungry. She'd missed plenty of meals since arriving at Stormbreak, but this was the first time it was nerves and excitement rather than grief and worry that suppressed her appetite.

She could see Apak through the open doors to the workshop, but she had no idea what he was doing. He was engrossed in his work, whatever it was, and he didn't spare a glance outside to spot her. That was good. She wanted to be unseen that day. Unseen until she'd finished everything she was setting out to do and had returned to this place with Reykas cured and safe.

Just down from the workshop was the front of the supply depot, and that's where she focused her attention. The barn doors stood open, slid back on their tracks, and two big men were pulling a wooden cart out from the building when she arrived. The men wore identical brown coats that reminded her of the one the attendant had worn while helping her move Reykas that morning, and she wondered whether someone in the castle might sew the things, turning out garment after garment for the rebels. The men strained with the weight of the cart, but they managed to get it rolling and turned it to the right, headed away from where Lizandra sat. After they'd turned, she could see the cargo in the back. There were a couple of wooden barrels, several crates, and a few lumpy gray sacks, all bundled together.

Where might that delivery be headed? She'd seen similar loads coming into the keep and disappearing into the supply entrance for distribution, but she'd never considered what happened with all those goods after they'd come in, or even where they might have been coming from. It made sense that an operation as large as the rebellion needed a steady flow of food, weapons, and other essentials, but until that moment Lizandra had considered only the supplies it took to keep Stormbreak running. That outbound load must have been headed for another hideout somewhere else in Teshovar. The Stormbreak Sanctuary was the rebellion's central headquarters, but how many other locations did they maintain? Were they all in abandoned Imperial fortresses? Unlikely. There just as easily could have been a rebellious village somewhere down south that wanted to throw off the Imperial leash, and they survived through the assistance of this supply depot far in the north.

Someone else moved in the supply doorway, and Lizandra slid forward on the wall, her shoulders suddenly tense. But no, it was Leyna Neron, that day wearing an olive smock Lizandra had seen her wearing a few times before. It hung down to her knees and was sleeveless, and beneath it showed the straps of the light brown coveralls the girl usually wore when she was working. Spots and streaks stained the smock, and Leyna wiped her hands down the sides of it just then. She stepped outside the doorway and looked down the path, in the direction the cart had gone. She had pulled her frizzy hair back and bound it so that it would stay out of her face, but it jutted out from the back of her head like a wild brown shrubbery.

Lizandra waited for the girl to glance her way and spot her, but Leyna called something about food back into the depot before she walked into the pathway and away from Lizandra. The kitchens were in that direction. She was going to eat, then, or at least to get food and bring it back. That should keep her away for long enough. Just to be sure, Lizandra waited until Leyna disappeared around the corner and then gave her another count of twenty. Finally satisfied, Lizandra stood and brushed the snow off her seat before she headed for the supply entrance.

It was midday, but the workshop where Apak toiled was mostly dark when she glanced inside as she passed. There were a couple of flickering lanterns far within, but it was too dim for her to see more than Apak's hunched shoulders moving over something he'd laid out on the table in front of him. In contrast, the light from the supply room shone brightly enough that Lizandra had to squint as she approached it. She'd been past plenty of times, but this was the first time she'd come in, and she paused next to the doorway, her hand resting on the edge of one of the open barn doors.

Shelves lined the walls inside, most of them piled full with parcels of all sizes and shapes. Five long tables ran parallel to each other down the width of the room, each of them loaded with bags and packages and boxes as well. A stack of papers sat on the nearest corner, and Lizandra picked up the top sheet. A schedule of departures and arrivals, and below that was another paper, this one listing who was traveling where and with what cargo. This was the heart of the rebellion, where all the small but essential decisions happened that made it possible for Vaino and Klavan and all the others to have their larger squabbles and to play at being revolutionaries.

The light came from lanterns that hung from the ceiling at even intervals, all of them working together to banish any sign of shadows from the room. This was a clean space, as tidy and organized as she'd seen, despite the abundance of supplies. She suspected a large part of that tidiness was thanks to the young man leaning over a broom between the last two tables on the right. He moved with a jerky motion, pulling the broomstick toward him, shuffling one leg forward, and then swinging the other to follow.

Lizandra slipped into the room and waited just inside the entrance. Time was short, but she didn't want to spook Oreth while he was at work. After a moment, he finished sweeping that row and turned at the head of the table, the broom in one hand and a rag in the other. His eyes caught hers, and he froze in place, an uncertain smile tugging at his mouth.

"Lizzie. Hi."

"Hi," she said and came farther into the room. "I hope I'm not bothering you."

"No," he said. He tossed the rag on the edge of the nearest shelf and propped the broom next to it. He turned back to her and came around the table, his injured leg stiff in a metal brace contraption.

"That's new," Lizandra said and immediately regretted it.

Oreth's quick smile reassured her she hadn't misspoken. "Not so new. Leyna made it for me shortly after I started helping her with the supplies. You just haven't been around."

"You've been spending a lot of time with her," Lizandra said and grinned.

Oreth gave her a shy smile and ducked his head, his hand coming up to ruffle the back of his red hair. It had grown longer than she was used to seeing it, and it suited him. When he looked up, his smile faltered, and he asked, "How's Reykas?"

Lizandra had planned on small talk. She'd intended to begin more casually, but there it was, with Oreth getting straight to the point of why she was there. "He's not well," she said.

Oreth limped to the end of the table nearest her and leaned against it, resting his weight on his strong leg. "I heard he's been sleeping."

She tilted her head and studied the bag on the tabletop next to her. It was coarse and woven, and someone had stenciled the word "NUTS" on it in black ink. She drew a finger down the side of the bag, feeling the rough texture, before she said, "He's not going to wake up as long as he has this illness." She glanced up at him, and he was looking down, his brows drawn together.

Back in Klubridge, Oreth had seemed much younger than he did now. In reality, he was only about a year younger than Lizandra was, but he'd always seemed more like a boy. Whether it had been his accident in the Downsteps or his time spent at Stormbreak, something had put new lines on his face and an awareness in his gaze that hadn't been there before.

"Is there anything they can do for him here?" Oreth asked, still not meeting Lizandra's eyes. In the past, it had been bashfulness that had kept his gaze averted, but now she could tell it was unease. He was as worried about upsetting her with talk about Reykas as she'd been worried about mentioning Oreth's leg. The two of them were dancing around each other like they'd never done before coming here.

"Nothing at Stormbreak," Lizandra said. "Have you talked with Samira? Did she tell you about Karsk?"

Oreth looked up at that, and Lizandra saw confusion in his eyes this time. He knew nothing about what had been happening since their arrival. "Karsk? What about it?"

"There was a man named Pelo Foyen. He was in the infirmary when we brought Reykas there. They shared a room, and they also shared a sickness."

"He has the same thing as Reykas?" Oreth's eyes were wide then with interest. All of them had speculated about what made Reykas sick, but none of them had seen anything like it before.

Lizandra nodded. "He said it's a disease the Empire created to kill mages. He called it a virus. It's supposed to spread among us, but it wasn't as effective as they'd hoped."

"But Reykas got it. And the other man. What else does he know about it?"

"Nothing now," she said. "Foyen is dead. He died in the infirmary."

"Oh." His eyes fell again, and his shoulders drooped. But he looked back up again and asked, "But what does that have to do with Karsk?"

"Before he died, Foyen said he knew about a cure for the disease. He said there's someone in Karsk who has the remedy."

Oreth's mouth opened and closed, and a hint of a smile played across his face. He looked as if he thought Lizandra might be making a joke and didn't know whether he should laugh to be polite. "There's a cure?"

"According to him. He said he knew someone else it worked on."

"Why didn't he get it himself?"

She shook her head. "That's a long story. Suffice to say that he wasn't able to get it, and he died. I don't want that to happen to Reykas."

"Of course not!" Oreth was smiling now, all uncertainty gone. "This is great news! I mean, if it's true. But it sounds like you trusted this man."

"I had no reason not to. I believe him. I believe there's a cure for Reykas, and it's waiting in Karsk."

Oreth waited for her to say more, but she held her tongue. It was better to let him work it out than for her to tell him herself. After a few seconds, his smile faltered. "They won't let you go after it," he said. "The rebels."

"I haven't asked," she said. "But no, I don't think Micah Vaino would let us go. We know too much about the rebellion, and it would be too big a risk to let us travel that far south."

"But it's so close! Karsk is barely even in Teshovar, it's so far north. It might as well be a part of these same mountains."

Lizandra gave a half shrug. "It might as well be in Meskia, for all the good that does us. If we mention this to anyone, they're likely to lock us up so we won't be at risk of leaving."

"That's not right," he said, frowning now. He moved to the shelves next to Lizandra, his foot sliding along behind him. "You have to do something."

"I want to, but I can't do it alone," she said, and she paused, waiting again for Oreth to catch up.

It didn't take long for him to cast her a sidelong glance. "You want me to help you."

She nodded, and her heart echoed in her ears. She had been more optimistic than worried until that moment, but this was the exchange that mattered. Just like the administrator could have put an end to the plans with a simple shake of her head, Oreth could dash all her hopes now. She had hung all her hopes on his being amenable to helping her, but doubt surged in her chest, and she held her breath as she watched him working it through.

"What do you need from me?" he asked.

"A cart for carrying Reykas and a horse to pull it," she said. "And some supplies to see us through to Karsk and back. Food, blankets, whatever you could spare. But it would have to be in secret."

Oreth's eyes darted to the side and then back to hers. He looked past her, toward the open door, and whispered. "I could get in trouble for that. Serious trouble."

"I know I'm asking a lot," she said. "I'm sorry." And she meant it. This was her task to do, her love to save, and if there had been any way she could do all of it on her own, she'd have done it. But she needed help, and they both knew it.

"They trust me here," he said, his voice still low. His eyes moved to the entrance again, and she knew he was watching for Leyna. "I finally have a place here. A real place."

"You had a place in Klubridge," she said. "You've always been one of us."

He barely shook his head, moving it just enough for Lizandra to see the regret in his eyes. "I know how it was there. I know how everybody saw me. How you saw me."

"Oreth! You're my friend. I've never thought badly of you."

"Not badly, but like I was a child. Like you needed to humor me." He held up a hand before she could protest again. "It's okay. I understand it. I know what I was like there, too. But things are different here. I'm not just the assistant. Not just the jokester."

The look he gave Lizandra was a plea, then. His eyes begged her not to ask him to risk what he'd built at Stormbreak, not to endanger the respect he'd earned on his own there. Not to threaten whatever was developing between him and Leyna. But, at the same time, those eyes also told her he'd agree to help her if she asked him just one more time.

Guilt tugged at Lizandra, urging her to find another way. Surely there was something else she could do that wouldn't involve Oreth. But no. Reykas was dying, and her time and options were limited. Before she could talk herself into backing down, she said, "This is the only chance Reykas has. If you help me and I'm caught, I'll deny that you had anything to do with this. I took everything myself, and I'm the one to blame."

She watched his eyes then, and she saw the worry melt into disappointment and then resignation. He sighed and looked to the door once more. "We have to do it at night, between guard shifts. And it'll have to be in between the mages' shifts. We have their schedule here, so I can see when the shield will be down and when no lookouts will see you leave."

Lizandra's heart thudded again, and she asked, "How soon can we go?"

"You just changed rooms. I saw the request come through. I'll tell everybody you're staying in there with Reykas and don't want to be disturbed. Stay there with him tonight, and I'll come find you."

"We're going tonight?"

"You're going tonight," he said, and the correction in his voice was clear.

"I didn't mean—"

"Tell no one about this," he said, his voice even lower now. He looked back toward the doorway one more time. "No one."

CHAPTER 21

"I suppose you're not here to hire me after all," Ergo Drass said.

The old sailor was much as Quentyn Wickes had imagined him, stout and gray-haired, his skin tanned and creased from decades of sea and the sun. Men who'd been on the ocean for that long often looked older than their years, but Drass had to be at least sixty, if he'd been at the job for as long as rumors told it. The locals had also said Drass rarely went without his old and battered naval jacket, but he was without it that day. Instead, the old man wore a plain beige shirt, stained with sweat around the neck and under the arms, tucked into the waist of similarly ordinary brown trousers.

"What makes you say that?" Wickes asked, standing as Drass came through the door. They were in a back room at a local tavern, and Wickes had secured their privacy with a few coins to the proprietor. It was a small room with barely space for the square table and the four chairs around it, but it was perfect for Wickes' purposes.

Drass glanced over his shoulder, but Jalla was there now, blocking the way behind him. The old captain sniffed and came the rest of the way into the room. "I know who you are, Quentyn Wickes. You're not the sort to hire me."

Wickes gestured to the chair across the table. "I apologize for the deception. Have a seat, Captain."

Drass took his time in coming to the chair and tossed his thumb toward the far corner, where Colm lurked in the shadows. "Doesn't your friend want a seat?"

"He's my attendant," Wickes said. "He's fine where he is."

Drass chuckled at that and waved in Jalla's general direction. "And that brute at the door's mine." He shook his head and finally lowered himself into the seat. His legs bent with effort, but at last he settled onto the chair and clasped his hands together on the table.

Wickes returned to his own seat and said, "You can close the door now."

Jalla snorted and said, "The door stays open." He hadn't enjoyed being left out of what had happened in the village, and he was determined to hear everything that transpired from that point forward. Wickes sighed and started to speak, but Drass was quicker.

"That deal with the Empire's going well, I take it?" His tone was dry, but Drass' gray eyes sparkled. He looked like he was enjoying this encounter more than Wickes was.

"That's done now," Wickes said.

Drass pursed his lips and nodded back toward the door. "Nobody told the Imperials, it seems."

"This is something different." The old sailor's easy manner put Wickes off balance. Wickes was the one in control here. He was the one who had called the meeting and who would ask the questions. With no preamble, he went straight for it: "Where is the Stormbreak Sanctuary?"

Drass' forehead crinkled when his eyebrows went up, and he had the nerve to laugh. Not a chuckle, but a great belly laugh that shook his cheeks and echoed in the small room. Jalla scowled in the doorway and glared at Wickes. This would be going better without that audience. It would be going better without the promise to Weylis, too.

"I know you know where it is," Wickes said. "Tell me, and we can all walk away from here in good health."

"I have no bloody idea where it is," Drass said. "You might as well ask me where Khealdir keeps his quiver."

"It'll do you no good to deny it, Drass. We know you smuggle for the rebels. We've ignored it for a long time, but we're not ignoring it today."

"'We,' you say. Are you an Imperial, Quentyn? I wasn't aware you'd signed up."

"You know why I'm here," Wickes said.

"You're here because you're still on Mediean's leash. He's the one leading you around these days, isn't he?"

"This has nothing to do with him." Wickes shouldn't have responded to that jibe at all, but something about this man was able to get under his skin. He wasn't afraid of Ergo Drass. The old man certainly had no leverage over Wickes, so what was it about him that was so unsettling? Wickes studied the old man's face, his rough hands, his belly that rounded the front of his shirt, and he saw what it was.

Drass was a man of the sea, just like Wickes was. But, where Wickes had chosen piracy and cowardice, Drass had sided against the Empire. He'd made a career of legitimate sailing, backed by smuggling for the rebels. He was doing what he could to oppose the very people Wickes himself should have been against from the start. Drass was who Wickes could have been and should have been, if he hadn't made every wrong decision and picked every wrong choice that had been laid before him.

And Wickes saw in Drass' eyes that the old man saw the same thing in Wickes, just in reverse. If Drass had lacked a backbone and if he'd valued his own skin more than he'd valued his honor and his principles, he'd have ended up in a situation very like the one where Wickes found himself. There was an appraisal in Drass' expression, and then there was something that had to be pity. Drass looked down and rapped his knuckles on the table. "In any case, I don't know where the place is. I truly don't. I wouldn't tell you if I did know, mind you, but I truly don't."

Wickes believed him. Somehow Drass did business with the rebels but didn't know where they hid when they weren't assassinating governors and blowing up stockades. But, still, Wickes

LIZANDRA'S DEEPEST FEAR

asked, "Did you take the wizard there? We know you gave Akithar passage from Klubridge."

Drass squinted across the table at Wickes, his lower lip pouting. Wickes had been right about his guess, and he had Weylis to thank for that, not that he'd have the opportunity. She'd been correct about the *Sephare* and about Drass, and now she was right about his having given passage to Akithar.

But Drass said, "I've never knowingly let a mage onto my ship. That would be me harboring illegals. You should know that, as close to the High Lord and his laws as you've been for the past few years."

"We know you did it, Drass. Just give us the details, and you're free to leave. Nobody even needs to know it came from you."

Drass' nose wrinkled at that, and he looked like he'd just smelled something awful. He pushed his chair back and said, "You're never going to be free of the Empire, Quentyn Wickes. No matter what you do for them, no matter how much you scrape for them. No matter how much you debase yourself, you're always going to be on their string. They'll never let you go."

Almost the same words Weylis had had for him, and they stung again. Less acutely this time, coming from a stranger, but they still stung. Wickes had no response, and he watched Drass pull himself up from the table and steady himself on legs that looked like they'd rather be at sea. "We're finished now," Drass said and turned to the door.

Jalla was still there and didn't move. The man was short but wide, and he blocked the way, and there was no way Drass could hope to get past. Jalla crossed his arms and squared himself in the doorway, but Wickes said, "Let him through."

Jalla's eyes flicked to Wickes' face for a moment, and he frowned a question back to him.

"Let him go," Wickes said again. "We've gotten everything we're getting." On another day, in another port, there would have been more conversation with Ergo Drass, and not all of it would have been verbal. But Wickes had his promise to Weylis, and he had every intention of keeping it.

Jalla stalled for another moment, no doubt loathe to take an order from one such as Wickes, but then he did move. He took a step back and to the side, and he turned to let Drass by. The old captain passed and disappeared into the outer room of the tavern, intact and not even visibly shaken by the encounter. Jalla watched him leave and stomped into the back room, slamming the door behind him. "You just let him go."

"We got what we needed," Wickes said.

"We waited here for two weeks for him," Jalla snarled. "We went into that blasted swamp. And for what?"

Wickes looked to the halflock in the corner. "You got it, Colm?"

The pale man bobbed his head and took a step into the light. Jalla sneered at him and looked back at Wickes. "I'll be reporting this," he said. "I promise you the General and the Admiral both will hear about this halflock."

Wickes had been counting on that. He never knew how Colm had come to live in his father's village, but his existence there had been little better than that of a slave. Back in the Empire's hands, he would at least be bathed and fed and properly kept. He wouldn't have been able to fare on his own after the Empire scrambled his brain, but he'd have a better life in the Imperials' hands than he'd had in servitude to Kosah Enwickesan.

"Where did Drass take the mage?" Wickes asked, pointedly ignoring Jalla's threats.

Colm kept his eyes cast down, and he flinched at the question, as if he expected to receive blows for a wrong answer. But he'd listened to Drass' thoughts, just like he was supposed to, and he responded, his voice quiet, barely more than a rasp. "North. He goes north. Went north. Docks there. Ships at docks, locks, knocks."

Wickes leaned forward, hoping to encourage the timid man. "Stormbreak is north from Klubridge?"

Colm shrugged one shoulder and ducked his head again. "Doesn't know. He tells the truth. He doesn't know. Knowsn't. Only goes so far."

It made sense. The rebels had Drass dock somewhere, and they picked up his goods without letting him near their actual base. But every bit of information was one step closer to finding the sanctuary. "Where are the docks, Colm?"

"Tresa," he said. But then, quickly, "No, not. Close. West. Tresa but west."

"West of Tresa? That's where the docks are?"

Colm nodded with his jerking head bob once more and said again, "He tells the truth."

Jalla had watched the exchange with a mix of interest and disgust on his face. He waited a beat after Colm had finished and said, "We go north, then?"

"We go north," Wickes said.

Jalla nodded and shoved his way through the door. Wickes stood more slowly and put a hand on the smaller man's thin shoulder.

"You did good, Colm. Just like we needed."

Colm nodded. "Truth he told, told the truth. Truth about you, too. True."

"The truth about me?" Wickes asked. "What do you mean?"

Colm met his eyes and said, "He said true. They'll never let you go. No. Row."

∼

The journey north would be a long one, and the *Gaillardia* had already put several days' worth of water between its stern and Inport when the dread came upon Wickes again. It had taken longer this time, likely because he was gladder to be away from that city and the swamp beyond it than he was afraid of sailing. But, just like always, the dread returned.

Wickes reckoned it was nearing midnight when he held the rail and hung his head over the side to watch the foam against the hull. The sky was clear that night, and the moon painted the jagged surface of the water with a broken oval that expanded and contracted in time with the ship's motions. Somewhere down there, she waited. Was she far below, down, down in the depths, lurking but biding her time? Or was she just beneath the black blanket of the sea, ready to emerge between white crests to rip the bottom out of the ship and drag them all down together?

For an instant, his father's face looked back up at him in the shimmering waves, stern and disappointed and betrayed. That was what Wickes had intended and had known would happen if his plan worked. And it had worked, but those sad eyes lingered in his mind and stared at him from the sea. This was the man who had tormented him since his childhood. The man who had filled the sea with fear, drop by insidious drop. His was the face Wickes hated the most when he lay awake at night, more even than he hated Mediean's or Bekam's. But Kosah Enwickesan still had the power to drag guilt and regret out of his son, even as the distance between them grew with every chop and lunge of the ship.

Wickes wiped a hand over his exhausted face, and when his eyes reopened, the ocean no longer bore his father's judging gaze. What had seemed to be Kosah's face had separated into a split reflection of the moon, golden and horrible in the otherwise empty blackness of the night. It now stared back at Wickes with the luminous and terrifying eyes that had opened before him as he'd struggled in the watery caverns beneath the village. In truth, those eyes had never left him after he'd emerged from his trial, but he'd been on the move and busy enough to distract himself from them. But now they glared at him with the same flaming fury that had scattered the serpents and freed him from drowning.

Was it Ikarna? Who else could it have been? Who else hid in those wet caves, living in every drop of water and seething with impatience now that she had Wickes in her clutches? But, if it had been her, why had she let him go? Why hadn't she put an end to his miserable life then and there?

"It weren't her."

The voice was one Wickes had known since he was a boy, and it didn't startle him, even though he'd believed himself to be alone on the deck that night. This voice was calmer than his father's, softer, and sometimes nonsensical, but always true and kind.

"What was that, old friend?" Wickes asked and half turned to see Colm standing behind him. The older man shifted with the deck, having taken to his sea legs quickly, even though Wickes knew he hadn't been on any sort of craft since the village had taken him in all those decades ago.

"T'weren't Ikarna you saw, saw, saw, saw." Colm bit off the looping word so hard Wickes could hear his teeth clamp together. Colm raised his arms and pressed the heels of his hands against his eyes, turning them until he could speak again. He came up to the rail then and put his hands on it, next to Wickes'. "You think you seen her, but t'weren't."

Even though he'd been acquainted with Colm his whole life and knew the man to be anything but malicious, it still sent a shiver down Wickes' neck every time he read his thoughts. He'd asked Colm not to do it long ago, before Wickes had left the village the first time. "Can't not, sot, wot, dot" had been the answer, and Wickes had had to accept it. Colm wasn't in control of his abilities, at least not since the Empire had cut his head open and done whatever it was they did with its innards to make him into a halflock. And who knew what he was like before that? Like all the others who went through the process, Colm had no memory of his life before. Not all of them went mad like Colm had done, but most of them did, and Wickes always wondered how the ones who stayed sane managed it.

"How can you know it wasn't her?" Wickes asked and looked back to the water. The reflections had shifted again, and no eyes looked up at him. Not his father's, and not Ikarna's now.

Colm shifted and was leaning now, matching Wickes' posture. "T'wasn't her. Was your brain under strain, grain. You were down there a long time. Nearly drowned yourself, drowned downed."

Wickes had already considered that what he'd seen wasn't supernatural and instead was a phantom image he'd conjured himself as his lungs burned and struggled. But, if the eyes hadn't been real, then what had scared away the serpents? Surely they hadn't been a figment of his imagination as well.

"The snakeys was real," Colm said, and Wickes had to shrug

his shoulders to keep the intrusion into his thoughts from making him shudder again.

Wickes pushed his hands together, threading his fingers one on top of the other. He let the conversation drop, replaced by the noise of the sea that long ago had become nothing but a background murmur to him.

When a few moments had passed, he asked, "Did my father mistreat you?"

Colm didn't answer, not even with his nonsense and rhyming. He stiffened, though, no longer leaning over the rail, and that was answer enough.

"You won't be mistreated again," Wickes said. "Not by me."

And he wanted that to be true. He'd kept his promise to Weylis, and Ergo Drass had gone free unharmed. The old sailor had given up the information Wickes needed, one way or another, and no blood had been shed. Getting the details in such a roundabout way hadn't been easy, and it had forced Wickes to face his father, but perhaps that was for the best. It was a confrontation that had built for decades. For all of Wickes' life, if he was being honest. And now, whatever else he might have gotten out of the encounter, Wickes had secured some sort of closure between them.

He'd also freed Colm from a lifetime of abuse. When he'd gone after the halflock, it had been as a means to an end. It was just a way to extract the information from Drass that Wickes knew the man wouldn't give up voluntarily. But now that that business was done, and Colm was still with him, it felt like he'd done something right for once. And, more or less, for the right reason. He'd kept his promise to Weylis. He might have betrayed every other person they'd both known and sent the lot of them to the gallows, but he'd at least kept the promise to Weylis, and that was a start.

A start to what, though? He still didn't know what he'd seen in the water during his trial, and he didn't know how this quest to find the Stormbreak Sanctuary would end. All that was certain was what everyone else seemed to know and agree on. It was the same thing he'd managed to not acknowledge during the years he'd spent hunting down his friends and crew.

No matter what he did, he'd never be free of the Empire. That wasn't their way. They didn't get their use out of a man and then live up to their bargain and let him go on his way. No, he'd keep running errands for them until the errands ran out, and then, once he was well and truly of no use to Mediean and Bekam and the rest of them, they'd either lock him up or kill him outright. Probably kill him, because that was simpler and didn't require maintenance.

So, what, then? He was on a ship bound north and surrounded by Imperials who no doubt had orders to murder him if he stepped out of line. There was no getting away, not while Jalla had his eye on Wickes. If escape had been hard before, it was all but impossible now that Colm was his responsibility, too. And, make no mistake about it, Colm was his responsibility.

Wickes had reasoned that the Empire could take the man in and give him a purpose now that he was freed from Kosah's zealotry, but not now that they were sailing together. Not now that they were talking. It felt like old times, when Colm was the only reasonable one in the whole village, his magical insanity aside. He was the only one who hadn't believed in Ikarna and hadn't feared her, and Wickes knew he wouldn't let this poor old man fall from one captive situation into another.

It was his responsibility to keep the man safe now. He'd done a poor job of keeping to his responsibilities the past two years, but he'd kept that promise to Weylis, and that was the start. Whatever came for them, Wickes would stick next to the halflock and bring him along whenever he finally saw the opportunity to run. But that wasn't now, and it wouldn't be soon. All he could do at this point was to see this current task through and hope a better option waited beyond Stormbreak.

~

Wickes crouched among bushes that were still green despite the cold that had set upon them. The farther north they'd traveled, the more persistent the chill had become. When they had at last angled west and passed Tresa, Wickes saw blankets of white topping the buildings in the distant city. Tresa wasn't where they were docking, though. Colm had pulled not just words but also images from Ergo Drass' mind, and he'd described a cove or a bay with an abandoned dock. It hadn't sounded familiar to Wickes, but one of the other crewmen said he'd seen such a place, directly west of Tresa. And so that's where they'd gone, and that's where they'd found this place.

Their arrival had been nearly a week ago, but they hadn't docked in the bay itself. Wickes had had the ship anchor farther north along the shoreline, and he'd taken out the dinghy with Jalla, Colm, and a couple of the other crew whose names he hadn't learned. They'd pulled it ashore north of the bay and trudged a route around the edge of the water through slushy snow and brambles to reach a vantage point in the woods, just above and south of that lone dock.

Wickes had noted a path they'd crossed on the way and took care to obscure their tracks. That had to be the route the rebels took when going inland from the dock. On that hill, Wickes had waited with Colm and the Imperials, provisioned for camping but careful not to light visible fires or expose themselves if their quarry arrived.

On the fifth day, their patience was rewarded. They took turns keeping watch from the line of greenery at the top of the low hill, and Jalla was back at their camp when the ship came into view. Wickes and Colm were on watch together then, along with a young Imperial they'd come to know as Kraden. He was skinny and pale, with large ears and thin brown hair that stuck to his scalp like wet yarn. Kraden was the first to see the ship and nudged Wickes, pointing.

"There! You see?"

Wickes pushed his arm down and shushed him. "I see," he whispered back and scanned the treeline for movement. All was still, aside from the sail that was on the horizon and drawing closer. The ship was coming into the bay and headed their way, no doubt about it. Wickes slipped the spyglass out of his pocket and extended it, pressing it to his right eye. The craft was still too far away for him to make out more than its shape and mast, but it was the *Sephare*. He was sure of it.

"It's Drass," he said, his voice low. If Drass was coming here, there had to be someone to meet him.

And, sure enough, Wickes heard hooves an instant before Kraden cocked his head toward the woods. The Imperial opened his mouth, but Wickes shushed him again and turned the spyglass downward, toward the edge of the forest. He had to wait only a few seconds before the horse clopped into sight, a white steed that moved along the snowy path at a measured pace.

The rider looked like a woman, but it was hard to tell with the heavy coat and the scarf wound around her face. Her hair was dark, though, and hung nearly to her shoulder blades. She pulled the horse to a halt at the head of the dock and dismounted, keeping the reins in her hand. She waited there, unmoving, as the ship drew nearer. The horse dug at the ground every once in a while, but it, too, remained calm and waited for the arrival.

"Go get Jalla," Wickes whispered as the ship turned and he saw the name burned into the hull: *Sephare*. He'd been right.

"He'll be back soon enough," Kraden said. "No way am I leaving you alone." His voice was louder than it should have been, and Wickes cringed, but the woman didn't react. A little more noise, though, and she'd be sure to hear.

Wickes put a finger to his lips. Satisfied that Kraden looked suitably chastened, he said, "Where do you think I'd go? Disappear into the forest and die of exposure? Stow away on Drass' ship?"

Kraden's brows drew low, and he said, "I've got orders to watch you, and I'm watching you."

Wickes cursed under his breath and returned the spyglass to his eye. The crew had tied the ship at the dock by then, and there was Drass himself, climbing down from the ship with surer movements than he'd shown back in the tavern at Inport. He had his naval jacket this time, the aged buttons gleaming dully in the sunlight. They were close enough by then that Wickes hardly needed the glass, but he kept it pressed to his eye, not wanting to miss anything about the exchange that was about to take place.

Drass walked up the dock toward the person waiting at the

end, and behind him, his crew began unloading what had to be supplies for the rebellion. Crates, tubs, baskets, all manner of containers and bags, laden with goods that were surely bound for the Stormbreak Sanctuary.

Wickes was suddenly glad Kraden hadn't gone for Jalla. If the other man had been with them on watch, he might have insisted on arresting Drass and the woman and the rest of the crew at the dock. He'd reason that they could interrogate her to get the location of the sanctuary, and Colm could pull the information from her head if she wasn't forthcoming. Wickes knew better. The rebellion hadn't kept its stronghold hidden for this long by being careless, and he'd bet his last seri that woman was but another intermediary. She'd see this cargo down the road a ways, and then it would change hands once more. There might be a dozen exchanges before it finally came into the possession of someone who knew the final destination. That's how Wickes would set it up, at least.

No, charging down the hill and laying hands on all these people would get them no closer to their goal, and there's no doubt it would result in violence. Wickes wasn't afraid of a fight, but he preferred to avoid them when he could. And he didn't want to break his promise to Weylis after he'd gone to such lengths to keep Ergo Drass healthy. He'd see to it the old sailor departed that dock in one piece, and it was for the best that Jalla wasn't there to spoil everything.

An attack wasn't the way forward, but a bit of snooping would suit him just fine. Wickes pocketed the spyglass and turned to Colm. "Stay here," he whispered. "Stay and watch. And go with the Imperials if they take you back to the camp."

The halflock was watching him with an open mouth but didn't respond. It was Kraden who hissed at him, still louder than Wickes liked. "What are you doing?"

"Going closer. We need to know what they're saying," Wickes said. He didn't wait for the Imperial to protest and instead kept low in the brush as he half-crept and half-slid down the hillside.

His boots kept their grip on the ground, despite the layer of snow that plowed ahead of him as he descended. He worked his way to the left and west, trying to circle around towards a cluster of trees that cast deep shadows that would be perfect for hiding. He glanced back just once and saw Kraden waving at him like an imbecile. It was a wonder nobody had spotted him yet. There was nothing to be done for it, and Wickes just had to hope the fool would settle down once he realized there was nothing he could do to bring Wickes back up that hill.

As he passed, now close enough to see her better, the woman tugged the scarf down from her face. Her warm breath fogged the air in front of her as she called out. "We didn't expect you back so soon."

The words came crisp and clear to Wickes through the cold air. He reached the edge of the treeline and squatted in the shade. The snow was up to mid-calf but hadn't fallen into his boots just yet, and he leaned against the largest trunk, straining to see around it without showing himself. Drass was nearly to the woman by then and said, "I have the supplies, but there's also a message."

The woman took a step away from the horse and looked back. For a terrifying instant, Wickes thought she'd seen him, but her gaze went past his position, back into the woods.

"I've only got the one horse. You need to see Daulet?"

"I do. I can walk. You know me and horses."

"I could go back and send the carriage."

"Let's just walk it. Might as well while I'm off the water."

And so the two of them set off into the trees, the woman walking beside her horse and Drass on her other side, keeping pace with her. They passed within thirty feet of Wickes' hiding place, and he held his breath until they'd made it far enough down the road. Where were they headed? Wickes hadn't seen any buildings or even a sign of civilization when they'd come around that bay a few days ago. There had been the path but nothing to indicate it led anywhere nearby. But there had to be something, and he couldn't let them get too far ahead of him.

He looked back toward the hill then, searching for some sign of Kraden or Colm, but there was nothing. He hoped Colm could tell Jalla what he was up to, but that fool Kraden would probably report that he'd run off.

Wickes sucked in a breath of cold air and looked back down

the roadway in the direction Drass had gone. He'd committed himself, and there was nothing to do at that point but follow through. He shoved himself away from the tree, freed his boots from the icy snow, and pulled himself through the forest, low again and as silent as the frozen undergrowth would allow.

CHAPTER 22

Hallways were easy, as were stairs. It was doorways that gave Bekam trouble. He tried angling his head to the left as he came onto the landing and approached the entrance to the second floor of the Robdwell Building, but he still misjudged and banged his left shoulder against the door frame. It was a hard enough hit to stagger him to the right, and he whipped a furious look behind him to ensure no one had seen the collision. He was alone in the stairwell, and he uttered a quiet curse as he renegotiated the doorway and passed through this time without incident.

Bekam squeezed his left shoulder and felt where the bruise would bloom later. The left side of his body had become a patchwork of marks that ranged from black to sickly green, all in various stages of healing. How long would it take for him to stop cracking his shin into low tables? How long until his elbow would stop hitting the corner of his desk? How long until he could pass through a door without ramming his shoulder into the wall?

His hand drifted up from his shoulder to trace the edge of the patch that covered his left eye. It was black and sturdy, the edges bordered in the blue of the Aerie to match his uniform, bound to his head with a thin black string that disappeared into his hair. He'd stared at himself in the mirror in his bedroom for nearly an hour the first time he'd put the thing on. It was better than the sight of the remains of his uncovered eye, at least, but would he ever get used to wearing the blasted thing? Would he ever get used to half the world disappearing from his view?

Cillan had told him the patch made him look dangerous, that he'd be more fearsome for wearing it. Bekam didn't feel fearsome or dangerous. He felt like a fool who'd let a mage get into his house and blind him, and there'd been nothing he could do to stop the attack. Marjiel hadn't looked at him the same since it happened. Pity had replaced her usual scorn, and he knew reproach lay beneath the pity, just awaiting its chance to emerge once the proper amount of time had passed. And she'd be right, though he'd never tell her that. He should have anticipated the spymaster failing. He should have expected Qae'lon would find out what he was up to. But he hadn't, and Bekam had paid dearly.

He'd failed to prevent the attack, but he would not fail to see it addressed in the proper way.

The page waited for him outside the room where he usually sat in anticipation of the Council's summons. Bekam wasn't sure whether it was the same page who'd led him through the building last time, but she wore the same black vest with white sleeves and greeted him with the same vacant smile and slight bow. "The Council is ready for you, General."

His step faltered, but he recovered in an instant. He'd never been ushered directly in to see them. They had always made him wait, whether they needed to or not. Perhaps they were taking his request with the seriousness it merited. He nodded to the page. "Lead the way."

She dipped her head into a slightly deeper bow before moving ahead of him down the hallway. They passed the same framed portraits and polished columns he always passed, and his mind barely registered them this time. How many of the Council would be there? They had eleven last time when they'd summoned him to chastise him. Would there be more or less this time, when he had done the summoning?

Bekam stopped outside the chamber doors and let the page go ahead of him. As always, his announcement came with an echo that spilled out through the open doorway and into the hallway: "General Tenez Bekam, Director of the Imperial Kites and Martial Appointee to Aramore." Oh, how the Council longed to strip him of at least one of those titles and probably both. They'd still do their best to see him disgraced and saddled with his Kites' failure, but not before he had his say.

He came through the doors and let his good eye study the faces arranged around the table that day. There were eight of them this time. Fewer than before, but still more than he was used to seeing. There was Prusik at the far side of the table, her hands folded beneath her chin and her mouth drooping in an eternal sag between her heavy jowls. General Milev was there again as well, tiny eyes shining in that overstuffed face. Teka Lacar was on the left again, the arrogant bastard having the nerve to give Bekam a nod and a smile.

Bekam tore his gaze away from Lacar and froze. His eyes widened, and his eyelashes on the left side brushed the inside of the patch. "What is he doing here?" Bekam asked, his voice tight and low. "What is he doing here?" He asked again, this time louder, fury and terror distorting the question midway through.

"Collect yourself, General Bekam," Prusik said. She spoke slowly, her tone almost bored. "General Qae'lon is here as a matter of formality, to address the very serious accusations you have leveled against him."

And there he sat, the smug creature, just to the right of Prusik, his white hair pulled back and the corner of his mouth turned up in an almost invisible smirk. He wore the same white gown he'd worn at Klubridge and again in Bekam's home, and for a dizzying moment curiosity consumed Bekam. Was that robe all the other man ever wore? Was it a uniform, or was it his own personal affectation?

"He blinded me!" Bekam said and halted his hand too late to stop his trembling fingers from touching the edge of the patch again. He forced his arm down and said, "He blinded me and endangered my family. He killed one of my servants."

"The Council will hear your complaints, General Bekam, but you will not remain out of order. Have a seat," Prusik said, sharper now. "Have a seat and collect yourself."

The same hard, wooden chair sat before him, facing the Council, but not a part of it. Not like the seat Qae'lon had taken behind the outer rim of the great, round table. Bekam hesitated and considered backing out of the room. He could go back into the hallway, back down the stairs, out of the building, and away from here. But if he did that, that would be the end of it all, wouldn't it? He'd have requested an audience with the Security Council and abandoned them in a panic, casting any chance of salvaging his career to the wind.

He willed his feet forward and lowered himself into the chair with a stiffness that came more from reluctance than from his bruises. Once Bekam sat before the Council, Prusik nodded, satisfied.

"You may proceed, General Bekam."

He took a moment to breathe and to look around the table again. Aside from Prusik, Milev, Lacar, and Qae'lon, he recognized only one other member in attendance, a younger woman with dark skin and a high, white collar trimmed in orange, the color of Tresa. He knew her face but couldn't recall her name. No matter. The other three were strangers to him, and they all stared at him with barely disguised disdain. All but Qae'lon, who studied him with something akin to amusement, as if he were waiting to see what trick Bekam would try next.

"This man invaded my home," Bekam said and extended his hand to point at Qae'lon. His fingers didn't shake now, but he lowered his arm before they could start.

The young woman from Tresa snorted but covered her mouth with her hand and masked her derision with a cough.

Bekam took a breath and began again. "I returned home from travels to find Qae'lon in my home, uninvited. He was in my dining room and had used magic on my wife and daughter."

"What sort of... magic?" Milev asked, saying the last word as if it tasted sour.

"They were seated at the dining table, and neither of them could move. They were rooted to their chairs and could not even speak."

"How do you know this was the general's doing?" Milev asked.

Bekam's eyebrows rose, and he glanced from Milev to Qae'lon and back again. "He was seated at the table with them! He had my butler under similar control and killed him in front of me."

"Killed your butler," the Tresa girl said, her tone flat, and her hands steepled beneath her chin now. This was an amusement to them.

"He took my eye!" Bekam said. He leaned forward in his chair and lifted the bottom of the patch to show them what had been done. To their credit, the ones who did look at his wound looked away quickly. Teka Lacar cut his eyes toward Qae'lon, who continued watching Bekam, his lips pursed and his eyes calm and unwavering.

"How did you lose your eye, General?" This was from an old man seated next to the representative from Tresa. He was pale like Prusik, his white hair receded to a fringe around the rim of his skull, and his head hung forward so that he looked over the top of his glasses from beneath drooping eyelids. He wore a suit with a red collar that might have meant he was from Dushouca, but it just as easily could have been a meaningless fashion choice.

"Qae'lon used his magic on me. He held me in place and…" Bekam felt cold sweat beading on his forehead, and he forced himself to swallow and breathe. "And he used a fork from the dining table. He stabbed me with it."

Prusik leaned back in her chair and tapped a finger on the table before looking toward Qae'lon. "You say he picked up a fork and—"

"No, Commissioner," Bekam said. "He used magic again. He levitated the fork and pushed it into my eye with his magic."

He let the silence settle after that last statement and watched the faces looking at him. The Council shared glances, some of them seeming bored and others uncertain, before Prusik at last looked to Qae'lon again. "What say you to these accusations, General?"

Qae'lon smiled at her, a keen smile with too-white teeth, and said, "I fear the general has suffered some sort of delusion.

Either that, or he believes he will gain something by serving these ridiculous tales to the Council."

"Then you call General Bekam a liar?"

"I say the general is mistaken in a most creative manner." Qae'lon shrugged and settled back into his chair.

Prusik watched him for another moment before turning her attention to Bekam. "Your wife and daughter are not with you as witnesses today?"

"My daughter would be unable to testify," Bekam said. And it was true. Even if Leonie got into the Council chamber without incident, she would be of no use. He'd tried talking with her about what had happened, and she seemed to have no recollection of any of it. Hardly unusual, given her ordinarily addled state.

"And your wife?" Prusik asked.

Bekam exhaled slowly. He knew they'd ask about Marjiel, and he still had no answer. What was he to tell them? That his wife was so ashamed of his performance on the evening of the attack that she wouldn't even speak to him, much less testify on his behalf? That she rarely had a kind word to support him, even in the best of times? "She is unavailable," Bekam said, and he saw Qae'lon's smirk from the corner of his eye.

Prusik folded her hands and shook her head. "Without witnesses, I'm not sure what you expect us to do, General."

"Arrest him!" Bekam cried. "He's sitting right there. He's a menace to the Empire."

"I understand you have a personal grievance against General Qae'lon, but that hardly qualifies as a threat to the Empire," Prusik said.

"He destroyed Klubridge. You ordered him to retake the city, and he tore it down. There's scarcely anything left but rubble. Is that not a menace?"

Qae'lon leaned forward at that, and Bekam stiffened, anticipating some sort of conjuring. Instead, the mage said, "General Bekam, the Council ordered me to bring Klubridge back under the wing of the Empire. Simply marching soldiers into its streets would not have accomplished that task. The citizens needed a lesson of obedience. Klubridge needed to be bowed before it would kneel. Examples had to be made of the rioters, and the nobles who allowed the rebels to take the city had to be punished. The city has fallen, and it's unlikely anyone still inhabiting it would try to stand against us again. I'd say I executed my order successfully. Wouldn't you?"

Bekam balked. "You executed the whole city!"

Qae'lon tittered a light laugh. "Let us not resort to hyperbole, General. There were deaths, yes, but most of the city lives and will recover."

Bekam opened his mouth to respond but found he had no words. No member of the Council had shown surprise at this newest exchange, and none of them had spoken to rebuke Qae'lon. Either they truly supported his actions, or he had them under his spells, just like he'd had Bekam's family.

"You condone this attack?" Bekam asked. He looked to Prusik first and then to Milev. To all of them, forcing every member to meet his eyes in turn. "You agree with the slaughter this man committed?"

It was Milev who finally responded. "What he says is correct, General. We ordered him to retake Klubridge. Granted, we did not anticipate the extent of his actions, but Klubridge is weakened, and no other city will dare repeat its revolt. Qae'lon accomplished what we set before him. You, General, have not. Klubridge is liberated, but we have received no report from you about your progress in locating the rebels."

"He has a relic," Bekam said. Surely they couldn't ignore that. Even government officials had to abide by the same restrictions on enchanted artifacts that the rest of the population did. "The Eye of Kelixia. That's what he used to bring down Klubridge."

For the first time, Prusik looked surprised. Her eyes shifted, and Bekam felt a hint of hope blossoming in his chest. She looked at the mage and asked, "Is this true? Do you possess a relic?"

Qae'lon nodded and favored her with a regretful smile. "It is true, Commissioner. I recovered the Eye from a smuggler my Herons had identified. The timing coincided with your orders, so I used it in the pacification of Klubridge."

"He can't keep it," Bekam said. "If he did this to Klubridge, what might be next?"

The woman from Tresa wrinkled her lip and asked, "What would you have us do? Take the Eye from Qae'lon and give it to you?"

"Of course not. I don't care what you do with it, as long as Qae'lon doesn't have it."

Qae'lon raised his hands, the palms open. "There is no need to argue this point. I had planned to deliver the Eye of Kelixia into Imperial hands, and I still intend to do so."

"Where is it now?" Prusik asked. A line marked her forehead, and there was another, deeper one between her eyes. She was finally taking some of this seriously.

"In my tower," Qae'lon said. "I will be returning there after this meeting, and I can retrieve the Eye. Shall I bring it to Salkire Keep in, say, a month's time?"

Prusik's lips twitched, and she looked to Milev. The heavyset man inclined his head, and she nodded back. "Within a month's time," she said. "That is acceptable."

Qae'lon nodded and smiled at Bekam as he settled into his seat once more. The meeting had gone his way at every turn. He'd had no intention of keeping the Eye after he'd used it at Klubridge, and he'd known he was in no danger of being punished for his actions there or in Bekam's home. The Council would not touch him, and Bekam had no retort. He had no way to object and no further recourse. His shoulders sagged as he watched Qae'lon behind the table. Would there be recompense for this meeting? Would Qae'lon come for him again, or had he accomplished what he'd set out to do?

Teka Lacar slid his chair back. "If there's no other business, then—"

"One additional thing," the representative from Tresa said. "I have a motion to propose."

Lacar had been halfway out of his chair but dropped into his seat once more, a flicker of annoyance on his face. "My apologies, Delegate."

"What is your motion?" Prusik asked.

"It has occurred to me that, while the rules of succession for enlisted officers of the Empire are clear, we lack formal guidelines of continuance for senior administrators who are under our purview. It is my motion that, if a senior administrator is ever incapable of performing their duties, their post will transfer to another official of equal standing."

The delegate looked at Bekam as she finished, and it all made sense. It was unclear how he'd done it, and Bekam didn't think it was through magic, but Qae'lon somehow controlled this Council. Or at least enough of them to make all the difference. Teka Lacar didn't seem to know what was going on, but this delegate from Tresa had clearly been compromised. Who else? Milev? Prusik herself?

"Do we have a second?" Prusik asked.

The motion was all Qae'lon needed. It was a broad move that would have sweeping consequences across the Imperial military, if anyone enforced it outside of this Council. But Bekam knew that wouldn't happen. The only place where it would matter was in this room, and the only officers it would affect would be Qae'lon and himself.

Qae'lon was his equal and opposite in the Imperial machine. Bekam managed the Kites, and Qae'lon managed the Herons. Their standings were equal in the eyes of the Empire, and no other officer was their match. If Bekam found himself displaced from his position, either through the Council's ruling or through a sorcerous cessation of his heartbeat, control of the Kites would fall to Qae'lon, and the magic hunters, Bekam's Kites, would be under the control of the most powerful mage in the government. The end goal remained unclear, but Qae'lon's ascension was evident.

"I will second the motion," Milev said, and just like that, the Council voted. Bekam's mouth turned dry as each member cast their vote, unanimously altering the Imperial charter of succession. They had the right to make changes like that on a whim, as long as the votes backed it, but they rarely exercised that option. Rarely wasn't never, though.

Bekam stared at a spot on the floor five feet in front of his chair. If he tried to vault the table and strangle Qae'lon with his bare hands, how far was he likely to get? Would he even make it out of his chair before the mage froze him in place again? And then? The Council would have every reason to strip him of his rank, hand his post to the mage, and send Bekam to prison, or worse. There was no play here.

Prusik was speaking again, and Bekam blinked and snapped his head up. She started again, "I was reminding you of your duty, General. The Empire lost Klubridge on your watch, while your Kites were in pursuit of a rebel spy. Your order to locate that spy and the information they were carrying still stands. I dare say that you need to make a compelling case for keeping your post, and delivering the Stormbreak Sanctuary to the Empire would be a good start."

Bekam squinted at her and wrapped his fingers around the arms of the chair. This was how they were going to do it, then? Make him out to be incompetent and wrest the position from him? "A good start?" he asked. "When last we met, locating that spy was the entirety of my mandate."

Prusik stared at him through her thick lenses as she closed the logbook before her. "Yes, General, it was. This concludes the Council's business, and I bid you good day."

CHAPTER 23

Oreth's arm and leg hurt worse when it was colder, and it was plenty cold that night. He was wearing a heavy coat with padding around the collar and at the ends of the sleeves, but that wasn't enough to keep the chill out. He had his left hand tucked into a pocket at the side of the coat, holding it steady so his arm wouldn't move too much, and that helped keep the coat shut as well. But even that wasn't enough, and his shoulders shivered as he came to the edge of the courtyard.

Was it the cold of the night, or was the chill rising up from inside him? Likely both.

He looked both ways down the hallway before he stepped again, his left leg moving better now that he had it in the brace, but his foot still dragged on the floor as he made his way past Vaino's office as quietly as he could manage. The man would be in his bed by that time, tucked away in the upper levels of the keep, but the fear lingered, insisting that every door he passed was about to slam open as someone stepped out to confront him.

The doors didn't open, and everybody was asleep, but that didn't banish the worry any more than the coat kept the cold away. There was no telling what kind of repercussions there would be if he got caught doing this, but he knew they wouldn't be good. The rebels were used to having him around, and he even had some of their respect now, thanks to the work he'd been doing in supply. He could probably explain any suspicions away if he did get caught. He was just going to check on some deliveries. He was getting an early start for the next day. He'd forgotten to do something before shutting the supply room down earlier in the day. There were dozens of excuses he could come up with, but how convincingly could he deliver them? And what would they think or say or do if they did figure him out?

What would Leyna do?

Oreth sighed at that, and a big plume of vapor appeared and disappeared in front of his face. He stopped at the last door and pulled his left hand out of his pocket, letting it dangle so the fingertips brushed the edges of the brace Leyna had made for him. If a guard caught him and figured out what he was doing, he might get tossed in a cell or interrogated. But if Leyna found out?

He scowled and shook his head. Reykas was dying, and this was his only chance. It wasn't a good choice, but Oreth had already made it, and he just had to hope it was the right one. If only he could tell Leyna what he was doing and make her understand. But she wouldn't understand. She'd been raised to believe magic was bad and anybody who could touch it was evil. If she knew Reykas was a mage, and that was why he'd gotten sick? She wouldn't understand. Or maybe she would.

Oreth shook his head again. He couldn't take that risk. Not after he'd already set everything up for that night. It was too late to back down now, and he'd have to deal with whatever came from it. The important thing now was to see it through and to save Reykas.

Oreth unlocked the door with a slender key on the ring he pulled from his trouser pocket. That ring normally hung on the wall in Supply, but he'd palmed it on the way out earlier in the day. Leyna had been standing right there, and he'd waited until she turned her back for just a second, and the keys went into his pocket. He'd deceived her that quickly and that easily.

One more head shake. No time to think or worry about all that now. Just get it done.

He pushed the door open, and the cart was sitting there,

waiting for him, just where he'd left it after he'd borrowed it from the infirmary that afternoon. Nobody had asked what he needed it for, and nobody had stopped him or even glanced at him when he'd rolled it out the front door of the hospital. And now he pulled it out from where he'd stashed it and eased it into the courtyard. He'd picked one that had four working wheels, but there was no preventing one of them from squeaking. Seemed like that's how it was with every one of the carts.

As he turned the cart and angled it in the right direction, a sudden gust of wind ruffled his hair and slipped beneath his collar, sending another shiver down his spine. He glanced up toward the tower and knew what that wind meant. Whichever mage had been on duty was gone now, and the shield was down. Based on tonight's schedule, they'd have about twenty minutes to get Reykas out, as long as the other mage didn't show up early. No time to waste, just in case.

He shoved the cart, and it wobbled down the walkway, the errant wheel giving a few whines Oreth hoped would disappear into the night with the sound of the wind. There was no one in the courtyard at that hour, and Oreth thanked his luck. Nearly the whole keep was asleep by that time of night, but there always could be someone out on a restless walk, and that might be all it would take to spoil his plan. But luck was with him, and he was alone when he slowed and stopped the cart in front of Lizzie's new room.

Oreth rapped his knuckles against the wood as softly as he could manage and waited. He couldn't see light beneath the door, but that meant nothing. Would he have even been able to see a single candle or a small lantern?

He shrugged the coat higher on his neck and squinted across the darkness of the courtyard behind him. Still no movement over there, and no movement at the door either. He turned back to the door and knocked one more time, still soft but a little firmer this time.

The wind whistled between the columns at the edges of the courtyard and rustled the branches of the tree at the center, and there was still no answer from the door. Had she changed her mind? Had she found another way to get the cure for Reykas? Had she given up?

None of those seemed likely, but Oreth's pulse quickened at the prospect of not having to smuggle Lizzie and Reykas out of the keep. Perhaps he wouldn't have to do it after all. Perhaps something else had worked out that didn't have to involve him at all.

But then the door did open, and Lizzie was there, looking small and afraid in the dark room. The moon lit half her face, and her eye glimmered wide and blue beneath her pale forehead and the tangle of yellow hair above it. Oreth remembered when her hair had been straight and fine and clean and nearly white. It had been the first thing he'd noticed about her when he'd come to the Chamberlain. She'd been hanging from a metal hoop suspended over the stage, and her hair had dangled beneath her as she pulled her feet over her head and bent backwards. Her spine had arched back impossibly far before she dropped from the top of the hoop to the bottom, coming upright then, her toes pointed down and her hair flipping around to settle on her shoulders and down her back. Oreth had thought then that he'd never seen anything more beautiful.

He saw her differently now, after he'd met Leyna. Differently, but he remembered how it had been and suspected there'd be a part of him that always remembered Lizzie that way. But that's not how she was just now.

"Did you get it?" she whispered.

He nodded. "We have to move fast. They have the shield down, but it won't last for long."

Lizzie took a step back into the room, pulling the door with her, but she stopped and stared at Oreth. She was in the dark, but he could see the light reflected in both of her eyes now. "Thank you," she said.

All he could think to say was, "I promised," and that was enough. She stepped out of the way, and Oreth pulled the cart behind him as he followed her into the room. There was a candle burning on the small table beside the bed, after all. The light it gave was weak, but it was enough for him to see Reykas' shape, lying motionless in the dark. If he hadn't known better,

Oreth would have thought his friend was already dead. He wasn't, was he?

Oreth's heart raced again as he took a jerking step towards the bed, and then he saw the sheet over Reykas' chest rise slowly. He was still breathing, at least, even if it was slow and shallow. "We need to get him onto the cart," he said, and Lizzie nodded.

The two of them lifted Reykas, Oreth at his shoulders and Lizzie at his feet, and they transferred him over onto the gurney. He weighed far less than Oreth had expected, and it wasn't hard to move him, even with his left arm weakened. Once they had him in place, Oreth crouched as much as he was able with the stiff left leg, and he pulled a heavy blanket out from the lower shelf on the cart. He spread the blanket over Reykas and ducked again to retrieve some cloth bags. He arranged them around the edges of the top of the cart. It wouldn't hide Reykas from anyone who got too inquisitive, but it should work from a distance for long enough to get them out of the keep. They shouldn't encounter anyone on the way, but it was better to be safe.

"I'll push the cart," Oreth said. "You walk at the front and make sure nothing's in the way. And keep watch for anybody who might be around."

Lizzie was out the door ahead of him without another word and led the way into the courtyard. Oreth pushed, and the cart rolled behind her, the wheels occasionally bumping on uneven stones and the back left wheel groaning and whining every once in a while. The bumps weren't hard enough to jostle the cargo, and the squeaks weren't loud enough to wake anyone, and Oreth pushed faster.

What would they do if they got him to the edge of the keep and couldn't go any farther because the shield was already up again? Give up and try another night? The way Reykas was looking, Oreth didn't think he'd have too many more nights for trying. No, it had to be that night, no matter what.

Lizzie hesitated at the archway leading out of the main keep, and she looked back at Oreth.

"To the stables," he whispered, and she nodded.

Oreth had access to the stable schedules, and he'd left a gap that night when the horses would be unattended. The stable hands wouldn't argue about having less time spent freezing their noses off in a smelly barn in the middle of the night, and nobody else should even notice that gap. He, Lizzie, and Reykas would have the place to themselves for at least as long as the shield was down.

"Do you know how to drive a horse and wagon?" he asked as they passed through the large doors. The wheels crunched on hay, and Oreth let the cart rest next to the inner wall, out of the direct wind.

"I've been handling horses my whole life," Lizzie said. Her voice was still low, and he had to strain to hear her. "My parents taught me when I was little, and I used to help drive their wagons."

"The circus," Oreth said.

She gave him a sad smile back. She'd told him about that circus and about her parents and all the places they'd traveled, and he knew she missed them. She'd had to leave them when Kites came looking for mages, just like they'd all had to leave Klubridge. She'd lost her family to the Empire's meddling, and now she might lose Reykas as well.

No, that wouldn't happen.

Oreth pointed across the barn, and Lizzie followed his shuffling steps as he guided her to the wagon he'd arranged earlier in the day. It was a good one and was sturdy, but no one had used it the whole time he'd been at Stormbreak. It wouldn't be missed, and neither would the horse he'd already set up to pull it. He'd adjusted some numbers, and nobody should think to question them.

"What's its name?" Lizzie asked.

Oreth blinked at her.

"The horse."

He frowned and considered the question. Why hadn't he ever wondered that himself? "I don't know," he said. "It's a girl."

"She needs a name."

"You can name her after you're away from here," he said. "I put supplies in the back. It should be enough to get you there and back, and then some. There are more blankets, too, and

LIZANDRA'S DEEPEST FEAR

kindling and some lanterns. Everything I could think you might need." He paused and looked toward the wide doorway ahead of them, the one that led away from Stormbreak. "It's dark, and the road's likely to be ice. Do you know where you're going?"

"I have a map," Lizzie said and pulled a folded parchment from inside her coat. He didn't ask where she'd found it but nodded back to her.

"You'll want to stick to the road. Don't go off it. If you get into the snow, the wagon'll get stuck, and you'll be stranded. You don't want that."

She shook her head and said, "I'll be careful." She tucked the map back into her clothes and put a hand on Oreth's arm. Just a few months ago, that gesture would have thrilled him, but now all he felt was worry that someone would show up at the last minute and catch them. Worry that the shield was already going back up. Worry that Lizzie would get lost heading south and would freeze to death in the snow. But he didn't say any of that. He put his hand over hers and nodded back to her.

"Just get the cure, Lizzie. Get it, and come back."

Lizandra had always thought of Karsk as being far, far to the north. It was a city that had somehow grown itself into a tangle of mountains, gnarled forests, and deathly cold, and the only way to get into it from the south was to follow a winding road up through an infamously treacherous pass. She'd had no desire to go that far north, but there she was, guiding a horse and wagon through mountains even farther north than Karsk.

She'd expected to have trouble the first night they were on the road. For one thing, she'd made the trip up to Stormbreak inside an enclosed carriage and had been unable to see any landmarks or even what the road looked like. For another, the season had turned since she'd been in the keep, and the way down probably looked very little like it had looked on the way up, now that it was covered in snow and ice that reshaped the roadway and the landscape around it.

The moon was bright the night she left, but she'd lacked

confidence that it would be enough to see them down from the castle and into the surrounding trees. And, once they'd made it that far, would the moon's light break through the dead branches enough to keep them on the path? The last thing she needed was to let the horse wander off and drag the wagon into a hip-deep snow drift. She was undertaking this mission to save Reykas' life, not to freeze them both to death.

According to the map she'd taken from the depot, there were at least a dozen ways in and out of the rebels' hideout and winding down towards civilization. She was more concerned with speed than losing any potential followers, so she was taking the most direct route south. And, despite her worries, the journey started easily enough. That's not to say it was comfortable.

Lizandra kept one hand on the reins and used the other to tug the scarf tighter around her head and face. The air was cold enough, but the night made it even more bitter, and the wind coming through the cliffs whipped sharp ice into her face with powerful and chilling gusts. She'd had to pull the horse to a halt less than an hour outside of Stormbreak so she could search through the clothes Oreth had packed for her and layer more on top of what she was already wearing.

She took the opportunity to check on Reykas and found him still sleeping, as well as could be expected. The wagon had jostled and rocked over the uneven ground, but it seemed that nothing could disturb whatever kind of slumber Reykas had fallen into. She'd covered him in several blankets, all of them tucked around his sides, but she'd left his face uncovered for the start of the trip. When she laid her bare hand on his cheeks and forehead during that first stop, they were so cold they almost burned her skin. She'd thought covering his face might have kept him from breathing properly, but breathing wouldn't be much of a worry if she froze him in the wagon.

It was with reluctance that she pulled another blanket up from the pile of supplies and wrapped it loosely around his head. She tugged at the fabric where it passed over Reykas' nose and mouth, and she formed it into a little tent that she hoped would help him breathe while still keeping him warm enough.

LIZANDRA'S DEEPEST FEAR

No matter what she did for him there, though, she had to get him south, and fast. He wouldn't last long in that wagon, even if the trip were not through the coldest lands of Teshovar.

But he did last, all the way from Stormbreak to Esterburgh, through nights of torrential snowfall, through days of lurching travel. Lizandra pushed their pace as much as she dared, but she was careful to keep the horse fed and rested, and she paid attention to the edges of the road, making sure they didn't veer a wheel off the path. She was less concerned with leaving a trail behind them. The persistent snowfall quickly covered any sign a horse and wagon had come that way.

Lizandra kept Reykas as warm as she could, but it did him no good to build a fire. She couldn't drag him out of the wagon for warmth and have any hope of loading him back into it by herself. So she went without fire as well and trusted they'd somehow make it together. Sleeping in the wagon whenever she couldn't go any farther and pressing forward as hard as she dared, sometimes through both night and day, left her with no sense of how long they'd been on the move. She'd intended to name the horse soon after they'd left Stormbreak, but she'd forgotten, and now it seemed too late. The horse was healthy and bore them safely down from the mountains, but she, too, was exhausted by the time the first sign of civilization breached the frozen wasteland before them.

Esterburgh was little more than rows of buildings lining the sides of a single main street and a few secondary ones, but it was the most tempting place Lizandra had ever seen. Her hands were stiff with cold, her upper lip felt frozen from where her nose had leaked on it, and her eyes felt drier than they'd ever been. Time was of the essence, but she couldn't press the horse so hard that she dropped dead in the road.

With that worry in mind, she guided the horse and cart toward a barn at the northern edge of town. They needed warmth and rest, but they didn't need prying eyes to see the young woman carrying an unconscious man bundled in the back of her wagon. The risk of word getting back to the rebels was bad enough, but the Empire had all their names by then and likely had descriptions of them, too. Did they also know she and

Reykas were mages? Anything was possible after what had happened in the square at Klubridge.

The barn turned out to be empty, possibly abandoned, but more likely just unused for that one night. Either way, Lizandra didn't question her luck and pulled the doors shut tight after she drove the horse and wagon through them. It was the first night since leaving Stormbreak that she'd have spent under a roof, and for once she wasn't worried about the falling snow covering them as she slept. Esterburgh was quiet when she'd rolled into town, and she even risked starting a small fire inside the barn, using a flint and kindling Oreth had included in the supplies. She set it near an open window so the smoke would drift outside, and she forced herself to stay awake while warming her hands over it. It wasn't until long after she'd stomped out the last embers that she allowed herself to fall asleep.

Once she closed her eyes, the sleep was deep and dreamless, a void of exhaustion that would have carried her through most of the next day if the sounds of the town awakening hadn't roused her just after sunup. Upon waking, Lizandra lay perfectly still, her eyes open and her ears waiting for any sign of discovery or another presence in the barn. But there was nothing. She and Reykas and the horse remained on their own. She went first to Reykas and checked his temperature and his breathing, as she did every time she awakened on that trip. He was much the same as he'd been ever since leaving Stormbreak, but the lack of a decline in his condition was not a sign of an improvement. They still needed to hurry. She scrambled through the straw on the floor to remove any sign of their passage and bundled the remaining kindling back into the cart. Ten minutes later, she was driving the wagon back out the doors on the north side of the barn, and she guided the horse around to the main road as if she'd just arrived and was passing through.

No one spoke to her as the wagon rolled down the road, and only a few early risers even glanced in her direction. These people had more pressing matters of their own and didn't care what a skinny girl driving a horse might be up to. They certainly didn't expect her to be a wanted fugitive of the Empire, but she pulled the scarf up over her mouth and nose to make doubly sure she wouldn't be recognized.

She didn't allow herself to relax into the rhythm of the road until they'd passed the last houses on the southern edge of Esterburgh, and even then she knew to keep her guard up. The wind was less insistent there, and the cold was less biting, but the danger was greater than ever. She'd descended from the unpopulated wastes of the north, and she'd brought Reykas into civilization. The journey became easier there, but as the road's condition improved, so did the number of travelers they passed. Lizandra kept her eyes on the path ahead and willed the miles to pass more quickly.

~

Klubridge was the biggest city Lizandra had ever seen, and coming to Karsk didn't change that. Karsk was huge in its own way, but it didn't sprawl along the coast like Klubridge had. It didn't bustle with promise and excitement and danger. It didn't gleam in the sunlight's reflection off the water.

Instead, Karsk hunkered at the base of a ragged mountain and hugged the foothills with its gray and solemn architecture. The mountains north of Esterburgh, where the rebels hid at Stormbreak, were sheer and cold and white, constantly covered with layer after layer of snow and ice. There was snow at Karsk as well, but it was different there. It capped the peaks of these mountains and piled at the sides of the road with white crystals that sparkled in the light of the day, but the road itself was so trodden that the brown dirt and black mud had mixed into the slush. The snow here was dirty and crusted, showing ruts where the clean powder had been sluiced away by the wheels, feet, and hooves that constantly moved in and out of the city.

Karsk was cold, no doubt, but it was a manageable cold. It wasn't the bone-chilling, murderous freeze Lizandra had experienced farther to the north. This was a slower and sadder sort of cold, the sky blanketed in clouds that constantly dulled the shadows of the trees she passed. Icicles clung to the face of the black wall at the north side of the city, white and dripping in the relative midday warmth, sure to freeze solid again as soon as the sky went dark. The gates stood open, and Lizandra glanced back into the wagon once more before urging the horse forward and through the square entrance.

She'd stopped the wagon at the side of the road less than an hour before and checked on Reykas again. There had been no change she could detect since they left Stormbreak, but she knew he was declining. That's just the way this thing worked. It wouldn't allow him to linger forever in this twilight between life and death, and he wouldn't be getting better this time. The only direction from here was downward, and it was coming soon. Lizandra couldn't see it in his face or hear it in his breath, but she felt it in her heart. Death was coming for Reykas, and it had pursued them all the way from Stormbreak, down through Esterburgh, and now into Karsk.

Lizandra hated wasting a single second now that they were so close to their destination, but she forced herself to make that final stop so she could pull more blankets on top of him. She dragged a couple of lightweight burlap sacks across him as well, covering the already flattened shape of his body. She arranged a couple of packs around the sides of his head and pulled one blanket higher, anchoring it to hide his face. She could still see the shape of his feet at the end of the wagon, the curve of one arm bent to the side, the rise of his chest, now shallower than ever. But no one else would see him. No one else would expect a man to be hiding beneath all that cargo, and she hoped the deception would hold until they'd found what she'd come for.

Most of the people congregating and buying and selling just inside the walls of Karsk were bundled for the winter, their clothes brown and dark and drab like those of the rebels Lizandra had left in the north. They did their business and moved through the streets without interacting more than they had to. Most of them had their heads hung low, their eyes cast down, and their hands in their pockets if they weren't laden with bundles or packages. She could hardly blame them, given how cold and stark this place was, but there was something more to it. This widespread melancholy wasn't solely due to the weather.

Lizandra watched a child in a threadbare coat slip between

the legs of two merchants and grab a pouch off the belt of one before darting back into the crowd. She thought of Dorrin, and a smile tugged at the corners of her mouth before that night came rushing back to her. She'd been on the roof of the dormitory, reaching for him, trying to grab his hand, but it had been no use. He'd made the jump toward her, and he'd caught himself with magic. The golden tendrils of light that had held him aloft between the rooftops were a sight she'd never forget. And she'd never forget what came after. The zip of the cable as it spun around Dorrin's neck and the horrifying snap as it pulled him backwards. The fierce scowl of the Kite when he reached Dorrin's body and stared down at it before he shifted his gaze up and across the empty expanse to meet her eyes. Hatred and madness had poured across the gap and would have struck Lizandra herself dead if his anger had carried weight. But Reykas had grabbed her hand and pulled her away, and the last thing she'd seen before she turned and ran was his red uniform. The red tabard with that accursed black bird on it.

The shape of the bird on the Kite's chest swam in her memory and clouded her vision, and it took a moment before Lizandra realized it wasn't just in her mind's eye. That same black bird stared back at her from the side of the road as the wagon wheels bumped over uneven pavers. Her eyes widened, and her breath caught in her throat. It was a Kite, no doubt about it. This one was tall and thin, a man with dark hair pulled back into a ponytail, his forehead severe and his cheeks sallow. He was talking with a woman, probably one of the city's merchants, and he hadn't noticed Lizandra. She tore her eyes away from him and pressed her gaze into the back of the horse's head, willing her to walk faster but keeping herself from urging her forward. Steady, calm, quiet. That was the way to not be noticed.

Still, her breathing came faster now, and she cursed the quick foggy plumes that would give her away.

Kites, here in Karsk. If there was one, there would be more, and that more than explained the somber air of the people she'd seen. Klubridge had responded to its occupation with indignation and revolt. Karsk seemed more prone to tucking its head and accepting whatever was thrown its way. This Kite wore a blue uniform, not the red of the ones who'd pursued them in Klubridge. She didn't recognize the man, but she knew those hunters. The Azure Kites were the ones who had monitored Klubridge for the entire time she'd lived there. The entire time Caius and Samira had been there as well, to hear them tell it. Their commander was a man called Tereth. He was Imperial, and he surely would have dragged them all out to be turned into halflocks if he'd known they were mages, but he'd still been a more reasonable man than any of the red Kites that had come to the city. Caius had even dealt directly with Tereth at some point, and the two had some sort of understanding or arrangement with each other. They'd all wondered why the Scarlet Kites were the ones who'd come to harass Caius, and perhaps this was the answer. The blue ones had been in Karsk instead. But why? And why were they still in the city, this long after?

As Lizandra turned it over in her mind, she spotted the second Azure Kite half a block south, along the right side of the road. She pulled the reins and guided the wagon left at the next cross street. She had to get off the main road and away from those uniforms. But where was she going? She had the name Pelo Foyen had given her and not much else. She was looking for an apothecary named Jod Padar, but who knew how many apothecaries there might be in this city? She needed to ask directions, but every person she spoke to was one more person who might spot Reykas in the wagon or recognize her from the description on the bounty that surely was posted by then.

If a merchant or a citizen or some other ordinary person spotted Reykas, it would be a curiosity and a topic of questioning. If a Kite spotted him, it would all be over. They'd arrest him and drag him out of the wagon and take him away for being ill. It wouldn't even matter whether he was a mage, and they wouldn't even have to know that she was a mage herself. They'd bring him in and lock him away until he died, so that he wouldn't spread whatever potential illness he carried to the rest of the population. That was as much a part of the Kites' mandate as hunting mages. But, of course, they'd know she was a mage before they got him halfway out of the wagon. Or at least the ones who found those first Kites' bodies would know. Either way, they'd be exposed, and Reykas would be dead.

That was the thought most present in her mind when she made another turn, this time to the right and directly into a roadblock. It was a single blue Kite, a woman with auburn hair that hung loose around her face in twisting tendrils, longer at the front than at the back. She waved the cart ahead of Lizandra through but held up a gloved hand as Lizandra approached. Lizandra pulled back on the reins and slowed to a stop beside the woman, her hands chilling inside her gloves. The cold crept up her arms and was well into her chest before the Kite spoke.

"When did you arrive in Karsk?"

Lizandra opened her mouth to speak, and her voice wouldn't come. Her dry tongue stuck to the roof of her mouth, and the insides of her cheeks felt like cotton. Her throat ached, and she realized she hadn't said a word in the days and nights since fleeing Stormbreak. She'd been so focused on caring for Reykas and hastening their descent through the mountains and keeping out of sight that she had said nothing to anyone, not even to Reykas or to the horse or to herself.

Lizandra coughed and swallowed and said, "Earlier today." Her voice sounded hoarse and false in her head, but the Kite glanced away from her and toward the wagon, seeming bored.

"Your business in Karsk?"

Lizandra blinked and looked at the Kite and away again. She was awful at lying and even worse at acting. Her place was bending and leaping and flying across the stage in silence, not concocting stories to save her from prison or worse. The last time she'd had to lie to Kites, it had been as a fine lady in the central bank at Klubridge. She'd gotten caught that time, and her prospects weren't any better when she was doing it as a bedraggled traveler with matted hair and a wind-reddened nose.

"Business," she mumbled and instantly regretted it. Something specific would have been better. So she added, "Antiques," and that was even worse. She squeezed her eyes shut but opened them again when she realized how guilty that would make her look.

The Kite was looking at her now, the woman's brows pulled

down and her face set with more interest than before. "What's in the wagon?"

Lizandra tried to swallow, but her mouth and throat were dry, and she made a gulping sound that was somewhere between a choke and a sob. The Kite looked behind her, toward the cart, and took a step in that direction. Lizandra's right hand dropped from the reins into her lap, and her fingers curled into a fist. She breathed through her nose and tried to steady herself, slow her speeding heart. But she knew what had to come next. She'd once sworn to Reykas that she'd kill anyone who came after him, and that time had come. Lizandra exhaled, and the power flowed into her fist. A dim green aura surrounded her hand, and she tensed to turn and sling light at the other woman.

"Mage!"

The shout came from behind her, and for a fleeting instant Lizandra thought it was the Kite. But no, it was a man's voice, loud and gruff. How had anyone known? How had they seen her? Her heart thudded hard and fast again, and the breath wheezed out between her lips, warming the scarf in front of her face. She turned in the seat and saw the Kite staring in the same direction, back toward the corner where Lizandra had turned just moments before.

The man at the corner was short and stocky, with a flat cap shoved on his head. A tangle of graying hair poked out from under it, and his face beneath the curls was round and pink, with stubble covering his cheeks and chin. "Mage!" he called again and pointed a finger back in the direction from which he'd come.

The Kite left the wagon and closed the distance between herself and the man with three brisk steps. She pulled back the edge of her long coat as she moved, exposing the hilt of the sword strapped at her waist. Lizandra watched with confusion as the man jabbed his finger toward the main street with more urgency. His eyes slid from the Kite to meet Lizandra's, and he mouthed something at her. She squinted and shook her head. He did it again, this time with his eyes wide. "Go!"

Lizandra hesitated and looked at the Kite, but the woman

was past the man now and moving toward the corner. She'd all but forgotten Lizandra.

"Go," Lizandra echoed to the horse in a whisper and shook the reins. The wheels crunched on the wet paving as the wagon rocked back into motion, and Lizandra cringed, certain the Kite would hear and change her direction. But no, they were rolling again, and the buildings of the side street swept past, faster and faster now, growing the distance between Lizandra and certain doom.

Two more quick turns off that street, and she was away from prying eyes but also entirely lost in the labyrinthine blocks of Karsk. The buildings all looked the same, each one a black or gray box like the one next to it, and mounds of snow capped all of them, sometimes sitting solid in the shadow of taller buildings and sometimes leaking down the sides and front as the sun turned the ice into slush. It was a miserable city, and Lizandra was close to tears by the time she slowed the horse and directed the wagon into an alley between two identical structures.

The map had taken her as far as the city gates, and she didn't know how to find the chemist after that. She hadn't expected that the city would be crawling with Kites, but she should have guessed it. Nowhere was safe now, not after what they'd done. Not after Klubridge. This would be their lives now, constantly running and hiding and fearing, unless the rebellion found them a way out of it. She snorted at that notion. Micah Vaino had no hope of leading his rebels to any sort of meaningful victory. Perhaps Naecara Klavan could have done better, but it hardly mattered who ran the rebellion. What could a handful of poorly trained rebel soldiers do against the might of the entire Empire?

Lizandra had considered simply fleeing with Reykas after she'd gotten him the cure. They could go somewhere else and make a life for themselves away from the Empire and the rebellion and all this nonsense. But now she knew that was nothing more than a dream. There was nowhere they could go, and she'd be fortunate at this point just to find that cure in time. If she did get it, she'd take him right back through Esterburgh and straight back up those mountains, and they'd wait at Stormbreak until something changed. Until it was safe to leave and have a life.

"Close one, eh?"

Lizandra lurched in her seat and looked down to her left. The man who'd distracted the Kite grinned up at her from the street, his hat now in his hands, and a bald spot showing atop his head.

"How did you find me?" she asked. Her voice was less raspy now, but her exhaustion and fear still muted it.

He shrugged with his hands to the sides, the hat wadded in one gloved fist, his fingers red from the cold and protruding from where the glove's fingers had been ripped or cut away. "I know this city," he said, the word "city" tumbling out with a lisp. "The Kites are no more welcome here than anywhere else."

She watched him as he pulled the hat flat again and pushed it back onto his head. "Thank you?" It came out as a question, so she said it again. "Thank you for your help."

He gave her a tight smile and looked out of the alley and toward the street. "If I might say, a bit of coin would go farther than a thanks, my lady."

"Of course," she said and leaned to fumble her hand into the pouch that had been riding at her feet. Oreth had included some money with the supplies, and it was more than worth a seri or two to make sure this stranger didn't decide she'd be better off under the watch of the Kites after all. She didn't take her eyes off him as her fingers dug into the bag, and it took her a moment to pull up a coin. She held it out to him but paused when she saw she'd taken two instead of one.

"You said you know this city," she said, still holding both coins.

The man's eyes were on her hand now, and he nodded, his cheeks shaking with the effort. "I do. I know Karsk from wall to wall and up and down."

"This is for your help earlier," she said and dropped one coin into his hand. "This second coin is yours, too, if you can help me find where I'm going."

"And where's that?" he asked, looking from the remaining coin to her face.

"I'm looking for a chemist named Jod Padar. Do you know him?"

The man's face split with a gapped grin. "Sounds like I'll be earning that second coin from you."

~

Paying the man an extra seri wasn't much, and Lizandra half wondered whether she'd been swindled after she got the directions and left him standing in that alleyway. But, true to his word, the stranger had given her directions that led directly to the apothecary's shop, and he told her how to get there while avoiding the main roads. He hadn't given her his name or asked her any questions, and she hadn't volunteered him anything beyond that extra seri. He'd seemed satisfied with that, and they'd parted ways.

Now, she stared up at the side of another building constructed from black stone, just like all the rest of them on its street. The only thing differentiating this one was an ancient wooden sign bolted to its face, just above the front door. The sign was so old and weathered she wouldn't have noticed it if she hadn't already known to be looking for it.

It must have been decades ago that someone stenciled something that looked like a flask on the left of the sign and something that looked like an herb or a leaf on the right side. The two symbols met and overlapped at the center, but much of the paint had given way to the elements. Below the pictures were letters that probably had once spelled "chemist," but now the H and M and T were gone. And above the icons, protected from the weather only a little better by the lip of the roof, were faded letters spelling out "Padar."

This was it. She'd reached the place she'd traveled so far to find, and now she was stopped before it, still sitting on the wagon seat and staring up at the sign. A breeze brushed across the exposed skin around her eyes, but she hardly felt it by that point. Inside that building was the man who could cure Reykas. After all this time and all this sickness, just when he was on the verge of death, Reykas could be healed.

Lizandra licked at her chapped lips behind the scarf before tugging the material down and off her face. She reached to drop the reins but stayed her hand as she glanced up the street. Padar's apothecary was on a back road, but there were still people moving along the street. She couldn't leave the horse and cart sitting in the roadway, not with Reykas bundled up and hidden in the back. There was a narrow space to the right of the building, between this structure and its neighbor, and that's where Lizandra directed the horse to take them. She'd have to back them out somehow when they were ready to leave, but this would be a sufficient hiding place until then.

Once she was sure the horse was content and the wagon was suitably tucked out of sight of the road, Lizandra rounded the corner and clasped her fingers around the metal doorknob. Even through her gloves, she could feel the cold pressing back. This was the moment she'd worked toward. The moment when she'd find out how much truth had been in Pelo Foyen's story. Her heart told her he'd spoken the truth, but her head stalled her with doubts. If there had been a cure to this disease, why wouldn't Foyen have accepted it? Why would he have let himself die in that lonely stone room, so far away from anyone and anything he knew and loved?

He'd said there was a price, and he wasn't willing to pay it. What price could be so great that he'd give his own life for it?

Lizandra exhaled as she turned the doorknob and pushed the door open. Whatever the price, she was about to agree to it.

The shop was dark, with only a single wall sconce flickering behind the counter. It wasn't a small space but seemed like it was tiny, cramped as it was with all manner of boxes and vials and flasks, all scattered across tables and countertops. The wooden shelves that lined the walls overflowed with sacks and packets, and leaves and twigs and powders spilled from some of them, trickling down onto the floor. The scent of unusual spices stung Lizandra's nose, and she thought for an instant that she would sneeze, but the urge passed after the door slid shut behind her. Her foot bumped against something, and she glanced down to see a book discarded on the floor next to the entrance. The whole place was in a cluttered disarray, and it matched the demeanor of the old man before her.

He stood hunched over the counter, his wiry frame backlit in the orange light of the sconce. The shadows deepened the lines in his skin and brought the dark bags that drooped beneath his eyes into stark relief. His eyes were tired and sad, brown but dull and sunken into his face. Gray hair hung long from his head, having receded but ended its march about halfway across the top of his skull. The remaining hair was stringy and unkempt, with individual white hairs flying away on their own, protruding as though they wanted to escape. He wore a dark yellow vest buttoned over a white shirt with long sleeves that ended in absurd and frayed borders of lace. The outfit looked like it had seen finer days and maybe even had been worn by a finer person. But now, here it was on this strange man in Karsk.

"I'm looking for Jod Padar," Lizandra said. Her voice was stronger now, and when it shook, it was no longer merely from the lack of use. The encounter with the Kite had frightened her, but reaching her intended destination and facing the man she believed she'd been seeking heightened her anxiety even more.

"You're looking at him," the old man said and sniffed. His voice was high and nasal, but soft enough that Lizandra almost had to strain to understand him. "What do you need?"

Lizandra stepped closer to the counter, and a movement to the right caught her eye. She squinted into the shadows and made out a form sitting in the darkness. It looked like an old woman, her hands busy at something in her lap. The firelight caught the glimmer of metal sticks, and Lizandra realized she was knitting. She sat silently in the dark, her needles clacking together every once in a while as they pieced together whatever she was making.

"What do you need?" Jod Padar asked again, and Lizandra looked back to him.

"I was told you could help my... my friend."

"Your friend," he said and leaned on the counter with his elbows, his curved back bending his head forward. He raised his eyes and was watching her now from beneath his sparse white eyebrows. He waited for her to say more, and so she did.

"He's outside in the wagon. Could you come see him?" After a second of conflict, she added, "He needs your help."

Padar exhaled through his nose and looked toward the

woman in the corner. He said nothing to her, though, and moved around a stack of shallow wooden boxes that had straw poking out the sides. He probably would have been an inch or so taller than Lizandra was, if he'd been able to stand upright, but his stooped posture thrust his head forward and dropped his eyes to chin-level on her. He waved toward the door, and she stepped back to open it again.

The daylight was blinding now, after only a few moments inside that dark storefront, and Lizandra squinted against the sun as she led Jod Padar out and around the side of the apothecary. As they stepped into the street, fear grabbed her heart, and she was certain the cart with Reykas would be gone when they reached the alley. But it was still there, and the horse huffed an impatient greeting when she saw them approaching.

"He's in here," Lizandra said. She looked out toward the street before reaching into the wagon and pulling the blanket back to expose Reykas' face. There in the daylight, it was easy to see how far his cheeks had sunken and how the skin around his eyes had hollowed. Reykas was only two years older than Lizandra, but lying there in the wagon, he would have passed for as old as Jod Padar.

The old man swatted Lizandra on the arm and motioned her out of his way as he came alongside the wagon. He had to lean up and forward, straining on his toes and pressing his weight into the side of the cart, in order to reach Reykas' face. He touched Reykas' cheek with the back of his hand and then moved it up to his forehead. Then he pressed his thumb against Reykas' right eye and lifted the lid. Lizandra gasped but managed to remain otherwise silent when she saw Reykas' dark eye exposed. It stared up toward the sky, unfocused and unaware.

Padar pulled his hand back and humphed under his breath.

"Can you help him?" Lizandra asked.

Padar looked at her, but instead of answering, he gestured past her, toward the back of the building. "Take him around there. I'll meet you at the back door." And, without waiting for a response, he limped back around the front of the shop.

Lizandra stared after him, blinking in the cold, and looked

down at Reykas. He lay as motionless and calm as he'd been when they first left Stormbreak. Even calmer? Her heart thudded, and she pushed her hand in front of his face, angling her palm under his nose. It took a few seconds, but she felt the soft puff of air as he exhaled. There was still time.

She grabbed the reins and gave them a gentle tug, walking ahead of the horse as she pulled the wagon into motion once more. The stone alleyway ended at an intersection, the back of another building in front of them and a dank walkway extending to both the left and right. Lizandra maneuvered the horse and wagon to the left, and as they made the turn, she saw a door open outward from the back of the apothecary. Jod Padar stepped out and beckoned her forward with a sharp motion, and she led the horse to him. As she came even with the door, Lizandra saw Padar had pulled a wheeled table up to the doorway, and he dragged it the rest of the way outside when the cart rolled to a stop once more.

"You'll help me with him," he said and rolled the gurney to the back of the wagon. It took a few minutes of shifting blankets and moving the remaining supplies out of the way, but they eventually cleared the way to move Reykas. Working together, they shifted him out of the wagon and onto the cart. With only the feeble man's strength to help, Lizandra wasn't able to be as gentle as she'd have liked, but the dragging and tugging and lifting and depositing hadn't disturbed Reykas' rest. She suspected nothing would ever disturb it, unless this cure worked.

They got him transferred, though, and only a couple of minutes later they had Reykas in the back room of the apothecary. It was brighter there than in the front room, these walls paneled in wood that looked like it had once been white. Three fat candles sputtered light from corners of the room, and a closed door in the far wall likely led back to the front room of the shop.

The gurney sat at an angle in the center of the floor, a rickety bookcase near the head. Lizandra's eyes roamed its shelves, looking for some answer, some clue to how this old man might cure Reykas, but there was nothing familiar. Just jars and small pots of various shapes, sizes, and colors, all arranged in neater rows than anything she'd seen in the front of the shop. This was where Jod Padar's real work was done.

"Do you know what's wrong with him?" she asked.

The old man had stooped over Reykas again, studying his face. His eyes flicked up to meet hers. "Do you?"

Before Lizandra could answer, the door to the front room opened, and the old woman was there. She looked every bit as ancient and decrepit as Padar, and he glanced back at her. "My wife," he said.

The woman wore a faded blue dress with sleeves too short for her skinny arms. The veins and tendons stood plain on the backs of her hands, and she curled her fingers into loose fists as she came into the room with a shuffling gait. The skin on the woman's face was crinkled and thin, looking more like the face of a puppet made from paper than an actual person. Her rheumy eyes stared ahead blankly, and Lizandra wondered whether she might be blind. Her hair was white and wild, standing out from her head, almost identical to the wig Lizandra's father used to place atop a scarecrow every time the harvest was coming in during those few dull months each year when the whole family wasn't traveling. As frail as the woman seemed, Lizandra wouldn't have been surprised to learn that she, too, had been constructed from straw and fabric.

Lizandra's eyes remained on the woman, but she asked Jod Padar, "Can you help him?"

He sniffed once, then again, and finally answered. "I can."

Lizandra looked at him then, her eyes widening. She'd brought Reykas all this way on the hope of finding a cure, but she realized that only at that moment, standing in the back room of a run-down chemist's shop, did she truly begin to believe and hope. Hope had fueled the journey, but it had been a false hope. Part of her had expected they'd arrive in Karsk to find no one named Jod Padar. Or that they'd find him, and he'd have no idea why she was bothering him with her nearly dead lover. But no, this old man knew what was wrong with Reykas. He recognized it, and he could fix it.

"He's not got long. Another day or two, and you'd have been

too late," Padar said. "Maybe even gone tonight." There was no emotion in the statement, and he seemed in no hurry as he came around the table to stand closer to Lizandra.

She held his eyes and waited, scarcely wanting to breathe. The solution was right here before her. Somewhere in those jars, those flasks, those boxes, this old man had the cure. The cure to a disease that had been taking Reykas' life by inches since before she'd known him. He was down to the last of those inches now, and this man could stop it.

"Help him," she whispered. "Please."

Padar stared at her through two breaths and then three. The lines at the corners of his eyes deepened, and he pressed his thin lips together, the bottom one protruding like a peevish child's. He exhaled one more time and blinked and said, "How bad do you want it?"

There was no hesitation in Lizandra's response. "More than anything." Her voice was still quiet, still almost a whisper, but it felt loud to her ears there in that unfamiliar room with this old man she didn't know. And the old woman as well. Lizandra had forgotten about her, but the woman was at her shoulder, having crept up from behind. Lizandra flinched at the woman's touch. The wrinkled and spindly fingers were cold against the side of her face as they stroked from the corner of her mouth back to the bottom of her ear.

Lizandra shuddered and pulled away, and the woman's hand lifted from her face, waiting, hovering an inch away. Lizandra turned her head to look at Padar's wife, and only then did she see how the woman's unruly hair fell in an unusual pattern down the back of her head. The horseshoe-shaped scar was barely visible, but it showed as a pink line amid the white tangles of hair.

"Your wife," Lizandra said. "She's—"

"A halflock," Padar said. "Hold steady now."

The woman looked at Lizandra, not quite meeting her eyes. She waited for Lizandra to give a slight nod, and then her fingers were back, the tips brushing against Lizandra's cheek. The invisible trails they left remained cold, and the skin tickled as though a feather had brushed it. Lizandra held steady this time, though, just like Padar had told her. She watched the old woman from the corner of her eye, and for an instant Magra's round face transposed itself over this woman's. Two halflocks, both victims of the Empire, both working toward Imperial goals. Only one of them had already betrayed her, but Lizandra had little confidence that she could trust this woman any more than she did Magra.

The woman's fingers passed under Lizandra's right ear and around to the base of her neck, digging beneath the scarf and sending another shiver through Lizandra's shoulders. She still held steady, and she fixed her eyes on the far corner of the room. Lizandra had gotten Reykas out of the keep and smuggled him south through snow and ice and ill terrain, and she'd kept him alive the whole way. She could sit still for another moment or two or however long it took this woman to do whatever she was doing.

Lizandra felt fingers running up her neck now and into her hair, sliding upward now, the cold palm cupping the back of her head, the thumb grasping at the bottom of her skull. She felt more aware than ever of the oily mess her hair had become during the journey. Not only then, though. She'd stopped taking care of herself long before they'd left Stormbreak, and she knew she must have looked pitiful at that point. Her hair, once sleek and smooth and nearly white, was a dark nest now, all wadded and woven around on itself. It was disgusting and dirty, but the old woman didn't hesitate to spread her fingers and run her hand higher up the back of Lizandra's head. Her hand squeezed gently, and Lizandra realized the old woman was cupping the same part of her head that the Empire had cut open on the woman's own. Before Lizandra had time to process that information, a jolt rocked her head forward with a loud popping sound, and her eyes swam out of focus, black spots invading her vision for an instant before everything settled itself again.

The woman's touch was gone, and Lizandra raised a shaking hand to feel the back of her head, sure she'd find herself injured. But there was nothing but the snaky mass of hair she knew she'd find. She looked at Padar and opened her mouth to ask what had happened, but he was watching the old woman who now stood just ahead of Lizandra.

"Well?" he asked.

"It's him," the woman said, her voice little more than a hollow croak. It was the sound of a leaf skittering across the floor in an abandoned house. The last breath of a dying person. But the woman lived, and she lifted her left hand to point a bony finger toward Reykas.

"What is it?" Lizandra asked. "What's him?" Fear fought to overtake her reason, but she swallowed hard and looked between the old woman and her husband, trying to reason out what had just happened.

Padar was still looking at his wife, though, and he snorted. "Him. Figured." Only then did he turn his attention to Lizandra. "What you want. There's a price for it."

The price. The damnable price that had been too much for Pelo Foyen to pay. "The price," she said before she realized it was aloud.

"You said you wanted this more than anything."

"I do," she said, leaning forward now. "Please help him."

"You can't pay the price I want," Padar said.

Lizandra sat motionless, her lips barely parted, and she was unsure she'd heard him correctly. "I can pay. I will pay. Just tell me what you want!"

"What I want's what you want the most. What's most precious to you. That's the price for the cure." He looked at his wife again. "Only, she says what's most precious to you is him. Can't very well heal him and take him at the same time, can I?"

"She read my thoughts?" Lizandra asked and fought against another shudder. This woman was just like Magra, down to her remaining abilities.

"Not so much. She can tell you what's important. What you live for. That's it, but it's generally enough." Jod Padar rubbed at his chin, and his hand passing over the stubble made a scratching sound that was impossibly loud in that small room. "It's usually the one who's been infected that comes for the cure. That's an easier bill to settle. They always have something they can give. Not you, though. He's what you live for. You can't pay me."

"That's... that's ridiculous," Lizandra said. She fought for control, but her voice was louder now. "I brought him all this way, and I'm willing to pay you. Tell me what I can give you. You can save him. Please, be reasonable."

Padar frowned at that. "You think this isn't me being reasonable, girl? You think I enjoy this job? I have rules, and I follow them, and that's how I live." His eyes flicked to his wife and back. "How we live."

Lizandra looked at the old woman and her blank expression, and she understood. "You work for the Empire, don't you? For Peregrine. It's why you have your wife. They made her a halflock, and they'll take her back if you don't do what they say."

Padar didn't give her a direct answer but said, "It's a barter. If they're going to suffer a mage to be saved and live, they need something equal in return. Easiest thing's to take whatever's most important to you. For some it's honor. For some it's money. Some, it's loyalty or their name or who knows what."

"How do you take someone's name? Or their loyalty? You're making no sense."

He cut his eyes toward the door. "You'll need help loading him back, I expect. Might as well let him rest here until he's gone, though. I don't imagine it'll be long."

Her heart thudded in her throat, and she shook her head. "No, please! They won't know. You can help him, and I won't tell anyone."

The old man scowled at her. "I don't know you, girl. You're asking me to trust you, and I don't. We have no barter, we have no deal. Take him or leave him until he's done. Either way, we have no business."

He opened the door to the front of the shop, and his wife moved toward it with slow, shuffling steps. Tears flooded Lizandra's eyes, and they stung from the sudden warmth replacing the cold that had haunted them all the way down from Stormbreak. She held the edge of the gurney and stiffened her arms so she wouldn't collapse if her legs gave way. This couldn't be the end. Not after all they'd been through together. Not after what she'd managed. Not when the cure was so close at hand, there, likely in that very room. She placed her hand on Reykas' chest and watched his motionless face. It looked the same as it had for those past days, when he seemed to already be gone, but she knew he was still there, still sleeping, just waiting for her to save him.

She slid her hand up to the side of his face, and her eyes widened.

"Wait!"

Padar turned an irritated frown toward her, and his wife halted her slow steps. The chemist watched Lizandra, waiting for her to speak.

"You said the ones who are infected are usually the ones who come to you. They're the ones who pay the price."

"And?" he said, his hand still on the open door.

"Let her touch him. Find out what's most important to him. We can pay that." She didn't know whether that would even work. Could the woman sense anything from Reykas with him in that deep slumber at the edge of death? It seemed doubtful, but it was all she had.

Padar's lips pressed together again, and he glanced at his wife. She had half turned then and was looking toward Reykas, but her eyes seemed focused past him, on nothing at all. "Say she does it. She might see you're what's most important. You might be the price," he said.

Lizandra moved her hand down from Reykas' face to his shoulder, and she stood steadier, firmer than she had since they'd arrived in Karsk. She knew her purpose, and she knew what she was willing to do. She'd told Reykas she would kill for him. Would she be willing to die for him instead?

She swallowed hard one more time and said, "Then I'll pay it."

PART III
THE PRICE

CHAPTER 24

Caius counted his breaths in the darkness. The ground beneath his feet was firm, but there might as well have been nothing else in existence beyond the flatness that pressed back up to support him. It was a blackness unlike any he could remember, and he touched his face to verify that his eyes were, in fact, open. Aside from his own breathing, he heard no sound, and there was nothing to smell beyond a faint and bitter scent that reminded him of the electrical wires he and Apak had installed in the theater.

He lowered his hand from his face and reached forward, outward, his fingers searching for a wall, a railing, anything that might moor him in space or give him any sense of where he was or what surrounded him. There was nothing but empty air, not cold but cool. Caius frowned and flexed his fingers in the space before him. His hand curled into a fist, but there was resistance, as if there was a thickness to the air. He inhaled again, this time through his mouth, and there was no mistaking the metallic sourness on his tongue. There was something in there with him. Something strange and hidden and possibly electric?

A thudding echoed from in front of Caius and reverberated at his sides and behind him, surrounding him with a chorus of clanks, with a high-pitched whine following in its wake. Out of the black nothingness, a blue light blazed into existence before him. It was far away, but he lurched backwards in surprise and turned his head, throwing his arms up to block his squinting eyes.

The cacophony of bangs and thuds died all at once, but the whine remained, a ringing in his ears that he might have believed was nothing more than his imagination if its tone didn't ebb and flow in time with the pulsing of the blue light. Hesitantly, he turned his head to face the glow once more, and he peeked between his outstretched fingers to see the illumination. It was triangular and almost resembled a brazier set into the distant wall. The light it emitted looked like it came from flames, but the flickering was blue, not orange, and its undulations were far too regular to be natural.

The triangular object remained the only source of light in the otherwise continual darkness, but it was enough for Caius to see that the shape of the room where he stood mirrored that of the light source. The walls angled up toward each other from the left and right, meeting somewhere far overhead and extending down the long corridor before him. Blue light rippled along the walls, giving hints of a rough but reflective texture, but the room was too big and the light too small for him to see more detail than that.

Caius let his hands fall to his sides, and he looked down to see hints of blue light flickering across the toes of his boots, just enough to confirm that he was standing on solid ground. He slid his right foot forward, slowly and carefully, still not trusting that there wouldn't be an unseen pit yawning before him. But the floor was smooth, and his step carried him forward, closer to the blue light by inches.

He shifted his weight to pull his left foot forward with the same careful stride, and that was when the room shook. Everything rocked left and then right, and he staggered, bending his knees to keep his balance. His breathing came faster then, and he stumbled with the next great quake, going down on his left knee and banging it hard against the floor. He caught himself with his hands and felt the ground against his palms. It wasn't rock, like he'd expected. His fingers rubbed against a texture that was both smooth and pitted, colder than the surrounding air. It was metal, like the walls and like the taste in his mouth.

The room gave one more pitch, and Caius tumbled backwards, and the ground was no longer there. He spun and spiraled, and his vision went white, and he squeezed his eyes shut. When he opened them, Samira crouched over him, her hands on his shoulders.

"Caius!" She raised her voice and wasn't quite shouting, but everything was loud then, rumbling and grinding. The room still shook and wobbled, but the floor beneath him was wood now. Wood, covered in something that felt like carpet.

Caius blinked and squinted toward the daylight streaming through the windows of the carriage, and he got his elbows under him as he pushed himself off the floor. "What happened?"

Samira slid one hand from his shoulder around to support his back, and she cupped the back of his head with her other hand, probably trying to keep him from banging it against one of the seats or some other fixture. Even as she wrestled him up and onto the seat opposite hers, the concern on her face was plain.

"You were sleeping," she said. "I knew you hadn't slept last night, so I tried to let you rest. But then you got up. You were on your feet, and I think you were trying to get out the door. I blocked the door, but then you fell over, and I thought—I don't know what I thought. What was that?"

He saw the concern in her eyes, and there was some fear mixed in, but what could he tell her? He looked away, out the window. "Where are we now?"

"No," she said, and she grabbed his chin to pull his gaze to meet hers again. "You're not going to keep brushing this aside. What was that?"

He stared into her eyes for a moment before he shook his head and said, "I don't know. A dream? I hardly even know anymore." He pinched at the bridge of his nose, as if that would make the mounting headache subside. "Every time I sleep, it's something bizarre. Not like any dreams I've ever had."

"And the only other time you've sleepwalked was that night you went up to the top of the keep," Samira said.

He considered letting that go with a lie of omission, but what good would that do? Something was clearly wrong with him. He shook his head again. "There was at least one other time since then."

They sat facing each other, their knees inches apart in the rocking carriage. Caius lowered his hands onto his thighs, and Samira put her hands over one of his. "Whatever this is, we'll figure it out. Do you remember the dream?"

"Just that I was in a tunnel. Or maybe a hallway? Some sort of enclosed space. It was dark, and there was a blue light at the far end." Was there more than that? He strained toward more details, but they fled, his mind fumbling through them and losing them to his waking consciousness. "That's all I remember."

He looked away again, no longer trying to avoid Samira's gaze, but confident that he had nothing else to contribute to that conversation. The landscape passed by the window, leaves flicking past in a blur of green, orange, brown, and red. He leaned closer to the glass and pulled his hands free from Samira's. "There's no snow."

"We're far enough south now," she said and glanced out the window. "We made the turn south of Salkire while you were sleeping. We're headed for Bria now."

"Bria," he said. He and Samira had spent many years traveling before they settled in Klubridge. It had been a long time since they'd been in Bria, but he remembered being there in the summer. The city was far inland and due west from Klubridge, so he expected the winter weather there would be something more like he was used to. Not as chilling and crushing as the wind and ice at Stormbreak had been.

"You're thinking about Klubridge," Samira said.

He gave her a slight smile. "In a way."

"How bad do you think it is there?"

"Bad," he said. "The city's still there, but I doubt we'd recognize it."

Samira frowned and looked out the opposite window. Just as she'd known he was thinking about Klubridge, he could see the worry in her posture and knew she was remembering all the people they'd known there and left behind when they'd fled on Drass' ship.

"There were a lot of survivors," he said. "Micah got reports of refugees."

Samira's lips tightened at the mention of Micah Vaino, and Caius added, "This is how we get away from him. Away from him and the rebellion and all the rest of it."

She breathed out and stretched her neck to the side. "I know. It's just... I never would have imagined any of this for us. Even in the autumn when the Kites were after us, this isn't what I thought would come next."

"We're going to get out of this," Caius said. "All of us. We're going to get this Gressam person, this scion or whatever he is. We're going to bring him back to Stormbreak, and that'll be the end of it."

Samira looked back at him. "Do you really think it's going to be that simple? When is anything that simple?"

She was right, but Caius said, "We'll be old news. We probably already are, now that they've attacked Klubridge. That was the Empire punishing the city for rebelling. They don't even need to make a public spectacle out of us. Out of me."

"Then why are there still bounties on all of us?"

It was a fair question, and there had even been posters with crudely sketched images of Caius' face hanging on the walls in towns they'd passed through. Probably in Aramore as well, but they'd been able to circumnavigate that city. "Reward for the Wizard Akithar and His Accomplices" is what the papers had said. The drawing had been of a black-haired man with a thin mustache, the face of Akithar but not of Caius Harrim. As much weight as he'd lost that winter and as scraggly as he knew his hair and beard looked by that time, it was unlikely that anyone would recognize him. But there was always the chance, and people knew what Samira looked like. They knew her and Apak and Lizandra and the rest of them. It was a problem, and it would continue to be one.

"We have to take him back to Stormbreak," Caius said. "It's the best chance we have of turning the Empire's attention on someone other than us. The rebellion's attention, too."

Samira pulled her mouth tight but didn't protest. She didn't have to. She knew Caius could read her, just like she could read him, and she wasn't happy with this plan, but there was no point in resisting it. They had no other options that offered them any chance at freedom. Any chance at leaving Stormbreak and picking up the pieces and starting some sort of new lives.

"We'll make this work," Caius said. "Once we get back to the castle, we'll work it out, and we'll come back south with everyone."

"Not everyone," Samira said and met his eyes for just an instant before looking down again.

"Reykas."

"Reykas," she said.

Caius took a deep breath and let it out as he looked out the window. There was no chance he'd still be alive when they returned to Stormbreak. He might even be gone already. "We left Lizzie there, alone with him."

"Oreth is there. And Aquin," she added, looking even sadder.

Caius hadn't pressed Samira for details about what was happening between herself and Aquin, and he let the topic rest.

But Samira said, "We can bring Lizzie with us. And probably Aquin. She doesn't want to be there any more than we do. And Fairy. But I don't know about Apak. He seems like he might not come as easily."

Caius nodded. "He wants to see this through. Maybe he'll be ready to move ahead after this is all done."

"He's with the Klavan woman now," Samira said.

"They'll be back at Stormbreak again, either before or after we return. We'll all be together, and there will be an end to this."

"Or his business with her will entrench him even more," Samira said. "He's becoming a rebel, Caius. It seems like he wants to be a rebel."

Caius wanted to disagree, but he'd seen the determination in his old friend as well. "What about Oreth? Would he leave if Oreth left?"

"I don't know whether Oreth will want to leave. He's found a place there."

"The girl, Leyna?"

Samira nodded. "He won't leave her easily now. And, even if he did, I don't know whether that would be enough to bring Apak with us."

"We'll have to—"

Samira held up a hand to silence him. "We're slowing down."

He looked back to the window, and it was true. The trees passed more slowly now, and the sound of the wheels was lessening as they rolled to a more measured pace and eventually halted with a crunch on the gravel that covered the road. "Where are we?" Caius asked and leaned toward the door, but it pulled open before he could touch it.

Dekan Hama's enormous face peered into the carriage, and he squinted at them in the relative darkness. "You'll want to come out and see this."

~

They could hear pounding before they even stepped down from the coach. It was metallic and repetitive, and for a disorienting moment, Caius was back in his dream, back in that dark hallway with the blue flame and the sound of metal striking at all too regular intervals. But this new sound was distinct from the one he'd heard in the dream. It was repeating but less regular, and it was tinnier, the strikes sounding high and echoing, multiple sources overlapping with each other.

"What are they building?" Hama asked once Caius and Samira were next to him at the crest of a hill off the left side of the road.

Caius squinted down the slope and toward the open field. The grass was probably lush in the summer, but the winter had turned it brown and coarse. Even without snow that far south, the season still turned, and the clouds still hung low and gray, casting shadows over the workers. There was a circular hole in the middle of the field, and it was hard to guess the diameter from that far away. It was big, though, likely big enough around to fit a decently sized house inside it. And it was deep, too. The curved wall opposite Caius' position descended into the ground, and there was no bottom in sight. Instead, some sort of scaffolding ringed the inside of the pit. People worked along that sunken platform, carrying tools and materials in and out of the hole, up and down two sets of stairs they'd built into opposite sides of the hole.

Protruding up from the center of the huge hole was a massive cylinder, black and metallic. Its walls were thick, and the center was hollow, a dark hole staring up from the end of the strange tube. The workers had constructed a wooden crane above the pit, and Caius recognized its various parts from similar cantilever designs Apak had created for moving large objects onto the stage for performances over the years. This crane was bigger than anything Apak had ever constructed. Much bigger and much stronger, anchored to the ground next to the hole with giant pilings that likely descended dozens of feet into the earth.

"What is it?" Samira asked.

Caius shook his head. "I don't..." He frowned and squinted at the construction site again. He glanced at Hama. "Do you have a spyglass?"

Hama grunted and handed him a compact device that looked like two short spyglasses connected side by side with a hinge between them. Caius turned it over in his hands and found soft padding around the lenses at one end. He began to lift one spyglass to his eye when Hama stopped him.

"Both eyes," the man said and mimicked pulling the device up to his own face.

Caius nodded and pressed the padded rings to his eyes. The distant workers jumped into his view and were so close he nearly stumbled backwards. He pulled away from the lenses and whispered, "Brilliant." This was every bit as ingenious as something Apak would have put together, but Hama didn't allow him a chance to marvel at the invention.

"It's bloody binoculars. Just look through them." The big man's tone was sharp, but when wasn't it?

Caius looked at the binoculars one more time before peering through the lenses again. He was ready for the images to leap closer this time, and he scanned the scene with slow movements.

Where was the shape he had seen? A bit to the left, and up now. Up a little more. There!

On the far side of the hole, huge metal poles lay in rows, waiting to be incorporated into the project. The magnified view confirmed what Caius thought he'd seen with his own eyes. Sunlight crept through the clouds to paint the twisting edges of the poles, and Caius said, "It's a drill. They're building a massive drill." It was just like tools they'd used backstage for building sets and props and tricks, but this one was enormous. It was hard to even imagine how far into the ground those spiral rods would cut. And what would power them as they went down? Certainly nothing as rudimentary as the cranks Caius was used to turning by hand in order to drill into a soft piece of wood.

Hama took the binoculars from him and pressed them to his own face. "Drill. What are they doing with it?"

"I don't know," Caius said.

"Quarrying rock?" Samira asked.

Caius shook his head. "That doesn't look like a quarry operation. They'd have blasted out a bigger space, and they'd already be working it with picks and shovels. Whatever they're going for, it's deeper than I've seen quarries go."

"Who are they?" Hama asked and shoved the device back into Caius' hands.

Caius looked through the lenses at the workers again. Many of them wore common clothes, trousers and shirts and aprons and boots like he'd expect at any work site. They dragged metal parts into the pit, handed tools up out of it, and toiled under watchful eyes above. Even though the air was cool, Caius could see the sweat on the workers. The ones directing the work above them, though, were in uniform. They were the ones standing at the rim of the hole and huddled around a table looking at what were probably blueprints. "Local workers in the pit, most likely," he said. "Villagers. The ones up top are Imperial."

Caius handed the binoculars back to Hama, but the man didn't take them. He stared down the slope and across the field toward the work site, his eyes squinted against the sun and his nostrils flaring.

"Hama?" Caius asked, but the big man ignored him and

whipped his head to the right, toward the Aescalan woman standing near him. Her name was Talit, and she was nearly as massive as Hama, maybe an inch or two shorter but just as broad at the shoulders. She'd pulled her dark hair back from her face and bound it in tight twin braids that hung down her back, exposing the triangular blue tattoos that sat high on her cheeks. Like the other Aescalan, she still wore the same furs she'd worn in the north, even though it had grown markedly warmer as they traveled south. She cut her dark eyes toward Hama.

"Arms," he said, his voice quiet but clear.

Caius looked to Samira on his left, but she was staring at Hama, her mouth half open. He turned back in time to see Talit nod before turning to the small caravan and jabbing her fingers at the packs tied atop the carriage. One of the other Aescalan, an older man called Lodar, was already off his horse and pulling at the green tarp that covered the cargo.

"What are you doing?" Caius asked, but Hama's attention was on the distant workers. "Hama," Caius said, louder this time, and the man finally looked at him.

"Can you shoot?" Hama asked, his eyes slipping from Caius' face to Samira's.

Caius' eyes widened as Lodar handed a bundle to another Aescalan, a younger man whose name Caius hadn't learned. The young man, just as tall as Hama, perhaps even an inch taller, dropped the covering on the ground and cradled the contents in his hands.

Caius blinked at the weapon and grabbed Hama's shoulder. "That's a firearm!"

Hama crinkled his nose and jerked his shoulder free. "Stay here, then." He reached back and took another gun from Lodar. It was a long one, the barrel a metal cylinder and the stock made from a thick chunk of red wood. It wasn't the first time Caius had seen something like this in person, but it was the first one with such a long barrel. He might not have seen such a weapon before, but he'd read plenty about the technology of firearms. Powder was powder, whether it was providing flashes on the stage or propelling projectiles at targets.

Samira finally spoke, and her voice betrayed the same fear

Caius felt rising in his own chest. "They're a work crew! This isn't the military."

"They're Imperial," Hama said. "They serve the Ruinbringer. Whatever they're building, it's for him. Hardly matters if they're military. Just means they won't fight back."

Samira looked at Caius, her eyes wide, and he said, "If you attack them, you'll draw attention to us. We're here to find your scion. We can't do that with the Empire hounding us. They already have bounties on the two of us."

Hama held his firearm aloft and peered down the barrel. "Why do you think we need the Tamrat scion, wizard?" His eyes shifted from the sight at the end of the barrel to squint at Caius. "Destroying the Empire is what we're here to do, and we'll do it brick by bloody brick if we have to."

"The Nightingales," Caius said. "Nahk said they'll be hunting us. We don't need this kind of attention, Hama."

The final Aescalan who'd traveled with them was a younger woman with light brown hair and a round face. She stood as tall as the rest but was slim, almost willowy in comparison to the others. She'd taken a weapon from Lodar as well, and Caius realized all five of the Aescalan were armed at that point. Vaino had told him he'd be the leader of this expedition, but there was no question who was truly in charge. Caius and Samira were at the mercy of these five giants.

"Hama, please, listen to reason. If the Empire finds us, they'll hound us. We won't be able to find this scion, much less bring him back to the rebellion."

The big man turned his back on Caius and pointed to Lodar. "Take Rikin. Get close." And then, to Talit, "You're with me, around the opposite side. Stay low and quiet." And, finally, to the younger woman, "Wait 'til we're in place. Then take the ones at the ledge." He pointed out toward the work site and traced the rim of the pit with his wide index finger.

She nodded and walked to the top edge of the hill, her gun propped on her shoulder. It was even longer than the others, a thin, metallic weapon with a small hole at the end. She dropped to her left knee and lowered the weapon so the stock rested on her right shoulder. The barrel dipped toward the ground as she settled into place.

"Right then," Hama said and waved his followers into action.

"No!" Samira moved to intercept the Aescalan, but Hama stopped her with a dangerous stare. His eyes shone a fierce greenish blue in the midday light, and he watched Samira and Caius for a long moment.

"If they interfere, kill them," he said to the younger woman, and she nodded back, still wordless as her captain dropped into a crouch and disappeared into the brush.

～

The Aescalan woman kept her attention divided between Caius and Samira to her left and the scene unfolding before her. Her eyes were quick and glowed amber beneath their heavy lids, and Caius had no doubt she'd execute both of them if either made a move to stop her. His own gaze moved between the woman and Samira. Surely she saw the same thing he did and knew they'd stand no chance, but Samira didn't look afraid. She looked frustrated and angry, a combination Caius knew to be formidable. Not as formidable as a firearm in the hands of a woman who knew how to use it, though.

Caius' hand found Samira's, and he squeezed it. She looked at him, and her brows drew together. He shook his head, and she blew out something between a sigh and a hiss. But she didn't move, and that's what mattered.

The woman looked away from them and saw something that made her shift her weight off her knee. She sat flat on the ground, her left knee raised now and her right foot tucked under it. She propped her left elbow atop the raised knee and rested the gun across the bend in her arm. She slipped into the posture with the familiarity of an expert, just like Lizzie and Reykas contorting effortlessly into one of their practiced poses after dozens of hours of training on the stage.

Caius searched the distant trees at the edges of the field but saw nothing. Either Hama's people were excellent at stealth or this young woman's eyesight was the keenest he'd ever known.

Possibly both. Even with that kind of vision, surely she didn't expect to hit anything from that distance. That's not how any gun Caius had heard about was built. Nevertheless, she tilted her head toward the firearm, her right eye in line with a small spyglass mounted atop the weapon. Was her role to provide a distraction while Hama and his people swarmed the site? Was she merely providing a signal for them to attack after all four were in place?

Caius realized he still held the binoculars at his side, and he raised them to his face, searching for whatever sign the woman had seen. It was then that the gun roared to his right, and he flinched away from it, the binoculars nearly dropping from his hands, but not quite. His eyes were still on the work site when, an instant later, one of the Imperials at the edge of the pit jerked upright before pitching headfirst over the edge. Confusion and fear rippled through the others, workers and managers alike, some of them scrambling up and out of the hole while others clambered down into it. None of them knew where they'd be safe or even what had happened to the first man.

And then there was a distant bang, almost like a clap of thunder miles away. A second and third followed it, and then there was a fourth. Bodies tumbled to the ground after each shot, and the shouts and screams reached the hillside a moment before the young woman fired her second shot. It flew as true as the first, downing another Imperial and sending him sprawling against and knocking over the table covered in documents.

Caius pulled his face away from the lenses, his throat tight with terror and shock and sadness, and he looked at the woman next to him. No firearm should have been that accurate at this distance. And it probably wasn't. This woman had trained for so long that she and the weapon were one. She knew how to compensate for the drop of the shot, for the wind, and for any number of other complications between the end of the barrel and her target. Caius would have thought he was witnessing magic in action if he hadn't already seen enough mages at work to recognize this as pure skill and familiarity. The woman's hands were moving quickly, breaking down the front of the gun and slipping new ammunition into it. Her eyes remained fixed on the chaos in the distance, and Caius took a shuffling step back, away from her.

"Stay," she said with an unnerving calmness as she brought the gun up once more and fired another shot. She would murder him and Samira as easily as she was dispatching the Imperials if either of them tried to run.

Caius' ears rang with the blasts, both near and far, and he looked to Samira. She hadn't seen the deaths as clearly as he'd seen them, but her face still contorted in rage. "They've done it," she said, just loud enough for him to hear. He suspected the Aescalan woman could hear her, too, but Samira didn't seem to care. "The Empire will know we're here now."

She glared at the woman with the gun, and Caius touched her hand again and shook his head. He turned so that his back was to the woman and flinched again as she fired another shot at the enemy. Hama's team replied with their own blasts, and the crackling cacophony seemed far away for that moment. Caius caught Samira's eyes with his own, and he tilted his head toward hers. "The Empire will know they're here," he whispered, just loud enough for her to hear. "They don't know about us. We can slip away tonight. We can find our own way."

"To where?" she hissed back. "We're in the middle of nowhere, and we have bounties on our heads."

"We can travel faster on our own. We find this Gressam person first and bring him back to Stormbreak ourselves."

"The assassins," she said, and her voice was finally low enough that the shooter probably wouldn't hear. "You said the Nightingales are after him."

"Nahk said they'd be trouble."

"We can't handle them on our own."

"But with your magic—"

"My magic won't help," she said and clenched her jaw. She looked away, toward the slaughter, but quickly turned her gaze back toward him. "Mollor nearly killed me in Klubridge. I only survived because of Apak. I can't hold off trained killers, Caius."

"What, then?" he whispered. "We stay with them?"

"You stay with us," the woman behind him said before ripping another bullet through another distant Imperial.

CHAPTER 25

"I've known him for more than twenty years. He's lived and worked here for more than two decades," Naecara Klavan said, but Apak scowled.

"That does not answer the question I asked," he said and sniffed at the air. There was something cooking ahead, the blended aromas of meat and smoke drifting to them through the cold air. He had hoped for warmer weather as they traveled south, but Esterburgh offered more of the same frigid temperatures he had experienced at Stormbreak.

Naecara glanced at him from the corner of her eye, and her mouth turned up in a half smile. "I trust him as much as I'd trust anyone I'd known for twenty years."

"And how much would that be?"

"Not a lot," Nahk said, riding at his left. "Not a lot."

The four rode south on horses Apak knew Oreth had supplied. Oreth had not been there to see them off, of course, but Apak knew his hand was the one who had arranged for their provisioning. He had hoped for an opportunity to speak with the young man before their departure, but there had not been time. There never was time, it seemed. A conversation would await their return, then.

Naecara had led the party down from the mountain, Nahk riding at her side for most of the descent. Apak was unaccustomed to horses, much to the amusement of Alev Adonar, the fourth in the group. Adonar had ridden alongside Apak the entire first day of the journey, advising him on the proper way to sit astride and guide his mount. Apak had bristled at the instruction, but the truth was that he was more likely to have fallen in the road than to have arrived in Esterburgh without it.

Adonar was one of the mages Vaino had sequestered in the tallest tower at Stormbreak. Along with a second one, Adonar maintained that accursed shield that encompassed the keep for more time each day than Apak liked to consider. With one mage gone, Stormbreak at last would have more time freed from its invisible prison and would be less likely to suffocate its inhabitants.

"What are you thinking?" Naecara asked, still looking at him.

"I am thinking it is cold, and I am tired and sore from riding," Apak said but immediately regretted his tone. Naecara Klavan was the good half of the rebellion's leadership. She knew the way to bring about change and recognized the threat the High Lord posed. Apak's discomfort was her fault only through her trusting him enough to include him on this mission. He turned his head to offer an apology, but she was smiling.

"You'll get some rest and some proper food, too," she said. "We're here." She nodded her head to the right, indicating a squat building at the side of the road. It slumped low just off the curb and would have reminded Apak of the slums in the East Ward if not for the mound of snow piled on the roof. A narrow chimney poked up from the white blanket, and smoke curled out the top. A weathered sign hanging on an arm above the front door read simply, "Inn." The place advertised no other name beyond its function. Apak might have turned his nose up at such a lack of presentation, but the aches in his neck and his legs and even in his backside were enough to persuade him to keep his silence.

There was shelter for the horses around the side of the inn, and the group of four riders walked through the front door only a few minutes later. It took several seconds for Apak's eyes to adjust to the dimmer light inside after a day of riding through the blinding white of the sun reflecting off the snow. Once he could see, he frowned. It was an absolutely ordinary inn, no different from any lower tier establishment he had seen in any of his travels. A flame burned in a large fireplace at the back of the room, and a disarray of various boots and shoes dried and warmed on the hearth before it. Several round tables with chairs had been scattered across the floor, but no one sat there at this time of the day. Or perhaps the inn had no guests. That was not an impossibility, given how far north this remote establishment was and how meager the entirety of Esterburgh seemed.

A short bar protruded from the wall on the left, just before an open doorway that should lead back into a kitchen. A narrow flight of wooden stairs ascended at the right side of the room, disappearing when it turned left at a small landing only a few steps up. It was to the bar that Naecara marched, stomping the loose snow from her boots as she went. Apak followed her and rubbed his hands together, wishing not for the first time that the gloves he had brought for the trip covered his entire hands and did not have the fingers snipped off. They were useful for maintaining his dexterity and allowing him to work with his fingers unimpeded, but they did nothing to stop the chill that crept into his hands and lingered.

Naecara knocked her knuckles on the surface of the bar three times, loud enough for anyone in the building to hear it. The cold seemed to have no effect on her. Little did. She was as impervious to the chill as she was to the ever-present threat Vaino posed. Apak had tried to talk with her about that rotten man, but she would have none of it. She had said Vaino wanted the same thing she did, but he had a different approach. Apak pursed his lips at that and grunted. Vaino's approach was to ignore the obvious danger of the High Lord Peregrine in favor of believing he could assemble an army of barbarians to wrest Teshovar away from the Empire on the battlefield. It was a short-sighted and ignorant approach, and it would get countless rebels killed for no reason. But it was clear Naecara wanted no part of that conversation as they traveled south, and so Apak had held his tongue. He was becoming better at that with every day that had passed since leaving Klubridge.

Nahk had wandered toward the fireplace, and Alev Adonar

joined her. Adonar pulled their gloves off and flexed their large hands toward the warmth of the fire. Apak considered lining up with them to warm himself while Naecara conducted her business, but his curiosity allowed him to endure the discomfort a while longer. He went to the bar and waited behind Naecara as a man shuffled in from the back room.

The proprietor was broad at the shoulders and short, his hair a messy tangle beneath a beret he'd pulled down nearly to his ears. He huffed as he came around the back side of the counter, small eyes taking in the strangers warming themselves at his fire before his gaze settled on Apak, standing back and waiting for whatever came next. When his eyes shifted to Naecara, he huffed a laugh, and his stubbly face split with a grin. His lips were thick and wet, and a gap at the front of his mouth showed where teeth should have been.

"Naecara Klavan," he said. "You should've told Brius you were coming!" His voice was thick and carried an accent. Apak frowned and tried to place it, but it was nothing he had heard.

"Brius," Naecara said, clasping his hand in hers. "It's good to see you."

"How long's it been?" The man asked and squinted at her, still grinning. "Must be a year or more by now, eh?"

"Could be," she said. She let his hand drop, and she glanced back at Apak before continuing. "I wish this were a social call."

"Always business, is it?" Brius asked, but he was still smiling, his grin curious, and the tip of his tongue finding the space between his teeth.

"I'm afraid so, at least this time. You heard about what happened in Klubridge?"

Brius blew out between his lips and shook his head. "Ugly thing, that. The whole city's been hurt. Destroyed, some might say."

"The Empire did it," Naecara said. "There was a weapon, something magical. They used it to raze the city."

The man's mouth was shut then, the corners pulled tight, and a crease between his eyes. He already knew this story. He knew exactly what had happened in Klubridge. If Apak could see through this fellow's expression so easily, Naecara surely could as well.

"You know everything there is to know about what's happening on the magic black market," Naecara continued. "We need to find that weapon and make sure they don't use it again. Can you help us?"

Brius nodded his head toward Apak. "Who's this, then?"

"Never mind him," Naecara said. "He's helping me. Them, too." She tilted her head toward the fire, and Apak saw Nahk was watching the conversation now. The fire still had Adonar's attention, and they continued wringing their hands before the flames.

Brius studied the two by the fire for a long moment before sniffing and looking back to Naecara. "You're thinking Brius knows enough to tell you where the Empire gets its toys?"

"I'm thinking Brius does." Naecara placed her hand flat on the bar, and Apak heard the clack of coins beneath it. She slid the seri toward Brius and held her hand over them for an additional second before lifting it. "And we would be appreciative if he could share what he knows."

Brius glanced down at the money, but not for long. He covered the seri with his own palm and dragged it off his side of the bar into his other hand. After pocketing the coins, he gave Naecara a closed-mouth smile and propped himself forward on his elbows. He leaned toward her, his eyebrows drawing down, and he asked, "Do you know the name Kam Dhaz?"

"Should I?" Naecara asked.

"I know the name," Apak said. Naecara gave him a look that could have been surprise, but surely it was not an indication to remain silent. He stepped closer to the bar and said, "Kam Dhaz was a gangster in Klubridge. He ran criminals while I lived there. He was known for his brutality."

"Well, well," Brius said, leaning on his left arm and thumbing the front of his beret with his right hand. "It seems never-mind-him knows more than you do."

"Kam Dhaz," Naecara said, ignoring Brius' slight. "What does he have to do with this?"

"You want to fill her in, or should I?" Brius asked, winking at Apak.

"I never encountered the man myself. The gangs in Klubridge were mostly cutpurses. Street thieves." He hesitated and swallowed, denying the grief and anger that tried to swell in his chest and up to his throat. What happened to Dorrin could not be changed, and he had seen the boy avenged.

"Kam Dhaz ran street thieves?" Naecara asked, mistaking Apak's sudden silence for a completion of his thoughts.

"No," Apak said. "His gang did not employ children. He worked the black market. He saw contraband in and out of the city."

"Contraband such as magical weapons?" Naecara looked back to Brius.

The shorter man gave her an emphatic nod. "Just so. Dhaz has had his hands in all kinds of nastiness for as long as I've heard his name. He runs his schemes beneath the notice of the Empire, but this time he was square in the Empire's sight."

"This time?"

"The Empire hired Kam Dhaz," Nahk said. Apak had not noticed her approach, but she stood just behind him and to the right. "Dhaz got a weapon for them, didn't he? They could have taken the city back with soldiers, but they wanted it to be showy. A display of power. So they had Dhaz use an artifact. Something from the black market."

"The Eye of Kelixia," Brius said. He held his hands apart, forming the shape of a ball just large enough for his fingertips to touch. "Supposed to be about, eh, this big? That's what the Empire went to Kam Dhaz to get, and that's what Brius would wager you're looking to find."

Apak shook his head. "This is not correct. Kam Dhaz is a businessman. He would hire brutes and acquire weapons, but he would not destroy an entire city himself, particularly one where he has a significant vested interest."

"And yet," Brius said, his hands opening as he shrugged.

Naecara was studying Apak, weighing what he'd said. "We don't know enough." She turned back to Brius. "Where can we find Kam Dhaz?"

LIZANDRA'S DEEPEST FEAR

∾

Alev Adonar cast a worried look toward the spires that were just becoming visible over the northwestern walls of Aramore. "We'll be better served to enter quietly and stay to the north."

"You know Aramore?" Apak asked, taking his attention away from his horse for an instant to look back at the mage riding to his left.

"I spent time there," they said. "In another life."

Apak nodded and returned his focus to the horse. He had grown accustomed to the steady rhythm and rocking beneath him, but he doubted he ever would feel fully at ease while riding that far above the ground. Horses were massive creatures, seen up close, and he had spent a lifetime being no closer to them than was necessary.

Naecara brought her horse alongside Apak's on the right. "Alev knows their way through the city. We should follow their advice."

"Have you been to Aramore?" Apak asked.

Naecara shook her head. "I traveled a lot, but I always avoided this place." She looked toward the towers that were growing in the distance, and she shuddered.

Apak could hardly fault her reluctance. Aramore was, for all purposes, the seat of Imperial power in Teshovar. The Imperial machine's cogs spun and levers moved throughout the land, but this was the heart of the mechanism. This was where the government held its meetings and passed its laws, and it was where all the wickedness was justified in courts and in council rooms. Apak pressed his lips together and allowed the horse to carry him ever nearer to the walls of that accursed city.

All four of them would have avoided Aramore if they could, but it was the only way through from Esterburgh to Ornamen, unless they wanted to go south through Karsk and then to Salkire. That roundabout journey would have taken too long, and Salkire was nearly as dangerous as Aramore. If the trek south through the mountains and through that blasted frozen Karsk did not kill them, passing through the High Lord's own ancient city of Salkire might. And so they had set out for Aramore under the strange innkeeper's instructions.

Kam Dhaz was a name Apak had heard for years, but he had avoided crossing paths with the man, just as he had avoided entanglements with all the other gangsters of Klubridge. Even though that was not his life, Apak still heard things. He knew Dhaz to be aloof and removed from the other gang leaders who prowled the slums of the city. He had positioned himself as something of a gentleman scoundrel, and everyone who lived in the city knew Kam Dhaz was the one to see if they needed anything that might raise Imperial interest. Enchanted items and magical artifacts were his primary trade, and there were tales about the sorts of relics Dhaz had let slip into unscrupulous hands. If what Naecara's contact had said about the Eye of Kelixia was true, this was the man's most egregious transaction.

Brius had told them Dhaz kept operations in Klubridge, as well as in Gramery and Ornamen and elsewhere. With Klubridge decimated, that was one place they knew he would not be found. He was said to make rounds between the various cities where he kept safehouses, and he used one of his own artifacts to make the trips between cities more quickly. Apak had heard talk of items that could transport the holder to distant lands, and he believed such enchantments would be possible, but he had never seen such an enchantment in person. If anyone would be in possession of such an item, it would be a scoundrel like Kam Dhaz.

Apak scratched at his beard, now longer than he had ever kept it, and considered how such an enchantment could even be rendered. It was likely to involve the connection of points in space similar to the portals Reykas could create. Imbuing an item with such an enchantment would strengthen and broaden that magic, making it easy to traverse many miles instead of simply reaching through space a few feet removed. Reykas' ability was impressive and had proven useful both in the stage productions and in the battle at Klubridge, but his reach was limited. Magic tended to become more potent when associated with solid objects, much like the focusing stone at Stormbreak was able to expand a magical shield to encase the whole castle. It stood to reason that whatever item Kam Dhaz was using to transport himself benefited from some similar expansion in energy.

When their party reached the gates, Apak felt his shoulders tense. The Imperial guards were visible at the end of the straight path, flanking the entrance to the city. Nahk rode just ahead of Apak and to his right, and he saw her shift her cloak as the group approached, no doubt readying herself for an attack if they were identified. Of the four, Apak suspected he was the most recognizable, having been at the center of the conflict in Klubridge. His face was probably on pamphlets from Tresa to Meskia by then, but his lack of shaving over the past weeks could work to his advantage. The others, either having spent years removed from society or living in the shadows, would be less known to the Empire.

Rationally, Apak knew it was unlikely they would have trouble entering the city, just four more travelers in a long stream of horses and carts, but he still held his breath as they passed between the guards and through the city gates. The guards paid them no attention, their eyes bored and unfocused and their hands slack and loose around the pikes they held at their sides. Once through the city walls, Naecara slowed to allow Adonar to lead the party, and they followed to the left, angling north from the gate.

Aramore bore a dusting of white, the snow falling in a light and airy descent, but it was nothing like the mounds of powder and ice they had traversed after leaving Stormbreak. It was cold, to be sure, but it felt nearly balmy after the time spent farther north. Apak flexed his fingers on his horse's reins, thankful that they were not stiff from the cold for once. He angled his head up to look at the buildings as they passed.

Clusters of shops and roadside vendors had gathered just inside the gates, nothing different than Apak had seen in Klubridge and in any other large city he had visited. Unlike in Klubridge, however, order reigned this street. He saw no guards patrolling within the first block, but there was a solemn air about the people that he was not used to seeing farther afield from the Imperial seat. Past these shops and merchants, the white walls of the government center arose, and it was that central complex that loomed over the rest of Aramore like a watchful eye. There was crime and disorder to be found in Aramore, no doubt. That was a fact of every large city. But it hid better there, lurking somewhere out of sight of the Imperial lords.

It took only a few minutes for the atmosphere to shift around their party as they worked their way north and away from the main streets. Adonar led the group up and around the edge of the city. The well-maintained cobblestones at the entrance soon gave way to cracked paving, and that eventually surrendered itself to a roadway so broken that some sections had crumbled to reveal the snow-crusted dirt beneath. The tidy rows of shops became streets of respectable houses, and those slouched into dirty taverns and ramshackle businesses, many with wood boarded over their broken windows.

The slums of Klubridge had sunk to the south of the city, but it was becoming increasingly evident that Aramore's poor districts were to the north, toward the mountains and barren lands outside the city. It made sense, given that Salkire and the rest of Teshovar awaited to the south, and the wealthy visitors would come and go through the southern gates. Still, seeing this disrepair and decrepitude even in Aramore creased the line between Apak's eyebrows. The Empire was unfit to take care of its citizens, even in its own most loyal city.

Adonar was looking back and must have seen the frown on Apak's face. How it differed from his usual countenance, Apak could not say, but the other mage gave him a sad smile. "It's not pleasant, but it'll get us through the city unseen," they said. "We'll pass the northeastern gate and go out the eastern one toward Ornamen."

Apak nodded back and slowed his horse as a filthy child ran across the street after a fleeing cat. Reminders of Dorrin, everywhere he looked. This one was younger than Dorrin had been, perhaps no more than seven or eight. He already had a fierceness in the gaze he shot back at Apak that Dorrin had managed to avoid. Somehow, despite his rough upbringing on the streets and despite his thievery and involvement with one of the East

Ward gangs, Dorrin had maintained his innocence and had wanted nothing more than to have a family and to belong somewhere. He had had that for a short time, and then the Empire had taken it away, as they did with everything of value.

Apak's fist tightened on the reins, and his ears warmed with fury again, as they did every time he allowed himself to dwell on what had happened these past months. On everything he had lost and that all the rest of them had lost. He had allowed that fury to drive him in the plaza at Klubridge, and he still was not convinced he had been in the wrong. His intention had been sound, and his execution of the plan had been successful.

Naecara slowed her horse ahead of Apak, and he pulled back on his own reins, jerked out of his thoughts to see the party stopping before a man blocking the roadway. He was a brute, and Apak recognized his type, from the sour snarl to the muscles that bulged in his crossed arms. He stood firm in the center of the lane, and it was clear he intended to allow no passage.

Nahk shifted on her saddle and looked back at Apak and past him, her eyes moving quickly. Apak followed her gaze over his shoulder as two more people stepped out from an alley to block the path behind them. Naecara's horse shuffled a nervous step forward before she pulled it to a halt.

"We have nothing you want," she said to the man in front.

"Doubt that," he replied, his voice low and harsh. "I see packs on them saddles." He sneered at her. "I see horses. All of that seems worth our time."

"Let us pass, and we'll give you some seri for your trouble," Naecara said.

"Better I don't let you pass and take it all, yeah?"

He stepped forward and reached for Alev Adonar's reins. Before his fingers could touch the leather, Nahk was off her horse, launched into the air sideways. Apak gasped and flinched back as she hit the wall of the building to the right, caught the impact with her bent right elbow and knee, and sprang off straight ahead, toward the robber. As she sailed past Naecara, Nahk flicked her right hand forward. A cable unsheathed from her wrist, shooting out from a zephyr spool so much like the one the Kite had used in Klubridge. Like the one he had wrapped around Dorrin's throat.

The cable zipped around the brute's extended arm, wrapping itself twice before the small blade at the end caught in the skin on the back of his hand. An instant later, Nahk's feet slammed into his chest, knocking him backwards. The two fell out of Apak's sight, so he could not see but certainly heard the path of the blade as it spun its way back around the man's arm. A line of red sprayed the darkened storefront on the left as the fallen brute began screaming, but Nahk was already up again and sprinting, moving fast and low past Apak on his left.

As soon as she was behind and clear of her companions, Nahk shot her arms forward, crossing them in front of her, and letting her barbed cables unspool in opposite directions. The one she flung from her right arm shot past the face of the nearest mugger and sparked against the wall near his head. The one from her left arm flew true, though, and sliced the side of the third man's neck before slipping back past him and disappearing into Nahk's sleeve once more. The wounded man clapped a hand to his neck, and blood leaked between his fingers as fear filled his eyes. The one who was still uninjured cursed and fled, leaving shallow footprints in the slushy mix of dirt and snow that coated the ground.

Nahk turned to pursue him, but Naecara called to her. "Let him go. We need to be gone before the guards come."

Nahk cast one more glance toward the corner where the third thief had disappeared, and she gestured to the two men moaning on the ground, one ahead of the horses and one behind. "What about these?"

"Leave them."

Apak thought Nahk might protest, but her nod was immediate, and she hurried back onto her horse. Seconds later, they were moving again, and Apak looked down at the lead brute as they passed. He sat half-propped against the side of an empty building on the left, his wounded right arm cradled in his left. He looked up as they passed, and his eyes met Apak's. The man's face was already turning a deathly white, and his lips moved soundlessly, no doubt begging for help. But Apak could see the damage. Nahk had severed the veins in his wrist, and the man had already lost too much blood. There would be no saving him, even if they had been inclined to stop long enough. This man would die on that dirty street, his blood staining the gray clumps of snow red. Apak felt no satisfaction, but some of his anger ebbed, yielding to something less familiar. Something that might have been regret.

∽

The four rode in silence through the slums. Apak watched Naecara riding ahead of him, Nahk beside her, and Adonar in the lead. None of them looked at each other or even acknowledged what had happened. The ground sloped downward, the farther north they went, until they reached what Apak estimated to be the midpoint of the city wall between the two northern gates. Then the elevation increased again, and with it the buildings became cleaner, the road in better repair, and the children who played alongside it rounder of face, healthier, and dressed in less tattered clothing. Every city had its slums, and every city hid them just the same as all the others.

The gate to the northeast came into view as they rounded the edge of the northern district, and Apak saw no guards posted on the inside of the walls. It was likely that they stood outside, just as they had been flanking the gate through which he and the others had entered. Aramore feared nothing that was already inside its walls. Anything to be feared was external, bearing down on the city and its rulers.

Naecara fell back into pace with Apak once they were past the gate that would lead to Tresa if they had taken it. The ride would have been long, and Apak expected the road would have skirted past the small cove where he, Caius, and the others had disembarked from Ergo Drass' ship what seemed like an eternity ago. But they did not take the road to Tresa, and they continued their circumnavigation of the city center. They had avoided the constabulary and any other agents of the Empire so far, and Apak hoped the civilians would continue taking no notice of the four travelers, especially after the attempted robbery.

"Are you all right?" Naecara asked. She rode so close on his left that her knee almost bumped Apak's. Her voice was low enough that anyone they passed would not hear her, but her words were loud enough for Apak to discern over the clopping of the horses' hooves.

He considered the question and studied Nahk ahead of them. She rode with her head down, the hood of her cloak pulled up, and her shoulders hunched. Her long sleeves hid the weapons Apak now knew she hid on her wrists. "Is she a mage?" he asked.

Nahk looked back, her dark eyes narrowed, and Apak knew she had heard the question. Her ears were better than he had expected. She made no comment but met his eyes and held them for a moment before turning back to face the road ahead.

"She's no mage," Naecara said. "The Empire took her when she was a child. They trained her and infused her with magic, but she's no mage."

What was that tone in her voice? Was it sadness? Pity? Apak considered Naecara's face in profile. She had a strong jaw and an angular nose that gave her a serious air, even when she smiled. A twisting lock of dark hair hung free from her hood, swaying beside her ear. She cut her eyes toward Apak and raised an eyebrow. He cleared his throat and asked, "What do you mean when you say the Empire infused her with magic? What is that?"

"I don't know how it's done, but it's what they did to her. You're familiar with the halflocks and how they're made."

It was not a question, but Apak nodded. "The Empire performs surgery on mages. Their brains are altered to diminish their abilities."

"What they did to Nahk is similar, but different. There was no surgery, but…" Naecara's voice trailed to silence, and Apak followed her eyes forward to see Nahk watching them again.

The younger woman slowed her horse to walk even with them on the other side of Naecara. She turned her eyes ahead again but said, "I'm not a mage, and I'm not a halflock."

"I'm sorry, Nahk," Naecara said. "I didn't—"

"It's all right." She looked past Naecara, to Apak, and said, "I was a child. They taught me to kill and trained me to use weapons. They taught me to be a weapon. And then they locked me in a..." She frowned and shook her head. "I don't know what it was. Like a coffin, but metal. They did something to me while I was in there. It was the worst pain I'd ever felt. And when I came out, I was different."

Apak let go of the reins with one hand and touched the rim of his glasses. This was remarkable. He was familiar with the Empire's practices concerning the creation of halflocks, and he knew how Herons were turned and imprisoned in metaphorically gilded cages. He had never heard of this infusion process, though. How was such a thing even possible?

"I don't know how they did it," Nahk said, her eyes still on him.

His eyebrows raised. "Did you hear my thoughts just now?"

Her lips curved into a sly grin. "That's not how this works."

"What can you do, then?" he asked. "How did they change you?"

She broke his gaze to look down at the road. "I can see at night, for one thing. And I can do this." She looked up at him again, but she was no longer Nahk. In place of her short, dark hair, there was long, blonde hair. Her skin was paler, and her eyes had grown lighter. Apak blinked, looked away, and looked again. He was looking into the eyes of Fairy.

"How," he began, but even as he questioned the transformation, the features blurred and shifted. Fairy's face disappeared, and Nahk was looking at him again, as if nothing had changed. "You can change your form," he said. He had seen magic done in many ways, but he had seen nothing like this.

But Nahk shook her head. "It's not me that changed. It's how you saw me. It's my Veil. I can influence people to see me differently than I am. It's weak, though. I can only trick a few people at a time. And, as soon as someone is skeptical, I start to lose them all. Just like what happened with you just now."

"What else could you do after this infusion?" Apak asked. He slid his glasses down the bridge of his nose and peered over them at Nahk.

She shrugged. "Nothing I couldn't already do."

"What about..." He hesitated, unsure of how to ask what he

wanted to know. "The things you did when those men stopped us."

"The Empire was training her to be a Nightingale," Naecara said, as if that would be explanation enough.

Apak looked past her, to Nahk, and the younger woman shrugged again. "I told you. They taught me to be a weapon."

CHAPTER 26

Lizandra was not the price for Reykas' cure. She was not what he held closest to his heart and not the thing that defined him.

The old woman had sensed that he was that for her, though, and Lizandra hadn't argued or disputed what she'd known to be true. But she wasn't that for him. Lizandra had known that, too, but it still stung to have the suspicion confirmed by the words of a stranger. A stranger with the ability to reach into Reykas' mind, even while he was unconscious and lingering on the edge of death, to retrieve what really mattered to him.

They were past Esterburgh now, riding north, and the cart wheels slowed in the mounding piles of snow that littered the road. It wouldn't be long before they were back at Stormbreak. She'd slip them back in under the cover of night, just like she'd slipped them out, and nobody would even know they'd been gone. Nobody but her and Oreth.

The cart hit a bump, and she glanced back to make sure it hadn't jostled Reykas. But he lay as motionless as ever, a slender, soft shape beneath the layers of blankets she'd piled atop him. Jod Padar had helped her load him back into the cart, but he hadn't lingered after that. The old man had given her one last look and a nod, and he was back inside his shop, their business finished and the door firmly closed behind him.

Lizandra hadn't seen whatever Padar had done to Reykas. He'd urged her out of the room so he could do his work, and she had allowed herself to be shuffled into the front of the shop, close behind the quiet old woman. Walking behind her, Lizandra studied the lines of the scar on the back of her head and felt desperation rising in her chest. This was, well and truly, her last hope. An old man who claimed to be a chemist and his halflock wife, both hidden away and working some deal with the Empire, far removed from the rest of Teshovar. Her last hope, and she'd been willing to pay anything for it.

When he'd finished, Padar had called Lizandra back into the room where Reykas still lay prone on the gurney, and that was when they'd moved him outside, back into the cold and back into the bed of the cart to be covered and hidden once more. Reykas hadn't stirred the whole time, and he'd looked as absent as he had when she'd first brought him. Lizandra hadn't known what to expect, but part of her had hoped Reykas would awaken as soon as Padar was finished. That he'd sit up and stand and walk to her, and the two of them would ride away from Karsk side by side. That they would turn south, not north, and that they'd forget all about Stormbreak and the rebellion.

She'd hoped, but she knew that's not how it would happen. If Reykas had awakened on that metal table, she'd have had to face his questions right away. She'd have had to tell him how she'd ignored his insistence that she not bring him to Karsk, and she'd have had to tell him the extent of her scheme. She'd have had to tell him what the cure had cost him.

But he didn't wake up when they put him back into the cart, and he hadn't awoken all the way from Karsk to Esterburgh nor even after they'd left Esterburgh and had begun the slow ascent up the mountain toward Stormbreak. She looked back at him once more and watched the steady swaying of the body beneath the blankets. She couldn't see his face from her seat at the front of the cart, but she knew his eyes were still closed and his hands still lay unmoving at his sides. Had Jod Padar even done anything? Had he tricked her into paying for something he never intended to deliver?

The fear that she'd been swindled needled her, but she knew

Padar had delivered. She didn't know the method of the cure or how it worked, but Padar had done something to Reykas. The fact that he still lived was proof enough of that. Without whatever remedy the chemist had provided, Lizandra had no doubt she'd have left Karsk alone, having buried her love in the cold ground of an unfamiliar city. But Reykas was alive, and she struggled to hold on to the hope that he would awaken, would see her again, would stand. She reached for the hope that everything would be all right. That he would forgive her.

As the day gave way to night and the sun sank below the horizon, the peak of Crowspire crept into view. It stood hard and stark against the darkening sky, its jagged peak ruining the illusion of its birdlike presence. How much farther? Lizandra considered stopping somewhere away from the road and making a cold camp for the night, out of sight of any rebels who might chance to travel up or down that path. But no, she'd come so far and was already so tired, and their destination seemed so close. She needed to arrive at night, anyway, in order to slip into the keep while the shield was down. There would be no delays and no camping. She would press onward and reach Stormbreak before sunlight.

As eager as Lizandra was to see actual progress after Jod Padar's work, she knew Reykas couldn't awaken until he was safely delivered back into his bed in the castle. Having him regain consciousness in transit would be as hard for her to explain as it would have been if he'd woken up in Karsk. But, if this cure had been real, Reykas would awaken, and every moment Lizandra delayed their return to Stormbreak was another moment she risked having to explain to him what she'd done.

She had asked Padar how long it would take for Reykas to recover, and the old man had shrugged. "I'm a chemist, not a physician," he had said, and that was his only comment about the matter. He'd known how to reverse or stop what the sickness was doing to Reykas, but that seemed to be the extent of the old man's knowledge. Lizandra had had to accept his ignorance and, with it, her own uncertainty about what would happen with Reykas after they left Karsk.

Lizandra tugged the scarf up around her face again as the familiar, biting cold stung her lips and numbed her nose. She looked back into the cart once more before they began the gradual ascent toward the looming mountains.

∽

Oreth quickly lost count of how many times he went up to the wall that overlooked the western path out from Stormbreak, but it was on the third night after Lizandra left that he ran into Leyna. It must have been just past midnight. The moon shone round and bright, unfiltered by any magical dome or clouds. That would have been Alev Adonar's shift for keeping the shield up, but they'd left with Apak and his group, and Vaino had yet to come up with a new schedule. That left the keep unshielded more of the time than it was shielded, which didn't seem good for security but was convenient for Lizandra's eventual return.

Even without an invisible shield in her way, Lizzie would need help getting back into Stormbreak unseen, and that's what drove Oreth up to the high walkways and made him squint down between the crenelations every day and night. Surely she wouldn't return before sundown, given that she'd used the darkness to mask her departure, but Oreth didn't want to count on guesses and chance. He watched that path descending from the keep as often as he could steal away to take another peek.

"I thought you were going to bed."

Leyna's voice came out of the darkness, and Oreth lurched and nearly fell over. He would have, if not for the leg brace that kept him upright. His heart thudding now, he looked over his shoulder and found her sitting on a chair in the dark, tucked into a corner just opposite the stairs he was about to climb.

"What are you doing?" he asked as he turned away from the steps. She had her arms folded and tucked inside her coat, and her curly mane of hair framed her face in the dim light.

"Couldn't sleep," she said. "Sometimes I come out here when I don't want to be awake but can't get my brain to stop."

A gust of wind whistled down the stairs from the open door above, and Oreth shivered. "Don't you get cold out here?"

She shrugged and tossed her head back. "You offering to warm me up?"

"I—" Oreth found his heart racing again, just like it had a moment ago.

"So what are you doing up and about?" Leyna asked, breezing right past the previous question. "You'd said you were dead tired."

And so he had. He'd made excuses to leave the supply depot early, and he'd used the opportunity to catch a couple hours of sleep before time to check the roadway again. That's how it had been each night since Lizzie left. Work, get a little sleep, and get up again to see if she was back. He didn't truly expect her back so soon, but he had to be ready whenever she did return, with or without Reykas.

"I slept a bit," he said, glad he didn't have to lie about that. He'd sidestepped Leyna's questions about where this and that had gone and where they'd misplaced the cart that he'd sent away with Lizzie. Leyna knew her job, and she knew the rebellion's inventory better than Oreth had expected. It hadn't taken her long to start noticing the supplies he'd pilfered were missing, but she didn't seem suspicious. Not yet, anyway. And Oreth hadn't had to outright lie to her about it. Not yet on that, as well.

"This must be the popular spot for midnight wandering," Leyna said. "You going up to the roof?"

"What?"

"You looked like you were headed for the stairs. You going up there?"

"Oh." He looked up toward the far end of the staircase, where the moonlight crept through the doorway and painted the top three steps in its yellowish glow. "I thought I'd just have a walk around the wall, see if it got me sleepy again."

"Want some company for that walk?" she asked. It was too dark there for him to see her clearly, but she shifted as if she were getting ready to stand up.

"I…" he started once more. Did he want Leyna up on the roof with him for a midnight stroll under a full, round moon? Oreth thought nothing had ever sounded more appealing to him. But if they went up there together, and this was the night Lizzie showed up with the missing cart and whatever was left of the supplies Leyna had been missing? "It's okay," he said. "I'll just make it quick and go back to bed."

"Ah," Leyna said and settled back against the chair. He still couldn't see her expression, but there was something in her voice that sounded like disappointment.

Oreth pressed his lips together and tried to think of something else to say. Something to salvage whatever moment she'd been hinting at. But no, the moment was gone, and he'd messed it up, whatever it might have been. "All right, then," he said.

"All right," she said back, and he left her there in that dark corner.

Of course, that hadn't been the night Lizzie had come back. Nor was the next night, nor the one after that. He continued watching the road, checking it as often as he dared, but he only ran across Leyna that one time. The rest of the time he saw her was during the day when they worked together on the supplies. Everything was as it had been, and neither of them mentioned the midnight encounter. Nevertheless, Oreth watched for Leyna, checking that dark corner every time he crept up to the roof during the night.

He wasn't sure how many nights had passed or how many times he'd climbed up to the battlements, but it was on a particularly calm night when the snow wasn't falling that he spotted movement down below. There, between the distant rocks, something dark moved over the white layer of snow that shone in the moonlight. Oreth held his breath and placed both hands on the top of the wall. He favored his right hand when he leaned forward, as if that little shift would allow him to see into the night any better than before. He waited like that, breath held, and neck stretched forward until he was certain. It was a horse, and behind it rolled a cart with a driver sitting at the front.

Could it be her? It had to be, didn't it? Who else would be approaching Stormbreak at that hour? Oreth knew the schedules, and no one was supposed to be on that road that night. Whether or not it was Lizzie, he had to do something.

He left the wall and took the stairs down as fast as he dared, his left leg dragging and almost tripping him on a few. He didn't slow until he was on the ground floor, though, and only then did he pause, breath sucked in once more as he listened for movement. Sometimes there'd be a few people milling about the courtyard in the night or wandering the hallways like Leyna had done. But, that night, he heard nothing but his own heartbeat echoing a muted drumbeat in his ears.

Satisfied that he was alone, Oreth slipped out the western gate and made for the stables, where he had said goodbye to Lizzie when she'd left on her mission. A lantern burned in the building, and he knew at least one stable hand would be in there. They probably were sleeping at that hour, but an unexpected cart rolling into Stormbreak would wake them fast enough.

Oreth hesitated outside the stable door. He'd been watching for Lizzie every night and day, but he hadn't given enough thought to what he'd actually need to do when she showed up. If that was even her on the road. It had to be. Who else would it be? The Empire coming to raid the rebellion with a single horse and cart?

The certainty that followed that thought spurred Oreth into motion, and he came in through the barn doors, intentionally banging the side of his leg brace against the door frame. That sent a shock of pain through his weaker leg, but he gritted his teeth against it as movement rustled a few feet away. A tousled head popped up from behind the low wall of one of the stalls.

"Oreth!" It was one of the younger stable hands. Leyna liked assigning the young ones to duty when they were less likely to have to deal with any important shipments. That's how this girl ended up asleep on a pile of hay.

"Sorry, did I wake you?" he asked as he rounded the corner of the stall. His left leg dragged again, sweeping straw along in his wake.

"No!" she said as she wiped at her eyes. "I wasn't asleep." A yawn tried to crawl its way out, but Oreth pretended he didn't notice.

"Why don't you take the rest of the night off? Go get some rest."

She frowned and looked past him at the door that led back into the keep. She glanced between it and him as if she thought this was some kind of test or trick. "For true?"

"For true," he said. "I was awake and felt like getting things done. It'll be a quiet night, so you might as well benefit from it."

She was on her feet by then and said, "If you're sure..."

"I'm sure," he said, and that was all the assurance she needed. She gave him a grin and was out the door and into the keep, and he was alone in the barn.

There were no horses in this one that night. They usually kept the animals in the other stable and brought them up to this one when they were ready for a trip. Oreth stood alone in the building now, and he tried to steady his breathing from a hitching irregularity that was not entirely caused by the cold breeze.

What if he'd been wrong? What if that wasn't Lizzie? What if it really was someone else coming back early from a supply run or, far worse, an Imperial spy or scout of some sort? He'd spotted them and had plenty of time to react, and all he'd done was ensure they'd have a clear path straight into the keep.

Oreth glanced back toward the door and wondered how many guards might be on duty that night. Vaino usually had fewer than seemed prudent. Would one of them make their rounds at just the right time to see that cart rolling across the covered bridge?

Oreth rushed to the opposite door and leaned around it, looking out toward the road that sloped down and disappeared into the rocks. The cart was close now and slowing. He could see the driver in silhouette as they pulled back on the reins and stopped the horse. The wheels rolled to a halt just outside the perimeter of where the shield would be.

Oreth squinted at the shapes of the horse, the cart, and the driver. It had to be her. Or at least someone who knew where to stop when the shield was in place. He had already taken a step toward the road when he realized he was in clear view of the person as he stood in the doorway with the lantern lighting the stables behind him. Too late to question it or to worry now that he was committed.

He left the building and jogged as best he could through the powdery snow until he reached the packed surface of the road, and he was surer with every step. It had to be Lizzie. There was no question. He waved the driver forward as he moved, and the cart rolled toward him, closing the space. Oreth ran to the side of the cart and fell into pace, a smile on his face until the driver pulled back her hood and looked down at him. He nearly stumbled and might have fallen under the wheels if he hadn't caught the edge of the wagon with his right hand.

The face that looked down at him, now visible in the wan moonlight and the nearing lamplight, was gray and gaunt, the eyes rimmed with dark skin and the hair filthy and tangled. She was almost unrecognizable, but he asked, "Lizzie?"

The smile she gave him was tight. "Can we get in safely?" Her voice was rough and hoarse, like she'd gone the whole journey without rest and without water.

Oreth nodded back and guided her into the barn. As the cart came to its final halt, Oreth looked up at Lizzie again. She sat forward, her shoulders hunched, and she stared at the floor beneath them. "I can't believe we're back."

There was no sign of Reykas. "We? Did it work?"

She dropped the reins and slid her feet over the side so she could drop to stand next to Oreth. "It worked," she said. "He's still unconscious, but it worked."

Oreth's breath caught. He'd wanted to help, but he'd hardly dared to hope the cure would be real. "Are you sure?" he asked. "Is he back there?" He moved toward the back of the cart without waiting for an answer, and then he saw the shape beneath the blankets. Reykas lay there, completely covered, just as he'd been when Lizzie had left.

"If it hadn't worked, he wouldn't have made it this far," Lizzie said. She was beside him now and rested a hand on the blanket that covered Reykas. "Will you help me get him back to our room?"

"Of course."

She cut a sharp look at him. "Has anyone noticed we're gone?"

He shook his head. "I told everyone you're waiting in your

quarters with Reykas. Waiting for him to…" He let the sentence trail off. She'd said the cure had worked, but the thought of Reykas dying was still there and still felt real to him. It would be a long time before it would feel true that Reykas' illness was gone.

"You still can't tell anyone we left," Lizzie said.

"What will they think when Reykas wakes up?" he asked. "What will Reykas think?"

"Let me worry about that. Just promise me, Oreth. Promise me you won't tell anyone what we did." She hesitated and then met his eyes. "What you helped me do."

He swallowed hard and nodded without even thinking. That last bit was right. He'd helped her. He had a hand in this as much as Lizzie did, and he'd be in trouble as surely as she would. "The important thing is, it worked," he said.

Lizzie took her hand off Reykas and placed it on Oreth's weakened arm. She smiled at him again, but it was different than before. Something had changed in her eyes, either since they'd come to Stormbreak or since she'd left and come back from Karsk. Oreth wasn't sure when it happened, but there was something harder there. Something colder, and the smile, sincere though it might be, stopped at her chapped and wind-reddened lips.

"You may have saved Reykas' life," she said. "I won't forget that."

She squeezed his arm in appreciation, and Oreth bit his tongue to keep from flinching at the pain.

~

Lizandra tugged the comb through her hair, and it snagged for the fifth time. She set her jaw and pulled again. The teeth tore themselves through the tangle, ripping hairs free from her scalp, but she reset and did it again. Again and again, each time pulling more hairs away but leaving the ones that remained a little straighter than before. She'd found the comb in a box of supplies in a storeroom near her quarters, along with a cake of soap and a basin that she'd filled with water.

Whoever had built the pump into the keep had done so in an interior room that remained warm enough to keep the pipes and their workings from freezing up. It was a wonder the parts that ran underground stayed unfrozen as well, but that was not her concern.

At the moment, all she wanted was to strip the past months out of her hair, off her face, and away from her body. The exhaustion, the stress, the grief, and the guilt had layered on top of her like the grime that she rubbed away until her cheeks were pink. She scrubbed and picked at her fingers until the black disappeared from under her nails. She massaged her feet with an ointment Oreth had given her, and the aching chill finally subsided from her toes.

When Lizandra had finished, she looked into the oblong mirror that hung before her, and she saw someone she recognized for the first time in a long while. A few new lines creased her face, framing her mouth and punctuating her forehead. Her lips remained red and scabbed from the harsh wind. But she knew those eyes. She knew that hair that was finally clean and straight. She knew those hands, pale and thin but strong.

Lizandra pressed her fingers into loose fists and rested them on her lap, and she held her own eyes in the mirror for as long as she could stand it. She recognized herself, but she was not the same woman who had come to Stormbreak on that ship. She had schemed in secret, and she had made Oreth an accomplice to her deception. She had ignored Reykas' wishes in the name of saving him, and in doing so she had paid a price that he could never know. No, she had forced him to pay that price.

Lizandra closed her eyes and broke the gaze. She might look more like the Lizandra who had performed on the stage with Reykas and loved him and cared for him, but that wasn't who she had become. She'd crossed a line in going to Karsk. If she hadn't gone, she'd have already lost Reykas, and she would go again without hesitation. But it was no use trying to fool herself into thinking she was the same girl who'd left Klubridge with him. No, that girl was left behind, buried somewhere in the rubble of the city.

This new person—this impostor—could never let them

know. She'd play the part as best she could, and she'd be the old Lizzie as much as she was able. None of them could know the price she'd negotiated, least of all Reykas. She'd never been a good actress and had never been able to lie effectively, but this is when she'd learn.

Lizandra was halfway across the courtyard before she realized someone was calling her name. "Aquin," she said, and stepped aside to let a man carrying baskets pass her.

"I haven't seen you in so long," the other woman said. "How have you been?" She touched Lizandra's arm, and Lizandra barely kept from pulling away. Something visceral tried to shrink from the compassion, but she tilted her head instead.

"I'm... all right. How are you?"

Aquin sighed and dropped her hand, and strange relief rushed through Lizandra's chest and head, almost dizzying her. "I don't know," Aquin said. "Everybody is gone. Samira tried to take me with them, but I told her I needed time. And now I have the time, and I just..." Her voice trailed to silence as her eyes dropped, but she shook her head. "But you don't need to hear my complaining. You have enough to deal with."

Lizandra nodded but could think of nothing to say that wouldn't sound false.

"Oreth told me you've been staying in your room with Reykas."

She nodded again but couldn't hold Aquin's eyes. Lizandra looked to the right, past her and toward a young man practicing with a wooden sword in the far corner of the courtyard.

"I've been thinking about you," Aquin said, and her voice was low, almost like a confession. "About you and Reykas. You shouldn't have to endure this alone."

Lizandra felt her brows draw together, and she looked back at Aquin. "What do you mean?"

"I don't know what your feelings are about faith. About religion." Aquin waited, probably to see whether Lizandra would protest. When she didn't, Aquin continued. "I believe in Ikarna, and I believe in her healing power. I also believe she helps carry us away from here when we are beyond healing."

"My parents believed in... something," Lizandra said. "They

didn't push me to it, and I haven't really thought much about it since I was younger."

"I'm not trying to convince you of anything," Aquin said with a smile. "But I was wondering if you'd mind..." She hesitated again, the smile turning awkward. Lizandra felt the hairs at the back of her neck prickle, and she looked away again. At last, Aquin finished, "Would you let me see Reykas? Would you let me talk with Ikarna in his presence?"

Lizandra blinked and almost laughed. "You want to pray over Reykas?"

"Something like that. I don't want to be an imposition. I know this is a difficult time, and I'd just like to help in my way."

"I..." Lizandra rubbed at the back of her neck, and the skin was still tender from the scrubbing she'd given it a few minutes earlier. She glanced to the right, toward her room where she knew Reykas lay unconscious, still sleeping and still alive. He'd needed help, but no one else had offered anything practical when it was time to act. Lizandra had done what Ikarna wouldn't. None of the absent gods had deigned to make their presence known, but Lizandra had saved him. And now Aquin thought she could make a difference by praying over him. Praying to her water god. But Lizandra swallowed and said, "Thank you. You can see him."

And she led Aquin the rest of the way across the courtyard and into the short hallway to her door. Unlike their previous room, this one had a lock, and Lizandra slipped the key into the hole and turned it, pushing the door open ahead of her.

A triangle of light pressed its way into the darkened room, first revealing the edge of the bed and then crawling up the sheets to where Reykas' head rested on a low pillow. Lizandra's breath hitched as she came into the room, and she felt her eyes burn with sudden tears. "Reykas!"

He stared back at her from the pillow, awake but with eyes shining half-lidded and bleary. His hoarse voice was just loud enough for her to hear. "Lizandra. My magic is gone."

CHAPTER 27

Drass and the rebel woman had been in the small house in the snowy forest for nearly ten minutes. It was a rickety wooden structure that looked like it might blow over if a strong gust of wind hit it just right, but Wickes suspected it had withstood many winters and would stand through many more. He wouldn't have seen the house from the roadway and would have passed right by it if he hadn't been following the two when they veered off the path and between the narrow black trunks of the trees.

Wickes felt certain they weren't alone in there, and there could be as many as three others with them. Probably no more than that, unless they were stacked atop one another. The woman had hitched her horse to a post to the right of the door before they'd gone inside. There was already another horse tied to a similar post to the left, and Wickes could see the edge of what looked like a carriage hidden around the other side of the building.

He hunkered in the snow, his feet wet now from the slush that had dumped into his boots as he'd chased after the old pirate. He'd been breathing hard by the time he'd reached this spot. It wasn't hard to keep pace with Drass and the woman, but it had been nearly impossible to do so without making noise and without slipping on a sneaky patch of ice. He had his breath now, though, and it came slow and steady as he watched the building.

Drass would be inside meeting with this Daulet person he'd asked for. He'd be telling him there was a dangerous man named Quentyn Wickes on the hunt for the wizard Akithar. He'd be telling him Wickes used to be a good man but had fallen to the side of the Empire and now was their hunter and was a damned good one. How long would it take him to tell that tale? Would he share all the details? Would he tell Daulet about how Wickes was so vicious he'd handed his own crew off to be slaughtered?

Wickes glanced toward the roadway, barely visible through the clusters of spindly trees. They had no leaves, but there were enough of the creaky old things to obscure most of the view and to cast that little cabin into a protective shadow. No doubt Kraden had convinced Jalla that Wickes had run off. They'd be coming after him before long, but they might not spot the house as they approached. It was certain anybody looking toward the road would see their approach, though, and then what? Three or four rebels plus Ergo Drass would ambush them, and they'd not be finding Stormbreak that day or any other.

Wickes shifted his weight, ready to head back toward his captors. He'd go just far enough to intercept Jalla and let him know what he was doing. Just far enough to reassure him he didn't need to come stomping down the path and alert everyone in the forest the Empire had arrived.

Wood creaked behind him, and Wickes turned again to face the little house. Someone had pushed the nearest window open. It swung outward from a hinge at the top, and they'd propped it in place with a wooden bar. Even in these frozen woods, a small room with enough people crowding it could get warm. But, even more than warm, they could get loud. Voices drifted out from the window, and Wickes picked up a word every few seconds. "Pirate" was one of them, and "Empire" was another. He was ready to creep back toward the road when "Stormbreak" reached his ears.

Wickes stopped and looked back toward the window. They

could be discussing the location of the sanctuary at that very moment. And, by the time he got to the road and back, they might have finished their meeting, and that carriage might have taken off for parts unknown. He cast one more glance back toward the road, its surface winking at him through the trees that swayed with the breeze, and he knew staying was worth the risk. If he could learn where Stormbreak was, they wouldn't even need to track that carriage. They wouldn't need to put Colm to work reading more minds, and they wouldn't need to keep chasing leads. They'd know where to go, and maybe, just maybe, Wickes would be a step closer to his freedom.

He blew out a warm breath and dropped into a crouch as he crept closer to the open window.

∽

Wickes stayed low and shuffled through the snow with as quiet a step as he could manage. He had to catch his weight with his hands a couple of times, once sinking in the powder to his elbows, but he continued moving and kept his eyes on the open window. The conversation continued as he crept nearer, but he knew he'd be finished if anyone took a look outside. They couldn't fail to see him, a dark form approaching low across the white snow.

He whispered a prayer to Ikarna that he'd remain unseen, but he knew it was futile. Ikarna would do as Ikarna wanted. It seemed unlikely she'd spared him from drowning amid the serpents, only to have him caught and slaughtered there in the snow. Her ways were inscrutable, though, and maybe she had no use for him and would be pleased to see him bleeding out there, stuck through with blades. Whichever way it would go, Ikarna would do as she willed. Prayers were as useless as ever, and still he whispered one last entreaty as he covered the final distance.

Wickes dropped to the ground, his back pressed to the wooden wall, as he caught his breath again. He'd made it that far, thanks to his own careful navigation and luck. Ikarna had neither helped nor hindered him, but she wouldn't leave the corners of his mind.

"I could eat," said one of the men inside the house. Wickes recognized the voice as Drass', and he frowned as he strained to hear the response.

"Take a seat," another man said, and there was the sound of wood scraping on wood. A chair dragging across the floor, perhaps. "No sense sending you back now with your belly empty."

There was a metallic scraping, like a utensil in a bowl. Had Wickes dragged himself all this way only to listen to a bunch of rebels slurping stew? He shifted into a crouch and slid his back up the wall, trying to angle his head so he could see through the open window without revealing himself to the occupants.

A shadow moved across the section of wall he could see, and when he leaned a bit farther, he could make out the back of a man's head. He was stocky, with dark hair and light skin, and he was bent over a table. Wickes couldn't see what he was doing, but another man spoke just then, confirming there were at least four people inside: two men he didn't know, the one woman, and Drass.

"Where'll you go after this?" the unseen man had asked.

After a pause, Drass said, "Back south. It's wisest if I stay out of your business for now."

The other man grunted his reply, but it was too low for Wickes to hear what he said. Wickes was leaning closer to the window when a flicker of motion past the corner of the building caught his eye. He slipped back into a crouch, his muscles tense now, ready for anything. What had that been? Perhaps an animal? He stared past the edge of the house, where he'd seen the movement, out through the trees, toward the road beyond, and his eyes widened.

The sound of a boot kicking in the door was unmistakable, and Wickes flinched away from the crash, nearly sprawling flat on the ground. He scrambled back under the window and risked raising his eyes above the sill as shouts arose from within.

There was a table against the left wall, and Ergo Drass was halfway up from the stool where he'd been sitting. His knee hit the underside of the table, toppling a metal bowl and sloshing out the broth. The woman was to his right, her back to the window, her right arm across her body, a sword half drawn from the scabbard at her left hip. The stocky man with dark hair was stumbling back from the table to the right, where he'd been bent when Wickes had seen him a moment before. The final rebel was another unfamiliar man, taller than the others, his hair run through with gray, and a green cape hung down his back.

And there, ahead of all of them, staggering through the broken door, was Kraden, that imbecilic fool who'd tried to stop Wickes from leaving the hill. His sword was in his hand, and his eyes were wide, his jaw hanging slack. The dolt looked surprised he'd managed to get the door open, and he clearly had no plan for what he'd do after he got inside.

The woman beside Drass knew what to do, though. Two quick strides closed the ground between them, and a fast slash opened Kraden across his stomach. The sword fell from his grasp, and he had just enough time to fumble his gloved hands at his wound before he collapsed to his knees and then his face.

Wickes sucked in a gasp, but it wasn't from the shock of the blood or the suddenness of Kraden's death. Wickes had seen plenty fall. Some of them went slow, some went fast, some went easy, and some died trying to hold their guts in. Nothing about what happened to Kraden rocked Wickes. It was the open door behind Kraden and Jalla running toward it. But, more than that, it was Colm's terrified face just past Jalla.

Wickes had no concern for whatever might happen to Jalla, but Colm had no place there. Why had they even brought him along? But, of course, he knew why. Kraden had reported that Wickes had fled, and Jalla knew they could lure him back with the halflock. Curse it all. Wickes lunged around the corner, slid on a patch of ice, righted himself, and ran toward the front of the building, his feet crunching in the hard-packed snow on that side.

Colm and Jalla both spotted him at the same time as he rounded the building. Jalla arrested his charge toward the door and pointed his blade at Wickes. He yelled something incomprehensible and sprinted at Wickes just as the stocky man came outside, sword in hand. "Keep one alive!" the older man bellowed as he followed, fumbling to unclasp his cape.

LIZANDRA'S DEEPEST FEAR

Wickes had no weapon and barely dodged Jalla's first wild swing. "Run!" he yelled at Colm. "Run, blast you!"

The halflock stumbled backwards a couple of steps, fear and confusion confounding his feet. Colm dropped backwards into the snow, sitting hard on the cold ground. Wickes cursed and had to turn his back on his old friend as Jalla came for him again.

The blade slashed at his torso, and Wickes danced back, clear of the edge once more. Jalla was no swordsman, but Wickes would tire from dodging long before Jalla's arm gave out. He bent his knees, ready to move again, when the younger and broader of the rebels crashed into Jalla from behind. The blow was hard enough to knock the wind out of the Imperial, and he collapsed forward, the sword flying free and disappearing into a mound of white powder.

Wickes leaped for the blade and thrust his hands into the cold, soaking his sleeves up to the shoulders as he swept the ground. Where had the damned thing gone? He'd seen it flung straight into the snow. It couldn't have gone far after disappearing!

A shout from the right snapped Wickes' head up, and Jalla was on his feet again. He'd gotten out from the rebel's grasp and, instead of standing to fight, was legging it for the trees, away from the fray and past Colm, who still sat bewildered in the snow. Both of the rebel men had their eyes on Jalla's back, and the older one was jogging after him.

Wickes knew when making an exit was more prudent than making a stand. He abandoned the search for the sword and scrambled to his feet, turning to run towards Colm.

"No," the woman said, and he slid to a halt, falling back into the snow and sinking to his elbows. She stood before him, dark hair whipping in the wind and her sword unsheathed and pointed at him. Red stained its edge, and a drop of Kraden's blood fell on the front of Wickes' shirt.

So, this was it. Ikarna had saved him from the serpents and the water, only to deliver him to the blade of an anonymous rebel in this accursed frozen waste. What does one say when faced with such a fate? Surely something eloquent would be appropriate, but the woman didn't give Wickes a chance. She stepped forward, turned her hand, and brief pain and blackness were all he knew.

CHAPTER 28

Fairy pulled a tool out from the box and leaned back in the chair, letting it tilt onto the two rear legs while she propped her feet up on the corner of the table. Oreth shot a glance in her direction but said nothing this time. He'd told her to keep her dirty boots on the floor enough times that he ought to know it wouldn't do any good, so he just sighed and went back to tracing his finger down the rows in one of his ledger books.

Fairy studied the tool she was holding and turned it over in her hands. It had a long, thin handle made of metal, nearly as long as her forearm. At the end, there was a round disc of metal with spikes on it, held in place with a pin through the center so it could spin around. It looked like the spurs she'd seen Imperial riders wearing when they'd come through Klubridge on their big stallions. This wasn't a spur, though. It was on the end of a stick, for one thing, and it looked like it was made to turn, for another.

"What's this?" she asked and thrust the thing out at arm's length.

"What?" Oreth looked up from the book again, blinking at her.

"This thing. What is it?" She waggled it in his direction, and the spiky disc jangled on its little metal pin.

"Where did you get that?"

She kicked the side of the wooden box and scooted it a couple of inches toward him. He frowned back. "All that stuff is for leatherworking. Put it back."

"What does it do, though?"

That line crinkled up between Oreth's eyebrows again, and Fairy could have sworn it was getting deeper every time he did it. "Just put it back," he said, and his voice was snappier now, too.

She snorted at him and dropped the tool back into the box, where it landed among other strange metallic instruments with a clank. Fairy waited for Oreth to say something else, but his attention was back on those numbers again, so she slumped back in the chair and tilted her head to look at the ceiling. Oreth had been grumbly when they'd first arrived at Stormbreak, after he'd gotten hurt in Klubridge and didn't want to talk to Apak and so forth. But he'd seemed better after he'd met Leyna. They'd spent more and more time together in the supply room, and Fairy wouldn't be surprised if they'd been spending time elsewhere too. Leyna had made that brace for his leg, and he'd seemed better. Happier. But lately he was back to the grump he'd been when they'd all first made that long ride up in the carriage.

Fairy pouted and looked back down the table at him. He was in a foul mood, but he didn't mind her company, at least. She didn't have anywhere better to be, so she'd been hanging around the supply depot. Every once in a while, she'd been able to help him get something down from a shelf or carry something across the room. It was hard for him to manage some of the heavier bags and boxes with one leg and one arm being weaker than the other. It felt good to be useful, but Fairy knew not to make a big deal out of it. Oreth was already in a foul mood, even without her poking at him and making it worse, and that was a fact.

She tried to think of something that could lift his spirits, and then it came to her. She sat up so all four legs of the chair were on the floor again and asked, "Did you hear about Reykas?"

Oreth had been writing, but that got his attention. "What about him?"

"He's better now!" she said. "I heard he was up and around." She frowned. "Well, sitting up, at least."

"Who'd you hear that from?"

"From Aquin. She saw him herself. She went to visit him, and he'd woken up."

Oreth stared at Fairy just long enough to make her look away, and then he said, "That's great news," but his voice was flat, and she could tell his heart wasn't in it.

If bringing him news that his friend wasn't going to be as dead as everybody had expected wasn't enough to bring him out of whatever mood Oreth was in, Fairy was at a loss. She slipped her feet off the edge of the table and stretched as she stood. "Aquin said she was going to pray for him," Fairy said. "Do you think that's what did it?"

"Did what?" Oreth asked. He was looking at the ledger again but hadn't picked his pencil back up.

"Made him better. Something had to've done it."

He looked at her one more time, and this time, his eyes looked tired. The kind of tired you'd get from worrying over something important, not from just staring at numbers in a book, and that's something Fairy knew about all too well after her days keeping records for Scrounger. "Must have been that, then," Oreth said, and it was clear he was done talking.

Fairy pulled her lips tight and watched Oreth for another moment before she pushed the chair back under the table and wandered out the big barn doors at the front of the depot. If Leyna had been around, it might have been worth talking to her to see if she had any idea what was up with Oreth. But Leyna was a little strange herself, so maybe it was for the best that she was off in some other part of Stormbreak, helping somebody fix something.

A cart sat just outside the doors, its big wheels sunken into the snow. Since Alev Adonar had left with Nahk and the others, the magic dome didn't cover the castle for as long each day, and that meant more snow was coming down. Fairy turned her face up to the midday sky, but there were no flakes just then.

"They usually fall earlier or later in the day, when the sun isn't as high."

Fairy had been squinting at the clouds, and it took a second for her eyes to adjust and see Magra watching her from beside the cart. "You knew what I was thinking," Fairy said.

Magra shrugged. "Hard not to."

"It doesn't bother me," Fairy said and came around the corner of the wagon. "What're you doing?"

"Checking over the grain sacks," Magra said and patted a big burlap bag that was piled in the back of the cart alongside several identical ones.

"Grain?" Fairy asked.

"We have too much of that and not enough of some other things. We take the extra grain out and trade it to get what we need."

"Who do we trade it with?"

"There are other rebels out there, away from this place. Also, other people who aren't quite rebels but aren't afraid to trade with us. They've had a whole supply network running for years. Decades, maybe? Who knows?"

"This is what Oreth does?"

"What he does, what that girl Leyna does, and now what I do, too. Others as well. Others like those two lazies I'm waiting on right now."

Fairy chewed at the inside of her cheek and looked at the bags of grain again. "I want to go with you."

Magra raised an eyebrow at her. "You do, do you?"

Fairy met her eyes and nodded. "I do. I've been stuck here with nothing to do, and now even Oreth's being a pain."

Magra snorted at that. "You ever ridden an open wagon before? It's not comfortable."

"Had you ever done it before we got here?"

"Don't know. Maybe I had," Magra said and gave her a sharp grin. "I could've been a noble, for all I know. Had people driving me around in my own coach."

Fairy had forgotten for an instant that Magra, of course, didn't know whether she'd ridden in a wagon or done anything else before the Empire got their hands and their knives on her. Asking the question had been a mistake, but Magra didn't seem too upset about it.

"Let me ride with you. I'll help out, and I won't be in the way."

Magra eyed her and said, "You don't even know where we're going. Could be a week-long trip."

"Is it?"

"No."

"It wouldn't matter if it was. Nobody here would miss me, and I'm sick of being here," Fairy said. She knew she sounded like a sulky little brat, but for the moment she didn't care about that any more than she cared about where the cart was going. She just knew she wanted something different, and this was her best chance at a change of scenery. Two men were approaching from behind Magra, probably the lazies she'd been talking about, the escorts that went with her on the supply runs. They'd be leaving soon, and Fairy intended to be with them when they went.

Magra was studying her then, her big eyes appraising Fairy. She pursed her lips and blew out a loud breath before shaking her head. "Fine with me. I could use company beyond these two silent meat heads. You have a heavier coat? You'll need something warmer than that."

~

The seat at the front of the cart was like a bench with a high back. Fairy sat on the left side of it, and Magra was on the right, holding the reins. The two men who'd accompanied them rode on their own horses, just ahead of them, side by side. Magra had called them Wik and Len, and she seemed fonder of them than she liked to let on. Calling somebody a meat head must have been her way of showing affection.

The wagon's wheels bumped over every little divot in the road, and after a couple of hours of riding, Fairy's backside was numb. Would it have hurt them to put a little padding on the seat?

She shifted again and squinted up at the white sky past the treetops. It looked like somebody had dragged a dirty gray sheet over them, blocking out the blue.

"That's where the snow'll come from," Magra said, keeping her eyes on the horse and the road ahead. "Just you wait and see."

"You heard me thinking again?"

Magra shrugged one shoulder and cut a glance at Fairy. "Doesn't seem to bother you."

Fairy shrugged back. "Anything I'm thinking, it seems like it'd be okay to tell you. You just save me the trouble."

Magra chuckled at that. "That's not how people usually feel about it. They don't like having their secrets laid bare. I suppose that means you don't have any secrets to hide?"

Fairy scratched at the side of her face and pondered that one. She'd had plenty of times when she'd had to hide things in the past. Lots of secrets she'd kept from Scrounger, things she hadn't told Skink, even things she'd thought it was better for Dorrin to not know about. But they were all gone now, and she was out of Klubridge and into a new life. There wasn't much to that new life, but there wasn't anything secretive about it, either. She shook her head. "Guess not. And anyway, I like you. You're easier to figure out than the rest of them."

"I am, eh?"

Fairy nodded. "Everybody else is all wound up in who they like or don't like or what's the best way to get at the High Lord or whatever else they're all worried about. Oreth was more normal, but even he's gotten all weird now."

"A girl will do that to a boy his age," Magra said.

"Leyna? That's what I thought, too. I don't know." She sighed. "Point is, you're not all messed up with all that, and I don't have to worry about you sending me off somewhere just to get rid of me. I like that."

"Who sends you away?"

"All of them. They just think I'm in the way. Apak wouldn't teach me anything, and now he's gone off to wherever with Nahk and the others. She wouldn't teach me, either. And Caius and Samira just basically forgot about me and took off to somewhere else."

"You feel like you don't have a place," Magra said. "That's something I can understand."

"You do?"

"Course I do. You don't get your brains dug out and get locked up by the Empire and feel like you fit in."

"I guess not." Fairy looked at Magra from the side and studied what she could see of the scar on the back of the woman's head. She'd still been keeping that part of her head shaved smooth, even though Caius had skipped shaving his face and even though the weather up at Stormbreak had to be bitter on her bare scalp.

"You know, it can be good to have people underestimate you," Magra said.

"That's all it feels like anybody does now. I mean, people did before, when I was back in Klubridge. But, even then, enough people knew I was smart. They knew I could take care of myself and could figure things out. But not here."

"It can be good," Magra said again. "Take me, for example. Most halflocks, the Empire burns out their common sense alongside their memories. I lost my memories but stayed in my right mind otherwise." She gave Fairy a sly wink. "As much as I'd ever been there, mind you. But I pretended to be like the others. I talked silly, I stared, I acted weird."

"Why'd you do all that? Wouldn't it have been simpler to just be yourself?"

"Simpler, maybe, but not smarter. The less somebody thinks you can do, the less they expect you to do. The Imperials didn't think I had the sense to even understand I was a prisoner, so they gave me a long leash. If I hadn't played dumb, I wouldn't have been roaming free when Samira found me and got me out of there."

Fairy supposed that made sense. "It still feels wrong, though, not doing everything you're capable of. Lying and hiding yourself."

"You do what you have to do to get by. I suspect you understand that part of it, at least."

And she did. She'd had to scramble to survive after Scrounger was dead, and after the rest of them were gone. She'd tried to care for the younger kids Scrounger had left behind, but in the end it had just been Fairy on her own, struggling to stay alive.

Magra gave her a sideways nod, and Fairy knew she'd heard those last thoughts, too. "Never let anybody know the full extent of what you're capable of. That's one to live by. Let them think less of you, and then you live on your own terms. You get more control, and you get to choose if and when you let them in on the secret."

"The secret?" Fairy asked and raised her eyebrows at Magra.

"That you're the most capable one of them all," the woman said back and smiled. She looked back to the road, and she gasped. "Child, get down."

Fairy asked, "What?" and then one of the men fell off his horse. She wasn't sure if it was Wik or Len, but whichever one just toppled right off into the deep snow piled on the side of the road.

Magra pulled back on the reins hard with one hand and shoved Fairy with the other. Fairy toppled off the seat and onto her knees on the floorboard. She scrambled to hold on to the edge of the cart to keep from falling out, and something thudded into the wood next to her hand. An arrow had lodged most of the way through the board, and the back end with the feathers was still vibrating.

The next arrow took Magra straight through the chest. She wheezed once before she fell to the side and off the seat, dragging the reins with her, and then the cart wheels were up on the side of the road, and the whole cart was toppling over, and Fairy didn't even have time to scream before it crashed down on top of her.

CHAPTER 29

It had been less than a week since Hama's people had slaughtered the Imperial workers. Every time she slept, Samira still heard the gunshots echoing across the landscape and saw the distant overseers' heads jerk as they collapsed to the grass or tumbled into the pit. She wasn't sure whether she'd actually seen red mists of blood exploding from their wounds during the attack, but that's how she remembered it. Fast, brutal, and loud, all repeating every time she closed her eyes.

Caius wasn't resting any better than she was, but that was nothing new. He mumbled in his sleep and occasionally thrashed, but he hadn't stood or tried to sleepwalk out of the carriage again. And sleep had been an ordeal for the past few days, after the two of them had become little more than glorified hostages. Hama had heard their protests and taken their lack of bloodthirstiness to be tantamount to betrayal of him, their mission, and likely the entire rebellion. Samira had little doubt that he'd have left their bodies behind with the Imperials if he hadn't felt like he needed them in order to convince the scion to come with them. The end couldn't come soon enough, now that things had gone the way they'd gone.

"Caius," Samira whispered. She knew the sound of the carriage bumping along the rough road should mask her voice, but Ranja was in the driver's seat, and Samira now knew better than to underestimate the strange woman's hearing. "Caius," she whispered again, and he turned his head away from the window to look at her.

"What is it?"

"I thought you might be asleep."

He shook his head. "I've been trying not to."

She leaned across the space between their seats and put a hand on his knee. He gave her a tight smile in return, and the creases next to his eyes seemed deeper than ever.

"Do you know where we are?" Samira asked.

"We passed through Bria while you were asleep."

"We didn't stop?"

"Not in the city. Good thing, too. I'd be surprised if the Empire didn't already have the word out about what happened at the drill site. They'll be on the lookout for us."

"For the Aescalan," Samira said. "And they're hard to miss."

Caius nodded and leaned to the side so he could get a better look at the passing landscape. "I'd say that was a couple of hours ago. We're heading west now."

Samira remembered the location the spy had provided. "It shouldn't be long, then. We're almost there."

Caius didn't respond for a moment but finally looked at her and asked, "What do you expect to find when we get there?"

She'd been giving that some thought all the way down from Stormbreak, but she still wasn't certain. "A man," she said. "Beyond that, who knows? You know as much about this Tamrat thing as I do."

"And that's not much," he said. "Do you think this Gressam man even knows about it?"

"He's living in the middle of nowhere, according to the spy. That could be intentional. He might be trying to outrun his ancestral legacy."

"Or he could have no idea about any of this, just like we didn't know. The Aescalan were raised from birth on stories about that family and how this scion would destroy Peregrine and help them overthrow Teshovar. That's not something we're taught here."

Samira leaned her head back against the padded top of her seat. "Either way, we need for things to move quickly once we get there. The more time we spend there, the more time the Empire will have to track us. They won't let that attack go unanswered."

"Don't forget the Nightingales," Caius said.

Samira closed her mouth and held her hands in her lap. The fact was, she had forgotten the Nightingales in the midst of everything else. And a determined band of assassins was something she couldn't afford to be forgetting. "Them, too. We have to get this man and get back on the road as quickly as we can."

The carriage bumped out of the rut in the road and swayed as it turned right, off the main way and onto a small and overgrown path. "That's our turn," Caius said, watching out the window again. "It won't be long now until we see how things go."

~

Samira was about to ask Caius whether he thought they should open the carriage door when it swung outward on its own. She'd had her hand resting against its window and jerked back, startled. Dekan Hama's frame filled the open doorway, and he had to stoop to look inside. His eyes lingered on Caius for a few seconds before shifting across to Samira. "Don't try anything," he said.

"We want the same thing you do," she said.

"Didn't seem that way." The other Aescalan were dismounting and talking behind him, and Samira could see the red painted wall of what looked like a farmhouse beyond them.

"It serves all of us to get this man and head back to Stormbreak as quickly as we can. We won't be doing anything to delay that."

Hama's mouth was closed, and he breathed heavily from his nose, making the hairs in his red mustache twitch. His small eyes, more grayish blue than greenish blue in the shadow of the carriage, studied Samira's face for any sign of betrayal. She forced herself to hold his gaze, and she kept her chin raised. He'd either have to trust her, or he'd kill them, and she was betting on the former. At last, he grunted and pulled away from the door, saying, "Get out, and behave." As he stepped out of their way, he said, "I'll do the talking."

Samira slid out from the carriage first and then turned to help Caius step down. His legs seemed unsteady at first, and he held her arm until he regained his balance. She watched him until she was sure he was stable, and he squinted past her, toward the house. She followed his gaze and saw the wooden building sat at the end of a short walkway paved with old bricks that might once have been red but now were dusty brown. The house itself was small, with a narrow porch along the front and a single door flanked by two windows. No one was on the porch, but someone was at work in the field to the left of the house. Green plants sprouted from the dirt, covering what Samira guessed might have been an acre, but Caius had always been better than she was at estimating space.

Dekan Hama stood to the side of the carriage, also looking toward the stooped figure toiling in the crops. He squinted and raised a hand to shield his eyes from the sun. Talit moved next to Hama, her eyes on the farmer as well. Her voice low, she asked, "Is that him?"

The other three Aescalan had gathered close, waiting for Hama's answer, and it was impossible to miss the mix of fear and hope on their faces. Samira looked back at Hama and blinked in surprise. The man's jaw trembled, and a tear escaped the corner of his left eye, clearing a wet trail down the side of his nose. He grunted and wiped at it with the back of the hand he'd been using to shield his eyes.

"Is it?" Talit asked again. She pulled at one of her braids with a trembling hand.

Hama cleared his throat and bellowed across the field. "Is your name Gressam?" His voice echoed for a long, tense moment before the man in the field straightened and looked in their direction.

"It is," he called back.

Samira squinted against the sun and could see the man had brown skin and dark hair. He looked tall and slim, but it was hard to make out more details from that distance. He stood motionless, the green leaves around his ankles, his hands hanging loose at his sides.

Something snorted, and Samira thought it was one of the horses until she saw Rikin, the youngest of the Aescalan, now on his knees in the grass, his hands planted on the ground, and his back heaving. He snorted again and looked up long enough for Samira to see his face wet with hysterical tears. Hama glanced at the younger man, and Samira half expected some reproach from him. Instead, he sucked in a quick breath and wiped his palm across his mouth. He looked to Ranja, standing just the other side of Rikin, and said, "See to him." Ranja's face remained impassive, even as her friends seemed on the verge of frenzy. Even old Lodar gaped at Gressam and put a hand against the carriage to steady himself. Ranja simply nodded to Hama and knelt to slide her hands under Rikin's arms so she could pull him away, out of sight of the farmer.

As she watched the awe and terror wash across the faces of these Aescalan, Samira realized they were seeing what amounted to a deity manifested. These people had lived in reverence of the Tamrat dynasty, and their people had predicted the rise of a scion and the overthrow of Peregrine for centuries, if not millennia. Now, here they stood on a remote farm west of Bria, staring at the man they believed would fulfill their prophecies. Their reactions couldn't be much different from if Ikarna herself appeared before Aquin or Apak.

Hama said to Talit, "Wait here." He turned back toward the field and took another heavy breath.

Samira took a step toward him. "Perhaps I should be the one to—"

The look Hama gave Samira silenced her, and she retracted her step. His face pinched into a mean and wrinkled scowl. "No. Wait here." Before Samira could make a move to follow him, even if she were inclined to do so, a firm grip on her arm held her in place.

"Wait here," Ranja said in that same even, quiet voice she'd used while killing Imperials.

Now that she knew she couldn't, Samira wanted to jerk her

arm out of Ranja's hand and follow Hama into that field. She wanted to be the one to talk to Gressam. In truth, she should be the one. None of the Aescalan were in any condition to tell a man he was the subject of centuries of legend and had to leave his life immediately because assassins were coming for him. Caius was barely in a state to stand, much less convince that man to leave his farm. It should be Samira, but instead, it was Hama.

She watched the big man stride into the field, his focus so set on the smaller man ahead of him that he didn't mind his steps. His huge boots tromped through the crops, stirring the dirt and tearing the leaves, and onward he went, his shoulders impossibly wide against the noon sky. If Samira had seen this man, an improbably massive stranger, coming at her with no introduction or context, she'd have fled. Hyden Gressam stood his ground, though, moving only to brush his dirty palms against his thighs.

Samira glanced to her left and caught Caius' eyes. He raised his brows and tilted his head, and she gave him the smallest of nods. They'd wait and see how this played out. What else could they do?

~

Caius could hear Hama's voice rising and falling behind the closed door, but he couldn't make out anything the man was saying. Hyden Gressam's voice was much softer, and from the other side of that door it sounded as if Hama were having a passionate conversation with himself. They'd been at it for nearly half an hour by then, and Caius had to force himself to stop peering out the window, toward the road where he imagined the Imperials or the assassins would be showing up anytime now.

Gressam was a farmer, just as Vaino had said, and he'd seemed to know nothing about the Tamrat or the Aescalan or any of the rest of it. He'd waved Hama into the side door to the house to continue the discussion out of the sun, and that had been the last they'd seen of either of them. What had been less predictable was the sudden emergence of a woman from the front door shortly afterwards, but they should have expected Gressam might have a family.

The woman was his wife, Phyla, and she was a tiny woman, made even smaller in the presence of the Aescalan visitors. Her hair was as dark as her husband's, and her skin was a shade darker. Her eyes were a light brown, and they almost seemed golden when she turned them on Caius. "Perhaps you'd like to wait inside?" And then, to the rest of the group. "All of you can come in from the heat."

The weather was hardly what Caius would call hot, but it was much warmer than what they'd left behind in the north. Caius, Samira, and two of the Aescalan had followed Phyla inside. Talit had waited outside with Rikin, ostensibly to keep an eye on the caravan. It had been clear that Rikin was not ready to interact with anyone, though, and Talit kept a hand on his shoulder as he whispered something that sounded like a prayer over and over.

And now Caius sat next to Samira on one side of a wooden dining table that looked like one of the Gressams might have crafted it. Lodar had taken the stool at the head of the table, to Samira's right, and Ranja was in the chair on the opposite side, to Caius' left. The young Aescalan woman slumped in the chair, her left foot up on the seat and her elbow propped on her knee. She looked entirely at ease, but Caius had no doubt she'd snap into action as soon as he made any move to leave. Lodar, on the other hand, had his attention fixed squarely on that closed door. The older man had been given no food, but his closed mouth worked constantly as if he were chewing something.

"Would you care for tea?" Phyla Gressam asked. She stood at the side of the room, a hopeful smile on her face that no doubt masked her confusion and unease. Caius wouldn't have wanted a bunch of strangers in his house unannounced, and he doubted this woman felt much differently about the situation.

Before anyone could answer, the front door banged open, and Caius flinched. Samira and Lodar had turned to look in its direction, but Ranja continued studying whatever had fascinated her on the toe of her shoe. A small form sped into the room but stumbled to a halt in front of the table full of people.

"We have visitors," Phyla told the little boy. And then, to the others, "This is our son, Danel. Say hello, Danel."

The boy stared at the two Aescalan, wide-eyed. They seemed too large for the house, like some sort of trick. Caius and Samira were of less interest to him, but Caius leaned forward and smiled. The boy was better fed and rounder, and his complexion was darker, but he still reminded Caius of Dorrin. He was about the same height and had the same look of wary wonder as he watched the newcomers. "Hello," the boy said.

"How old are you?" Caius asked.

Danel glanced at his mother before answering. "Ten."

Dorrin had been eleven. The memory tugged at Caius' chest. Dorrin's death had hit all of them as hard as if he'd been one of their own all along, and they'd hardly known the child. It was no wonder Fairy had had such a hard time in the aftermath.

Caius slipped a hand into his pocket, and Ranja's eyes flicked to follow it. He drew a single coin out, showing it in his open palm, both so the boy would see it and so Ranja would know he had no designs on attacking anyone. "This is for you," he told Danel.

The boy looked at Phyla again but took a step toward Caius, his hand outstretched. Just before he took the coin, Caius closed his fist over it, turned his hand, and fanned his fingers open quickly, one at a time. Danel frowned and then gasped when he saw the coin was gone. It was the same reaction Caius had seen hundreds of times, but it never got old. He smiled at the boy and said, "Tastes funny, doesn't it?"

Danel frowned again, but then his eyes widened with realization. He opened his mouth and stuck out his tongue, and there was the coin, sitting head-side up just like it belonged there. Danel grabbed the coin and turned it over again and again, studying both sides before he looked at Caius. "How'd you do that?"

Caius winked and said, "Magic."

Of course, it wasn't magic. It was one of the earliest tricks he'd learned, even before he'd recreated himself as Akithar.

Samira had seen this one too many times to count, but she still favored him with a smile. Lodar's eyes were as wide as the boy's, and Caius knew he'd be trying to work out whether he'd used real magic or how he'd done the trick. Ranja's eyes registered no surprise, though, and they flicked from Caius' face down to his opposite hand, the one he'd been careful to keep in his lap. The corner of her mouth twitched upward, but she said nothing.

It was then that the door opposite from them swung open, and Dekan Hama ducked to pass through it without cracking his head on the frame. Lodar and Ranja looked at him, but Ranja's attention returned to her own boot before the big man said anything. Caius knew she'd registered the same thing from Hama's scowl that he had. Gressam had remained unmoved and had no intention of going anywhere with this odd group.

~

Even though he made it clear that he wouldn't be joining them on their journey back north, Hyden Gressam invited the group to stay for dinner before they resumed their travels. There was no offer of shelter for the night, and it was evident that his hospitality would see them through a meal and no further.

Talit volunteered for Rikin to help with the food preparation. The young man had done some of the cooking during the journey down from Stormbreak, but it seemed less likely that Talit was interested in showcasing his culinary skills and more likely that she hoped to keep him busy with chores so that he didn't collapse into a weeping mess again. Each of the Aescalan had reacted differently to facing and interacting with what amounted to a legendary hero, and keeping Rikin from prostrating himself before Hyden seemed to be a primary concern.

Caius stood outside the house with Samira as the sun went down, and they watched the figures moving through the windows.

"This isn't good," Samira said.

Caius cast a sidelong look at her. "Hopefully, it'll at least be edible."

"You know what I mean." She hugged herself against a sudden breeze, and Caius suppressed a shiver. There might be no snow on the ground this far south, but nature had its ways of reminding them it was still winter.

"I do," he said. He looked past her to where Ranja stood on the porch, her back propped against the front wall of the house. "We're being watched."

"Let her watch. I'm sure she can hear us from that far away, too. The girl has the ears of a gabac."

Caius smiled at that. "You're right, though. This isn't good."

"You have to do it," Samira said without looking at him.

"Do what?"

"What Vaino sent you to do. You're here because you're Akithar. You're the hero of the rebellion, and you're going to win this man over better than Dekan bloody Hama could do."

Caius wanted to protest that he wasn't Akithar any more than she was, but it was true. He'd spent ten years building a mythology around himself, and now it had taken on a life of its own. The name alone was inspiring songs in taverns, and the people believed he had single-handedly dismantled the Imperial regime in Klubridge. That was before the Empire decimated the city, but that detail had yet to work its way into the ballads. Still, he shook his head. "We didn't know he'd have a family. He won't leave them behind."

"He can't leave them," Samira said. "The Nightingales are as likely to slaughter them as they would be to kill him. All three of them have to be gone from here before they arrive."

She was right, as usual, but Caius asked, "How are you so sure I can convince them? They probably haven't even heard of Akithar all the way out here."

"You already won one of them over," Samira said with a smile. "The boy would follow you to Meskia and back."

"It's a shame he's not the one making the decisions, then."

The dinner table had accommodated four of them while Hama was meeting with Hyden Gressam, but it was too small for a party of four Aescalan plus Caius, Samira, and the family of three. Still, they all crowded around it, some sitting on chairs and others on stools, as Rikin ladled a vegetable stew into their bowls with a shaking hand.

Before he'd finished with the last bowl, Samira leaned into the table and asked Hyden at the far end, "Do you know the name Akithar?"

Dekan Hama straightened and scowled at her, his mouth opening to spit some sort of rebuke at her, but Ranja, sitting to his left, rested her fingers on his forearm. He looked down at her hand and then shot a glare directly at her. Ranja didn't acknowledge that glare, but Hama closed his mouth and settled back in his chair.

Hyden seemed to have missed that exchange and was shaking his head. "I can't say I know it."

They'd expected as much, and Samira said, "There are songs and stories being sung and told about him. He was a mage in Klubridge when the Empire laid siege to the city. The stories say he routed the Imperials and freed the city."

"This is an ancient story?"

"This is a recent story. And it's true. It happened just a few months ago, and we were in Klubridge when it happened." She stopped long enough to tilt her head toward Caius. "This is Akithar."

"I don't understand," Hyden said. "When I spoke with Dekan Hama, he said I was supposed to go with you and that I would lead an army." He had a bemused grin on his face and looked from Samira to Hama, who looked anything but entertained.

Before anyone else could speak, Caius clasped his hands together on the table and asked, "What do you know about your family's history?"

"I never knew my father," Hyden said. "My mother died many years ago. I didn't know much before her time."

"Did Hama tell you about the Tamrat?"

"He mentioned it, but I don't understand what that has to do with any of this. It sounded like some sort of religion his people follow?"

Hama looked like he wanted to respond to that, but Ranja's hand tightened on his arm, and he kept his silence.

Caius said, "I didn't know any of this until recently, so this is new for me as well. Before the Empire, a monarchy ruled here."

"A monarchy," Hyden said. He looked at his wife to his right, but she was watching Caius and said nothing.

"The Tamrat family was the ruling dynasty at that time," Caius said. "The Empire displaced them."

"The Ruinbringer destroyed them," Hama said, finally breaking his silence even as Ranja shot him a stern look. "He arose and killed the king and scattered the heirs. That was the end of the dynasty and the start of Teshovar." The way he said the name of the place carried all the hatred Caius imagined he could muster.

Caius resumed his story. "The Tamrat were your ancestors. You are descended from ancient royalty."

Hyden laughed at that. "If only that were true."

"It's true," Caius said, and the smile faded quickly from Hyden's face. "Imperial records have confirmed that you're the last remaining descendant. The Empire systematically wiped out the rest of your family. I'm sorry to be the one to tell you this."

Hyden frowned back. "This makes no sense. My mother hardly even knew my father. He left before I was born, and we had no idea where he'd gone. And my mother died from sickness. The Empire played no part in any of that."

Caius opened his hands on the table. "That may be the case, but they have worked hard over hundreds of years to end your family line. Maybe they lost track of the recent generations, or maybe they were responsible for whatever happened to your father. Either way, they know about you now. They've sent..." Caius hesitated and looked at Danel's round eyes staring up at him from his small stool. "They've sent people to find you. We don't know how long it will take for them to get here, but they are dangerous people. They will find you. That's why we're here."

Hyden ran a hand down the short whiskers on his cheek. "Dekan Hama, you told me none of this."

"Dekan Hama's priorities are different than ours," Caius said before any of the Aescalan could respond. "I want to save you and your family, and the only way to do that is to take you away from here before the people who are looking for you find this place."

"This is our home," Hyden said. "We're not going to abandon the farm. The house. Everything we have is here."

"It'll still be here after all this is over," Caius said. That was the first lie he'd spoken since arriving. He had no assurance the property would remain intact any more than he'd known the fate of his own theater before the Kites ransacked it. For that matter, he had no assurance that any of this ever would end. It was impossible to think of a day when the Empire wouldn't threaten them, but he had to sell that dream if any of them were to have a chance at surviving. "There's a rebellion against the Empire. They are building an army, but it's not enough. They don't have enough allies willing to move within Teshovar."

"Then it's hopeless?" Hyden asked.

"Not quite. Dekan Hama and his people are Aescalan. They come from outside of Teshovar, across the Madigus Sea. They have a massive army of their own, and they're willing to come here and help overthrow the Empire. They'll only come if they know you are with the rebellion."

"This is ridiculous," Hyden said. "I'm just a farmer. I'm not royalty. I'm no soldier. I've never even held a sword."

"You won't have to," Caius said. "The Aescalan revere the Tamrat dynasty. They believe in removing the Empire and reinstating your family's monarchy. They didn't know about you personally until very recently, but their culture has a prophecy saying the scion of the Tamrat will lead them to victory in Teshovar. You don't have to fight, but they need you as a figurehead. If you're with the rebellion, they'll send their ships to Teshovar, and the Aescalan will join the fight." Caius left out the part about Hama wanting to destroy Teshovar rather than free it. One issue at a time.

"Ridiculous," Hyden said again. "I've never had anything to do with politics or history or the military or any of this. I'm a farmer. I'm a father and a husband. I have no place in this rebellion."

"I wish that were the case," Caius said, and he meant it, truly. "I wish it were the case for me, too. You and I both have been pulled into this thing against our will. If we're going to survive, we both have to see this through." He looked down at the bowl of stew that was cooling before him. "If you come with us, Samira and I will help you for as long as you need it. The Empire has bounties on the two of us, so there's not much we can do until this succeeds, anyway."

"But they can't know about me. There's no way they would. I'm not a part of this," Hyden said.

Caius reached into the inner pocket of his coat and pulled out the paper Nahk had brought back from Tresa. He unfolded it and handed it down the table. "This is the contract on your life. They don't have your location yet, but they will soon. The people hunting you are called Nightingales. They—"

"They're a myth," Phyla said, speaking up for the first time. Hyden was reading the contract, and she looked at it from the side. "This can't be real."

"It's real," Caius said. "One of our friends has experience with the Nightingales, and they are as dangerous as they're supposed to be. They're coming here. Maybe not tonight, and maybe not tomorrow, but they'll come."

Caius let that sit in silence, and he hoped it would be enough. He took a look around the table. All eyes were on the Gressams, aside from Samira, who gave Caius a reassuring nod, and Ranja, whose head was tilted to the side as she stared at Caius. She looked as if she were appraising a horse before a long journey.

"We can't—" Hyden said.

"This is real," Phyla said. "This document is sealed and signed. It's official." And then, to Caius, "I worked in legal affairs before coming here."

"But it can't—"

"It is," she said again. "We have to go with these people, Hyden. This is absurd, but it's true. We are in real danger."

He pressed his lips together and looked up at the ceiling, then the walls around them. "I built this house, Phyla. This farm. This is all we have."

"Tregin will tend the animals when he sees we're away. He's done it before."

Hyden opened his mouth to protest again, but Phyla stopped him.

"Who will tend the farm if we're all dead?" she asked. "Will anything matter if these people find us? If they find Danel?" Without waiting for her husband to answer, she looked to Caius. "We'll go with you. We'll leave tonight."

CHAPTER 30

Fairy's eyelids fluttered a few times before they opened. It was dark above her, and everything was wet and cold. She shifted, but something was holding her down. She groped in the dim light and tried to look down, and her fingers glided over something that felt like rough fabric. She pushed at the heavy weight across her chest, and as she struggled against it, she realized where she was. The cart had turned over, and the big bags of grain had tumbled out. One of those had pinned her to the snow and was keeping her from sitting up.

She pressed her right hand against the bag and shoved with all her might, but her left arm wouldn't cooperate. She frowned and turned her head, raising her neck as much as she could. Nothing was holding her left arm down, but everything was very much not dice over there. She couldn't see the arm itself, hidden beneath the layers of coat and shirt, but she was fairly sure it had an extra bend now where one shouldn't be, right between the elbow and wrist. She'd seen plenty of kids get hurt in the East Ward—broken bones, cracked heads, smashed noses. There was no question her arm was broken, but it didn't hurt. Not yet, anyway.

So, one arm it would be. She couldn't get enough leverage to rock the grain bag off to the side, but she felt it sliding forward and down. She groaned as it moved off her chest and onto her

LIZANDRA'S DEEPEST FEAR

stomach. It was easier to draw a deep breath then, but it felt like all her innards were getting squashed about. She'd have to shift it again, and soon.

Fairy could sit up just enough to pull her elbows under to support her. The left one still worked just fine, but the rest of that arm dragged behind it, useless. She sat like that for a moment, collecting her strength, before she gave the bag another shove. It did slide to the side that time, and she was able to rock her hips enough to pitch the heavy thing off and into the snow. The bag sank next to her with a soft crunch, and she sat upright, her head barely clearing the inverted bed of the cart above her.

She was beneath the wagon, and there were other bags of grain under there with her, but she was otherwise alone. The one escort, possibly Wik, had fallen off his horse and was probably dead. She hadn't seen the arrow and didn't know what was happening at the time, but it seemed clear now. The same thing likely happened to the other one just after. And Magra must have been thrown clear when the cart overturned. Fairy could see no sign of her, but she knew she was dead. There was no surviving that arrow.

Fairy squeezed her eyes shut. She couldn't afford to lose it just now. It was like when Dorrin had died. She'd had a task to do. There would be tears and grieving and horror later, but right then she had to get herself free and find out—

"It's another sack of grain."

Fairy held her breath and remained as still as she could. Her backside was numb from being soaked in the snow, but she ignored the discomfort and waited and listened.

A second voice nearby said, "This one, too. It's all grain."

The first one cursed, and there was a thud, like a kick. "All this for some bleeding grain." That man sighed and said, "Might as well collect it up. Grain's worth taking."

Bandits. It had been bandits on the road, and they'd taken Magra and her escorts as a merchant wagon, and it had been Fairy's rotten luck to pick this as the time she just had to get out of the safety of Stormbreak and roam around the wilderness.

Now she was stuck underneath a wagon with killers three feet away from her.

They were to her left, and the gap between the front wall of the cart and the snow was so narrow that only a sliver of sunlight came through. The space was bigger on her right, where the rear of the cart had come down. She studied the opening and saw another bag of grain wedged between the corner of the cart and the ground. The sack had tumbled in such a way that it had caught the weight of the wagon and had probably saved her life. Without it, the whole thing would have crashed down on her, and there would have been no waking up, broken arm or no.

Fairy looked back down to her left and slid her right hand under her left forearm with all the carefulness she'd have used to pick up a newborn kitten. She could bend and use her left elbow, but everything below that just flopped like a fish. She'd have to be careful not to make it worse with careless movements. But, just then, no movement at all seemed wisest. The bandits were still crunching around in the snow, and they were grunting as they hauled up the heavy sacks that had fallen free.

Fairy looked again at the sack that was holding up the cart and the other one she'd just pushed off herself. Had the robbers seen her when they'd attacked? Did they know she was under this thing? Did they think she was already dead? More importantly, did they know there was more grain down there, and would they be coming for it?

A sudden, sharp pain flared in her left forearm, and Fairy winced, grinding her teeth against it. She wouldn't cry out. Things were bad enough without her giving herself away.

It subsided to a throbbing ache, but that pain would be coming back.

Fairy listened to the two men working and mumbling to her left, and she stared at the triangle of light to her right. She could try to slip through the gap and crawl away, but they were sure to spot her. She couldn't run in that snow, not with a broken arm flopping about. And if she tried to slink away, they'd see her for certain. The snow was too bright, and she was wearing dark clothes, and she'd be all too easy to pick out. She might make it five feet before they pinned her down with an arrow or two of her own.

So, what was left to do? Nothing but wait and hope they didn't come for those additional bags of grain.

Fairy cradled her broken arm in her lap, drew her knees up as close to her chin as she could get them, and tried to ignore the pain and the cold and the fear.

∾

It was impossible to know how long it took the bandits to finish collecting the grain, but it felt like much longer than they needed. There had been no sign of them before the arrows started flying, but they must have had their own cart they were loading the sacks into. Every time they walked back toward Fairy's hiding place, she tensed up, and that sent another shot of pain through her broken arm. Each time, she was certain they'd come around the opposite side of the wagon and take the bag that was propping up the cart. Or they'd come for it and find her. She wasn't sure which sounded worse, so she just kept her eyes closed and her breathing as steady as she could.

Fairy breathed in and out and in and out and listened to her breath and tried to keep it as quiet as possible. After a while, it wasn't her breathing that was the loudest in her ears, but rather her heartbeat. She could hear it thudding away, faster than normal, and she tried to tell it to slow down, but it just kept hammering at the inside of her ribs. She'd tucked her chin into her chest, and she could feel the heartbeat in her throat as she sat that way. It bumped its way down her arm, and every beat became hot pain all the way to her fingertips.

She couldn't and wouldn't let the bandits find her, and she focused all her attention on that pain and the sounds of her breathing and the feeling of her heart beating. Those were the things that mattered and filled her world, and she squeezed her eyes shut until all she could see were the bursts of light behind her eyelids. Everything narrowed down to Fairy and her pain and keeping herself alive.

Fairy jerked her head up.

She sniffed and looked to the left, toward the thin crack of light, but it was gone. She could barely see that side of the wagon in the gloom. Her eyes widened as she whipped her head to the right, where the grain sack still held the side of the cart far enough off the ground that it wasn't pinning her. The gap on that side was still there, but it was smaller, the snow having piled higher, to where only a small triangle of light shone through.

Somehow, impossibly, she'd nodded off to sleep in the middle of her ordeal. Nodded off? More likely passed out again. How long had it been? It felt like only a moment, but sometimes what seemed like a quick nap really lasted for hours, and that was a fact.

Fairy shifted, and the numbness left her backside all at once. She sucked in a breath and fell over on her right side, vaguely glad she hadn't collapsed on her left arm. The coldness rushed into her soaked legs, and it felt like a million tiny bees were stinging all the way from her waist down to the soles of her feet. The muscles in her thighs started cramping just then, and everything in the lower half of her body hurt worse than her broken arm had even dared to.

She scrambled to the right, pulling herself along with her right arm and dragging the left behind her, snaking her way toward the narrowing gap under the right side of the wagon. Just before she reached the bag of grain, she forced herself to stop. Were the bandits still out there?

Fairy gritted her teeth against the pain and strained to listen. There was the sound of the wind outside, and there was the thumping of her own heart in her ears, but that was all she heard. No voices, and no movement.

She pulled herself a little farther and straightened her legs in a way that the cramping subsided just enough for the pain in her arm to become the worst thing once again. Fairy held her breath for another few seconds before she thrust her hand through the gap, sweeping away the mounding snow to make a hole big enough she could crawl through.

Getting through the gap was less of a crawl and more of a wet and cold slither, but she came out headfirst, fit her shoulders through, and then pulled the rest of her body behind her. Once she was out from under the wagon, Fairy allowed herself to collapse face-first into the snow. It was still daylight, but the snow was coming down hard, and there was no telling how long she'd been out. Long enough for the bandits to finish what they were doing and disappear.

She gasped and pushed her knees under herself. Magra!

Fairy's legs and feet still ached with pinpricks across the cold numbness, but she raised herself up and stumbled around the side of the wagon.

She was alone. Magra was gone, as were Wik and Len. There wasn't even a sign of the horses. The bandits had loaded them all up and carried them away, leaving no sign that anything had happened, aside from the overturned wagon. And even that would be buried in the snow, off the side of the road, before night fell.

Fairy scowled as she leaned against the corner of the wagon. It made sense that the bandits had taken the grain, and even the horses made sense. But why would they have carried away three corpses? Why would they have tried to hide what had happened on the road?

Her eyes widened, and she stumbled back a step into the roadway. They didn't want to leave a warning, because they were still watching the road, and they were waiting to do it all over again to the next wagon that rolled by. They could be watching her that very instant.

Fairy sucked in a quick gasp of air and pushed away from the cart, willing her feet to shake the numbness out and support her. She took a second to orient herself. Which way had they come from? The cart had rolled over on the left side of the road, so they had to have come from behind her. Or had the cart turned around while falling over?

She squinted in both directions but had to decide fast. Standing there and getting run down by those same killers would be even worse than choosing the wrong direction. She turned her back on the cart and ran, powered by the desperate hope that the road ahead led to Stormbreak and not deeper into the wilderness.

Night came upon her fast. She knew maps, and she knew directions, but figuring out which way you were going when everything around you looked the same was something entirely different. At some point, Scrounger had told her about how she could tell which way was east and what was west, but she'd barely paid attention and couldn't remember the details with any certainty. The sun went up on one side and down on the other, and moss grew in some specific direction, and water flowed one way or another, but none of that was helpful when she was lost in the snow with darkness all around.

The flakes had continued falling, and it hadn't taken long for the road to cover over with a thick layer of white. Fairy had been able to see where the sides of the road sloped upward, though, and she'd followed that until she realized she was no longer on the road at all. Trees tangled ahead of her and to the sides and behind, and the snow fell even faster and thicker.

She stopped moving for the first time since she'd left the cart, what seemed like hours ago. Terror had driven her to run until exhaustion had slowed her, but stubbornness had driven her onward. Onward straight into this dead end.

Fairy stood motionless, staring at the trees in front of her and at the blackness beyond them. Snowflakes settled into her hair now that she'd stopped moving, and they tickled her ears that were burning from the cold. Her cheeks felt like they were on fire, too, and her lips were desperately dry. Her breathing came fast, in and out, and her lungs ached with every inhalation.

She turned and looked back the way she'd come, and it was so obvious now that she'd left the road. Sometime along her flight, she'd veered off and had been pushing through a forest for what must have been hours. She hadn't felt the full weight of her tiredness while she was moving, so certain she was going the right way, but it crashed down on her all at once now that she'd stopped. She didn't know where she was or even whether she'd been going in the right direction all that time. Nobody else even knew she was missing or that they'd been attacked or that Magra and the others were—

Fairy closed her eyes against those thoughts again, but they shoved their way into her mind, anyway. She'd watched three people die, and she'd barely escaped with her own life, only to get herself lost.

She was going to freeze to death.

She tried to keep that thought away as well, but it insisted on joining the others and took the last strength out of her legs. Fairy dropped to her knees and didn't even care that she sank to mid-thigh in the snow. It didn't matter. Nothing would matter before long. She was lost and alone and cold and injured, and there was nothing she or anybody else could do about it.

Tears burned her eyes then, but they didn't roll down her cheeks. She guessed they must have dried up or frozen or gone back inside her head to hide. It was that cold, and she could really and truly feel it now. When she'd woken up under the wagon, her legs had stung from the wetness of the snow, and she'd thought that was as bad as it would get. But now she was learning the real meaning of cold, and it wasn't anything she could have imagined. It was a painful and desolate thing, and it felt more like her skin was on fire than that she was freezing. She couldn't even feel her left hand at all.

With trembling fingers, Fairy felt for her left arm with her right hand. It was still there, just dangling. The fingers on that hand would probably be blue if she could see them. Blue, just like the rest of her would be before long.

"No," Fairy whispered. She'd come too far and gone through too much to give up. She'd lived when so many other people had died. Dorrin and Scrounger and Skink and now Magra, and she wouldn't be the next on the list. She pulled her right leg forward and pressed her foot into the packed snow, willing herself to stand up again. She made it midway before her knee buckled, and she pitched forward onto the ground. Her face turned just before the impact, and the firm snow hit her left cheek like a slap.

Fairy groaned and tried to press herself up again, but she had nothing left. All the strength had left her, and she didn't think she could have gotten herself back up again even if she'd had the use of both arms. But she didn't, so she'd never know, and she slipped into nothingness as the snow hurried to cover her.

∼

The next time Fairy's eyes opened, she wasn't facedown in the snow. She wasn't in the snow at all or even facedown, and both of those things felt wrong. She was supposed to have been dead by then, frozen and lost in the wilderness at night, but it was daytime, and the sun was so bright above her she had to squint.

"About time you woke up."

Fairy sat upright and flailed at the tangle of blankets wrapped around her. "What? What? Who—"

"Easy there," the stranger said from the other side of the fire. "You'll hurt your arm again."

She hadn't gotten herself loose from the blankets but stopped to stare at him. He sat on a fallen log, a hood pulled up over his head, and his shoulders hunched forward so he could warm his hands. A wooden token hung from his neck on a thin string, and it had a strange carving of what looked like a tree with a face in the middle of it that stared back at Fairy as she tried to make sense of things.

The man had a scarf wrapped around his nose and mouth, but the skin around his eyes was pale and reddened from the cold, much like Fairy expected her own to be. His chubby cheeks glowed rosy over the edge of the scarf, giving him a jolly appearance. His eyes pressed into thin slits as he smiled back at her. "You all right there?"

"Who are you?" she asked and found the top edge of the blankets with her right hand. When she pulled it down, she found her left arm bound close to her body with a sling wound around it and tied across her body.

He kept smiling at her with his eyes but didn't answer. "I found you last night. Lucky thing, too. Another half hour, and you'd have been an icy treat for the wolves."

"Wolves?" Fairy scanned the small camp and the snowy landscape beyond but saw no wolves or anything else.

The man shrugged. "They come out at night. Pick that up," he said and pointed to the ground next to her.

Fairy frowned and picked up the coin that lay atop a leaf, as if it had been placed there with care on top of the snow. She turned it over, expecting something special, but it was just an ordinary seri.

"Now give it to me," he said, his palm open.

Fairy hesitated, searching what she could see of his face for any sort of trick, but he waited patiently, his hand open. She put the coin into his palm, and he closed his fingers over it.

"You hungry?" The coin now forgotten, he held a bowl toward her, and she snatched it out of his hand before she had a chance to talk herself out of accepting food from a stranger. She was starving, and it felt like that was a more literal thing than usual. Fairy turned the bowl up and downed the thin, warm broth in a few messy gulps.

"Go slower," the man said between chuckles. "You need it, but you'll make yourself sick if you go too fast."

"Thank you," she remembered to say and then wiped the back of her hand over her mouth before handing the bowl back. "I don't know where I am."

"Where are you trying to go?"

"I..." But she stopped herself. She'd be dead without this man, no doubt, but he was still a stranger. He didn't need to know any more about her or what she was doing out there than he already knew. "I got lost. Do you know which way I'd go to get to Esterburgh?"

He pointed past her. "That way's to the south. It's a bit of a journey, especially with a bum arm."

Behind her was south, which meant ahead of her was north, and that's where she needed to be heading to get back to Stormbreak. "I should be going," she said and extracted one leg and then the other from her coverings. "Thank you for finding me, really."

"You're welcome to rest here a while," he said. "And I'm happy to help you get where you're going. I know the way to Esterburgh."

"It's all right," she said. "I should be on my way."

He watched her scramble to her feet, awkward with one arm tied to her. It didn't hurt as much as it had, at least, and she wondered how much of that was due to the help she'd gotten from this man and how much of it was because her arm had just given up hope of ever doing anything again. "You can take the blankets with you, at least," he said. "You don't want to get caught out at night again without them."

"I won't," she said, but she eyed the blankets.

"Esterburgh's more than a day's travel on foot," he said. "Take the blankets, girl."

She almost told him she wasn't going to Esterburgh but remembered to keep her mouth shut at the last instant. Instead, she scooped up the blankets with her good arm and slung them over her shoulder. They were warm and thick, but not so heavy that they'd weigh her down. She might as well take them. "Thank you," she told the man again.

"The road's just past those trees," he said and nodded off to his left, toward what Fairy now knew had to be the east. "You sure you don't need more help?"

"I'm sure," she said, and she left the stranger at the fire.

Once she got to the trees, she looked back to see if he was following her, but he was still sitting there, still tending the flames. She stepped around the trees, moving faster now, and it was only a moment later when she found the road. How had she wandered off it last night? It was packed hard and should have been unmistakable. However she'd done it, she was on it again now and had a rare second chance.

Fairy glanced to her right, south, toward Esterburgh. After one more look back toward the camp, now hidden by the trees, she headed north toward Stormbreak, her feet crunching on the softened snow.

CHAPTER 31

Nahk let the small blade slide out from the bracer on her left wrist, and she pulled it into her right palm, listening to the cable zip as it spooled out. She held the metal up before her face, turning it so it caught the light. It was no bigger than the head of an arrow, but she kept both edges far sharper than any arrow she'd ever handled.

She angled it and peered down the length of the blade on one side and then the other. There were no bumps or imperfections. She knew there wouldn't be. She polished and sharpened the blades in both bracers more frequently than was probably necessary. She was wearing down the metal faster than ordinary use would have done, but she'd rather have to change out the blades every once in a while than be caught with a dull weapon.

She crossed her right leg so her foot was propped on her left knee, and she slid the blade along the edge of her boot's sole. A tiny fleck of leather peeled away and drifted to the floor in a wispy spiral. Satisfied, she let that blade slip back into the bracer and crossed her leg the other way so she could inspect the other tiny knife hidden up her right sleeve.

Nahk had seen many people testing their blades on their own skin. Foolish practice, and one she hadn't done herself since leaving her education. Pricking their own skin left them with tiny cuts that healed over quickly, but the minor sting stayed for at least a few days, if not longer. The nicks and scrapes didn't look like much, but they were unnecessary distractions, and any distraction could get you killed. Nahk wasn't about to risk her life that way, and so she trimmed a thin sliver of material off her boots or trousers or cloak whenever she needed to confirm that her blades were as sharp as she could make them.

Satisfied with the second blade, she let the cable retract into the second zephyr spool, and her hand slid across to her side. She pressed at her ribs with her palm and prodded at the tissue and bones with her fingers. The ribs responded with a dull ache. She'd mostly recovered from the fight in Tresa, but she'd need to continue being careful for a while longer. That was another distraction she didn't need, but there was nothing she could do to prevent that one, aside from fighting better next time. That Nightingale had nearly finished her.

Nahk scowled at the memory and stepped through the combat once more in her mind. She remembered every thrust and spin and dodge. She'd made obvious mistakes, but the Nightingale had, too. By all rights, she should have been dead on that ballroom floor, and she wouldn't let that happen again.

"You're doing it again," Naecara said. She was sitting at an angle in the chair, her right arm propped on the back of it so she was twisted halfway around to face Nahk. Her other hand rested on the table next to the empty pint she'd just finished.

"Doing what?" Nahk asked, but there was no use in playing dumb with Naecara. The woman knew her moods as well as she knew her own.

"You're thinking about the Nightingales again."

"I shouldn't be here. I should have gone with the Aescalan. With Akithar."

Apak sat across the table from Nahk, just to the right of Naecara, and he straightened a bit at the mention of his friend, but he didn't say anything. He wore that same frown he always wore. Sometimes it meant he was pondering something. Sometimes it meant he was hungry. Sometimes it meant nothing at all. Nahk hadn't known him long enough to recognize the differences in all his frowns, but he always seemed to carry one with him, even here in Ornamen, while they waited in this hastily rented room for an update.

"You should be exactly where you are," Naecara said. "I need you here."

"If the Nightingales find the Tamrat—"

"They won't. They don't have his exact location, and our people do. Akithar will get there before the Nightingales find them, and they'll probably be back at Stormbreak even before we are."

"You don't know that," Nahk said, half out of worry and half just wanting to be obstinate. She didn't like being dragged away from the best opportunity she'd had for taking down her old masters, but she'd do anything for Naecara. And Naecara understood every nuance of that balance and the conflict it presented to her.

The sound of footsteps stopped Naecara from responding, and she sat straight in the chair. She leaned forward, looking ready to spring away from the table.

"It's Alev," Nahk said.

"You're certain?"

"It's Alev," she said again and uncrossed her legs. She knew the sound of the mage's steps by then and could identify them, even muted from outside the door. Naecara had said she didn't have Nahk's talent for picking up those kinds of details, but it was no more than paying attention to the things that everyone else ignored.

The door opened, and there was Alev, casting a fast glance over their shoulder before stepping into the room and pushing the door shut behind them. Naecara's arms dropped, some of the tension leaving her shoulders, but she still stood from the chair quickly enough to bang the edge of the table with her thigh. The cups jostled, but nothing spilled.

"What did you find?"

Alev exhaled and closed their eyes before answering. "I found my friend. She's still working at the constabulary, but it wasn't easy to get in. They had guards on all the entrances."

"Trouble in the city?" Naecara asked.

Alev shrugged. "I don't think so. Ornamen is the same as it

always is. Nothing much going on, nobody much passing through. The guards seemed like standard procedure."

"But you were able to bypass them," Apak said, his voice tight and his eyes squinting an impatient glare through his glasses.

Alev gave him a curt nod. "I did. She said Kam Dhaz is in the city now. He always stays at an inn called The Jaded Wolf."

"He doesn't have his own base of operations here?" Naecara asked.

"She said he does a lot of business here, but he always stays at that inn."

"Maybe he owns it," Nahk said. It would make sense for an unscrupulous businessman to own some legitimate establishments, just in case the law came prying.

"She was certain he's in Ornamen now? And at this inn?" Naecara asked, not bothering to comment on Nahk's suggestion. That could mean any number of things about whether Naecara thought the theory held water, but it still made sense.

"He's there, but she doesn't know for how long. He travels frequently, and he doesn't do it by foot or by horse. She said the same thing Naecara's friend said. He has some sort of artifact that takes him where he wants to go."

Naecara glanced at Apak in the brief pause, and his eyes flicked toward her. "Did your friend know anything else about this artifact?" Apak asked.

"It's round and flat. There's a design on it, circles within circles. She's seen him with it several times. That's all she knew."

Apak made a grunting sound, one of his many frowns accompanying it.

That was one frown Nahk could decipher. "You recognize the description."

"The Seal of Metarr," Apak said, his voice a low grumble.

"You know about this thing?" Naecara asked.

"Only by reputation. It is ancient and has been the subject of much speculation. It is said to have unique and miraculous abilities, but no one I have encountered has known what those were." He pursed his lips and stroked his chin with his thumb. "I suppose we now have an answer to that."

Naecara had a frown of her own now. "So Dhaz is a mage?"

Apak shook his head. "I would think it unlikely. These sorts of artifacts usually do not require magic to activate them." He hesitated before adding, "Sometimes certain magics can enhance their abilities, but I am inclined to believe that is not the case here. The magic resides in the object, not in the man."

That was a relief, at least. The last thing they needed was to go up against a mage without knowing what he could do. Nahk frowned at that thought. "If he has this Seal, he could have others. Things he could use to fight us."

"Aside from the one he used to destroy a whole city?" Alev asked. Their mouth had crooked into a half smile, but Nahk was in no joking mood.

"We need a plan. We can't go after him without knowing exactly what we're going to do and how to handle whatever he might throw at us."

Naecara tilted her head in Nahk's direction. She agreed with the need for a plan, at least. Even after all these years at her side, some of her expressions were still hard to read, but that one was unquestionably a tilt of approval.

"We must secure the Seal first," Apak said. "Dhaz could use it to transport himself and escape us if he felt threatened."

"And once we have the Seal, we make him give us the weapon," Naecara said. "Preferably before he blasts Ornamen off the map as well."

The four sat in silence around the table for close to a minute before Nahk drummed her fingers on the edge of the wood. Naecara raised an eyebrow at her, and Nahk said, "I know how we can do it."

∾

Apak tugged at his shirt collar and ran a thumb over the button holding it shut. Satisfied, he smoothed both hands down his chest and belly, letting his fingers glide over the embroidered black designs woven through the green fabric.

"You look fine," Naecara said, keeping her voice low. "Stop fidgeting."

Apak began formulating a retort when Alev interrupted his thoughts. "This is the place."

The inn was at a dead end, where a short street culminated in the building. Other structures, all dark at that late hour, flanked the group of three as they moved toward their destination. The sign above the door showed the silhouetted head of a wolf, its jaws open to howl, and the name of the inn had been stenciled in blocky black letters beneath the illustration. The Jaded Wolf.

"Dhaz could have people in any of these buildings, watching us," Naecara said. "I don't like this."

"It's fine," Alev said, but they looked less than certain when Apak glanced up at them. "He's agreed to meet with us, so he probably does have people checking us out. But he's interested in whatever we're offering him, so he'll be in there waiting for us."

Even as they spoke, the door to the inn swung inward, and two people stepped through. One was tall and broad, his thick arms crossed over his chest. The other was a woman who stood just as tall, her hair nearly shaved to the scalp on the sides and braided at the top. Apak met the woman's eyes and forced himself to hold them until he stood before the pair. They were undoubtedly some of Dhaz's hired thugs.

There had been plenty to hear about Kam Dhaz in Klubridge. He had run the black market for artifacts for as long as Apak could remember, and his reputation was even less savory than the other gang leaders. Barween Drach and the others had been content to send children out to pick pockets and run minor scams, but Kam Dhaz always had his eyes set on bigger prizes. There were plenty of tales about unfortunate citizens who had carried the wrong parcel through the city and ended up beaten or worse.

It was with that preparation and expectation that Apak held the thug's eyes as she grabbed his right hand, ran her palms along his right sleeve, and then did the same on the left side. As she felt his waist and legs, Apak saw the man was doing the same to Naecara. None of them had brought weapons, having anticipated this sort of search.

The tall woman stepped back from Apak and said, "Clean,"

before she pushed the door to the inn open and gestured for him to follow her inside.

Naecara and Alev moved to follow, and the other guard stopped them with an outstretched hand. "Where you think you're going?"

"They are my bodyguards," Apak said, his voice even and more patient than he felt. "I am certain your employer would have no objection to their going where I go."

"You can go in. They wait out here," the man said and placed a big boot in Alev's path. It was doubtful whether that would impede Alev if they decided to pass anyway, but Apak refrained from commenting. All of them had been prepared for the likelihood that Dhaz would allow only Apak inside the inn. This affair would be easier and more comfortable with all of them together, but they were ready for either scenario.

Apak was about to nod his acquiescence when a voice called from within, "Let them all in. He can have his bodyguards."

Without hesitation, the guard stepped out of Alev's way, and the other one waved all three toward the door. Apak spared not a glance at the other two before he led the way into the inn.

It looked much like every other tavern he'd encountered. The front room was expansive, a fire burning in the hearth on the side wall and tables spaced evenly throughout the room. Stairs toward the back rose toward the upper levels of the building. There were two floors above this one, and Alev's contact had said Kam Dhaz kept his temporary residence on the top level.

The front room was empty of patrons, aside from one man sitting alone at the side of a table toward the middle of the floor. He had a keen look, his cheeks prominent in the flickering firelight, his eyes narrow and mean. He had black hair pulled back from his face and secured into a ponytail that hung down his back. Not even Micah Vaino kept his hair that long. The man rose from his seat as Apak came through the door, and he gave a half bow as he extended a hand toward the only other chair at his table.

"Please forgive the precautions. I'm certain you understand the need for them."

"Just so," Apak said and pulled the chair out from under the edge of the table. "You are Kam Dhaz?"

Dhaz nodded. "And I'm afraid our mutual friend didn't give me your name."

Apak grunted and dropped into his chair. He kept his eyes on Dhaz as the other man studied him. A strange scar marked Dhaz's left temple. It was not new, but it had not yet healed to the point that it blended with his skin. Dhaz blinked and touched a fingertip to the edge of the crooked pink line as he sat across from Apak. The two guards from the front of the inn moved behind him, taking silent positions to his right and left, their hands clasped behind their backs in a practiced stance.

Apak broke Dhaz's gaze long enough to glance over his shoulder, where Alev stood to his right, and he knew Naecara would be to his left. Alev stood with their hands behind their back, not quite mimicking the stance Dhaz's guards had taken, but close enough to match their air of disinterested malice.

Dhaz raised two fingers, and a young girl with wide eyes came around the bar. Apak had not spotted her before that moment, likely because she was as small and as silent as a shadow. She carried a tray with two glasses and placed one before Dhaz and the other before Apak, before she uncorked a bottle she had been carrying under one arm.

"None for me," Apak said, waving his hand over the top of his glass.

"Pour for both of us," Dhaz told the girl. And then, to Apak, he said, "We are doing business. It's only proper that we share a drink."

Apak pressed his lips together in a frown but elected to give no argument. Whatever conversation happened in this room was a pantomime. It hardly mattered whether they had drinks or ate a meal or climbed atop the bar and danced a jig. What truly mattered was happening above their heads at that very moment.

Once the glasses were poured full, the girl shrank behind the bar once more and disappeared from view. It was unclear whether she had left them entirely or merely settled into silence somewhere out of sight. Either way, the only sounds in the room were the crackling of the fire and the clink of Kam Dhaz's glass as he lifted it from the table and took a long drink. The gangster's eyes stayed on Apak's, but Apak did not touch his glass. He sat patiently and waited for this act to play out.

At last, Dhaz placed his glass on the table and steepled his fingers together. "I'm told you've acquired an interesting piece. A puzzle box?"

Apak nodded and leaned forward, his own hands clasped on the table before him. "It is made from wood and metal, with many intricate levers and springs within. It—"

"What does it do?"

Apak stopped, his forehead crinkling. "Do?"

"It's not just a puzzle box, is it? We're discussing magic, are we not?"

The flippant manner with which Kam Dhaz broached the subject was illustrative of his years of living above or away from the scrutiny of the Empire. Most men would blanch at the idea of even mentioning such a topic so openly in a public establishment. But how public was this place, truly? There were no other patrons, and there appeared to be no other employees aside from that one wispy girl. Perhaps Nahk had been correct in her assessment that Kam Dhaz owned the building.

Apak gave a half nod. "We are discussing the puzzle box, and, as you say, magic is an inherent part of this conversation."

The corner of Dhaz's mouth raised a fraction of an inch, showing his upper teeth in a half sneer. He leaned forward and said, "Let us be candid. There's no need to mince words here. You have a magical artifact you want to sell. You can tell me what it can do, or we can end this conversation now."

Alev shifted behind Apak, and Dhaz's eyes flicked up toward their face. "Your bodyguard seems nervous."

One of Dhaz's guards, the man, chuckled and tilted his head back. "I can relieve some of that tension."

Alev shifted again, but Apak kept his eyes on Dhaz and said, "As you said, we are here to do business."

"Rightly so," Dhaz said and snapped a glance over his shoulder. "You'll stay quiet, and you'll be professional. We can discuss this later if you disagree."

"No disagreements," the guard said and straightened his back. He lifted his chin and closed his mouth, but he stared at Apak with eyes that burned with disdain.

Before the conversation could resume, the boards above them shook with a thud, and dust trickled down from the beams overhead. Kam Dhaz swore as he looked up toward the sound. Apak kept his face impassive and his gaze leveled on the gangster. That sound had to have come from Nahk. Her plan had involved stealth, not tumbling around the second floor. What in blazes was she doing?

"Go see what that was," Dhaz said, and the male guard made a sharp turn toward the stairs at the back of the room.

"Surely you are being overly cautious," Apak said.

"There's no such thing in my line of work," Dhaz said. "I'm sure you can understand." He nodded toward Alev and Naecara, and Apak dipped his head in allowance. He would have to trust that Nahk would be able to hide from or handle that guard. There was nothing more he could do to stall the man's ascent to the second floor.

"And, speaking of my line of work," Dhaz said, at last settling his attention back on the meeting, "you were about to tell me exactly what you're trying to sell me."

Apak nodded. "As I said, it is a puzzle box built from wood and metal. When the correct sequence of presses and turns is applied to it, a spring-loaded door hinges upward at the top. It—"

"What does it do?" Dhaz asked again, this time enunciating each word with crisp punctuation.

"It is engineered to—"

Dhaz sighed and shook his head. "I have no use for engineering, unless there's something magical about it. Surely you know my reputation?" He waited, but Apak said nothing. "Are you wasting my time, little man?"

Apak bristled at that and straightened in his seat to answer the insult, but the sound of the guard's boots descending the stairs halted him. He forced himself to look away from that staircase, and he turned his head to the left, focusing his eyes on the most distant corner of the ceiling.

"What now?" Dhaz asked, following Apak's gaze. Apak knew Naecara and Alev would have averted their eyes by then as well. The fewer people looking at the guard, the better.

The footsteps stopped just short of the table, and the other guard, the woman, had just enough time to make a curious grunting sound before a whistling thud drew everyone's attention away from the ceiling and toward Dhaz's thugs. The woman was on her knees now, toppling to the floor, and the man stood over her, a weighted leather sap in his hand.

Apak couldn't stop himself from looking at the man's face, and he knew everyone else was doing it by then as well. The features blurred and ran together, and the effect was similar to the way an image contorted and shifted when one's focus moved past it and allowed it to distort. Just as quickly as the man's face faded, Nahk's sharply dimpled chin and keen nose appeared in its place.

Kam Dhaz managed to say, "What—" in the instant before Nahk grabbed the back of his neck and shoved him forward. His head turned, and his cheek bounced against the table hard enough to rattle the two glasses. With her other hand, Nahk gripped his wrist and pulled it around his back. She lunged forward, applying pressure, and Dhaz winced and grunted.

"You have it?" Naecara asked.

"I found the disc," Nahk said and jerked her head downward. The edge of something round and gray was visible in the waist of her trousers.

Dhaz struggled against Nahk's grip, but she leveraged his wrist up higher, and he moaned. "I know what you are," he said, his mouth pressed sideways against the tabletop. "I've seen your kind of magic."

"It's not magic," Nahk said.

Dhaz barked a quick laugh. "Of course it is. You're a Nightingale."

Nahk's mouth closed, and her eyes went to Naecara. She was breathing hard through her nose, and her eyebrows twitched with what Apak thought might be fury. Surely Nahk would not kill this man outright, but the anger was clear enough for any of them to see.

Alev had moved around the table by then, and they slid the disc out from Nahk's waistband. They cradled it in their hands with the carefulness of a giant handling a baby before they held it out for Apak to take. "Is this what you were talking about?"

Apak took the disc and held it before him, one hand grasping either side. It was perhaps nine inches in diameter and around two inches thick at the center. It tapered down to thin, blunt edges all around, forming a perfect circle. The outer edges were gray and streaked with scratches and the wear of hundreds or thousands of years of handling. A black ring was inset an inch in from the edges, a blue circle concentric within it. At the middle of the disc, emblazoned atop that blue circle, was a pattern of gold lines that formed crosses and crosshatches in a sequence Apak did not understand or recognize. Although he could not read the meaning of those markings, there was no question about what he held.

"The Seal of Metarr," he said with a slow nod.

"Take it," Dhaz said, his eyes wide and trying to roll far enough upward to see Nahk. "Take the blasted Seal and let me live."

"We're not here for the Seal," Naecara said. "Where is the weapon?"

Dhaz blinked, and his forehead creased. "Weapon? What weapon?"

Apak sat the Seal of Metarr on the table before him with the same care Alev had exercised when handing it to him. Given the centuries of scars on the face of the relic, it was unlikely that a bit of jostling would activate anything undesirable, but it was better to be careful with these sorts of things. Apak rested his fists on the wooden tabletop on either side of the Seal, and he leaned forward, forcing Kam Dhaz's eyes to meet his own.

"The Eye of Kelixia," Apak said, his voice low and even. The Seal was unlikely to cause harm if mishandled. If the Eye were on the premises, that would be another story entirely. Apak's nostrils flared as he stared into the other man's face. Was this gangster to blame for the destruction of Klubridge and the death of what would likely prove to be a sizable portion of its population? This trembling criminal?

Dhaz blinked again. He should have cowered then. He should have begged them for mercy and protested his innocence. Instead of doing any of those things, Kam Dhaz laughed. "Of course you want the Eye. I'm sorry to disappoint you, but you're a few weeks late."

Apak frowned. "Late? What do you mean?"

The man's eyes flicked from Apak to Alev and finally settled on Naecara. He gave her a closed-mouth smile, and his brows drew down. "You're the boss," he said. "Call off your Nightingale, and we can discuss this in a civilized manner."

"There is nothing civilized about what happened in Klubridge," Apak said, his words clipped, and his face heating.

"As it happens, I agree with you," Dhaz said, his eyes still on Naecara. "Now, can we have a respectful conversation, or are you going to have your Nightingale eviscerate me?"

"I'm no Nightingale," Nahk said, so quietly it almost was a whisper, but Apak could still hear the malice in her voice. He looked up at her just as she looked at him, and they shared a silent moment of fury. It was scalding and enraging, but the intimacy of that moment somehow cooled Apak's face, and he saw Nahk's shoulders relax downward a fraction of an inch.

Dhaz saw none of the exchange, his eyes still on Naecara, and the edges of his lips still turned up into a placid smile. He knew Nahk would not be killing him. Not while they knew he had information they needed. And, if there was anything Kam Dhaz knew, it was how to bargain when he had the upper hand.

"Let him go," Naecara said, and Nahk gave Dhaz's face a final shove against the tabletop before releasing him. She stepped back as the man sat up, but she stayed close behind him, her eyes never leaving the back of his head. Apak knew she could and would end Dhaz at the first sign of a threat.

But Kam Dhaz presented no threat. As he sat up, he pulled at the lapels of his jacket and straightened his cuffs. He shrugged his shoulders once, settling into his chair, before leaning back to cross his right leg over the left. That done, he tilted his head toward Naecara. "Why do you want the Eye of Kelixia?"

Apak's upper lip curled, and he said, "We shall not—"

"We want it to prevent another Klubridge from happening,"

Naecara said. Apak closed his mouth and refrained from looking up at her, standing by his side.

Dhaz's hand raised, and Nahk tensed behind him, no doubt ready to puncture some part of his body. But he merely cupped his chin in the valley between his thumb and index finger. "You're rebels," he said. He looked from Naecara to Apak, and his eyebrows raised in an expression of what might have been surprise. "You're Apak Brem! Of course you are. The posters got the general likeness right, but they missed the surly scowl." No, it was something more than surprise. Was it delight?

Apak's eyes narrowed, and Dhaz was smiling then with his lips parted just enough for the edges of his white teeth to be barely visible. He said, "They didn't have your name for the first few days, you know. The first week, at least. They knew the theater manager already, and they had descriptions of some others. It wasn't until the bounties were posted that they got all your names and started putting up the sketches. Apak Brem, Samira Tandogan, and whoever else it was. All notorious cohorts of the rebel wizard Akithar. They never did get his real name, mind you. All the rest, but not the ringleader." Dhaz's smile widened, and his hand dropped to the table, his fingers tapping a quick rhythm before he flipped an errant strand of black hair behind his ear. "The ringleader, they said. But I wonder."

Where was this monologue going? Apak wanted to respond, but he scarcely dared open his mouth, lest he say too much. How much did Kam Dhaz know about what had happened in Klubridge? More than anyone else in the room other than Apak, it seemed. And so Apak remained silent and watched the man across the table from above the rims of his eyeglasses.

"You're wondering how much I know," Dhaz said, and Apak failed to prevent himself from swallowing. "I know everything about what happened that day in the plaza. They said it was Akithar who bombed the buildings. Akithar who killed the Imperials. Akithar who tipped Klubridge into full revolt. That's not the way I remember it."

He had been there. Kam Dhaz had been in that accursed

plaza when the Imperials had dragged Caius out in shackles. Apak looked up at Naecara and said, "Perhaps we should—"

"I had agents there," Dhaz said. "They recall the Great Akithar lying motionless in a heap. He was in no condition to prop himself up, much less lead a revolution. Apak Brem, on the other hand..." Dhaz was talking to the others, but his eyes remained on Apak's face. "He was the one to see that day. Apak Brem, laying waste to an entire unit of Kites and destroying a chamir as well, if you can believe that."

Nahk's eyebrows drew together, and she cast a look at Apak, but he did not meet her eyes this time. He stared at Dhaz, waiting for the conclusion of whatever tale the man was building.

"As I recall, this Apak Brem was armed with a box of some sort on that day. Something that obliterated lines of soldiers in a blazing white cone of light. Am I telling this correctly?" He did not wait for a response. "The Apak Brem I have heard about has an affinity for these artifacts. These... weapons." Dhaz clasped his hands and waited just long enough for a dramatic beat, exactly like Caius was wont to do before a theater full of patrons who hung on his every word. And, finally, Dhaz said to Naecara, "I think I understand why you want the Eye of Kelixia now, rebel."

Apak's mouth had gone dry, and he could feel the pulse in his neck. The very notion that he would desire such a weapon was ludicrous. The suggestion that he would want to wield the very device that had ruined Klubridge was unthinkable. But this man had thought it and had spoken it, and the trust Apak had built in this party teetered on Naecara's response.

"Do you have it or not?" she asked, and Apak exhaled a slow breath.

Kam Dhaz wore a smirk as he looked up from Apak to Naecara, and he paused again, just long enough to let the silence settle. Then he slapped his palms on the table, causing Apak to flinch, and the Seal of Metarr to wobble, but Nahk moved not a muscle. "I do not. But I did, and I can tell you where to find it."

"We're listening," Naecara said.

"A client commissioned me to find it for him, and it was no simple task."

"But you found it."

Dhaz's brows lowered, and he touched his fingertips to his chest, affronted. "Of course I found it. I met with him in Ordport and made the transaction."

"Who was your client?" Naecara asked, her voice holding even, but even Apak could detect the note of impatience in it.

"Qae'lon," Dhaz said and leaned back in his chair. It creaked with his weight, and his eyes moved to each of them in turn.

Kam Dhaz's demeanor suggested they should know the name, but Apak was the first to speak. "What is Qae'lon?"

Dhaz huffed a breath. "You can't be serious."

"Not a what. It's a who. He's an Imperial," Naecara said.

"He's a bastard," Dhaz added.

"Qae'lon runs the Herons," Nahk said.

Apak scowled. The only thing worse than Kites hunting mages was a band of Herons hunting mages. The Kites at least had no sense of magic. They were not mages themselves, and they had no concept of what it meant to have magic. Herons, on the other hand, knew all too well. They were mages who had betrayed their own. Whether the betrayal arose from fear, self preservation, a misplaced sense of duty, or some other origin, the reason hardly mattered. The result was an entire branch of the Imperial military staffed by mages who hunted and killed other mages. Apak had heard of them through the years, almost as rumors, but he had seen them with his own eyes in Klubridge. He had killed them with his own magic, most likely. So many had died in Klubridge, it was hard to be certain.

"Qae'lon is a mage himself, then?" Apak asked.

Naecara's eyes flicked toward Dhaz and then over to Nahk and Alev before she answered. "He's probably the most powerful magic user in Teshovar, short of Peregrine himself. He's not limited to any one discipline. He's a monster."

Apak grunted at that. It was true that most mages were limited in how they could use their powers. Apak could imbue enchanted artifacts with his power, enhancing and expanding their capabilities. Lizandra could shape light into form, and Reykas could open holes connecting disparate points in space. But none of them could roam very far away from their central and core abilities. The limitation had never seemed innate and immutable to Apak, though. He had always believed his lack of magical breadth was due to a lack of knowledge and wisdom. If he had proper training or stumbled upon a breakthrough on his own, he felt certain he could do more.

Samira could do more. She did not know how or why, but she could form invisible shields, and she could also heal wounds. The two abilities came naturally to her, but Apak had always believed she had unwittingly taught herself to range farther than the rest of them had done. The High Lord Peregrine's power appeared limitless, likely because of his seemingly endless lifespan and the opportunity and resources to teach himself all manner of arcane knowledge. And now this Qae'lon had emerged, unfettered by the limitations that held most other mages back from their full potential. Was he also as ageless as Peregrine?

"What makes him a monster?" Apak asked aloud.

"There are stories about Qae'lon," Naecara said. "He's been in power for a long time. He seems dedicated to the Empire but even more dedicated to the magic."

"That makes no sense," Apak said. "The Empire's mandate is the eradication of magic."

"Not all of it," Naecara said. "The Herons are allowed a lot of leeway. They're the only ones allowed to touch magic without having their abilities dulled, and Qae'lon is the head of them. He's powerful, both politically and magically."

"Powerful in what way?"

Naecara lifted her shoulder in a half shrug. "Qae'lon is amoral. I've heard about him obliterating whole buildings full of innocent citizens. And—" Her face darkened, and she looked to Dhaz. "You're not lying. It was him, wasn't it? He's the one who attacked Klubridge."

Dhaz raised his eyebrows and gave her a small shrug.

"Qae'lon has a reputation as a sadist," Naecara said. "And you handed him the Eye of Kelixia."

Dhaz raised his hands, the palms toward Naecara. "I didn't know what he was going to do with it."

"What did you think he wanted with a weapon like that?" she asked. "You knew who Qae'lon was, and you gave him something that powerful."

"Sold it to him, if we are being precise."

"And you call him a bastard."

Dhaz's smile faltered, and he glanced to the side. "I lived in Klubridge before this happened. It's where I ran my operations. I had a storehouse there with all my merchandise in it. And now? Now, it's all gone." He flicked his hand into the air and pulled his lips tight. His gaze shifted past all of them, toward something unseen and distant. Likely toward his warehouse full of magical artifacts, now lying in ruins beneath the crumbled buildings of Klubridge.

"My heart bleeds for you," Naecara said, her tone dry now. "You took the risk, and you're paying the consequences. Where is Qae'lon now?"

Dhaz pulled his attention back to her. "What do you plan to do once you know where he is?"

"We're going to find him, and we're going to get the Eye."

"We will make him pay for what he did," Apak said. His voice was quieter than the others', and they all looked at him. He felt the weight of their stares, but they said nothing until Kam Dhaz broke the silence.

"Well," he said. "I can tell you where you can find him, and more beyond that. But first, I have one condition."

Naecara sighed. "What's your price, Dhaz?"

"You take me with you. If you're taking Qae'lon down, I want to be there when he falls."

"I don't trust him," Nahk said and glanced over her shoulder at the two men still seated across the room.

Naecara followed her gaze. "Apak?"

"I meant Dhaz." And she had, but that gave her pause. How much did they really know about Apak Brem? He'd shown up at

Stormbreak while she was away in Tresa, and by the time she'd returned, he and his friends seemed to have won the trust of the whole rebellion. She'd trusted them, too. Even the girl, Fairy, after a fashion. But there was so much they didn't know about what these people had done before leaving Klubridge, if the conversation with Kam Dhaz was any indication.

Naecara nodded when Nahk looked back at her. "I don't trust Dhaz, either, and that's a healthy way to be. His reputation is not one to be ignored."

"And Apak?"

Naecara looked toward the men once more and gave a slight shake of her head. "I believe he's on our side. That's the most we can hope for from most of the people we know."

"What about Kam Dhaz? Is he on our side?"

Naecara gave a low chuckle. "Not in the least. Kam Dhaz is on Kam Dhaz's side. But, for now, his goals are aligned with ours. We need that weapon, and he wants revenge on Qae'lon. If there's anything we can trust, it's that Dhaz will act in his own interest."

"I will, indeed," Dhaz said, his head cocking in their direction. "And it's time we discussed how we're going to do this."

Nahk exchanged a brief look with Naecara before leaving the side of the bar where they had been propped. "How do we find him?" she asked as she approached the table.

"Qae'lon has a tower where he…" Dhaz's sentence trailed off, and he waved a hand. "Where he lives or lurks or does whatever sort of malicious nonsense mages get up to."

"You have seen this tower?" Apak asked.

"I have not," Dhaz said. "I know it's west of Teusas. That's all flat grassland, but there's one low hill, and that's where his tower is."

"How do you know this?" Naecara asked, joining the group and putting her hands on the back of the chair next to Apak.

Dhaz wagged an index finger at her once and shook his head. "I have my sources. The important thing is that they are reliable."

"So you say," Apak added, and Dhaz frowned in response.

"I do say, and I also say the tower can't be missed if we can get into that general area. It's summer weather year-round there, even now, during winter. There's talk of strange creatures, too. Things like deer and rodents and birds like you'd expect in nature, but they're not like any you've seen. Birds with feathers like rainbows. Fanged gophers. Two-headed fawns."

"Fanged gophers?" Alev asked, a smile lingering just behind their otherwise neutral eyes.

"I have heard about this sort of thing," Apak said. "Where one can find a concentration of magic, one often finds... strange results."

"Like that chamir you destroyed," Nahk said and watched Apak for a reaction.

He looked at her, but his face revealed no emotion. Their eyes met for the briefest of moments before he inclined his head and looked back at Dhaz. "Teusas is weeks away by horse or carriage. Perhaps months, as we would be avoiding Imperial patrols. It is too far to travel by road in a timely manner, particularly in this season."

"How else do you expect to get there?" Dhaz asked before his eyes dropped from Apak's to the table. He smiled in apparent understanding and shook his head. "No, that wouldn't work."

"What?" Nahk asked.

"You can take us there using this," Apak said to Dhaz and placed his fingertips on top of the Seal of Metarr. It sat motionless on the table, looking like nothing more than a dull plate with strange ornamentation.

"It wouldn't work," Dhaz said. "The Seal will only take you to places you've physically been to and seen with your own eyes. I haven't been to Qae'lon's tower."

"But you have been to Teusas?"

"Of course I have. It still wouldn't work, though. It can transport one person at a time. Sometimes two, but the second person should not be overly attached to any particular limbs or organs prior to the travel."

Naecara said, "It's no good, then. If the Seal could reliably take two at a time, one of us could bring it back and forth to ferry the others to Teusas. But it only works for one, and there are five of us now. We'll have to go by road."

Naecara shifted as though that were the end of the conversation, but Apak's stillness held Nahk's attention. What was he thinking? Whatever he might have done and hidden from them, there was no doubt a brilliant mind lived inside the strange little man's head.

"We will not travel by road," Apak said.

Naecara frowned back at him. "What do you mean?"

"I can take us to Teusas. It was many years ago, but I have been there, and I know the geography. I can take all five of us at once, and I can do it as soon as you are prepared to travel." He said all this while staring down at the disc on the table, his voice even and passionless and factual. There was no sign as to how he might pull off this feat, but Nahk felt compelled to believe in his confidence.

"How will you do this?" Naecara asked.

And then Apak looked up at her, but his eyes shifted to Nahk's before he answered. "There are things I have not told you. Things I should tell you now."

His hand slid over the disc, and his palm rested on the center of the Seal. As Nahk watched, the air shimmered around the artifact, almost like the ripple you'd see on a paved roadway in the middle of a blistering summer day. The surface of the disc glowed with a faint redness. When Nahk looked back to Apak's face, his eyes stared back at her through his spectacles, the pupils now invisible, the irises burning crimson.

CHAPTER 32

Lizandra watched him from the back, hardly hoping to believe what she was seeing. Reykas sat upright in a chair for the first time in weeks. His frame was still thin, his face gaunt, and his arms spindly where they used to be strong and full, but he was alive, and he was getting better. Day by day, his improvements became more pronounced and more obvious. There was no doubt now. Whatever Jod Padar had done had healed him.

Reykas reached for a cup of water on the table before him, and his hand shook as his fingers wrapped around it. It was a tremble of weakness, a shake Lizandra knew all too well. First, his hands would shake, and then the strength would leave the rest of him, and eventually he would be covered in sweat and unable to rise from his bed. But not this time. This time the shake accompanied the return of strength, and it would lessen without the illness. It would, in time, subside, never to return again. For now, though, his hand shook, and water sloshed over his wrist and onto the table.

Lizandra moved to his side and put her hand over his. "Let me help."

His hand loosened from the cup, but he didn't look at her. His head drooped, and he asked, "What has become of me?"

She had the cup midway to his mouth and almost spilled it

LIZANDRA'S DEEPEST FEAR

herself. Instead, she put a hand on the back of his neck, as much to steady herself as it was to reassure him, and she held the rim of the cup to his lips. She felt his spine, the ridges pressing up through skin that seemed impossibly thin. His whole body was like that now, thin and hollow, the bones more visible than the muscle. It would all come back, and everything would return to how it should be, but how long would that take? How long would he be a skeletal shade of his former self?

Reykas sipped at the water slowly at first but then gulped at it, and it was no wonder. He'd gone so long without food or drink. Lizandra had tried to give him water after he'd fallen into that long sleep, but her efforts had become useless after a while. He'd not only shrunken, but he'd dried out as well, and his voice was now low and raspy, a contrast to the deep and confident sound she knew so well.

He swallowed greedily and pulled away from the cup when a coughing fit hit him. She sat the cup on the table once more and put a hand on his forehead. It was cool and dry, so different from the scorching, soaked skin she was used to feeling when he took ill. "Not so much all at once," she whispered as he caught his breath. "You'll choke yourself."

He sat panting for a long moment, his head leaned into her hand, but he finally looked up. His eyes, sunken over protruding cheekbones, shone wet in the light that came through the room's only window. Lizandra might have been fooled into thinking his coughing had summoned the wetness until a tear broke free and rolled down his cheek. She slid her palm down the side of his face and wiped at it with her thumb. It left a damp streak on his dark skin.

"What has become of me?" Reykas asked again.

"You woke up," she said and squatted beside him. "No one believed you would, but I did. I stayed with you, and you came through it. You woke up."

"The magic," he said and looked down at his hand, now clasped in a feeble fist. The knuckles stood out like rounded spikes.

"Perhaps it will return," she said, but she knew it would not. It never would again. Reykas would never summon another portal or vanish another item, but he would live. The exchange was a fair one.

Reykas worked his fingers, opening and closing his hand as if testing himself or feeling for something. He closed them again and looked into her eyes once more. "It was always there. I could feel it. But not now." His shoulders sagged. "It's gone."

"But you're not sick now," Lizandra said. She sounded like she was pleading, but she had to take away the desperation and sadness she saw in his face and heard in his voice. She had to reassure him that everything was going to be fine. That the trade was for the best, even if he knew nothing of the deal and had had no say in it.

"It will come back," he said. "It always does. This time it took my talent."

"No!" Lizandra took his hand in both of hers and leaned low to find his gaze. "This time is different. You'll see." What could she tell him without revealing what she'd done? How could she bring him any kind of assurance?

"Pelo Foyen, the man who was in the room with you," she said.

Reykas didn't comment but raised his head a fraction of an inch.

"He said the illness was intentional. That the Empire created it to make mages sick. If your magic is gone, it stands to reason that the sickness would be gone, too. Doesn't it?"

The edges of his mouth raised just enough for her to see the hint of a smile, but it faltered. "Why would the magic have left? After all this time, why would it choose to leave me? And why would that cure me?" He breathed and then continued, "I know you want there to be purpose to this. For all this to be true. But you've known me long enough, my love. You know how this sickness goes."

She did know how it went, and she'd have been inclined to believe him if she didn't know the truth. A truth that made no more sense to her than anything did to Reykas at that moment. It had taken a team of four Herons to attempt to silence a single man's magic back in Klubridge, and they had not even been successful. How, then, could the chemist have removed Reykas' magic in an ordinary back room in the space of a few minutes, all by himself and with no magical intervention?

Lizandra didn't understand science, and it seemed improbable that science and magic could meet at any sort of intersection that she could comprehend, but it had been done. Jod Padar had done something to Reykas in those few minutes, and his magic was gone, and with it the illness. She had agreed to that exchange without even considering how the work might be done or how improbable it seemed. And, when she'd seen Reykas again, the work was complete. He would live a healthy life, and he was a mage no longer.

She opened her mouth to speak, but the rush of footsteps running outside the door halted her. "What was that?" Reykas asked, his head rising again.

"I don't know. Wait here," she said and regretted it right away. What else could Reykas do at this point other than wait there? She pushed to her feet and leaned into the hallway.

"What's happening?" she asked one of the rebels she recognized, a young man with sandy hair and a short beard.

"We found someone outside the keep," he said, breathing hard and looking toward the entrance to the courtyard. "A child."

She followed his gaze as a man hurried through the archway, a limp form in his arms. Lizandra gasped at the pale hair swaying with his steps. "Fairy!"

The rebel carried Fairy through the courtyard and out the back, and Lizandra hurried to follow. She was right behind the man when he pushed through the front door to the infirmary and brought Fairy inside. A wave of dread washed over Lizandra as she followed down the hall and into one of the empty rooms for patients. It wasn't the same room Reykas had been in, but it was close enough, both in proximity and in design, to make her lose her breath for a moment.

The nurse that had led them to the room stepped aside, and the man placed Fairy on the bed with a gentleness that pulled at

Lizandra's heart. The girl's face was pink from the cold, and her lips were chapped, much like Lizandra's had been when she returned from the trip to Karsk. Fairy's left arm had been bound to her chest with a cloth sling that looked rudimentary but neatly wrapped.

"What happened?" Lizandra asked. "Where did you find her?"

"She'd gone out on the supply run with the halflock. They were due back later today, but I found her by herself when I was on my patrol. She was unconscious on the road just before the final turn." He wrung his hands together and glanced from the girl's prone form back toward the door. "I'd best let Vaino know about this."

"We'll take care of her," the nurse told him. "You did well."

He gave her a quick nod and was back out the door, and Lizandra blinked after him with her mouth hanging open. "The halflock. Magra?"

"Sorry?" the nurse asked, tilting her head.

"He said she was on a supply run with the halflock." She turned to face the nurse, aware that her voice was growing louder than it should have been in that room. "Do you know who she was with?"

"I don't know anything about that. Would you mind waiting with her? I'll fetch the doctor."

"Of course." The nurse was gone then, and Lizandra stood alone in the room with Fairy. Even though it wasn't Reykas' old room, it was similar enough that she felt that shudder of dread once again. There was only one bed in this one, but she couldn't stop herself from looking across the room to where Pelo Foyen would have been. Where he'd died after unintentionally sending Lizandra on her mission.

Fairy groaned, and Lizandra dropped to her knees at the bedside and took the girl's uninjured hand in hers. "Fairy? Are you awake?"

She shifted on the mattress, and her eyes opened slowly. "Lizzie?" It came out as a murmur, but it sounded more like someone just awakening from sleep than from someone truly in danger.

"You're at Stormbreak," Lizandra said. "You're in the infirmary. Do you remember what happened?"

Fairy took in the room with a sweep of her eyes and pulled her right hand free to wipe it over her face. "I was coming back. I thought I could make it. I was so close." Her words trailed to silence, and her eyes squeezed shut.

"You're okay now. You're safe." Lizandra said and laid her hand over Fairy's again.

Before either of them could say anything else, the door opened again, this time so swiftly that it swung inward and knocked against the inner wall. Lizandra flinched and looked up, expecting the doctor. Instead, Micah Vaino stood at the foot of the bed, his dark hair hanging loose around his face and his expression uncharacteristically intense.

"Is she all right?" he asked Lizandra.

"The doctor hasn't seen her yet," she said. "But her arm—"

"Is she awake?" he asked. He came around the opposite side of the bed and stood facing Lizandra, looking down at Fairy.

"I'm awake," Fairy said, opening her eyes again. She pushed herself up the bed with her feet, raising her head enough to sit up against the wall behind her.

Another man had followed Vaino into the room, this one broad and pale, his eyebrows thin and high on his forehead, making him look as if he were in a constant state of surprise. "The nurse said the doctor is on the way."

"The doctor can wait a moment," Vaino said, sterner than Lizandra liked, but he was smiling when he turned back toward them. His eyes settled on Fairy, and he lowered himself to perch on the edge of the bed. "Now," he said, "I'm told you went with the supply cart yesterday."

Fairy nodded, awake now but wary. She answered Vaino, but her eyes were on Lizandra. "Magra said I could go. It was her and me and two others. Wik and Len were their names."

Lizandra swallowed at the past tense Fairy was using, and she knew Vaino would have noticed as well. But he nodded, encouraging the girl to go on. Fairy opened her mouth, but her forehead creased, and she closed it again. She blew out a breath and at last looked at Vaino. "It was bandits. They jumped us after we'd been on the road a while. We didn't even see them coming. Well. I think Magra must have seen them or heard them or sensed them or something. She saved me." At that, Fairy looked down at her lap and fell silent.

Lizandra's heart thudded hard in her chest. She knew what would come next, and she dreaded it. As much as the halflock had vexed her, betrayed her, and insulted her, this is not what she would have wanted for the woman. Lizandra had wished her gone and away so many times, but never this. The quiet moment stretched longer, and Lizandra hoped her guess was wrong and that the worst was not true. But Fairy dashed that hope when she looked up again and broke the silence.

"They killed them. All of them, Magra and Wik and Len. And they took the horses and the grain and everything. They didn't see me, and I stayed quiet. I waited until they were gone."

If Lizandra hadn't already been kneeling, her knees surely would have betrayed her balance. But she kept her hand on the edge of the bed and looked from Fairy to Vaino. The man didn't respond immediately. He breathed slowly as he watched Fairy, and he blinked with a slowness that must have been deliberate. When he spoke, his voice was soft and measured. "Did you see the bandits that attacked you?"

Fairy shook her head. "The wagon turned over, and I was under it. I waited for them to be gone before I crawled out. I never saw them."

Vaino frowned and looked to the other man, the one who'd come in with him. He stood, Fairy all but forgotten by then. "This was no bandit attack. Those were Imperials."

The other man managed to look even more surprised than he already had seemed. "Imperials, sir? This far north?"

"We know the bandits in the north. Most of them are on our coin." He held his fist over his mouth and exhaled into it, his thin shoulders heaving with the effort. When he lowered his hand, he said, "We've been betrayed, Bayor. I want an accounting of every soul who has left Stormbreak in the past ten days. No, twenty days."

"Twenty days, sir," Bayor repeated.

Vaino nodded. "Someone has betrayed us, and I mean to find the spy."

Lizandra's hand tightened on the bedsheet as her dread crept toward panic.

~

Lizandra slid and nearly fell on a patch of ice just outside the door to the infirmary. She regained her balance and checked behind her. No one seemed to have noticed her haste, but she needed to be more careful. Better to take her time and not careen into someone important or pitch face-first into the stone walkway. Still, it was hard to keep from running as she passed through the courtyard and out the door toward the supply depot.

Rebels had been killed, Magra had died, and they'd nearly gotten Fairy, too. Vaino was certain Imperials were behind the attack, and that made more sense to Lizandra than a roaming pack of bandits. But, with that, came Vaino's certainty that someone had betrayed the rebellion. That there was a spy in their midst. All this, just after Lizandra had sneaked out of the keep under Vaino's nose. If anyone learned about her excursion, she'd be the first name on his list of suspects.

No one knew that she'd gone, not even Reykas. No one but Oreth. She had to get to him before he heard about it from someone else and started getting nervous. Surely he wouldn't be nervous enough to tell Vaino about how he'd helped her, but that wasn't a risk she could take.

Lizandra was trying to find the right words as she exited the keep again and jogged down the path toward the depot. A woman carrying a wooden box had to skip out of her way, and Lizandra slowed long enough to apologize. That pause brought laughter to her from two voices inside the open supply doors.

Oreth wasn't alone. Of course he wouldn't be alone. It was the middle of the day, and he'd be working supplies, just like always. And, more and more, Lizandra felt certain the time of day and the needs of his work had no bearing on when she might find him in the company of Leyna Neron.

She still hadn't found the right words to say to Oreth even if he'd been on his own, much less with Leyna there. Lizandra forced herself to stop outside the building, her hand pressed against the cold of the wall, and she chewed at her lip. The sound of more voices behind Lizandra propelled her forward once more. She couldn't stand and fret so long that somebody else brought the news to Oreth, and he spilled the details about helping Lizandra. She hoped his guilty conscience wouldn't lead him to betray her, but she had to get to him first.

Leyna spotted her as Lizandra rounded the corner and came through the open doorway. The girl sat on a stool at the opposite side of the depot, her shoulders resting against the back wall and the front legs of the stool kicked back in a precarious lean. She rocked forward as Lizandra entered, and Oreth stopped whatever he was saying mid-sentence and turned to see her, his eyebrows raised.

He grinned at her. "Lizzie! I didn't think—" He stopped again. "What is it? Is it Reykas?"

Lizandra shook her head and stopped a couple of steps inside the door. "It's not him. Something has happened." She glanced from Oreth to Leyna and back before continuing. Lizandra knew she was no good at deception and at keeping secrets. She never had been, but she had to navigate this conversation carefully. "Fairy just came back to Stormbreak."

"Fairy?" Oreth asked. "She went out with Magra's wagon."

"I know. She came back alone." There was no way forward but through, so Lizandra pushed the rest of the words out in a rush. "Magra is dead, Oreth. The riders who went with them, too. Fairy is the only one who made it back."

Oreth's face paled, and he dropped a hand onto the nearest worktable to steady himself. Leyna was on her feet, the stool forgotten behind her. "Was it the Empire?"

Lizandra dropped her eyes. "Fairy said it was bandits, but…"

"All the bandits around here work for us," Leyna finished. She leaned forward on the edge of the table, her jaw set in an angry scowl, and a tangle of brown hair fell free to hide her eyes.

Oreth shifted, and Lizandra looked up to see the pain in his face. It was so much like the anguish she'd seen that night in

Klubridge when he'd learned Dorrin had been killed. "What did she say?" he asked, but it came out almost as a whisper.

"She said bandits ambushed them. Fairy was hurt in the attack. I think her arm's broken. But whoever attacked them didn't find her. They killed the others and took the cargo and the horses. She waited until they were gone, and then she fled."

"Did she see them?" Leyna still stared at the scarred wood on the table before her and didn't meet Lizandra's eyes.

"No."

Leyna blew out a breath hard enough to stir the papers stacked to her right. She snapped her head up toward Oreth. "We have to talk to Micah."

Oreth blinked a couple of times before turning toward Leyna. "What? What do you mean?"

"He'll want to know how the Imperials found that cart. That's something I'd like to know, too."

Oreth said, "You don't think someone here—"

Leyna came around the table, her brows drawn down. "There are dozens of roads through these mountains. They're all winding and twisting and icy. And these Imperials just happen to set up an ambush on the one road we're using at exactly the time we're using it?" She shook her head. "We rotate through the different routes so this won't happen."

"We have to talk to Vaino. We have to tell him," Oreth said, shifting his stiff leg so he could follow Leyna.

She was already at the door and paused just long enough to look between Oreth and Lizandra and back again. "I'll tell him." And she was gone, leaving Oreth staring after her, his chin shaking.

Lizandra seized her moment and put her hand to his cheek, turning his face toward hers. She lowered her voice and leaned close. "Oreth, are you all right?"

"I... Does Leyna think I had something to do with this?"

"She's scared and confused. Everybody will be."

"But surely nobody would have—"

"Oreth, listen to me. Are you with me?"

His eyes were wide and scared, but he shook his head up and down in a frightened nod.

"If anyone knew I left Stormbreak with Reykas, they'd tell Vaino, and they'd suspect me. Do you understand?"

"Nobody would—"

"They would. And if they knew you helped me, they'd suspect you as well. We're new here. All these people have known each other longer. They have bonds. We'd be easy targets if they became suspicious. Do you understand what I'm saying?"

"But we could explain it to them," he said. "Anybody can see how Reykas is better."

"No," she said. She lowered her hand from the side of his face to rest on his shoulder, and she gripped him tight. She held him in place so he'd understand. So he'd have to see how important this was. "If they knew I went to Karsk, somebody would remember Pelo Foyen had been there. They'd remember he didn't accept the healing because the price was too high. I accepted the price, Oreth. The chemist healed Reykas, and I agreed to his terms."

"Lizzie, no. Nobody would believe you'd do that. You could tell them the truth!"

"No, Oreth," Lizandra said again. She held his other shoulder now, her hands tight, her eyes compelling him to listen. "No one can know the truth. If they do, we're both finished."

She stopped and glanced back at the open door, still empty, and her heart hammered in her chest. She looked back to Oreth and said, "And they'd be right. It was me. I traded Magra for Reykas."

PART IV
HER DEEPEST FEAR

CHAPTER 33

Bekam rubbed a weary hand down his forehead and across his face. As they tended to do these days, whenever he wasn't wearing the patch, his fingers lingered over his left eye. The fingertips laid gently over the closed eyelid and felt the shape of the eyeball beneath.

The eye itself was still there, more or less. He had pulled the eyelid up with his fingers a few times when looking into a mirror, and the eye it revealed beneath hardly seemed to be his. It was cloudy and still and misshapen, the wounds from the fork's tines still visible across its center. He couldn't see through the blasted thing, but it sat there in his head, a scarred and permanent reminder of Qae'lon.

Qae'lon, who had not shown himself since the meeting where his interference had made a mockery of everything Bekam had accomplished. He could feel his grasp on all of it slipping away, bit by bit. Qae'lon had stolen his redemption at Klubridge. Qae'lon had invaded Bekam's home, blinded him, and shattered whatever semblance of family he had. And now he'd taken away Bekam's respect and influence with the Council. If there had been any question during that meeting, the letter that now lay on Bekam's desk put the uncertainty to rest.

Bekam dropped his hand to the desk and drummed his fingers atop the paper, but he couldn't bear to read it again. It said everything he'd suspected, and there was no comfort in being right. At least there was still some loyalty in Teka Lacar, the only member of the Council who had reached out to Bekam after that charade of a hearing. The letter had come from Lacar, but it did not bear his office letterhead. The man would send a warning to his old mentor, but he was not sturdy enough to stand behind the words and do anything of substance to help.

Bekam swore and looked at the paper once more before shoving it across the desk's surface to the left, out of sight. In truth, he wouldn't have risked his own neck, if he'd been in Lacar's position. In the real truth, he doubted he'd have even sent that letter. But the letter was sent and received, and, in no uncertain terms, it said the Council had called into question Bekam's fitness to serve in his capacity and station after the revolt in Klubridge and his recent behavior at the meeting. They intended to strip him of his rank and hand the Kites to Qae'lon. The structure of the guillotine had been obvious, and Bekam had just been waiting for the blade to fall. And fall, it had.

Where was Qae'lon? If not for this evidence of his complicity in whatever scheme the Council was supporting, Bekam might have thought the mage had disappeared with the Eye of Kelixia, his ties to the Empire unbound. A man of Qae'lon's skill and notoriety could live any life he wanted in Teshovar, especially when he possessed the most potent weapon that had surfaced in more than a century. But no, he was too enmeshed in the Imperial machinery that even now turned its cogs toward Bekam's destruction and Qae'lon's elevation.

So, where was he? Was he lurking somewhere nearby, waiting to finish Bekam himself? Was he hovering just outside the office window at that very moment?

Bekam cursed himself for swiveling to look out that window. All he saw against the black glass was his own lopsided reflection staring back. Paranoia was tightening its grip on him, and Bekam shook his head. He was becoming as bad as Gieck, and he had no intention of meeting a similar fate, felled on bloody cobblestones by an agent of his own side.

What was there to do, then? Bekam sat back in his chair and clasped his fingers beneath his chin. He had enough seri in the various Aramore banks to see him safely out of the city and into a new life. That was provided, of course, that he could make it through the gates without being arrested or worse.

He settled his hands into his lap and surveyed his office. This was what it came to, then? Decades of service, all dismantled and disheveled by a greedy magician with a penchant for politics. Such was the way of the Empire. Bekam had seen countless Imperial servants rise and fall at the whims of their betters. He'd always known his time might come, but it had felt unlikely and distant. But now it was here, and he had to get ahead of that machine before it crushed him beneath its weight.

"Cillan," he called and picked up the patch from where he'd discarded it on the right corner of his desk. He was settling the string around the back of his head when the office door rattled and opened.

"Sir," Cillan said as he entered, but he dropped his gaze to a stack of ledgers piled on a cabinet to the side of the desk. Bekam grunted and slid the patch over his closed eye. Having the cursed thing uncovered unsettled Cillan, even if the wound itself was hidden behind his eyelid. Knowing it was there was enough to turn his secretary's weak stomach.

"I have some banking business I need you to attend to," Bekam said.

"Banking, sir?" Cillan looked up at that, his hands clutching tighter on the notepad he held to his chest.

"Nothing official. It's a private matter."

Cillan nodded his head once. "The banks will be open again in the morning." The man hesitated.

"Was there something else?"

"Well, sir, I didn't want to bother you with it at such a late hour, but there was a message just a moment ago from, well, the prison."

"The prison?" Bekam frowned and leaned forward. "Who sent it? What do they want?"

"The message came from a soldier. Someone called Galen Marabe?"

"I remember him."

"He said they have someone in the prison infirmary you'll

want to see."

~

"We found her in the north," Marabe said. "Closest town was Esterburgh, but she was out in the wilderness, quite a ways from there."

"What was she doing?" Bekam asked and looked through the window at the strange woman again. They had her strapped to a bed with bandages wrapped around her right arm and upper torso, but she hardly looked the type that needed those many restraints.

"Riding a supply run. We recovered grain and some other goods from her wagon."

"Was she by herself?"

"No, sir. Two escorts with her on horseback. She was driving the wagon, and they were ahead. They didn't see us coming."

"Where are the escorts?"

"Dead, sir. They were armed, and we took them down in the first volley."

"No other survivors? It would have been nice to have more than one half-dead halflock to question," Bekam said, but having that one halflock was a sight better than anything else he'd had in his grasp these last few weeks.

"She was in Klubridge when the revolt happened," Marabe said. He rested his hand on the hilt of the sword at his hip, no doubt thinking he could have kept order in the city if he'd only been there. More likely, he'd have been dead with most of the rest of the Imperials unlucky enough to be in that plaza, but Bekam left his thoughts unspoken. Marabe looked away from the window and added, "One of the fugitives turned her over."

Bekam's eyebrows rose at that. "One of the Klubridge fugitives? One of Akithar's crew?"

"The acrobat girl. She dealt with a chemist in Karsk and traded secrets with him. One of our reliables." Reliables. That's what the soldiers called them, and that was always a tidy way of describing citizens on the Imperial hook with some sort of bribe or blackmail holding them in place.

"Lizandra Daedan," Bekam said. He'd authorized the sketch that went onto her poster, and he recalled the way the artist had drawn her eyes. Defiant and wary, like she'd do anything to keep herself free. He didn't know who had provided the description for the sketch, but it seemed an accurate portrayal considering what she'd done. "She turned on her own? Is she in custody now?"

Marabe shook his head. "The chemist didn't know her importance when he gave us the information. He traded her some healing services for information, and she gave him this halflock. Seems the mage's gang took her with them when they left Klubridge." He paused and said it again: "They took her with them." The weight of that last detail was not lost on Bekam. All indications were that Akithar had fled directly back to the Stormbreak Sanctuary after leaving Klubridge. If he'd had this woman with him, she'd know where they had gone. She would know where the rebels were hiding.

Bekam looked through the glass again. The woman was awake now, her eyes open wide enough to cause alarm, and her head creaking this way and that on the pillow. The bandages around her chest were bound tight and likely restricted her breathing even more than the straps that crossed her torso and wrapped around her limbs. She wasn't sitting up, thanks to the belts holding her down, but she might not have been able to anyway, given her injury. Marabe's men had nearly killed her, but that could be addressed later. "Has anyone talked to her?"

"Not to any degree. Her brain's cooked, like most of them."

Bekam humphed his understanding. She would have been easier to interrogate if her mind had been intact, but he would work with what he was given. "I'm going in."

Marabe nodded and moved aside so Bekam could pass through the entrance into the patient's room. Bekam pulled the door shut behind him and glanced around the room for a chair before giving up and standing at the foot of the bed. The halflock's head rolled toward him, and her enormous eyes took a second to focus on him.

"What's your name?" he asked.

She wrinkled her nose and stretched her closed mouth wide

before she said anything. When she spoke, it was what could be expected, but Bekam had hoped for better.

"Name same tame game," she said, her voice raspy and childlike.

"You're with the rebels," Bekam said. "Where were you coming from?"

"Rebels pebbles," she said, and her wide mouth opened into a dark grin that made Bekam look away.

He took a deep breath and exhaled before looking back into her vacant gaze. She pursed her lips and blew, bubbles of spit popping and drooling down her chin.

"Right, then," he said. He turned back toward the window, a mirror from this side, and motioned toward the glass. It only took a couple of seconds for Cillan to get the door open, and then he was ushering three more people into the room. Two women and one man, all taking in the prone form on the bed with interest. The man and one of the women had the backs of their heads shaved, just like this injured halflock did. The other woman wore her dark hair pulled up into an oblong bun that she'd held in place with thin sticks. No halflock, that one.

"You know what to do," Bekam said to the Heron.

She nodded back. "These two can hear thoughts, to a degree. If they have trouble with her, I have my own methods." Bekam didn't know her name, but Cillan had found her within minutes. She was an Aramore Heron, still under Qae'lon's purview, but not one of his lackeys. She had more loyalty to the Council than she did to her master, whatever that loyalty might be worth these days.

The woman on the bed made a harsh, humming noise, and Bekam smiled down at her. "It's all right. I'll know what you know, even if you're not inclined to tell me." And then, to the Heron woman, "Send for me as soon as you have results."

Cillan followed him out the door and asked, "Is there anything else you need tonight? I can take your banking details for the morning."

Bekam hesitated and shook his head. "The bank errand is no longer necessary. Everything I need is in that room, and I'll have it soon enough."

CHAPTER 34

Fairy slid her fingers under the edge of the plaster cast and scratched at the itchy spots on her arm she couldn't see. The doctor had wrapped her arm up only a couple of days earlier, but it already felt like forever.

She'd seen plenty of broken bones in the East Ward. Some of them had healed up straight and proper, and others had been all bent and weak. She'd never given much thought to why some ended up one way and some another, but this doctor had assured her that binding up her arm like he did would make sure it healed up all proper. He'd apologized for not having a mage on hand who could heal her, but given the way Oreth had ended up after Samira had tried to help him, Fairy thought she might have been better off with the non-magical option, anyway.

It would be worth it to have her arm back and usable again, but in the meantime it felt like a bunch of ants had been wrapped up in there with it. Still better than losing the arm altogether. Better than dying out there in the snow, too, and that was a fact.

Fairy sighed and barely noticed the white wisp in front of her face. She'd been in the north for long enough that that was just a part of breathing now. She wouldn't get used to how bleeding cold it got up there, though. That was something she wouldn't be sad to leave behind her whenever she managed to get somewhere better than this place.

She shivered as thoughts of the cold took her back just a few nights to when she was positive that coldness was about to be the thing that would finally do her in. She'd given in and collapsed face-first into the snow, and some little part of her had been all right with that. All right with dying alone out in the wilderness, with nobody to know what had happened to her. Anything had seemed preferable to crawling on aimlessly through the darkness as she slowly froze to death. Better to just get it over with all at once.

But it hadn't been, had it? Better, that is. The woodsman had rescued her and fed her and bundled her up and sent her on her way. If he hadn't been there, there was no doubt she'd be dead out there, stiff and cold under the snow or warm and chewed up in some wolf's belly.

She remembered the man's kindly eyes and his big laugh. She remembered how he dodged telling her his name. But, most of all, she remembered that wooden amulet that hung from his neck and the tree with the face on it at the center. That carved face had been in her dreams every night since she'd gotten back to Stormbreak, and she reckoned she could have carved it herself by then, if she had the proper tools. It had been familiar when she first saw it, but it had taken several days before she remembered it was Khealdir's symbol. The god of the forests.

"What're you pondering?"

Fairy blinked and realized she'd been staring at the cast on her arm while the snowflakes came down and settled on her ears and in her hair. She probably looked a proper fool. She tried a sheepish grin at Leyna and said, "Just thinking about things."

"Could you think about things while you help me with your good arm? There's a bucket over there, and you could stack those two packets on top of it."

Fairy followed Leyna's finger and nodded while she stooped to get the supplies together. Leyna already had both arms laden with several burlap sacks that were bulging and tied at the tops with twine. She nodded at Fairy after she'd hoisted up the bucket with her right hand, and the two set off together up the path.

Neither of them said anything until they were just short of the supply depot. That was when Fairy said, "What do you know about Khealdir?"

Leyna snorted. "The god of the woods? I know he's not real."

"How do you know that?" Fairy asked and regretted her tone as soon as she'd spoken. Leyna hadn't experienced what she had. It was natural she'd be skeptical.

"I know it because he's supposed to be a god. There's nothing like that that I've ever seen in this world. Just a lot of people." Leyna shifted the weight of the sacks and gave Fairy a crooked grin. "Some of them think themselves to be gods, sure enough. But that doesn't make it so."

"But people do believe in them. That the gods exist," Fairy said. "Apak's clever, and he believes in Ikarna."

"Being clever about some things doesn't mean you can't be a fool about others. The two aren't mutually exclusive."

They came through the wide doorway, and Fairy swung her bucket up onto the nearest table. It thudded against the wood, and something inside sloshed but didn't leak out.

"Careful with that," Leyna said and moved past her to drop her own bundles on the neighboring table.

"What do you think, Oreth?" Fairy asked. "About the gods, I mean."

Oreth sat at the far end of the table where she'd put her bucket, but he hadn't looked up when they came in. He did glance up then, though. He looked at her and shook his head before bowing it to the papers in front of him once more. He'd always been odd, ever since she'd known him, but he was getting odder by the day. True, he'd been unconscious and nearly dead when she first met him, but it's hard to get odder than that, and somehow he was managing. He'd hardly spoken to her since she'd gotten back to the keep, and she'd barely seen him talking to anybody else. Sometimes to Leyna, but of course he'd be talking to her.

"What's this about gods?"

Fairy looked behind her and saw Aquin just inside the depot

and to the right of the doorway. Even when she was stacking cans, Aquin had an elegant way about her, and it wasn't just the way she wore all those colors nobody else could pull off. She'd paused just then, a can in one hand and the other hand propped on her hip.

"Fairy's become a believer," Leyna said and crinkled her nose. It was a joke, and she didn't mean anything by it, but Fairy couldn't help but let it set her on the defensive.

"That's not what I said. I was just wondering what you thought," Fairy said.

"I think it's all ridiculous," Leyna said. "There's us, and there's what we can do while we're alive, and that's all that matters. Gods don't matter. Magic doesn't matter."

"You don't believe in magic, either?"

"Of course I believe in magic. Doesn't mean I like it or trust it or think it could benefit people in any way. But I suppose magic does have an edge on the gods, seeing how it's a real thing." Leyna put a hand on Oreth's shoulder as she passed him, and Fairy was certain Leyna didn't notice the way he flinched when she touched him. Did Leyna even know it had been magic that had saved Oreth's life before they left Klubridge?

Fairy didn't have a chance to follow up on that line of reasoning, though. Aquin had set aside the can she was holding and said, "I don't see anything ridiculous about faith. Sometimes that can be all we have, and it's still enough."

Leyna rolled her eyes, and in that instant Fairy knew she was going to have to dislike the other girl. It was one thing to have your own opinions about something, but it was another to be openly disrespectful. Especially to somebody like Aquin. Turning her disapproving eye away from Leyna, Fairy asked, "What do you believe, Aquin?"

Aquin looked like she wanted to answer, but she looked at the door first, and her mouth pulled tight at the corners. Fairy knew a nervous person when she saw one. "It's all right," she said. "If you don't want to say, you don't have to."

Aquin shook her head. "I am simply unaccustomed to being able to discuss these kinds of things openly. Where I came from, it was wise to stay silent and to remain as discreet as possible."

She slid her fingers along the neck of her shirt and pulled at the chain around her neck. A medallion of some sort slid out and rested on her chest.

"Ikarna," Oreth said. He was still moping, but that necklace had his attention. "Apak has an icon like that."

Aquin nodded. "I follow her ways."

"What about Khealdir?" Fairy asked. She didn't look at Leyna but could feel another eye roll happening.

"He is a sibling of Ikarna's. She is his sister."

"So you believe both of them exist?"

"If I believe in one, it's hard not to believe in the other," Aquin said with a smile.

"Do you believe they're real?" Fairy searched for the right words. "Not real like you believe in them but don't see them. But real like you can see them and they can talk to you?"

Aquin traced a finger over the icon she wore and frowned. It wasn't an unfriendly sort of frown but was more like she was trying to decide how best to answer. At last, she said, "I don't know. I have heard stories of Ikarna appearing in the surface of water and speaking to her followers. They say she gave them guidance or told their future or answered some pressing question."

"But it's never happened for you?" Fairy asked.

Aquin shook her head. "It has not. But I still—"

Fairy heard the footsteps behind her just as Aquin went silent, and she turned around to see three people coming in that she didn't recognize. Two of them were brawny men who looked so similar with their scruffy beards and bulky arms they might've been brothers. The other was a smaller woman who looked nothing like them, but she was clearly the one in charge.

"Aquin Mirada?" she asked, not bothering to apologize for interrupting the conversation. Fairy decided she didn't like this woman at that moment, either. Politeness was an easy thing to have, and there was no sense in not having it.

"That's me," Aquin said, curiosity and a little bit of wariness on her face.

"Get her," the woman said.

As the men moved forward, Fairy took a step toward the door in protest, and Oreth asked, "What is this?"

The woman answered, no emotion registering in her eyes or her voice. "Micah Vaino sent us with orders. This woman is a spy for the Empire and has betrayed our cause." And, to the men, "Take her away."

CHAPTER 35

For the first time since all this began, Caius knew he was dreaming.

When he looked down, he had no body. He felt his hands and raised them, but they were not there. Nor were his feet or legs or torso, and he was certain his face would not look back at him if he peered into a mirror.

He knew he was dreaming, but it made little difference. This dream felt every bit as real as all the others had. He could feel the breeze against his body that didn't exist, and he could smell the aroma of some flower he couldn't identify. He stood in a field of violet grass, where red and green blossoms swayed a lazy and foreign dance.

He moved forward, borne bodiless by feet that were not beneath him, and the sensation was more like floating than walking. At first, he'd thought he was dreaming of the sunset, but as his eyes rose to the sky, unbidden, he saw the sun blazing at its full height. The surrounding sky was a burnished red, streaked with clouds tinted orange.

Caius stopped midway across the field at the top of a gentle rise, where the breeze blew stronger. He knew peace, then, even with all the colors wrong and with no trace of familiarity around him. He knew peace in the solitude, and yet... he was not alone. The sense of someone at his back was unmistakable, but he had no power to turn and see them. He remained in place, staring up into the sky, until the voice spoke. It was feminine and full, and it said, "Do you not still hunger, Inter—"

The voice was gone, trampled under the sound of the wheels turning and the road passing beneath. Caius rocked on his seat, dizzy, and had to catch hold of the door handle to stop himself from spilling onto the floor. But Samira was there next to him, and she put a hand on his leg, and that was enough to steady him and bring him out of the dream stupor.

Caius blinked at the sudden moonlight streaming through the carriage windows and then at the Gressams, seated across from himself and Samira. Hyden sat directly opposite Caius and wore a pensive frown as he stared at the passing countryside. Phyla was on the other end of that bench seat, with Danel between his parents. The boy was leaning against his mother, and she had one arm around his shoulders as the other stroked his hair in an absent but determined manner that made Caius wonder whether it was more soothing to Danel or to Phyla.

The wheels were slowing, probably the cue that awakened Caius from his strange sleep, and it wasn't long before the caravan was stopped at the side of the road. It was nighttime, but in the light of the full moon, they could see trees lining the road out both sides of the carriage, with a break leading to a small clearing on the right. Caius leaned toward Samira and asked, "How far have we gone?"

"Not far," she said. "Only an hour or so. We're not back to Bria yet."

He nodded as Lodar pulled the door open on the right side, next to Caius and Hyden. "We plan to drive straight through," he said. "No more stops until we're clear of the city. We rest here tonight."

It was a smart decision, given the forces that were aligned against them. There was more chance of their being spotted inside a city than on the outskirts, and it made sense to rest now that they were away from the farm but not yet to Bria. Once the decision to leave the Gressams' home had been made, Phyla had pressed her husband with urgency. They'd abandoned the stew, not even taking time to dispose of it, and had been on the road with empty bellies in minutes. There was food in the caravan, though, and Caius would be glad for the chance to eat something. Sleep was something he'd already had enough of, though.

"I'll take the first watch tonight," Caius said.

"You will not," Dekan Hama said as he passed the carriage, and that was that.

They cooked over a small fire in the middle of the clearing, and Rikin toiled over a cookpot for the second time that night. In the end, he produced something akin to the stew he'd made back at the farm. The food smelled good, but, despite feeling hungry when the caravan had stopped, Caius could not eat anything.

"Are you all right?" Samira asked, keeping her voice low. She sat next to him on a log at the edge of the clearing, well away from the others but still within view of the watchful Aescalan.

Caius stirred his spoon in the bowl on his lap but didn't try tasting it. "I don't know," he said. And then, after a moment, "I don't think so."

"Tell me," she said and sat her own bowl aside, half finished.

He looked toward the fire and tried to find the words to express the dread that had been creeping into him ever since he awakened on Ergo Drass' ship. The best he could manage was, "I think I'm going mad."

"Is it the dreams again?"

"Again, still, always. It's every time I sleep now. I had another one when I fell asleep in the carriage after we left the farm."

"What was this one about?"

He'd tried to withhold the contents of most of the dreams he'd had and had shared only the basic concepts and generalities. Telling all the details would be a sure way to convince anyone he was well along the road to insanity. But he'd just admitted he thought he was going mad, so what did he have left to protect?

"I was somewhere... I didn't recognize it. Something strange had happened, and the sky had turned red. Everything was different and wrong." He paused, remembering. "I had no body, but I was present. And someone else was there. A woman."

"Did you recognize her?"

"I didn't see her. She spoke to me just before I woke up. She... she asked if I was hungry." He looked down at the bowl in his lap once more and put it aside with a sigh.

They sat in silence for a few moments, and it was nice. It was like things had been before all the death and running and politics. Before coming to Klubridge, even. It had been just the two of them, traveling together from town to town, performing for what little seri they could scrounge before they moved on to the next place. They'd had so little, but none of that had mattered. It had been a good life, traveling and working and surviving with his best friend, and there had been so many nights like this one, when they'd sat under a full, fat moon and watched the flames of a campfire lick at the cooling night air.

"You're not going mad," Samira said. Caius looked at her and could see she was looking back at him, the distant flames flickering light and shadows across her face. "You almost died in Klubridge. We all did, but what you went through is nothing I've even heard about."

"The silencing," he said.

"The silencing. If you'd been a mage, you'd have lost your power. The Herons would have burned it out of you, and that would have been the end of it. But you weren't a mage. You had no magic to lose. I don't even know what effect that ceremony might have had on you. Whatever it was ended up being their own undoing. They created a creature that destroyed them and ate its fair share of the Kites."

She'd told him about the chamir, but he still had a hard time believing such a creature could exist, even if it had been created by magic gone awry. "You don't think I'm mad, but you think they broke me."

"I don't think you're broken, either, but I do think what you experienced is unprecedented. When soldiers see horrors, what they witnessed lingers with them. It's trauma that doesn't go away once the battle has ended. I think something similar happened to you in Klubridge. What the Herons did to you is what's affecting you now. It's no wonder you're having the kinds of dreams you're having. Or that your appetite has grown so fickle," she said, eyeing the discarded bowl at his side.

"But it's getting worse," he said.

"That's because you've had no time to process what you've been through. What we've all been through. I'm just amazed the rest of us aren't experiencing what you are."

"Lizzie will," Caius said, and in that instant he dreaded returning to Stormbreak.

Samira breathed the night air for a few seconds before asking, her voice even softer, "Do you think, by now... Is Reykas..."

Caius didn't answer immediately. He watched the flames again and finally said, "We'll be back before long. We have to be there for her."

When Samira didn't respond, he looked at her again, and she was frowning toward the group around the fire. They were eating and talking, their low murmur carrying across the clearing as an indecipherable mumbling. Samira pulled her eyes away from them and leaned closer to Caius, so close her lips brushed his ear. She whispered, "I don't think we're going to Stormbreak."

"What—"

She silenced him with a finger across his lips, and he sat still, waiting for the rest of it.

"The Aescalan have no reason to go back. They have their scion now."

He looked at her, and she stared back. She was serious, and her eyes told him this was something she'd been considering for longer than the brief time they'd been sitting on that log.

"I've watched Hama," she whispered. "I don't know whether he means to abandon us or take us with them. Or worse. But I don't think he has any plan to go back to Vaino."

Caius looked away and found Hama, sitting on the near side of the fire, his back to them and his head tilted toward Lodar. The older man said something, and Hama laughed a throaty chuckle that cut through the air. Caius' eyes drew past Hama and past the fire, to where Ranja sat on the opposite side. As he watched, she cocked her head in his direction. Caius would have sworn her eyes locked with his, even at that distance, and the skin at the back of his neck prickled.

Even though Hama had denied him a turn at the watch, Caius got no sleep that night. Samira had wrapped herself in a blanket Talit had given them, and she lay on the grass next to him, sleeping soundly. Caius was wide awake, though, sitting with his back against the log where they had sat and conspired. Rikin had regained enough of his composure for Hama to name him as the first watch, and, as far as Caius could tell, he was the only other member of the party still awake at that late hour.

The fire had burned low to little more than embers before the others went to sleep, and the darkness made it easy to see the approaching horseman with a torch held aloft. He was coming along the road from the east, and they'd camped far enough into the clearing that the trees along the roadway should have provided ample cover to block them from his view. Caius expected him to ride past them without incident, but the torch's progress slowed and then halted, just on the other side of the trees.

Caius sat forward and strained his eyes in the darkness. The rider was visible through the gaps in the branches, just barely. He was dismounting, and his horse huffed a low whicker as he slid to the ground and raised the torch. Its light caught his chest, illuminating the black emblem of a diving bird embroidered on the yellow tabard. The symbol of the Kites. Caius reached for Samira without taking his eyes off the moving form ahead of him. He caught her shoulder and gave it a quick shake.

She shifted beneath his hand before opening her eyes.

"Shh." He pointed to the trees, and he didn't have to look at her to know she was sitting upright and had seen the soldier.

Samira leaned close from behind him. "What is he doing?"

"Nothing yet," Caius whispered back, but then the Kite dropped to a knee and felt the ground with his palm. "We didn't cover our tracks. He's going to find us."

"They're looking for us," Samira said after a pause. "After what happened at the drill site."

"Help you, sir?" The voice was nearer, but still on the other side of the trees. Rikin. Caius was on his feet then, squatted next to the log, and he turned to find the young man in the darkness. He could barely make out his form looming at the edge of the road.

Caius glanced at Samira and saw that she was no longer looking at the road. Her eyes were on the bundles near the campfire, farthest from the treeline. She was watching the Gressams sleep. She caught Caius' look and nodded toward them. "We have to warn them."

He grabbed her wrist before she could move away. "What are you planning?" he whispered.

"I don't know," she said and pulled her arm free. She looked at him once more, then toward the road, and left him alone at the log. She disappeared into the darkness as she half-crawled, half ran toward the family.

Caius cursed and moved to follow her. The Kite was responding to Rikin, but the sound of Caius' own heartbeat thudding in his ears distorted the words. The warning tone was obvious, though. Trouble was on the way.

Samira was halfway to the Gressams with Caius two steps behind her when the shout went up from the treeline. He couldn't tell whether it was Rikin or the Kite, but the roar of a gunshot came less than a second later. "Guns!" shouted an unfamiliar voice, and still more took up the cry. The Kite wasn't alone.

Dekan Hama scrambled to his feet as Hyden Gressam raised a groggy head. "Kites," Samira told Hama and then, "Imperials," when he frowned at her in confusion. That was all it took to move him into action. He grabbed the rifle that lay near his bedroll and leaped over Lodar, who had raised onto one elbow and was blinking drowsy eyes at the others.

"What is it? What's happening?" Phyla asked, sitting up and reaching for Danel.

"Get up," Samira said. "The Imperials found us."

Hyden's eyes were wide in the meager glow of the dying fire. "What do we do?"

Samira looked over her shoulder to Caius and then toward the road. Gunshots cracked amid screams and the sound of metal meeting metal. All five Aescalan were already in the battle, and there was no telling how many Kites were up there. "Do we help them?" Samira asked.

Caius watched the shapes moving and struggling through the trees for a moment and shook his head. "We go. The five of us. We're not going to have another chance. Either the Kites kill them and then come for us, or—"

"Or the Aescalan kill them," Samira finished. "Get up," she told Hyden. "We have their horses."

They had three of the horses, to be exact. One was still harnessed to the carriage, and there'd be no maneuverability with that thing. The others were tied closer to the treeline and were pulling at their tethers with increasing urgency every time a rifle echoed through the night. Caius ran for the nearest horse and began untangling its reins. Hyden was doing the same with the next horse, and Phyla was headed for the third. Samira grabbed a pack from the ground, and Caius thought it might have been Talit's. She slung it over her shoulder and turned to say something when her eyes widened.

"Caius!" she yelled at him, pointing. He was turned halfway toward the road when he saw Ranja just this side of the trees, down on one knee, staring at him down the barrel of her gun.

The rifle roared, and Caius flinched, turning away from the shot, but Samira was faster. Her invisible shield deflected the rifle slug, sending it ricocheting into the grass. Ranja tilted her head at that but sighted down the rifle again, this time aiming slightly to the left.

"I've got her," Samira called as she shielded herself from the next shot. "Get the horses."

"Already there," Caius said. Samira had always been the better rider, and he moved aside for her to mount up first.

She shook her head. "I have to keep this up. Get on and I'll come behind you."

Hyden was already on his horse and held Danel in place ahead of him as Phyla was slinging a leg over the third mount, past them. Caius pulled himself up and onto his horse, and extended a hand for Samira. She ignored it and grabbed at the saddle with her right hand while her left arm remained extended. The barrier she projected was translucent, but Caius could see its curved edges occasionally reflecting green under the moonlight. A third shot had bounced off the shield by the time Samira was astride the horse, her right arm now wrapped around Caius' waist.

"She's reloading. Go!" she shouted.

"Where?" he asked. The clearing only had one defined exit, and he wasn't about to ride into the battle.

"Anywhere but here!"

Hyden leaned forward, kicked his heels inward, and galloped what Caius reckoned was south, away from the road and toward the forest. Phyla followed, and Caius pulled his own horse into line with far less skill. It was clear the Gressams knew how to ride and had experience at it that Caius lacked. He couldn't remember the last time he'd been on horseback, but he couldn't worry about that now. All that mattered was getting clear of the Kites and the Aescalan, and he spurred the horse between the trees and into the night.

CHAPTER 36

Wickes kept his eyes closed, even though it hardly mattered with the blindfold bound around his head. He couldn't see anyway, so he shut his eyes and tried to rest as the carriage rumbled over the bumpy road.

How long had they been on the road, anyway? They would drive all day, pausing only long enough for a midday break and food, before they'd drive even farther and end up in a different barn each night. The days and nights were interminably dull, and Wickes was alone inside the carriage, as well as he could tell. They'd bound his hands and feet and shackled them together, so he couldn't raise his arms far enough to pull the blindfold down. He probably could have leaned forward far enough to work it off his eyes if he'd really wanted to, but again, what was the use?

He'd been caught and tied up, and now he was headed for some unknown destination, leaving his Imperial watchdogs far behind. Despite his predicament, this was the most he'd been able to relax in months. Years, perhaps. The Empire probably thought he'd defected and joined up with the rebels. That fool Jalla certainly would believe it, and he'd relay the word back to Bekam and Mediean. Would they send hunters to bring him in, or would they write him off as a casualty of their crusade?

Either way, he was of no use to the Empire now, and every mile that rolled beneath that carriage stretched the strings that

LIZANDRA'S DEEPEST FEAR

tied him to them, popping and snapping them one by one. By the time the rebels got him to their destination, he'd be blessedly free of Imperial interference, for once. The worst imaginable scenario had been that the Empire would turn on him and jail him and execute him if he didn't do exactly as they ordered him. Well, no. It had been that they'd find out Weylis was still alive and do the same to her. But now Wickes was out from under their thumbs, and everything would change. It could only be a change for the better, couldn't it?

Unless the rebels decided to kill him, too.

They'd probably question him first. They'd want to find out what he was doing in those snowy woods and what his ties were to the Empire and who those other fools were that had blundered around in the snow with him. Wickes frowned at that. Ikarna could swallow Jalla and the others, as far as he cared, but Colm had been his responsibility. He'd bound himself to protecting the man, and now where was he? Had the rebels taken him, too? If not, surely the Empire would round him up and put him back into service. He'd once been a halflock, and now he'd be right back where he started.

Wickes sighed and traced the outside edge of his hand along the carriage door. He could probably get it open, and he might even free himself from his bindings and tumble out of the coach without the driver being any wiser until he'd gotten a long way down the road.

But what then? Would he run shackled all the way back from wherever he was, just on the chance Colm was still there? If the rebels hadn't collected him, that poor man was long gone. As long and as far gone as Wickes was, just in a different direction. There was nothing to be done now but to sit and await whatever was coming at the end of this journey.

Would the rebels torture him?

Not unless they took joy in it, and that had always been more the Empire's style. Wickes would tell them anything they wanted to know. What loyalty did he have to Bekam or any of the rest?

The great irony was that they'd dispatched him to find the Stormbreak Sanctuary, and that's exactly where these rebels were most likely to be taking him. Sometimes fate had a funny way of giving Wickes what he wanted at the time and in the way that was least useful to him.

Nothing to do but wait and see what happened after they got there, and so that's what he did.

~

When the carriage jostled to a halt, Wickes shifted forward on his seat, and that was enough to wake him from one of his many naps. He blinked behind the blindfold, disoriented for a moment, but he soon remembered exactly where he was and what was happening to him. Well, not exactly where he was, but the circumstance rushed back with clarity.

There was the sound of the door to his left jerking open, and a cold breeze washed over him.

"Getting out here," the guard said, his voice as rough as ever. All the way from the rebel hideout to wherever they had taken him now, Wickes had failed to learn even the guard's name. The driver was Mawin, and he only knew that much because the man had a tendency to refer to himself in the third person when he was gossiping with the guard when they thought they were out of Wickes' earshot or thought he was asleep.

The guard grabbed him by the arm and pulled, and Wickes went with him, ducking his head to avoid cracking it on the top of the door frame. He'd done that the first few times they'd unloaded him from the car and had eventually learned to negotiate his exit without banging against anything.

This time, the guard gave him an extra yank, and Wickes came out of the carriage stumbling and nearly falling. The jolt was enough to knock the blindfold down, the cloth falling from his face and hanging around his neck with the knot tied in the back.

"Cursed thing," the guard said and reached to pull the fabric back over Wickes' face. In the few seconds of brightness, Wickes turned his eyes upward, and he barely withheld a laugh.

Crowspire.

He'd never been there, but there was no mistaking that broken-off bird-looking heap of a mountain overhead. And they

LIZANDRA'S DEEPEST FEAR

were leading him through the outer walls, right into the keep. Of course the Empire hadn't been able to find the rebels. They'd been hiding up here in the icy north where nobody wanted to go, and they were doing it on the Empire's own property. It was ridiculous. Stormbreak Sanctuary was nothing more than the rubble of an old Imperial fort.

They were dragging him along again, and his feet shuffled through the snow. The blindfold was over his eyes again, but the guard had done a poor job of tucking it all around, so Wickes could see out the bottom. Not much to see there, but he watched his own feet trudging through the white that had piled up on the paving stones. He shivered when another breeze hit him. Just one more reason he'd avoided the north himself and had spent most of his life sailing more tropical climates.

There were voices and the sounds of movement after they were through the doors and into the keep. Wickes couldn't see anyone, but there was no doubt the place was busy. If a blindfolded man being led through their corridors was an odd sight for these rebels, none of them seemed to pause and acknowledge it. The rebels continued their business, and the guard pulled Wickes along by his arm.

"Sit here," the guard said when they were in a room where the sounds of the keep were more distant. Wickes slid his feet back until he felt the edge of a chair behind him, and he sat. The chair was hard and a good deal less comfortable than the coach seat where he'd spent the journey to Crowspire. He suddenly found himself missing that padded bench and shifted his weight on this new chair.

"Hold still." The guard was down at his side, and he yanked Wickes' feet a few inches forward. The metal shackles were gone, but the man was pulling ropes around where they'd been. Then he was up again, and he pulled the blindfold up and off his head. "You wait here."

Wickes blinked around the bare room and glanced down to where the guard had tied his ankles to the legs of the chair, which were already bolted into the floor. His hands remained bound, and a rope connected them to his feet, bound by that same rope. "I won't go anywhere," Wickes said with a faint smile.

The guard looked at him one more time, his eyes surveying the bindings, before he left the room, pulling the door shut behind him. There was the sound of a big key turning in the lock, and then Wickes was by himself once more.

The room was a small one, the walls plain and built from the same stone he'd seen in his brief glimpse of the outside walls. It was all held together with the same ancient mortar that had kept this place standing for centuries. The stories had the castle in ruins, but reality, as always, told a different story. How long had the rebels been hiding up here? Whose idea had it been to claim this desolate place, anyway?

Wickes stretched, turning in the seat as far as his bindings would allow, and his spine gave a satisfying crack. He settled back into the chair and looked down at his feet again. The bolts at the legs of the chair were telling. This was a room for interrogations, and it probably had been for much longer than Wickes had even existed. There were no bloodstains on the stony floor. No racks with implements of pain. This was a room for conversations, not torture. That might have been another story when this place was Crowspire, but Wickes suspected Stormbreak operated on a different set of rules. The rebels' softness was likely to lose them this revolt, but for the moment he was glad to see no blades and needles in waiting.

The lock clicked open again, and Wickes looked back to the door. It pushed inward, and a new man stood in the entry, his hand still on the doorknob as he examined his prisoner. The man was pale, his face angular and his hair long and dark. He wore a black suit that looked fancier than anything Wickes would have expected to see here. He'd assumed the rebels had been leading a hardscrabble life, holed up in the ruins of Crowspire, but this man looked more like a ballroom dandy than a desperate refugee.

"Quentyn Wickes," the man said. He stood there for another moment before he came fully into the room and pushed the door shut behind him. He didn't bother locking it. Wickes wasn't going anywhere. "Quentyn Wickes," he said again and waited.

What was Wickes supposed to say to that? The man knew

him. That wasn't unusual, given what Wickes had been up to the past couple of years and for the rest of his life prior to that. So Wickes kept his silence and watched the man watching him.

The man sniffed when Wickes didn't say anything and glanced around the room, as if there would be anything to see in there other than the prisoner tied to a chair. "Ergo Drass told me your name. He said you're a pirate."

Wickes' eyebrows rose at that. So this fellow didn't know him after all. It was a rare thing when his reputation didn't precede him these days, but it was not necessarily an unpleasant feeling.

"You work with the Empire, he said. You ambushed him and several of my people." These were all statements so far. The man was asking no questions, but he'd already told Wickes more about himself than he probably suspected. This man was no mere interrogator. This was the head of the rebellion, or something near to it.

"How many Imperials were with you?" the man asked.

"It was me, and then the fool who got himself killed, and another one named Jalla," Wickes said. "He was the one holding my leash." He hesitated. "There was another man, Colm. A halflock. Do you know what happened to him?"

"Were you part of the other ambush as well?"

Wickes frowned. "What ambush?"

"Who knows where we are?" the man asked, ignoring all of Wickes' questions. "Does the Empire know where Stormbreak is?"

Wickes did laugh at that. "If they did, don't you think they'd be beating down your walls by now?"

"Then how did they know when and where to find the supply wagon?" The man was glaring down at him now, the pulse in his neck visible.

The smile dropped from Wickes' face, and he shook his head. "I truly have no clue what you're talking about."

The man stood there for a moment longer, his hands in fists at his sides, and a long strand of hair hanging down his forehead. At last, he swiped at his face, tucking the hair back behind his ear, and he pulled the door open. "We're finished in here," he called outside. He added, "For now," looking back at Wickes.

This time, they pulled a sack over his head before they unstrapped him from the chair. It was rough and brown and had a strong, earthy smell. Did it speak more to the rebels' disdain for him or to their meager supplies that they had tucked him into a potato sack before leading him back out of the interrogation chamber?

As it had been with the blindfold, Wickes could see out the bottom of the sack as they walked. That's the only reason he didn't stumble when they took him to a set of stairs and began leading him upwards. They turned at a landing and continued up, and then they headed down a long corridor. Wickes had a good sense of direction on the water, but they'd gotten him utterly turned around in this keep. He'd known Crowspire to be one of the Empire's smaller castles, but he'd still gotten lost in it.

He might not have known the layout of the place, but the sound of a key scrubbing into metal was familiar enough, as was the grating screech of the cell door being pulled back. Someone dragged the sack off his head before giving him a hard shove in the back, and he staggered into the cell, nearly falling with his feet still tied together.

"Surely you can undo these," he said, holding his bound hands toward the guard at the door.

The man sneered at him and slammed the door shut. He gave Wickes one last look through the small barred window set in the center of the door before he disappeared, his footsteps receding back down the hallway toward the stairs.

Wickes sighed and dropped his hands. At least the sack was gone, and he hadn't had to endure the questioning for too long. The questions had confused him more than anything else. What sort of ambush had there been? The Empire couldn't already know where Stormbreak was located, that much was true. If they did, they'd have already disassembled the place brick by brick.

That thought in mind, Wickes ran his fingertips along the blocks in the outer wall of his cell. Too sturdy and too thick to break through from the inside, and the bars in the window that looked out across the snowy mountains would not budge, either. It was a well-built prison, and he wouldn't be getting out of it until someone let him out.

"It's a long drop, even if you get out the window."

Wickes started and looked to the left, through the wall of bars that separated his cell from the neighboring one. It was dark in there, and he'd assumed it was empty, but now he saw the eyes looking back at him. It was a woman, strikingly beautiful, with skin even darker than his own. She sat on the edge of a cot like the one in his own cell, and she watched him with a casual boredom that he recognized as poorly disguised anxiety.

Wickes smiled back at her and took a seat on the edge of his own bed, facing her through the bars. "So," he said. "Come here often?"

CHAPTER 37

The Robdwell Building was colder than last time, especially near the window where Bekam stood, his hands behind his back and his eye following the trails below where footprints cut through the snow. Despite the chill, a trickle of sweat ran down his temple, and he swiped at it with a quick flick. His pounding heart threatened to betray his anticipation for this meeting.

The Council thought him finished. Qae'lon thought he'd cornered him and taken his position. All of them had counted him out. Today he'd show them what happened when they came after Tenez Bekam.

The corner of his mouth tried to turn upward in a sneer, but he forced it down, stoicism the order of the day. Qae'lon himself was likely to be in attendance again, curious to see why the erstwhile general had requested another convening. None of them knew what he knew, and it was impossible to keep from thrilling at the surprise he'd be seeing on their faces in just a few minutes.

"What in the hells are you doing here?"

The question came whispered at his shoulder, and Bekam allowed himself to smile at the reflection behind him in the window's glass. "Hello, Lacar."

The young man wore the same light blue doublet as last time,

LIZANDRA'S DEEPEST FEAR

but today his sleeves were a pale green. Always bearing his colors, always ready to insert himself into whatever would advance his own career.

"Why are you here?" Teka Lacar asked again. He shot a quick look down the hallway before leaning even closer. "I thought you'd be out of Aramore by now, not prancing into the middle of the bloody Council."

Bekam tilted his head toward Lacar, still not turning away from the view of the white courtyard. "Everything is in hand, my friend. And I will not forget your loyalty."

Lacar huffed something else under his breath, but it was too low for Bekam to hear. The other man's steps receded down the hall and disappeared with the opening and closing of the chamber door. The Council was assembling, and the rest of them were probably as confused as Lacar had been. Bekam smiled with anticipation and straightened his back when he saw the page approaching in the reflection.

"The Council is ready for you, General."

There was the usual announcement, the awkward pomp that seemed more appropriate for a ballroom introduction than for a round room full of bureaucrats. But the introduction was made, and Bekam settled himself into the hard chair before the round table that arced before him. This time, the seat felt decidedly more comfortable than in the past.

The Council had filled eleven of its fifteen seats the last time he'd been there. They'd all wanted to see him brought low, to witness the subjugation of Tenez Bekam. Today, they filled only six seats, and Qae'lon was not among them. There was less interest in seeing a man they believed they'd already beaten.

Prusik was there again, seated directly before Bekam. She had been writing on a tablet when he entered and gave him only a quick glance over her half-lenses before returning her attention to her scribbling. Milev was there, too, his shaved head shining under the gaslamps that flickered above. He nodded once to Bekam, but there was no smile of greeting. His small eyes seemed even narrower today, curiosity plain on his face.

Teka Lacar sat to the left, several chairs away from Milev. Lacar was the newest member of the Council, raised by Bekam's own influence, and he hadn't been there long enough to assume a seat toward the center of the curved table. Still, he was in the room, and every voice counted the same once you made it there. That's what they told each other, at least.

Bekam recognized two of the others, both women from some office or another. They hadn't been in the room the last time he was there, and they watched him with more open interest than the others. This was their first time at the show, and they were ready to watch him struck down after having missed the last round. He met the younger woman's eyes, and she looked away, but the older one stared with unabashed intrigue.

The sixth person in the room was new to him. Between Lacar and Milev sat a tall woman with stern eyes and a firm set to her jaw, her face unlined despite the white hair she'd bound behind her head in a severe bun. She looked at him, but her eyes moved on, appraising the women sitting opposite her, then moving to Prusik. She turned her head to take in Milev on one side of her and then Lacar on the other. Who was this woman whose interest spread as evenly across the Council as it did toward Bekam?

"General," Commissioner Prusik said, looking up from whatever she'd been writing. No one had been talking, but the room fell even more silent at this commencement. "You have requested this meeting, much to the surprise of the Council. I can only assume that means you have significant progress to report? Perhaps you have taken it upon yourself to reclaim Klubridge, now that General Qae'lon softened it for you?"

The question might as well have been a rhetorical one, and a smile played around Milev's mouth. They knew damned well he had done nothing toward retaking that accursed city. They'd denied him the resources he would have needed to properly make any moves in that direction, much less to pursue his actual mandate of finding the rebels. And yet...

"I have not," Bekam said. "Klubridge remains in the hands of whatever cockroaches have crawled out of the rubble to claim it."

Prusik scowled at that and eyed him once more before

glancing at Milev. They'd expected him cowed. They'd been sure he would beg for some sort of leniency or to grovel once more for his station. They hadn't predicted his defiance.

"Then," Prusik said, her voice hard, "why have you wasted our time today?"

All eyes were on Bekam, and Lacar's were especially round, like he'd just swallowed something bigger than he could get down. He no doubt feared the consequences of his own connections to this condemned general, but Bekam would remember his promise. After Bekam was lifted above the rest of these fools, he'd remember the man's loyalty.

"I have not pursued Klubridge," Bekam said, "because I've found something more significant." He let the statement settle in the room and managed to keep a smile off his face.

Prusik twisted her creased mouth downward. "I suppose you could enlighten us about this discovery?"

Bekam's smile betrayed him, and he said, "I know the location of the Stormbreak Sanctuary."

∼

Bekam let the Council doors close behind him, and he suppressed any sign of satisfaction until he had reached the end of the hallway and stood before that window once more. Only after he was certain he was on his own and saw only his own reflection in that glass did he allow himself to exhale the breath he'd been holding all the way down the marbled walkway.

They had been skeptical, of course. One did not presume to win the confidence of an antagonistic body with a bold assertion alone. That's why he'd brought Galen Marabe and summoned him from the outer waiting area. Milev's disdain had softened when another soldier entered the room, and Marabe's testimony had been convincing. Bekam had watched all the politicians' faces as Marabe described the trading of intelligence that had happened in Karsk, the acrobat girl's betrayal of her own people, and the ambush that had netted them the halflock who had turned out to be called Magra.

When Marabe's part of the story was finished, Milev was a believer. Prusik was harder to crack. She'd had no part in the military, and the words of a dedicated soldier were less convincing to her than numbers in a ledger would have been. After they'd dismissed Marabe, she'd said, "That was an exciting diversion, General. Where is your proof of the location of Stormbreak?"

Milev had frowned at her, and that had been enough for Bekam to know he'd already won the rest of them over. But Prusik was the one who mattered most, and she was the one he suspected had the strongest ties to Qae'lon. And so he had said, "I suppose it would take someone of higher standing to convince you, Commissioner. It's a shame my counterpart is absent from this meeting."

That had brought a rare smile to Prusik's face. "A shame, indeed."

"Although Qae'lon is not here, I do have one of his lieutenants on hand," Bekam had said. "Page, could you bring us Rozin Gadhi, Captain of the Aramore detachment of the Imperial Herons?"

And that's how Bekam brought a fully credentialed Heron, answerable directly to Qae'lon himself, into the Council chamber to corroborate his claims. Gadhi had answered Prusik's questions and testified that she had verified the claims made by the two halflocks she'd brought to interrogate the prisoner. Both of them had pulled the location of Stormbreak out of her head with some difficulty likely borne of the halflock's madness, and Gadhi had validated the truthfulness of their statements. Her magic was in truthfulness, and she'd found no lies in what her two halflocks had reported.

"Stormbreak Sanctuary is at Crowspire," Prusik had said when the Heron was finished, reluctant belief in her voice, and Bekam had known he had them all.

"Clever." That had come from the older woman Bekam had recognized. "They've been hiding in the last place we'd look. One of our own abandoned fortresses."

"Too cold to go up there on a whim anyway," Milev had said.

Lacar and the younger woman had held their tongues after

that, letting the more senior members of the Council have their discussion, and the stern-faced newcomer had stood and left the chamber after it was clear Bekam had proven the credibility of his claims. None of them had said it, but the purse strings were as good as open. Bekam would get his funding, and he'd be marching north instead of east. Klubridge could rot, as far as these bureaucrats were concerned. The true prize was north of Karsk now, tucked into the mountains at the top of the world.

Bekam allowed himself another moment at the window, savoring his victory, before he headed for the steps that would take him back downstairs and through the streets to his estate. He had preparations to make, and perhaps Marjiel would even deign to acknowledge his presence, now that he was back in the favor of Aramore.

He would remember Teka Lacar's loyalty, as he had promised. A rising officer needed those around him he could trust, and Lacar had risked his own standing by alerting Bekam to the Council's intentions. Bekam would remember that, but he'd also remember that Lacar gave him no warning prior to the previous meeting, where Bekam was called to account before Qae'lon. Favor was a fine instrument and an even better weapon, when wielded with caution.

Bekam pushed through the front doors of the Robdwell building and breathed the cold air with an enthusiasm he'd lacked for the past few months. Ever since Klubridge fell to Akithar's revolt, the Empire had been drawing Bekam closer and closer to the cliff's edge. A few more steps, and he'd have been pitched over, plummeting to his doom. He'd forestalled that progress and set himself on a new path. He was the man who had brought Stormbreak to the Empire. The possibilities were endless, and his ascent was just beginning.

He followed a narrow path through the snow, his boots sinking to mid-foot as he passed between the government buildings. On another day, he might have taken a coach back to his gates, but the sun was bright, and the air was crisp and clear, and Bekam wanted to see every face he passed. He wanted to remember how these people beheld him on the last day before they knew he was the one who would bring down the rebellion.

Smiling, he glanced over his shoulder just in time to see a figure slide off the street and into an alcove on the right. He hesitated and watched the front of that building, waiting for the figure to emerge again, but there was nothing. Was he being followed?

His forehead creased, and he turned back to his walk and tried to keep himself from looking over his shoulder again. He made it half a block before he could stand it no more, and he checked the street behind him. There was a figure in a long coat, a hat pulled low on their head, and their hands shoved into deep pockets. They were half a street back from him, and when he turned, they slowed to peruse a shop window.

Bekam's pulse quickened. Who would be following him? Who knew what he knew, aside from the few people in that Council room? The halflocks and the Heron, certainly, but those were the only ones. Not even Cillan or Marabe knew the truth of the knowledge Bekam had gleaned.

Could it be Qae'lon?

No, Qae'lon would be more direct. He would be more theatrical with his approach. Bekam shivered less at the cold air than at the memory of that night in his own dining room. His eye ached, and his good spirits evaporated in the cold air.

Perhaps an agent of Qae'lon. An assassin? A hidden spy from the rebels? Someone who learned about his intentions and wanted to stop him before he could assemble an army to take back Crowspire?

Breathing heavier now, Bekam quickened his pace. If they knew to follow him, they'd likely know where he was headed. He couldn't go directly back to his estate.

Bekam ducked into a side street, intending to circle back to the government square. He could wait this out in his office with his own guards until he was certain the threat had passed. Those thoughts were foremost in his mind when another figure moved into the alley ahead, blocking his progress.

His feet slid to a halt on the icy ground, and he frowned at the familiar face beneath the white hair. "You," he said.

The stern woman from the Council room glared at Bekam without a word as a strong arm slipped around his throat from the back, and a hand pressed a soaked rag over his face. He had just enough time to recall he'd been trained for situations like this before the dizziness claimed him and the daylight faded.

∽

Bekam awakened to the smell of alcohol. He shifted and sniffed, and it took him a moment to open his eye. When he did, everything was still dark. Dear gods, had he lost his other eye as well?

He jerked upright and nearly tumbled out of the chair where someone had propped him. It was every bit as hard a seat as the one in the Council chamber had been, but he lacked the confidence he'd felt while sitting in that other one just a few moments ago. Hours ago? How long had it been?

Bekam blinked, and light slowly crept into his vision, dim though it might be. A single lantern hung from a chain above his head, dangling from the ceiling and casting a wide and solitary circle of light on the floor. The rest of the room remained dark, and he could make out no features that might tell him where he'd been taken. He turned to crane his neck and, belatedly, realized his hands were not bound. His feet were free as well. He sat on a strange chair in a strange room, but nothing kept him there. He leaned forward to rise.

"Stay."

The woman's voice cut through the darkness with sufficient weight to force him back into the chair. He sat back and squinted ahead, toward where the woman must have been, but he could discern nothing.

"Who are you?" he asked. "What do you want?"

Her shoes clicked on the floor as she took a couple of steps toward him, stopping just outside the circle of light. He could see her now, her hair white in the darkness and her chin raised, her jaw set.

"You were in the Council chamber," Bekam said. "What is the meaning—"

His words died on his lips as two more figures stepped closer to him, one on either side of the woman. They moved a step closer than she had, fully revealing themselves to him. Each wore a tight black suit with long sleeves and legs. Over each suit draped a black cloak, the hood pulled up. And, within each hood, Bekam saw black leather masks with holes at the eyes and a beak to cover the nose.

"No," he whispered as a chill ran up his arms. He should have stood and run. He should have attempted anything to escape, but his feet shuffled against the floor, pressing him backwards, pushing him harder against the back of the chair. Fear rooted him to the seat, but his legs wanted him as far away from those masks as possible.

"I have money," he said, his voice trembling now. "I can pay you. I can grant you favors. What do you want? It's yours. I—"

"Be silent," the woman said, and his mouth shut, the teeth clacking together.

The two Nightingales stood ahead of her and at either side but did not move closer than the positions where they had stopped before him. Both of them watched him through the holes in their masks, but the shadows their hoods cast hid anything that might have been identifiable. They stood motionless, as still as sculptures. As still as death itself.

"Is Akithar at Crowspire?" the woman asked.

Bekam blinked at that and coughed before speaking. "Crowspire," he said.

"Crowspire is where the rebels have been hiding, yes? That was your statement to the Council."

"Yes, but—"

"Is the mage called Akithar at Crowspire? Is he with the rebels?"

"I believe so," Bekam said.

"How certain are you?"

"He left Klubridge on a ship that we believe was bound for Stormbreak. Crowspire," he said. "That was the same day the revolts happened. A lot of time has passed since then. He could have gone there and left. He could be anywhere by now."

"But you believe he's still there."

"I do."

The woman nodded. "We think so, too. He left for a time,

though. We have descriptions of him and a small party that traveled south. They passed through Bria and caused some trouble for your Kites."

"Bria... The Amber Kites." Bekam had received word that several of his yellow Kites had been ambushed on a road somewhere near Bria. He'd assumed bandits, but could it have been Akithar?

"He traveled with a party to find the Tamrat scion," the woman said. "They found and retrieved the scion, and we believe they returned to Stormbreak with him."

"The scion... You're not here for me. You're still on the Imperial contract." Bekam felt like laughing, but if he started, he might fall into hysterics and never stop.

"We are hunting the scion," the woman said. "We have a contract for him, not you. Not for Akithar. But finding Akithar will find the scion, so it seems your goals are aligned with ours."

Bekam opened his hands with a half shrug. "You know where they are now. Why don't you just go get them? Kill the Tamrat, kill Akithar, kill all of them, if the urge strikes you."

"Our contract is for the Tamrat scion," the woman said again, and her tone brooked no argument.

Bekam watched her for a long moment, but her face betrayed nothing. The subtext of this conversation was becoming clear, though. "You didn't take me so you could kill me. You're trying to threaten me because you need me. You can't get into Crowspire on your own."

"The Nightingales are resourceful," she said.

"I have no doubt about that. But can they invade a castle full of rebels and find one man inside without alerting the rest of them?" He nodded his head to the side. "Maybe. But I'd wager it would be a lot simpler if you had an army leading you there."

The woman's mouth moved, frowning as she ground her teeth. Finally, she spoke. "As I said, our goals appear to be aligned."

"I will be assembling an army, all right," Bekam said. "Soldiers, Kites, Herons, all pointed north. And you can come along for the trip."

"I sense a bargain coming," she said.

"Just a simple request. I'll help you if you can help me."

"What do you want, General?" She frowned again and shifted, her weight on her back foot now.

"If you will execute a contract for me, I'll bring you to Crowspire. Nobody else has the authority I have right now."

She sighed and said, "It is true that the Council will fund you again. Prusik will receive her orders by the evening." She tapped her front foot once, twice, and asked, "Who do you want killed?"

Bekam licked at his mouth, his lips suddenly dry. "Qae'lon. Kill Qae'lon, and I'll march you straight through the front gates at Crowspire."

CHAPTER 38

Oreth ran his finger under the final number on the page, checked it against the total on the prior page, and shook his head.

"Trouble?" Leyna asked. She'd been sitting at an angle from him for the past half hour, her stool slid back so she could prop a foot on the table.

"The totals are wrong. There should be twenty more pounds of salt." He breathed a weary sigh. "I'll do it again."

"You've done it four times already. I've been watching you stare at that same page for so long you should have memorized it by now." She leaned across and put her hand on the page, covering the numbers so he had to look up at her. "You've been in a mood."

"It's not a mood," he said. Or was it? "She shouldn't be locked up."

Leyna's eyebrows raised. "Aquin Mirada?"

"She didn't do it. She shouldn't be locked up."

"Who else could have leaked the route to the Empire? Who else would have? She started coming here just before the ambush. She had access to all the maps and schedules right under our noses." Leyna pulled her hand back and frowned. "It's infuriating."

"She's just been trying to find her place here. Surely you can't believe what Vaino's saying," Oreth said, even though he already knew she did. He remembered how Leyna had left the depot after Fairy brought news of the attack. Leyna might even be the one who had suggested Aquin to Vaino.

"She's a newcomer here. Nobody knows her," Leyna said.

"I'm a newcomer."

"But you haven't been ranting the whole time you've been here about how you hope the Empire wipes out the rebellion."

Aquin hadn't adapted to Stormbreak as well as Oreth had. At least, not as well as he had until Lizzie upended everything he'd been trying to build there. He shook his head. "She didn't mean all that. Aquin's had a hard time, and—"

"I'd say you had a harder time than she did! You arrived half disassembled and nearly dead. And look at you now."

Look at him now. Betraying the very people who had welcomed him and given him a role. "But this wasn't Aquin. She wouldn't do this. She doesn't even know any Imperials!"

"And you're willing to wager all our lives on that?"

Oreth met Leyna's eyes across the table, and he held them for a few seconds. He was the one to break the gaze when he looked down at the ledger once more. "There might not even be a spy at all."

Leyna chuckled and reached across the table again, this time putting her hand over his. Her palm was warm and soft, but her fingers were harder, calloused from years of tinkering with machinery in the cold. "There has to be a spy, Oreth," she said. Her voice was lower now, and it was slow, almost like she was talking to a child. "How would they have known exactly when and where to wait with the ambush? And to have the right number of people to take the horses and carry off the bodies? This was planned to precision. They knew our route."

"It might not even have been the Empire," he said, but he knew the protest was weak. Of course it had been the Empire. No bandits would have raided a single cart for grain and murdered three rebels. Not when they made better coin than that, acting as lookouts and messengers on Stormbreak's payroll.

Leyna didn't even bother answering that. Instead, she squeezed his hand, gave him a sideways look, and slid off her stool. "I'll give you some time and space to get your thoughts together. We need these ledgers finished by tonight."

He waited until after she was out the door before he let his shoulders slump, and he clasped his hands together on top of the book. Vaino had taken Aquin away, and she'd hardly even protested. Now she was shut away somewhere in the keep, probably behind a barred door, accused of a crime she hadn't committed. A crime Lizzie had done and had admitted to him while making him her accomplice. Magra and Wik and Len were dead, and it was partly Oreth's fault. Mostly his fault. The rebels had trusted him with their most sensitive information about getting supplies in and out of the keep, and he'd guarded the charts and diagrams and timetables just like he was supposed to.

Just like he was supposed to until he'd given supplies to Lizzie and let her roam freely in the depot where she'd stolen a map and seen their schedule. How stupid he had been to trust her. She'd hated Magra ever since Klubridge, when the woman had tricked her and gotten her captured by the Kites. They'd even quarreled several times in the keep, but Oreth never would have imagined Lizzie's anger would have led to this. Not to what amounted to murder.

He pressed his forehead into his hands and tried to force back the headache that had been threatening him all afternoon. It wouldn't be stopped, though, and it wasn't long until his temples throbbed and his eyes ached.

What was he going to do?

He knew the truth and had played a role in the betrayal. Even if he hadn't known Lizzie would give Magra to the Empire, he knew the risks of letting her leave the castle with Reykas that night. He'd fretted over it and over getting caught every moment she'd been gone. He'd told himself it was worth the risk when she came back with Reykas healed, but even that had felt wrong. Was it even what Reykas himself had wanted? Betraying his friends and the rebellion surely wasn't how he would have chosen to be healed, and Oreth had known it.

Should he report them to Vaino himself? Trade his and Lizzie's freedom for Aquin's? That seemed like the just thing to do, but was it the right thing? He could tell Leyna instead and see what she'd say. But no, he knew what she would say. She'd hate him, and she'd tell Vaino herself. Whatever there was between them wouldn't stretch so far as to have her side with him in this matter. Should he stay quiet, then? Let Aquin rot in whatever room Vaino had put her until he decided what to do with her?

If they'd been back in Klubridge, Oreth knew who he would ask about this. He knew who he could trust with the most sensitive of questions and who would never betray his trust. But Apak was far away, off on whatever mission he'd chosen with Naecara Klavan, and there was no use wishing he hadn't gone. Even if Apak had been there, could he have asked for help? Had Oreth already ruptured that friendship irreparably when he had blamed Apak for what had happened in the workshop in Klubridge?

Oreth dropped a hand to his leg and traced his fingers down the crooked bones. That hadn't been Apak's fault. It had been what Apak had warned him about time and time again. The explosion had been Oreth's own clumsiness or carelessness or willful ignorance. Whatever he called it, it had been Oreth's fault. He'd been wrong to blame Apak, but knowing that did him precious little good now.

There was no one at Stormbreak he could truly trust.

Oreth closed his eyes and clenched his fist against his knee. No one other than the person who had gotten him into this situation to begin with. He slid his chair back and pushed himself up from the table, testing his injured leg before putting his full weight on it.

He second guessed himself all the way into the courtyard, through it, and up the stairs, but he made himself push ahead. He'd made his decision, and hesitating would only unmake it. His mind was halfway to allowing that unmaking when he found her in the corridor on the second floor, a bundle of linens in her arms. Lizzie's eyes opened wide when she saw him coming, and she opened her mouth to speak, but he cut her off.

"We have to talk. Now."

LIZANDRA'S DEEPEST FEAR

Lizandra had no time to drop the linens or even to respond. Oreth caught her arm at the crook of her elbow in his surprisingly strong right hand and dragged her along in his wake. Her feet barely kept up with the pace he set, even with his left leg stiff and creaking in its metal brace. They were up two flights of stairs and through the door to the battlements before she pulled herself free and spun to face him.

"Oreth, what's happened? What is this?"

He shoved the door shut behind him and took a second to look past her, toward the empty walkways, before he answered. "What's happened? We've killed three people, Lizzie. We've covered up what we did and lied about it, and now Aquin is paying for it."

"We didn't kill anyone. This isn't your fault. You—"

"I helped you slip out of Stormbreak, and I covered for you while you were gone. I deceived everyone. I lied to Leyna." His face twisted at that last declaration, and he tilted his head away from Lizandra. "I helped you sneak back into the castle, and I kept your secrets. How can you say that's not my fault?"

"You were only doing it to help Reykas. It was only because I asked you to do it."

He snapped his eyes back toward her, and she saw how tired they were. He'd missed sleep and was looking as worn as Lizandra herself had been before she'd made the trip to Karsk. Oreth narrowed his eyes and said, "I'd never have done it if I'd known what you were going to do. How could you agree to that? You let them kill Magra! I know you hated her, but Lizzie... And the others as well. You didn't even know them!"

"That was not the deal I made," she said. And that's what she'd been telling herself for the past few days, after Fairy had returned with the news of the attack. But it was the truth, even if it didn't feel that way now. "I told them I knew where there was an escaped halflock. They were going to recapture her, not kill her."

"Because the Empire is so compassionate," Oreth said. "You

had to know what they would do, Lizzie. You saw it firsthand when they…"

He stopped himself, but she knew what he was going to say. When they killed Dorrin right in front of her. She'd been inches away from saving him, and the Empire had pulled him away and slaughtered him, just like they'd slaughtered Magra and the two others. Why couldn't she even remember the others' names? She was responsible for their deaths. Surely she could give them the dignity of knowing their names.

But she shook her head. "I didn't know, Oreth. You have to know I'd never intentionally do that. I didn't trust Magra, and I didn't like her, but I'd never have sent her to die. They were going to capture her and return her to the Empire."

"She knew where Stormbreak was!" he said, and Lizandra's chest filled with ice. How had she not even considered that the Empire would interrogate the woman and use her to find the rebellion?

Desperation. That's how she hadn't considered it. She had been in Karsk, frozen and distraught, and a cure for Reykas had been within her reach. She had agreed to the terms without giving them half a thought. In that moment, would she have agreed even if she had known how things would end?

That was not a question Lizandra could answer or even wanted to answer. She covered her mouth with her free hand, hugging the bundle of linens to her chest with the other. They were sodden from the snowfall by then, and she'd have to get new ones once she was back inside, but none of that mattered for the moment. "I didn't think," she said. "I made a mistake, Oreth. This wasn't my plan. You know that's not the kind of person I am."

He stared at her for a long moment. Too long, and her heart ached from the sting of betrayal she saw in his eyes. "You tricked me," he said. "You used me and tricked me."

"I didn't—"

"You gave them your map. And you knew where Magra would be because I trusted you enough to not hide the supply schedules when you were around. You knew when and where she would be, and you gave that to them."

LIZANDRA'S DEEPEST FEAR

All of that was true, and there was nothing she could say to make it any better. She'd described only a portion of the supply route and had given the old chemist nothing on paper, but that hardly mattered. She searched Oreth's face for any kind of understanding or compassion, but all she saw was hurt and accusation.

"I don't know what kind of person you are," he said. "Not anymore."

She dropped her eyes and closed them. A single tear escaped and traced a line down her cheek before the chill wind dried it. "What would you have me do? How can I make this right?"

"They've jailed Aquin. They think all this was her. You have to get her out and clear her name. We owe her that."

Lizandra gripped the sheets tighter, and her breath came quick. "You want me to confess to Vaino."

"You have to," he said, but his voice was less sure now. He wouldn't meet her eyes.

"If he knew what I'd done—"

"You can't let Aquin suffer for this. The Empire already tortured her in Klubridge. And now the rebels have jailed her here. Samira wouldn't stand for this."

"Samira isn't here, is she?" Lizandra clamped her mouth shut as soon as she asked the question. "I didn't mean that, Oreth."

He watched her as the wind whipped at his hair, now shaggy and longer than she'd ever seen it. She was barely a year older than Oreth, but he had always seemed so much younger. Not anymore, though. Whether it was his accident or his new role at Stormbreak or his growing relationship with Leyna, something had aged him and matured him. The boy she'd joked with and teased in the back halls of the theater was gone, and the man who stared at her now was someone she didn't know any more than he probably felt he knew her.

"If I tell Vaino, I'll be jailed," she said. "You probably will, too," she added a moment later and hated herself for the addition. But he had to understand what he was proposing. No matter what assurances she'd given him a few moments earlier, Oreth was nearly as guilty as she was. She would not be the only one punished for these acts.

Oreth looked away from her again, and she knew she'd reached him with that plea. "We don't know what they would do with us. And Leyna," she said, the words tumbling out. "How could she ever trust you again if she knew what you'd done?"

He looked at her after that, and she shuffled a step backwards, her feet sliding through the snow mounded on the stone walkway. "Aquin is not going to pay for this," he said.

"There's nothing we can do without being imprisoned ourselves."

"There's one thing you can do," he said. "You're going to tell Reykas what we've done. And, if you don't, I'll tell him myself."

~

Lizandra leaned against the crumbled wall at the side of the castle and studied the snow covering the uneven ground where the rubble had settled. When the top of the mountain looming over Crowspire had fallen countless years ago, it had sheared away this section of the keep and dragged stone and wood and probably soldiers over the face of the cliff to disappear into the icy mist far below. The Imperials seemed to have abandoned the place shortly afterwards, and nobody had ever repaired the damage.

The crushed rooms and collapsed wall gave the place an abandoned air that served the rebels who had been hiding there for the past decade or so, and the view across the mounds of snow and beyond the edge of the cliff took Lizandra's breath. More mountains hovered in the distance, looking as though they floated in the pale blue sky atop the low-hanging clouds that masked the valleys. It wasn't snowing that day, and she could see for what must have been miles.

Reykas stood at the edge of the cliff, his back to her. His stamina had increased quickly over the last few days. The tremors in his hands had faded first, and his appetite had returned shortly after. Then he could sit upright for longer periods, and before long he'd been able to stand and then walk. It would take time for him to regain the weight he'd lost and for his full strength to come back, but there was no question he'd get there. He was cured, and every day showed improvements.

He wore a tan shirt, the sleeves long, the fabric hanging loose off his frame. He had to be chilled to the bone in that thin shirt, but he showed no sign that he felt it. The shirt was an ill fit because of his weight loss, but it reminded Lizandra so much of the billowing shirts he had worn when they would perform together on the Chamberlain's stage. They had soared on wires and twisted and leaped, and they had trusted and supported each other through all of it. That seemed so long ago now, and it was so far away.

The last time Lizandra saw the theater, the Empire had claimed it, and the Scarlet Kites were ransacking it. That night, on the streets with Samira and desperate for a way out, she'd wavered. She had suggested betraying Caius to save the rest of them. She'd never forget the way Samira had looked at her when she'd made that suggestion. Samira hadn't mentioned it again, but Lizandra knew she remembered it and probably thought about it often. Is that who Lizandra truly was? A woman who would betray her friends so easily to save herself? Someone who had been willing to sacrifice Magra to save Reykas?

She shook her head, trying to banish the doubt and the questions, but they lingered. The only way forward was standing at the edge of that cliff, and she knew what she had to do. Lizandra stepped over the low lip of the wall where a layer of ancient bricks remained, and she picked her way across the snow covered rubble.

Still facing away from her, Reykas slid his right foot back and raised his left hand. His fingers curled, and he swept his hand in an arc to the left, drawing a circle in the air. He held the position for a moment before dropping his arms to his sides, bringing his feet together, and starting over again.

"Aren't you freezing?" Lizandra asked as she approached from behind. As she drew nearer, she saw the sweat staining the shirt under the arms and down the center of the back. "How long have you been out here?"

Reykas slid his foot back and extended his hand once more.

"It will come back in time," he said. His voice was still weak, but it was so much closer to the reassuring one she knew and loved.

"What are you doing?" she asked, stopping next to him. His jaw was set, and his eyes stared across the emptiness, toward the distant mountains, with determination. Lizandra glanced at the point where the ground disappeared into nothingness, and a quick wave of vertigo passed over her. She was used to heights in her performances, but this was something else altogether.

He lowered his hand and looked at her with a grin. "The magic. I can feel it just outside my reach." He looked back toward the mountains and raised his hand again, sweeping that same arc.

Lizandra watched him go through the routine twice more, and she saw the hope in his eyes fade to disappointment and back again every time he made the attempt. He curled his fingers at the end of his raised arm a third time, and Lizandra could take no more of it. She stepped closer and placed her hand on his forearm. "It's not coming back," she whispered.

She didn't think he'd heard her at first, but then he allowed his arm to drop again. "The magic will return," he said, "and my health will fail again. It will be as it always is."

"Not this time." She closed her eyes against the words she knew had to come next, and when she opened them again, Reykas was watching her, a concerned frown creasing his face. Confusion played at the corners of his eyes, and Lizandra didn't give him a chance to ask the question she knew was coming. Instead, she said, "I took you to Karsk."

The confusion fled, giving way to a mix of emotions Lizandra couldn't read, even after all this time. He turned away from the cliff's edge to face her and asked, "What did you do?"

There was no doubting her. No surprise or questioning the truth of what she had told him. There was only a mounting dread made manifest in his question.

"You were going to die," Lizandra said. "Pelo Foyen had already died, and everyone was leaving. Caius and Samira and Apak. They were all leaving us, and I was going to be alone here to care for you. I couldn't let you go. You were all I had, Reykas. All I have."

She reached for his hand, but he pulled his arm back just far enough to evade her touch. Again, he asked, "What did you do?"

"I asked Oreth for help. He gave me a cart and supplies, and he helped me slip you out of the castle in the night. No one knows we left. I took you south, and I found the chemist Foyen told us about. All the way there, I didn't even know whether he'd been telling the truth, but he was. It was a man named Jod Padar. He had the cure."

Reykas opened his left hand and gazed into his palm as he flexed his fingers. He made a fist and turned his hand over, looking at the tendons and the veins along the back as if it were the first time he'd seen them. Lizandra could see he wanted to protest, to deny that what she was saying was the truth, but he knew she'd done it. There was no other explanation for his condition. No other explanation for his even being alive.

"This is not what I wanted," he said. His voice was so low the wind nearly carried it away, but Lizandra heard him.

She had no response. What could she say? Nothing other than the one truth that had pushed her to do what she'd done. "I love you, Reykas."

He looked away from his hand and met her eyes, and Lizandra thought she'd never seen anything as sad as the way his mouth formed the words once more. "This is not what I wanted." His lips parted again, and he blinked at her. "My magic. You said it will not come back. The man who died said there was a price he wouldn't pay. You traded my ability for my health."

"No," she said, but then, "Not quite. Pelo Foyen was right when he said the disease was something that comes for mages. Most of us seem to be immune, but if it affects you, it'll always be there for as long as you have your magic. The process of curing you took your magic with it. The sickness can't infect you again."

Reykas crossed his open palms on his chest and looked down, as if he were feeling his own body for the first time. He slid his hands over and down to his elbows until he stood, hugging himself. Lizandra wanted to step forward and embrace him but knew that wasn't what he needed or wanted from her. He needed the rest of the truth, and she couldn't stop there.

"Losing your magic was part of the cure, but it wasn't the price."

He didn't ask her what she had paid, but she had to tell him. She had to be rid of the secret, and Oreth would tell him if she didn't.

"The chemist was an old man, and his wife was a halflock. She could sense things. She could sense what matters most to you. What's most important in your life. I allowed her to sense you."

"You..." Reykas began, but he didn't finish whatever he was about to say. He closed his mouth and angled his head down so he was looking at the snow and not at her. He seemed as if he couldn't look at her and might never again.

"I was ready to sacrifice myself," Lizandra said. "I would have gladly given my life to save yours, and that's what I was going to do if she said I was what was most important to you." Even in this telling, as she bared her crimes before him, she still felt the sting of the old woman's confirmation, and she couldn't keep the edge of bitterness out of her voice. "But it wasn't me."

"You should not have done this," Reykas said, but he still wasn't looking at her.

"It was your loyalty. That's what she said was most important to you. That was the price."

He frowned and did look up then, and he said, "I don't understand."

Lizandra forced herself to hold his eyes as she said, "I betrayed the rebellion on your behalf. I told them how to find Magra."

She'd never be sure whether he looked at her with hurt or disgust or horror in that moment or if it was something else entirely. Whatever he felt, it caused Lizandra to reach for him again, and he pulled back, quicker this time. "You were the one," he whispered. "You traded her life for mine."

"They weren't supposed to kill her," Lizandra said, but the words sounded hollow and weak even as she said them. "They were going to take her back as a prisoner. I didn't know they'd do this."

"Three people are dead," he said. "Nearly four. And this is the

LIZANDRA'S DEEPEST FEAR

price for my life?" Reykas groaned and dropped to his knees, heedless of the snow soaking his trousers.

Lizandra went to him then and touched his shoulders. He jerked away so hard he tumbled onto his side in the snow, and she saw the tears on his face. "This is not what I wanted!" he shouted at her, and she recoiled from him. "What have you done?" he asked, but she knew there was no answer she could give him. He knew everything now, and every tear he shed drowned her soul.

Reykas staggered to his feet, his hands still clutching his arms. He stumbled through the snow and over the uneven stones, his shoulders rounded in a quivering arc. Lizandra watched him go and waited until he'd passed beyond the ruined wall and was out of sight before she cried her own tears. She had been too afraid of losing Reykas, and she'd betrayed everything he stood for and believed in making sure he wouldn't leave her. And now she stood by herself on a frozen cliff behind a decrepit castle, and she'd never felt as alone in her life.

The sadness boiled into rage, and she screamed as she kicked one of the ice-marked stones and sent it careening over the edge of the cliff with a trail of snow following it. She curled her fingers into fists at her sides and poured her anguish into her hands, letting them glow so brightly she had to close her eyes. She bent at the waist, wailing into the void as she thrust her hands forward, fingers wide. A vicious swathe of sharp green light flared out from her body, chasing her cries across the valley. For an instant, Lizandra wanted nothing more than to follow that stone's trajectory and allow the wind to dash her against whatever fate waited at the bottom of the cold mist below, but she knew she wouldn't do it. She was a coward, and that very cowardice had engineered the manifestation of her own deepest fear.

She was alone. More utterly and completely alone than she'd ever been.

CHAPTER 39

Apak had been to Teusas, but that was many years ago, and his visit had been brief and constrained to the outskirts. He had not ventured farther into the city than the inner gates, and his business certainly did not take him up the stairs that wound around one of the sprawling city's square brick towers. But now he sat atop one such tower, unexpected greenery surrounding him in the midst of the urban constructions.

It was midday, and it was comfortably warm that far south. Nearly too warm, if he were being honest. It was hard to believe that winter continued to freeze Stormbreak far to the north, but Apak had lived for so many years in Klubridge that he was used to the seasons changing at a milder and more leisurely pace.

A breeze blew through the rooftop garden where he waited, ruffling the leaves in the broad tree that grew at its center. A gardener, stooped and tending to weeds at the far side of the roof, put a hand up to steady her hat, the brim flapping and threatening to take flight.

"How long have you been able to do that?"

Nahk's question pulled Apak's attention back to the present, and he grunted. "I have never done that. This is my first encounter with the Seal of Metarr." His hand slid to his side and cupped the brown bag that hid the artifact. He had carried it into the city with the strap slung over his shoulder. Dhaz had tried to convince him to let him carry the disc, but Apak was no fool.

"Not the Seal," Nahk said. "Not specifically that." Her voice was low, and it was unlikely anyone would hear her in the emptiness of the garden, but she dropped to a whisper before saying, "The magic. How long have you known you had it?"

Apak squinted against the sunlight that gleamed on the many glass windows scattered across the buildings below them. A low brick wall circled the perimeter of the rooftop, and beyond its edge he could see the western end of Teusas and beyond, as the streets gave way to a flat, green expanse of waving grass. There were no hills in view, and there was no tower to see. Had Dhaz spoken the truth, or was he playing some sort of game with them, wasting their time while he hatched a scheme of his own?

"Apak," Nahk said, and he looked at her once more.

"Always," he said. "I did not understand its nature until I was nearly twenty years old. It has always been with me, though."

"Do your friends know you can do this? That you're a mage?"

Apak wanted to laugh at the absurdity of the question, but he pressed his lips together. Of course they all knew. They had kept each other's secrets for nearly a decade. Samira, with her shields and healing. Lizandra, with her blades of light. Reykas, with his portals. Even Oreth, with his own strange brand of magic augmentation. Oreth had seemed a natural fit as Apak's apprentice. Apak could manipulate magic within inanimate objects, and Oreth manipulated it within living mages. The boy could bend the very magic itself and might have been the strongest of all of them, if he could only learn to harness and apply his gift in the right ways. Apak had taught him the lessons of engineering and machinecraft, of course, but the true schooling had been more arcane.

"They know," Apak said at last.

Nahk did not respond to that and instead stared across the garden and toward the blankness of the grasslands. Perhaps that was the extent of her interest.

But no. A moment later, she asked, "How does it work?"

"Work?" Apak asked, glaring at her beside him on the bench.

"I have no idea, and it is not my place to question, and nor is it yours."

"You think magic is divine."

He did not dignify the implied question with any reply beyond a low snort as he returned his gaze to the horizon.

"You touched the Seal, and you made it work in ways it didn't before. Is that how it works for you? You put power into enchanted artifacts?"

"No," he said. "Well, yes, but it is not limited to artifacts."

Nahk was looking at him again, her eyebrows raised this time. "You can create your own. You can turn ordinary objects into enchanted ones."

"Not as you are thinking of them. The enchantment is temporary." Apak leaned forward and plucked a small stone from the ground. He turned it between his thumb and finger, feeling its smoothness and studying its divots and imperfections. "This rock is perfectly ordinary," he said. He shot a fast glance toward the gardener, but she was still bent with her back toward them. A slight push, and the familiar tingle moved through his hand. The stone heated where he touched it, and a faint red light pulsed from its surface, illuminating the rock and flowing through to all sides. "It now is extraordinary."

Apak rotated his hand, letting the stone roll into his palm, and gave it a gentle push. It floated upward, no more than an inch, but enough to illustrate his point. Nahk watched the display with her lips parted and a line between her eyes. It was not unlike the way Oreth looked when he was trying to grasp some particularly esoteric point in his lessons. Oreth, back in Stormbreak, no doubt satisfied with his new position and purpose as an agent of the rebellion.

Apak sighed and closed his hand, moving it away from the levitating rock. As soon as his hand was clear, the light faded from the stone, and it dropped into the grass with a soft thud. "And so," Apak said, "it is ordinary once more."

Nahk's eyes followed the stone as it fell, and then she sat forward and looked into Apak's face with an intensity she had not previously shown. "Tell me what happened in Klubridge."

Apak wanted to look away, but her eyes held him and called

him to account for the things he had seen and the things he had done. The things he saw and did again night after night in an unceasing repetition in his dreams. He sighed once more. "What would you like to know?"

"The things Dhaz said. Are they true?"

Apak nodded once. "They are true."

"What was the weapon he mentioned? Was it something you enchanted?"

Apak's mouth twisted. "What I do is not enchantment."

"You said that already. Whatever you do, is that what the weapon was?"

"It was a mechanical device I had built for stage productions. For special effects. It…" He stopped and started again. "Its prior purpose is unimportant. I repurposed it to be a weapon, both mechanically and magically."

Nahk listened to his explanation without interrupting. When he had finished, she said, "He claimed you killed people. Imperials. Kites. Was that your purpose when you built the weapon?"

"It was," he said, without hesitation. This was more than he had admitted to anyone, save Oreth the night Apak had unburdened himself to the poor boy as he lay broken and unconscious. The night Apak had sworn to do the very killing he had later done.

"Do you regret it?" Nahk asked.

That question caught him by surprise, and he sniffed in a breath before asking, "Regret the design?"

"The killing."

Did he regret it? He considered his answer, but for less time than he might have expected. "I do not. My friends were in danger and would have died if I had not done what I did. There was justification in my actions."

Nahk's elbows were on her knees, and she clasped her hands, the fingers interlacing. She looked down, either at her hands or past them toward the grass, where the stone had fallen. "Even when it's justified, you can still have regrets."

Apak weighed the truth in the statement before saying, "If the Kites came again and threatened my friends again, I would act exactly as I did in Klubridge. If I had the opportunity to repeat that day, and I could change my actions, I would not. It was through necessity that I destroyed the Kites. It was through necessity, but it was also anger, and it was a promise I made to a friend. Those are consequential factors."

Nahk kept her elbows on her knees but turned her head to look at him. "But you can still feel sorry it had to happen. Even if there's no way around it, and even if it's the only way to keep your friends safe, you can still regret the killing."

There was a strange and plaintive tone in her voice. Apak frowned as he tried to disentangle the implication from the context and from the statements. It was all too woven together, and so he said, "You are not a Nightingale, but you have the training of one."

Nahk nodded, still watching him.

"Killing is a thing you do, and you live with it. You kill for the rebels so that your friends might live. You killed for us as we traveled to Ornamen. It is something you understand must be done, and you are capable of doing it. I doubt Naecara could do it as readily. Alev could not, and I have doubts Kam Dhaz has killed. He has had underlings to do that work for him." Apak considered Nahk, so much younger than he was but in possession of an understanding only the two of them shared.

"You and I are the only ones of this group who understand what it is like to kill out of necessity and without remorse. We have the capability they do not."

Nahk's face darkened, and something changed in the space between her and Apak. She did not move, but the fracture was apparent, even if Apak did not understand what was different. Nahk drew a breath, and she seemed on the verge of some explanation when Alev interrupted from the top of the stairway.

"They're back."

In the years since Apak had been to Teusas, the city had spread farther outward but not upward. The brick towers that housed the local government and many of the local businesses had stood even then, looming over the smaller structures.

As Apak came down the final few steps, his aching knees assured him he would avoid those towers and likely all of Teusas in the future.

Naecara waited at the bottom, a brown cloak around her shoulders with the hood pulled up. Kam Dhaz waited behind her, his hair pulled back in a severe ponytail and a sheen of sweat sparkling on his forehead. He mopped at it with a handkerchief and swore. "You'd hardly know it was winter."

"The temperature is the least of our concerns at the moment," Apak said, keeping from huffing the words out after the long descent from the garden. Nahk had gone down a few steps ahead of him, and she waited with Alev, watching as Apak paused at the bottom of the final step. He ignored the obvious concern in Alev's demeanor and turned to Naecara. "What did you learn?"

"Not here," she said and took his arm. His shoulders stiffened, but he allowed her to pull him into the street. They stepped into a break in the foot traffic and moved west along one of the city's central roads. "Too many eyes," Naecara said, her own gaze shifting from face to face as they walked.

"In here," Dhaz said from their right. "We'll at least be out of the blasted sun."

Naecara guided Apak by the elbow, and he restrained himself from shaking off her grip. He was a wanted man and had a sizable bounty on his head, and he had no desire to draw attention to himself in a crowded city. And so the two of them followed Kam Dhaz off the street and through the open doorways. It was a squat building constructed from the same brick as the towers, but this one was painted white and gleamed so brightly in the sun that Apak had to squint until they were through the doors.

"What is this place?" Alev asked from behind them, but Apak already knew.

Glass displays flanked the entry, and within the one on the left stood a suit of ancient armor. The metal was dull with age, but the gold accents and leafing along the chest shone, even in the relative gloom of the chamber. To the right, a pillar behind the glass case held a tea set that looked as if it might have been porcelain. A blue and swirling design along the upper rims of the cups placed it somewhere in the twenty-second century, if Apak's recollection served him correctly. "This is a museum," he said.

"The Teusans do love their history," Dhaz said. "I sold them some of the pieces in here, not three years ago."

"That speaks volumes about their standards," Apak said and wrinkled his nose at a stack of scrolls behind glass on a wall-mounted shelf, all of them bearing the seal of the High Lord's Aerie.

Dhaz led them through the first chamber and then through two more display rooms, continuing the procession through the labyrinthine building until they were in a space that had to be toward the back of the museum. A few patrons and several students had wandered the displays toward the front, but no one else was this far into the building, back where the old and unpopular displays sat in derelict cases covered in dust.

"My friend knew the tower," Naecara said after scanning the room and seeming satisfied with their solitude. Still, she kept her voice low and tight.

"You seem to have many friends," Apak said.

"This is my part in the—" She stopped herself, clearly about to say "rebellion" and instead continued with, "organization. I cultivate relationships wherever we can. You never know when they'll come in handy."

"Such as now," Apak said and nodded for her to continue.

"Dhaz was mostly right about the tower's location."

"Give me more credit than that. I told you it was to the west," Dhaz said. It was impossible to say whether he took actual or feigned offense from Naecara's slight, but Apak found he did not care either way.

"It's to the southwest," Naecara said. "To our recent ward's credit, it is on a hill, and the fields are strange around it, just like he said. Qae'lon spends a lot of time there and is reclusive whenever he's in residence."

"Is he there now?" Dhaz asked.

"Weren't you there to hear all this firsthand?" Nahk asked.

Naecara rolled her eyes. "He was there, but he was more

interested in the barmaid than the conversation." And then, to Dhaz, she said, "He's there. He's been taking occasional audiences, and he sees visitors by appointment. He's selective about who he sees, though. We're as likely to get turned away as we are to be let in, if we try that approach."

"He knows me," Dhaz said, but his voice held some uncertainty.

"Be that as it may, there's a complication." Naecara hesitated and looked at Nahk before she started again. "There's a contract on Qae'lon's life. The Nightingales are coming for him."

Nahk's eyes went wide at that. "Who hired them? What do they want?"

"That's unclear," Naecara said. "It's likely another Imperial, though."

"Dissent in the ranks," Alev mumbled. "This could be good."

Dhaz was shaking his head, though. "I heard nothing about this. Why didn't you tell me this bit?"

"You would have heard it if you'd had your nose out of that poor woman's cleavage for half a moment," Naecara said.

"They are coming for the Eye of Kelixia," Apak said. It was the clearest explanation. "Qae'lon used the weapon at Klubridge, and now another Imperial envies the power."

"That does make sense," Naecara said. "We can count on the Empire to eat itself from the inside if we're not able to stop them from the outside."

Dhaz had his hand on the edge of a column where an old and neglected urn stood amid a nest of cobwebs. "I say we let them have him."

"You what?" Naecara asked, turning on him.

"This changes everything," he said. "Going after Qae'lon is one thing. The likelihood of success there is slim enough. But getting between him and a crew of Nightingales?" He shook his head again, so vigorously his pony tail wagged behind his head and nearly slapped him in the face. "Let the Nightingales kill him, and we can be done with him. That's our job done."

"What about your desire to be there when Qae'lon goes down?" Alev asked.

"That was before. I'm fully content to watch this play out from afar now that the Nightingales are involved."

"We still need the Eye," Apak said.

"I don't," Dhaz said. "The Nightingales will take it after they do him in, and Qae'lon won't have it anymore. He's the problem, not the Eye. The Eye's existed for… however long that thing has existed. It didn't obliterate a city until it was in his hands."

"And if the Nightingales take it to another Imperial? To the person who hired them?" Naecara asked. "Who's to say they're not as bad as Qae'lon?"

But it was Nahk who responded. "They won't do that." She was studying a display on the wall with two crossed sabers mounted behind a glass box. "If the Nightingales get the Eye, they'll never turn it over to anyone else. It'll be theirs, and that is truly the worst-case scenario. Worse than another Imperial getting it, and it's even worse than Qae'lon having it."

"What do you mean?" Dhaz asked, taking his hand down from the column so quickly the urn shuddered and threatened to rock off its base.

"Qae'lon is devoted to a cause. He has a side in this conflict," Nahk said. "As extreme as his methods are, we know his ultimate goals will align with the Empire. He's predictable. The Nightingales aren't. They can be bought, and there's no telling what they could target if they got possession of this thing."

"But surely anyone who doesn't have the Imperial agenda is better to have it than an Imperial zealot," Dhaz said.

Nahk opened her mouth, but Naecara placed a hand on her shoulder. "Nahk's right. There are things you don't know about the Nightingales. Things nobody should have to know. If they got hold of the Eye…" She shook her head and said again, "Nahk's right. We have to get to Qae'lon before they do."

Dhaz spread his hands. "And how do you propose we do that?"

~

Shortly after lunchtime, a group of students filed into the back rooms of the museum, a lecturer leading them and pointing out various points and pieces of interest. The older man eyed the strange group huddled in the side corner with suspicion, and Naecara shrugged her hood up and led the way back out and into the street. She knew an innkeeper only a couple of blocks away, and that saw them into a private dining room on the first floor of a three-story lodging.

Alev stood by the door, their arms crossed and their mouth turned down in thought. Apak and Dhaz sat across from each other once more, an echo of their first meeting in Ornamen. This time, Naecara sat to Apak's right, hunched over the table with her fingers drumming a nervous rhythm. Nahk stood from her seat across from Naecara and said, "We have to do it now. The Nightingales must be nearby. If we catch them on their way to the tower, they won't suspect anything. We could take the whole team. I could take the whole group."

"How do you plan to do that?" Dhaz asked. "There's nothing deadlier than a Nightingale, and, as I recall, you're not one of them. How are you going to take on a full squad of them?"

"They'll be moving by night," she said and held up a finger to count. And then a second finger as she said, "There will be no more than four in the group. Probably three. They're tough when they know you're coming and they have time to prepare, but we'd ambush them." And a final finger. "If things turned bad, we have the Seal of Metarr. Apak could get us away safely."

Apak shifted in his seat. The role into which Nahk was trying to draft him was not one he could fill with confidence. Before he could protest, Naecara shook her head. "We can't go after the Nightingales, Nahk. That's not why we're here."

Nahk had paced away from the table but rounded at that. "Why are we here, then?"

"To get the Eye of Kelixia. Without the weapon, all of this is for nothing. And we'd be no closer to getting the Eye, even if we took down the whole group of Nightingales."

Nahk's jaw worked as she stared at Naecara across the table. She drew a quick breath and said, "This isn't right, Naecara. This isn't what you promised me."

"I promised you'd get your revenge, and you will. This isn't the time for it. There will be time later."

"You always say that," Nahk said back, her voice rising. "When is later going to be? When it's convenient for you? When you've already taken down the whole rest of the bloody Empire? When you don't need me to kill anybody else for you?"

Naecara sat up, her face softening. "Nahk—"

"No," Nahk said. "I've had enough of this. It's always your priorities. Your schedule. Enough." She spun away from the table and took two steps toward the door before she was toe to toe with Alev. She craned her neck up to meet their eyes and said, "Move."

Alev looked toward Naecara but did not hesitate in shifting to the side. Nahk pulled the door open and slammed it behind her hard enough to rattle the walls in the small room.

"And now we're down our best blade," Dhaz said. He leaned back in his chair, his arm draped casually over the back.

"She'll be back," Naecara said. "It will take some time, but she'll return with a cooler head."

Apak believed her, but something did not sit well with him about that exchange. It was like the unease he felt after the brief conversation he had had with Nahk in the rooftop garden. The pieces still would not fit to show him the entire picture, but it was clear there was something he did not understand about Nahk and her relationship with Naecara and perhaps with the rebellion as a whole. Regardless of that, they still had planning to do.

"It is not a blade that we need," Apak said. "It is intelligence."

"Go on," Dhaz said, and Apak ignored the smirk that tilted the corner of his mouth upward. Apak was accustomed to being mocked, and it discouraged him as little now as it ever had.

"We are unlikely to defeat either Qae'lon or the Nightingales in a direct confrontation," he said. "We need something more clever. Something that they will not see coming."

Naecara tilted her head. "It sounds like you have a plan in mind."

Using subterfuge would need to be at the core of any plan they followed. Apak's eyes scanned the small room, taking in the cutlery piled on a shelf, the bundle of fabric shoved into the back corner, the wires tangled at the ceiling from an aborted attempt to run electricity into the establishment. He inventoried all the parts and pieces, all the elements that could come together into a—

No. Apak was a builder, not a planner. He had planned the incursion into the library at Klubridge, and that had resulted in disaster. A child had lost his life because of Apak's poor planning, and that was not something that would leave his conscience. Just as he had told Nahk, he felt no remorse for killing the Imperials in the plaza that day. No sorrow for the many lives he had taken with the machine he had constructed to obliterate their armor and destroy their weapons. What sat heavy on his shoulders was the one life that had been lost on the rooftop that night in Klubridge. He could never forgive himself for what happened to Dorrin.

"I have no plan," Apak said and dropped his eyes so they would not meet Naecara's and so they would not see the satisfied scorn that no doubt sat on Kam Dhaz's face.

"Qae'lon must have servants," Alev said, breaking the brief silence with a fortunate interjection.

"He does," Dhaz said. "He's a proper dandy. Every time I've seen him, he's had a gaggle of attendants with him."

Alev took a step closer to the table and uncrossed their arms. "We could disguise ourselves as servants. They probably have some sort of common uniform or livery, yes? We get into the tower that way, and we should have the run of the place."

"And how are you going to get these costumes?" Dhaz asked. "Are you in the business of murdering servants now?"

"We could pay them off," Alev said. They looked to Naecara. "We have the seri for that, don't we?"

Naecara's response was hesitant. "We have the seri, but—"

"The risk is too great," Apak finished. "Qae'lon could know all his servants by name and by sight. Even if he does not, could we truly take the chance that coin alone would be enough to buy the servants' silence? Perhaps they are loyal to him. Perhaps he has bound their will with magic."

"Is that even possible?" Naecara asked, her eyes round.

Apak shrugged. "The older I become, the less surprised I am by anything I learn."

"I knew someone who could influence will," Alev said. "If Qae'lon is as powerful as he's said to be, it's not unreasonable to think he could do what Apak is describing."

"We won't do that, then," Naecara said. "What about making some sort of distraction to draw Qae'lon out of the tower? We could sneak in while he's not inside. A fire, maybe?"

Dhaz laughed at that. "These plans are becoming worse by the minute. Qae'lon isn't going to waste his time coming out to investigate a brush fire. That might pull a few servants out to deal with it, but Qae'lon would still be inside for you to handle."

Naecara sighed and propped her chin on her hand. She turned her head toward Apak. "Is there anything you could do? Any kind of magic you could use that would help?"

Apak huffed and shook his head. "I would need some sort of device or artifact or object to enhance. We have nothing other than the Seal of Metarr, and we cannot use it to take ourselves inside the tower. I can increase the Seal's capacity to transport us, but the limitation Kam Dhaz described persists. I would need to have been inside and seen the interior of the tower. The Seal has already taken us as far as it can go."

"What about the tower itself? Could you do something to it?" Dhaz asked.

Apak favored him with a smile of the same sort he gave Oreth when he asked a particularly stupid question. "That is not how it works."

Dhaz rolled his eyes and leaned back in his chair again, his arm draped across the back. He tilted his head back, appearing to study a dark corner of the ceiling, while Naecara sat back and stretched. Disappointment and frustration filled the room as the group's ideas dwindled. Would anything short of a frontal assault be advisable? And would such an attack be at all effective, even with Nahk's skills?

"It's a shame we can't just negotiate with Qae'lon and set a meeting," Alev said. "Naecara's contact said he accepts audiences."

"She said he's as likely to turn one away as he is to accept one," Naecara said.

"We have nothing he would want, aside from each other," Apak added.

Naecara nodded and slouched in her seat, her eyes finding the door. Apak glanced in that direction as well, but it remained shut. He looked back to Naecara, and she still stared at the door, seeming to will it to open. Wherever Nahk had gone, Apak doubted Naecara would rest until she had returned.

Dhaz exhaled a long and loud breath, and his chair creaked as he sat up. He opened his mouth, closed it, and opened it before closing it once more.

"Say something if you have something to say," Apak said. "Stop gulping like a fish."

Dhaz rubbed a hand down his face and shook his head. "I have an idea, but I don't like it."

This pulled Naecara's attention away from the door. "What is it?"

He took another deep breath before he leaned forward. "I can't believe what I'm about to propose."

CHAPTER 40

The innkeeper gave Samira a suspicious eye as she passed through the common room, but she kept her head down and pushed through the crowd. He'd already taken more seri than she'd planned to give him the previous night, thanks to the shortage of lodging in Bria. She wasn't about to waste more of the coin she'd found in Talit's bag, just to keep his tongue from wagging. What did he know, anyway? That a man and woman had arrived with a family of three and rented a cheap room at the top of the stairs. They'd made for an odd group, but he'd soon forget about them, as crowded as the city was getting.

Caius had wanted to ride straight through Bria and find a place to rest farther along the road, but he was barely hanging onto the horse by that point. Samira had seen that kind of exhaustion taking him many times before, and she knew he'd push himself until he couldn't ride another yard, much less past the city. He'd collapse in the saddle, and there'd be nothing she could do for him at that point. It was much better to argue him into agreeing to stop in Bria, and he'd proven easy to sway on that point. Having a ten-year-old boy along for the ride made for a compelling argument for stopping sooner than later as well. Danel Gressam had fallen asleep in front of his father, and Hyden had been keeping the boy upright with one hand while managing the horse with the other. That was another task that would prove easier after a proper night of rest.

Samira stepped aside to let two surly men come in through the front door, and then she was out and into the street. The morning was already bright, later than she'd expected. She squinted down the crowded road and saw the sun well above the edge of the city wall. The city watch lined the sides of the street, but it was clear the passing carts and riders and pedestrians outnumbered them by a large margin.

Most of the passersby shared the same distant, haunted eyes as they stumbled down the street in soiled clothes, their shoes showing holes. A round woman with red cheeks huffed next to Samira and said, "Sorry lot, they all are. Won't be here for long, though, just you see."

"Who are they?" Samira asked, not wanting to stare at the people but unable to keep herself from watching a man leading a forlorn mule with a tiny, filthy girl trailing behind.

"Refugees," the woman said. "They come all the way from Klubridge. Gramery couldn't hold them all, and Craydon wouldn't take them, so this is where they march. They won't find Bria any more welcoming than anywhere else."

Samira swallowed hard and watched a pale woman pass with a ratty valise in one hand and a crying child clinging to the other. All these people had been her neighbors for a decade. They'd lived in the city where she and Caius had settled, and they'd lost everything. It hadn't been her fault or Caius' or even Apak's, but it was hard to keep from feeling the guilt. It hadn't been their faults, but it wouldn't have happened if they hadn't been in Klubridge. Or would it? Would the Kites have found someone else to harass? Probably so, but would they have found someone else who would have fought back as hard as they did? Would they have found others who would incite a full-on rebellion and draw sufficient ire for the Empire to lay waste to the entire city? Unlikely.

Samira saw the contempt in the other woman's eyes as they tracked one poor soul after another. "Where would you have them go?" Samira asked.

"Back where they came from would be fine with me," she

said before she spat into the street and headed back into the shop she'd been tending.

There was food in that shop, but Samira wasn't about to support that woman's kind of selfish bigotry. Another store across the street had a loaf of bread painted on the front window, so she headed that way, weaving through the crowd that was moving from east to west. She dodged the nimble fingers of a cutpurse midway through the crowd. It had been rare for the street kids to try and rob her in Klubridge, but she'd still been savvy enough to avoid any attempts. The people of the Theater District had known her and recognized her, and that had usually translated into an unwillingness to lift her purse. Not so in Bria, even from these refugees, some of whom might still recognize her if they weren't so desperate themselves. Imperial bounties had a way of jogging memories, though, and she ducked her head once more and pulled the collar of her coat a little closer to her face. It was unlikely anybody would spot her, even among these Klubridge travelers, but she'd rather be safe about it.

Samira opened the front door to the shop and immediately smelled the bread that had been painted on the window. It was a warm and wholesome smell, and it reminded her, oddly, of the kitchens at Stormbreak. The food there was not exceptional, but there was always something baking in the ovens. The aroma was welcome every time she passed near the kitchens, and she felt a tug of nostalgia for that terrible and remote keep. Not for the keep, but for the people she'd left there. What was Aquin doing in her absence? Would things be better after Samira returned? And what would have become of Lizzie by then? Samira stopped herself before her thoughts could turn to Reykas. Grief was a luxury she couldn't allow herself just then, so she focused on the display ahead of her and the assortment of warm pastries on display behind the glass.

"Help you?" the short man behind the counter asked. He wore a white apron and was bald but for a fringe of gray hair around the back of his head. His nose twitched above a matching mustache as he wiped flour on a dark rag.

Samira looked through the glass, appraising the loaves, but

hesitated. "Has it been busy in here?" She glanced to the side, seeing that she and the baker were alone in the shop.

He shrugged and sat the rag aside. "Slow business today, yesterday, every day," he said. "And still I bake."

"There are so many people in the streets."

"None of them with coin. They left everything behind or lost it when Klubridge fell. And anything they didn't lose then, they've lost since, on the way here." He shook his head and pursed his mouth. "Sad thing, the displacement of a people."

"What do you think will happen to them?" Samira asked.

He shrugged again and leaned forward against the counter. "That, I can't say. They have no future in Bria, though. The watch'll send them away. They can go north, they can go south, but they can't stay here."

Samira frowned at that. "On whose orders?"

"The mayor's, I expect. Or the watch captain? Someone who knows more than I. Now," he said, "do you have coin, or shall I have to send you on your way as well?"

She had coin and left the shop with three loaves wrapped in parchment and tucked under her arm. It wasn't the finest dining, but it would keep them fed long enough to plan their next move. If Caius would even eat it. He'd said he was hungry the night before but hadn't touched his food. He'd been growing weaker and more tired with every mile they traveled. She could see the exhaustion coming on him day by day and, despite her assurances to him, did not know what was happening to him or how she could help. The most she could do at the moment was see him safely back to Stormbreak, where they at least had doctors who might recognize this sort of thing.

Samira rapped three times and then once more on the door and glanced down the dark hallway. It was well into the morning, but the other visitors hadn't yet arisen from their rooms. It was a cheap inn in a cheap part of town, and there'd been a lot of drinking happening in the common room past midnight. Some of those beds might not vacate until well into the afternoon.

She heard the chair slide away from the door before Hyden pulled it open and peered into the corridor. There were no locks here, so they'd done the best they could with pushing furniture against the door as they slept.

"You found food?" he asked as he pulled the door open.

"I did." She handed him two of the loaves and came inside. Phyla and Danel sat on the edge of the bed to the right. Danel looked tired and bored, but his mother's eyes were wide and sought Samira's.

"You must tell us now," Phyla said. "What happened last night? We have to know."

Samira looked at Caius, a lumpy shape under a thin sheet, still sleeping in the bed on the left. He was on his side, turned toward the wall, and he let out a soft moan when she sat on the corner of the mattress. His sleep tormented him, but he needed the rest. She would let him slumber for as long as she could before they had to leave. It wouldn't be for long, but every bit helped.

She crossed her hands on her lap, holding the third loaf of bread, and said, "The Aescalan were going to abduct you. I don't know what they were going to do with... Akithar and me, but it was probably something dire."

"I don't understand," Hyden said. "You're all part of the same rebellion, aren't you?"

"We all want the Empire to fall, but there are a lot of different thoughts about the best way to get that done. There's an organized rebellion with soldiers, leaders, all of that. They're waiting for us at the end of this journey."

"And you still can't tell us where that is," Phyla said. Danel leaned into her side, and she rested her arm around his shoulders without taking her eyes off Samira.

"It's safer for you if you don't know," Samira said. "The Empire has mages who can hear your thoughts. If you don't have the information, they can't take it from you. We're going to get you to the rebels' hideout, and you'll be safe there until this is done. They call the place the Stormbreak Sanctuary."

"You said there were different thoughts about how to see it done," Hyden said. "What is the Aescalan's way?"

"They care only about you. Not about your family, and certainly not about the rebellion here in Teshovar. They come from people who hate this realm and everything and everyone in it. They want to use you to inspire their armies, and they plan to invade Teshovar and destroy everything."

"Not just the Empire," he said.

"Not just the Empire."

Caius shifted, and Samira looked over her shoulder at his sleeping form until he settled again before she continued. "They had no intention of bringing you to Stormbreak. They were going to get rid of us and take you wherever they wanted to take you. Possibly back over the sea to where they came from. They see you as some kind of savior, Hyden. They think they're unbeatable with you at the front of their armies."

"This is absurd," he said. He sighed and handed one loaf to Phyla. "And now we will have Dekan Hama and his people hunting us, along with the assassins and whoever else you said already wanted us."

"If they survived the fight," Samira said. She had little doubt Hama and his people were more than a match for those Imperials, even if they were Kites. There was always the chance the Aescalan were dead, but they couldn't and shouldn't count on it. "Either way, we need to get back to Stormbreak as quickly and as quietly as we can. Hama had maps of the back roads we took when we came to Bria, but we don't have those. We'll have to travel the main roads to Karsk, and that means going near Salkire."

"Salkire," Hyden said. "I thought we were avoiding the Empire, not riding straight into it."

"Salkire should be all right, as long as we're careful. There's an old fortress on a hill, but the true power is north from there, in Aramore. That's the city we'll be avoiding. We're going to slip past Salkire and head west."

Hyden accepted her decision but looked at his wife. They shared some unspoken communication Samira couldn't decipher, and he looked back at her. "Is he ill?" He nodded toward Caius.

"No," she said. "He's just exhausted."

Hyden held her eyes for a long moment and asked, "Will he be able to make the trip?"

"Of course he will," she said with what she hoped sounded like conviction, but she broke the gaze first.

～

The traffic along the main road north became congested after a couple of days' travel. They should have been a few hours away from where the road forked, but the way was nearly impassible by then. Samira didn't know the name of the woman who drove their wagon, and she didn't know the names of any of the three children she assumed were the woman's or of the man who seemed to be an older brother or uncle. What they didn't share in names or stories, they did share in haunted stares up the road clogged with displaced people, animals, and vehicles. Packed together, they all crawled forward at an achingly sedate pace, gradually nearing the point where the road would split north to Salkire and west to Karsk, but taking twice as long to get there as they normally would have.

Samira sat in the back of the wagon, her back bumping against the sideboards every time the wheels rolled over another rock in the road. She looked back and nodded to Hyden on the horse just behind them. He returned the nod but kept his face impassive, his back straight, and his hands wrapped around the reins. The other two horses they'd taken from the Aescalan were pulling the wagon, their heads bowed as the caravan made its slow way up from Bria. It had been a fair trade. Two horses to pull the woman's cart, in exchange for a ride in the wagon, extra clothing for all of them, and the anonymity of traveling among the endless line of refugees.

"This is too slow," Caius said. He sat beside Samira, his knees tucked close and his arms wrapped around his legs. They'd made it far enough to feel winter again, and the first snowflakes had settled on his knees a few minutes earlier. The two of them shared the space with Phyla and Danel, sitting across from them, and all the refugee woman's worldly belongings piled around them.

"We wouldn't be making any better progress if we'd stayed on horseback," Samira said. She kept her voice low, but it was unlikely the woman or anyone else would hear her amid the rumble of voices and footsteps and creaking carts and whinnying horses.

She studied Caius in profile, ready to look away if his eyes turned in her direction, but they remained fixed on the lumpy bag of the family's clothes that sat between his feet. It was hard to tell whether the sleep he'd gotten in Bria had helped or hurt him. He seemed more alert now, but also more haunted. Every time he slept, it was as if he awoke with another piece of himself chiseled away.

Samira was about to ask if he was all right, a question she already knew was useless, when the wagon lurched forward again, and the woman in the driver's seat mumbled something. "What was that?" Samira asked.

"Checkpoint at the fork," the woman said. "Bloody Imperials."

Phyla grabbed Danel's hand and turned toward the back of the wagon, toward her husband. Samira reached across the bundles and bags to touch her shoulder. "Calm," Samira said, her hand gentle but firm enough to push the other woman back to where she'd been sitting.

"Are you mad?" Phyla asked, her eyes wide. "Didn't you hear what she said?"

"I heard, and there's nothing we can do about it. We're almost to the fork now." Samira shot a quick look past the driver's head. She couldn't see the checkpoint yet, but it was coming soon if the driver had already seen it. "If we jump out now, they'll see us. We'd have nowhere to go, anyway."

"What, then?" Phyla pulled Danel against her, and he frowned up at his mother.

Before Samira could conjure an answer Phyla would accept, Caius spoke. "We do like Samira said. We have to be calm. We're just refugees. We've been run out of our homes, and we're trying to find somewhere safe."

Phyla hesitated but finally said, "That's not exactly untrue."

"Not for any of us," Samira said. For what must have been the hundredth time, she watched the people moving slowly ahead of, behind, and around their wagon. How many of them had she crossed paths with in Klubridge? How many of them might have even come to the Chamberlain and seen their performance? Those thoughts bound her to these people with a desperate kinship, but they also reminded her to keep her face down and her voice low. The refugees were desperate, too, and claiming a bounty on a woman they suddenly recognized from some magic show they'd attended last year would go a long way toward setting any of them on firmer ground.

"Something's happening ahead." The voice at her back startled Samira out of her thoughts, and she half turned to see that Hyden had brought his horse even with their cart.

"An Imperial checkpoint," Samira said. "We're going through just like everyone else. Stay calm, and stay quiet, and everything will be fine."

"Intercessor," Caius said.

Hyden frowned, and Samira blinked at him. "What did you say?"

Caius' eyes were back on the bag at his feet.

"What did you mean?" Samira asked and put a hand on his arm.

Caius swayed with the slow rocking of the wagon wheels and studied the cargo before him but had nothing else to say.

Caius tugged his coat tighter around his shoulders, but it wouldn't quite close at the chest. He'd gotten it as part of the bargain with the refugees, and he suspected it had belonged to one of the woman's older children before it came to him. It was woolen and heavy and rough, and even though it wouldn't fasten in the front, it still kept him warm enough to venture out the front door of the inn and into the cold darkness. It hardly mattered that it was night. During the day, the sun should have cut through the chill, but they were in Karsk now. They'd spent enough time in the north for him to know the winter clouds conspired against any sort of warmth the sky might offer. He'd been just as cold when they'd arrived in the city that afternoon

LIZANDRA'S DEEPEST FEAR

as he was now, just past midnight. At least it wasn't actively snowing, but how long would that last?

They had made it safely through the checkpoint south of Salkire and into the mountains, according to Samira. Caius remembered little of the journey, although he believed he'd been awake the entire way. Time had blurred somewhere between Bria and Karsk, but he remembered rolling into the city and through the open gate in the big, black walls. He'd become untethered again, but Samira had told him they'd found an inn with a compassionate owner who was taking refugees. The family from Klubridge had decided to stay there and go no further, and that was the end of the journey for all of them. They couldn't very well make the trek from Karsk up to Esterburgh on foot and then from there up to Crowspire. Not with a young boy. And not with whatever Caius was becoming.

That's not how Samira had said it, but that's how it felt. It was like he was leaving his body and losing all form of consciousness, and it was coming more frequently. When it had started, it had only been every few nights, and then it had become every night. More and more, he'd been keeping himself from falling asleep, but the periods of blankness still found him whenever his eyes inevitably slipped shut during the daytime. The dreams came every time now, and sometimes they propelled him out of his bed and into action. Exhaustion dragged at every bone and every muscle, but he refused to rest. Sitting meant relaxing, and relaxing meant sleep, and sleep meant... something different now than it always had before.

Samira was asleep, though. She had taken a room for herself and Caius and the Gressams. The innkeeper believed all of them had been run out of Klubridge as well, and that wasn't really a lie, was it? The Empire had chased Samira, Caius, and all the rest of their troupe out of the city just before they'd destroyed the rest of the population. It was just a small fib to bring the Gressams in with them. And the Empire had seen to it that they were as much without a home now as all the rest of them were. But, for one night at least, all these people had a place to sleep in peace, and Caius had slipped out once he was sure Samira's breathing was too regular to be faked.

It was too easy to fall asleep there in the darkness, while the others slept an arm's length away from him. Forcing himself out into the cold of the night was sure to keep him awake, at least until sunrise. Samira wouldn't have approved of his nighttime jaunt, and she wouldn't have to know about it if he returned to the inn before she woke.

Bria had been packed day and night with people, everyone jostling shoulder to shoulder as the refugees piled into the city. It had been like a more desperate and compressed version of everyday life in Klubridge, all funneled into a city that was not ready for that influx of hope and misery. Karsk at midnight was an entirely different place, both literally and figuratively.

When Caius stood outside the inn, the emptiness of the street chilled him nearly as much as the winter air did. Gas fueled the lanterns that hung outside buildings up and down the roadway, but there was no sign of another person in either direction. Granted, this inn was off the beaten path, and the main streets probably saw more traffic, but for the time being, Caius stood alone in silence.

He exhaled again and ran a hand over his face. If he could hold on until they got back to Stormbreak, he would consult the doctors, but how much could they truly help him? Samira had found no injury that she could heal, and it was doubtful that what was happening to him was any sort of persistent disease. If it were his own mind devouring him, what then? What could he do about such an invisible and internal predator?

Caius dropped his hand and glanced up the street to the right as a bitter wind creaked the hanging gaslamps against their mountings. The gust ruffled his hair and tugged at his collar, and he was halfway to pulling the coat tighter around his neck when he heard the whisper in his ear.

He stopped moving entirely, his hand just brushing the front of the coat and his head cocked to the left. He held his breath, and his pulse thudded loud in his head. Caius waited, certain he'd imagined it, but it came again.

The whisper, definite and present but incomprehensible.

The words formed loosely, sibilant, drifting away even as they were spoken, but he was certain they were there. He spun to the right and back to the left, sure someone would be at his back, but he still stood alone at the edge of the street. His heart beat faster, and he took in a deep breath of the night air. He was awake. He was positive about that. But that whisper had all the unreal and incorporeal qualities of the dreams that had been haunting him since they left Klubridge.

Caius stepped into the empty street and stood at the middle of the road, and he turned, scanning the buildings and their windows and the rooftops for any sign of life. For any indication that someone was toying with him. And still he stood alone, no—

The whisper came again, this time borne on still air and without the wind pressing it forward. He couldn't understand the words, but somehow the intention was clear. It pressed him forward, guiding him down the street to the left and away from the inn.

It was more an instruction and less an urge of his own, though the lines between the two were blurring. That was the correct way to go, and his legs would carry him to where he needed to be. Caius frowned as he walked, and he hunched his shoulders and cupped his palms over his elbows, hugging himself against the cold. This made no sense, and he did not know what was guiding him or where it was taking him, but he felt no desire to resist the pull. The need to walk hummed in his veins. He doubted he could have resisted it even if he'd wanted to.

Caius took a right at the first cross street and walked up the middle of the empty road toward the next intersection ahead. Two squat buildings made from rough stone sat at the corners ahead of him. The whole city seemed to have been pieced together, block by block, with that same black rock. It glimmered with a wet sheen in the pale moonlight, pitted with uneven shadows and streaked with frozen runoff from the snow-mounded roofs. The wind whistled down an alley to Caius' right and stung his cheeks, but he pushed onward toward the intersection.

The sound of the wind gave way to an unfamiliar grinding sound, and Caius stopped, one foot sliding an inch on an icy patch on the road. The urge to move forward had abated with the introduction of that new noise, and Caius stepped out of the street, putting his left hand against the side of the building at the corner. The grinding was louder there, and it increased in volume as it neared. He risked a glance around the corner to the left and saw a cart approaching, pulled by two huge horses, blinders shielding their eyes. Lanterns swung from both sides of the wagon, casting maddening shadows over the driver.

Caius pulled back from the corner and into the shadow of the building as the cart reached and passed his street. The horses clopped ahead, their hooves crunching through piles of snow and ice, and the cartwheels spun behind them, making rickety progress down the road. The grinding noise followed the cart, and Caius squinted at the heavy, angular block dragging behind the cart, attached to the rear with heavy chains. The chains jangled as the construction bumped over uneven spots in the road, but they remained mostly taut as the wood dragged along the street, its shape wildly similar to the prow of a ship. And, much like a ship split the sea, the wide block of wood cut through the fallen snow and ice, shoving the slush out of the middle of the road and depositing it onto the curbs at either side.

Obviously, they'd need something like that plow for clearing the streets this far north, and it made sense they'd do it in the middle of the night, when every sensible person was indoors and avoiding the night chill. Caius wasn't alone in the frozen streets of Karsk that night, after all. He took a step off the curb as the cart passed, ready to round that corner, but pulled his foot back before the horseman behind the cart spotted him.

A single rider followed the snow wagon, his horse walking the cleared street with care. The man held the reins with black-gloved hands that matched the thick, dark fabric of his pants. What drew Caius' eye, though, was the blue gambeson the man wore with the black bird insignia on his chest.

"Kite," Caius whispered and covered his mouth as soon as he'd spoken. The noise of the plow had been loud enough to mask the single word, and the rider kept his eyes ahead,

LIZANDRA'S DEEPEST FEAR

watching the cart's progress. He didn't look to the right to see Caius shrinking back into the darkness.

It had been the Scarlet Kites that came to Klubridge and destroyed his life, but seeing one of the soldiers in blue filled Caius with nearly as much dread as seeing one in red might have done. The Scarlet Kites had been strangers, interlopers into Klubridge, and their inability to understand the city had gone a long way toward ensuring their own downfall. Caius knew the Azure Kites, though, and their commander. He was a reasonable man named Tereth who'd never caused trouble for Caius or any of the rest of the troupe. As reasonable as Imperial mage hunters could be, at least. He and his Kites had been missing from Klubridge when the Scarlets arrived, and Caius had tried in vain to find out where Tereth had gone. He had his answer now. Where one Azure Kite rode, all the others were sure to be near.

Caius looked back down the darkened street, back toward the inn. He knew the Azure Kites, and many of them knew him. They'd be likely to recognize his face, even outside of Klubridge, and the bounty on his head made recognition even more probable and even more dangerous. The smart thing would be to return to the inn, wake Samira and the others, and find the fastest way out of the city. That was the smart thing, and it was nearly what Caius did.

As the plow and the rider behind it disappeared into the night, though, the buzzing returned to Caius' veins and pulled him around that corner. He would return to the inn later, after he'd finished... whatever he was doing. Something called to him, and he followed. The path took him up the street and through a couple more turns, eventually bringing him into one of the city's major thoroughfares. Taverns had their windows lit there, and music poured into the street as late-night drinkers staggered past him, out one door and into another a few buildings down.

Caius scowled at the people who shared the street with him and glared at the glowing windows. He shouldn't be there among these people. He should be back at the inn, hidden from sight and telling Samira about the Kites. But his legs pulled him onward another thirty feet before turning him into an alley on the left. He wouldn't have spotted the break between buildings if he hadn't felt compelled to walk into it.

Dirty gray piles of snowy slush and ice packed into the corners where the walls of the neighboring buildings met the alley floor. Discarded refuse had frozen onto the cracked paving stones, leaving the whole narrow corridor in disarray. The far end of the alleyway was black, but light from the street behind Caius helped him make his way without stumbling on anything. His shadow loomed long in front of him, and it obscured a pile of filthy rags heaped against the building on the right until he shifted, letting the light hit it.

The hairs on Caius' arms tingled beneath his sleeves. It felt like the static pull of the electrical devices he'd studied in the backstage rooms of the theater before the Kites came and ruined everything. Were those machines and gadgets still in those workrooms? Was the Chamberlain even still standing? His thoughts drifted toward Klubridge, and he didn't realize he'd been walking toward the heap of stained fabric until he stood over it and was already leaning down to grasp the corner of one of the rags. He pulled it back, and gleaming, wild eyes stared up at him.

Caius stumbled backwards, his back colliding with the opposite wall. He would have cried out in surprise, but his throat locked and allowed no sound to escape.

"You." The man hissed at Caius as he shifted and pulled himself to his feet. "You!" he shouted, his voice hollow and harsh. A long beard covered most of his face, and his hair hung in tangles around his head. It was hard to tell where his ruined clothing ended and the heap of rags where he'd been sleeping began. The man raised a thin arm, the fabric falling back to show the dirt staining his thin and wrinkled skin. "You!" he yelled once more and staggered toward Caius.

Caius tried to speak, but pain stilled his voice. He wrapped his arms around his midsection and fell to a knee on the hard, wet ground, as his stomach seized. A cramp unlike anything he'd ever experienced squeezed at his guts and felt like it was tearing his insides apart.

"Demon!" the man bellowed as he moved forward another

step. Spit hung from his lips, stringing into his beard, and a manic fervor ignited his eyes. It was impossible to tell how old he was behind all that filth and hair. "Demon!" he shouted again, and Caius lurched away from the man, falling backwards on the cold pavers.

Repulsed, Caius got his knees under him again and pushed most of the way to his feet, but the pain still gnawed at his stomach and kept him stooped. He steadied himself with a hand on the wall and shuffled away from the screaming man, backwards toward the busy street and the lights. Anything to get away from this confrontation. The man growled something that sounded like a curse in a language Caius didn't know and was still coming after him, still pointing with that rail-thin arm.

Caius' fingers wrapped around the corner of the building, and he was at the edge of the alley, almost back into the street. He tried to turn his head to look behind him, but his eyes locked with the crazed man's, and the cramp in his gut became something definable. Hunger rushed outward from that pain. A hunger worse than he could remember rooted him in place, and his mouth wet with anticipation. The hunger was urgent and scrabbling for purchase, and its focus was on the man stumbling up the alley.

There was just enough time for Caius to see the mad shine in the man's eyes that matched the vague golden aura that glowed from his filthy, extended hand before the man lunged. His bony hands were at Caius' throat and then on his face, shifting and scrabbling toward his eyes, his nose, anything that could be grabbed or torn. The light of whatever magic the man carried was blinding when shoved in his face, and Caius fell backwards. The man was on top of him, his face above Caius' and his breath reeking like sulfur.

The madness of fear and anger and hunger drove Caius to scream back into the man's face. It was a mournful keening, a wail that came from deep in Caius' throat and deeper, up from his belly. Before Caius could stop himself, he turned his head and clamped his teeth on the man's hand. The magic flared and peeled off the man's body, flowing into Caius' mouth and up his nose as he sucked in a quick breath. He bit through the dirt and through the skin and into the soft meat at the base of the thumb and chewed, still screaming around the torn flesh and blood that now wet his face. The hunger was primal and cannibalistic, and the two men's shouts mingled into one furious howl.

As quickly as it had happened, the other man lifted away, hauled up and off Caius, and Caius saw the shock in the man's eyes as hands pulled him back. "Demon!" the man screamed once more, shaking his bloody hand at Caius. "A demon rides him!" A bigger man had his arms around Caius' attacker now, pulling him away and shoving him against the alley wall. Caius shifted up onto his elbows and scrambled to his feet. He touched his face and rubbed his fingers over his mouth, and they came away red in the light from the street.

"Are you all right?" the newcomer asked Caius. Without waiting for an answer, he spun the man from the alley around and slammed him face-first into the side of the building, one hand on the back of the man's neck and the other twisting his bloodied hand behind his back. "Bloody halflock," the bigger man said, and Caius saw the vague outline of the scar woven into his wild hair. "Must have escaped somewhere nearby."

"I think I'm all right," Caius said, not at all certain that was the truth. His jaw and teeth ached, and he spat the other man's blood onto the ground. He glanced at it, half expecting it to glow with whatever golden power he'd seen. But no, it was just flesh and blood, as ordinary as anyone else's would have been. Caius wiped a hand over his face again, and he saw the blue of the uniform before him. The Azure Kite's back was to him, but there was no mistaking the cut of that gambeson or the weave of the fabric. The black-haired Kite had the other man's chest pressed against the wall, and he turned his head toward Caius.

Commander Tereth locked eyes with Caius, and every emotion fled aside from fear. Was it dark enough at the edge of that alley to make Caius a stranger to Tereth? Did Caius look different enough from Akithar, now gaunt and bearded and with blood covering half his face? The men regarded each other for a long moment before Tereth nodded. "Get off the streets, then."

Without another word, Caius turned away and forced himself to walk until he was certain he was out of the Kite's view. He then broke into a loping run that carried him all the way back to the abandoned streets, where the darkened inn waited.

∼

When Caius woke Samira, the room had been too dark for her to see the state he was in. She'd just felt his cold hand on her arm and sensed the urgency in his voice. Just a few minutes later, however, they were downstairs with the Gressams, all of them yawning and trying to shake themselves awake, and Samira saw his face by the light of the fireplace.

"You're hurt! What happened?" she'd asked.

"I'm fine," he'd told her, but his tone was anything but convincing. "It's not my blood."

That was less than a reassuring response, but she knew him well enough to know that's all she would get out of him that night. She'd made him wash up before they'd left the inn, and they'd slipped out the side door without alerting the innkeeper or any of the other guests. They had left their one remaining horse in the stable attached at the back of the inn, and the other two horses they'd traded to the Klubridge family were back there as well. Samira had paused only a few seconds before telling the others, "They won't need the horses now. They're staying here." Phyla had seemed skeptical of the logic of this thievery but hadn't acted to stop the actual theft. Not long after, they were on the road again and headed north through the Karsk gates, black and towering against a sky that was nearly as dark.

Clouds hid the moon and the stars the rest of that night, and they rode as much by intuition as by keeping their horses on the path between the dim impressions of snowbanks at either side of the road. The journey to Esterburgh was rough, with Caius sharing the horse with Samira again. Once they reached the town, they stopped for just long enough to have a meal and trade the last of their seri for another horse. Progress was quicker once Caius could ride on his own, but Samira kept him in her sight, not liking the recent prominence of his cheekbones or the way the skin pulled tight over his forehead. His whiskers were going white at the chin, a distinguished look under other circumstances, but not something she wanted to see developing in her friend alongside his other troubles. Despite his evident exhaustion, he stayed alert and upright on his saddle, and he didn't seem to have any more of his dreams or hallucinations or whatever they were for the rest of the trip. None that he told her about, at least.

It was with some trepidation that Samira rode north, but the roads became too tricky for her to worry about Caius more than she worried about her horse's footing. There were switchbacks and sections of the road that ice had made impassable. There were side paths and steep inclines where they had to dismount and lead the horses upward. There were days of wind so sharp she was certain it would cut her face to ribbons, only for all of them to emerge unscathed aside from some pinkness in their cheeks.

And then, just before their meager food supply would have run out, that ugly and misshapen summit emerged from the cloudy haze ahead of them. The suggested shape of the bird with a broken head stood against the gray sky, the top jagged and angled where the peak had fallen ages ago. It was a foreboding and ugly and desolate thing, and Samira was sure she'd never felt as glad to see a landmark in her life.

"The shield's down," Caius said, riding next to her now.

"What?" she asked, peering ahead, but then she saw it. There was no telltale arc of snow above the keep. The invisible barrier was gone. "Apak must still be gone with the others. Vaino only has one barrier mage now."

Samira squinted against the sun that backlit the ramparts. The silhouettes of what must have been two sentries stirred between the old blocks at the top of the wall, and one moved out of sight. They'd spotted the approaching party.

The four horses crossed the narrow covered bridge without challenge, and they'd nearly reached the stable to the left of the main gate when a sturdy man wrapped in heavy wool came out the door to the right of the gate. His hand strayed toward the sword he wore at his hip, but he relaxed his arm after he saw the sorry state of Samira and Caius and the others.

"What's your business?" he asked, his voice gruff but bored. He knew they were rebels of some sort, but duty obligated him to ask the question.

"This is the mage Akithar," Samira said. "Micah Vaino sent us to find these people and bring them here."

The guard's eyes passed over each of them in turn, lingering for an extra second on the family of three before he called toward the stable. "Iza, there's visitors." And then, to Samira, "She'll handle the horses. You wait here." He left them there beside the stable and went back through the door and into the keep.

A teenage girl rushed out the barn doors, hay stuck to her sleeves and shoulders and sleepiness still tugging at her eyes. "In here! In here!"

Samira shot a quick glance at Caius, and he gave her a brief shrug in response. They rode through the big doorway into the barn, and Samira slid off her horse first. She moved to help Caius down, but he was already halfway out of his saddle.

Samira turned to Hyden Gressam and said, "We should see Vaino. He's the leader of the rebellion and will want to talk with you."

"What am I supposed to do here?" Gressam asked.

"That's something Vaino can tell us," she said. And then, to Caius, "How are you?"

He gave her a tired but honest smile. She still wasn't used to his too-thin face and the beard going white at the chin. "I'll survive," he said.

"I want you to see a doctor."

"I will, but Vaino first."

She pressed her lips together. She could argue, but it would be a losing battle. "Fine," she said. "But you see the doctor immediately after."

He nodded his reply, and that was good enough. Something over Samira's shoulder caught his attention, and she turned to see the guard coming through the door on the opposite side of the barn. "Vaino wants to see you," he said and jerked his head back toward the keep.

"That was quick," Caius whispered.

Samira motioned for the Gressams to follow, and she walked behind the guard, leading the group out of the stable and into the keep itself. The place was as busy as it had been before they'd left, but only a few of the faces were familiar. Did rebels come and go that quickly? Several sets of eyes, most of them from strangers, tracked their progress along the edge of the courtyard. The guard motioned them toward the closed door to Vaino's office.

Samira turned to speak to Caius, but his attention was on the opposite corner of the square. She followed his gaze, and her eyes widened. "Ranja," she whispered.

The Aescalan woman sat on a bench, her left foot propped on her right knee. She'd paused in sharpening a knife, the whetstone in one hand and the blade in the other. She sat with her shoulders hunched, her hair dangling at the sides of her head where it hung loose, her amber eyes piercing Samira's. Ranja sat motionless and didn't reach for the rifle propped casually against the side of the bench. That had to be the same rifle she'd used to try to murder at least two of them. Her gaze was intense but emotionless, and she didn't blink when a quick breeze stirred her hair across her face.

Phyla put her hand on Danel's shoulder and pulled him against her side. The boy looked up at his mother and tried to squirm out of her grasp, but she held him tight.

Samira should have known the Aescalan had come back here. They'd known exactly where she and Caius would take the Gressams. All they'd had to do was follow the path north and wait for their scion to arrive.

Samira flinched as the guard rapped his knuckles on the office door. Three quick bangs, and he sniffed and scratched at his face, oblivious to the drama playing out behind him. Samira looked back toward the Aescalan woman, and she still hadn't moved. She sat silent on that bench, her foot crossed over her knee and her hands poised with the knife and the whetstone, as if she could hold that position forever.

LIZANDRA'S DEEPEST FEAR

It only took a moment for the office door to swing inward, but it might as well have been hours. Samira let the breath she'd been holding out in a deep exhale that as soon as she saw Vaino in the threshold.

He wore a black suit, the collar open just enough to show white lace on the shirt beneath the high-buttoned vest. He'd pulled his dark hair back from his face and bound it with a loose tie that left a messy ponytail hanging between his shoulders. Vaino looked first at the guard who'd knocked, but his eyes darted to the left, past Samira, to Caius.

His eyes wide now, Vaino grasped Caius by the arm and pulled him into the office. "They told me you'd returned, but I hardly believed it. We all—Well, I feared the worst. Come in."

The guard moved aside, and Samira motioned the Gressams through the door ahead of her. She waited until Hyden had gone inside and risked one more glance back at Ranja. The woman remained motionless, her eyes still trained on Samira's, and that's how she sat even as Samira slipped into the office and pushed the door shut behind herself.

"When Hama returned without you, I wanted to send a search party," Vaino was saying to Caius.

"Hama betrayed us," Samira said.

Vaino halted mid-speech and raised an eyebrow at her. "That's not the story he told."

"It's true," Caius said. He moved to the side and nodded to the family, standing just to the right of the closed door. "This is Hyden Gressam. His wife, Phyla. Their son, Danel. Hyden is the Tamrat scion. He's the one you sent us to find."

Vaino took a quick step forward and extended his hand. "Please excuse my lack of manners. This is all quite sudden and unexpected. I'm Micah Vaino."

Gressam looked like he wanted to step back out the door to the courtyard but took Vaino's hand after only the briefest hesitation. "I would say it's a pleasure to meet you," he said. "I'm not much of a liar, though."

"You didn't know, then? About your family or any of this?"

Hyden shook his head. "None of it. I'm a farmer. I've never known anything about politics or any of the rest of it."

Vaino released his hand and turned back to Caius. "What is this about Hama, then?"

"What did he tell you?" Caius asked.

"He returned with several of the Aescalan. They were one short when they got back, and they were missing some of the horses."

"The horses are in the stable," Samira said. "We used them to escape from him." And then, "One of the Aescalan didn't return with them?"

"Rikin," Vaino said. "The youngest one. Hama said the Imperials ambushed you, and Rikin died in the scuffle."

Samira remembered the young man and his tentative way. He'd made stew for them, and she'd watched him weep on his knees at the farmhouse. He'd been awestruck when he met Hyden, and he'd had no business going along on that mission. Now he lay dead somewhere to the south, probably run through with a Kite's sword.

"The Imperials found us, but it was only after Hama instigated the conflict," she said.

Vaino's eyebrows went up again, and he shifted his attention back to Caius. Annoyance gnawed at Samira, but she closed her mouth and looked away.

Caius shot her a quick and apologetic glance before he picked up the narrative. "We came across an Imperial work camp on the way south. They were building some sort of giant drill and had excavated a huge hole in the ground. We could have passed by with nobody seeing us, but Hama stopped the caravan and ordered his people to attack the workers."

"I've heard about similar sites," Vaino said. "The Empire has been constructing these drills for at least a couple of years now."

"What are they drilling?" Samira asked.

Vaino responded with an exaggerated shrug. But then he frowned. "You said Hama attacked the work crew. What did he want to do that for?"

"They're maniacs," Samira said, not caring that Vaino was directing all the questions to Caius. "Hama and the rest of them. They're obsessed with their hatred, and they slaughtered all the

Imperials. We tried to stop them, but it was no use. From that point forward, we were their hostages."

"Hostages," Vaino said, his voice hardly a whisper. "This was before you found the Gressams?"

"It was," Samira said. "We continued on after that, and we eventually came to their farm. We knew the Empire would be hunting us then, though. We tried to make a quick trip back here, but yellow Kites found us while we were camping in the night, just outside of Bria. That's when the attack happened."

"We didn't see Rikin die," Caius said. "We heard the shouting and the swords through the trees. That's when Samira and I got the Gressams, and we stole the horses. Ranja tried to stop us, but we got away while the rest of them were fighting."

"Hama said you were separated in the chaos," Vaino said.

"I suppose that's true, from a certain perspective," Caius said. "If we'd stayed, Hama might have killed us or just abandoned us. He had no intention of bringing the Gressams back here."

"What was his intention, then?"

"We don't know," Samira said. "But it wasn't good. We got away, and we made our way back here." She glanced back at the closed door. Ranja was still out there. Samira couldn't see her, but she could feel the other woman's eyes, even through that door.

Vaino crossed his arm across his body and propped his right elbow on the back of his left hand. He rested his right thumb against his lower lip and watched Samira for a silent moment before shifting his eyes to Caius and then to the Gressams and back again.

"You don't believe us," Samira said.

Vaino dropped his arms and shook his head. "That's not what I said. That's not it at all. I simply find myself in a confounding position."

His eyes went back to the Gressams, still standing in a small cluster next to the door, and Hyden said, "It's because of me."

Vaino tilted his head and gave a subtle nod. "It's because of what you represent. Dekan Hama speaks for his people. Not just the ones he brought with him. He is here on behalf of all the

Aescalan." Vaino finally directed a question to Samira. "Do you know how many that is?"

She stared back, her lips tight, and offered no answer.

"I don't know, either," Vaino said, continuing as if she had responded. "Tens of thousands. Hundreds of thousands. Maybe even millions. They're a militant society, and their technology is beyond what we've even imagined."

Caius straightened at that. "What do you mean?"

"They're not limited like Teshovar is. They've never lived under the rule of a tyrant that suppresses research and discovery. They've been free to explore avenues that have been closed to us for centuries. Can you imagine what they've come up with in that time?"

Samira watched Caius' eyes and knew the spark she saw there. Did Vaino already know that was the way to keep him on the hook? She could see Caius' brain turning over the possibilities, considering the things he and Apak had worked on in the back rooms of the Chamberlain, and extrapolating what might have been if they'd had access to the discoveries the Empire had denied them.

"You really think the Aescalan can defeat the Empire," Caius said at last.

"I do. And they're willing and eager to do it, as long as they know they're going to win. They won't commit to something they don't feel they're preordained to win."

"And they think they'll win as long as they have..." Caius trailed off and looked over his shoulder.

Hyden said, "Me. They believe I can make them win. I saw it in the way they talked to me and looked at me. They think I'm something I'm not."

Vaino shook his head. "They know exactly what you are, Mr. Gressam. Perhaps even more than you know yourself. You're descended from ancient royalty, and, as far as anyone knows, you're the last in the Tamrat line. You and your son. Nobody even knew the line persisted until recently. That's what is important to them. It's the continuation of something that came before the Empire. Before Teshovar became what it is. They don't care if you know how to actually lead them."

"They want me as a symbol."

Vaino nodded and spread his hands. "As advanced as they might be, their society is religious. Their culture has a long memory of being thrown out of these lands, and they want back in. They believe Peregrine was to blame for their expulsion, and they believe restoring the Tamrat dynasty is the way to defeat him. They'll come here, and they'll fight for us now that they know you're here to continue the line."

Hyden snorted and shook his head. "I have no interest in leading an army. I have no interest in ruling anything or leading anything. My family is my only concern. I'm only here because staying on our farm was not an option. We intend to return there as soon as it's safe."

Samira watched Vaino's face and saw a hint of the truth that she expected. These people weren't ever going home. Not back to that farm, at least. Their lives would never be the same again, regardless of how this rebellion turned out. But that's not what Vaino said in that moment. What he said was, "You don't have to lead anything. They just need to know that you're on their side. You won't be fighting. You won't be doing anything but sitting here and staying safe until it's all done. And you won't have to rule anything after the dust settles." It was so similar to the lines he'd given Caius when they'd first arrived at Stormbreak.ABies to make his pawns complacent until they were of use to him.

Vaino didn't elaborate on that last bit, but Samira's eyes narrowed as she searched for the ambition in his tone. Did he fancy himself the next king of Teshovar? Did he intend to insinuate himself into the post-war politicking, presuming everything else followed his plans and design?

"That's why you're hesitant," Caius said to him, dragging Samira's attention back to the present. "You know Hama is ambitious and treacherous, but it doesn't matter. You need him, because he's the way you get your army."

"He's the way we defeat the Empire," Vaino said. Something like regret tinged the edge of his voice, but Samira no longer trusted anything about this man's motivations.

"How will they defeat Peregrine?" Phyla asked, speaking to Vaino for the first time.

Vaino gave her a smile that landed just this side of patronizing and said, "They have plans. This is something they've prepared to do for as long as they've lived across the Madigus from us. I'm not worried about their capabilities. They'll come in such numbers and with such armaments that the Empire can't withstand them." And that was his final word on the matter. He didn't tell her that Peregrine didn't even exist, and he must have assumed neither Caius nor Samira had had that conversation with the Gressams.

"So we do what?" Samira asked. "We tiptoe around this keep until your war is done and hope the Aescalan who already tried to kill us don't give it another go?"

The corners of Vaino's mouth turned down, but Samira had no interest in how he might spin an answer to that question. She forestalled his answer with, "We've been traveling and are exhausted. Akithar has things to attend to." She eyed him, signaling that she had every intention of seeing that he went to the doctors straight away. "And I need to see Lizandra."

Vaino blinked at her. "Lizandra?"

"She needs us. We were gone when... Reykas..." Samira couldn't even finish the sentence. They'd been through so much while they were away from Stormbreak. When had Reykas died? Had it been while they were traveling south? Perhaps while they were at the Gressams' farm? Surely not after they were on their own and coming north again. Whenever it had happened, her friend was gone, and she should have been there in his last moments. The regret gnawed at her, but when she looked back to Vaino, his eyes were wide, and he showed a hint of a smile.

"You don't know. Of course you don't," he said. "Reykas Kozic is alive. He's better than just alive."

Samira's mouth dropped open even as she felt the hairs on her arms prickle and a flood of warm hope stinging her eyes. She looked to Caius, and he stared back at her. "How is that possible?" he asked Vaino.

"Nobody knows," Vaino said. "He had been ill since you all arrived here, and Lizandra stayed with him night and day. She refused the doctors after a while, and I was certain..." He looked at Samira with unease, at least having the grace to not speak of what she'd been certain would happen. "But then he recovered. We have no explanation. He's up and about and seems—"

"Reykas is alive," Samira said, her voice shaking. It was impossible. She trusted nothing Vaino said about anything else. How could this thing be the truth? "I have to see him. I have to see Lizzie." She put a hand on Caius' shoulder and said, "See the doctors. I'll find you later. I have to see them. And I have to see Aquin."

She was halfway to the door when Vaino stopped her. "Wait, Samira. Please."

Her fingers rested on the doorknob, but she forced herself to look back at him instead of barreling ahead into the courtyard.

"There's more that has happened while you were away," he said. "You need to hear this from me. It's about Aquin Mirada."

CHAPTER 41

"My parents never wanted me to be a librarian," Aquin said.

"No?" Wickes sat on the floor of his cell, his shoulders against the wall. With his hands still bound to his feet with that short length of rope, he had to bring his knees up close to his chest so that he wouldn't have to sit with his back hunched in that position.

"No," she said, sitting on the edge of her cot, her chin cupped in her palm and her elbow on her knee. "But I imagine they'd rather that than where I ended up."

Wickes laughed at that. "I can't imagine my father cares much what happens to me."

"I'm sure that's not true."

"I'm sure it is," he said.

"When did you last see him?"

Wickes tilted his head. "A few weeks ago? I don't even know what month it is now."

"But you saw him recently."

"It was the first time since I was a kid," Wickes said. "It was a brief visit and not a pleasant one. He tried to drown me, I scammed him. You know how it goes."

There was no immediate response, and Wickes looked at

Aquin through the bars. "If you're waiting for a punchline, there isn't one. It's just the way things are."

Aquin sighed and sat back, her hands propping her up on the thin mattress. "What about your mother?"

"Never knew her, to be honest. She could have been any of the women who laid with my dad. He always said I was birthed from Ikarna, but I suspect my origin was less abstract."

"Ikarna," Aquin said, and something in her voice made Wickes turn his head to look at her again. She was sitting forward now. "Your father. He's a believer?"

"I am, too," Wickes said. "We don't agree on the best way to foster that belief, but... yes, he's a believer."

Aquin slid off the bed and onto the floor, and she crawled toward the bars until she was next to him. "Put your hands through the bars."

"Put what?"

"Just do it."

He frowned but complied, pressing his hands together and flattening his palms against each other so they'd fit through the narrow space. Aquin shot a furtive glance at the door to her cell before she reached into the edge of her sleeve and drew something out between her fingers. It gleamed in the meager light from the windows, and he saw the edge of the razor's blade.

Wickes pulled his hands back. "I don't—"

"Shush," she said and grabbed his wrists, holding him in place. "Don't move."

It took a bit of sawing, but she cut through the rope that bound his hands to his feet within just a few moments. "There," she said, and she slid the razor back into her sleeve.

"You've had that the whole time, and you haven't tried to get out of here?" he asked, incredulous.

"It's in case things become dire."

"Dire how? You're already locked in a cell in the middle of nowhere."

"It could be worse," she said. "Vaino could decide he's tired of questioning me and had rather dangle me from the end of a rope. He won't get that chance."

"Do they do that here?" Wickes asked.

"How should I know? I don't know any of these people or what they're capable of doing. I won't be caught unprepared, though."

Wickes nodded and stretched his feet out before him on the floor, letting his knees relax. He looked at his hands, still clasped in his lap. "Think you could cut the rest of these ropes off me?"

She shook her head. "They might not notice that one missing, but they'd surely notice if your hands and feet were free. Can't risk that."

He had to admit she made a good point, but he'd work his way toward convincing her to let him borrow that blade sooner or later. "Where did you come from?" he asked.

"Klubridge. I worked at the school there."

"The university."

She nodded. "That's where I was a librarian."

Wickes chewed at his lip and finally asked, "How long have you been here? Do you know... Have you heard what happened there?"

"I know as much as anybody up here does, I imagine. The Empire destroyed the city."

"It's not all gone, but near enough," he said. "You must have left just before it happened. How did you get here?"

She sighed and tucked her knees under her chin and pressed her back against the wall next to him, the bars between them. "I fell for someone. Or she fell for me. Or... I don't know. It's complicated."

"Most love stories don't lead to one of the lovers being a prisoner of the rebellion."

"I suppose this one is unique," she said. "I didn't have a say in it, but I came here by ship, right after the revolt in Klubridge."

Wickes sat forward and turned toward her. "Ergo Drass' ship. You came here with Akithar."

"How do you know them?" She was frowning now, suspicion in her eyes.

"It's a long story. Suffice to say that I ended up here for much the same reason you did, but without the tragic love tale. Is he still here? The mage?"

"Akithar?" The disdain in her voice was clear. "Not lately. And he's called Caius. Caius Harrim."

"Caius Harrim," Wickes said. The Empire would surely love that bit of information, but they wouldn't be getting it from him. "Was your family there, in Klubridge?"

"No," she said. "What about you? Where is your family?"

"Aside from the old man? I don't know," he said, and that was the truth.

"Do you have family? Aside from your father?"

"A daughter. Once."

"When did you last see her?"

"When she was small. It had to have been ten years ago now. Fifteen, maybe."

"What happened?"

Wickes clasped his hands together and leaned against the wall again. The uneven stones were cold through his shirt. "A lot." Unbidden memories tried to take him, and so he asked, "Why did they lock you up?"

Aquin blew a frustrated breath through her lips. "Vaino thinks I'm a traitor. There was an ambush, and he thinks somebody here sold out the rebellion to the Empire."

"Vaino is…"

"He's the one who runs things here. Well dressed, dark hair."

"Looks more at home at a ball than in this keep."

Aquin smiled. "That's the one. Don't let him fool you, though. They say he's a brilliant strategist. He used to be an Imperial himself."

"Really," Wickes said. He hadn't considered it, but it made sense. The way the man had held himself, the ease with which he'd accepted the subjugation of another. The pieces fit.

"I heard them say he graduated from the academy in Aramore, was on track to be a general, all the usual things."

"What brought him to this side?"

Aquin shrugged. "I hear things, but I don't hear everything."

Wickes nodded. "He thinks I was part of that ambush, too. He asked me about it and didn't take it well when I knew nothing."

"It was bad," she said, and then she went quiet, and Wickes let her sit in her silence. After a minute or more, she said, "The Imperials were waiting on a road south of here. The rebels had a supply wagon going that way, and they jumped it." She went quiet again, and the silence was thicker this time.

"You knew people who got hurt?" Wickes asked. "The woman you mentioned—"

"Not her," Aquin said. "But yes. There was a woman who came here with us from Klubridge. A halflock. Her name was Magra."

"They killed her?"

Aquin nodded, and Wickes dropped his head. Had Colm escaped? Had the Empire rounded him up and pressed him back into service? Wickes had sworn to protect the poor, addled man, and now he had no idea what had become of him.

"There was also a girl with the wagon," Aquin said. "She came with us from Klubridge, too. She'd lived on the streets and had to be no more than fifteen, I'd imagine."

Wickes looked at her. "Not her, too?"

"She's still alive, but they hurt her. She came back here with a broken arm and half dead. I don't know how she made it." Aquin sighed. "It was bad. And Vaino thinks I was party to this."

They sat together without talking for long minutes as the sunlight became thin, and Aquin finally spoke again. "Vaino thinks I'm a spy, but what does he think you did?"

"He thinks I'm an agent of the Empire, and he's right enough."

"What did you do?"

How much should he say? Would she think poorly of him if he told her the truth? Would she think even less of him if he told her less than the truth?

"I was a pirate," he said at last. "A good one. I'd been at it for more years than we need to discuss, and they caught up to me."

"The Empire," she said.

"The Navy. They were going to execute me, but I cut a deal with them. I betrayed everything and everybody, and I saved my own neck."

"Was it worth it?"

"No," he said. "I've recently come to wish I'd let them hang me or sink me." He hesitated and added, "I lacked the courage for that, though."

"How did that bring you here?" Aquin asked.

"The Empire sent me after Akithar. Caius Harrim, I suppose. Things didn't go as planned, and here I am."

"If they had gone according to plan, we'd have been on opposite sides of this conflict," she said.

"I suppose we would. But things went as they went."

"What are you going to do when you get out of here?"

"When I get out of here? You have more confidence in our longevity than I do."

"I have confidence in your propensity for self preservation," she said and cut a sharp look at him. "What will you do? Go back to your Imperial masters?"

He couldn't bear that look, so he turned his head. "I don't know what happens after this."

"The Empire won't let you go, no matter what you do for them."

"I know," he said, and it was starting to feel like he meant that.

"They nearly killed the girl, Fairy."

"Fairy?"

"That's her name. Your daughter would be about her age by now."

He nodded.

"They nearly killed Fairy," Aquin said, "and they'd do the same to your daughter if they took a notion."

Wickes wanted to give her a reply, but he had nothing to say. In all his traveling and scheming and betraying, he'd known it was all to save his own skin. He'd had nobody else to worry about, with Weylis hidden and presumed dead. But what Aquin said was true. If the Empire knew he had a daughter, they'd find her, and they'd use her. And the worst of it was, he knew it would work. The Empire would break her to break him, and there was no amount of hunting and killing that he could do to ensure those ledgers were balanced.

It had been a week since Aquin had said it, but Wickes still couldn't get it out of his head. It was the same thing Ergo Drass had said. The same thing Weylis had said. The same thing everyone knew and the same thing he had known in his gut this whole time.

It didn't matter how many of his friends he hunted down. It didn't matter how far he traveled, how many confidences he broke, and how far down he bent himself. Teshovar had him in its grasp, and Teshovar didn't let go of anything. By its very definition, the Empire survived by finding and exploiting resources, and Quentyn Wickes had been one of its most reliable resources for the past few years. No matter what he did, none of it would be enough, and the Empire would relax its grip on him only when he was dead and cold beneath the waves, of no more use and drowned in Ikarna's embrace.

Had he ever truly believed it would end otherwise? He must have. There had to have been some resolution he saw at the end of this journey that was not just his own end. He couldn't have done all the things he'd done just to buy himself one more day of the Empire's grace at a time, could he? It was time to accept that he hadn't done it for Weylis, despite what he might have told himself. She'd tried to set him straight on that notion.

Then what had it all been for?

The lock clicked, and Wickes looked up from his seat on the floor as he shifted his hands down near his feet. They hadn't marched him out of the cell more than a couple of times since bringing him in, and nobody had noticed where Aquin had cut the rope. He didn't plan on being caught unaware now.

But no, it wasn't his door. The door to Aquin's cell opened with even less regularity than his own did, but that was the one swinging inward now. A new woman was standing there, her pale skin glowing pink either from the cold or exertion or both, and her brown hair lay tousled around her head, wind whipped and in disarray. She wore heavy traveling clothes and indeed looked as if she'd just arrived from a journey.

"Aquin," she said and was into the room and kneeling on the floor in the space of a breath. Her hands were on Aquin's shoulders, her back, her face, and she was pulling Aquin into her arms.

"Samira, what—" was all Aquin got out before the guard was into the room and pulling the new woman back by the collar of her coat.

"None of that. This is a prisoner," he said as he dragged the woman, Samira, away.

She spun on him and yanked her coat out of his grasp. "Don't touch me," she said, and the venom in her voice was enough for the guard to hold up his hands and back away.

"All right," he said. "Okay, but just don't do that again. Vaino'll have my hide."

Wickes was sitting less than two feet away from the exchange and slid himself away and up onto his bed without drawing attention. He was no part of this reunion and shouldn't have even been a witness to it. Circumstances made him a captive audience in the most literal sense, but he could at least give them some semblance of privacy.

Samira was on her knees again, on a level with Aquin, but she wasn't touching her. "Are you all right? What have they done to you?"

"There is no 'they,'" Aquin said. "This is Vaino. Imperials attacked while you were gone. They... They killed Magra. Fairy was hurt."

Samira closed her eyes and dropped her head at that. "And he thinks you had something to do with it," Samira finished for her, her voice low now.

"He thinks I'm a spy for the Empire."

"How could he believe something like that? This is ludicrous."

Aquin shrugged. "Locking people up seems to be a recent hobby of his." She glanced in Wickes' direction, but Samira kept her eyes on Aquin.

"Why would he think that? What did he say?"

She gave another shrug and said, "I'm the only one of our

group who hasn't been in lockstep with his rebellion. I haven't been twisting myself in knots to make them happy."

"I haven't—"

"You haven't been here," Aquin said. "I know I told you to go, but you don't know what it's like here. This whole rebellion is a farce. Vaino is…" Aquin shook her head and then looked back at Samira. "You have to get me out of here."

"I will," Samira said. "I need to know everything. What makes him think there's a spy?"

"Magra was out on a supply run. Just a standard trip, like she'd been doing with them regularly. Fairy just happened to be along for the ride that time. But the Imperials knew exactly when and where they would be. Someone had to have told them."

Samira frowned through the explanation, and Wickes could see her mind turning through the facts and the possibilities. "Do you know who the spy could be?" she asked.

Aquin pulled back. "Of course I don't. I had nothing to do with this, Samira."

Samira started to reach for her but stopped her hands midway. "I know. I know you didn't. But have you seen or heard anything? Has anything been suspicious? Who would do this?"

"I don't know," Aquin said, sullen now. "I didn't do anything. I'm not complicit in anything."

"I know you're not. I just—"

"Just go," Aquin said.

"Aquin—"

"Go," she said one more time, and she turned her head away from Samira.

The other woman's face fell, and that was the first time she looked through the bars and toward Wickes. Their eyes met for the briefest instant, but it was long enough for him to see the sadness and the fury and the worry in them. She looked away as she stood. She moved as if to go back to the door but hesitated, looking down at Aquin on the floor one last time. "I'll get you out of here," she said, and then she pushed past the guard, and he pulled the door shut with a hard clang. The lock turned once more, and the cells were quiet again.

Wickes waited a few minutes, but Aquin said nothing and didn't look at him. Should he even say anything? If he hesitated, he'd talk himself into the coward's path, just like he'd been doing these past years, so he said, "That woman loves you."

"What?" Aquin turned her head toward him, and he sat forward on the edge of the bed so she could see him in the darkness.

"She's the one you told me about, isn't she? She cares deeply for you, and I can tell you feel it for her, too."

Aquin opened her mouth but closed it again without speaking.

Wickes said, "You need to handle whatever's bothering you and let her help you. Finding somebody like that is a rarity in this world."

"You know nothing about her," Aquin said. "Or me. Or any of this."

"I know enough," he said. "Don't be a fool."

"A fool!" She was on her feet by then, her hands wrapped around the bars separating them. In that moment, Wickes was thankful for those metal rails. "You call me a fool after what you've been doing? You've been bowing to the Empire and killing on its behalf."

"Not anymore," he said. "I don't know what lies ahead for me, but it's not the Empire anymore. We have to learn from our mistakes and make the best choices we can make. For you, that's this woman. She's your way out of here. Out of all this mess."

"How can you know that?" Aquin asked, but her grip on the bars had loosened, and some of the anger had melted from her voice.

"I've made enough mistakes of my own to recognize when somebody else is about to do the same." Wickes pulled his feet onto his bed and rolled away from her. "Don't be me."

∼

The next time one of the cell doors opened, it was Wickes', and it was the following morning. This time, the form in the doorway was Micah Vaino, his hands clasped behind him and his hair once more pulled back from his face. Wickes was sitting on his cot, his knees already pulled up close to his chest, so it wasn't hard to hide the severed rope.

"I need a word," Vaino said.

"Is there any word I could tell you that you'd believe?" Wickes asked.

Vaino came into the room and closed the door, more gently this time. "I believe you're not in league with her," he said, gesturing toward Aquin with his head. She was on her bed, sitting up with her back against the wall. She didn't react when Vaino nodded in her direction.

"What convinced you?" Wickes asked.

"The guards. They've been listening, and I'm satisfied that you didn't know this woman before you came here. You were not involved in the first ambush."

Wickes' skin heated as he tried to recall everything he'd discussed with Aquin. Everything they had talked about and shared, believing it to be in the confidence of each other. Naturally, Vaino had posted guards to listen to them. Why else would he have had them share cells with nothing but a barred wall between them? It had all been a test.

Vaino sniffed and turned his head to the side before he said, "We have the man you asked about. The halflock. He's safe here in the keep."

Relief washed through Wickes' body, but he kept his face as impassive as he could. "Does this mean you'll let me out of here?" Wickes didn't look at Aquin when he asked. In the past, he'd have abandoned her without a second thought. Anything to win his own freedom. And that was the game he had to play for now, but he had no intention of walking out that door without securing her freedom as well.

"You weren't involved in that attack, but you certainly were there for the ambush near Tresa. You'll tell me about that," Vaino said. "This time, you'll tell me everything."

And so he did. He started with the piracy, and he told about his crew and how they were his family. He omitted his fraught relationship with his father and the Ikarna cult in the swamp, but he told how the Imperials caught him by luring him to attack a baited ship.

He told about the trial and the selfish deal he'd struck and how he'd sworn to find and deliver all his mates for their own trials and executions. He left out the truth about Weylis, but he told the rest. The guards had probably heard most of this already, and they'd surely passed it along to Vaino. So Wickes talked.

He described his pursuit of Dhasho Keats and the delivery to Mediean and the new deal with Bekam. He told of his hunt for Akithar and following Drass' trail. He left out Weylis' part once again, and he concluded the story with his trailing Drass through the snowy forest, where he'd hidden behind the lone cabin until that brainless rookie Kraden had stormed the place.

"And that's everything," Wickes said when he was done.

Vaino had listened to all this, standing motionless by the door. He held one arm across his chest, and the other elbow was propped there so that his thumb was against his chin. He watched Wickes' face after the story was finished, no doubt looking for any sign of deception or anything that might have been left out.

"All of this was because you're the Empire's errand boy," Vaino said.

Wickes gave a half nod. "Until recent circumstances amended that deal."

"What do you mean by that?"

"I'm obviously not going back to them. You're either going to kill me or keep me here or free me. And, if you free me, there's no way they'd trust me again. If I went back to Bekam, my neck would soon be a few inches longer."

"Hmm," said Vaino, his thumb still at his chin.

Wickes waited for more, but there was nothing coming. He asked, "Have you heard enough to convince you?"

Vaino watched him for another moment before saying, "I have not."

He tapped at the door, and one of the guards opened it and closed it again once he'd left. Wickes watched the door shut and listened to the key turn the lock before he looked across the cell to where Aquin sat. Their eyes met, and he knew they were both thinking the same thing.

Neither of them would get out of there alive.

CHAPTER 42

Petitioners milled about the clearing before the mage's tower, none of them speaking above a murmur but all of them casting anxious and impatient glances toward the windows in the upper levels. Nahk walked as one with the crowd, her riding hood pulled up but her appearance otherwise undisguised. The place felt more like a crowded marketplace than the entrance to the den of one of the most dangerous wizards in Teshovar, and it was amid that throng that she felt comfortable enough to not worry about seeming out of place.

Every fifteen to twenty minutes, the guards opened the double doors at the front, and a stocky man in dark livery stepped outside. The murmuring died as soon as the doors began to creak open, and everyone was silent by the time the man emerged. He always frowned across the hopeful faces before pointing a stubby finger at one and motioning for them to follow him, waving his hand impatiently.

Qae'lon was in the tower, and he'd been taking audiences that day. From what Nahk had overheard, he acted as something like an unofficial lord in these parts. He decided squabbles between the citizens, he advised important business dealings, and he even leaned in the direction of local politics. Nahk was uncertain whether it was through reverence or fear that these people came to seek his word, but it was likely to be a little of both.

There were servants outside as well. Some of them tended to the grounds, some departed for nearby errands, and others kept surreptitious eyes on the crowd as they pretended to busy themselves with other work. There were armed guards ranged at the front of the gathering, all of them dressed in the black armor of the Heron guards, but the real keepers of the peace were those servants, likely mages in disguise.

All the servants other than the man who came to summon the supplicants wore similar white tunics with tight trousers dyed a shade between gold and green. Nahk noted the intricate lacing along the sleeves and studied the embroidery that decorated the shoulders and fronts of the garments. She also paid special attention to one particular servant who left through a side entrance, loaded sacks of something heavy into a cart, and rode away on the path to the east.

That one was a young woman with a fierce look about her, her nose keen and her eyes even sharper. She had dark hair pulled back into twin braids that hung down her back, and she spared no smile for anyone awaiting entry or for any of her fellow workers. The others gave her a wide berth and watched after her with wary eyes as she left. An outcast among her own, and she was perfect for Nahk's purposes.

It had to be getting close to time for Dhaz's plan to commence, and Nahk sidled toward the edge of the crowd, lingering just outside the huddled mass so she could see the roadway approaching the tower from the south. And there, right on time, came the cluster of familiar faces. Apak led them, and it struck Nahk once more how little he looked like himself with his beard shorn. A barber in Teusas had given him a proper shave, and he seemed a decade younger, even as he still squinted through the same small spectacles and wrinkled his nose as if everything he saw offended his sense of smell.

Naecara and Alev followed close behind him. Apak held the end of a thin rope wound around his hand. At the opposite end of that rope, stumbling along behind the other three, came Dhaz, trussed up like an animal on its way to auction. He had dirt smeared under one eye, and his hair hung in tangles, but it was clear to anyone who knew him that this was Kam Dhaz, delivered to the doorstep of the mage who'd been his client until recent events put an end to their business dealings.

The approaching group had the crowd's attention, and Dhaz's name lifted from many of the whispers, but Nahk's attention was on Naecara. The woman walked with her head held proudly, her focus on the tower ahead. This plan was as absurd as any Naecara had ever proposed to Nahk, but somehow, they always had a way of working out for the better. Almost always, at least. But how many more of these plans would there be? How much longer would Nahk suffer the endless delays?

She owed Naecara her life. There was no question about that. But at what point would that debt be repaid? It was not a debt Naecara reminded her of in any overt way, but it hung between them with every turn of a deal and with every shift of a priority. Naecara had promised Nahk would have her revenge and that they'd take down the Nightingales. She'd promised Moghadan would pay for what he'd done to Nahk and what he continued to do to the others. But when would he see his justice? There was always one more diversion. Always one more task that needed doing for the rebellion.

Nahk's patience grew shorter with every mission. She was a trained killer, and she did it better than anyone else at Stormbreak, but Naecara knew how she felt about it and what every life she took did to her own soul. And, even so, there was always one more person who needed to die, all for the sake of the rebellion.

Nahk pushed those thoughts down and forced them into her gut, where they always grumbled but didn't interfere. She'd find an end to this deal, but this was not that day. Today she would enter that tower while Apak distracted Qae'lon, and she would recover the Eye of Kelixia. Not because Naecara wanted it and certainly not because the rebellion needed it. Nahk didn't trust anyone with that much power. If the opportunity and means presented themselves, she'd see that nobody left the tower in possession of that weapon. She'd destroy it with her own hands if she could. For now, though, the task was to get in and find the blasted thing.

Apak had reached the guards at the front now, and he was telling them something. Their attention was on him, and Nahk chose her moment. She slipped out of the crowd and around the corner of the tower while no eyes were on her. As she moved into the shadow of the structure, she concentrated on that servant who'd left with the delivery. She was headed toward Teusas and shouldn't be back for hours. That should be long enough.

As always, there was no physical change, but Nahk knew the Veil was in place. She produced a scowl, just as she'd seen the other woman do, and she pushed her way through the side door. It opened into a short hallway with doors opening on either side, leading into a kitchen to the left and a storage room to the right. Servants were at work in the kitchen, but none of them looked her way as she slipped past the door. If one or two spotted her, she'd be all right. She could maintain the Veil with even three people looking at her, as long as they weren't suspicious. More than that, though, and she'd have trouble.

At the end of the hallway, she pulled open a green wooden door, and an older woman in the serving uniform met her eyes for an instant before dropping her head and shuffling backwards with a muffled apology. Nahk grunted something unintelligible and swept past the woman, thankful there hadn't been a few others waiting with her.

She came into a small, round room, the walls smoothed brick but not the same sort of brick they had throughout Teusas. This was yellow, and it didn't look painted. Something the wizard had had hauled here from elsewhere and piled up to build his tower. Or perhaps he'd summoned the materials up from nothingness and assembled it all together in the air himself. Could mages even do that? If any of them could, it would be Qae'lon.

Winding stairways made their way up and down from that point. Nahk went to the bottom of the stairs that led upward and peered along the wall. The stairs turned as the tower curved, and she couldn't see the next landing. There was a narrow slit of a window in the outer wall, but that was the only thing remarkable about the stretch of the stairwell she could see. There were voices above, but they didn't sound like they were descending.

Up or down? Apak should be inside by then, and he'd have Qae'lon distracted, but for how long? Nahk needed to search quickly and find the Eye as fast as she could. The plan hinged on her being able to locate the bloody thing and then get to wherever the others were meeting with the wizard. Kam Dhaz's life no doubt hung in the balance, and that mattered to her, even if she didn't want it to.

"Where do you think you're going?"

Nahk's shoulders tightened, and her legs tensed. She half turned toward the voice, her right arm flexing and her fingers working just out of sight of the speaker. The point of her blade dropped into her palm, and she readied it.

"Well? Answer me, or have you gone daft?"

It was the stocky man who'd been managing the front doors to the tower. Now he stood in the small chamber behind her, his fists on his hips and a disapproving frown on his face. But there was also familiarity in that expression. Her Veil was intact, and he suspected nothing.

Nahk murmured, "I was just—"

"You were just going to Teusas, is what you were just doing," he said. "You were to have been away already."

"I was just about to leave," she said. She hadn't heard the other woman speak, so the best she could do was dropping her own voice into her best guess at what the servant might sound like. Bitter, a bit petulant, maybe a little weary?

The butler squinted one eye at her and paused for just long enough to convince her the game was up. Her fingers tightened on the blade, and she tugged it just enough to pull a half inch of the cable free from its spool. But then the man shook his head and said, "Be about it, then. The master's not one to suffer delays. You know that as well as I do."

Without waiting for a response, he brushed past her and took the stairs upward at a lurching gait. Nahk blew out a tense lungful of air and released the small blade. It slid back into its housing on her wrist, the cable retracting into the spool.

Luck wouldn't be on her side forever, and she had to get moving. She waited until the butler was out of sight before she followed up the steps, taking them as silently as she could, her black padded shoes soft on the stones despite the Veil's appearance that she was wearing hard-soled brown boots. The stairs curved up and to the left, and she followed the inner wall of the tower up to the next landing.

It was another round room, this time with doors opening in three directions. The stairs continued up from there, but she moved to the nearest door and pulled it open. Nahk's breath caught when she saw the long hallway stretching before her. A blue carpet ran the length of the floor, and windows on both walls afforded views of the countryside all the way down. She stepped back from the open door and placed her hand on the curved wall of the tower. That hallway should not exist. There wasn't room in the round tower for such a thing, but there it was.

She pushed that door shut and moved to the second one. She was less surprised this time, but her head still reeled with a strange vertigo when she beheld the wide stairway sweeping upward on the other side of that door. The architecture was impossible. This whole tower was a thing of sorcery. It felt and looked real, but how much of it was an assemblage of magic, cobbled together into strange geometries to house Qae'lon and whatever business he held here?

Nahk stepped away from the second door and eyed the first one again. Would that hallway still be there if she opened it a second time, or did the geography of this place shift as unpredictably as the tower occupied space? It was with hesitancy that she grasped the doorknob again and pulled. The door swung toward her, and the hallway was still there. It was as she had seen it the first time, but now it wasn't empty.

"You there. Girl!"

Nahk froze and watched the man approaching from about midway down the corridor. He wore an unnecessarily gaudy, flowy robe, exactly the sort she would have expected from his kind. There was no mistaking a Heron, even when he wasn't throwing his magic around. His chin was up, aloof, and his eyes burned a challenge into her, even from that far away. Behind him came two more Herons in conversation with each other, and a fourth trailed behind those two. The mage in front was the only one who'd noticed her, but the other three would see her soon enough, and that was too many. Her Veil would falter, and she'd be exposed. She might have been able to take on three arrogant mages, but that wasn't something she wanted to test.

Nahk shoved the door shut and turned, running back toward the stairs. She hesitated and looked toward the steps going up before angling to the left and taking the descending stairs. She knew what was below her and couldn't afford any more surprises just then.

She was nearly back to the first landing when the door above opened with a bang. The Herons' voices echoed down the round stairwell, but it was impossible to make out what they were saying. Without waiting to see whether they'd follow her, Nahk slipped around the column at the center of the stairs and moved farther down, descending below ground level now. She took the stairs with quick, small steps that carried her to a final chamber with no windows. The stairs stopped there, but closed doors surrounded her on all sides of the curved walls, each made of heavy dark wood and seeming identical to the next.

If this were any ordinary building, she'd believe these were storerooms or vaults. They'd be the perfect place to store valuable items of power. But in this place, there was no telling what might be behind those doors.

It was no use guessing or waiting, so she went to the first one and pulled it open. A second door, this one more ornate and forged from dark metal, waited behind the wooden one. Nahk sighed in frustration and grabbed the new door's handle, giving it a tug. The door did not budge, but the arcs of metallic embellishment she'd taken for ornamentation swirled into motion. The rough suggestion of a face formed before her.

Nahk gasped and lurched backward, but her hand would not

release the door's handle. Nothing held her in place but her own fingers, but they refused to release the cold rod of metal. Her heart thudded as she pulled harder, but her hand remained tight, the muscles betraying her.

The face, now fully formed, was monstrous. It was like the gargoyle visages she'd seen on the high places in Aramore, far from the streets and visible only to the birds and to women foolish enough to climb into twelfth-story windows. Even as she stared, metal eyelids rolled open with a clank, exposing the hard black orbs of eyeballs.

"Forbidden." The word came like a hiss, malevolent but ephemeral, and she was almost convinced it hadn't been spoken until it happened again. "Forbidden," the door said once more.

"Let me go," she said back, scarcely believing she was talking to a door, but the panic rising in her chest allowed her this ridiculousness. Someone would come down those stairs, probably sooner than later. Maybe the Herons, maybe the butler, and she was well and truly stuck.

"Forbidden," the door said one more time.

Nahk threw herself away from the door, but her hand still held fast. Her arm popped with the jolt, and she forced an even breath into her lungs. She probed her shoulder with her free hand and, satisfied that she'd done no damage, she licked at her lips and turned once more to the face on the door.

"Let me go. Please," she whispered.

"Forbidden," it replied in the same otherworldly voice. The tone was unchanging, exactly as menacing as before, and not a bit more or less.

"You're not real, are you?" Nahk asked. "You're just an enchantment."

"Forbidden."

This wasn't a demon or some other creature Qae'lon had placed in the tower. The familiar and sour taste of something mystic filled her mouth, the same as it had every time she'd been on the receiving end of spellwork. It was magic Qae'lon had worked into the door to prevent the wrong people from breaching it. That meant it was a device and not a monster, and that meant whatever was behind the door was worth protecting.

LIZANDRA'S DEEPEST FEAR

Her eyes traveled the surface and perimeter of the door, but there was no visible keyhole. No lock she could pick. Not that she'd expected there to be one. When dealing with magic, you couldn't get around it with ordinary means. You had to play by the magician's rules, or you didn't play at all.

She turned her attention away from the edges of the door and toward the face at its center. This guardian was an artificial menace, cast into place to keep the wrong people out of that room. And, presumably, to let the right people in? How would it know the difference? The handle?

Nahk knelt and leaned in toward the door. She was careful not to touch any other part of it, lest she become even more trapped, but she examined the point where her fingers made contact with the handle. Touching the door had awakened the magic, but that wasn't the part that evaluated the visitor. It was only after the face had formed that the door had said she was—

"Forbidden."

Nahk bit at her lip, hesitated a moment, and raised her free hand. Still being cautious to not even graze the metal with her skin, she moved her hand to cover the beast's eyes.

A moment passed, and then another. Longer than it had gone without saying she was forbidden. With ginger care, she wiggled the fingers on her right hand, and they came loose from the door handle.

With a laugh, Nahk shifted back, away from the door. As soon as she dropped her left hand and exposed the eyes again, the door said, "Forbidden."

She was free, and escaping from that basement felt all too tempting, but Nahk stood firm before the door. It was guarding something, and she wasn't leaving without seeing whether that something might be the Eye. But how would she get through? The rules were clear, and she was not the right person. The magic could see that, and it would not let her through. Unless...

Nahk looked at the grotesque face for another second before she stepped to the left, behind the open wooden door and out of view of those cold, dead eyes. She closed her own eyes and recalled the butler. The short man with broad shoulders and gray hair. The way his jaw squared at the sides, but the chin rounded. The way his nose turned up at the end, looking not quite like a pig's snout but not entirely dissimilar. All these details came back to her, and she recalled them into being. She willed them into the Veil.

Nahk opened her eyes and stepped around the wooden door. She stared directly into the metal creature's eyes. The moment felt like it stretched into an eternity. After what she supposed were truly just two or three seconds, the same ghostly voice said, "Permitted."

There was no sound of a lock disengaging or of any other sort of mechanism releasing the metal door. The beast's face swirled and faded in silence, and the door swung inward on silent hinges.

It had worked! Nahk's heart was beating too hard for her to savor the victory. Wasting not a second, she stepped through the entryway, still being careful not to touch any part of the door, even after it had let her through. She knew she'd be safe while she wore the butler's face, but the cold aftertaste of magic still sat on her tongue.

The room within was so dark Nahk couldn't see her own hand ahead of her as she reached forward. She closed her eyes again and felt something surge behind her eyeballs. She'd never been quite certain what that was. Blood? A muscle spasm? Some form of arcane energy? Whatever it was, once she opened her eyes again, she could see, even in that deep blackness.

She took a step forward and squinted, trying to make out the shapes before her. Was that…

"Oh," she said, her pulse harder and even faster in her neck now. "Oh, no."

∾

The weather had been warm in Teusas, but it truly seemed like summer as they approached the tower. That was one thing Dhaz had not been lying about. Apak twitched his brow, and a bead of sweat ran down from his forehead, beside his nose, and onto his upper lip. He wiped at his mouth with the back of his hand, rubbing away the sweat and feeling discomfited at the smoothness of his skin.

How long had it been since his face was cleanly shaved? Not since he had moved to Klubridge, certainly, so it had to be well over a decade. He had endured the treatment at the barbershop, acceding to Naecara's insistence that he would be less recognizable without the facial hair. It seemed unlikely that such a change would mislead anyone determined to claim the bounty on him, but Apak was learning that going along with Naecara's requests and urgings was often easier than seeing her annoyance when she did not get her way.

And so he led the group as the tower came into view, a warm breeze colder on his face than it had been in many years. The tower rose from the top of a low hill at the center of a wide field, just as Kam Dhaz had said it would. It was a round tower, more ordinary than expected. It was a brick construction, the blocks formed from some pale stone and stacked into place with a matching mortar. Narrow slots of windows climbed the tower in a spiral, all the way from the ground up to the top. It was difficult to estimate how many floors were within, given the staggering of the windows and the awkward angle from which Apak viewed the tower. Whatever its internal design, the exterior was plain and functional and shorter than a mage of Qae'lon's repute might have desired.

The scale of the structure became more apparent as the group climbed the hill, and the gaggle of people clustered outside the doors came into view. The curved walls climbed upward from them, and for an instant the tower looked far taller than it had on the initial approach. Had its size changed? Apak shook his head and tugged on the rope in his hand, making Dhaz stumble and swear behind him. It was nothing more than an illusion. The landscape was playing tricks on his eyes with its expanse of flatness, with no sense of scale for anything.

There were no trees, no shrubs, not even a log or stump. Green fields with swaying grass poured away from the hill on every side. No animals scampered through the growth, and not even a bird sang. There were no creatures of the sort Dhaz had described and none of the more ordinary variety, either. Apak squinted to the right, north of the road, and there was nothing. More grassland that eventually faded from green to yellow to brown. Dhaz had told the truth about the area around the tower seeming like eternal summer, but he had been wrong about the magical fauna.

Had that been a lie? Something to entice Apak toward the tower? If so, how much of the rest was a lie as well? Was this excursion nothing more than an elaborate scheme for Dhaz to claim the bounty on Apak and to turn in the others?

The murmur of the crowd reached Apak's ears, and he shot a fast look over his shoulder at the others. It was too late to alter their plan. A plan Kam Dhaz had proposed, no less. Nahk would be in place, watching them from somewhere near the tower, and some of the crowd had seen them by now. Apak watched conversations die as heads turned in their direction, eyes falling inexorably to the leash he held and then to Kam Dhaz, appearing beaten and bound behind him.

No voices called out for him to halt. None of the people shouted his name. Apak rubbed at his face again. Perhaps the shave was more effective than he had expected. It would not be long before the extent of the subterfuge would be tested. Qae'lon was an agent of the Empire, and surely someone among his attendants and guards would have seen the posters and heard the descriptions and would be on watch for any of Akithar's cohorts from Klubridge.

The crowd drew back, parting as the group approached. Apak scanned the faces but did not see Nahk. She would not have a new face in that mob. There were too many eyes that would see through her deception. She would be watching from afar and would make her move once the distraction was in place.

"What's this?" one of the two men standing guard before the great doors asked.

Apak did not stop walking until he was at the bottom of the four steps that led up to the entrance. He looked up at the guards, and another trickle of sweat ran off his scalp, this time down the back of his head and down his neck to his collar.

"This is Kam Dhaz," Apak said and gave the rope another tug.

LIZANDRA'S DEEPEST FEAR

He did not look back to see the result, but he heard Dhaz stumble to his knees on the dirt roadway.

The guards looked at each other and then past Apak, toward the others. Apak glanced to the side and saw he had the attention of the whole throng. Before he looked back to the guards, a dark-haired woman near him whispered, "Kam Dhaz," to a bearded man who might have been her father. Similar whispers spread through the crowd.

"Why are you bringing him here?" the guard asked. And then, again, "What is this?"

"This man seeks revenge on your master. Qae'lon destroyed Klubridge, and now Dhaz is ruined. His business is in shambles, and he has plotted to exact his vengeance through murder."

The shorter of the guards chuckled. "He wants to murder Qae'lon? Heap of luck to him."

Apak inclined his head. "May I remind you that Kam Dhaz has proven to be a resourceful man? I trust you have heard about his collection of artifacts? He is quite well known for hoarding some particularly nasty pieces." Apak looked back toward Dhaz, and the other man scowled at him from where he knelt in the dust. Alev and Naecara stood to either side of him, their faces expressionless as they watched the exchange. Apak turned back to the guards. "He planned to destroy Qae'lon and this entire tower, and he had the means to do it. He no longer has those means, and I seek an audience with your master to deliver the prisoner and to discuss the terms of my reward."

"Reward," the shorter guard said and chuckled again, but his eyes were less certain now. He sniffed and looked to the taller man next to him. The other man looked at him, and they both glanced at Apak with an unease that was impossible to mistake.

Before either of them could speak, the door on the right slid open with a groan. A man even shorter than the shortest guard stepped through, his shoulders broad and sloped downward and his white and wispy eyebrows drawn together in what had to be a constant frown of disapproval.

"Let them through," he said and beckoned to Apak.

"All of them?" The guard on the left asked.

"All of them."

The other guard stepped to the side but asked, "They're getting a reward for this?"

The squat servant, dressed in a dark suit that contrasted with the uniforms the guards and other attendants wore, turned his cold eyes on the other man. "That's for him to decide. For now, he's intrigued, and that's not for me to question, nor for you." Without waiting for a response, he shifted his gaze back to Apak and waved his hand toward the door with more vehemence. "Come on in, then."

Apak took the stairs one at a time, pulling Kam Dhaz along behind him. He did not pause to ensure the other two were following, but he heard their footsteps shuffling on the brick stairs behind him. Both guards followed the procession with hard glares, but Apak passed between them without further acknowledgment. Three more strides forward, and they were through the entry and into the tower.

"This way," the servant said and headed for an open archway on the left without waiting to see whether they would follow.

The foyer was large and round, the walls seeming to follow the curvature of the exterior, and the floor laid from the same pale stone as the rest of the tower. Where the walls were rough and textured, however, the polished floor reflected the light from the gaslamps affixed around the sides of the room. A curved staircase led up to the right and descended to the left. Apak observed all of this as he made a quick passage through the room, his short legs moving fast to keep up with the man leading them.

As they passed through the arch on the left and into a long but narrow hallway, Apak grunted. This hallway should not exist if his earlier observation of the tower's area and volume had been accurate. It was magic of some sort, but it was not a display like any Apak had seen prior to this visit.

"You'll wait in here," the attendant said as they reached the end of the hallway and came into a large room with smooth white walls and a vaulted ceiling. Apak craned his neck as they entered and observed the tapestries hanging along the walls. The large skylights in the high ceiling had permitted sunlight to fade the weavings, leaving what probably had been colorful creations to be sad hangings now composed of mostly muted yellows, greens, and browns. The original patterns were barely perceptible in the decayed textiles.

"How is this possible?" Naecara whispered to Apak after the attendant had disappeared back into the long hallway. "This room is enormous."

Apak nodded and dropped his end of the rope. He placed the bag with the Seal of Metarr against the wall next to the entrance as he eyed three columns at opposing sides of the round gallery. A single orb floated above each white plinth, motionless in the air. All the orbs were black, but occasional hints of violet and blue swirled in their surfaces.

"Magic," he said and pointed at one of the orbs. "Do you know what that is?"

Alev took three hesitant steps toward the column before halting and retracting one of those steps. "It's some kind of focal artifact. It's like the stone at…" Their voice trailed off before they could speak the name of Stormbreak, likely a wise omission in this place. "It amplifies magic."

Apak nodded. "I see three in this room. I suspect there are more throughout the tower."

"That's what makes this place bigger inside than outside?" Naecara said and stared at the nearest orb with something like fascination.

"That's what holds this whole bloody place together," Kam Dhaz said. He still looked suitably bedraggled, as they had intended, but he rubbed at his wrists with an indignant frown at Apak.

"What does that mean?" Naecara asked.

"Precisely what he said," Apak replied. "The tower is not a normal, physical construction. It is bound together with magic, and Qae'lon holds the entire structure together through focusing energy into these spheres."

"He'd have to be sending power to them continually," Alev said. "That's how the focusing stone works up… there, anyway."

Apak nodded. Kam Dhaz had described Qae'lon's power, but the implications of the constant upkeep this tower required were staggering. The man had to maintain his focus on these orbs at all times, even when far away from this place. And he still had the residual focus, energy, and talent to wield sufficient magic to destroy Klubridge and carry on whatever other business Peregrine set before him.

"Kam."

The voice was high and clear, with almost a lilt. Apak turned his attention away from the columns to behold the speaker. The man wore a white robe, its patterning similar to the uniforms the guards and other servants wore. Intricate but subtle patterns ran down the front and along both sleeves. The man's hair hung long and nearly silver, framing his long and slender face. Smooth, white skin covered cheekbones that gave him a skeletal look, particularly when he pulled his thin lips back into a rictus that fell somewhere between a grimace and a smile. Despite his skeletal appearance, it was impossible to guess how old this man might be.

"Qae'lon," Kam Dhaz said. He stood with his chin up, proud and defiant, but some of the bluster had gone from his bearing. "We do have to stop meeting like this."

The mage narrowed his eyes at the smuggler. "I don't recall meeting exactly like this. The last time I saw you, it was to pass a bag of seri your way."

"Just before you destroyed my livelihood."

Qae'lon clucked his tongue. "You are smart enough to know my actions had nothing to do with you. We've had an amicable arrangement for many years, and I had no reason to harm you."

"And yet," Dhaz said with a shrug.

"And yet," Qae'lon echoed, his grin sliding into a half smile. "Perhaps you'd introduce me to your friends."

Apak met the other mage's eyes for an instant before Qae'lon's gaze moved to Alev and eventually to Naecara. He sized each of them up in a matter of moments before turning his eyes back to Apak.

"You come here as the leader of this merry band," Qae'lon said.

Something was in his voice that Apak could not identify. Was it amusement? Mockery? Regardless, Apak had the mage's attention, and none of them had died just yet. In that respect, everything was going according to the plan. He simply had to keep that attention until Nahk found the Eye of Kelixia and came to them. She would use it to gain their freedom and possibly to end Qae'lon. It would be up to Alev's shield to protect them and up to Apak's facility with the Seal to effect their escape.

Apak's eyes flicked to the nearest orb for an instant. If Nahk killed Qae'lon with the Eye, as she undoubtedly intended, his power over those focus spheres would end. Would that bring the whole tower crashing down atop them? Would the room where they stood simply cease to exist, dropping them into a fold between the spaces of reality itself? They might soon find out.

Unless the Eye was not in the tower at all.

Apak frowned, banishing that unproductive thought. Of course it was in the tower. A personality like Qae'lon would keep something that powerful near at hand. It was in the tower, and Nahk would surely find it in time.

"This man swore vengeance on you," Naecara said, and Apak blinked, pulled out of his thoughts. Qae'lon had been watching him, but his eyes flicked toward Naecara, his head unmoving. "He has grievances against you, and we captured him. We're here to do you a kindness, and we hope you'd do the same for us."

Qae'lon folded his arms, his mouth pressed into a thin line now. A flicker of that inscrutable thing that might have been mockery still lit his eyes. "A reward, is it? You've come here for a reward."

The mage raised one hand to his pointed chin. "While I do appreciate being made aware of threats against my life, I have some doubts about the threat Mr. Dhaz might pose." He walked toward Dhaz, stopping when he was less than an arm's length away, and leaned forward. "Did you intend to do me harm?"

Dhaz met Qae'lon's eyes for only an instant before breaking away and seeking Apak.

Qae'lon made a sound like a musing snort or half of a giggle. It was unlike anything Apak expected to hear from such a man, and it unsettled him. The mage walked past Dhaz, pacing the floor, his head turned back toward Naecara but his eyes tracking Apak. "I'm afraid there is no bounty for this man. I was unaware that he considered me, a longtime patron, an enemy. As such, I have no reward to offer you."

Qae'lon slowed and stopped his walk next to a strange piece of furniture that stood next to the door where they had entered from that long hallway. Apak had not noticed the piece until just then, either because it was painted the same creamy off-white color as the walls or because he had been so taken by the focusing orbs when they had first come into the gallery. Whatever the reason, the tall, square thing had his attention now. It stood on four tall legs that supported a small, flat surface at the top. It was like a desk with the proportions all wrong, its surface coming up even with Qae'lon's chest. A segmented shell formed a domed covering at the top, reminiscent of a roll-top writing desk Apak had brought into the back rooms of the Chamberlain many years ago.

"On the other hand," Qae'lon said, "there is quite a sizable bounty for Apak Brem. And I imagine there would be something in the offing as well for Naecara Klavan, puppeteer of the rebellion." His eyes slid to Alev, and he said, "I have no idea who you are, but I'm certain all of you will appreciate this."

His hand turned a lever at the side of the strange furniture, and the shell rolled back at the top, exposing the surface of the thing.

Apak sniffed once and smirked as he covered his beardless mouth with a cold hand. He beheld the object as Qae'lon picked it up and, even in the face of certain death, appreciated the irony of the moment.

~

The first body hung from the wall, but there were no visible ropes or wires. Nahk took a trembling step toward it, her eyes narrowing in the darkness of the vault, and she reached a hand toward the wall. Before her fingers could touch the torn fabric hanging from the corpse's arm, the body shifted. The shoulders lurched away from her, and the head lolled toward her, the eyes open now and burning pink through the holes in the mask.

LIZANDRA'S DEEPEST FEAR

Nahk flinched back, barely stifling a yelp, and the man's mouth dropped open. He coughed, and blood peppered his chin and sprayed the air in front of his face. Nahk danced back a step and moved her feet before the wetness could stain her shoes.

The Nightingale dangled in place, held aloft by some invisible force that secured him to the wall. He might have been able to pull himself free if he'd been at full strength, but he was clearly nowhere near that. His body sagged, the shoulders straining with his weight, and he could only emit a wet, hissing gurgle when he tried to speak.

Nahk looked past him to where the second one hung in a similar position. She wondered for an instant whether that one might still be alive as well, but then her eyes traveled down the torso, and she became certain this one was dead. As was the one on the opposite wall and the fourth one dangling nearest the entry. How had she missed that one when she came in?

"Qae'lon did this," she whispered, more to herself than to the assembly of carnage, but the living Nightingale moved his head a fraction of an inch upward and then let it fall again.

She stood amid the slaughter, her back to the open door, and her eyes shining in the blackness. Her thumbs and forefingers rubbed together as indecision rooted her to the ground where she stood. She had pushed Naecara to allow her to go after these Nightingales. She had longed to end them and to follow their trail back to their masters. But now, standing among their remnants, she knew Naecara had been right. The Nightingales were not the most urgent threat.

The one who still lived stared at her. Did he know her? Did he recognize her, even through her Veil?

Nahk relaxed her hold on the disguise, and the face of the butler faded away, revealing her own. She stood in silence for a moment, allowing the Nightingale to observe her, but he had no reaction. There was no spark of recognition or even a twitch of surprise when she shifted her appearance. There was nothing but the misery of a man who'd already accepted his doom.

Nahk's hand moved with quick precision, the blade between her fingers drawing a thin, dark line beneath the man's chin. The blood that poured down his chest looked black in the room's dimness, but Nahk did not look away until his head sagged a final time, and the glow faded from his eyes.

This was not an act of rancor or vengeance. This was the first time she had ever killed in mercy.

Her fingers, so steady when ending the man's life, shook now as they released the blade. It slid back into its housing, the blood still fresh on its edge. She'd have to clean that later, after she was out of this place. After they all were out of it.

Nahk's eyes widened. Naecara was with Apak and Alev, all of them somewhere in the tower and waiting for her to bring them the Eye of Kelixia. It was too late for that, and Qae'lon was far more dangerous than she'd anticipated. Anyone who could do this to four Nightingales...

She had to warn them, and they had to be gone from this place as quickly as possible.

Nahk turned and ran for the door, slowing for only an instant when she reached it. She closed her eyes and did her best to summon the butler's features to cover her own once more. Her thoughts were scattered, her heart raced, and the likeness wouldn't hold for anyone who knew the man. It had to be enough for now.

When she emerged from the vault, the round room full of doors was gone, and the staircase leading upward had disappeared. She now stood at the entrance to a long corridor, the walls white like the rest of the tower and the floor covered with a plush blue carpet that ran all the way down the center of the hallway. She stumbled to a halt, her feet deep in the thick fabric, and she spun back toward the vault. The door was gone. A solid wall of white brick blocked her way. The tower had altered around her.

She looked back toward the hallway, half expecting it to have changed, but it was just as she had seen it when she emerged from the vault. There was no way out but forward, and she took it at a run, her feet silent in her soft shoes on the cushioned fibers of the rug.

The dizzying thought that the hallway would continue lengthening ahead of her caused her to stumble once, but it was untrue. The other end was nearing, and when she glanced over her shoulder, she saw that blank wall receding behind her. She reached the end of the hall before she realized it, and she was off the carpet, her feet slapping against the hard floor and her arms pinwheeling to keep her upright. She half ran and half stumbled into a much larger room, round and bright with skylights in the ceiling.

Apak stood nearest to her, but Naecara was the one who called her name in surprise.

"We have to go," Nahk said, her breathing ragged. "He killed them. The Nightingales already got here, and he killed them."

Naecara's gaze drifted past Nahk, and Nahk stopped the stream of words. She pressed her eyes closed and forced a deep breath into her lungs. She knew what she'd see before she even turned to look, but the sight of the mage, resplendent in his white gown, still set an ache into her stomach.

His wide mouth split open, so like the throat on the man Nahk had just turned into a corpse, but instead of blood, this one gave her a grin.

"Welcome, little Nightingale. I trust the tower showed you the way? We were so anticipating your arrival."

He stood just beside the door where she'd entered. She'd stumbled past him without even seeing him, and now she was trapped in this big room with him. They all were. She scanned the walls and ceiling for some means of escape, but there was nothing. Of course there was nothing. Qae'lon had designed this place, and he altered it to suit his needs by the moment. The whole tower was made from his magic.

Nahk's eyes came back to Qae'lon and the strange pedestal next to him. It was an unusual platform with something that looked like a wooden shell retracted at the top. Whatever had been inside was now missing, and Nahk looked from the piece of furniture to the mage standing beside it.

Qae'lon smiled at her again and lifted his hands. "Is this what you were looking for?"

The round stone he held was scarcely bigger than a grimbit ball but white and streaked through at the surface with veins of red. The lines swirled and coalesced at the center, held between Qae'lon's slender hands. The patterns spiraled into the unsettling shape of an unblinking red iris. At the middle, the colors fell into blackness, looking for all the world like a huge, vile pupil.

He'd been waiting for them. He'd known they were coming and that they wanted the Eye. It had been a trap, and this is where they'd all die. Nahk didn't even have time to fling a single blade at Qae'lon before she tasted the sour flavor of magic flooding the room.

PART V
INTERCESSOR

CHAPTER 43

Fairy flexed her arm, and it worked all right. Lots better than it had when she'd been dragging it around behind her through the snow like a cat with a sore tail, and that was a fact.

She moved it up and down and bent it at the elbow and waggled her wrist and wiggled her fingers, and everything seemed pretty normal, aside from a little tingling on top of her hand. The skin still looked all bruised up, but that would probably get better in time, just like all bruises did. She'd had her share of them in the East Ward, and a few more wouldn't kill her.

That's one thing that had gone right, at least. Time to see to the ones that hadn't yet.

Fairy took the stairs two at a time and was on the second floor in no time. She rushed past people coming down, but none of them even glanced her way. They were used to people hurrying back and forth, and they were all probably used to seeing her in particular by now.

She knew where the cells were, thanks to exploring every inch of this place shortly after arriving, but she hadn't expected to be going there to see a friend. That was one thing that hadn't gone right, but she'd make sure it did.

The cell doors were on the left side of the hallway, opposite the wall with all the decorative holes in it that looked down into the courtyard if you pressed your face up against it and peeked through. You could tell which doors were the prison ones by the little barred windows set up high in them. There were two guards outside the cells, one of them sitting on a stool and looking bored from all the waiting. The other one was leaning on the wall next to him, looking just as bored from waiting but maybe bored from sitting, too.

The sitting one glanced Fairy's way with disinterest but looked back at her right quick after he saw how fast she was coming down the hallway. It might have been the determined set to her face, too. She'd been working on that in the mirror in her room in the infirmary and had gotten that serious glower just right.

"Hey, now," the sitting guard said and held up a hand.

"I'm here to see Aquin Mirada, and you can't turn me away," Fairy said, all her determination coming out in a rush of words. "Let me in to see her."

The standing guard was looking at her now, too, and he had started to smile, and that just made her angry. Angrier. "Nobody goes through that door without Vaino's saying they do."

She'd expected that. "Well, he said I do." Anticipated it, but she hadn't come up with a good solution.

The guards shared a grin that just infuriated her more, and the sitting one made a shooing motion. "Get along, now."

"I will not. You're going to let me talk to her."

"What do you want with her, anyhow?"

"She's locked up in there because they say she's a spy and got me hurt. She's not, and I want to see her."

"Sorry, little one," the one who was standing said. "You're not getting in, and that's that."

"Which door is hers?" Fairy asked.

"This one," the sitting one said, jerking his thumb over his shoulder to indicate the door on the left. "But you're not going through it."

"Fine," she said, and she grabbed the stool the standing guard wasn't using and dragged it across the hard floor with a loud and screeching groan of wood on stone.

"Hey!" said the guard who was now missing a stool, but it

was too late. The stool was in front of the door, and Fairy was climbing atop it. He'd have to grab hold of her and pull her down himself if he wanted her down that badly. Fairy flashed her teeth at him, and he moved back a step. Adults were bigger and stronger, but they knew kids could kick and bite. That was usually enough to buy some leeway.

"Aquin," Fairy called through the window. The stool had boosted her up enough to see through it, but the room was dark through the bars. There was a little window on the opposite wall, but that only made things in the cell seem even darker, with the sunlight coming in and glaring in Fairy's eyes. She squinted and called again, "Aquin, are you in there?"

"Fairy?" And then Aquin was there, looking as unusual and as pretty as ever with her big dark hair and her flowy purple dress. She looked tired and dirty and not like she'd been having a good time of it, but she was all right.

"It's me. I wanted to see you, but they tried to keep me from it."

Aquin smiled back at her. "I see you would not be deterred." And then she looked at the bottom of the window, where Fairy had her fingers all hooked over the edge so she could pull herself up an extra inch or so. "Your arm!"

Fairy looked down at it and gave it another waggle, like a chicken wing at that angle. "It's all good now. Samira fixed it for me after she got back."

"With her magic," Aquin said. She was talking quieter now, like maybe she didn't want the guards to hear her, but they were right there beside Fairy and could probably hear everything, anyway.

Fairy nodded, not sure how much more she should say about it with that kind of audience. Samira had kept her magic a secret for a long time, and she might want it to stay that way.

"How is Samira?" Aquin asked. Her voice was still lower, but it didn't sound secretive now. It sounded more like she was unsure whether she should be asking, like how Gad would sound when he needed to ask Scrounger something but didn't want to risk a backhand across the face.

"She's okay," Fairy said. "I think she's angry, though. She

seemed that way." She paused and bit at her lip before adding, "I think she misses you."

Something about Aquin's expression changed a little then, and she asked, "She and..." Aquin's eyes cut to the left, like she was anticipating the guards listening in. "Akithar. They both came back from their trip all right?"

"They did, and they brought some new people back with them. A man and a woman and a little boy. I think the man is the one they all went off to find, and they ended up coming back with a whole family."

"Have you seen them?" Aquin asked. "What do the new people seem like?"

Fairy shrugged as much as she could while hoisting herself up on her toes. "They're fine. Normal, I guess. The man seems serious, and his wife looks like she worries a lot. The little boy seems scared most of the time. He holds onto his mum's sleeves a lot."

Something shifted in the room, off to the right, and Fairy squinted in that direction. There was a wall of bars along that side of the cell, and a man was standing on the other side of them, watching the conversation. It was hard to see him in the dim light, and he was mostly just a silhouette, but Fairy grinned.

"You're the pirate, aren't you?" she asked. "I heard they had you in here, too!"

The man leaned into the bars, and Fairy could see his smile in the darkness. "Quentyn Wickes," he said. "You must be Fairy. I have heard about you."

"You have?" she frowned and looked at Aquin for a second before looking back at him. "I heard about you from some of the kitchen people. They said you used to sail the whole sea, and you stole all kinds of things. They said you got rich off it!"

"You can believe two-thirds of that," he said, and his voice was deep and seemed like the kind that could be scary if he wanted it to be, but that's not how it sounded just now.

"Pirates are fully dice," Fairy said. "I came here on a ship with one. Aquin, too."

Wickes smiled again, this time at Aquin, even though she wasn't looking at him. "You were right. She reminds me of my daughter. How I hope she'd be by now, at least. Perhaps without such a love for piracy."

Aquin glanced over her shoulder and smiled back at Wickes. Fairy smiled, too, because it seemed like things might not be so awful in there if Aquin could make a new friend in the middle of all this mess.

"I know you didn't do it," Fairy said, and Aquin looked back at her, her eyebrows up. "They say you're the spy and told the Empire where to find us, but I know it wasn't you. I'm going to find out who did it, and I'm going to get you out of there."

Aquin raised her hand and put her fingers on top of Fairy's, at the bottom edge of the little window. "You're a good person, Fairy. Thank you."

Fairy beamed back, but then she leaned closer. "What should I do first?"

"The best thing you can do is go befriend that little boy," Aquin said.

Fairy frowned at that. "How's that going to help you?"

"It will help me, because I'll know the two of you are not alone and that you are not getting into trouble. We all need somebody we can count on in this chaos."

~

It took a bit of roaming, but Fairy finally found the Gressams in the dining hall. It was the first time she'd been back in there since she came back from the doomed supply run, and she eyed the rafters as she came through the front door. They hung tantalizingly high above the tables, and she was tempted to test her newly healed arm with some climbing and swinging and hanging, but there'd be time for that later. Anyway, the attendants in the dining hall already had their eyes on her, and it wasn't with a kindly look that invited her to scale the walls.

The hall was emptying by the time she got there, just past lunchtime, and the Gressams sat at a table of their own, a good distance from anyone else. The man was picking at his plate, but the woman and the boy looked like they'd finished and were ready to be up and about.

"I'm Fairy," she announced and dropped herself onto the bench next to the boy.

His parents shared a look before the woman said, "Hello, Fairy. My name is Phyla. This is my husband, Hyden."

"I'm Danel," the boy said but right away looked like he wished he hadn't.

"You came here with friends of mine," Fairy said. She almost named Caius but caught herself in time to say, "Akithar and Samira."

The two adults nodded, and all three of them watched her, but they said nothing. Fairy had agreed to befriend this boy, and she wasn't about to be deterred by their guarded looks and tight lips. "All of this must be weird," she said. "I know I never expected to be here."

The man, Hyden, asked, "Where did you come here from, Fairy?"

"Klubridge," she said. "I grew up there, and I met Akithar and his friends just shortly before everything in the city went sideways. We got out just in time, I guess."

"I suppose so," he said. "I was sorry to hear about what happened to Klubridge. I'm glad you weren't there."

"Me too," she said, and she meant it. She had no genuine love for the place, but the thought of the entire city coming down with all those people still in it was terrible. She had nights when she still saw Miri and the other kids after she laid down and closed her eyes. Had they gotten out before the city fell? Probably not. They were probably all there when the whole place blasted apart. There was nothing she could do for them now, but she could help this one boy, just like she'd promised Aquin. "What was it like where you came from?"

The woman, Phyla, said, "We have a farm. It's a quiet place. The nearest city is Bria, but it's rare we go there. We're not accustomed to this many people in one place."

Fairy glanced around the room, less than half full by that time. If these people thought Stormbreak was crowded, it's a good thing they'd never made it all the way over to Klubridge. "I'm used to the people," she said, "but not to the cold."

"That's new for us as well," Hyden said with a smile. He had finished his food and pushed his plate back, but he hadn't gotten up to leave yet.

Fairy wanted to jump straight to the part where she started being friends with the kid, but she couldn't help but ask first, "What's it like, being so important all of the sudden?"

Hyden's eyes widened a little, and he said, "I don't know. It all seems…"

"Silly," Phyla said. "We've never believed in prophecies or mysticism or any of that nonsense. We live a simple life, and the thought that Hyden would be this person they're looking for—"

"The Tamrat scion," Fairy said with a sage nod. Those were words she'd just recently learned, but they felt weighty, and she liked saying them.

"Whatever that is," Phyla said.

"Well," Fairy said, "whatever it is, it seems important. Everybody here got excited when they found out about him."

Hyden looked toward the entrance to the dining hall, scanned the tables throughout the room, and finally leaned in toward Fairy. It looked like he was about to say something secretive, and that was always exciting, so Fairy leaned in, too. "Fairy, what do you know about these Aescalan people?"

"Not a lot," she said. But, not wanting to disappoint him, she added, "They're big and come from across the sea. I guess there's not supposed to be anything over there, but that's where they came from."

"Do you know why they're here?" he asked. "Do you know what they want, or if any of them can be trusted?"

Fairy sat back a little. She didn't know as much about any of that as she wished she did. She shook her head. "Nobody tells me much. I don't think Samira and Akithar like them much, but I don't know why. Everybody seems tense around them, like they're just waiting for something to happen."

Hyden nodded, and then he sat back, too. He looked down at his empty plate and slapped his thighs in the friendly way Fairy knew people did when they were ready to leave but didn't want to be rude.

Phyla said, "It was nice meeting you, Fairy."

"One more thing," Fairy said. "I was wondering if Danel

might want to see some of the castle. I could take him around." She tried to make it sound casual, like she was just suggesting it off the top of her head, but it probably sounded just like the plan that it was.

Hyden had been about to stand, but he stopped then and looked at Phyla, and she looked back at him, and they both looked at Danel sitting across from them. Hyden looked at Fairy then, and he said to Phyla, "I need to talk to Micah Vaino about all this. I'd like you there with me."

Phyla was looking at her then, too, and it felt like when somebody would eye you in the street and try to decide whether you were about to lift their purse. Fairy didn't like it, but she kept a plain smile on her face. Phyla sighed and said, "I suppose you won't be going anywhere we couldn't find you." And then, to Danel, "Do you want to go with Fairy for a little while?"

If the boy didn't want to tag along with her, all this would have been for nothing, but at least she'd have tried. But, no, he was all smiles and nodded, so that's how it would be. Fairy hopped off her bench and offered a hand to the boy. He took it and jumped up beside her.

"Please have him back before dark," Phyla said. "We have a room on the first floor."

"He'll be in good hands," Fairy said. She thought to add that she'd watched after plenty of kids in the past, but then she'd have to add that all of them had disappeared or died, so she just smiled instead and pulled Danel along with her.

The boy walked beside her, his hand loose in hers, and he craned his neck to look up at the rafters.

"Do you like to climb?" Fairy asked him.

He shook his head.

"Have you ever tried?"

Another shake.

"You've got to talk to me," she said. "You can't just follow me around shaking your head all day."

"There's nothing to climb back home."

"You're from a farm. Aren't there trees with... fruit or... vegetables or something?"

"Little trees," he said. "I've never climbed them, though." His round eyes told her the prospect scared him, so she shifted tactics.

"What about tools? I'd bet you got to handle plenty of those on the farm."

He shrugged. "I guess."

They were on the walkway between the dining hall and the side entrance to the courtyard, and Fairy diverted them toward the back. "I'll show you something you might like."

Danel didn't say anything between there and the narrow roadway out back that ran to the supply depot. Just this side of the depot was the entrance to the workshop where Apak had done his tinkering before he'd gone and disappeared, just like everybody else had done. The front doors stood open, and Fairy led Danel inside.

"This is where the rebels make things," she said. She pointed at the rows of instruments along the side wall. "Tools over there." She pointed the other way. "Things on that side, too." If Apak had agreed to teach her, she'd have had more to share, but with no instruction, most of this stuff just looked like curvy metal with round wooden handles. She knew hammers and saws and such, but she didn't know what most of the rest of it was or what it could be used for.

"Do you work here?" Danel asked.

"No," Fairy said. "I don't work anywhere. I just run around and make a nuisance of myself." She looked at the racks of tools one more time. "Do you recognize any of this stuff?"

He shook his head, and she said, "Me either. This was a bad idea." She was still holding his hand, so she let go of it and knelt next to him. He was probably four or five years younger than she was. Fairy didn't think of herself as being tall, but she had a good head and more in height on this boy. "What do you like?"

Danel narrowed his eyes at the tools on the walls and at the worktables and the sawdust on the floor. After a long deliberation during which he chewed at his bottom lip and then the top one, he looked at Fairy and asked, "Animals?"

"You like animals?"

"Animals," he said, this time with more certainty.

"Do you like horses?"

He nodded, and his eyes looked a little brighter at that question. She should have guessed he'd like animals. He grew up on a farm and probably saw them all the time. He probably had animals back home that he was missing.

"I know where we can see horses," she said, and she offered her hand again, standing up. He took it, and they were back out the door.

The straightest shot to the stables was through the courtyard, but Fairy felt like walking, so she took them around the side of the keep. This was the path not many people took, so the bushes along the side had gotten all brambly and looked like something terrifying from a story. She enjoyed going that way and pretending they were full of goblins or treasure.

Danel gazed at the monstrous brambles with his mouth open, and for just a second, Fairy felt a heaviness in her heart, and she had to swallow hard to keep her eyes from leaking. "You remind me of a friend I used to have," she said, once she was sure she could say it without blubbering.

"Yeah?" he said and looked up at her.

"Yeah. He was good at climbing, though."

CHAPTER 44

Naturally, it had to be in the north in the dead of winter. Bekam cursed as the wind whipped his cloak out of his hand, and he struggled to draw it back around his body before the blowing snow soaked his uniform through. He already had ice crystals in his mustache, and his eye ached behind its patch.

Karsk had civil servants that were supposed to keep the streets clear, even in weather like this, but there had been no sign of them since he'd arrived the previous day. He had spent the night rubbing his hands before the fireplace in his inn while Cillan sat nearby, apparently undaunted by the temperature and scribbling with fury on his notepad.

"The Council's representatives will be here tomorrow," Cillan had said, and Bekam had stopped rubbing his hands long enough to raise an eyebrow at him.

"The Council is sending someone? Here?"

"Commissioner Prusik, most likely. Oversight for the budget and allocation and so forth."

The thought of Prusik freezing her jowls off in this forsaken place was enough to put some warmth into Bekam's hands and a grin on his face.

That had been last night. Today, the fire was gone, and Cillan had already forged ahead to make preparations, and Bekam was trudging through calf-high piles of snow in the streets. By the time he reached the Linden building, he'd slipped and dumped snow into his boots twice, and the left leg of his trousers was so wet it was stiffening.

The warmth that hit Bekam when he stepped off the street and into the building was a surprise and came upon him so suddenly it made his joints ache. It was a pleasant burn, though, and certainly preferable to the mess he'd just come through to get there.

"General," Cillan said, waiting just inside the door. "I prepared a fresh uniform in the cloakroom, if you would like to change."

Bekam shook his head. "No need. Is everyone here?" Best to get things started. If he took the time to change clothes and made himself comfortable, he wouldn't want to venture back out into the blizzard, and that was coming after this meeting, whether he liked it or not.

Cillan nodded and gestured toward the big wooden door on the right of the entry hall. "They're all here, just waiting for you."

"Right, then," Bekam said and gave his hands a quick shake before pulling his cloak off and tossing it to Cillan. "See to that, will you?"

He stopped before the door and took a deep breath, savoring the moment. How different it felt to be the one summoning these people to an uncomfortable meeting for once, rather than being the one summoned. Letting the breath go, he shoved the doors open and set a grim look on his face as he came into the war room.

The space was lit with torches affixed to the walls, casting a flickering orange glow on the rough-hewn stone. No gaslamps in here. Tradition held that only technology contemporary to the founding of the Empire would appear in official war rooms, in deference to the High Lord Peregrine or some such nonsense. No such concessions were made in the way of comfort, as the modern furniture evidenced. Even that was styled to look old, though, like they were meeting in a chamber out of step with time itself.

A long wooden table dominated the space. It was made from a dark, rich timber and had been polished to a high shine. High-

LIZANDRA'S DEEPEST FEAR

backed chairs, their pieces also hewn from the same dark wood, surrounded the table. They were cushioned with thick, red velvet, abandoning all pretense of utilitarianism. Strategists would be at work in those seats for hours, and their backsides evidently had no concern for ancient propriety.

Maps, parchment, and pens littered the table. At the nearest end lay a large map of Karsk and Esterburgh and everything north, at least to the best of the Imperial cartographers' reckoning. No one had ventured up into those mountains on Imperial business for decades, as far as Bekam knew. Markers scattered across the map showed their best guesses at the enemy positions. At the other end of the table sat an ornate hourglass, the sand inside trickling steadily down. There was always an hourglass in every war room he'd seen. It didn't matter that even some of the common soldiers carried their own timepieces in their pockets now. There would always be those symbolic hourglasses, visual reminders of the moments slipping past as leaders like Bekam planned and schemed.

The air was thick with the smell of burning wood, wax, and the faint scent of leather. A fireplace, large enough to fit five men inside, blazed on the wall opposite the door. The fire was crackling, and the heat was palpable, making the room feel alternately welcoming and stifling. The firelight danced with shadows on the walls and cast dark illusions around the twin rows of plain chairs that sat apart from the table.

General Milev stood at the far end of the long table, in conversation with one of his soldiers, his hand resting atop the hourglass. He broke off mid-sentence when Bekam entered and dipped his chin in a quick bow. Prusik didn't favor him with so much as a nod, but she looked like it was all she could manage to restrain her misery. A huge coat hid her scrawny arms, which she had wrapped around herself, shivering even in the heat of the building. Outside of her own meeting room, her frailty was apparent, and it felt good to see her hating every moment of this visit.

Other officials, politicians, and soldiers Bekam recognized from all corners of Teshovar nodded or bowed or murmured a greeting when they saw him. This was as it should be. At last, when things had seemed their bleakest after Klubridge, the world was righting itself.

"Thank you all for making the journey," Bekam said as the room fell silent. He strode to the front and waited for the assembly to take their seats, the commissioned leaders around the table and the rest of them packed into the additional chairs. There were too many bodies for the room, and some of the junior officers were left standing along the walls, all waiting for their orders.

"We are days away from crushing the rebellion and restoring order to Teshovar," he said. Heads nodded in agreement, and a few faces smiled at each other. This campaign would be historic, and being here for this meeting was not a moment any of those he'd summoned would willingly miss, even if it meant dragging themselves through snow and ice to the worst corner of the Empire. "Today we will discuss the resources available to us, and I thank the gracious Council for its generosity in that matter."

For the first time since Bekam had entered the room, Prusik turned her attention to him and favored him with a glare. Seeing her this dejected was extra sweetening for this treat. He smiled back at her, ever the humble servant of the Imperial forces. His attention shifted to her left, where Milev had settled himself in an oversized chair that still looked uncomfortable.

"General Milev, I trust you brought every tool available to you?"

Milev nodded. "I did, General. We've filled a camp north of Karsk with nearly every available conscripted soldier from here to Meskia. I dare say the barracks have never been this empty throughout the realm."

Bekam looked past Milev, to where an array of color punctuated the otherwise drab uniforms in the room. Yellow, green, orange, a veritable prism of order. "And my Kites? Everyone is accounted for?"

"All companies have arrived in Karsk, sir." That was Cavia, commander of the Violets. She continued, "Commander Tereth was already here with his Blues, and the rest of us have been assembling for the past week."

"Good," Bekam said. "Excellent."

"What of the Herons, General?"

Bekam looked back at Milev, and his lips twitched. "I brought the loyal Herons of Aramore north with my caravan."

"And the rest of them?"

"Rest of them?" Bekam asked.

Milev shifted and glanced at Prusik. What was that look? "We've heard nothing from Qae'lon, so I took the liberty of sending a general summons for all available Herons to come north. They've been arriving for the past week as well."

"The Herons?" Bekam blinked at him. "All of them are coming to Karsk?"

"Coming or already here. They're being housed in the government facilities. I've assigned my own regiment to keep watch over them, and the Herons' guards came with them, to make sure they don't get up to anything we don't want them getting up to."

Milev had taken liberties, indeed. He would need correcting and reminding of who led this campaign. Now was not the time to inject uncertainty into the forces, though. That would be for later, after the rebellion lay beneath their boots, and Akithar and his compatriots sprawled dead before them. That would be when he reckoned with Milev and Prusik and all the rest of the Council who had plotted against him. Plotted against him with Qae'lon.

"Have you heard from Qae'lon?"

Bekam's attention snapped back to Milev, and he frowned. "I've heard nothing from Qae'lon." That much was true, at least. There had been no sign of the mage, and there had been no report from the Nightingales. Was Qae'lon already dead? Did he survive and was even then holed up somewhere plotting Bekam's demise?

Milev pressed his lips together and cast an uneasy look Prusik's way. Was that suspicion in the traded glance? Certainty? Did they know about the deal he'd made with the Nightingales? Did they know something more about Qae'lon's present condition and location?

"What?" Bekam asked. Better to be out with it than to let it fester this close to battle.

Prusik looked at Milev once more, and her shoulders fell. She turned her gaze to Bekam, and her voice was low enough to be barely audible. "We find ourselves on the unexpected brink of warfare. The Herons are a resource we can ill afford to squander. As such, the Council's provisional law is clear about the terms of leadership."

"What does that mean?" Bekam asked, but as soon as the words left his lips, he knew what it meant. His eyebrows raised, unbidden, and he placed his hands flat on the table before him, so as not to betray his emotions. Could it be that Qae'lon himself had unwittingly delivered victory into Bekam's hands?

"You were present for the Council's vote," Milev said. "The amendment states that, in the event that one senior officer is unable to execute their duties, their counterpart will assume command."

"In the absence of Qae'lon," Prusik said, "and only until his return, you will lead the Herons."

And, just like that, Bekam became the most powerful man in Teshovar. With both the Kites and the Herons under his command, no one would ever question him again.

"General?" Milev had spoken.

Bekam cleared his throat and stood, bringing his hands behind his back. "What was that?"

"We have the Kites, the Herons, and the army accounted for. What other resources need discussion?"

Bekam looked to the left, toward the map of the north. "The siege machines."

"Engineer Holger," Milev called, and a short man with thick eyeglasses stood from the second row of chairs. He wiped a quick hand over the top of his head, smoothing his hair into place, and nodded. "What will we need to breach Crowspire?"

The engineer sniffed and said, "I understand the keep is already partially destroyed, General. Is that correct?"

Milev turned to Bekam, deferring the answer. Bekam nodded. "I haven't been there myself, but all the stories say it was crushed in a landslide. It's been sitting abandoned for centuries, or so we believed."

"Do we know anything about its exact condition?" Holger asked.

"Not yet." Bekam needed scouts, and he needed information. The engineer's implication was correct. They couldn't simply march north without knowing what they would find there. But taking the time to send someone all the way into the mountains and back was a delay they could ill afford, with the great bulk of the realm's military already clustered in the frozen wind outside the walls of Karsk. Word would reach the rebels sooner than later, and the element of surprise would be gone. "We need options, and we need something we can transport into the mountains in this blasted weather. What do you have?"

The engineer bit at a thumbnail, and his eyes unfocused past Bekam. After a moment's thought, he said, "We can manage something that will work. I can provide you a full report tonight, after I've conferred with my team."

"Fine, then," Milev said. And then, to Bekam, "Anything else?"

Movement at the back of the room, in the shadows beyond the rows of chairs, caught Bekam's eye. He stared into the dark corner as the figure glared back, the shock of white hair recognizable even in the gloom. Weeks of no word at all, and this was how she chose to return?

Bekam stared at her long enough to cause the officers seated before her to shift nervously. At last, she bobbed her head once. Bekam nodded back. She had done it. Qae'lon was dead, and the Nightingales had come to Karsk.

Still watching the woman, he said, "Just a few final additions to our party, and we'll be ready for the journey."

CHAPTER 45

The night wrapped Reykas in its cold hands, its fingers as brittle and sharp as his body felt. He rocked with the motion of the wagon, an irregular swaying that might have lulled him into the blackness of oblivion, but sleep eluded him. And so he pressed his back against the wooden rails at the side of the cart and pulled his knees closer to his chest. He'd already slept long enough for a lifetime, anyway.

He squinted back the way they'd come, and his eyes picked out the vague shape of the mountain standing against the gray clouds that hid a sickly yellow moon. The ragged line at the peak glowed with its snowy cap, but the rest of the form was lost, mingled with the surrounding rocks and hills. She was back there in the castle beneath that mountain, probably asleep in the room that had been theirs. If she slept, what was she dreaming?

The wind stung Reykas' eyes, and he pulled them away from Crowspire. The next time he looked back, only a few moments later, the mountain was gone, disappeared around the turn they'd taken in the road. He rubbed a hand over his face, and only then did the weariness settle into his bones. It came with a suddenness that dropped his chin to his chest, and his head lolled with the motion of the wagon, and he slept.

The sun burned his eyes when he opened them again. He squinted once more, this time against the glare from the white snow piled at the sides of the road, and he craned his neck to look past the driver at the front of the cart. His shoulders ached with the effort after being slumped in that half-sitting, half-leaning position all through the night. His movements must have alerted the driver.

"We're making good time," the man said over his shoulder.

Reykas grunted something back that wasn't a word but should have sounded neutral enough to put an end to any morning conversation. He settled back against the wall of the cart and rubbed his hands together. His palms were smooth, and the skin felt thinner than he could ever remember it being. He'd gone too long without using them. The sickness might have been fading from his body, but all that time he'd spent in bed had left its marks. Not just in bed, though. He'd also been out and on the road, this very same road he now descended behind a rebel whose name he didn't even know. The man had a small pack of papers stowed at the front of the wagon bed, just beside Reykas' knees, but there was nothing about that satchel that told Reykas his name or anything else about him.

Reykas considered the curve of the man's shoulders and the way he sat forward, his hands on the reins and his head bobbing with the bumps in the road. Is that how she'd looked when she brought him down from the mountain? Had she stopped often, or had she driven straight through the nights? As frantic as she'd been to get him to Karsk, she would have gone through the nights until she couldn't go any farther. And then she'd have rushed her sleep so she could be on the road again.

And, all the while, Reykas had lain in the back of a cart, waiting to die.

He should have died.

He bit at a thumbnail and stared at the wooden crate against which he'd pressed the toes of his boots. Something had been stenciled across the side of the crate, but the black ink had faded from having been handled over and over again. Whatever was in the box this time was a mystery, as were the contents of the other crates, the single barrel, and the stack of burlap sacks that shared the wagon with him. Supplies the rebellion was sending somewhere, but what they were and who was receiving them were details Reykas didn't need to know. All he cared about at that moment was that the wagon had left the mountain, and it had gotten him past the guarded perimeter of the keep unquestioned.

The driver hadn't even questioned him when he'd said Vaino sent him to ride along. It had been a lie, but, after what had happened to Magra and her companions, anyone making a supply run to or from Stormbreak appreciated an extra body for security. Even a body as frail as Reykas'.

They stopped twice that day but kept their pace down the mountainside into the following night, and Reykas slept again with the rocking of the cart. That was the way it went, all the way down the mountain. Reykas had offered to drive the cart, but the driver had declined. It was probably for the best, given that Reykas was still regaining his coordination. He probably wouldn't have ended them up in a snowbank on the side of the road, but it was better to not find out. And so Reykas had sat in the back and dozed while the driver carried them farther away from Stormbreak and closer to civilization.

Esterburgh crawled into view as the sun dipped low, and the driver nodded to a barn sitting to the left of the road. "We'll stop there."

"Your contact is in there?" Reykas asked, watching the closed doors as they approached.

The driver shook his head. "We leave the cart in there, and we bugger off somewhere to get a warm meal. When we come back, it'll be unloaded and restocked with parcels for us to take back with us."

"Who unloads the cart?"

"That's something I don't know and don't want to know." He pulled at the reins, stopping the horse just outside the barn.

"What's in the new parcels that will be in the cart?"

The driver smiled back at Reykas as he slid down from the seat. "Again, not something I need to know. Give me a hand with these doors, will you?"

And so Reykas climbed over the wall of the wagon and stretched his legs for a moment before helping. The snow piled up outside gave resistance, but they got the doors open after some dragging and grunting. Reykas was sweating by the time they had the path cleared for the wagon, and night had fallen in earnest, but it felt good to use his muscles again. It felt good to know he could still use them at all. His strength was returning, a bit at a time.

As the driver pulled the cart into the barn, Reykas stepped to the side and flexed his right hand. Nothing. His physical strength might have been returning, but there was still no magic. And, according to her, there never would be again.

When he'd first awakened from his long sleep, the realization that the magic was gone was a sudden shock. There had been a keen, stabbing pain every time he had reached for the power. That pain had dulled to an ache until it was now a numbness. There was a hollow place inside that felt like nothing. The pain was gone, but it was impossible not to sense that something had once been there and was now missing. He'd heard stories about people missing limbs but continuing to feel their phantom ache for decades. Was that anything like this severed echo?

"That's a job done, then," the driver said, and Reykas blinked at him through the open barn doors. "Off to the pub, then?" the man asked.

Reykas gave him a tight smile. "You go ahead. I will catch up."

"Don't be too long about it. Dinner crowd'll be piling in soon. They might run out of stew." When Reykas didn't have a response to that, the other man nodded to him and trundled out through the barn's side door, letting it slam shut behind him. The horse neighed and scuffed at the ground.

Reykas had no intention of finding the driver again or of climbing back into that wagon to make the return trip to Stormbreak. He closed his eyes against that thought but couldn't keep himself from turning back to face the north. When he opened his eyes again, he saw the mountains rising before him, building their slopes above the town. Somewhere past them, far up the frozen roadway, lurked the broken bird, and she waited beneath it.

She had to know he'd left by then.

Something else ached, this time in his chest, and he closed his fist against it. He pressed his hand hard there, but the ache persisted, even after he turned away from the mountains and toward the town again. Had he been too hasty in leaving? Most likely. There was no question that she had betrayed him. She had intentionally worked against his wishes and had made him complicit in acts to which he never would have consented. Those acts were done now, and there was no going back to change what she'd done. Even if she could go back, it was doubtful that she'd do anything differently. It had been love and fear that had motivated her to save him, even at the expense of everything and everyone else.

And, despite all of it, he still loved her. He always would, but he couldn't look at her. He couldn't awaken in the same room with her or see her lingering at the periphery, waiting for him to forgive her. Waiting for a forgiveness that was unlikely to ever come. Despite all that, he loved her.

A sharp wind whipped at the thin coat Reykas had salvaged from the keep's laundry, and he pulled it tighter around himself as he moved away from the barn. Reykas tucked his head against the cold and crossed the street toward an inn. He had made no plans before leaving the keep. He'd seen an opportunity to leave and had taken it, but he had no notion of where he might go from there. There were decisions to make, and there was no sense in trying to make them while standing in the middle of the road.

The noise from the inn hit him before the heat did, and then he was in among the press of more bodies than he'd expected. Despite the freezing night that was descending outside, there was laughter within, and Reykas found himself in a din of shouts and cheers and the clink and clatter of cutlery and plates. Musicians played in the far corner, near the blazing hearth, and the scent of food wafted from the kitchen doors to the right.

Reykas' stomach gave a painful rumble, and he craned his neck to see whether the place had a menu posted. As his strength returned, so came his appetite, and there hadn't been a decent meal on the way down from Stormbreak.

"What do you want?" The barmaid yelled at him.

"What do you have?" He yelled back, his throat straining with the effort.

She eyed him up and down and gave a nod. "Got something'll put some meat on those bones. You got coin?"

He fished a handful of seri out of his pocket and flashed them to the woman. She gave another nod and disappeared into the back room. As she left, a man slid off a stool at the counter, and Reykas took his place, thankful for a place to sit. He was getting used to being up and around, and his legs worked better than they had when he'd first awakened in the keep, but his endurance was still a long way from where it had been just a few months ago.

Reykas rested his forearms on the bar, his shoulders rounded like the driver's had been in the wagon, and stared at the scarred wood before him as the noise of the inn washed over him. The voices and sounds of furniture and food mingled into a low roar, and the music rose over all of it, a banjo striking up a quick tune now. Reykas closed his eyes against the brightness of the room.

What would Samira think, learning he'd left just after she had returned to the keep? He hadn't even spoken with her or Caius after their return. He'd abandoned all of them by taking that wagon south. Samira, Caius, Apak, Oreth, everyone. Who knew when they'd all be together again? Whenever it was, it would be without him. He couldn't—

Reykas frowned and angled his head. The woman sitting next to him grinned back, her hands clapping out the rhythm of the tune.

"Do you know this song?" he asked. Surely he couldn't have heard what he thought he'd heard.

"Course I do," she said back, still slapping her palms together.

He hesitated just long enough to consider the ridiculousness of his question before asking, "What was the name he just sang? It sounded like Akithar."

"And so it was!" She beamed at him. "You mustn't get about much if you don't know this one."

"I've been... away," he said. He raised his head to look over the crowd, toward the singer. There it was again. Every few words were lost in the jumbled singing of the audience, but the roar of "Akithar" was unmistakable now. "What is he singing?"

"It's about the wizard and how he took Klubridge," she said.

She looked away from him to yell incoherent lyrics along with the rest of the crowd before she glanced toward the door. "I'm surprised they've the guts to play it here, especially on this night."

"Why's that?" he asked, his eyes scanning the crowd. Every mug was lifted, every voice raised. All these people were singing, and it was a song about Caius.

"Not smart to poke the Empire when they're in your town, is it?" the woman said with a smirk.

Reykas turned to face her. "The Empire? What do you mean?"

"They've been coming into town for a week steady. Started down in Karsk, but they've got a camp between here and there. And now they're all coming north."

"Coming north," Reykas said. His heart beat hard enough for him to hear it above the music.

"Something big," she said. She shrugged. "I've seen soldiers in town myself, I have. They say there are lots more coming, and there's Kites too. Herons. All of them coming north."

Reykas pushed away from the counter, and a wave of dizziness swayed him as he stood too quickly. He steadied himself with a hand against the stool, and then he angled his shoulder, pushing his way back through the crowd, out toward the door. The woman called something after him, but he ignored her and kept moving forward until he was through the door and out into the cold again.

The Empire moving north could mean only one thing. They knew. Somehow, they knew where Stormbreak was. It had to have been something about the attack on the supply wagon. They'd followed Fairy back. They'd figured it out themselves. However they'd done it, they knew, and they were coming.

He stepped into the street and looked down the road in the direction the driver had gone. The man had to be warned and had to get back to Stormbreak to let the others know.

Reykas' feet slid on the cold ground, and he locked his legs in place. Figures moved under the lamplight down the street, more than a block away. There was no mistaking the silhouette of Imperial uniforms, even from that far.

He judged the distance across the road to the barn. Could he make it without being spotted? He could wait there for the people who were coming to unload the supplies. Perhaps they'd know where the driver had gone and could summon him back to the—

The shouting began, and the soldiers were pointing. Reykas stiffened, certain they'd spotted him, but no. They were dragging someone else out of a building and into the street. He squinted through the dark and saw the man's features as they pulled him past one of the streetlights. Reykas swallowed and stumbled back a step. They had the driver in the street now, and they shoved him down to his knees. Reykas shifted his weight. Back in Klubridge, he could have closed the distance and taken down all three of the soldiers before they had a chance to move on him. But now? His strength had just begun to return, and his speed was untested. Worst of all, his magic was gone. But he had to do something. He couldn't allow the driver to be taken.

Before Reykas could act, one of the soldiers swung a sword. It flashed for an instant in the lamplight, and then it was over. The driver lurched to the side before falling forward, his face smacking into the icy slush on the road.

Reykas huffed a soft protest but held his ground. It was too late to help the driver, and the only thing he'd accomplish by charging down the street now was his own death. His life had been recently bought for too precious a price to throw it away in such a fashion.

What, then?

The soldiers were talking to each other, two of them raising their voices to the one who'd killed the driver. That one had one hand raised, trying to placate them, while the sword hung from his other hand, the tip nearly touching the ground. The three of them had their attention on each other, not on Reykas' shadowy form, watching them from down the street. He chose his moment and shuffled out of the roadway and behind the cover of the barn.

Another breeze ruffled his coat, and this one set his teeth to chattering. Or perhaps it was fear. Whatever the cause, his jaw quivered as he took one more look around the corner of the building. More people were in the street now, gathering where the driver had fallen. The soldiers were ordering them back, shouting at each other and at the onlookers in equal measure. Reykas pulled his head back and slid the barn door aside with shaking fingers. It came open easier this time, without the pile of snow to impede it.

The horse eyed him from the darkness and whinnied once. The cart was still attached, but had the rebels swapped the supplies yet?

Reykas left the door ajar, allowing the dim light of the moon into the barn. He placed a reassuring hand on the horse's neck and gave a pat as he walked past and peered into the wagon. The cargo they'd brought down from the mountain was gone, replaced by several wooden barrels and a fresh pile of brown bags, all tied at the tops with yellow cords.

Reykas looked from the fresh supplies to the back of the horse's head and past the barn doors, out into the cold night. He could unhitch the horse and leave the cart in the barn. He could slip past those soldiers on horseback, making quick time as he headed south, away from Stormbreak. He could avoid their camp and skirt around the edge of Karsk. He could continue south, making slow but steady progress until he was past the danger and free. The Empire would take Stormbreak, and they'd think they had all the rebels. He could fade into ordinary life and find something to keep himself busy. The illness was gone, and the magic was gone. The Empire would have no reason to pursue him.

Freedom was just outside that door and a brisk ride through the night.

His eyes slipped past the doorway again and searched the distant hills to the north. The road climbed and disappeared among the rocks and trees, and at its eventual end stood that enormous and accursed crow. And, somewhere beneath the crow, she slept. She had no idea the Empire was on the march, and she'd be caught by surprise, along with all the rest of them. They would be slaughtered, just like the driver.

Reykas sniffed against the cold and wiped a smooth palm down his face. He let out a long, low breath and cursed once more. The chemist in Karsk believed he'd taken Reykas' honor and loyalty. That was the price he'd asked her to pay, and she thought she'd paid it. What neither of them knew was that virtues were no currency, and anything they thought had been spent had been ephemeral. The choice Reykas now faced was no choice at all.

Curse it all. He had to save them. He had to save Lizandra.

CHAPTER 46

The sour taste of magic flooded Nahk's mouth, but she kept her eyes on Qae'lon and swallowed the urge to vomit. She scowled, half from the disgusting flavor of the air and half from actual offense.

"I'm no Nightingale," she said. How many people had she spoken those words to? How many of them even cared? She had learned to kill, and she had the abilities. All she was lacking was a completion to her lessons and a mask, and she'd be among their ranks. That, and a defined lack of conscience.

Qae'lon's smile grew at her outrage. "It hardly matters at this point, don't you think? Nightingale or not, you'll die the same."

"Not exactly the same," she said. "I saw the bodies. I saw what you did to them."

His smile faltered for an instant but returned with a chuckle. "Of course. You wore someone's face to get through the door. Who was it? Was it me?"

"I've never seen you in my life. I couldn't do your face."

"Ah," he said. "It was a clever move. I salute your ingenuity. But we have—"

"Who wanted you dead?" Nahk didn't look at Apak but hoped he knew to stay quiet and let this play out. It's the only way any of them would get out of that room alive. Naecara knew her well enough to see when she had a plan, and Alev...

Well, they *were* the plan. Kam Dhaz had looked too frightened to interject anything.

"Who doesn't?" Qae'lon asked. "I would venture to guess that no one in this room would be sad to see me gone. A person in my position collects enemies like your Master Dhaz collects relics." There was something mean and mocking in the glance he flicked toward the gangster.

"Who sent the Nightingales?" Nahk asked.

He sighed. "I couldn't tell you with certainty, but I suspect they were a gift from my counterpart."

"Your counterpart?"

"I oversee the Imperial Herons. My counterpart oversees—"

"The Kites," Apak said, and Nahk gave him a hard look. He ignored it. "Tenez Bekam oversees the Kites. He is the one who wants you dead."

Qae'lon gave a half shrug, and it caused the Eye to tilt in his hands, the pupil shifting upward to stare at the skylights far above. "We have had our differences."

"How did you kill them?" Nahk asked. "Four Nightingales against you. My seri would have been on the Nightingales."

"And you would have lost that wager. Dealing with them was merely the superiority of magic over martial training."

"Did you—"

Qae'lon frowned and cut her off. "You didn't come here to interrogate me about Nightingales. My patience grows thin, and I have other things to attend to." He gave the Eye a little toss to bring the pupil back to bear on them, this time pointing it directly at Nahk's chest. "I would say it has been a pleasure—"

"Wait," Nahk said, and, much to her surprise, he did stop mid-sentence. He didn't look happy about being interrupted, but he stopped, curiosity creasing his unnaturally smooth brow. Surely she'd stalled him for long enough, but she looked at Alev to make sure. "You got him?"

"I got him," they said and graced Nahk with a small smile without taking their eyes off the other mage.

"What..." Qae'lon began, but realization dawned, and he shifted the weight of the Eye into his right hand as he reached out with the left. His fingers probed the air, and he took a step forward before his hand halted, pressed against something invisible and immovable. He traced the inside of the shield with his fingertips, running his hand from side to side and then up as far as he could reach. "Well," he said. "My weakness seems to be monologues."

Naecara moved forward, fast on her feet, and she placed her hands on the outside of the bubble, looking like she was trying to give Qae'lon an absurdly wide hug from a foot and a half away. She pushed back from the bubble and gave Alev a vicious smile. "You got him." And then to Nahk, "Both of you."

"For now," Qae'lon said. "How long can you hold me, mage? An hour? Two hours? Five minutes? You'll grow tired. Your strength will ebb. Your concentration will break. And do you know what happens as soon as you falter?" He lifted his hand with the Eye toward Alev. "That's when you all die."

Nahk watched Alev's face, and it was impassive. They gave Qae'lon no response, either because they didn't want to give him the satisfaction of seeing them afraid or because maintaining the shield took every bit of their focus. Nahk hoped it was the former. If it were the latter, things could go very badly very soon.

"Or perhaps we'll see how well this thing works against your magic," Qae'lon said as he lowered his hand and laid it atop the Eye once more. He rotated it so that he held it from both sides. "Perhaps I end the suspense now and bisect you where you stand."

"You would be just as likely to end yourself," Apak said.

"You think so?" Qae'lon asked, his eyes still on Alev.

"I have seen a shield of this sort in a combat scenario. It was surprisingly resilient against all manner of weaponry and conflagration."

Qae'lon shifted his gaze to Apak. "You tested it with the Eye of Kelixia, too, then?"

"Of course I did not," Apak said, sounding perturbed. "You know very well I did not, and that is the reason for my uncertainty. Perhaps you would destroy the shield and all of us. Perhaps you would destroy yourself. That is a gamble you must weigh for yourself. I merely advise that these constructs are sturdier than I previously suspected."

"Can you shrink it?" Kam Dhaz said, speaking for the first time since Qae'lon had arrived. "Can you crush him?"

"Doesn't work like that," Alev said. "I could alter it if I were inside it, but not with me outside, not like this. Once the shield is in place, it's in place. If I try to move it, it could fail altogether."

Dhaz huffed his disappointment. "You should've cut him in half with it to begin with, then."

Alev's face contorted with disgust, but they kept their eyes on the trapped mage.

"We can just leave," Nahk said. "Alev, you can keep the shield up until we're out of the tower, can't you?"

Naecara turned on her. "We're not leaving without that weapon."

"Naecara," Nahk said, but Apak interrupted her.

"We are not leaving at all," he said.

Nahk didn't need to ask what he meant. He had walked around the side of the shield and had his hand on the wall next to the door that led into the hallway. He trailed his fingers along the outer edge of the bubble as he rounded it. Both sides of the bubble intersected the walls, blocking the only exit from the room. There was no moving the shield without letting Qae'lon out, and there was no getting past it to the door.

Qae'lon was trapped in the bubble, and the rest of them were trapped in his gallery. Nahk looked from Qae'lon to Alev and didn't have to wonder which of them would blink first.

CHAPTER 47

It was still as cold as ever, but at least it had stopped snowing long enough for the preparations to be made. It had been a week since they met in the war room, and Bekam stalked through the camp the soldiers had assembled north of Karsk, the white-haired woman at his side. His cloak dragged in the slush at his feet, but he had long since stopped caring about soiling or even freezing his garments. This was Karsk, and things would only get worse, the farther north they went.

The woman wore a wool coat dyed dark blue, and it looked almost black against the white-covered land around them. She had tucked her hands into the sleeves so that she walked with them together in front of her, as if her arms were bound. Her face was as stern as ever, her eyes flicking from one tent to another, taking in the orderly chaos of an army preparing to march. It was the first time Bekam had seen her in full light, and her eyes were as piercing a blue as he'd ever seen, just as frozen as the rest of this awful place.

Trailing behind was Cillan, his head down as he studied lists clipped onto a wooden board and made notes in the margin as he walked. Flanking him were his constant companions for the past several days, the two halflocks Bekam had brought up with him from Aramore. They had been the responsibility of the Heron,

LIZANDRA'S DEEPEST FEAR

Rozin Gadhi, until Bekam had sent her ahead to Crowspire. The woman who still refused to give him her name had sent one of her Nightingales north as a scout, and it felt better to have a familiar set of eyes accompanying the strange assassin than to trust anything a Nightingale might report independently. And so the halflocks had become Cillan's charges, and they followed him with vacant stares, looking more like forlorn puppies than dangerous mages.

"You're certain he's dead?" Bekam asked, tilting his head toward the woman so she would be the only one to hear the question.

She cut her eyes toward him, and he nearly flinched. "Four Nightingales breached his tower. Of course he's dead."

"How did it happen? Were you there?"

She squinted up at him, more from her own wrath than from the midday sun, and said, "Qae'lon is dead. My end of the bargain is fulfilled. That's all you need to know."

That was bloody well not all he needed to know, but there was no time to protest. They had reached the large tent at the edge of the easternmost cluster, and the woman yanked its flap back and ducked inside. Bekam motioned for Cillan to wait outside as he followed her in.

It took a moment for Bekam's vision to adjust to the dimness of the tent, but the woman seemed unhindered by the change in light.

"What did you see?" she asked, straight to the point.

Bekam had to blink a few times before he could make out the form of the Nightingale sitting on a crate in the far corner of the tent. The black bird mask hid her face, but even if she hadn't been wearing it, the gloom of the tent would have obscured any details. She leaned forward, and her hood cast her face even farther into shadow.

"The rebels are there, just as the general reported," the Nightingale said. Bekam had known they would be, but hearing the confirmation sent a thrill through his body that he hated to admit was a surge of relief. He'd been positive Stormbreak was at Crowspire, but if he'd been wrong and had dragged the Council and most of the Imperial military up to Karsk... Thankfully, that was not something he needed concern himself with any longer.

"They have sentries on the walls," the Nightingale continued. "The keep looks intact from the front. All the damage appears to be within the walls, probably toward the cliff face."

"Crowspire has been inhabitable all this time," Bekam said. The legends had said the entire top of a mountain had fallen, crushing the whole fortress and leaving countless Imperials dead. "Why did we abandon it?"

"Likely because nobody wants to stay anywhere this cold," the Nightingale said and flashed her eyes in his direction. They glowed with a faint pink light, and Bekam exhaled only after her gaze moved back to the white-haired woman. "They have guards on the walls night and day. There's a stable in front of the keep, just across the bridge. It appears unguarded. There was one attendant watching over it while we were there."

"A girl," a second voice added, and Bekam squinted toward the other corner. Rozin Gadhi sat on another crate, hunched forward with her hands clasped before her. "They have a young girl watching their horses, and nobody else is guarding them."

"What else?" Bekam asked.

"They have mages in the keep," Rozin said.

"We expected that."

"We didn't expect a force shield around the entire keep," she said.

"A... how is that possible?" Bekam had seen rogue mages who could create invisible barriers, but they were never larger than a ball big enough to surround a person. Only the Imperial mages at Salkire had managed barriers like that. The thought of a rogue conjuring a shield big enough to encase a whole fortress was ludicrous.

"I don't know how they're doing it, but they're doing it," Rozin said. "There's snow settled on top of it. They must keep it in place constantly."

"Have you heard of anything like this?" Bekam asked the white-haired woman, but she shrugged.

"You got what you needed," she said. "Now leave me. We have business."

Bekam wanted to summon a proper retort, but Rozin stopped him with a subtle shake of her head. He looked from her to the Nightingale lurking in the other corner and sighed. Rozin pushed the tent flap open and ducked back out into the bright and cold day. Bekam followed her out, and Cillan looked up from his notes long enough to nod a greeting to them.

"Those kinds of shields are impenetrable," Rozin said.

"How much experience do you have with them?" Bekam asked.

"A decent amount, for the normal ones. I've never seen one that large before. At least not in the wild."

"A large... shield?" one of the two halflocks said, his head tucked so his chin almost touched his chest.

"Big enough to surround an entire castle. Do you know of such a thing?" Bekam asked.

The halflock shivered and tilted his head, not quite meeting Bekam's eyes. "Heard of it. Never seen it. Is there a focusing stone?"

"What is a focusing stone?"

The halflock opened his mouth but closed it again, repeating the movement several times. He made only a clicking noise as frustration colored his face. Finally, instead of speaking, he grabbed the board from Cillan and flicked through the pages pinned to it, sending several spiraling to the ground.

"Stop that!" Cillan said, reaching for the board, but Bekam raised a hand, wanting to see where this would lead.

"Here," the halflock said at last before clicking one more time. He thrust the board forward, and Bekam looked down at what seemed to be a map or an architectural rendering of some sort.

"What is that?" Bekam asked.

"It's the last sketch of Crowspire's floor plan before the fortress fell," Cillan said. He stooped to recover the discarded pages, snatching them off the ground before the snow could soak through all of them.

"Do you see what you were looking for?" Bekam asked the halflock. "This focusing stone?"

The robed man jabbed a dirty finger at the paper, poking at one corner of the map. "Right there. That's it."

Bekam leaned over the diagram and could make out a diamond shape drawn in the middle of a circle that seemed to be a tower. It looked entirely ordinary and not worth the excitement it was inciting in this addled mage. Bekam looked up to Cillan. "Do you know what he's talking about?"

Cillan shoved his recovered papers back onto the board, clipping them beneath the map of Crowspire before he slid his glasses up his nose and studied the corner with the diamond shape. He made a "hmph" sound and then an "oh" and looked up at Bekam, peering at him above the rim of his spectacles. "This is very interesting." He looked from Bekam to Rozin and said, "This is an antephon. It must still be in the keep."

Rozin's eyes widened, and she leaned in for a better look. "Are you certain?"

"This is how they marked them on the old maps. I was not expecting that, so I was not looking for it. That's an antephon," Cillan said with more certainty.

"What does that mean?" Bekam asked.

"In the early days of the Empire," Cillan said, "mages had more leniency. They were encouraged to study ways to harness and enhance their abilities. They built antephons."

"They're objects," Rozin said. "Usually stone or metal or wood. Anything natural. Anything that came from the ground. I don't know how they work, but they enhance magic. They make it… bigger."

"Bigger," Bekam said and looked back at the map. "This thing is allowing them to surround Crowspire with an impenetrable barrier. And it's inside the barrier, so we have no way of getting to it."

"I wouldn't say that," Rozin said, color rising in her cheeks. She grinned and tapped her own finger on the drawing. "That's our solution, right there. I have to consult with the others. I'll let you know as soon as we've worked it out." And she was gone before he could respond.

Bekam watched after her until she disappeared around the

third tent at a run. Once she was out of sight, he pulled at Cillan's sleeve. "Let's walk."

The secretary stumbled along beside him in the snow and didn't speak until they were well away from the tent with the Nightingales. Then he leaned closer and said, "She's lying."

"Rozin?"

"No, the woman with the Nightingales. The white-haired woman."

Bekam stopped and looked back toward the tent, where she remained with the assassin who had scouted the keep. "Qae'lon is alive?" he asked.

"Perhaps," Cillan said. He nodded toward the two halflocks, both of them now standing with their heads tucked down, their eyes on the snowy ground and the scars at the backs of their heads showing through their patchy hair. "They both told me she was lying. She sent assassins after Qae'lon, but they never came back."

"They didn't get him. He killed them first," Bekam said, rage boiling in his chest but fear following soon after in his gut.

"Maybe," Cillan said. "There could be any number of explanations. But the woman doesn't know anything. As far as she knows, he's still alive. She sent four Nightingales and doesn't know where any of them are."

Bekam's stomach ached, and he put a hand to his mouth to stifle the sudden nausea. Qae'lon could be out there, knowing Bekam sent Nightingales after him. He could be in Aramore, and Marjiel could be as dead as her servant. Worse still, Qae'lon could be in Karsk. He could be coming straight for Bekam, seeking his vengeance.

Bekam looked back at the tent once more, just as the white-haired woman came out of it. She stood at its entrance, her chin raised and her hands tucked into her sleeves once more. Her eyes traveled across the encampment and stopped on Bekam. With a growl, he spun away from Cillan and stomped back toward her through the snow, fury rising.

"General," a voice called from his left. Bekam spared a look in that direction and broke his stride. Milev had a hand raised, and Prusik stumbled through the snow behind him.

"In a moment," he said, and he was already back at the tent, the white-haired woman staring up at him with her usual disdain but a hint of curiosity now as well. Milev and Prusik stopped just to the left, lingering but saying nothing.

Bekam stared into the woman's cold eyes, and she stared back, neither of them speaking for a moment. He forced his anger down and turned to Milev. "Are your troops ready to march?"

"They will assemble on your order."

"Get them ready," Bekam said. "We march before sundown. The Nightingales will be the first insertion. They'll infiltrate the keep with stealth. The Herons will have a solution to get us past that shield, but the Nightingales will be the first to scale the walls. They will bring down the guards without raising an alarm."

"General Bekam," the woman said, "this was not our agreement."

"Do you lack faith in your assassins?" he asked, snapping his head back toward her. She bristled at the question, and he said, "Someone has to go first." He turned to Milev again. "After the Nightingales are in, the engineers will bring their siege machine to bear."

"Provided they can get it up that mountain," Milev said, looking toward the peaks looming on the horizon.

"We may not need the siege machine," Prusik said.

"They have a functional gate," Bekam said, speaking slowly, as he would to his daughter. "We have to knock it down with something."

Prusik pursed her lips and as if she were contemplating an argument, but then she shrugged. "As you say."

Bekam watched her, trying to find meaning in her capitulation, but it was impossible. Between Prusik and the white-haired woman and Rozin running off to pursue some unknown plan, he had more than enough to worry about. In the end, he turned his attention back to Milev, the only one of them who made any sense to him.

"Organize your troops, and assemble the full company," he said. "They march on my order, and we don't stop until we reach

Esterburgh. No travelers pass us on the road. We risk no messages reaching Crowspire ahead of us. Tomorrow night, we take the keep." Bekam waited for Milev to nod his acknowledgment before he turned to leave. He paused mid-stride and came back for a final word.

"When we reach Crowspire, tell your troops to destroy the rebellion. There will be no prisoners. There will be no parley. I will see every rebel dead, and we will bring that castle down on top of them. Do you understand?"

"I do," Milev said. He swallowed, his eyes dropping. "Every rebel dead."

"Everyone except Akithar. Leave the wizard for me."

CHAPTER 48

Lizandra sat alone in the dark, just like she had yesterday and the day before. And the day before? How many days had it been? Had she eaten today? Was it even time to eat yet? There was an emptiness that wasn't hunger, and yet the guilt filled her so completely that she couldn't think of taking a bite of anything, even if she had felt hungry.

What she felt was nothing.

Lizandra had done what she'd thought was right. She'd saved the life of the best person she'd ever known. She'd known it was right. Hadn't she? Wouldn't the world have been a lesser place without Reykas in it? She had said she would do anything to save him, and so she had. She'd done what was right.

Hadn't she?

Something swam at the edges, gnawing at the guilt. Acknowledging it would be disaster, but every time it came in for another bite, it became clearer it was doubt.

Lizandra covered her face with her hands and bowed her chest into her lap, willing the tears to come, but they wouldn't. There was nothing inside but the guilt and now the doubt as well. There was no room for anything else. If there had been, self loathing might have made an appearance. Whatever she held inside, there were no tears, and so she sat in silence in her room, alone and folded into her own lap.

The knock at the door startled her upright, and she was across the room and pulling the door open before she could second guess herself. It wouldn't be Reykas, but... perhaps?

Samira was looking down the hallway when Lizandra opened the door, and for an instant, she thought about shoving it shut again. But now Samira was looking at her, and there was sudden concern. "Lizzie, are you all right?"

"Just a little under the weather," she said. "I think it was something I ate. I'll be fine." Once she'd started lying, it was hard to stop. She'd never been good at it, but one lie compounded another and another until she didn't even realize she was speaking untruths anymore.

"Is Reykas here?"

A great knot of something hung in Lizandra's throat, and she coughed and almost laughed, her despair wanting to give way to something like panic. "Not right now." He'd left her on the cliffside and had disappeared into the castle. She didn't know where he'd been sleeping or what he'd been doing. Was he even still at Stormbreak? He certainly wasn't there with her.

Lizandra moved to push the door shut, but Samira was talking again. "I was looking for you, too. Vaino has called some sort of meeting for all of us."

"We have to go to it?"

Samira rolled her eyes. "You know how he is. Caius is already there. Best to get it over with."

Lizandra managed a nod and looked down at herself, still wearing the same clothes she'd had on for the past two days. "I should change."

"You're fine," Samira said. "This shouldn't take long."

Lizandra took a step outside, and Samira stopped her again. "You should get your coat, though. It's cold out here."

She nodded again and struggled her arms through the sleeves with a weakness that was more spiritual than physical. She'd done what she'd thought was right, and it wasn't. It wasn't at all.

Magra was dead, and Fairy had nearly died. Aquin was jailed, and who knew what Vaino had planned for her? Reykas was healed, but even that fact was a hard one to accept, given that Lizandra couldn't even look in his eyes without seeing the disappointment and horror she'd caused. She'd thought watching Reykas dying was her greatest fear. How did all of this now seem so much worse?

They were halfway across the courtyard now, and Lizandra had no recollection of even closing her door. Samira was talking again, but the words meant nothing. Nothing meant anything.

Just before they reached the door to Vaino's office, Lizandra caught Samira's hand and stopped her. Samira was mid-sentence, but Lizandra cut her off. "I have to talk to you. I have to tell you something."

Samira looked at her then. She really looked at her, and she squeezed Lizandra's wrist. "After the meeting. Let's get this over with, and then we can talk."

And the moment was gone, and Samira had opened the door to the office, and they were going in, and a silence heavier than any weight Lizandra had ever felt settled around her.

Vaino sat behind his desk, his elbows propped on the surface and his hands clasped before his mouth. Caius stood behind him, his hand over his own mouth, and he looked at the door as the two women entered. His eyes were strained, lines at the corners, and it wasn't just the ordeal of whatever sickness he'd been dealing with ever since Klubridge. It was something more painful than any of that.

The girl, Leyna, stood to Caius' side, her arms crossed, and she turned a furious gaze toward Lizandra as the door closed. And Oreth sat in a chair to the side of the desk, his head bowed, and his hands folded together. He looked at Lizandra, too, but his face was sorrowful, not angry. "I'm sorry, Lizzie. They know."

Lizandra looked from him to Leyna to Vaino to Caius. They all knew. All of them. A cold thrill rushed through Lizandra, and her breath caught in her chest.

"Know what?" Samira stood between Lizandra and the others, and she looked from them to her and asked more directly, "What does he mean, Lizzie?"

But it was Leyna who answered. "How could you? How could you do it at all, but then to make Oreth a part of it? And—"

"Leyna," Vaino said, and she fell silent, but it was with effort.

LIZANDRA'S DEEPEST FEAR

Her jaw clamped shut, and she was breathing hard through her nose.

Vaino was calm where Leyna was not, and he turned his dark eyes on Lizandra. "Oreth unburdened himself to Leyna, and she brought this story to me. I have to admit, it's quite a tale, and I'd like to hear the truth of it from you."

Samira snapped her head back around to Vaino. "I won't have this. Whatever you're accusing Lizzie of doing—"

"No," Lizandra said, and Samira stopped and looked at her. But Lizandra's mouth slammed shut after that. Every eye in the room was on her, and her pulse thrummed in her throat, heavy and accelerating. In the courtyard, she'd been an inch away from admitting it all, from telling Samira what she'd done. She'd been on the precipice, ready to take the last step over the edge, and now she'd been pushed.

Lizandra managed a shaky breath before she said, "Samira, it's true. I did it. It was me."

Samira took a step back, her forehead creasing. It was doubtful that she understood the breadth of it, but it was coming together. It showed on her face.

"I betrayed the rebels. I betrayed everybody," Lizandra said. "I stole the supply route from Oreth. It was me, not him. I traded it to the Empire, and they saved Reykas. They saved him."

Samira's mouth was moving now, but Lizandra could hear none of what she was saying. Caius had his hand over his eyes, and Oreth's head hung low again. Leyna was talking, yelling, but there were no words. A rushing sound flooded Lizandra's ears, replacing everything else, and for an instant it was the noise of the sea, just as it had been on the ship before any of this had happened. Before she had done any of this. Before Stormbreak, before Karsk, before this moment. Her vision narrowed to a dark pinhole in the next seconds, just before her balance failed and her knees gave way. She pitched forward and welcomed the hard floor as it rushed toward her.

Reykas drove the wagon hard and fast through that first night. The sky was clear enough for the moon to light the road ahead of him, but the travel was still treacherous. Snow covered the trail, giving him a dimly glowing path to follow, but it also mounded at the sides of the road. Speeding through the dark, Reykas had no perception of depth or distance, so he kept the horse pointed straight ahead and whispered entreaties to the wheels that they'd stay on the packed powder.

His face was numb, and his fingers were aching by the next morning when they stopped to rest. Taking the horse to the side of the road risked upending the whole cart in the snow, so they remained in the center of the roadway. They'd been stopped there for only a moment, the horse's breathing slowing and Reykas blowing into his cupped hands, when there was movement ahead.

Reykas blinked into the bright whiteness of the morning light, and he squinted up the path, toward the ascending hills. Had he imagined it? He stared past the treeline, up to where the sunlight hit the base of the mountain, but there was nothing. He couldn't have imagined it. There had been a definite motion far ahead, something black against the white of the snow. Something too big to be a bird flitting past the edge of his vision.

He squinted into the distance, but there was nothing but the road and the snow and the trees and the hills. His brows drew together, and he glanced behind his back, certain for an instant that whatever he'd seen ahead had somehow doubled back and was creeping up on him. But there was nothing behind him aside from the empty road he'd already traveled. The snow covered the road in a smooth blanket, broken only by the twin tracks of his wagon's wheels and the hooves of his—

Reykas frowned and turned all the way around, standing now. The hairs on his forearms stood as goosebumps pimpled his flesh. His horse's tracks marked the center of the road, between the cartwheels, but two more sets of hooves headed in the same direction on either side. He turned forward again and peered over the front edge of the cart. Those hoof tracks to the left and right marched forward, ahead of him and past the point where his own horse's tracks ended. He blinked into the distance again. He might not see them now, but he hadn't been wrong. There were two more horses ahead on the road.

Rebels? Who else would be taking that remote road north from Esterburgh? Who else would be heading toward the Stormbreak Sanctuary?

The only rebels he'd seen coming and going from the keep were pulling wagons like the one he was driving. These could be messengers or some other outliers, but Reykas would have bet the full cargo of his cart those were Imperials ahead of him. Scouts snooping ahead of the army, most likely.

He sat hard on the seat as his mind flew through the possibilities. If he continued up the road, he'd eventually encounter them or maybe even pass them, if they saw him coming and hid off to the side. And then what? He was in no condition to fight anyone.

Reykas flexed the fingers on his right hand, no longer expecting the magic to be there, but something about the motion was reassuring.

No, he couldn't come upon them. The Empire had the element of surprise on its side, and they'd kill him to keep him from reaching Crowspire with news of the impending attack. He couldn't ride past them, but he had to get around them. What, then?

Reykas half turned and reached behind the seat to where the driver's pack sat at the front of the wagon. He dragged the satchel up by its straps, and he had it open before it was even onto the seat. There were rations in the bottom, but he ignored those, despite the sudden hunger rising in his gut. His long fingers flipped through the papers inside until he found the one he'd hoped would be in there. He pulled the map out and spread it across his lap.

A series of black lines ascended, crossed, and curved over and around the mountains. It was a messy jumble of a drawing, but Reykas recognized the straight one at the bottom that led from the town north. That was the road he was on. The tangle of lines described all the other ways through the mountains. The rebellion probably took different routes at different times, just in case they needed to evade Imperial suspicion. Just in case of a time like this.

Reykas traced another line with his finger, following it from where it split off to the right and wound around in a great half loop. He followed a third one, an offshoot from the second, and then he was on to a fourth, then doubling back to the third. He sat in silence for ten minutes or more, studying the map until he found his way. It would take extra time, but it was the only thing he could do. He tossed the satchel back into the bed of the cart but kept the map on his lap as he urged the horse onward.

They reached the first offshoot about half an hour later. The twin sets of tracks continued north along the original road, but Reykas guided his horse to the left. The snow was deeper here as he rode along a shadier path, and the cart's wheels protested but turned. The way forward was more difficult, but he had to press for speed now that the other riders were no longer directly ahead.

Trees crowded in, their bare arms stretching a canopy over the roadway as he reached the third path and took it northwest. The road angled up there, something the map hadn't shown but that he should have anticipated. The sun was dipping low once more by the time they'd made it a mile on that increasingly steep incline. They weren't going fast enough. If those had been Imperial scouts on the main road, they'd have time to reach Stormbreak and report back before Reykas even made it halfway back.

He pulled on the reins until the horse slowed and stopped once more. The beast huffed a frustrated breath and shook his head twice. "I know, friend," Reykas said.

Reykas looked back at the cart. Whatever was in those bags and barrels was probably important, but it wasn't important enough to risk the whole rebellion. It was heavy cargo, and the cart itself had more weight than the horse could pull up that hill with any kind of speed. They'd have to stop to rest too many times, and they'd never make it in time.

Should he look through the cargo, just in case?

Reykas slid down from his seat and caught the side of the cart with his hand. His feet crunched in the snow, and he nearly slipped. The hill was steeper than it had seemed from up in his seat. The map had shown this path to be a quick way back to the keep, but that speed must have been bought with a faster ascension.

He gave the supplies one last glance and grabbed the driver's pack, slinging its longest strap diagonally across his body. Those rations might save his life on the journey ahead. He didn't know whether the pack might also hold papers the Empire shouldn't see, but better to be careful than not. The bag secured, he crouched in front of the cart, careful not to put his body too close to the backside of the horse. Getting kicked in the head would do no good for him or anyone else.

He'd never hitched a horse to a cart before, but it was easy enough to follow the gear from the wagon up to where it attached to the complicated straps and bindings secured around the animal. Those straps looked like they were separate from the saddle and reins, but Reykas still pulled at all the buckles with care until he was certain he was only pulling the cart loose. The horse gave a couple of annoyed steps backward and forward as he worked, but Reykas finally released the last fastener, and the gear dropped into the snow.

The cart shifted as soon as it didn't have the horse holding it in place, and it rolled out of Reykas' grasp. There was nothing to do now but watch as it picked up speed, heading backwards down the hill. Reykas flinched as it bumped off the edge of the road and dropped out of sight. There was a distant cracking that sounded like tree branches, but the great crash he expected from the upended cart never came. The wagon was gone, swallowed by the wilderness as if it had never been there in the first place.

"Let's go," Reykas said, pulling his eyes away from the spot where the cart had disappeared, and he dragged himself up astride the horse. He lacked Lizandra's facility with horses, but he'd ridden a few himself in the time before they'd come to Klubridge. He leaned forward and urged the horse ahead, and it wasn't long before they were headed up the hill once more, this time at something near a trot.

The trip back to Stormbreak was quicker than the one to Esterburgh had been. Stretches of the road were nearly impassible because of mounds of snow and fallen branches, but

Reykas made the journey with a speed that surprised even him. His strength and endurance were still returning, but they saw him all the way up the mountain and into the shadow of the giant stone bird.

As he rode out of the trees and onto the main road again, he hesitated, his eyes sweeping the ground. There were no fresh marks from hooves or feet. Whoever had been ahead of him had not reached the keep yet. Or they had arrived and were watching from afar.

Reykas looked over his shoulder as he moved onto the path, but he tried to make the glance a casual one. He didn't need Imperials to set upon him this close to his destination. But there was nothing to see. No riders waited behind him, and nothing disturbed the powdery snow for as far as he could see it, down to where the road turned behind a huge rock.

He turned back to the keep and spurred the horse onward. They were halfway across the covered bridge when he realized he'd forgotten to check for the shield. Nothing had blocked the path. That was convenient for his return but would be a problem when the Imperials came up that mountain unimpeded any day now.

A teenage boy blinked at him, his mouth open, as Reykas rode into the stable. "Has anyone else come through here today?" Reykas asked.

The boy shook his head and took the reins when Reykas handed them down but said nothing else. Reykas shifted his weight and dropped from the horse. When his feet met the ground, his knees buckled, and he nearly collapsed. The boy catching him under his arm was the only thing that kept him upright. It felt like his arm nearly came out of the socket, but he did not fall.

"Thank you," Reykas said, rising shakily to his feet. The trip had been more taxing than he'd realized. He was used to weakness coming upon him, but this was different from the sickness. This was pure exhaustion from riding a horse up a frozen mountain day and night, just after lying in bed for ages. It was a wonder he made it back at all.

Back on his feet without his legs giving way, Reykas nodded

to the boy and headed out the back door of the stable and crossed to Stormbreak's open gate, keeping his steps slow and steady. The guard at the gate raised his eyebrows in recognition as Reykas approached but didn't try to stop him. Instead, he nodded his head toward the inner walkway, and Reykas followed him. The walk across the courtyard to Vaino's office felt longer than the entire journey up the mountain had been, but he made it step by step, the rebel with a sword strapped to his hip keeping half a step to his side.

The door was already open when they reached it, and Vaino rose from his desk, his eyes blazing. "Where have you been?" he asked before Reykas had even come through the doorway.

Reykas could have answered the question directly. He could have told Vaino what Lizandra had done. He could have told him about the driver, murdered in a street not far to the south. He would fill in some of those details later, and he'd likely never speak of others. For now, though, it sufficed to be succinct.

"The Empire knows where we are. They are coming."

CHAPTER 49

Samira stormed up the stone steps and took the turn at the landing with her feet hardly touching the ground. Shock and betrayal and confusion swam together in her head, but her heart was full of determination and anger.

Lizzie was the leak. She was the one who had betrayed the rebellion, gotten Magra and her two guards killed, and seen Fairy nearly maimed. She'd caused these horrible things, and she had confessed to all of it. That was bad enough, but when Samira had immediately demanded that Aquin be released, Vaino had said he preferred to wait for a proper investigation. What more needed to be investigated? Aquin was innocent, and she had sat rotting in that cell for far too long.

Samira reached the second floor, and she paused, her hand steadying her against the wall, as she remembered the way Lizzie had collapsed. It had all been for Reykas. Lizzie had made a horrible decision in order to save the one she loved. She was to blame for every bit of this, but would it have been that much different if Caius had been the one at risk? If Aquin had?

Samira frowned at that and slowed her breathing. The thought of willfully condemning someone in order to save someone else sent a chill down her spine, but could Samira truly say there was anything she wouldn't do to save the people she loved?

Looking down the hallway, toward the cell doors where the two guards stood on duty, Samira knew she had no space for condemnation. What Lizzie did was wrong, but what Samira was about to do might be just as terrible an idea. That didn't deter her for an instant, though. She pushed away from the wall and strode down the hallway, only now drawing the guards' attention.

"I want to see her," she said.

Vaino would not keep Aquin locked away for a crime she had nothing to do with. Samira had no qualms about countermanding and betraying him in order to see justice done. She had no loyalty to the man, despite Caius' belief that Vaino knew what he was doing. Caius had told her Vaino was right about the best way to hold together the rebellion, that he was probably right about Peregrine being a specter manufactured by the Empire, that he knew what they needed to do to see themselves free once more in Teshovar, able to live without fear of their bounties.

Some of those things might be true, but Caius' trust in an untested leader was not enough to stay Samira's hand. It wasn't enough for her to accept as a justification for Vaino's incompetence when it came to this current intrigue.

One of the guards was shaking her head. "We can't just—"

"Let her in," the other one said. "Vaino's allowed her in before."

Samira was unsure whether it was the prior access she'd been allowed or the murder in her eyes that convinced the first guard, but the sullen woman pulled the metal key from her pocket and fitted it into the lock. Samira said nothing more to the guards and didn't even wait for the door to finish swinging open before she pushed past and into Aquin's cell.

It was exactly as it had been the last time she'd visited: a tiny room with stone all around, bisected down the center with a wall of metal bars. Aquin lay on the small wooden cot someone had shoved into the far corner, and she started and looked over her shoulder as the door swung shut.

"Samira?" She blinked herself out of her sleep and looked around the chamber, disoriented.

"Lizandra was the mole," Samira said and dropped to her knees next to Aquin.

A voice behind her made a shushing noise, and Samira looked toward the bars, where Aquin's neighbor stood with one hand on the dark rungs and the other at his mouth, his index finger pressed to his lips. She frowned at him, and he pointed back toward the door. Toward the guards.

Samira nodded. It only made sense that a man as paranoid as Vaino would instruct his guards to listen to any conversations among his prisoners. She leaned closer to Aquin and whispered, "Lizzie admitted it."

Aquin's eyes went wide, and she pushed herself back on the mattress, sitting up against the wall. "Why would she do that?"

"I don't know the details, but she traded information for a cure for Reykas. She must have gone to Karsk." Samira exhaled as the plan assembled itself in her head. It was all so obvious, but it was too late to change or fix any of it. It made sense that Lizzie had gone to Karsk. There was the chance of a cure there, and nothing would stop her from helping Reykas. Not Reykas himself telling her he didn't want to go, and least of all Samira telling her going to Karsk was the wrong thing to do.

"She went to Karsk," Samira said with more conviction. "She made a deal with the Empire and traded them Magra for Reykas' cure."

Aquin's mouth dropped open. "That's…" She hesitated and blinked a couple more times but then looked back at Samira. "That makes perfect sense."

"After she confessed, I demanded that Vaino free you."

"And he wouldn't," Aquin said.

"He says he wants a full investigation, whatever that means."

"It means he still thinks Aquin was complicit," the man in the neighboring cell said, his voice as soft as Samira's.

Samira nodded once.

Aquin shook her head. "Then there's no hope. They're going to execute me."

"They are not," Samira said. She hesitated and looked once more at the door before ducking her head so her lips were even closer to Aquin's ear. "I'm coming for you. I don't have a plan yet, but I'm breaking you out of here. It will be within the next few days, and I'll come at night."

Aquin pulled away, her mouth twisted and her brows drawn together. "Don't be absurd. How would you get me out of here without getting yourself caught and locked up alongside me?"

"Let me worry about that. I have tools they don't know about," Samira said, and she raised her hand between them, the faint glow of magic radiating from her palm.

"Even if you got me free, what then? Where would I go?"

"We go south," Samira said. "Away from here. First to Esterburgh and then to Karsk. From there, we continue south. We get new names, we change our appearances. We fall into Teshovar, and nobody has to know who we are or where we came from."

"No," Aquin said. "We're in the middle of nowhere, and there's snow and ice all around. How would we even make it out of the mountains? And you can't go with me. You have Caius and—"

Samira pressed her finger to Aquin's lips. "You are my priority. I've ruined enough of your life, and I'm not letting this stand. Caius has Apak. He has Reykas and the others. He'll need to be there for them through whatever happens with Lizzie. You and I have each other. Whatever you might think of me for getting you involved in all this, let me help you now. Hate me later, but trust me now."

Aquin sat with her mouth half parted, and she had no response. The man shifted behind them and said, "If you do this, you'll be moving against the rebellion. Vaino will take it as a confirmation that Aquin is an Imperial sympathizer and that you are, too. You need to be prepared for the consequences."

Samira heard and understood every word of the warning. She didn't dismiss it, but she couldn't acknowledge it, either. The moment called for planning and action, and any doubt could derail either or both of those. She stood from the floor next to Aquin's bed. As she backed away toward the door, she said, "Be ready. When I come, it'll be at night."

∼

"How do you feel?"

Caius weighed the question briefly before saying, "Better."

Samira eyed him and noted the dark patches under his eyes, the lines on his face where they hadn't been before all this began, the gray sprinkled through his hair where it used to be brown. He caught her looking and gave her a weak smile. "I didn't say I was good. I said I'm better."

She sat on the chair next to his bed. He was sitting on the corner of the mattress, his shoulders rounded and exhaustion clear in his movements, but something did look better about him. Getting back to Stormbreak had done him good, even if they were surrounded by Aescalan now.

"You don't think you should be in the infirmary?"

"What more are they going to do for me?" he said. "The doctor tried to give me some kind of powder to help me sleep. Sleeping's not the problem. It's the dreaming. The dreaming and the hallucinations and who knows what else?"

"It's all still happening like it was?"

"It is. Maybe a little less since we got back here, but it's more or less the same as before."

She frowned and studied his face again. Behind those tired eyes and that haggard growth of beard, he was the same person he'd always been. He was her best friend, and he'd been beside her through so much. "What happened with Lizzie?" she asked.

He sighed and shook his head. "She came around after you left. I don't think she knew what was happening even then, but Micah had his people carry her to a room."

"A cell?"

"Just a room. Somewhere she could stay until he figures out what to do with her."

"What do you think he'll do?" Samira asked.

Caius met her eyes but didn't have an answer. "Do you know where Reykas is?"

"No. He should know about this."

"I suspect he already does. That could be why nobody can find him."

Samira raised her eyebrows. "You think he left? That he's gone from Stormbreak?"

"I don't know where he would go, but it's possible."

"The guards would have seen him leave."

"Maybe," he said, but he didn't sound convinced.

Samira considered how to ask her next question before she asked it outright. "What's going to happen with Aquin?"

"I imagine she'll be let out soon."

"You heard Vaino. When I asked him, he said he wanted to investigate more."

The slight smile formed on Caius' face again. "I don't recall you doing much asking."

"Well," she said. "In any case, she's still locked up, and it's not right."

Caius opened his hands. "We can't do anything. Micah is the one who gives the orders here. We have to wait until he's satisfied, and then he'll let her go."

"But what if he doesn't? What if he decides she's in league with Lizzie?"

"She's not, though. Lizzie said it herself. She acted alone."

Samira wanted to press the issue further, but it would do no good. Caius saw the rebellion as the only way they'd all be free, and that meant bowing to Micah Vaino and his incompetent rule. She clasped her hands in her lap and looked at them as she said, "You have to help Lizzie, Caius. You can't let Vaino execute her."

He nodded. "What do you have in mind?"

"You have sway with him. You can convince him to be lenient."

"She betrayed him and the whole rebellion. The Empire could have found Stormbreak because of what she did. They could have followed Fairy back here."

Samira looked up at him. "You think she deserves to be killed for that?"

"Of course not. But he's going to order that something be done. We can't expect her to just walk free."

"We need Reykas here," Samira said.

Caius dropped his head, and they sat in a familiar silence.

Samira looked at him from the corner of her eye. He sat hunched, tired and weakened, but he would be all right. He was getting better, and he'd be able to shoulder whatever was ahead of them. Was this the last time they'd share this kind of silence? After so many years, was this where their paths diverged?

She reached across the space and put her hand over his. "Caius, you need to know something."

He looked at her hand and then up at her. "What is it?"

"You've always been my best friend. You taught me how to take care of others, and I'm a better person for knowing you."

His smile was uncertain now, but he put his other hand on top of hers. "You know I feel that way about you, too, but what is this? Is something wrong?"

Samira surprised herself with a laugh. "Everything is wrong. But we both have to do whatever we can to make it right again."

He nodded, his eyes still questioning.

She opened her mouth and was an inch away from telling him her intentions. From telling him how she planned to free Aquin and flee south with her. From telling him how she'd try to find him after all this was finished, but she couldn't be certain she'd ever be able to emerge from hiding. Those words nearly came, but uncertainty stopped them. How much did Caius believe in Vaino and the rebellion? Would he try to talk her out of this? Would he succeed?

So, instead, she said, "There's just so much pulling at us right now. If something happens... If we're ever separated. If I'm not here," she said and waited until she was certain her voice wouldn't tremble. "If I'm not here with you, you still have to take care of all of them. Lizzie, Reykas, Oreth, Fairy now. Even Apak whenever he comes back."

"We'll both do that," he said. "Nothing is going to separate us. What do you think—"

"I don't think anything. I just need to say this, just in case." She swallowed hard and looked away from him. If she held his eyes for another instant, she'd either spill her whole plan to him or she'd backpedal on the entire thing. She couldn't risk leaving Aquin captive for a moment longer than necessary, so she looked at the wall. "We don't know what might happen. I need you to know that, no matter where we are, I'll always care about you. I will always love you, and nothing will change that. Not space or time or the entire bloody Empire and the rebellion and the Aescalan dragging us apart."

"Nothing's dragging us apart," he said and squeezed her hand. "We're going to be all right."

She risked a look at him again and matched his smile. "Just promise me you'll remember that. If I'm ever not here, you have to take care of the rest of them. Don't let them hurt Lizzie, and don't let things go badly for anyone else."

"I promise," he said. She could tell he meant it, but his eyes were still uncertain. That was as good as either of them would get. She nodded and slid her hand out from between his, and her heart ached for what she knew she had to do.

CHAPTER 50

Lizandra must have been unconscious for only a few seconds, but it was long enough to throw the room into turmoil.

Suddenly Caius had been there, squatting on the floor and holding her head and saying it would be all right. And Samira was yelling at Vaino and jabbing her finger at him, saying something about Aquin. Leyna was yelling back at Samira and pointing at Lizandra. Vaino sat in the middle of it, saying nothing until he shook his head and told Samira something about an investigation, and that just made everything worse. Samira had yelled words at him and at Leyna that Lizandra had never heard her use, and then Samira was gone, the door slamming behind her.

The minutes after that were a dizzy smear of hands and voices and cold and shame. Hours, likely, given the angle of the sun and the dimness of its light through the single window that opened into this chamber. Lizandra couldn't remember exactly how she got from the floor of Vaino's office to the room where they put her, or even where that room was, but that's where she was sitting, once again alone, when she realized there were tears. After all that time and all that emptiness, she was finally crying.

Lizandra raised a shaking hand to her face and touched her fingertips to the wet trails beneath her eyes, hardly believing

LIZANDRA'S DEEPEST FEAR

what she was feeling. And that caused even more tears to fall, and they kept coming, bending her over double on her seat, her shoulders shaking and her arms wrapped around her stomach. She cried all the tears she could imagine crying, and then she cried more.

It all poured out in a torrent of shame, guilt, and fear. Reykas abandoning her. The horror in Samira's eyes. The misery in Oreth's. The hatred in Leyna's. Only Caius had shown her compassion, and that only made it worse. Why should anyone feel sorry for her, when she'd built this disaster with her own cunning?

When the tears and the shaking had stopped, she ran a hand through her hair and pulled it back from where it had spilled down her face and stuck in wet strands to her cheeks. She sniffed and wiped at her nose with the heel of her palm, and her head ached with the effort of drawing a simple breath.

They hadn't tied her up. They hadn't even scolded her, as far as she could remember. They'd just taken her to this room and tossed her inside and told her to wait.

She stood, her legs unsteady for only a moment, and she went to the door. She didn't have to try it to know it was locked, but she still put a hand on the doorknob. She was a prisoner now. She'd confessed to her crimes, and she would pay for them.

Lizandra hugged her arms around herself again and looked up at the narrow window placed high in the wall behind her. There was no glass in it, and she could feel the breeze coming through, cold and bitter. It was high on the wall, but it was reachable. It was probably even wide enough to fit through, maybe even an inch taller than the window she'd escaped through in the bank back in Klubridge. A high enough jump, and she could be through it and out and away.

She considered all the angles and her trajectory in a couple of seconds, but it was an academic exercise. She had no intention of escaping this time. This was the one time she'd stay, and she would face whatever might come through that door for her. Reykas must hate her now, and none of the rest of them would ever trust her again. The chance that she could regain any of their trust was slim. But that chance was nonexistent if she allowed herself to give in to fear, as she always did. If she let herself bound up that wall and slide out that window, she'd be on her own forever, and there'd be no coming back.

She would stay, if only for the hope that she could somehow regain some semblance of respect from Reykas and thereby find some trust in herself once more.

Lizandra was still looking up at the window, watching snowflakes dance past it in lazy spirals, when the door slammed open. She flinched at the noise and spun to face it, even as a chunk of splintered wood dropped to the floor, the doorknob soon following with a dull thud.

The Aescalan, Dekan Hama, had to stoop as he entered, and even then, his head barely cleared the top of the doorway. He wore a scowl behind his thick beard, and in his right hand he held the hatchet he'd used to bash the door open.

"Is it true?" he asked her.

If Leyna had hated her, there was no word for the way Hama looked at her. His tiny eyes swam with malice, wet with fury. "Is it true?" he asked again, louder this time, and he banged the backside of the hatchet against the wall so hard it knocked pebbles of rock loose.

Lizandra backed away, fear now eclipsing everything else she'd felt in the instant before Hama arrived. "Please," she said.

Hama snarled at her and advanced, juggling the small axe up so he held it higher on the haft. "Is it true?"

She could do nothing but nod. The words were stuck in her throat, and her mouth was dry, so she nodded.

Hama turned his head and spat on the floor, a great glob that looked oily on the stone. "You filthy traitor," he said, his voice shaking now. His hand shook, too, his anger making the axe quiver in his grip. "You helped them. You helped Peregrine."

"Dekan Hama." The voice came from outside the door, and it was unfamiliar and carried no tone of command, but it stopped Hama in his tracks. "Dekan Hama, you will leave this woman alone."

Hama was breathing hard, and the look he gave Lizandra was murder, but he didn't move any closer to her. The axe hung

LIZANDRA'S DEEPEST FEAR

loose in his fingers. "She's a traitor," he said. "She deserves death."

"She deserves a fair trial," the other man said, and Lizandra could see him through the door now. He was tall, with light brown skin, and he looked exhausted. "Leave her alone."

"I—"

"You say I'm your scion," the other man said.

"The scion of the Tamrat," Hama said. The correction seemed slight but significant to him.

"If you want my help, you'll leave this woman alone."

Hama looked from the scion to Lizandra, and his lip curled at her in hatred one more time. With a final snort, he turned away and ducked through the door again, his axe slapping against the ruined door's frame as he left.

Lizandra's hands trembled, and she placed them on the back of her chair to keep her whole body from rattling. "Th—Thank you," she managed to say without her teeth clacking together.

The man—the Tamrat scion—watched her for a long moment before he looked down the hallway to his left, toward the direction Hama had gone. "I'll let Micah Vaino know about this. Hama won't do that again." And then he was gone, and Lizandra lowered herself onto the chair with shaking legs, and she sat facing the shattered door.

CHAPTER 51

Apak sat on the edge of a desk at the center of the gallery. The surface was higher than it had seemed, and he had had to hoist himself backwards onto it, a task he had managed with minimal shuffling and grunting. His fingers drummed on the desktop, tapping a rhythm against what seemed to be a white marble composite. It had been less than an hour since Alev trapped Qae'lon, but it was becoming increasingly evident that every minute that passed brought Alev closer to exhaustion.

Nahk stood between Apak and the blocked doorway where Qae'lon stared at them from within the transparent bubble. He caught Apak's eye, and his smirk sent a shudder through Apak's shoulders, forcing him to avert his gaze. Nahk was looking at Apak now, her arms crossed, and a crease between her eyebrows. She turned away from the trapped mage to approach the desk where Apak sat.

Nahk angled her head to keep Qae'lon in her field of view but leaned close to Apak's ear to whisper, "The Seal of Metarr. Do you have it?"

Apak sighed and looked back toward the doorway. His small satchel sat against the wall, less than a foot on the opposite side of the bubble, but fortunately not within it. "It is there," he said, and Nahk followed his gaze.

Qae'lon glanced at the floor where the bag sat, just outside his reach. "And what might that be?" he asked, his voice betraying a genuine curiosity.

"Nothing we need right now," Naecara said. She turned to Nahk and Apak. "We're not leaving here without that Eye." She did not try to lower her voice as Nahk had done.

"How do you think we're getting it now?" Nahk asked.

Qae'lon watched the exchange with a placid smile, the Eye of Kelixia still in his hands. "Drop the shield, and perhaps we can discuss terms," he said.

"Could you drop this shield and kill him with a new one?" Naecara asked.

Alev blanched and shook their head. "Don't even ask me to try that. It's all I can do to hold him in place with this one."

"Kam Dhaz," Qae'lon said. Naecara's attention came back to the mage, but he was looking in the other direction now, toward the white wooden chair where Dhaz had been sitting for the past half hour, his elbows on his knees and his head down. He looked up when Qae'lon called his name.

"We have enjoyed a mutually beneficial relationship," Qae'lon said, his voice now saccharine, like Samira sounded when she needed a favor from Apak. "I see no reason for that relationship to end, despite our present impasse."

"What are you talking about?" Dhaz asked. He looked more miserable than Apak could have expected. The man had volunteered himself for this mission and had been the one to lead them directly to the tower, but he seemed to have underestimated the true risk.

Qae'lon smiled, and his white teeth were vicious behind his thin lips. "Kill the mage, and you can go free. I will not pursue you, and I will compensate you for the loss of your facility in Klubridge."

Naecara opened her mouth, but Apak spoke first. "Qae'lon lies."

Dhaz looked at him, a line forming between his eyebrows. Would the foolish man actually consider this offer? For the moment, Dhaz had not moved from his seat. Apak spoke again before he had a chance to consider the terms. "Qae'lon will kill all of us as soon as the shield drops. In fact, I suspect he could have killed any of us at any moment but has chosen not to. He wants to do it with the Eye. He is toying with us. He is toying with you, Dhaz. He wants to watch you break."

Naecara frowned from Apak to Qae'lon and back again. "What do you mean he could kill us?"

Apak nodded toward the mage. "He is able to extend his magic outside the shield. I have never seen that done before, but he is able to do it."

"That's not possible," Alev said. "I know how my shields work, and that's not how they work."

"It is now," Apak said. He pointed to the nearest orb, floating silently above its plinth. He moved his arm to point to the second one, and then he pointed at the third. "These spheres maintain the structure of this tower. There probably are others somewhere in other rooms. Qae'lon focuses his magic into them and maintains the magic that holds the building together. If he were not sending his energy into the orbs, they would not be levitating as they are." He raised his arms and looked up toward the skylights. "This tower would not continue to stand." He lowered his arms and looked back toward Qae'lon. "He is able to use his magic outside the shield. I suspect the shield diminishes his abilities, but that is supposition. There is a very real chance that he could kill us on a whim."

Nahk had been staring at Qae'lon the whole time and said, "It's true. Apak's right."

Qae'lon shrugged inside the bubble, his palms turned up and the Eye resting in his right hand. "What can I say? I do enjoy a bit of drama." His thin lips turned upward in an expression that could have been amusement or disgust or some mixture of the two. "You are determined to take this weapon from me, and I am determined to hold on to it. I'd like to see how this plays out."

"He might be able to use his magic out here, but he still can't pass through the shield," Alev said. Their voice was strained. How much longer would they be able to hold the barrier in place?

"Getting tired?" Qae'lon asked with a sneer. "I'd say you have less than an hour left. What do you think?"

"I'll hold you as long as I need to," Alev said.

"And then? What is your plan? You'll drop your guard sooner or later."

Alev had no reply to that. They all knew it was the truth. Alev was tiring, and as soon as they let the magic slip for even an instant, Qae'lon would be free. He had not attacked them yet, but it was certain that he would move once the shield did not separate him from his victims. Would he obliterate all of them in a single blast from the Eye? What a disappointing death, all things considered.

"Might I introduce an additional complication?" Qae'lon asked, his smile devilish now. "What do you think your friends are doing right now, while we have this parley?"

None of them responded, but Naecara's back stiffened. Qae'lon surely noticed and said, "I would imagine they are trying to keep warm in that frozen fortress where you've been hiding. It's just north of Esterburgh, yes?"

Naecara's face twisted with anguish, and she looked at Nahk. Nahk returned the look, but the message they communicated in silence was lost to Apak.

"Oh, yes," Qae'lon continued, rolling the Eye from his right palm to the left. "We know where your precious Stormbreak Sanctuary is located. Plans have been laid, an army has formed, and I can assure you that all hope for your rebellion is lost."

"You know nothing," Naecara said, but her hand trembled at her side.

"I know all. I know you've been holed up in Crowspire for years now, and I know it is woefully undefended." He leaned toward her, his head pressing so close to the shield that his hair displaced against it. "I know General Bekam leads his forces there, even now. By the time you returned from here to the north, all your friends would have been dead for weeks. But you won't be returning there, will you? I think you all know how this exchange will end."

Naecara met Apak's eyes, and he saw despair there. Any doubt that Qae'lon was bluffing had fled. He knew exactly where Stormbreak was located, and that meant, despite any rivalry between the two men, that Bekam and the rest of the

Empire knew as well. He was correct. They were doomed, all of them.

Qae'lon saw his victory in their eyes. He leered at Alev. "I remember when the first brick was laid at Crowspire, child. You underestimate my patience, and you have no idea who you're dealing with."

Naecara said to Apak, "What do we—"

"Ha!" Qae'lon's eyes blazed. Apak followed them to the bench where Alev sat, facing the wizard. Alev, whose head now lolled forward, their eyes slipping shut, their mouth hanging open in exhaustion.

A rumble sounded, similar to the growing hum that had filled the theater whenever Apak threw the switch for his electrical lights. Qae'lon had a tight grip on the Eye of Kelixia, his own furious stare nothing compared to the red glare that built inside the artifact, glowing around the ball. "I knew you would—No!"

At Qae'lon's exclamation, Apak looked back to Alev. Their face blurred, and he blinked twice, unable to resolve their features until their eyes and mouth steadied once more, as firm and intently focused on Qae'lon as ever. Nahk stood at their side, glaring at Qae'lon with determination.

Apak was not looking at the wizard in the instant the Eye of Kelixia erupted, too late for Qae'lon to stop it, but he heard the brief crashing sizzle of destruction and saw the flash of red light reflected off all the white surfaces in the room. Alev yelped and bolted to their feet as Apak spun back toward the mage. The bubble was visible now, tinted red but otherwise empty. It lost its form when Alev staggered a step forward, and the red hue resolved into a fine mist that settled to wet the floor. It was the last remains of Qae'lon, now nothing more than vapor.

"What…" Naecara stammered, "What?"

"I did what I had to do," Nahk said, stepping away from her position next to Alev. "It was the only way out."

"You Veiled Alev with their own face," Apak said.

"You can do that?" Dhaz asked, now coming to his feet as well.

"Apparently so," Nahk said. "For just long enough to trick him, at least."

Alev stammered before saying, "My barrier was still up when he activated the Eye. It blew back on him, just like Apak said it would."

Naecara blinked at Nahk and gasped. "The Eye! He was holding the Eye!"

"He was, and now it's gone just as much as he is. The Empire won't have it anymore. Nobody will have it," Nahk said, her gaze level on Naecara.

The two women were still staring at each other when the first floating orb dropped. It hit the top of the column beneath it with a sharp crack, splitting into shards that looked like black glass before they evaporated into a dark smoke. Then the second orb fell, and the floor shifted, tilting just enough to throw Naecara off balance.

"The tower is unmaking itself," Apak said. "We have precious little time."

He moved fast, careful to avoid the slick spot on the stone where Qae'lon had stood, and he scooped his satchel from the floor. He looked through the doorway and down the long corridor. A corridor that was becoming shorter by the instant as the far end rushed toward him. Apak ripped the Seal free and tossed the satchel aside. "We must go now."

The third sphere fell, and a wave of dizziness hit Apak. He closed his eyes against it and forced himself backwards, toward his companions. "Put your hands on me. Hurry!"

He opened his eyes as Nahk grabbed his arm, Naecara taking hold of his wrist an instant later. Alev had a hand on his shoulder, and Kam Dhaz was just behind them, reaching for them.

"No, not Dhaz!" Naecara said, her voice rising over the din that built around them as reality spun and tore itself apart. "He's not coming to Stormbreak!"

"A bit late for that," Nahk said.

Apak frowned at Naecara and grabbed Dhaz by the forearm. "I will not leave him. I will leave none of us."

The world extruded, and Apak closed his eyes, and everything went red again.

CHAPTER 52

"How well do you know this Lizzie? Lizandra?" Wickes asked. Samira had called her by the nickname, but Aquin had used her full name.

"Not well," Aquin said. "I just met her shortly before we all left Klubridge. I like Reykas. He's her... I don't know what he is now. He is a good man and honorable, and I can't imagine him taking this lightly."

"You don't seem overly surprised by all this."

"After the last few months, not much surprises me anymore," she said with a sigh. "But no, I did not see this coming. I thought there might not even be a mole. That it was all just in Vaino's head."

"It made sense that somebody talked. The Empire wouldn't patrol this far north without reason."

"Even so, Vaino seems incompetent enough to have cooked up this whole thing himself. A paranoid delusion."

Wickes tilted his head. "I wouldn't discount him out of hand. People are rarely what they appear to be at first glance."

"Clearly," she said and shot a glance at him.

He smiled and shrugged. "People can change." He and Aquin were sitting on the floor, the bars and a couple of feet of space separating them, but he slid a bit closer to the bars before he

LIZANDRA'S DEEPEST FEAR

asked, "What about Samira? Is she capable of doing what she said?"

"Breaking me out of here?" Aquin smiled and gave a low laugh. "She once broke me out of an Imperial interrogation room in the middle of Klubridge."

Wickes' brows drew together. "How often do you find yourself in this situation?"

"More than I did before I knew Samira," she said, but a hint of the smile was still there.

"If she does get you—" A low rumble halted Wickes' words. "What was that? Did you feel that?"

Aquin shifted and put her hand to the floor. "It was shaking. What—"

It came again, louder this time. Wickes hadn't felt the ground shake the first time, but there was no question of it now. It heaved once and twice, rocking him to the left so hard he had to put his own hand on the floor to keep from tipping over.

"Earthquake?" Aquin asked and pulled herself to her feet.

"This far north? I've never heard of that," Wickes said, but it truly did feel like the ground itself was quaking. What else could it be? He grabbed the bars and heaved himself to his feet, his eyes going to the high window as if he'd find any answers there.

The room shook one more time, and with it came a great groaning sound, like the keep itself cried out in protest. "More likely a landslide," Wickes said. "Not the first time that's happened here."

Aquin held the bars with both hands now, her eyes turned upward to the ceiling. It was intact, but would it stay that way? Had the rest of that giant ugly bird of a mountain decided now was the moment when it needed to crumble itself into the remains of Crowspire?

There was a shout from outside, and Wickes shuffled his way to the door and pressed his face to the small window so he could see between the bars. "Hey!" he called through the opening. "Guards!" But no one answered. There was another shout, and another, a chorus of voices rising in fear or anger or both, all drifting to him from outside, maybe from the building's central courtyard. From where he stood at the door, Wickes could see light through the decorative holes in the wall opposite him, but he could see nothing of the courtyard itself.

"Something is wrong," he said and turned from the door. "You need to cut my hands and feet loose." He shuffle-walked back to where Aquin clung to the bars and held his hands through the bars, just like he had on the day when she'd shown him her blade.

"The guards will see," she said, sending a nervous look toward the doors.

"The guards are gone. Something bad is happening out there."

She hesitated only another instant before sliding the razor out from her sleeve and beginning to saw at his bindings.

"Aquin!" The voice came as soon as the rope around Wickes' hands snapped. He grabbed the razor from her before she rushed to the door, and he set about cutting his feet free himself. The blade had dulled, and it took some dedicated sawing to get through the wiry hemp, but the ropes finally fell away.

"I can't get in," Samira said, her face at the window in Aquin's cell door. "The guards are gone."

"What's happening out there?" Wickes asked as he pulled himself to his feet again.

"We're under attack," Samira said, her eyes wide. "The Empire is here."

The room shook again, and ancient mortar crumbled from the ceiling, settling as a fine dust in the shaft of light that came through the outside window. More voices raised, and now there was a persistent booming that sounded like it was coming from all around them.

"What are they—" Wickes began, but that was when the whole room shifted. The floor rocked back, sending him tumbling against the outer wall, and a huge stone fell from the ceiling, crashing into the ground where he'd stood a moment before. He opened his mouth to shout to Aquin, but got no further than that before he felt the wall at his back shaking, sliding, coming unbound. The room was disintegrating around him.

Wickes pushed away from the wall with all his strength and launched himself forward, over the fallen rocks and past the crack where the floor had already given way. A great and horrible tearing noise called at his back, but he ignored everything aside from those metal bars between the two cells. Both his hands wrapped around them, even as they tilted toward him.

He held fast to the bars and felt the floor continuing to pitch outward, angling toward the wall as it fell behind him. When he could look over his shoulder, he could see snow and mountains and clouds. All the things he very much should not have been able to see from within that cell.

Aquin was at the door, her own hands hanging onto the small bars in its window, and Samira was shouting something through the opening. None of that would matter if Wickes couldn't keep himself alive for the next few moments, and all of that hinged on his keeping himself in that cell and not flying out the new opening that threatened to eject him through the side of the castle.

He held to the bars until the room stopped shaking, and it was just like hanging onto the rigging in a storm, waiting for the waves to settle and for the ship to stop heaving enough to allow him to find his footing. And find it, he did, albeit on a floor that now sloped dangerously toward that gaping maw in the wall.

"Aquin," he called from where he held onto his side of the bars that separated their cells. "Climb to me. Get on the other side of these bars."

"What?" she yelled back, terror filling her eyes as she clung to the door.

Samira had stopped her shouting and was looking at him, and he could tell she'd put it together. "He's right. Aquin, get to the bars. He can get to you that way."

"And then what?" she asked, panic in her voice.

"Just do it!" Wickes shouted. He let his hands slip down a few bars, bringing himself to the brink of the hole in the wall. Without risking a look down, he let go with his right hand and pulled at the stones that had not fallen yet. He strained and pried and leveraged his weight against them, and one of them finally pulled loose. Then another and another, and he let them tumble out the hole toward whatever awaited below.

The keep shook again, and more blocks fell of their own

accord. Enough had gone now that Wickes could swing himself around the end of the bars, and he was in Aquin's cell. The floor was tilted on that side of the room as well, but it was not as far gone as on his side. As he glanced back at his side of the divided cell, the floor where he'd just been standing trembled and gave way, sliding out into the white light of the day.

"We can't stay here," he said.

"Where would you have us go?" Aquin shouted back.

He looked from her toward the opening in the outer wall.

"No," she said, shaking her head, her hair wild and bobbing with her movements.

"Go with him," Samira said. "There's a balcony at the end of this hall. He can get you around to it. I can meet you there."

"Samira!" Aquin called. "Wait! Don't leave me!"

"I'm not leaving you. I'll be waiting for you on that balcony." Samira slid her fingers through the small gap between the bars in the window and touched Aquin's hand. "Don't make me wait long." And she was gone, running away to the right. The voices were louder outside now, and there was the sound of metal and stone and wood hitting against each other in such a great cacophony, it was no wonder the whole place was coming apart.

"We have to do it now," Wickes said. "These rooms won't last long."

Aquin looked at the door once more, and when she turned back to Wickes, determination had overtaken the fear on her face. The fear was still there. Wickes would have doubted anyone who didn't fear this predicament. But she was ready now.

He retreated to the hole in the wall and leaned his head out far enough to see the stone ledge that stretched out to the right. It looked like it had been an ornamental addition in the original construction. It certainly wasn't anything people were expected to walk on, but it was all they had. The whole thing couldn't be more than a foot wide, and there was no telling how sturdy it was. It had protruded out the side of the castle in the frozen elements for centuries. He might step on it and find that the whole thing crumbled under his weight, or his foot might shoot off the edge after hitting an invisible patch of ice. It was all they had, though, and he wasn't about to speak his fears into Aquin's mind.

"Follow me," he said instead. "Press yourself against the wall, face first. Don't look down. We'll go sideways and slowly. Don't rush it."

Her throat moved as she swallowed, and some uncertainty came back into her eyes, but she nodded. Wickes nodded back, and he went out the opening first.

His right boot sought and found the ledge. He followed his own advice and did not look down. He kept his eyes ahead, tracking the cold stone of the outer wall as he edged his way to the right. Once he had gone far enough that he had to let go of the edge of the opening, he called to Aquin again. "Come now. Go slow."

She came out from the cell, to his left now, and her hair whipped in the icy wind. She squinted her eyes against it and pushed herself against the wall, just as he'd told her. Her arms spread wide against the stone, her fingers seeking purchase on something, but there was nothing to hold. The wall was smooth and regular, and there were no handholds or footholds aside from that one narrow ledge.

"You've got it," Wickes told her, even as he felt the wind tug at his own clothing. The key was to keep moving. It would be so much harder to start again if they stopped, and that made it easier to fall. They had to keep going. They couldn't stop, and they couldn't look down.

But Aquin did look down.

She had made it barely three feet out from the hole in the wall when she turned her head to look at Wickes, and her eyes tracked past him and down. They widened, and her mouth opened, but he couldn't hear what she was saying, if she were saying anything. The terror was clear, though, and Wickes couldn't keep himself from turning his head to the right and looking down in the same direction.

"Ikarna help us," he whispered to the wind, but he knew Ikarna wouldn't hear or care.

The entrance to the keep lay below them and to the right, and the stable near the bridge was in flames. Past the burning building, rows and rows of heads and arms and bodies pushed forward toward the keep. The line of soldiers stretched back across the bridge and as far as he could see, disappearing around the bend in the road. As he watched, the army surged forward through the opening where the front gate had once been.

The Empire had come to Crowspire, and Wickes had no more reassurances for Aquin when he turned his head back toward her. All he could say was, "Keep moving. Don't stop."

∽

Bekam braced himself against the wind that whipped off the side of the mountain and sent sheets of snow and ice pelting down on his army. They had traveled up the winding roads and through the precarious passes at as fast a speed as they could safely make it, and the trip saw them to within sight of the hideously huge birdlike formation Bekam knew loomed over the castle. They now slowed as the end of the road neared, and the army approached the shadow of the final peaks where it would wait, hidden from the castle itself.

The army crawled forward, a grumbling mass of soldiers and mages, all too cold and uncomfortable to be anything but angry and impatient by then. Rozin Gadhi waited for Bekam just before the last turn in the road.

"The Nightingales are inside," she said, coming to meet him at the head of the winding line of troops. They had compressed into a march no more than five shoulders wide, snaking its way up the slopes. "There was a focusing stone, just like the map showed."

"You were able to counteract the shield?"

She nodded. "It's a weakness in them. They can enhance magic directed at them, but there's a limit. If you try to push too much power into them…" She balled her fists together and then splayed her fingers while she blew out between her pursed lips.

"How big was the explosion?"

"It wasn't an explosion at all. Not an actual one, as you'd know it. I have a shield mage of my own. He worked his magic into the barrier, and the combined power was too much. All that power poured out of the stone and into whatever poor mage they've had maintaining the shield. That's when the barrier dropped."

"It killed them?"

"Maybe," she said. "Probably not. In theory, it should knock them out but shouldn't be fatal. When they wake up, all their memories will be gone, and their mind will be scattered."

"Like a halflock."

She cut her eyes at him with a half smirk. "Something like that." The smirk disappeared an instant later. "They know we're coming."

Bekam frowned. "How could they?"

"Unknown, but they do. They've braced the gates, and they put extra guards on watch above the walls. They don't have a large force, but they have them all prepared to defend against a siege. Someone got a warning to them before we arrived."

"And the Nightingales?"

"Two of them got in after we disabled the shield. I don't think the rebels have even noticed it's down. The Nightingales cleared a stable just outside the keep, and they got over the walls after that."

"Over the walls?" Bekam blinked at her. "They climbed the face of the walls?"

She shrugged. "Milev told them to get in, and that's what they did. They took out all the guards at the top, quiet as you'd please, and they sent the signal down that they'd done it without being detected."

"How long ago?"

"Minutes," she said. "They know we're coming, but they won't know we're here yet."

"Someone will find those corpses. We go in now." He raised his hand, and the troops moved forward again, rounding the final turn. Anyone looking down from Crowspire would see them now, a black carpet of death trudging their way through the snow and crossing the bridge that connected the keep to the rest of Teshovar. The alarm would go up at any moment, but it hadn't happened yet. Luck was with them, as was the element of surprise.

The engineers were at the head of the army, twelve of them lugging a long machine of wood and metal between them. They'd designed it for portability, but getting it up those mountains had been no easy feat. They had made it, though, and they had it assembled before the massive wooden gates within moments of reaching their destination.

Bekam craned his neck and scanned the top of the wall. The Nightingales had taken out the guards, but surely someone else would be up there soon enough. Surely the rebels had enough foresight to stock boulders on the walls to hurl down on the heads of anyone brazen enough to launch a frontal attack. But there was nothing. Nothing moved on the walls above, and even the army behind him was so silent he had to look over his shoulder to reassure himself they were still there. The soldiers stared back with hard eyes and grim frowns, ready for battle. They were ready to end this and go home. Bekam could hardly blame them.

"We're ready, General." It was Holger, the engineer who had been in the war room at Karsk. A smudge of frost clouded the left lens of his eyeglasses, and he swiped at it with a handkerchief as he awaited the order.

Bekam surveyed the machine at the castle door and saw the twelve breachers, six on each side, all with metal handles in their grips. They looked back at him, their muscles tense and their breaths blowing fast plumes of vapor in front of their faces.

"Do it," he said, and the engineer raised his hand and lowered it again, pointing to the gate.

The central part of the machine pulled upward and halted at the end of its backswing, the twelve handlers struggling with its weight. Once it had locked in place, they stepped aside, and the two at the back threw twin levers. The whole contraption jolted, and for a terrifying moment, it looked like nothing was going to happen. Had they hauled the thing all the way up from Karsk for nothing?

But then a gear spun, and something locked or unlocked with a loud clang. The ram flew forward, propelled by whatever mechanisms the engineers had devised, and it met the gate with a roar that shook the ground. The wood held firm, but the rest of the castle shook, mortar trickling out from between its ancient stones. There'd be no hiding their approach now. The attack had begun.

Bekam turned his head away from the sound and cast a wary glance upward. Too much of that noise, and they'd be just as likely to pull down the rest of the mountain on top of the keep. Perhaps that would be for the best. Bury the rebels in their own stolen fortress.

"The gate still stands," Bekam said.

Holger said, "It will take more than one hit, General. It's more efficient than a traditional ram, but it still requires multiple charges."

As the engineer spoke, the twelve breachers moved back into position and pulled the central ramming body back to lock it for another attempt. Holger's arm went up and down again, chopping through the air, and the two men shoved the levers again. The ram thundered into the gate for a second time, causing the whole thing to shudder, but it still held solid. Shouts arose inside the walls. The rebels knew they'd arrived, and the counterattack was coming.

"Engineer Holger," Bekam said, a warning tone in his voice.

"Just a few more hits, General. We'll have it," he said, but his own voice trembled. Whether it was from the fear of Bekam's impatience or an uncertainty about the efficacy of his machine, it was hard to tell. Either way, he turned back to his team and raised his arm again, but it stayed in the air, wavering before he lowered it and looked back at Bekam.

Bekam scowled and stepped forward, ready to chastize the engineer, but he stopped just short of him and stared at the wall before them. It rippled. That was the only way it could be described. The whole thing shifted, moving like waves through water.

An enormous block trembled and fell from the top, dropping just to the right of the ramming team. The handlers on that side lurched out of the way, but it was a good ten feet clear of them. Was this the start of the rebels' defenses?

Bekam squinted through the snowy haze at the gap where that block had been. Movement just down and to the right pulled his attention, and he frowned at the wall again. Surely, it was an illusion of some sort. His eye was tricking him, seeing a distorted image in the dry cold.

But, just as quickly, it was clear that everyone else saw it, too. A block, even larger than the first one, was sliding forward, inch by inch. It pulled itself free from the wall and tumbled downward, striking the edge of the cliff with a crash before spiraling down into the valley below. And now another block was doing the same, and another and another. To the left, now. The wall was disassembling itself, the mortar crumbling and its great stones falling away.

"What is this?" Bekam asked the engineer. Not waiting for an answer, he turned to Rozin, and he saw Prusik beyond her. The dowdy commissioner had trudged all the way up here for what? Surely to see Bekam fail, but she would be disappointed in that regard. "What is this?" he asked again.

Prusik had been watching the wall disintegrate before them, but she looked away from it to meet Bekam's eyes. A slow and knowing smile spread on her face, and Bekam didn't like that at all. He took a step toward her, but she was leaving. She turned her back and pushed her way through the front ranks of soldiers and disappeared into the armored bodies as she headed back down the mountain.

"What—" Bekam began again, but Rozin's hand on his shoulder stopped him.

"General," she said, the word whispered and harsh. She was still watching whatever was happening to the wall, but now her mouth hung open, and Bekam watched tears bead in the corners of her eyes and roll down her cheeks.

He glanced back at the wall and was about to turn away, about to demand an explanation for this, when what he saw froze him in place. His heart thudded in his chest, and he staggered around to face the keep. His knees wobbled, but he stayed upright, his face slack and his own eye watering now. A chill so cold that it burned ignited in Bekam's chest, and he tried to speak, but his mouth moved without words.

He gasped as his brain and mouth tried and failed to work in concert. Stones and blocks, each larger than the last, continued

LIZANDRA'S DEEPEST FEAR

falling from the walls, and now whole sections of the keep were crumbling without their structural supports. He watched all of this, and he saw the truth of how it was happening. It was terrifying and maddening, and his mouth at last formed and spoke the only words he could summon.

"It's him."

~

The first crash washed into Caius as a dream, prodding at his mind behind his half-closed eyes. When the second one came, his eyes flew open, and he sat upright on the mattress. He'd put his head down for just a moment, just to rest briefly. How long ago? What was happening?

He pushed off the bed, and his feet hardly felt like his own, his legs nearly tangling with each other. Another thunderous boom shook the castle, and he staggered across the darkened room to throw the door open. Shouts flooded into his room then, and rebels rushed past his door, all headed for the stairwell at the end of the hallway.

"Samira," Caius whispered and rushed into the hallway, hesitating just long enough to pull his door shut. As it latched closed, the keep shook again, and a grainy block of gray stone tumbled loose from the ceiling, cracking the floor at his feet.

His brain, still swimming in a half slumber, awakened at that, and he followed the flow of feet to the second-floor landing. Most of the ones going upward carried bows, arrows, crossbows, and even rocks with them. The ones heading down the stairs were mostly unarmed.

Caius watched the chaotic division at the stairs, and he knew in an instant what was happening. The Empire had found them. Stormbreak was under siege.

"Samira," he said again and took the stairs downward faster than he'd thought possible upon first waking up.

The courtyard swarmed with rebels hurrying to defensive positions. They'd had training, but it was unlikely many of these people had faced an actual battle before this day. How could they stand against the Empire?

In the middle of the courtyard, just this side of the immense tree, Vaino was shouting orders. As he pointed and directed his people this way and that, he pulled a leather jerkin over his head, tugging it down to cover the black suit he was wearing. He glanced down at more pieces of leather armor at his feet but abandoned them as he crossed the snowy ground toward Caius.

"Get to safety," he said.

"Have you seen Samira?"

"No," Vaino said and flinched as the invaders slammed against the gate again. "That thing won't hold for long. Either pick up a sword or get somewhere safe."

Caius squinted up at the clear sky. "How did they get past the shield?"

"I have no bloody idea, but they did it, and we had no warning other than Reykas' vague message."

Caius blinked at him. "Reykas? You've spoken to—"

"Caius!"

He spun, and Lizandra came through the doorway at a dead run, panic on her face. "Caius!" she called again, and he caught her by the arms, steadying her before she slid down on the icy ground.

"What happened? How did—"

She caught her breath, but her voice still trembled. "He came for me, but the scion made him leave. But then he came back when the castle started shaking. I had to run! I wanted to stay in the cell, but I had to run, Caius. I—"

"Who? Who do you mean?"

But he needn't have even asked. The giant Aescalan followed through the back entrance, a small axe wrapped in his enormous fist. When Hama spotted Lizandra, his eyes narrowed, and he pointed the hatchet at her. "Give her to me."

"Absolutely not," Caius said and pushed Lizandra behind him. "Run," he said, and she did.

Hama snarled at Caius and stomped toward him as the rebels lined up at the gate with their shields and spears and swords.

"Hama, by the gods," Vaino said, stepping between them. "Now is not the time."

"She betrayed you," he said. "Now is the time."

"Hama," Vaino said, his voice hard now. That was all he had time to say before the first block flew out of the wall, just above the gate, and slammed into the third row of rebels, crushing two men and knocking over a third.

Voices raised in new shouts, this time of alarm, as a second block shook itself free from the mortar and ejected itself into the courtyard. This one clipped a woman in the side of the head, felling her with a sickening crunch before it tumbled to rest next to the tree.

All eyes were on the wall now and the gate it surrounded. The battering ram had resumed its assault, but it couldn't be responsible for the rocks that continued to fly free, large ones and small ones, some peppering the rebels' shields and others smashing through their lines and breaking bones.

"Mages," Vaino said. "Herons."

"No," Hama said, the axe hanging at his side now. The big man's lower lip trembled. It was the first time Caius had seen fear in any of the Aescalan.

A great ripping sound drew Caius' attention back to the wall as the entire gate shook once, twice, and tore itself free from its supports. The wood splintered down the center, spraying sharp spears of oak at the rebels, who now cowered behind their shields. They moved back, wary now, and some of them dropped their weapons and fled as the gate hovered in the air. With a clap like thunder, the gate split in two, and both halves hurtled into the courtyard, scattering more of the terrified defenders and crushing the few who stood nearest the front.

Caius' breath caught as the first Imperials poured through the archway, swords drawn and death in their glares. A few arrows arced down from above, and one took an Imperial soldier in the back, but a scream from the ramparts ended that volley. Caius looked up in horror as two dark forms moved quickly among the archers, slicing at some and simply pitching others off the walkways. They were black against the sky, and Caius knew what they had to be.

"Nightingales," he said, and Vaino followed his gaze upward.

Metal crashed against metal as more soldiers pushed through the opening, but the rebels pressed forward, shields ready and spears prodding ahead of them. The Imperials stalled and staggered back a step. They'd expected to overwhelm an unorganized militia, but Micah and Naecara had prepared these people to defend Stormbreak with their very lives.

Hope swelled in Caius' chest, allowing him to believe for an instant that it would be that simple. But then there was a flash of sudden color, and the Imperials shoved the rebels back again. First there was yellow, then green, and then there was a flash of purple, all the colored uniforms setting dread into Caius' heart.

"Kites." Vaino spoke Caius' fear aloud. The red ones had destroyed their lives in Klubridge, and there had been only a handful of them. It was impossible to count the number of Kites than now followed the enlisted soldiers into the keep. They stabbed, slashed, and parried with vicious expertise, and blood painted the white snow and melted the ice on the courtyard ground.

"Go," Vaino said to Caius as he pulled his sword across his body, releasing it from the scabbard on his hip.

The Kites were overwhelming the rebels, and now a new wave of attackers followed, these not wearing any discernible uniforms. Caius shifted back, about to follow Vaino's order, when the face at the head of the newcomers arrested his movement. The dark skin of the man's shaved head was what caught his eye, but when he heard the man's baritone chant cutting through the chaos, there was no question. This was the lead Heron from Klubridge, the man who had tried to silence magic within Caius and instead unleashed a monster upon the city. All the people coming through the broken wall now were Herons.

Caius moved to warn Vaino, but he stuttered to a halt once more, as something new filled the space in the wall where the stones and gate had been. Vaino saw it, too, and he raised a hand to cover his mouth, nearly dropping his sword. Hama remained motionless near them, but he made a sound Caius knew he'd never forget. It was a whine, not quite a moan and not quite a word. It was terror made audible.

The thing in the gate was at first without form. A black void that filled space and seemed both corporeal and not. Intangible at the edges, black tendrils rippled and peeled away from it, dissipating into the air like smoke. As it drifted into the courtyard, the shape coalesced into something like a human but somehow taller, longer, clad in the silhouette of a black and hooded robe. Even if there had been a face to see, the rippling suggestion of the hood hid it. The very air seemed to peel away from the thing, surrounding it in a blurry haze that hurt Caius' eyes. If this thing had ever been human, it was now something else.

"It's him," Vaino said, audible only because the other rebels had lost their voices and gaped at the creature, standing still just long enough to fall to the blades of the Kites or the magic of the Herons. "It's him," Vaino said again, sounding both awed and stricken.

Caius felt something unhinge at the back of his mind. Something that had been there for months, waiting just beyond his consciousness. Something that felt both alien and familiar. His hands and feet tingled, and he sagged, a silent wheeze leaving his lungs. An insubstantial force kept him upright and directed his eyes at the thing in the gate. It was terrible and strange, but there was no question about what had entered the courtyard.

The High Lord Peregrine had returned to Crowspire.

∾

Death was all around. Fairy ran down the hallway on the second floor, dodging more people than she'd seen in one place the whole time she'd been at Stormbreak. She had to hop over a man sitting on the floor as he counted arrows, and she spun around another man trying to wrestle his way into some kind of metal shirt made of chains that looked like it was about half as big as it needed to be to fit him.

She took the corner with a skid and stopped there. The cell doors were gone. Not just the doors. The cells themselves and everything else had just disappeared, and there was nothing but open space where they'd been. She could see all the way to the outside, and some snow had blown in and collected on the floor where the guards had stood. One of their stools was still there, but the other one was nowhere to be seen.

Fairy gulped and forced herself to turn back around and head for the stairs. Aquin hadn't been in there. She'd gotten out somehow before all this happened.

As unlikely as that might be on any other day, that had to be the truth on this day. That's what Fairy told herself as she ran down the stairs, ducking around more people, some of them going up and some going down. When things got bad, you could tell yourself whatever you needed to hear, and you could even make yourself believe it for just long enough to get through to the other side. Some people said you needed to deal with what you were dealt, but those usually weren't people who needed to act fast if they were going to live. Those were people who had the time to sit around feeling bad.

Fairy had stuffed everything deep down inside when Dorrin had died, and that was how she'd lived long enough to get out of Klubridge. She'd had to think about it later, and she'd thought about it a lot since then, and it was probably even worse for having put it off. But if she'd let herself stop and roll around in all that sadness right when it first happened, she wouldn't have made it onto that ship and would be a flatcake under some building in Klubridge, and that was a fact.

And she'd tell herself Aquin was okay, and that nice pirate man was, too, and that's how she'd get through this day. She still had someone other than herself to worry about, and that was another thing that kept her going. She hadn't been able to save Dorrin, but she'd promised Danel Gressam she'd watch after him, and that was one little boy who wouldn't die on her watch.

Fairy came out into the courtyard and stopped in her tracks again. Pretty much everybody else was doing the same thing this time, so she didn't feel too awkward just standing there and staring. Some big, fuzzy blob was floating in the courtyard, just inside the entrance to the keep. The whole wall behind it was wrecked, and that was probably how it and all the soldiers and mages had gotten in. As Fairy watched, the floating thing moved, and what looked like an arm raised on its left side, and black, inky swirls unspooled from it and wrapped one of the rebels up.

"There's another thing we're going to deal with another day,"

Fairy said, and she forced herself to look away from whatever that thing was doing to the man it had grabbed. Her inventory of things to handle later was growing, but she could keep going as long as she kept shoving them in there.

"Danel!" she called, but it was no use. There was too much screaming and shouting and clanging and roaring happening everywhere. She barely heard herself, much less anything understandable from anybody else. Danel wouldn't hear her calling for him, so she'd have to look for him.

The courtyard was too full of people, all of them pushing and stabbing and killing, and she'd be sliced up if she even tried to go farther that way. Instead, she ran along its perimeter and scanned the crowd from the outside. If the Gressams were in that shoving bloody huddle, there was precious little she could do for them, so they weren't in there. They were somewhere else, because she'd promised to watch after Danel, and that was what she was going to do.

She stopped, breathing hard and peered across the top of the crowd one more time, and her eyes traveled up the inside walls of the courtyard, up to where a section of the wall had already crumbled away. And there, improbably, stood Danel Gressam. He was on the second floor, right around the corner from where she'd just been, and he was staring down at the carnage through a hole that was newly blasted in the wall.

Fairy looked back at the stairs she'd just come down, but they were choked with people now, too crowded for her to go back up. She turned back toward the courtyard and narrowed her eyes at the wall beneath the opening where the boy stood. The holes in the stonework were more than decorations now, and she'd kick anybody in the head if they tried to pull her down this time.

A woman yelled at Fairy as she ducked under her arm, barely missing skewering herself on a blade the woman was carrying. She skipped around a man with a shield and sprinted to the base of a column at the far edge of the quad. Fairy dropped into a quick squat and launched herself upward, her fingers scrabbling and finding purchase between the bricks. Nothing to it. Far easier than climbing up the Imperial tower in Klubridge, but nobody was actively murdering each other beneath her when she'd done that.

Fairy's legs pumped upward, and she dug her toes into the bricks and shoved her body up so she could hook her fingers through the first holes in the stone wall. From there, the climbing truly was easy. Hand over hand and foot over foot, her fingers and toes finding convenient places to grab and pull, moving her up to the second floor faster than she could have made it if she'd taken the stairs.

Something exploded behind her, and the wall shook once and nearly threw her off, but she held to it with all her might, and she scurried up the last few feet before the whole thing could disintegrate beneath her.

Danel was leaning out of the hole for a better look, one hand supporting him on the remains of the wall. He glanced down and jumped back in surprise when he spotted Fairy heading up to him. Pieces of stone pulled loose as she leveraged herself up and over the edge of the hole, but she'd made it. Her feet dropped onto the floor of the second-story hallway, and she took a second to catch her breath before she grabbed the boy's hand.

"Where are your parents?" she asked, pulling him away from the demolished wall.

He didn't answer but squeezed her hand with his small fingers, and she held on tight. "We'll go find them," she said. Her head tried to tell her it was too late to find anybody else, but that was the unnecessary part of her brain. She shoved that thought right down in the bundle for later, alongside everything else that was already making it bulge.

"Where are we going?" the boy asked, looking up at Fairy, and she stopped to think. She'd been in charge of kids many times before. She'd done a good job of it, too, and the things that had gone wrong hadn't been her fault. Still, she'd lost everybody who'd trusted her, one way or another. That would not happen this time, so she had to think hard and make smart choices.

They needed to get clear of the fighting, and that meant getting out of the castle. They couldn't stay up here. Much more of that blasting and booming, and the whole rest of the place would come down. The courtyard was a horror story, and they needed to avoid it, but there was no other way out. Not unless Fairy could suddenly sprout wings and fly them out one of the holes that had gotten knocked in the side of the building.

"We're going downstairs," she said. "We have to go near the fighting, but try not to look at it. We'll stay clear of it and get around the edge of it. All right?"

He nodded at her, not quite looking certain, but she could tell he trusted her, and that was enough. "All right, then," she said, and she pulled him along toward the stairs.

The rebels who'd been blocking the way a few minutes earlier were gone now. Still, Fairy went down slower this time with Danel holding onto her hand, so it took longer to reach the exit into the courtyard. Things looked even worse now than they had before. The fighting was still happening, but it might as well have already ended. There were more Imperials than rebels, and, even though she knew nothing about fighting herself, Fairy could tell the bad guys were better equipped and better trained.

"This way," she said and headed left, where there was more space between the inner wall of the courtyard and the writhing mass of people and sharp things. That big black blob was still floating at the front of the courtyard, and now she could see it looked a little like a person. That felt completely wrong, so she shoved that observation down in the later bag as well.

They slipped through the gaps, and they turned right at the corner, and straight ahead of them, there was the doorway that would take them out back. They could make it to the infirmary, or maybe to the workshop or the supply depot. Maybe Oreth would be back there and could help them. Maybe Aquin was even back there.

Fairy's hopes shriveled when one of the bad guys stumbled into the walkway ahead of them, his blade red and wet and his hair tousled and sweaty. He wore a uniform just like the ones the red Kites had worn in Klubridge, but this one's tabard was green. It had the same awful black bird on the chest, though, and that meant nothing good at all.

"They make rebels littler every day," he said with a sneer and flicked his sword, slinging a spatter of blood across the ground.

Danel's hand trembled in Fairy's, and she squeezed it tighter as she backed them away. What could she do to protect them? She had no weapons. They couldn't run. She could have, and she probably could have made it through the crowd and gotten out another way, but she couldn't do it with Danel tagging along. And she wasn't about to leave him. There was nothing she could do, and what could she possibly say to this man to make him not kill them? That was the whole reason he'd come all the way up here. To kill them and everybody else.

And then the green Kite slammed against the wall and dropped his sword, and the man who'd shoved him grabbed the sword up and stuck it right through his side, leaving it skewered into him.

"Quentyn Wickes!" Fairy shouted. Of all the outcomes she'd expected, having the pirate barrel out from the middle of the courtyard to tackle the Kite was far from the most likely.

"Are you all right?" he asked as he shoved the Kite onto the floor. The man was still alive and pawing at the sword and saying something, but Wickes ignored him and pulled at the sleeve of a confused-looking older man who'd been stumbling along behind him. The man craned his neck to look upward, and the horseshoe-shaped scar on the back of his head explained his strangeness. Wickes kept one hand on the halflock he was leading and reached for Fairy with the other.

"We're alive," Fairy said. "How did you get out? Where's Aquin? Is she okay?"

"She's fine and is with Samira. Come with me."

That was all she needed to hear, and it was one less big thing that she had to keep pushed down in that bag for later. Wickes led them ahead, and there, right in front of the door where they'd already been heading, stood Samira. She saw them and said something to someone behind her, and then, even more improbably, there was Phyla Gressam, covering her mouth with her hands and then shouting for Danel to come to her. Fairy released his hand and let him run the rest of the way into his mother's arms.

That's when the new noise came. It shouldn't have been called a voice, because it sounded more like a big metal chain being dragged across rocks or the biggest door being opened on the loudest hinges in the world. Maybe both at the same time, while some kind of huge angry animal was growling and hissing. It was all those things at once and even worse than those could describe. It was the sound of something speaking that shouldn't have had a voice.

TAMRAT

That one word rumbled through the castle, and Fairy felt it down deep in her chest, vibrating so hard she thought her heart might jump out.

"Hyden," Phyla said, fear in her eyes. "They're here for Hyden."

It looked like they were here for a lot more than Hyden, but Fairy wasn't about to argue that fact. Especially not when Danel's eyes grew wide, and he pointed.

There, in the middle of the fray, stood Hyden Gressam, back to back with the big Aescalan man, Dekan Hama. Hama held a small axe in his left hand and a sword in his right hand, and he was swinging with both of them, yelling and growling and spattered with blood. Hyden looked tiny behind him and terrified. Hyden held a sword, too, but he wasn't slashing with it and looked like he barely knew which end was supposed to stick the bad guys. He was jabbing with it, more like it was a pitchfork than something with a blade on each side.

TAMRAT

The voice made Fairy shiver, and she knew she should get out of there and lead Danel to safety, if such a thing still existed in those mountains. Something rooted her to the spot, though, and in the moment, she wasn't even sure whether it was her fear or if she was just mesmerized by this thing that was unlike anything she'd ever seen. She could push a lot of stuff down, but this was one thing that wouldn't wait to be dealt with later.

"It's Peregrine," Wickes said, and Fairy knew it was true. What else could this thing be? The halflock moaned and covered his face, and Wickes put an arm around the man's shoulders and tried to turn him away from the terror.

It flickered in the late afternoon light, insubstantial one moment and solid the next, and it hovered higher, now above the heads of the nearest fighters. By then, everybody had figured out they couldn't stop fighting for long enough to be amazed. Doing that was the surest way to stop fighting for good, so they kept swinging their swords and shouting and killing. But the High Lord floated over their heads like a black specter, and some of them looked like the fear of what was above them had caused them to lose all control and fight even harder and wilder. Peregrine wasn't concerned with them, though.

"Hyden!" Phyla screamed as the blackness approached him. He probably couldn't have heard her in all that noise, but he still turned and looked up, seeing it as it loomed closer. Black tendrils peeled away from it, and the form raised its left arm again, and this time a slender and gnarled thing like a finger uncurled at the end to point at Gressam.

TAMRAT

The word sounded like a gong and a horn and breaking glass, all the loud things all at once, and it was awful. Fairy gaped and felt a trickle of sweat roll down her back, even though she felt as cold as she'd felt that night in the forest. Her skin was ice, and there was nothing she could do when two of those black and swirling appendages shot out from Peregrine, looping toward Hyden Gressam, getting ready to wrap him up just like that other rebel.

Dekan Hama saw them coming, and he swung the sword at one of the undulating black things, but the blade passed right through, and he stumbled and nearly fell flat on his face. The woman Hama had been fighting stepped forward in the second he had his back to her, and she swung, and a terrible red gash opened at the back of his left thigh. He roared, and then he did tumble forward and was on the ground. He was on his back then and jabbed his sword up just as the woman came for him again. She didn't see the attack coming, and Fairy didn't see the sword go in, but she knew the big man had gotten her when the woman flinched back before dropping her sword and falling to her knees.

Hyden Gressam jumped back from the smoky tendrils and tried to escape, but there was nowhere to go. They were right there on him, and he was caught. He dropped the sword, for all the good it had been doing him, and he crossed his arms over his face like he could ward off the thing like that. More black energy tore itself away from Peregrine and shot toward Gressam in long whips and spears, and there was nothing he could do.

It didn't wrap Hyden like Fairy thought it was trying to do. It didn't envelop him like it had done with the other man. No, it shot straight through him, jabbing through his left shoulder. Another one stabbed through his right leg, and he cried out, nearly falling. The black spears held him up as a third one caught him in the stomach. The final one swooped in from the side and passed straight through his neck.

There was no blood, and there were no wounds, but when the High Lord's magic released him, Gressam fell forward, and Fairy knew he was dead. He was as dead as Scrounger had been, toppling forward on the floor. As dead as Skink on that Kite's blade in Klubridge. As dead as Dorrin, and Fairy grabbed Danel around the shoulders and pulled him back before he could run to his father, tears streaming down his face.

Hyden Gressam was dead, and Peregrine shifted in the air, his ragged cloak of dark nothingness swirling in the bitter wind.

CHAPTER 53

A flash of red, and the world swam into brutal clarity. Apak stumbled into Kam Dhaz but kept his grip on the Seal of Metarr until a quick survey showed everyone had arrived intact. They were intact upon arrival, at least, but the bloodshed that surrounded them suggested that would not last for long.

Indeed, a soldier in black armor saw them a second later and was already in the backswing with his mace. Alev had enough time to cover Apak in a shield before the weapon carried through its arc, and the soldier's whole body vibrated with the unexpected impact against the invisible barrier.

"Thank you, Alev," Apak said and shifted the Seal into his left hand as he pushed his glasses up his nose with the right one. "Please continue protecting us as—"

A shout from Nahk stopped Apak's instructions and aborted any semblance of organization. She leaped away from the group, tiny blades unsheathing from her sleeves and cables whipping about her. Two Imperials were down and bleeding before her feet touched the ground again.

"I'll find weapons," Naecara said, and then she, too, was gone, disappearing behind them into the keep.

"What do we do?" Kam Dhaz was inside the shield with Apak and Alev, and he flinched as another blow glanced off the barrier. The taller mage kept their hands up and their concentration on the casting.

"We find our friends," Apak said and put a hand to Alev's back. "You said you can maintain the shield while we move?"

Alev nodded. "As long as I'm inside it."

Dhaz asked, "Friends? What friends do we have here?"

"You have none," Apak said. A flash of green, ahead and to the right, caught his eye. "We have many. Alev, please follow."

The group of three moved ahead as one attack after another bounced back from the protective bubble. They walked with slow steps, and Apak frowned when his foot slipped, not on ice but in blood. As they pressed forward and into the melee, Alev's barrier pushed against bodies. Soldiers tripped and jumped aside, always looking back at the small group in confusion. Apak had no concern for them and no time.

A large woman with dark hair, one of the Aescalan, spun to face them, her eye peering down the long barrel of a firearm. She squinted but moved aside, taking aim elsewhere, and there, just beyond her, Apak saw Lizandra.

Beset from the front and sides, she pressed her back against the tree at the center of the courtyard and flung magic at her attackers. Her green blades flashed under the shade of the branches, and her hands moved with incredible speed. The Imperials blocked most of the energy shards with their shields and their armor, but a few splinters were getting through, one of them slicing a groove in the shoulder of a Kite in yellow. He cursed, turning away from her, and another of her blades struck him in the side, just below his armpit, and he fell.

"Lizandra!" Apak called, and the word left his mouth too quickly for him to consider its repercussions.

She turned her head in his direction and spotted him between the other combatants, but she could not see the uniformed woman coming at her from the right. Micah Vaino saw the soldier, though, and he was there in an instant, his sword blocking and parrying the attack. He turned the Imperial away with his elbow, and then his own blade came up and caught her through the stomach.

"You're back," he said to Apak with a casualness belied by his trembling hands.

"You saved me," Lizandra said to Vaino, a question in her eyes that Apak could not comprehend.

"I'm not a monster," Vaino answered and shoved another Imperial away as he fought his way toward Apak. The man looked as if he had been wearing leather armor, but only the jerkin remained, and it hung in tatters. Beneath it, he wore one of his impractical black suits, this one ragged with tears. "Where's Naecara?" he asked.

"She went to find weapons," Alev said. They then added, "I don't know if I can extend my shield to hold you as well."

"Don't bother," Vaino said. "I need to be out here, fighting. Get yourself and Apak to safety."

Alev nodded and turned, but Vaino stopped them. "Wait. Did you find it? Did you find the weapon?"

Apak had no time to consider his words before he said, "We found it, and it was destroyed. No one will use it again."

Vaino held his eyes for the briefest second and nodded. "It's for the best." And then, to Alev, "Get them out of here. It's safer toward the back. Take Lizandra with you." And he sidestepped into the throng, his sword flashing once more.

Alev kept the shield aloft as they pressed past the tree and toward the back of the courtyard, its rear exit now visible over the fighting. Lizandra followed close behind, walking in the wake of the barrier and slashing with her green daggers whenever someone crept too close.

The keep was in ruins, even more than it had been before Apak and his group had departed. Even as he watched, a section of the roof collapsed, spilling masonry onto rebels and Imperials alike. It reminded Apak of the devastation he'd caused in the plaza in Klubridge. This was not the sort of damage an ordinary clash between armies would create. Powerful magic was at work here. Apak had believed Qae'lon's final assertions, but seeing the destruction wreaked by this kind of power still astounded him.

"There," Alev said, and Apak saw Samira's face through the crowd. They shoved forward, faster now, and Aquin was there, her arm around a stranger, a woman weeping on her knees as a young boy held fast to Fairy, his face buried in her chest.

Samira looked up as they broke free of the crowd, and she stood. "Apak! How—" But her question halted when her eyes shifted past him. "Lizandra. This is her doing."

Apak looked from one woman to the other, expecting a protest from Lizandra, but she said nothing. Her hands dropped, the magic withheld, and her head hung low. "What does she mean?" Apak asked her. And he repeated the question to Samira when Lizandra had no answer. "What do you mean? How is this her doing?"

"She betrayed us to the Empire." Samira looked down, her hand now on the crying woman's shoulder. "This is Phyla Gressam. Her husband was Hyden Gressam. He was the Tamrat scion. We found him, and we brought him back here. He's—" Her voice trailed to silence as she looked toward the courtyard. But she looked back to Apak and said, "Peregrine is here. He's real, and he's here."

"I know," Apak said, and what more was there to say? He had no solution to this siege. He was ill prepared this time, and there had been no opportunity to plan. He had constructed no weapon in secret. All he could do was nod and look at the woman and what he presumed to be her son with an expression he hoped conveyed sympathy.

"Oreth!" Lizandra's shout broke Apak free of his thoughts, and he found the boy alongside the crowd.

Oreth, wild-eyed, limped along the perimeter of the fighting, his face dirty and his collar torn. He pulled the girl from the supply depot with him. She staggered and held an arm tight against her side, blood soaking her shirt and running down to her trousers. She looked up through a tangle of wild hair, and her face was pale, her eyes distant.

Lizandra ran to meet them and pressed past them, hurling more magic as she went, buffeting back the Imperials unwise enough to challenge her. Oreth reached their sad huddle near the back corner of the courtyard and stumbled, nearly falling over. Alev dropped their shield as the two approached. The wounded girl slipped from Oreth's grasp, and Apak caught her before she could fall.

"Are you harmed?" Apak asked Oreth. It served no purpose

to ask the same of his companion. The girl was clearly injured but might yet live, if they could get her clear enough of the fighting for Samira to tend her wound.

"Caius," Oreth said, his breaths coming in gasps. "Caius."

Samira snapped her head to face him. "Caius? Where is he? Did you see him?'

Oreth pointed a shaky hand toward the fighting, and Apak followed his finger, seeing nothing of his friend. But then Oreth's hand raised, and Apak's eyes tracked it, scanning up the inner wall of the courtyard and focusing on what remained of the third floor, the roof already having caved inward.

"What is this?" Apak asked.

Black whips of energy, almost like tentacles, writhed in the air, striking and retreating, originating from some unseen source. It had to be Peregrine, but tumbled columns and piles of rubble blocked Apak's view. What he could see was the way a blue energy mixed with the black, high above the crowd. A different force, shimmering in the air and identical to Peregrine's smoke-like tendrils in every way but color, held the attack at bay.

Apak followed the trail of blue through the air, watching as wisps of energy poured off it, dispersing even as the magic renewed itself. He craned his neck, tracing the winding light back and over the heads of the fighters to the opposite side of the fray, where a figure hung in the air. Blue light surrounded and pulsed around the man who dangled there, his arms and legs slack, his toes pointing downward, toward the tops of the heads below him, and his head tilted back as if he were asleep. His body moved not at all, but blue light poured out of him in a continuous stream.

Samira took two steps forward and covered her mouth. "Caius!"

And it was. It was Caius Harrim, Apak's oldest friend and the man he trusted the most. It was Caius Harrim, Akithar, who had never possessed any hint of magical ability, now levitating in the courtyard and holding back the High Lord Peregrine with an undeniably clear show of power.

"Liar," Fairy whispered from behind Apak.

LIZANDRA'S DEEPEST FEAR

∾

Caius Harrim was there, but not there. His eyes, half-lidded, stared at the white sky above the keep, but he could also see everything around and beneath them. It might have been more accurate to say he could sense everything. Samira on her knees, her hand on Phyla Gressam's shoulder. Hyden Gressam lying dead among the other bodies. Dekan Hama pulling himself to his feet and struggling to stay upright as his boot filled with blood. Apak stepping into the courtyard from nothingness. Reykas stumbling his way through the chaos and shouting for Lizzie. Imperials of all ranks and uniforms filling the castle, murdering rebels, staining their uniforms red.

The tingling in Caius' hands and feet had spread to his arms and legs and eventually throughout his body, leaving him numb from head to toe. It was a strange sensation, but not unpleasant. He hung in the air, suspended by forces he couldn't understand, but he felt no fear. The wind billowed his jacket around his back and blew through his hair, but the cold was distant and didn't touch him.

It was the way he felt when he dreamed. When he ventured through sleep and into that other, foreign perspective, piloting a body that wasn't his. As he dangled high above the fight, he knew it didn't just feel that way. It was that way. This was whatever had been tormenting him. This was whatever had been a passenger in his body and in his brain ever since he'd left Klubridge. It had been waiting, and it had been guiding him in its own haphazard way, and now he was the passenger. The thing piloted Caius, and he could do nothing but hang in the air under its control.

The blue energy that rippled out from Caius' body was what came closest to inspiring any sort of sensation, but even that was distanced. The flesh and bone and blood that levitated inside the flickering and sparkling cloud of magic was Caius' body, but it was not Caius. His mind was somewhere else, aware and watching, but disengaged. His body was now host to something else. Something vicious that was not him, but he couldn't help but think of this thing, this body, as his, despite the unfamiliar power that emanated from it.

Arrows flew from bows far below, and he swatted them aside with ease, the blue energy swelling for an instant to block each attack before the arrows reached him. Tendrils of blue peeled away, translucent and shimmering, to shoot downward, skewering Imperials where they stood. The tendrils flew down two at a time and then four and then eight, multiplying and extending and parting and receding with dizzying speed and precision. The archers fell first and then a line of Kites, and there was even a Heron mage struck down while summoning her own attack.

Caius existed within and without that cocoon of magic and laid waste to soldiers and Kites and Herons without moving so much as a finger. He couldn't move if he'd wanted to, but at that moment he felt no inclination to do anything but continue existing in the back of whatever force inhabited him.

It was something sentient. There was no doubt about that. It was angry, and it hungered, and that was a relief, at least. The hunger hadn't been Caius. All those bizarre sensations and hallucinations had been this other thing—this stowaway that had remained hidden until now.

It was hidden no longer, and it took only another moment before malevolent eyes turned on Caius. The eyes were invisible and blank, hidden in the blackness of the ghostly hood that tapered to a smoky and insubstantial cloak, but Caius knew they were watching him, and he knew what this thing was that wished him harm. Vaino had been wrong. They'd all been wrong to believe him, as certain as he'd been. All but Apak, who had known the High Lord was no myth. None of them were prepared, and this was the reckoning.

Black, swirling spears shot forth from the folds of the High Lord's cloak, speeding across the courtyard toward Caius. A new swath of blue poured from Caius' chest, mingling with the cloud of energy that already surrounded him. It extended, catching Peregrine's attack and twisting it, entwining and dispersing the magic.

More whips of dark energy flew out of the entity that was

the High Lord, some of them arcing high, some low, some wrapping around from the sides. Caius blocked, shattered, and dissolved all of them, but they kept coming. The upper levels of the courtyard flashed and sparked with the clash of magic as black flowed into blue and blue into black, each winding around and shearing apart and rebuking the other until a mass of crackling light and twisting, inky tendrils joined Caius to Peregrine, the two of them floating higher above the rest of the combatants.

INTERCESSOR

The voice came from Peregrine but sounded like no voice Caius had ever heard. It was a mountain sliding into the ocean. It was the sky itself, ripping apart and swallowing the land. It should have terrified Caius, but he heard it and accepted it and didn't struggle against what was happening. Could he have even struggled if he'd tried? But he didn't try. If he somehow broke free of this entity—this Intercessor—what, then? And so he remained, somewhere between knowing and unknowing. Midway between existing and ceasing.

Caius felt Samira seeing them now. She gaped and stared, and Lizzie was there, looking up beside her. Oreth had his hand on Apak's arm, and Apak cradled Leyna, bloodied, in his arms as he stared up at the confrontation. Fairy glared up, her eyes squinting when the energy flashed too bright, and Danel Gressam shrank from the fighting, his face hidden. Phyla had her hand on the boy's back, but her eyes were on Caius. Reykas was not with them, not yet, but he was on the way.

Even as he saw his friends and felt their fear and their awe, he saw more Imperials coming through the ruined gate behind and beneath the thing that was Peregrine. There was a sturdy man in a dark blue uniform, a patch over one eye and his own look of terror in the other. He was shouting something to the bald Heron Caius had recognized from Klubridge. Farij Basos. The name came to him now. Was Basos the cause of what was happening now? Had his mages created this thing inside Caius, just like they created the beast that had ravaged the onlookers?

The other Imperial newcomers stared, slack jawed, and that brought Caius' attention back to the conflict everyone else was watching. The one between himself and the most powerful force Teshovar had ever known. And Caius was winning.

It was a slow thing. Slow, and Caius imagined it was exhausting for one or both of them, but he felt none of the exhaustion himself. He watched, detached, as the blue energy crawled forward, inch by inch, swallowing the black. It pulled Peregrine's power in and devoured it, and, for the first time in months, Caius was not hungry. That existential craving he'd felt for so long had not been for food. It had not been for meat or grain. It had been for this raw, chaotic stream of energy. He had hungered for magic.

Peregrine roared, and the keep shook again. An inner corner fell free from the roof and crashed into the courtyard, crushing two Imperial soldiers and three rebels, but the High Lord's focus never wavered. The shrouded sorcerer reached toward Caius with its skeletal left hand, the arm and hand and all digits composed of swirling black smoke. It reached and opened its palm, and more magic poured out, joining the torrent, but it was no use. Caius drove the High Lord back, the blue energy continuing to consume the black.

"How are you doing this?"

The voice swam through Caius' mind, and he recognized it. It was Farij Basos. The man was below him, much too far away to be heard, but his voice was as clear as if he'd been standing a foot away.

"I don't know," Caius said, but inaudibly, his mouth still slack and his head still tilted backward.

"You had no magic in Klubridge. You are no mage."

"I never had magic," Caius said.

"What is this?" Basos asked, his voice petulant now, the demand of a child who didn't understand the way some basic thing worked.

When Caius had no answer, Basos reached his arms up and shouted a chant with his voice—his real voice. Whatever he said was Aevash. Apak would have understood it, and maybe Aquin too, but it was gibberish to Caius. It was effective, though.

Even as Basos spoke, Caius saw the turn of the tide. Peregrine lunged forward in the air, his assault renewed, and blackness slithered out from his hand and spiraled around the blue. This force—this Intercessor—could hold back Peregrine and press the attack, but withstanding Farij Basos at the same time was too much.

A shard of blue energy broke free and streaked downward. Caius watched its flight as it whipped away, still tethered to Caius with a shining and wavering beam of light. The blue spear, insubstantial all the way down, plunged through Basos' chest and passed out his back. There was no sign of entry, no torn garments, no pierced skin. No blood flowed from the wound, but Caius felt Basos dying at the end of that tether. Or the Intercessor felt it, and Caius witnessed it.

Basos dropped to his knees, and with his dying breath, he whispered something else in the old tongue. The Aevash words were lost to Caius, but he saw Basos' arms raise, and the man's fingers wrapped around the blue tendril that had speared him. It had been intangible and ephemeral, but now Basos had hold of it. Something left his body as he died, and the blue darkened. Caius' magic released Basos, and the Heron tumbled forward, lifeless, but it was too late.

The rot climbed its way back toward Caius faster than the magic could dissipate. The tendril of energy turned to physical dust behind the ascending disease, and still it came. When the darkening wave reached the apex, it spread around Caius, reducing the bright blue aura around him to a pulsing and weak midnight glow. And then that, too, turned to dust.

Sensation returned to Caius in the space between two instants. There had been the numb nothingness of being wrapped in the magical cocoon, and then there was an explosion of gray powder all around him and a rush of cold, and the wind whipped at Caius' face as he fell from the sky.

∼

Basos collapsed dead, and an instant later Akithar dropped from the sky. Bekam spared a quick look at the Heron at his feet before unsheathing his sword and heading into the fray.

Basos was dead, and there was nothing to be done for him, but Akithar might yet live.

It was the first time Bekam had fought since losing his eye, and his left flank was vulnerable. He stayed well to the left of the battle, keeping the inner wall of the courtyard at his side as he made his way toward the rubble where the wizard had fallen. He kept his eye ahead and pointedly did not look up. Peregrine floated somewhere up there, and Bekam's heart thudded in his throat at the mere thought. He didn't need to look upward and wet himself from fear. He'd barely kept his wits outside the keep when the High Lord made his first appearance and disassembled the wall and the gate.

Some of the soldiers closest to the front hadn't been as sturdy. Several had fallen to their knees and wept as stones flew free from the castle. One had torn his helmet away from his head and thrown himself wailing over the edge of the cliff. Peregrine's appearance had nearly undone the whole siege, not that the High Lord appeared to need the rest of them. He could have rendered the entire place to ash single-handedly, if not for Akithar's sudden magic. And yet the Kites and the Herons and the engineers and the enlisted troops remained. Those who had not gone mad at the sight of him.

Prusik had known the whole time. Her coy speculation that a siege engine would be unnecessary. Her smirk just before the High Lord appeared. She had known he existed, and she had let Bekam wallow in his ignorance. How many of the rest of them knew and had been laughing at him behind his back? Milev? Surely he knew. And Teka Lacar? Bekam scowled at the thought that his own protegee had so deceived him.

Where had Bekam even first heard that Peregrine was a myth? It was a known fact to so many in the upper ranks, and all of them had laughed at the ignorance of their underlings and the population of Teshovar. They'd believed he was a specter, made up to control the masses. What fools they'd all been.

Bekam squeezed the hilt of his sword harder and slashed at a rebel who came screaming at him from the right. The blade caught her across the chest, and she fell, and he stalked onward.

No one would be under any delusion about the nonexistence

of the High Lord after Stormbreak. He had revealed himself to end the Tamrat line once and for all, and everyone present would remember the horror of his arrival and the shape of his power.

Bekam had marched an army north to destroy the rebellion and to ensure Akithar was dead, so that he could maintain his lie about what happened in Klubridge. All of that seemed at once insignificant and of paramount importance. Nothing would be the same now that he knew and had seen the true power of Teshovar. But he no longer reported to a simple Council made of human bureaucrats. Peregrine, whatever he or it was, existed, and that's who Bekam reported to now. And that was not someone he was eager to disappoint.

Bekam studied the far side of the courtyard, where he'd seen the man drop. The debris was piled nearly a whole story high by then, in scattered mounds and hills, with valleys dug between them. He glanced up at the shape of the keep and didn't like what he saw. The whole place would come down before the end of that day, and he wasn't eager to be trapped beneath the ruins. Akithar had to be just to the right, behind that center heap of stone and wood. Bekam set off again across the uneven ground but halted when a giant blocked his path.

The man was enormous, easily the tallest Bekam had ever seen. A wild mane of orange hair framed his face, joining to a beard that was full of blood and dirt. He held a sword in one hand and an axe in the other and struck a fearsome stance atop a rampart that had fallen into the courtyard.

"You're Aescalan," Bekam said.

Instead of answering with words, the brute lunged forward, blood already running down his leg as he came. Just like these savages. Let them into Teshovar, and this was the trouble they'd bring.

Bekam sidestepped the first swing of the axe, and he parried the first strike from the man's sword. The giant was undoubtedly a ferocious fighter, but he lacked technique with the sword, and he was already wounded. Hardly a fair fight, but this wasn't a man Bekam relished the thought of facing at his freshest.

Another swing from the sword, another sidestep, and Bekam

swung his own blade up and across. The Aescalan grunted, dropping both weapons, and held his hands to his gut as he fell. Bekam kicked the axe out from under the beast and pressed his boot against the man's shoulder, giving him a hard shove. The Aescalan rolled over, murder in his eyes, his face going pale. He snarled something at Bekam in his native tongue and bared his teeth, now bloody.

Bekam kicked him in the jaw and left him there, bleeding out in the rubble. He had a more pressing target, and he would not risk leaving Akithar alive long enough for him to utter a single word to anyone else.

Bekam climbed the center hill of fallen stone, pulling himself up with his left hand, the sword still in his right, and at its peak he looked down and beheld The Great Akithar, the mage of Klubridge.

The man looked entirely ordinary, dressed not in the formal suit he'd worn for his stage shows but in a heavy coat and plain trousers. Not fighting gear, but not the costume of a showman, either. His face was pale and bearded, his hair brown going gray. He lay on his back and stared up at Bekam with confusion and fear. He showed no sign of pain or awareness that his left leg was crumpled and broken beneath him. After that fall onto hard stone, his spine was probably in a similar condition.

Bekam came down the other side of the hill, his boots sliding the last few feet until he stood over the prone body of the mage who had caused all this trouble.

"You're Akithar," Bekam said.

The mage coughed and had the audacity to smile, his lips red now. Something terrible had broken inside him. Barring any last ditch magic, this man was not getting up, even without Bekam's intervention.

"You're the one who's been offering the bounty," Akithar said. "Are you allowed to collect the seri from yourself?" His voice was unsteady, and he laughed, but it turned into another cough. He turned his head and spat blood onto the rubble.

"Stop me," Bekam said. "Use your magic."

The man rolled his head back toward Bekam. "I have no magic. Your Herons took it in Klubridge."

"They took nothing." Bekam tapped at Akithar's broken knee with his boot, and the man didn't flinch. His spine was done for, truly. "Why don't you patch yourself up? Fly yourself out of this pit and strike me down like you did to Basos."

Akithar closed his mouth and stared into Bekam's eyes, and a chill of fear ran down Bekam's own spine. Perhaps he'd underestimated this man or overestimated Basos' ability. Perhaps Akithar had been a mage all along and still had his magic and would do exactly what Bekam had just suggested. Bekam settled his weight on his back leg, ready to move at the slightest provocation. He raised his sword arm and held it ready to defend.

Akithar opened his mouth to take a breath, and Bekam flinched, driving the sword down with all his strength and fear.

∽

Samira started running as soon as she saw Caius fall. Wherever he'd fallen, he'd be injured, but she could help him. She could fix him.

She dodged swords clashing, she weaved around people grappling with each other, and she blocked a crossbow bolt with a quick flash of her shield. Nothing stopped her as she clambered over and around and through the ruins of the courtyard even as more of the keep fell in on itself.

On her hands and knees, she scrambled over a low heap of rock, and she caught sight of Caius on the ground as she came to her feet. She saw the man standing over him with the sword. She watched it happen, and she was too slow to raise her hands. Too slow to block the descent of the blade with her magic.

Caius' name caught in her throat, and it came out as an anguished scream that drove her back down to her knees. The scream turned to sobs, and her hands clawed at the stones as she tried to pull herself up and toward him. She must have seen it wrong. The angle was bad. It wasn't what it seemed.

Quentyn Wickes was there. He picked her up from the ground, one arm wrapped around her chest, pulling her back, saying her name. She screamed again and beat at him with her fists and reached for Caius. She flung her hand at the swordsman, willing her shield to eviscerate him where he stood, but Wickes was too big, and he pulled her away, her feet kicking and dragging, one of her shoes coming loose. The magic flew wide and missed the Imperial entirely.

Wickes pulled her tighter, squeezing her, and she pressed her face into his chest and wailed, her weak fists beating at his shoulders, all the strength gone from them. She tried to turn away and reached back for where she'd been, where she'd seen it happen, but Wickes had her back on the other side of the courtyard by then.

"Can you take her?" He pushed Samira forward, and Aquin was there and wrapped her in her arms.

"Here," Aquin whispered, her breath warm in Samira's hair, her hand stroking the back of Samira's head, and that was all it took. Samira's knees gave way, and she fell forward, and Aquin sank to the ground with her, softening her fall.

Someone said, "We have to go." Someone else said, "This whole place is coming down." Another voice said, "Where is Naecara?" The last was Apak, and Samira tried to look up at him, but her eyes stung, and her vision was blurred, and he was just a dark shape standing above her.

"She hasn't come back," Nahk said.

Apak turned toward Samira and asked, "Where is—"

Aquin shook her head, her hair brushing Samira's face, and Samira squeezed her eyes shut and shuddered, fighting nausea. Before Apak could say anything else, Nahk said, "I'm not leaving Naecara."

"There is no time," Apak told her.

But she said again, "I'm not leaving her." She shifted as though to go, but she turned back to Apak. "I'll find you again." And Nahk was gone, running away, her feet slapping the ground in her soft shoes, the footsteps receding into the clamor of the battle.

"What is that?" Aquin asked, looking up now, and Samira pulled her own gaze up. Apak held something round in his hand, and it shimmered with a soft red glow.

"It's how we're getting out of here," an unfamiliar man with long hair said. He grabbed Apak's arm. "Take us out of here."

LIZANDRA'S DEEPEST FEAR

"A moment," Apak said, turning. "Everyone, gather close. Lizandra—"

"No!" Samira's eyes widened, and she jerked free of Aquin's grasp. "No! She caused this! She brought the Empire here! She... she killed..." Her words failed, and she saw Lizandra on the other side of Apak, looking back at her, stricken. Samira shook with fury. "You wanted to give him up in Klubridge! You wanted to turn him in to save yourself."

Lizandra shook her head, her eyes wide. "That's not... Samira, I would never—"

Apak silenced her with a raised hand. "We do not have the time for this. This disc is an artifact that can bring us to safety. I believe I can take all of us, but you must be close, and you must be touching me or the disc. I—"

"Apak, no!" Samira was on her feet now, her eyes burning and her face wet. "She's not coming. She killed him, Apak. She's not coming with us."

Apak frowned at Samira and grabbed her hand, pulling it to rest on the disc. "How many times today must I refuse to abandon a comrade? Lizandra is coming, and we are out of time."

Something exploded in the courtyard, and the great tree at its center creaked, half of it leaning outward as the trunk split down the middle. Voices cried out, some screaming in fear, some shouting in anger, all of them raising in volume as the keep shook anew. The opposite corner of the courtyard trembled, and the roof fell, collapsing into the third floor, cascading down to the second and the first, and the rest of the structure roared with devastation, spewing dust into the air and enveloping all the fighters who remained standing.

Fairy asked, "Where are we going?"

Before anyone could answer, Samira tore her eyes away from the chaos, looked at Lizandra for a hard moment, and told Apak, "Go."

Apak nodded back to her, and his focus shifted to the disc. He squinted at it, the strain clear on his face. "Oreth, I need assistance," he said, his voice tight.

Oreth tightened a hand on Apak's wrist, his other arm barely holding Leyna upright. As Oreth closed his eyes, his own face tense, the red glow intensified, pouring light out from the disc. Samira felt no heat, even though the artifact blazed as brightly as Apak's eyes. The world around them tinted red, and it was then that Lizandra shrieked. Her hands slipped off Apak's shoulder, and Samira's head jerked in her direction. A soldier had her by the hair, dragging her back, even as her hands scrambled for purchase.

"Lizzie!" Oreth yelled, his strong hand still wrapped around Apak's wrist and the other arm weakly pushing Leyna's limp form against Apak's back. Leyna's eyes blinked open at his shout, and she rolled her head in confusion. Her eyes widened when they turned to face the disc blazing with magical energy. Everything was too loud by then for Samira to hear the girl's screams, but Leyna's mouth was wide, terror on her face, as she struggled against Oreth's grasp, pulling away from Apak.

Samira opened her mouth to shout something at Apak, but what would it be? Horror chilled her veins as she watched Lizandra dragged away, and there was no satisfaction, despite the fury that still raged inside her. But then, impossibly, Reykas was there. Reykas, just past the Imperial, a sword in his hand, slicing downward, cutting into the space where the soldier's neck met his shoulder. The man fell, and Reykas lunged forward, shoving Lizandra, and she staggered forward, her hands slapping onto the disc in the instant before it blazed its brightest, and a wave of vertigo spun Samira's head.

Her eyes widened and met Reykas' as the courtyard faded. He was two steps away from them, but it might as well have been a world away. He was too far, and he was still reaching for Lizzie even as he disappeared. Oreth shouted something as Leyna thrashed hard enough to pull his hand off Apak's wrist. Oreth disappeared, blinking away as if he had never existed. The world folded on itself, and everything was red and silent.

CHAPTER 54

Apak placed the Seal of Metarr on the scarred wooden table and traced the indented ring on top with his fingertip. The disc was cold and plain and silent now, lacking any trace of the immense amount of magic he had poured into it. Lacking any indication of the enormous effort it took for him to maintain his connection to the artifact while not losing or dismembering anyone during the transit. Lacking any sign of the way Oreth had bolstered Apak's own insufficient power to complete the journey. The rest of them knew or suspected they would not have made it out of the Stormbreak Sanctuary without Apak's intervention, but it was doubtful that any of them knew how he had accomplished the feat. It was not something he wished to do again, and it was unlikely to be something he even could do again.

What mattered was that the ones who had arrived were all safe, more or less. Apak closed his eyes and allowed himself a moment to remember the tangible separations he had felt when the ones who had not made the journey had dropped away. Naecara and Nahk had stayed behind. Reykas had been mere feet away. Oreth.

He sniffed and opened his eyes once more. He looked at the closed cabinet at the back of the room and at the familiar shelf next to it before he left the Seal and ducked under the tattered fabric that separated him from the others. It hung in shreds of red, the edges frayed and even burned in places, but it held together well enough for him to push it aside without having it fall to pieces in his hand.

Micah Vaino sat on the nearest chair, his leather jerkin half ripped from his body, and his forehead in his hands. His long hair, ordinarily pulled back in a severe ponytail or arranged into a fashionable style, hung thick and sweaty, obscuring his face. He looked up when Apak came near, and he said, "They're all dead. It's my fault, and they're all dead."

Apak stopped to stare at him. "You were foolish and incompetent. You did everything the wrong way, and there is nothing to be done for that now."

Apak moved onward, stepping around Kam Dhaz, who patted Vaino on the back with a ginger touch, saying, "There, now. It can't be as bad as all that, can it?" Alev Adonar gave Apak a look he did not quite understand, but then they nodded to him, and he nodded back.

The woman he took to be Phyla Gressam sat on the floor, not far from them, her son curled in her lap and a distant, glazed look in her eyes. It was the look of loss that was not yet real and that had not yet solidified into the eternal weight it would become. The boy shivered in her arms and hid his face from Apak. Fairy stood near them and turned her sorrowful eyes toward him. Apak gave her shoulder a quick pat and stepped past the girl before she could begin crying. Apak was competent at many things, but responding to a child's tears was not among his set of skills.

Apak's gaze shifted left, back toward a darker corner, where Lizandra sat with her knees pulled close to her chin. She had her hands clasped before her shins, and her haunted eyes stared at the wet spot on the wooden floor, the place where Leyna had staggered out of the huddle and collapsed into her own blood.

Lizandra looked up at Apak standing before her. She wiped at her face and said, "I didn't mean any of this. None of this should have happened."

"Recriminations can wait for another day," Apak said.

"Do you know where Reykas is?"

Apak exhaled. He had expected for Reykas' illness to have claimed him by the time he returned north with Naecara and the others. He had expected that nothing could be done for the man. But Reykas was not gone when they returned. Nothing was as any of them had expected.

"He remained behind," Apak said. "He was the one who saved you."

Apak gave Lizandra a moment to respond, but she said nothing, and he left her alone in that dark corner with her guilt.

He walked to the farthest side of the wide floor, toward his eventual destination. Two men stood together, one the sturdy man Aquin had called Wickes and the other a trembling halflock named Colm, who kept his face turned downward. Apak followed his gaze and saw the thin man was staring at Leyna, now healed but unconscious atop a curtain Wickes had torn down and piled in a heap for her.

The big man had lifted Leyna and carried her to the makeshift bed on his own, but it had taken the combined efforts of Kam Dhaz, Apak, and Aquin to pull Samira's shaking hands over the girl's wounds. The healing had come, but Samira had moaned and shuddered and finally collapsed when it was done.

Wickes nodded to Apak as he approached, and Apak gave him a perfunctory nod in return. So many new people, and Apak had saved as many of them as he could. All of them had lost something, but they had kept their lives, whatever those might be worth.

Aquin sat just past them, her back against the wall and her legs stretched before her on the floor. Samira lay next to her, her knees tucked in and her head in Aquin's lap. Aquin stroked her hair in silence as she watched Apak approach. Leyna's blood had dried on Samira's fingers, but she had taken no notice.

He stopped before them and squatted, his knees protesting the posture, but it felt important that he bring himself down to Aquin's eye line. "How is she?"

Samira shifted and opened her eyes, streaked red from crying but now dry. "You saved us," she said, her voice hoarse.

Apak looked away. Why did that feel like an accusation?

Samira had been unable to stand immediately after they had

arrived here. After she had healed Leyna, Wickes had lifted her with a gentleness Apak would have guessed impossible for the big man, and he had carried her to the side of the room where he stood vigil with the halflock while Aquin held her.

Samira pushed herself up from Aquin's lap and sat at an angle on the floor, with her left arm supporting her weight. She studied Apak's shoes before she looked up to meet his eyes. "Caius is gone."

"He is," Apak said. A thickness was in his chest, similar to the one he'd felt after losing Dorrin. The ache was becoming familiar in a way it never should for anyone.

"Reykas, too. And Oreth," she said.

"I believe they still live." And he did, at least for the moment. The certainty that Oreth still drew breath somewhere far north of them was what kept the despair at bay.

"The whole rebellion is gone," she said. "Peregrine won. It's all over." She took a breath with great effort and said, "We're finished."

Apak's eyebrows rose. "We are far from finished. Nothing is finished."

"What do you mean?"

Apak reached forward, unsure whether he should offer such support but doing it, anyway. He placed his hand over Samira's and said, "We have much to do. There is much we must set right. There is much to rebuild." He released her hand and stood, looking around the stage and up at the roof that had endured intact, the electric lights even having survived the doom that came to the city. Looters had vandalized the theater, but the structure itself was stable.

"How?" she asked, her look plaintive.

"You and Caius rebuilt this theater once before. You and I will do it again. It will be our home once more. We will rebuild the rebellion as well. We will find our friends and bring them back here, and we will enact justice. No one has answered sufficiently for what happened to Dorrin. To Hyden Gressam. To Caius. To all the others we have lost. But we will build an answer together here in Klubridge. And, this time, we will do it the right way."

CHAPTER 55

The metal room was cold and familiar. The man's boots rang against the smooth black floor, and he waited at the end of the room for the beacon to light. At last, it flared to life, the blue flame igniting the triangular symbol in the opposite wall that matched the shape of the room itself. The walls angled inward from both sides of the floor, meeting at the top far above the man's head, but the angles always made the room feel small and constrained, as if it were about to shrink and squeeze around him.

The device in the wall clanked with a hollow and percussive unlatching, and the triangular wall before him lowered, disappearing into the floor, the point at the top vanishing last. The man waited until the gate had finished opening before he walked through it.

The chamber beyond was round, a cylinder constructed from black metal like the entry had been. The man had stood in that room many times but still didn't know how far the cylindrical room rose above him. It disappeared into shadow, the ceiling somewhere farther above him than the light would reach.

Blue light sparked before him, illuminating the Keeper on her raised chair that had been forged from the same metal as everything else in the room. She frowned at him but waited for a similar light to ignite beside her, bringing the Builder's identical throne into view. He sat with his chin in his hand, his elbow on the arm of the chair as he regarded the man before them. "Bargainer," he said.

"Builder," the man responded with a quick bow.

The other sconces lit around the room, one after another, as the others arrived and took their seats. The Bargainer saw the Mediator to the right of the Builder, his eyes half closed. He always appeared disinterested, but the Mediator would miss no detail of these proceedings. The Foreseer sat far to the left, almost at the end of the array of seats. A dark veil of embroidered lace covered her eyes, and her mouth remained open just far enough for her lips to part.

"The Intercessor has overstepped its bounds," the Keeper said. "You should have prevented this."

"I have no control over the Intercessor," the Bargainer said.

"And yet you still interfered."

"I did not control the Intercessor, but I agreed with its decision."

The Keeper's nostrils flared, but her voice was steady. "It took a human host, and not just any human. It took Caius Harrim."

"It took him after Peregrine's mages attempted to silence Caius Harrim's magic."

"You told us Caius Harrim had no magic."

"He did not. When they tried to silence him, their work was inept. Butchers performing a surgery. Part of Caius Harrim was lost in the act, and the Intercessor moved into that void."

"Part of him was lost," the Builder said, leaning forward. "Are you referring to a soul?"

"Of course not," the Bargainer said, not bothering to disguise the contempt in his voice. "But something was lost, and Caius Harrim would not have survived the ritual if the Intercessor had not taken him."

"And now he is dead anyway," the Keeper said, her own disdain present in her voice.

"It had to happen. He had to die in order for—"

"In order for your plans to come to fruition?" she asked. "You interfered directly with the humans. You posed as a human yourself. That is not our way, Bargainer."

He huffed and stared back at her. "I followed our ways. I did nothing wrong, and none of them knew I was among them."

"What of the girl you helped in the forest?" the Mediator asked, breaking his silence.

The Bargainer turned to face him. "She would have died if I hadn't helped her. Her part is essential in what's coming." And, turning back to the center, he said, "I offered no help without payment. Every one of them compensated me. I followed our ways, Keeper. Nothing for free."

"It was too great a risk," the Keeper said. "And this girl already knew you. You had dealt with her in the past, before you found her in the forest. You truly believe she did not recognize you?"

"They see what we allow them to see," he said. "Especially in times of crisis. Everything I did was in service to ensuring our goal. And it almost worked." He bit the last sentence off, regretting it as soon as he'd said it.

"Almost," the Keeper said.

"The Intercessor killed many of Peregrine's soldiers. It even held Peregrine at bay in the battle."

"For a time. But now Caius Harrim is dead, and the rebellion has failed. Ultimately, it was all for nothing."

The Bargainer shook his head. "I disagree. The end of one era has opened the door for another."

It was always a risk to push back against the Keeper in this way, so he stopped there. After a moment, the Builder said, "Continue, Bargainer."

"The rebellion had been mismanaged and was doomed to begin with. Its leader did not even believe in Peregrine's existence."

"And now the rebellion has been destroyed," the Keeper said. "I fail to see how this benefits anyone other than Peregrine."

"Allow me to continue what we have started, Keeper. Everything had to happen exactly as it happened. New leaders will rise."

"You sound so certain," the Keeper said. "But yours is not the power of prognostication."

"It is not," the Bargainer said, "but it is the Foreseer's."

All eyes turned to the woman seated to the left, her face still shrouded. She did not move until the Keeper spoke to her. "Well, Foreseer?"

And then she bowed her head. Her breaths were loud in the metal room, coming fast through her nose for a full minute before she exhaled through her mouth. Her head came up, but she did not look at any of them. She said, "The Bargainer speaks truly. Caius Harrim had to die. The child had to survive. The rebellion had to fall. These are all links in the chain we have been assembling."

The Keeper watched the Foreseer for another moment, waiting for more. When it was clear that no more was coming, she looked back to the center of the room, where the Bargainer waited.

"We will allow you to continue," she said.

He ducked his head in another quick bow. "Events will unfold as we have been guiding them. It will take more time and more guidance, but I will ensure our victory."

The Keeper laughed. "You will bring us victory by your hand, Bargainer? When the rest of us have failed?"

"Not by my hand, Keeper, but by my influence. A new Stormbreak will rise, and Peregrine will fall."

AFTERWORD

In the afterword for *Akithar's Greatest Trick*, I promised you I had a plan for the Teshovar series and that I'd be sticking to it. *Lizandra's Deepest Fear* is the second big piece in the story I'm building, and it's the dark middle chapter in the first of three trilogies. Not everything turned out happily in this one. Well, not much turned out happily. But, as the Foreseer said, all the things that happened are links in the chain. The upcoming third novel will complete this first story arc and will finish laying the groundwork upon which the rest of the series will sit.

The first Teshovar book released in mid-2021, but it didn't truly find its audience until early the following year. I would be remiss if I didn't acknowledge the enormous impact BookTok has had on my career, starting in 2022. The authors and readers I have met through that community have become lifelong friends and some of the very best supporters I could have hoped for. Regardless of whether you found my books through BookTok or elsewhere, I appreciate every one of you who has joined me on this fantastical journey.

We are now two novels and one novella into this epic saga, and there are seven more full novels to go. I've already outlined all the remaining books to varying degrees, and I can't wait to show you where the story takes us. Along the way, there will be

AFTERWORD

more novellas and other side stories that will show you the unexplored corners of Teshovar and beyond. You can keep up with my writing online at JasonDorough.com, and I look forward to seeing you next time. In the meantime, as always, remember to be kind, be generous, and have empathy.

ABOUT THE AUTHOR

Jason Dorough is the author of the epic fantasy Teshovar series, including *The Gem of Tagath*, *Akithar's Greatest Trick*, and *Lizandra's Deepest Fear*. Originally from Georgia, Jason now lives in Florida, where he works as a voiceover artist when he's not writing. You can visit him online at JasonDorough.com.

Made in the USA
Columbia, SC
15 February 2024